Modern Stories in English

Modern Stories in English

Fourth Edition

Edited by

W. H. New
University of British Columbia

H. J. Rosengarten
University of British Columbia

Toronto

Canadian Cataloguing in Publication Data

Modern Stories in English

4th ed.
ISBN 0-201-70939-2

1. Short stories, American. 2. Short stories, Canadian (English).* 3. Short stories, English. 4. American fiction—20th century. 5. Canadian fiction (English) — 20th century.* 6. English fiction —20th century. I. New, W.H. (William Herbert), 1938– . II. Rosengarten, Herbert.

PR1309.S5M62 2001 823'.0108091 C00-932159-4

Previous editions published by Copp Clark Pittman, Ltd.
3rd edition of *Modern Stories in English* copyright 1991.

ISBN 0-201-70939-2

Vice President, Editorial Director: Michael Young
Editor-in-Chief: David Stover
Marketing Manager: Judith Allen
Developmental Editor: Lise Creurer
Associate Editor: Susan Ratkaj
Production Editor: Susan Adlam
Copy Editor: Cheryl Cohen
Production Coordinator: Peggy Brown
Page Layout: Janette Thompson (Jansom)
Art Director: Mary Opper
Interior Design: Lisa LaPointe
Cover Design: Sarah Battersby
Cover Image: PhotoDisc

1 2 3 4 5 05 04 03 02 01

Printed and bound in Canada

Contents

Introduction

Good stories entertain us: this is the main reason we listen to them or read them. But "entertainment" comes in many guises. For some listeners and readers, narrative is everything—they like a quick-moving tale, a thrilling plot, mystery, adventure, suspense. Some want to identify with the characters of a story, perhaps to share their experiences vicariously, or perhaps because such empathy enlarges their understanding of the complexities of human behaviour. For other readers, plot and character are subordinate to a story's educational purpose or moral point; they want fiction to teach a lesson about life. A different group of readers is less interested in a separable "moral" or "subject" than in the manner in which the story is told: its formal qualities. For this last group, the form that the story takes—meaning the cadences and textures of its language, as well as its structure—constitutes a "subject" in its own right. Readers look to a story variously for escape, for instruction, for a mirror of the world, for a work of artifice.

Just as there is a multiplicity of readers, so the modern short story draws on a multitude of forms that have long been a part of narrative tradition: myths, legends, fables, folk tales, ballads, fairy tales, and oral "exempla." Since the first half of the nineteenth century, when authors such as Edgar Allan Poe and Nathaniel Hawthorne began producing models of narrative suspense and psychological drama in short story form, American writers have been among the short story's foremost practitioners. But the same era saw the development of short fiction elsewhere as well—in France, Germany, England, Russia, China, Spain, Italy, and Brazil—and the new perspectives brought by these different cultures and traditions gave additional vigour to the short story, strengthening its claim to be regarded as a fictional form in its own right. Such cross-fertilization has continued into our own time. Twentieth-century writers in English were influenced not only by their own cultures, but also by innovative writers in other languages: by the folk writers of Asia and Africa, for example, and the Gothic authors of Quebec, the political fabulists from Czechoslovakia, and the "magic realists" of Latin America.

Yet in English alone there is a rich variety, reflected by the stories in this collection. They display diverse views and contrasting styles; they are representative of the twentieth century's main technical developments in short fiction; they also come from many different parts of the world: mostly from the United States, Britain, and Canada, but also from Africa, the Caribbean, South Asia, and the South Pacific.

They have in common the English language; to make this assertion, however, is to cover a wealth of specific differences; for in the relation between language and culture something happens that affects the shape and substance of stories. The way writers use images, for example, derives not so much from literary or linguistic precedent and example (though these play their part), as from the way the writers see their own world—from their particular experience, their own observations of places and people. Faulkner's South and Achebe's Nigeria are fictional locales, rooted in specific cultural and political observations. The social patterns of American and Nigerian families are not the same. Comparing stories from different cultures, therefore, can provide an opportunity to study ethnic differences, and to delight in the linguistic variety to which such differences have given rise. It can also reveal elements of social disparity and inequity, even while it underlines the common humanity of the experiences that the writers have depicted.

There are many shared human experiences—love, hate, work, war, birth, death, dreams—which recur from author to author, from country to country, in all forms of literature, and these can serve as points of comparison. The number of stories about parenting and growing up, for example, or about the relations between men and women, or about coming to terms with disease, testifies to the similarity of everyday emotional and intellectual life around the world. Stories about political or racial oppression ("Dry September"), or about the problems arising out of modern scientific progress ("Report") can awaken comparable responses in readers from a wide range of backgrounds. But even here a reader must be sensitive to differences, and avoid making facile connections. The roles of men and women vary from society to society, as they have varied within a single society over time; attitudes to communal and individual values differ (individualism is not universally regarded as socially desirable or necessary); and generational conflict in a culture that reveres tradition will obviously carry different overtones from those it possesses in a society committed to novelty and change.

Although all the writers in this anthology have in common the cultural and linguistic heritage of English, that heritage has been altered by time and place. During the twentieth century, many national literatures founded on English patterns and traditions moved away from them in order to reclaim older indigenous traditions, or because new experiences, landscapes, and cultural mixes led to a need for different words and different ways of using them. Walt Whitman's efforts in the mid-nineteenth century to articulate a new language for the United States provided something of a model; Whitman wanted American

English to mirror his "new" nation's expansionist, democratic, colloquial politics. The American writers in this book, from Faulkner and Hemingway to Proulx and Vonnegut, convey the characteristic sounds and rhythms of the language that subsequently evolved. In Africa and the Caribbean, where the tradition of oral storytelling developed into a sophisticated folk art, the tensions of modern life are still couched in a characteristically "oral" form. Achebe and Naipaul rely extensively for their effects on the rhythms of speech and the contrasts between different orders of vernacular fluency. Achebe's "Civil Peace" deals with the collapse of communal solidarity during the Nigerian civil war, while Naipaul's "My Aunt Gold Teeth" affirms the value of a tradition the narrator admires even while he can no longer participate in it; in both cases, it is the oral character of the culture that preserves the values and forms of a civilization once strong and now lost.

As with patterns of speech, so with thematic concerns. In Australia and New Zealand, writers found new subjects in responding to a set of social preoccupations born out of their separate South Pacific contexts and their relations with the colonizing power, Britain. Katherine Mansfield's deliberate, class-conscious individualism in "The Doll's House" looks back to a time when English conventions were still strong, while the satire of Peter Carey's "Do You Love Me?" questions the ways a post-colonial society defines its identity. Canadians have also sought their own voice: though living in an environment in many respects similar to that of their American neighbours, they have determinedly celebrated the differences that distinguish their social organization and social values from those that pertain in Britain and the United States—in the process developing a lively rhetoric of regional identities. Atwood, for example, vividly records the sounds and sights of a particular locale, emphasizing how her characters' lives and language are inextricably intertwined with their environment. Similarly, Rohinton Mistry's "Swimming Lessons" and "When Mr. Pirzada Came to Dine" by the American writer Jhumpa Lahiri place characters in cross-cultural circumstances in order to reveal the constraints of speech and the presumptions of culture. All these stories evoke the language of place, some in dialogue, some through narration or description, some in transformations of everyday speech into political or social symbol.

In one way or another then, whether through setting or subject or language, a sense of place pervades all the stories in this collection. In many, however, that awareness is rooted in feelings of exile or alienation from an older tradition. Such exile, during the twentieth century, proved to be an opportunity to discover freedom on the one hand, and an experience that is spiritually debilitating on the other. People chose to emigrate, or were driven to do so; they willingly embraced a different kind of life, or had one forced upon them. Whichever is the case, such moves inevitably brought with them a sense of something left behind, something lost. Katherine Mansfield reveals this divided consciousness: she rejected what she considered the provinciality of New Zealand, and yet her stories sometimes look back wistfully to a colonial childhood. V.S. Naipaul experienced a twofold alienation: from his Indian heritage, and from his Trinidadian upbringing. For Ernest Hemingway and Paul Bowles, exile was a deliberate choice, dictated by a need to find fresh values. Working in Paris in the 1920s, Hemingway sought to break away from outworn modes and empty rhetoric, to give literature new force and meaning by portraying life in starkly realistic terms, and yet he could never wholly shed the ideal of heroic individualism that marks his American tradition.

The experience of alienation is not restricted to individuals. The Salish writer George Clutesi, for instance, observes that indigenous peoples in North America are dispossessed without even moving from their homeland. Writers from ethnic minorities (Alice Walker, David Wong Louie, Thomas King), using or responding to the language of the "majority" culture around them, live with an isolation of a related kind. For many writers, therefore, fiction becomes a way of challenging or subverting social conventions, a means to shape in artifice an alternative vision of the world. Feminist writers (Grenville, Thomas, Walker) have attempted to combat the presumptive values inherent in linguistic conventions as well as in social ones. And there is another kind of alienation—intellectual and artistic, such as we find detailed in Rudy Wiebe's "Where Is the Voice Coming From?" which dramatizes the struggle by a member of one culture to reach some understanding of another, and to find ordered utterance for his confused and painful impressions.

The language of the modern short story, then, can be not only a means of reporting on experience, but also a way of charting alternative perceptions of experience, sometimes realistically (Proulx, Ford), sometimes in fable (Carter, Ballard). Whatever the goal, the writer can call on a multitude of devices through which he or she may pattern the experience: through realistic description, for example, or through fantasy, through satire, through myth. In a story such as "Hills Like White Elephants," for example, the writer's intention is to make us believe we are direct observers of the action; Hemingway creates the illusion of reality by focusing on dialogue, so that we have the sense that we are listening in on a real conversation. Stories like this move us from the page to the world; we recognize the action as a comment on or description of life, a projection of psychological disturbance or a dramatization of social conflict. But other writers ask readers to look at the word as much as at the world. Writers like Barthelme and Vonnegut (writing "reports"), Helprin (writing "letters"), and Wiebe (copying out phrases from historical archives) adapt forms that, in part, paradoxically stress the limitations of documentary realism. Their stories challenge readers to acknowledge the empirical world and then to use their imagination to transcend its obvious restrictions. They ask readers to be co-creators of the story. They are celebrants of language-in-process, taking pleasure in language at play, exploring its boundaries.

Language takes narrative shape in other, more traditional ways. For writers like Callaghan and Bowles, a concern with moral behaviour takes the form of parable or fable. In stories such as those by Jacobs and Forster, it is the pattern of fantasy or myth that structures experience; the reader enters the world of dream or nightmare, with its associative leaps of logic and its symbolic or psychological implications. For writers of satire—King, Gallant, and others—the story is patterned by a comic irony that exposes the flaws and foibles of people who live their lives in two dimensions, blinkered to other possibilities and unaware of their own follies.

Several stories in this anthology incorporate elements of myth as a structuring device, either the kind of myth that articulates directly a society's moral tradition, or the kind that is used as a literary means to sound "archetypes," to arouse in the reader a recognition of enduring patterns of human experience. Both kinds of myth can serve didactic purposes. Clutesi's "Ko-ishin-mit and the Shadow People" comes from a tradition in which such tales were designed (in the author's own words) "to teach the young the many wonders of nature; the importance of all living things, no matter how small and insignificant." In contrast, Bowles's "Allal" merges the conventions of myth with those of realism to produce a social fable that comments on modern human beings. It is ironic, oblique, spare; its eye is on contemporary behaviour all the while it seems to be concerned with events of pure fantasy. We are asked to believe in the truth of what the story tells us but not necessarily in the reality of the events it portrays—they are a means to a different end. That such stories are in one way or another "fantastic" does not make them any less relevant to our own daily lives; it simply makes us more conscious of the artifice that characterizes all works of literature, and by means of which writer and reader are able to share the pleasures of the imagination.

For the Instructor

We are very pleased to announce that, for the first time ever, we have an *Instructor's Manual* (ISBN 0201-70940-6) to accompany *Modern Stories in English*. This supplement has been authored by Kevin G. Stewart of the University of British Columbia.

The *Instructor's Manual* provides a comprehensive package of pedagogical resources for instructors to use in conjunction with the fourth edition of this text. Recognizing the many challenges that instructors often face when teaching short fiction, we provide instructors with useful teaching ideas and practical resources that can be readily used (or adapted for use) in the classroom. *The Instructor's Manual* offers:

- sample course outlines
- ideas for exercises
- sample essay and exam questions
- alternate Tables of Contents for the anthology (chronological, thematic)
- handouts on essay writing, reading short stories, and documenting sources
- a glossary of terms used in discussing short fiction
- a punctuation review
- web resources
- a bibliography for further reading and research

We hope the strategies and resources included in the *Instructor's Manual* will maximize the discussion in your classroom and inspire your students to explore various aspects of reading and writing outside the confines of the lecture hall.

The Publishers

Chinua Achebe

Born in Ogidi, Nigeria, in 1930 and educated at Umuahia, Ibadan, and London, Chinua Achebe has become established not only as an editor and publisher, but also as one of the most respected literary voices in contemporary Africa. He has written verse, books for juveniles, two books of short stories, and five novels, of which the first three won particularly enthusiastic reviews. *Things Fall Apart* (1958), *No Longer at Ease* (1961), and *Arrow of God* (1964) render different aspects of the conflict between European and African civilizations. The powerlessness of the traditional culture to remain intact in the face of European enslavement and colonization, the inability of a modern young African to reconcile his family attachments with his sense of independence and his observation of political corruption, the incapacity of both the lay African society and the European colonial bureaucracy to understand the role and identity of a traditional priest: these are Achebe's topics. His aim is openly political and didactic. In "The Novelist as Teacher," he asserts: "Here, then, is an adequate revolution for me to espouse—to help my society regain its belief in itself and put away the complexes of the years of denigration and self-denigration." In so doing he fulfills one of the traditional roles of the writer in African society: to educate the young to an appreciation of the moral truths of their own culture. His method, too, derives from traditional techniques; he relies on simple narrative structures, using speech idiom and the formal patterns of Igbo proverbs to suggest how the present can still learn from the received wisdom of the past. "As long as one people sit on another and are deaf to their cry," he writes, "so long will understanding elude all of us."

"Civil Peace" is the concluding story of the volume *Girls at War and other stories* (1972), which, like his most recent novel, *Anthills of the Savannah* (1987), reflects the civil war that disrupted Nigerian life in the late 1960s. Though the fatalistic ironies that permeate the story are not untouched by humour, the work is fundamentally serious and reveals Achebe's continuing account of his deeply held commitment to freedom. In exploring its nature, in attempting both to communicate to a national audience and to reach across cultural and racial boundaries, he shows himself to be an acute and humane observer of human behaviour.

Civil Peace

Jonathan Iwegbu counted himself extra-ordinarily lucky. "Happy survival!" meant so much more to him than just a current fashion of greeting old friends in the first hazy days of peace. It went deep to his heart. He had come out of the war with five inestimable blessings—his head, his wife Maria's head and the heads of three out of their four children. As a bonus he also had his old bicycle—a miracle too but naturally not to be compared to the safety of five human heads.

The bicycle had a little history of its own. One day at the height of the war it was commandeered "for urgent military action." Hard as its loss would have been to him he would still have let it go without a thought had he not had some doubts about the genuineness of the officer. It wasn't his disreputable rags, nor the toes peeping out of one blue and one brown canvas shoes, nor yet the two stars of his rank done obviously in a hurry in biro, that troubled Jonathan; many good and heroic soldiers looked the same or worse. It was rather a certain lack of grip and firmness in his manner. So Jonathan, suspecting he might be amenable to influence, rummaged in his raffia bag and produced the two pounds with which he had been going to buy firewood which his wife, Maria, retailed to camp officials for extra stock-fish and corn meal, and got his bicycle back. That night he buried it in the little clearing in the brush where the dead of the camp, including his own youngest son, were buried. When he dug it up again a year later after the surrender all it needed was a little palm-oil greasing. "Nothing puzzles God," he said in wonder.

He put it to immediate use as a taxi and accumulated a small pile of Biafran money ferrying camp officials and their families across the four-mile stretch to the nearest tarred road. His standard charge per trip was six pounds and those who had the money were only glad to be rid of some of it in this way. At the end of a fortnight he had made a small fortune of one hundred and fifteen pounds.

Then he made the journey to Enugu and found another miracle waiting for him. It was unbelievable. He rubbed his eyes and looked again and it was still standing there before him. But, needless to say, even that monumental blessing must be accounted also totally inferior to the five heads in the family. This newest miracle was his little house in Ogui Overside. Indeed nothing puzzles God! Only two houses away a huge concrete edifice some wealthy contractor had put up just before the war was a mountain of rubble. And here was Jonathan's little zinc house of no regrets built with mud blocks quite intact! Of course the doors and windows were missing and five sheets off the roof. But what was that? And anyhow he had returned to Enugu early enough to pick up bits of old zinc and wood and soggy sheets of cardboard lying around the neighbourhood before thousands more came out of their forest holes looking for the same things. He got a destitute carpenter with one old hammer, a blunt plane and a few bent and rusty nails in his tool bag to turn this assortment of wood, paper and metal into door and window shutter for five Nigerian shillings or fifty Biafran pounds. He paid the pounds, and moved in with his overjoyed family carrying five heads on their shoulders.

His children picked mangoes near the military cemetery and sold them to soldiers' wives for a few pennies—real pennies this time—and his wife started making breakfast akara balls for neighbours in a hurry to start life again. With his family earnings he took his bicycle to the villages around and brought fresh palm-wine which he mixed generously in his rooms with the water which had recently started running again in the public tap down the road, and opened up a bar for soldiers and other lucky people with good money.

At first he went daily, then every other day and finally once a week, to the offices of the Coal Corporation where he used to be a miner, to find out what was what. The only thing he did find out in the end was that the little house of his was even a greater blessing than he had thought. Some of his fellow ex-miners who had nowhere to return at the end of the day's waiting just slept outside the doors of the offices and cooked what meal they could scrounge together in Bournvita tins. As the weeks lengthened and still nobody could say what was what Jonathan discontinued his weekly visits altogether and faced his palm-wine bar.

But nothing puzzles God. Came the day of the windfall when after five days of endless scuffles in queues and counter-queues in the sun outside the Treasury he had twenty pounds counted into his palms as ex-gratia award for the rebel money he had turned in. It was like Christmas for him and for many others like him when the payments began. They called it (since few could manage its proper official name) *egg-rasher*.

As soon as the pound notes were placed in his palm Jonathan simply closed it tight over them and buried fist and money inside his trouser pocket. He had to be extra careful because he had seen a man a couple of days earlier collapse into near-madness in an instant before that oceanic crowd because no sooner had he got his twenty pounds than some heartless ruffian picked it off him. Though it was not right that a man in such an extremity of agony should be blamed yet many in the queues that day were able to remark quietly on the victim's carelessness, especially after he pulled out the innards of his pocket and revealed a hole in it big enough to pass a thief's head. But of course he had insisted that the money had been in the other pocket, pulling it out to show its comparative wholeness. So one had to be careful.

Jonathan soon transferred the money to his left hand and pocket so as to leave his right free for shaking hands should the need arise, though by fixing his gaze at such an elevation as to miss all approaching human faces he made sure that the need did not arise, until he got home.

He was normally a heavy sleeper but that night he heard all the neighbourhood noises die down one after another. Even the night watchman who knocked the hour on some metal somewhere in the distance had fallen silent after knocking one o'clock. That must have been the last thought in Jonathan's mind before he was finally carried away himself. He couldn't have been gone for long, though, when he was violently awakened again.

"Who is knocking?" whispered his wife lying beside him on the floor.

"I don't know," he whispered back breathlessly.

The second time the knocking came it was so loud and imperious that the rickety old door could have fallen down.

"Who is knocking?" he asked then, his voice parched and trembling.

"Na tief-man and him people," came the cool reply. "Make you hopen de door." This was followed by the heaviest knocking of all.

Maria was the first to raise the alarm, then he followed and all their children.

"Police-o! Thieves-o! Neighbours-o! Police-o! We are lost! We are dead! Neighbours, are you asleep? Wake up! Police-o!"

This went on for a long time and then stopped suddenly. Perhaps they had scared the thief away. There was total silence. But only for a short while.

"You done finish?" asked the voice outside. "Make we help you small. Oya, everybody!"

"Police-o! Tief-man-o! Neighbours-o! We done loss-o! Police-o! . . ."

There were at least five other voices besides the leader's.

Jonathan and his family were now completely paralysed by terror. Maria and the children sobbed inaudibly like lost souls. Jonathan groaned continuously.

The silence that followed the thieves' alarm vibrated horribly. Jonathan all but begged their leader to speak again and be done with it.

"My frien," said he at long last, "we don try our best for call dem but I tink say dem all done sleep-o . . . So wetin we go do now? Sometaim you wan call soja? Or you wan make we call dem for you? Soja better pass police. No be so?"

"Na so!" replied his men. Jonathan thought he heard even more voices now than before and groaned heavily. His legs were sagging under him and his throat felt like sand-paper.

"My frien, why you no de talk again. I de ask you say you wan make we call soja?"

"No."

Na = it is.

"Awrighto. Now make we talk business. We no be bad tief. We no like for make trouble. Trouble done finish. War done finish and all the katakata wey de for inside. No Civil War again. This time na Civil Peace. No be so?"

"Na so!" answered the horrible chorus.

"What do you want from me? I am a poor man. Everything I had went with this war. Why do you come to me? You know people who have money. We . . ."

"Awright! We know you say no get plenty money. But we sef no get even anini. So derefore make you open dis window and give us one hundred pound and we go commot. Orderwise we de come for inside now to show you guitar-boy like dis . . . "

A volley of automatic fire rang through the sky. Maria and the children began to weep aloud again.

"Ah, missisi de cry again. No need for dat. We done talk say we na good tief. We just take our small money and go nwayorly. No molest. Abi we de molest?"

"At all!" sang the chorus.

"My friends," began Jonathan hoarsely. "I hear what you say and I thank you. If I had one hundred pounds . . ."

"Lookia my frien, no be play we come play for your house. If we make mistake and step for inside you no go like am-o. So derefore . . . "

"To God who made me; if you come inside and find one hundred pounds, take it and shoot me and shoot my wife and children. I swear to God. The only money I have in this life is this twenty-pounds *egg-rasher* they gave me today . . . "

"O.K. Time de go. Make you open dis window and bring the twenty pound. We go manage am like dat."

There were now loud murmurs of dissent among the chorus: "Na lie de man de lie; e get plenty money . . . Make we go inside and search properly well . . . Wetin be twenty pound? . . . "

"Shurrup!" rang the leader's voice like a lone shot in the sky and silenced the murmuring at once. "Are you dere? Bring the money quick!"

"I am coming," said Jonathan fumbling in the darkness with the key of the small wooden box he kept by his side on the mat.

At the first sign of light as neighbours and others assembled to commiserate with him he was already strapping his five-gallon demijohn

anini = coin (1/10 of a penny)

to his bicycle carrier and his wife, sweating in the open fire, was turning over akara balls in the wide clay bowl of boiling oil. In the corner his eldest son was rinsing out dregs of yesterday's palm wine from old beer bottles.

"I count it as nothing," he told his sympathizers, his eyes on the rope he was tying. "What is *egg-rasher*? Did I depend on it last week? Or is it greater than other things that went with the war? I say, let *egg-rasher* perish in the flames! Let it go where everything else has gone. Nothing puzzles God."

Thea Astley

Born in 1925, in Brisbane, Australia, Thea Astley graduated from the University of Queensland in 1947 and went on to teach English at Macquarie University in Sydney. Author of more than a dozen books of fiction—including such novels as *The Slow Natives* (1965), *An Item from the Late News* (1982), *Reaching Tin River* (1990), and *Coda* (1994)—Astley has won numerous literary awards in Australia, and she has slowly acquired an admiring, discriminating readership for her verbal economy and for her unsentimental renderings of ordinary people. In her writing, she fastens shrewdly on their ambitions, weaknesses, lusts (for power, most notably), and their desperate refusals to deal with these drives and shortcomings except through violence. While she is often characterized as a caustically witty writer, Astley is far more sympathetic to human weakness than such a portrayal might suggest, but she is never tolerant of stupidity, in women or in men.

If her novels, as one reviewer commented in 1990, tread the "fine line between going crazy and going on," so do the stories in *Hunting the Wild Pineapple* (1979). Along with the other stories in this collection, "A Northern Belle" is told by a single narrator, a cynical, one-legged misfit whose own youth is recounted in *The Slow Natives* (1965). In the short stories, the narrator has grown old but not exactly up. He now runs a seedy motel in what might be called "remote" Queensland (Astley's recurrent setting). Through these stories, he filters to his listeners the lives of his fellow citizens, strangers who dwell together in the same small town. Developing incrementally, as one set of contraries breaks into another, "A Northern Belle" tells of the corrosive presumptuousness of "superiority" and of the devastating consequences of one Aboriginal man's gesture of concern. In its stylistic dexterity, and in its cogent analysis of the insidiousness of race and class "categories," the story invites comparison with William Faulkner's "Dry September."

A Northern Belle

The night Willy Fourcorners sat with me, awkward in his Christian clothing, he told me, between the clubbing blocks of rain, what it was like sometimes to be black in these parts. He's sat with me other nights as well and what he told me of this one or that, this place or that, was like taking a view from the wrong side of the fence. Wrong's not the word. Photographing in shadow, the object that is? No. I'm still hunting the wild simile. It was . . . it was like inspecting the negative, framing and hanging its reversals, standing back to admire, then crying in despair, 'But it's all different!'

People I knew, he knew, but he knew them some other-how — as if he saw Lawyer Galipo and Father Rassini from the lee side of the banks of heaven. I asked him once why he'd ever left his little house on the outskirts of Tobaccotown, and he was silent a long time. I coddled his silence and at last he told me. I put his story onto their stories and still I get one story.

This is Willy's story, my words.

■ ■ ■

She was born in one of those exhausted, fleetingly timbered places that sprang up round the tin mines of the north. Not in the poverty of a digger's shack, let it be understood, but in the more impressive veranda'd sprawl of one of those cedar houses that loiter in heavy country gardens. How capture the flavour of those years? Horse-rumps, sweat, hard liquor, crippled shanties, all forgotten in the spacious hours after lunch and before tea when baking fragrance settled as gently as the shadows across and into the passion-vined trellis.

A porky child with a fine cap of almost white dead-straight hair, her body gave no indication of the handsome bones that were to emerge in late adolescence. Skip some years. Now we have her at fourteen bounding confidently across the town hard-court, shimmering with sweat, her hair longer now, darkening now, still fine and unmanageable; but it's still no pointer to the strong-minded Clarice of nineteen who, despite a profile of pleasing symmetry, still boyishly racquet-scooped balls, served low and hard, and later dispensed lemon squash in the tin side-line shed where other acceptables of the town gathered each Saturday afternoon.

She had early the confidence of her class. Her father was a mine manager and owner. 'AG' they called him, and he knew to a nicety what line of familiarity to draw with the blacks who still hung about the perimeters of town, even instigating a curfew for them, but was less certain when it came to men of his own colour. Which was either bright red or mottled white. In snapshots from the period he, heavily moustached and mutton-chopped beside his wife, dominated rows of sawney after-picnic guests. She always appeared formidably silked and hatted and her bust was frightening. 'Breasts' is somehow too pretty, too delicate a word to describe that shelf of righteousness on which many a local upstart had foundered. Along with the bust was a condescending familiarity with the town's priest, two ministers of other religions, and four members of parliament whom she had seen come and helped go. Clarice was an only child, not as much of a son as the father had hoped for and something less of a daughter; but with the years her looks fined and softened; and if she was not in fact a beauty privilege made her just as desirable in a country where a fine bank account is as good for launching a thousand ships as a face: it's even better.

Her mother was determined Clarice would marry well, but no one was ever quite well enough.

Motor-cars and Clarice's teens created small tensions. There were various young men; but the town had little to offer beyond bank- and railway-clerks, or the sons of Italian tobacco farmers whose morals the mother suspected to be doubtful. Should too long a time elapse between the drawing-up of a young man's car and Clarice's flushed entry to the house, her mother would tighten her mouth, draw up that juridical bust, and struggle to find words that were at once proper and admonitory. She was rarely able to draw that nice balance and one afternoon, as she worked with her daughter in the kitchen crumbing butter and flour for scones, she said without preamble and quite formally:

'I was once attacked by a sexually maddened blackfellow.'

Clarice was startled.

'That is why.' Her mother shut her lips tightly and a little line was ruled.

'Why what?'

'Why you must keep men — all men — at a distance.'

'All men?' inquired Clarice. 'Or just sexually maddened blackfellows?'

'You are too young, Clarice,' her mother said sharply, 'to use such words. Girls of sixteen should not even know such words.'

'But I don't understand,' Clarice persisted. 'Were you —?' she hesitated. 'Harmed' seemed not an exact enough word. 'Were you carnally known?'

Her mother fainted.

'I do not know where,' she later gabbled to Clarice's father, 'where this — this child — could pick up such . . . I have done all . . . appalling knowledge . . . how the good nuns . . . wherever . . . she must be protected from. . . .'

She spoke at length to her daughter on the necessity of virtue, the rigours of beauty, of chastity, the clean mind, and the need to expunge lust. She went so far as to summon Father Rassini to give spiritual advice. She read her daughter an improving poem. Clarice listened to all this with an expression on her face as if she were trying to remember a knitting pattern. Young men were discouraged from calling. Her current bank-clerk went away in the army and Clarice, after dreadful scenes in which she finally proved herself her father's daughter, took the little branch train to the coast, caught the main line south, and burrowed into essential war industry.

The city was only partly strange to her, for she had been educated at a southern convent where her only achievements had been to stagger the nuns by the ferocity with which she played badminton and Mendelssohn's *Rondo Capriccioso*. She revealed no other talents. They taught her a little refined typing and book-keeping, insufficient to addle or misdirect any feminine drives; enough French to cope with a wine list in the better restaurants; and some basic techniques in watercolours. She had a full and vigorous voice that dominated, off-key, the contralto section of the school choir for three years, but even this mellowed into suitable nuances before the onslaught of the mistress in charge of boarders.

'My dear Clarice,' she would reprove icily, 'you are not a man.'

'Non, ma mère,' Clarice would reply dutifully, giving the little curtsey this particular order required.

'And further, you seem to forget that men do not. . . . oh, never mind!' Mother Sulpice rolled her fine brown eyes upwards, a kind of ecstatic St Teresa, and swished off with her beads rattling.

The boarders pondered Mother Sulpice.

'You can see she was quite beautiful,' Clarice's best friend, a thumping girl, commented doubtfully, 'Quite Renaissance.'

'Do you think she was jilted in love?' The students spent much time in these speculations.

'Oh, I heard. I heard.'

'What? What did you hear?'

'I shouldn't say.'

'Oh, come on! What?'

'My mother told me something.'

'Told you what?'

'I shouldn't really say.'

'Oh, yes you should,' Clarice insisted. She kicked quite savagely at the iron railing of the terrace that looked out over Brisbane hills. 'By not telling me you are creating an occasion of sin.'

Thumper went pink. 'I'm not. How could I be?'

'Who knows what I shall think,' Clarice said cunningly. 'I could think almost anything. In fact, I do think almost anything.'

She looked slyly at her friend and observed the moral contortion with interest.

'You've got to promise,' Thumper said, 'that you won't tell.'

'Well?'

'Do you promise?'

'Of course.'

'Well,' Thumper said with a pretty play of hesitancy, 'well, she was engaged. Before she entered.'

'And what then?'

'He died. He was killed in France. It wasn't,' she said, lowering her voice in horror, 'a true vocation.'

'Oh, stuff that,' Clarice said. 'How did it happen?'

'Mummy said it was quite tragic.' Clarice saw her friend's eyes grow moist and noticed she was getting a new pimple. 'He was running to regain the trenches and he ran the wrong way. He was dreadfully short-sighted.'

Clarice wanted to laugh. Instead, she looked at her friend hard and asked, 'Do you think they'd had sexual intercourse?'

'Now you *will* have to go to confession!' her friend said.

'Poor Mother Sulpice!' Clarice sighed.

But it was for her, perhaps for the wrong reasons, transfiguration.

She studied the nun's graceful walk, imitated the Isadora-like arabesques of her hands, modulated her voice, and began training her hair into expressive curves across her ears.

'How Clarice has changed!' the nuns observed with relief. 'She's growing up at last.'

In class, her mind closed to the finer points of the redundant *ne*, she sought for and thought she discovered the delicate prints of tragedy on Mother Sulpice's completely calm face.

'That will be the way I will bear it,' she said to herself.

After she left home the first job she obtained was as an office assistant in a factory supplying camouflage tents to the troops. She left the day the senior accountant, who was married, suggested they take in dinner and a show. When she leapt offendedly onto a tram, an American serviceman asked could he help her with her bag. She had no bag but was so confused by the nature of his offer that before she had gone three blocks she found herself in conversation with him. He told her many lies, but those she most vividly remembered were about a cotton plantation in Georgia, an interrupted semester at Yale, and no engagement of the heart, legal or otherwise. As she dressed in her YWCA cubicle for her third outing with him, she kept telling herself it was Mother Sulpice all over again, and she dropped her firm tanned neck, glanced back into the speckly mirror, and lowered her eyes in unconscious but perfect parody.

On the sixth outing seven days after they had met, he attempted to take her to bed, but she resisted with much charm. On the seventh he told her he had been drafted to the Pacific and they then exchanged deeply emotional letters that she read again and again, all the time thanking God for the good training which had prevented 'that' from happening. 'That' was happening all about her. Thumper was pregnant to a marine who had crossed the horizon without leaving any other memento of his visit. Men were all like that, Thumper assured Clarice between her sobs. Clarice thought it a pity her nose got so red when she cried.

Clarice managed to repress her feelings of righteousness and exultation that she was the one spared, and after she had seen her friend take a sad train back to her stunned parents up country she slid into Thumper's job in an army canteen. She was totally unprepared for a letter some months later from Roy telling her he had married a nurse in Guam because he had to. 'Honey,' he wrote, 'you will always be very special to me. You will always be my one true love, the purest I have ever known.' He was lying again, but she was spared the knowledge of this.

She was not built for pathos. The troubles of others found in her a grotesque response of incomprehension. She kept meeting more and more men, but they all failed to please, were not rich enough or wise enough or poor enough if wise, or were too worldly or unworldly. And through all of this, growing steadily older and handsomer, she bore her singleness like an outrageous pledge of success.

At parties when other girls more nervous than she spilt claret cup or trifle on the hostess's carpet at those endless bring-a-plate kitchen teas she seemed always to be attending, she would say offhandedly, 'Don't worry. It's not *her* trifle,' and go on flirting tangentially and unconsummatedly with this or that. She was moving up the ranks and knew a lot of colonels now.

When the war was over she settled more or less permanently into a cashier's desk at a large hotel where for half a dozen years she was still courted by desperate interstate commercial travellers who, seeing her framed between the stiff geometry of gladioli, found a *quattrocento* (it was the hairstyle) mystique which they did not recognise as such but longed to explore. She accepted their pre-dinner sherries with every symptom of well-bred pleasure, went to films, dog-races, and car-trials with them, but always bade them firm good-nights outside her own apartment.

Then her hair began to show its first grey.

Her father died suddenly shouting at a foreman; and after Clarice had gone home to help out her mother held onto her for quite a while, determined to see her daughter settled. Rallying from grief, she arranged picnics, dances, barbecues, musical evenings, card suppers; yet even she gave up when Clarice returned home far too early from a picnic race-meeting with a *fin de siècle* languor about the eyes.

'Where's that nice Dick Shepworth?' her mother demanded from a veranda spy-post.

'At the races, I suppose.'

'You left him there?'

'Yes. He is suffering from encroaching youth.'

'But, my God!' cried her mother. 'He's the manager of two cane mills with an interest in a third.'

'He holds his knife badly,' Clarice said, picking up a malformed piece of knitting.

'You must be mad,' her mother said.

'And he chews with his mouth open.'

'Oh, my God!'

She was dead by the end of the party season. Clarice got Father Rassini to bury her alongside AG, sub-divided the property, sold at a profit and, having invested with comfortable wisdom in an American mining corporation, retired into her parents' house and spent her days in steady gardening. It became a show place. It was as if all her restrained fertility poured out into the welter of trees and shrubs; and if the rare and heady perfumes of some of them made occasional sensual onslaughts she refused to acknowledge them.

The day she turned forty she bought herself a dog.

He was a fine labrador who established his rights at once, learnt smartly to keep away from the seedling beds and to share her baked dinner. They ate together on the long veranda which stared down at the mined-out hills beyond the garden, and the tender antithesis of this transferred the deepest of green shadows into her mind, so that she found herself more and more frequently talking to Bixer as if he had just made some comment that deserved her reply. Her dependence on him became engrafted in her days: he killed several snakes for her, barked at the right people, and slept, twitching sympathetically with her insomnia, by the side of her bed. She only had to reach down to pat Roy, a colonel, a traveller, or even Dick Shepworth, and they would respond with a wag of the tail.

Although so many years had passed since her parents' deaths, Clarice still believed she had a position in the town and consequently gave a couple of duty dinner parties each year — but not willingly — to which she invited old school friends, townsfolk who still remembered her father, and occasionally Father Rassini. He dreaded the summons, for she was a bad cook; but attended, always hopeful of some generous donation. Aware of this, she would keep him sweating on her Christmas contribution till it was almost Easter; and when she finally handed him the envelope they both remembered her stoniness as he had talked to her, thirty years ago now, about the sins of the flesh. He'd been young, too; and whenever he sat down to an especially lavish meal at some wealthy parishioner's home he recalled her cool look as she had asked, 'Are you ever tempted, Father?'

As her muscles shrank the garden acre flexed its own, strengthened and grew more robust than a lover. There were rheumatic twinges that worried her. One day when she went to rise from where she had been weeding a splendid planting of dwarf poinsettia, the pain in her back was so violent she lay on the grass panting. Bixer nosed around, worried and whimpering, and she told him it was nothing at all; but she thought it was time she got a little help.

She was fifty when she took in Willy Fourcorners as gardener. He was an elderly Aborigine, very quiet, very gentle, who had been for a long time a lay preacher with one of the churches. Clarice didn't know which one, but she felt this made him respectable. Willy wore a dark suit on Sundays, even in summer, and a tie. He would trudge back from the station sometimes, lugging a battered suitcase and, passing Clarice's house and seeing her wrenching at an overgrowth of acalypha, would raise his stained grey hat and smile. The gesture convinced Clarice that though he was a lesser species he was worthy, and she would permit herself to smile back, but briefly.

'Willy,' she said one day, emerging from the croton hedge, 'Willy, I wonder could I ask your help?'

Willy set down his bag in the dust and rubbed his yellow-palmed hands together.

'Yeah, Miss Geary. What's the trouble then?'

She came straight to the point.

'I need help with the garden, Willy.' She was still used to command and the words came out as less of a request than she intended. She was devastated by the ochreous quality of his skin so close to hers and a kindliness in the old eyes she refused to admit, for she could not believe in a Christian blackskin, preacher or not. 'It's all getting too much for me.'

Willy's face remained polite, concerned but doubtful. He was getting on himself and still worked as a handyman at the hardware store. On week-ends he preached.

'Only got Saturdays,' he said.

'Well, what's wrong with Saturday?'

'I like to keep it for m'self.'

Clarice struggled with outrage.

'But wouldn't you like a little extra money, Willy?'

'Not that little, Miss Geary,' Willy said.

Clarice's irritation riveted at once upon the simple smiling face, and unexpectedly, contrarily, she was delighted with his show of strength.

'I'm a fair woman,' she said. 'You'd get regular wages. What I'd give anyone.'

Willy nodded. He still smiled through the sweat that was running down his face, down his old brown neck and into the elderly serge of his only suit.

'Please,' Clarice heard herself pleading. 'Just occasionally. It would be such a help, Willy. You see, I can't handle the mowing these days.' And she produced for him what she had managed to conceal from almost everyone, a right hand swollen and knobbed with arthritis, the fingers craned painfully away from the thumb into the beginnings of a claw.

Willy looked at her hand steadily and then put out one finger very gently as if he were going to touch it. She tried not to wince.

'That hurts bad, eh?' he said. 'Real bad. I'll pray for you, Miss Geary.'

'Don't pray for me, Willy,' Clarice said impatiently. 'Just mow.'

He grinned at that and looked past her at the thick mat of grass that was starting a choking drive about the base of the trees.

'Saturday,' he said. 'Okay.'

He came every few weeks after that and she paid him well; and after a year, as her right hand became worse and the left developed symptoms, he began to take over other jobs — pruning, weeding, planting out, slapping a coat of paint, fixing a rotted veranda board. She grew to look forward to the clear Saturday mornings when with Bixer, ancient, dilapidated, sniffing behind her, she directed him down side paths as he trimmed and lopped the flashy outbursts of the shrubs. Although at first she tended to treat him and pay him off as she would imagine AG to have done, gradually she became, through her own solitariness, aware of him as a human; so that after a time, instead of returning to the veranda for her cup of tea after taking him his, she got into the habit of joining him at the small table in the side garden.

'Where is it you get to, Willy,' she asked one Saturday morning as they drank their tea, 'when you take the train down to the coast?'

'Don't go to the coast, Miss Geary.'

'Where do you go then?'

'Jus' down as far as Mango.'

'Mango?' Clarice exclaimed. 'Why would you want to go to Mango?'

'Visit m'folks there,' he said. 'Got a sister there. Visit her kids. She got seven.'

'Seven,' Clarice murmured. 'Seven.' She thought of Thumper. 'That's a large number, I must say.'

'They're good kids,' Willy said. 'My sister, see, she'd like me to go an' live down there now they're gettin' on a bit.'

'She's younger than you, then, Willy?'

'Yeah. Fair bit younger.'

'And have you any, Willy? Any children, I mean?' She knew he lived alone, had done since she had come back to live.

'Two,' he said. 'Two boys. Wife died of the second one. But they been gone a long time now. Real long time.'

'Where to?'

'South,' he said. 'Down south.'

'And what do they do? Do they write?'

'Yeah. Come home sometimes an' stay with m'sister. One's a driver for some big factory place. Drives a truck, see? Other feller, he's in the church. He's trainin' to go teachin' one of them mission places.'

'Well, he's certainly done well,' Clarice said. 'You must be very proud of him.'

'Pretty proud,' old Willy said. 'Teachin' up the mission when he's through. Up Bamaga way he'll be. Might get to see him then, eh?'

'Do you get lonely, Willy?' she asked. But he didn't answer.

Bixer developed a growth. When Clarice noticed the swelling in his belly she summoned the vet from Finecut who took one look and said, 'I'll give him a shot if you like.'

'Get out!' Clarice said.

She cared for him as far as she was able, but he could only shamble from bedroom to veranda where he'd lie listless most of the day in the hot northern sun, not even bothering to snap at the flies. He lost control of his bladder and whimpered the first time he disgraced himself on the bedroom floor. Clarice whimpered herself as she mopped up.

Willy found her crying over the dog one Saturday morning. Bixer could hardly move now, but his eyes looked their recognition as Willy bent over him.

'Best you get him put away, Miss Geary,' Willy advised, touching the dog with his gentle fingers. 'Pretty old feller now.'

'Help me, Willy,' she said. 'I can't do that.'

He brought along an old tin of ointment he'd used for eczema on a dog of his own, and though he knew it wouldn't help he rubbed it in carefully, if only to help her.

'There y'are, Miss Geary,' he said looking up from where he knelt by the panting dog. 'That might do the trick.'

She was still tearful but she managed a smile at him.

'Thank you, Willy. You're a good man.'

It didn't do the trick; and when finally on one of the endless bland mornings of that week she found he had dragged away to die under the back garden bushes she could hardly bear it. She sat for a little on the veranda, which became populous with the ghosts of the endless summer parties of her youth. The smack of tennis balls came from a hard-court.

The blurred voices of bank-clerks and railway-clerks and service men and travellers, and even the sound of Dick Shepworth eating, hummed and babbled along the empty spaces where her mother still sat in her righteous silks.

She put on her sun-hat and walked down town to the hardware store, where she found Willy sweeping out the yard.

'You've got to come, Willy,' she said. 'He's dead.'

'Strewth, Miss Geary. I'm real sorry. Real sorry.'

'You'll have to help me bury him, Willy. I can't dig the hole.'

'Strewth, Miss Geary,' Willy said. 'Don' know whether I kin leave.'

He propped himself on his broom handle and regarded her awkwardly. She was trying hard not to cry. He felt all his age, too, leaning there in the hot sun thinking about death.

'I'll fix that,' she said. She was still AG's daughter.

After it was over she made some tea and took it out to the garden. Willy looked hopelessly at her with his older wisdom.

'Don't you worry none, Miss Geary,' he kept saying. 'I'll get you a new little pup. A new one. Me sister, she got plenty. Jus' don' worry, eh?'

But she was sobbing aloud now, frightful gulping sounds coming from her as she laid her head on her arms along the table.

'Please, Miss Geary,' Willy said. 'Please.'

He touched her hand with his worn one, just a flicker, but she did not notice, did not look up, and he rubbed his hand helplessly across his forehead.

'Look,' he said, 'I got to be goin' soon. But true, me sister she's got these two dogs an' they jus' had pups. I'll get you one of theirs, eh? You'd like that. There's this little brown feller, see, with a white patch. He's a great little dog. You'd like that, eh?'

Slowly she lifted her head, her face ruined with weeping, and saw the old black man and the concern scribbled all over his face.

'Oh, Willy,' she said, 'that's so kind of you. It really is. But it won't make any difference.'

'But it will,' Willy argued, human to human. 'Nex' time I come to mow I'll bring him back. You see. You'll love him.'

He pushed his chair back, came round the table and stood beside her, wanting to cry himself a bit, she looked that old an' lost. She looked up at him, messy with grief, and Willy put his old arm round her shoulders and gave her a consoling pat.

'There,' he said. 'Don' you mind none.'

He'd never seen a face distort so.

She began to scream and scream.

Margaret Atwood

Margaret Atwood's international reputation stems from the forceful, witty, analytic character of her style, from the intellectual substance of her feminist argument, from the literary tension she establishes between the humane and the sardonic, and from her sheer productivity. Since 1961 she has published numerous books of poetry, fiction, criticism (including the influential *Survival*, 1972), children's literature, and social commentary. Her volumes of poetry include such feminist texts as *Power Politics* (1971) and an evocative reading of Canadian women's history called *The Journals of Susanna Moodie* (1970); her novels include *The Handmaid's Tale* (1985), a dystopian satire of academic inertia and American fundamentalism. Born in Ottawa in 1939, Atwood moved to Sault Ste. Marie and Toronto as a child; a graduate of Victoria College (Toronto) and Radcliff College (Harvard), she has taught and has been writer-in-residence at a number of universities, an editor for the House of Anansi, a cartoonist for *This Magazine*, president of the Writers' Union of Canada, and an active supporter of Amnesty International. She now lives in Toronto.

"Death by Landscape," which appeared first in *Saturday Night*, is from a collection called *Wilderness Tips* (1991). In one sense, it tells straightforwardly of the force of loss and the power of memory, as a character disappears into the landscape. The author's interest is less in the particulars of this experience, however, than in the resonances. While the "landscape" of the title refers to the surroundings of this particular canoe trip (the story of the accidental death—or was it murder?—of the painter Tom Thomson is not far from the surface here), "landscape" refers at the same time to the ways in which Canadian culture in general—the image of what constitutes Canadian culture, perhaps—has "disappeared" into Group of Seven landscape paintings. The story asks: has the way we see the environment around us been conventionalized by how the Group of Seven painted it? Recurrently, Atwood writes about how people distance themselves from both the horrors around them and the horrors they are reluctant to recognize in themselves. As Rosemary Sullivan writes, in *The Oxford Companion to Canadian Literature*, Atwood has, in her stories, "designs on our psyches—we are to be instructed through the underdarkness so that we can become saner and more resilient."

Death by Landscape

Now that the boys are grown up and Rob is dead, Lois has moved to a condominium apartment in one of the newer waterfront developments. She is relieved not to have to worry about the lawn, or about the ivy pushing its muscular little suckers into the brickwork, or the squirrels gnawing their way into the attic and eating the insulation off the wiring, or about strange noises. This building has a security system, and the only plant life is in pots in the solarium.

Lois is glad she's been able to find an apartment big enough for her pictures. They are more crowded together than they were in the house, but this arrangement gives the walls a European look: blocks of pictures, above and beside one another, rather than one over the chesterfield, one over the fireplace, one in the front hall, in the old acceptable manner of sprinkling art around so it does not get too intrusive. This way has more of an impact. You know it's not supposed to be furniture.

None of the pictures is very large, which doesn't mean they aren't valuable. They are paintings, or sketches and drawings, by artists who were not nearly as well known when Lois began to buy them as they are now. Their work later turned up on stamps, or as silk-screen reproductions hung in the principals' offices of high schools, or as jigsaw puzzles, or on beautifully printed calendars sent out by corporations as Christmas gifts, to their less important clients. These artists painted mostly in the twenties and thirties and forties; they painted landscapes. Lois has two Tom Thomsons, three A.Y. Jacksons, a Lawren Harris. She has an Arthur Lismer, she has a J.E.H. MacDonald. She has a David Milne. They are pictures of convoluted tree trunks on an island of pink wave-smoothed stone, with more islands behind; of a lake with rough, bright, sparsely wooded cliffs; of a vivid river shore with a tangle of bush and two beached canoes, one red, one grey; of a yellow autumn woods with the ice-blue gleam of a pond half-seen through the interlaced branches.

It was Lois who'd chosen them. Rob had no interest in art, although he could see the necessity of having something on the walls. He left all the decorating decisions to her, while providing the money, of course. Because of this collection of hers, Lois's friends — especially the men — have given her the reputation of having a good nose for art investments.

But this is not why she bought the pictures, way back then. She bought them because she wanted them. She wanted something that was in them, although she could not have said at the time what it was. It was not peace: she does not find them peaceful in the least. Looking at them fills her with a wordless unease. Despite the fact that there are no people in them or even animals, it's as if there is something, or someone, looking back out.

■ ■ ■

When she was thirteen, Lois went on a canoe trip. She'd only been on overnights before. This was to be a long one, into the trackless wilderness, as Cappie put it. It was Lois's first canoe trip, and her last.

Cappie was the head of the summer camp to which Lois had been sent ever since she was nine. Camp Manitou, it was called; it was one of the better ones, for girls, though not the best. Girls of her age whose parents could afford it were routinely packed off to such camps, which bore a generic resemblance to one another. They favoured Indian names and had hearty, energetic leaders, who were called Cappie or Skip or Scottie. At these camps you learned to swim well and sail, and paddle a canoe, and perhaps ride a horse or play tennis. When you weren't doing these things you could do Arts and Crafts and turn out dingy, lumpish clay ashtrays for your mother — mothers smoked more, then — or bracelets made of coloured braided string.

■ ■ ■

Cheerfulness was required at all times, even at breakfast. Loud shouting and the banging of spoons on the tables were allowed, and even encouraged, at ritual intervals. Chocolate bars were rationed, to control tooth decay and pimples. At night, after supper, in the dining hall or outside around a mosquito-infested campfire ring for special treats, there were singsongs. Lois can still remember all the words to "My Darling Clementine," and to "My Bonnie Lies Over the Ocean," with acting-out gestures: a rippling of the hands for "the ocean," two hands together under the cheek for "lies." She will never be able to forget them, which is a sad thought.

Lois thinks she can recognize women who went to these camps, and were good at it. They have a hardness to their handshakes, even now; a way of standing, legs planted firmly and farther apart than usual; a way of sizing you up, to see if you'd be any good in a canoe — the front, not the back. They themselves would be in the back. They would call it the stern.

She knows that such camps still exist, although Camp Manitou does not. They are one of the few things that haven't changed much. They now offer copper enamelling and functionless pieces of stained glass baked in electric ovens, though judging from the productions of her friends' grandchildren the artistic standards have not improved.

To Lois, encountering it in the first year after the war, Camp Manitou seemed ancient. Its log-sided buildings with the white cement in between the half-logs, its flagpole ringed with whitewashed stones, its weathered grey dock jutting out into Lake Prospect, with its woven rope bumpers and its rusty rings for tying up, its prim round flowerbed of petunias near the office door, must surely have been there always. In truth it dated only from the first decade of the century; it had been founded by Cappie's parents, who'd thought of camping as bracing to the character, like cold showers, and had been passed along to her as an inheritance, and an obligation.

Lois realized, later, that it must have been a struggle for Cappie to keep Camp Manitou going, during the Depression and then the war, when money did not flow freely. If it had been a camp for the very rich, instead of the merely well off, there would have been fewer problems. But there must have been enough Old Girls, ones with daughters, to keep the thing in operation, though not entirely shipshape: furniture was battered, painted trim was peeling, roofs leaked. There were dim photographs of these Old Girls dotted around the dining hall, wearing ample woollen bathing suits and showing their fat, dimpled legs, or standing, arms twined, in odd tennis outfits with baggy skirts.

In the dining hall, over the stone fireplace that was never used, there was a huge moulting stuffed moose head, which looked somehow carnivorous. It was a sort of mascot; its name was Monty Manitou. The older campers spread the story that it was haunted, and came to life in the dark, when the feeble and undependable lights had been turned off or, due to yet another generator failure, had gone out. Lois was afraid of it at first, but not after she got used to it.

Cappie was the same: you had to get used to her. Possibly she was forty, or thirty-five, or fifty. She had fawn-coloured hair that looked as if it was cut with a bowl. Her head jutted forward, jigging like a chicken's as she strode around the camp, clutching notebooks and checking things off in them. She was like their minister in church: both of them smiled a lot and were anxious because they wanted things to go well; they both had the same overwashed skins and stringy necks. But all this disappeared when Cappie was leading a singsong, or otherwise leading. Then she was happy, sure of herself, her plain face almost luminous. She wanted to cause joy. At these times she was loved, at others merely trusted.

There were many things Lois didn't like about Camp Manitou, at first. She hated the noisy chaos and spoon-banging of the dining hall, the rowdy singsongs at which you were expected to yell in order to show that you were enjoying yourself. Hers was not a household that encouraged yelling. She hated the necessity of having to write dutiful letters to her parents claiming she was having fun. She could not complain, because camp cost so much money.

She didn't much like having to undress in a roomful of other girls, even in the dim light, although nobody paid any attention, or sleeping in a cabin with seven other girls, some of whom snored because they had adenoids or colds, some of whom had nightmares, or wet their beds and cried about it. Bottom bunks made her feel closed in, and she was afraid of falling out of top ones; she was afraid of heights. She got homesick, and suspected her parents of having a better time when she wasn't there than when she was, although her mother wrote to her every week saying how much they missed her. All this was when she was nine. By the time she was thirteen she liked it. She was an old hand by then.

■ ■ ■

Lucy was her best friend at camp. Lois had other friends in winter, when there was school and itchy woollen clothing and darkness in the afternoons, but Lucy was her summer friend.

She turned up the second year, when Lois was ten, and a Bluejay. (Chickadees, Bluejays, Ravens, and Kingfishers — these were the names Camp Manitou assigned to the different age groups, a sort of totemic clan system. In those days, thinks Lois, it was birds for girls, animals for boys: wolves and so forth. Though some animals and birds were suitable and some were not. Never vultures, for instance; never skunks, or rats.)

Lois helped Lucy to unpack her tin trunk and place the folded clothes on the wooden shelves, and to make up her bed. She put her in the top bunk right above her, where she could keep an eye on her. Already she knew that Lucy was an exception, to a good many rules; already she felt proprietorial.

Lucy was from the United States, where the comic books came from, and the movies. She wasn't from New York or Hollywood or Buffalo, the only American cities Lois knew the names of, but from Chicago. Her house was on the lake shore and had gates to it, and grounds. They had a maid, all of the time. Lois's family only had a cleaning lady twice a week.

The only reason Lucy was being sent to *this* camp (she cast a look of minor scorn around the cabin, diminishing it and also offending Lois, while at the same time daunting her) was that her mother had been a camper here. Her mother had been a Canadian once, but had married her father, who had a patch over one eye, like a pirate. She showed Lois the picture of him in her wallet. He got the patch in the war. "Shrapnel," said Lucy. Lois, who was unsure about shrapnel, was so impressed she could only grunt. Her own two-eyed, unwounded father was tame by comparison.

"My father plays golf," she ventured at last.

"*Everyone* plays golf," said Lucy. "My *mother* plays golf."

Lois's mother did not. Lois took Lucy to see the outhouses and the swimming dock and the dining hall with Monty Manitou's baleful head, knowing in advance they would not measure up.

This was a bad beginning; but Lucy was good-natured, and accepted Camp Manitou with the same casual shrug with which she seemed to accept everything. She would make the best of it, without letting Lois forget that this was what she was doing.

However, there were things Lois knew that Lucy did not. Lucy scratched the tops off all her mosquito bites and had to be taken to the infirmary to be daubed with Ozonol. She took her T-shirt off while sailing, and although the counsellor spotted her after a while and made her put it back on, she burnt spectacularly, bright red, with the X of her bathing-suit straps standing out in alarming white; she let Lois peel the sheets of whispery-thin burned skin off her shoulders. When they sang "Alouette" around the campfire, she did not know any of the French words. The difference was that Lucy did not care about the things she didn't know, whereas Lois did.

During the next winter, and subsequent winters, Lucy and Lois wrote to each other. They were both only children, at a time when this was thought to be a disadvantage, so in their letters they pretended to be sisters, or even twins. Lois had to strain a little over this, because Lucy was so blonde, with translucent skin and large blue eyes like a doll's, and Lois was nothing out of the ordinary — just a tallish, thinnish, brownish person with freckles. They signed their letters LL, with the L's entwined together like the monograms on a towel. (Lois and Lucy, thinks Lois. How our names date us. Lois Lane, Superman's girlfriend, enterprising female reporter; "I Love Lucy." Now we are obsolete, and it's little Jennifers, little Emilys, little Alexandras and Carolines and Tiffanys.)

They were more effusive in their letters than they ever were in person. They bordered their pages with X's and O's, but when they met again in the summers it was always a shock. They had changed so much, or Lucy had. It was like watching someone grow up in jolts. At first it would be hard to think up things to say.

But Lucy always had a surprise or two, something to show, some marvel to reveal. The first year she had a picture of herself in a tutu, her hair in a ballerina's knot on the top of her head; she pirouetted around the swimming dock, to show Lois how it was done, and almost fell off. The next year she had given that up and was taking horseback riding. (Camp Manitou did not have horses.) The next year her mother and father had been divorced, and she had a new stepfather, one with both eyes, and a new house, although the maid was the same. The next year, when they had graduated from Bluejays and entered Ravens, she got her period, right in the first week of camp. The two of them snitched some matches from their counsellor, who smoked illegally, and made a small fire out behind the farthest outhouse, at dusk, using their flashlights. They could set all kinds of fires by now; they had learned how in Campcraft. On this fire they burned one of Lucy's used sanitary napkins. Lois is not sure why they did this, or whose idea it was. But she can remember the feeling of deep satisfaction it gave her as the white fluff singed and the blood sizzled, as if some wordless ritual had been fulfilled.

They did not get caught, but then they rarely got caught at any of their camp transgressions. Lucy had such large eyes, and was such an accomplished liar.

■ ■ ■

This year Lucy is different again: slower, more languorous. She is no longer interested in sneaking around after dark, purloining cigarettes from the counsellor, dealing in black-market candy bars. She is pensive, and hard to wake in the mornings. She doesn't like her stepfather, but she doesn't want to live with her real father either, who has a new wife. She thinks her mother may be having a love affair with a doctor; she doesn't know for sure, but she's seen them smooching in his car, out on the driveway, when her stepfather wasn't there. It serves him right. She hates her private school. She has a boyfriend, who is sixteen and works as a gardener's assistant. This is how she met him: in the garden. She describes to Lois what it is like when he kisses her — rubbery at first, but then your knees go limp. She has been forbidden to see him, and threatened with boarding school. She wants to run away from home.

Lois has little to offer in return. Her own life is placid and satisfactory, but there is nothing much that can be said about happiness. "You're so lucky," Lucy tells her, a little smugly. She might as well say *boring* because this is how it makes Lois feel.

■ ■ ■

Lucy is apathetic about the canoe trip, so Lois has to disguise her own excitement. The evening before they are to leave, she slouches into the campfire ring as if coerced, and sits down with a sigh of endurance, just as Lucy does.

Every canoe trip that went out of camp was given a special send-off by Cappie and the section leader and counsellors, with the whole section in attendance. Cappie painted three streaks of red across each of her cheeks with a lipstick. They looked like three-fingered claw marks. She put a blue circle on her forehead with fountain-pen ink, and tied a twisted bandanna around her head and stuck a row of frazzle-ended feathers around it, and wrapped herself in a red-and-black Hudson's Bay blanket. The counsellors, also in blankets but with only two streaks of red, beat on tom-toms made of round wooden cheese boxes with leather stretched over the top and nailed in place. Cappie was Chief Cappeosota. They all had to say "How!" when she walked into the circle and stood there with one hand raised.

Looking back on this, Lois finds it disquieting. She knows too much about Indians: this is why. She knows, for instance, that they should not even be called Indians, and that they have enough worries without other people taking their names and dressing up as them. It has all been a form of stealing.

But she remembers, too, that she was once ignorant of this. Once she loved the campfire, the flickering of light on the ring of faces, the sound of the fake tom-toms, heavy and fast like a scared heartbeat; she loved Cappie in a red blanket and feathers, solemn, as a chief should be, raising her hand and saying, "Greetings, my Ravens." It was not funny, it was not making fun. She wanted to be an Indian. She wanted to be adventurous and pure, and aboriginal.

■ ■ ■

"You go on big water," says Cappie. This is her idea — all their ideas — of how Indians talk. "You go where no man has ever trod. You go many moons." This is not true. They are only going for a week, not many moons. The canoe route is clearly marked, they have gone over it on a map, and there are prepared campsites with names which are used year after year. But when Cappie says this — and despite the way Lucy rolls up her eyes — Lois can feel the water stretching out, with the shores twisting away on either side, immense and a little frightening.

"You bring back much wampum," says Cappie. "Do good in war, my braves, and capture many scalps." This is another of her pretences: that they are boys, and bloodthirsty. But such a game cannot be played by substituting the word "squaw." It would not work at all.

Each of them has to stand up and step forward and have a red line drawn across her cheeks by Cappie. She tells them they must follow in the paths of their ancestors (who most certainly, thinks Lois, looking out the window of her apartment and remembering the family stash of daguerreotypes and sepia-coloured portraits on her mother's dressing table, the stiff-shirted, black-coated, grim-faced men and the beflounced women with their severe hair and their corseted respectability, would never have considered heading off onto an open lake, in a canoe, just for fun).

At the end of the ceremony they all stood and held hands around the circle, and sang taps. This did not sound very Indian, thinks Lois. It sounded like a bugle call at a military post, in a movie. But Cappie was never one to be much concerned with consistency, or with archaeology.

■ ■ ■

After breakfast the next morning they set out from the main dock, in four canoes, three in each. The lipstick stripes have not come off completely, and still show faintly pink, like healing burns. They wear their white denim sailing hats, because of the sun, and thin-striped T-shirts, and pale baggy shorts with the cuffs rolled up. The middle one kneels, propping her rear end against the rolled sleeping bags. The counsellors going with them are Pat and Kip. Kip is no-nonsense; Pat is easier to wheedle, or fool.

There are white puffy clouds and a small breeze. Glints come from the little waves. Lois is in the bow of Kip's canoe. She still can't do a J-stroke very well, and she will have to be in the bow or the middle for the whole trip. Lucy is behind her; her own J-stroke is even worse. She splashes Lois with her paddle, quite a big splash.

"I'll get you back," says Lois.

"There was a stable fly on your shoulder," Lucy says.

Lois turns to look at her, to see if she's grinning. They're in the habit of splashing each other. Back there, the camp has vanished behind the first long point of rock and rough trees. Lois feels as if an invisible rope has broken. They're floating free, on their own, cut loose. Beneath the canoe the lake goes down, deeper and colder than it was a minute before.

"No horsing around in the canoe," says Kip. She's rolled her T-shirt sleeves up to the shoulder; her arms are brown and sinewy, her jaw determined, her stroke perfect. She looks as if she knows exactly what she is doing.

The four canoes keep close together. They sing, raucously and with defiance; they sing "The Quartermaster's Store," and "Clementine," and "Alouette." It is more like bellowing than singing.

After that the wind grows stronger, blowing slantwise against the bows, and they have to put all their energy into shoving themselves through the water.

■ ■ ■

Was there anything important, anything that would provide some sort of reason or clue to what happened next? Lois can remember everything, every detail; but it does her no good.

They stopped at noon for a swim and lunch, and went on in the afternoon. At last they reached Little Birch, which was the first campsite for overnight. Lois and Lucy made the fire, while the others pitched the heavy canvas tents. The fireplace was already there, flat stones piled into a U. A burned tin can and a beer bottle had been left in it. Their fire went out, and they had to restart it. "Hustle your bustle," said Kip. "We're starving."

The sun went down, and in the pink sunset light they brushed their teeth and spat the toothpaste froth into the lake. Kip and Pat put all the food that wasn't in cans into a packsack and slung it into a tree, in case of bears.

Lois and Lucy weren't sleeping in a tent. They'd begged to be allowed to sleep out; that way they could talk without the others hearing. If it rained, they told Kip, they promised not to crawl dripping into the tent over everyone's legs: they would get under the canoes. So they were out on the point.

Lois tried to get comfortable inside her sleeping bag, which smelled of musty storage and of earlier campers, a stale salty sweetness. She curled herself up, with her sweater rolled up under her head for a pillow and her flashlight inside her sleeping bag so it wouldn't roll away. The muscles of her sore arms were making small pings, like rubber bands breaking.

Beside her Lucy was rustling around. Lois could see the glimmering oval of her white face.

"I've got a rock poking into my back," said Lucy.

"So do I," said Lois. "You want to go into the tent?" She herself didn't, but it was right to ask.

"No," said Lucy. She subsided into her sleeping bag. After a moment she said, "It would be nice not to go back."

"To camp?" said Lois.

"To Chicago," said Lucy. "I hate it there."

"What about your boyfriend?" said Lois. Lucy didn't answer. She was either asleep or pretending to be.

There was a moon, and a movement of the trees. In the sky there were stars, layers of stars that went down and down. Kip said that when the stars were bright like that instead of hazy it meant bad weather later on. Out on the lake there were two loons, calling to each other in their insane, mournful voices. At the time it did not sound like grief. It was just background.

■ ■ ■

The lake in the morning was flat calm. They skimmed along over the glassy surface, leaving V-shaped trails behind them; it felt like flying. As the sun rose higher it got hot, almost too hot. There were stable flies in the canoes, landing on a bare arm or leg for a quick sting. Lois hoped for wind.

They stopped for lunch at the next of the named campsites, Lookout Point. It was called this because, although the site itself was down near the water on a flat shelf of rock, there was a sheer cliff nearby and a trail that led up to the top. The top was the lookout, although what you were supposed to see from there was not clear. Kip said it was just a view.

Lois and Lucy decided to make the climb anyway. They didn't want to hang around waiting for lunch. It wasn't their turn to cook, though they hadn't avoided much by not doing it, because cooking lunch was no big deal, it was just unwrapping the cheese and getting out the bread and peanut butter, but Pat and Kip always had to do their woodsy act and boil up a billy tin for their own tea.

They told Kip where they were going. You had to tell Kip where you were going, even if it was only a little way into the woods to get dry twigs for kindling. You could never go anywhere without a buddy.

"Sure," said Kip, who was crouching over the fire, feeding driftwood into it. "Fifteen minutes to lunch."

"Where are they off to?" said Pat. She was bringing their billy tin of water from the lake.

"Lookout," said Kip.

"Be careful," said Pat. She said it as an afterthought, because it was what she always said.

"They're old hands," Kip said.

■ ■ ■

Lois looks at her watch: it's ten to twelve. She is the watch-minder; Lucy is careless of time. They walk up the path, which is dry earth and rocks, big rounded pinky-grey boulders or split-open ones with jagged edges. Spindly balsam and spruce trees grow to either side, the lake is blue fragments to the left. The sun is right overhead; there are no shadows anywhere. The heat comes up at them as well as down. The forest is dry and crackly.

It isn't far, but it's a steep climb and they're sweating when they reach the top. They wipe their faces with their bare arms, sit gingerly down on a scorching-hot rock, five feet from the edge but too close for Lois. It's a lookout all right, a sheer drop to the lake and a long view over the water, back the way they've come. It's amazing to Lois that they've travelled so far, over all that water, with nothing to propel them but their own arms. It makes her feel strong. There are all kinds of things she is capable of doing.

"It would be quite a dive off here," says Lucy.

"You'd have to be nuts," says Lois.

"Why?" says Lucy. "It's really deep. It goes straight down." She stands up and takes a step nearer the edge. Lois gets a stab in her midriff, the kind she gets when a car goes too fast over a bump. "Don't," she says.

"Don't what?" says Lucy, glancing around at her mischievously. She knows how Lois feels about heights. But she turns back. "I really have to pee," she says.

"You have toilet paper?" says Lois, who is never without it. She digs in her shorts pocket.

"Thanks," says Lucy.

They are both adept at peeing in the woods: doing it fast so the mosquitoes don't get you, the underwear pulled up between the knees, the squat with the feet apart so you don't wet your legs, facing downhill. The exposed feeling of your bum, as if someone is looking at you from behind. The etiquette when you're with someone else is not to look. Lois stands up and starts to walk back down the path, to be out of sight.

"Wait for me?" says Lucy.

■ ■ ■

Lois climbed down, over and around the boulders, until she could not see Lucy; she waited. She could hear the voices of the others, talking and laughing, down near the shore. One voice was yelling, "Ants! Ants!" Someone must have sat on an ant hill. Off to the side, in the woods, a raven was croaking, a hoarse single note.

She looked at her watch: it was noon. This is when she heard the shout.

She has gone over and over it in her mind since, so many times that the first, real shout has been obliterated, like a footprint trampled by other footprints. But she is sure (she is almost positive, she is nearly certain) that it was not a shout of fear. Not a scream. More like a cry of surprise, cut off too soon. Short, like a dog's bark.

"Lucy?" Lois said. Then she called "Lucy!" By now she was clambering back up, over the stones of the path. Lucy was not up there. Or she was not in sight.

"Stop fooling around," Lois said. "It's lunch-time." But Lucy did not rise from behind a rock or step out, smiling, from behind a tree. The sunlight was all around; the rocks looked white. "This isn't funny!" Lois said, and it wasn't, panic was rising in her, the panic of a small child who does not know where the bigger ones are hidden. She could hear her own heart. She looked quickly around; she lay down on the ground and looked over the edge of the cliff. It made her feel cold. There was nothing.

She went back down the path, stumbling; she was breathing too quickly; she was too frightened to cry. She felt terrible — guilty and dismayed, as if she had done something very bad, by mistake. Something that could never be repaired. "Lucy's gone," she told Kip.

Kip looked up from her fire, annoyed. The water in the billy can was boiling. "What do you mean, gone?" she said. "Where did she go?"

"I don't know," said Lois. "She's just gone."

No one had heard the shout, but then no one had heard Lois calling, either. They had been talking among themselves, by the water.

Kip and Pat went up to the lookout and searched and called, and blew their whistles. Nothing answered.

Then they came back down, and Lois had to tell exactly what had happened. The other girls all sat in a circle and listened to her. Nobody said anything. They all looked frightened, especially Pat and Kip. They were the leaders. You did not just lose a camper like this, for no reason at all.

"Why did you leave her alone?" said Kip.

"I was just down the path," said Lois. "I told you. She had to go to the bathroom." She did not say *pee* in front of people older than herself.

Kip looked disgusted.

"Maybe she just walked off into the woods and got turned around," said one of the girls.

"Maybe she's doing it on purpose," said another.

Nobody believed either of these theories.

They took the canoes and searched around the base of the cliff, and peered down into the water. But there had been no sound of falling rock; there had been no splash. There was no clue, nothing at all. Lucy had simply vanished.

That was the end of the canoe trip. It took them the same two days to go back that it had taken coming in, even though they were short a paddler. They did not sing.

After that, the police went in a motorboat, with dogs; they were the Mounties and the dogs were German shepherds, trained to follow trails in the woods. But it had rained since, and they could find nothing.

■ ■ ■

Lois is sitting in Cappie's office. Her face is bloated with crying, she's seen that in the mirror. By now she feels numbed; she feels as if she has drowned. She can't stay here. It has been too much of a shock. Tomorrow her parents are coming to take her away. Several of the other girls who were on the canoe trip are also being collected. The others will have to stay, because their parents are in Europe, or cannot be reached.

Cappie is grim. They've tried to hush it up, but of course everyone in camp knows. Soon the papers will know too. You can't keep it quiet, but what can be said? What can be said that makes any sense? "Girl vanishes in broad daylight, without a trace." It can't be believed. Other things, worse things, will be suspected. Negligence, at the very least. But they have always taken such care. Bad luck will gather around

Camp Manitou like a fog; parents will avoid it, in favour of other, luckier places. Lois can see Cappie thinking all this, even through her numbness. It's what anyone would think.

Lois sits on the hard wooden chair in Cappie's office, beside the old wooden desk, over which hangs the thumb-tacked bulletin board of normal camp routine, and gazes at Cappie through her puffy eyelids. Cappie is now smiling what is supposed to be a reassuring smile. Her manner is too casual: she's after something. Lois has seen this look on Cappie's face when she's been sniffing out contraband chocolate bars, hunting down those rumoured to have snuck out of their cabins at night.

"Tell me again," says Cappie, "from the beginning."

Lois has told her story so many times by now, to Pat and Kip, to Cappie, to the police, that she knows it word for word. She knows it, but she no longer believes it. It has become a story. "I told you," she said. "She wanted to go to the bathroom. I gave her my toilet paper. I went down the path, I waited for her. I heard this kind of shout . . ."

"Yes," says Cappie, smiling confidingly, "but before that. What did you say to one another?"

Lois thinks. Nobody has asked her this before. "She said you could dive off there. She said it went straight down."

"And what did you say?"

"I said you'd have to be nuts."

"Were you mad at Lucy?" says Cappie, in an encouraging voice.

"No," says Lois. "Why would I be mad at Lucy? I wasn't ever mad at Lucy." She feels like crying again. The times when she has in fact been mad at Lucy have been erased already. Lucy was always perfect.

"Sometimes we're angry when we don't know we're angry," says Cappie, as if to herself. "Sometimes we get really mad and we don't even know it. Sometimes we might do a thing without meaning to, or without knowing what will happen. We lose our tempers."

Lois is only thirteen, but it doesn't take her long to figure out that Cappie is not including herself in any of this. By *we* she means Lois. She is accusing Lois of pushing Lucy off the cliff. The unfairness of this hits her like a slap. "I didn't!" she says.

"Didn't what?" says Cappie softly. "Didn't what, Lois?"

Lois does the worst thing, she begins to cry. Cappie gives her a look like a pounce. She's got what she wanted.

■ ■ ■

Later, when she was grown up, Lois was able to understand what this interview had been about. She could see Cappie's desperation, her need for a story, a real story with a reason in it; anything but the senseless vacancy Lucy had left for her to deal with. Cappie wanted Lois to supply the reason, to be the reason. It wasn't even for the newspapers or the parents, because she could never make such an accusation without proof. It was for herself: something to explain the loss of Camp Manitou and of all she had worked for, the years of entertaining spoiled children and buttering up parents and making a fool of herself with feathers stuck in her hair. Camp Manitou was in fact lost. It did not survive.

Lois worked all this out, twenty years later. But it was far too late. It was too late even ten minutes afterwards, when she'd left Cappie's office and was walking slowly back to her cabin to pack. Lucy's clothes were still there, folded on the shelves, as if waiting. She felt the other girls in the cabin watching her with speculation in their eyes. *Could she have done it? She must have done it.* For the rest of her life, she has caught people watching her in this way.

Maybe they weren't thinking this. Maybe they were merely sorry for her. But she felt she had been tried and sentenced, and this is what has stayed with her: the knowledge that she had been singled out, condemned for something that was not her fault.

■ ■ ■

Lois sits in the living room of her apartment, drinking a cup of tea. Through the knee-to-ceiling window she has a wide view of Lake Ontario, with its skin of wrinkled blue-grey light, and of the willows of Centre Island shaken by a wind, which is silent at this distance, and on this side of the glass. When there isn't too much pollution she can see the far shore, the foreign shore; though today it is obscured.

Possibly she could go out, go downstairs, do some shopping; there isn't much in the refrigerator. The boys say she doesn't get out enough. But she isn't hungry, and moving, stirring from this space, is increasingly an effort.

She can hardly remember, now, having her two boys in the hospital, nursing them as babies; she can hardly remember getting married, or what Rob looked like. Even at the time she never felt she was paying full attention. She was tired a lot, as if she was living not one life but two: her own, and another, shadowy life that hovered around her and would not let itself be realized — the life of what would have happened if Lucy had not stepped sideways, and disappeared from time.

She would never go up north, to Rob's family cottage or to any place with wild lakes and wild trees and the calls of loons. She would never go anywhere near. Still, it was as if she was always listening for another voice, the voice of a person who should have been there but was not. An echo.

While Rob was alive, while the boys were growing up, she could pretend she didn't hear it, this empty space in sound. But now there is nothing much left to distract her.

She turns away from the window and looks at her pictures. There is the pinkish island, in the lake, with the intertwisted trees. It's the same landscape they paddled through, that distant summer. She's seen travelogues of this country, aerial photographs; it looks different from above, bigger, more hopeless: lake after lake, random blue puddles in dark green bush, the trees like bristles.

How could you ever find anything there, once it was lost? Maybe if they cut it all down, drained it all away, they might find Lucy's bones, some time, wherever they are hidden. A few bones, some buttons, the buckle from her shorts.

But a dead person is a body; a body occupies space, it exists somewhere. You can see it; you put it in a box and bury it in the ground, and then it's in a box in the ground. But Lucy is not in a box, or in the ground. Because she is nowhere definite, she could be anywhere.

And these paintings are not landscape paintings. Because there aren't any landscapes up there, not in the old, tidy European sense, with a gentle hill, a curving river, a cottage, a mountain in the background, a golden evening sky. Instead there's a tangle, a receding maze, in which you can become lost almost as soon as you step off the path. There are no backgrounds in any of these paintings, no vistas; only a great deal of foreground that goes back and back, endlessly, involving you in its twists and turns of tree and branch and rock. No matter how far back in you go, there will be more. And the trees themselves are hardly trees; they are currents of energy, charged with violent colour.

Who knows how many trees there were on the cliff just before Lucy disappeared? Who counted? Maybe there was one more, afterwards.

Lois sits in her chair and does not move. Her hand with the cup is raised halfway to her mouth. She hears something, almost hears it: a shout of recognition, or of joy.

She looks at the paintings, she looks into them. Every one of them is a picture of Lucy. You can't see her exactly, but she's there, in behind the pink stone island or the one behind that. In the picture of the cliff she is hidden by the clutch of fallen rocks towards the bottom, in the one of the river shore she is crouching beneath the overturned canoe. In the yellow autumn woods she's behind the tree that cannot be seen because of the other trees, over beside the blue sliver of pond; but if you walked into the picture and found the tree, it would be the wrong one, because the right one would be further on.

Everyone has to be somewhere, and this is where Lucy is. She is in Lois's apartment, in the holes that open inwards on the wall, not like windows but like doors. She is here. She is entirely alive.

J.G. BALLARD

James Graham Ballard was born in 1930 to British parents and raised in Shanghai, China. When the city fell to the Japanese in 1941, he was briefly separated from his parents, then interned in prisoner-of-war camps until the end of the war. In 1946 he and his parents moved to Britain, where he studied medicine at Cambridge for a couple of years before working as a porter in Covent Garden, then joined the Royal Air Force to be trained as a pilot. His writing career began in the 1950s, with science fiction stories that took as their subject catastrophes and cataclysms overtaking the modern "civilized" world, a subject that would dominate his writing. Early novels like *The Wind from Nowhere* (1962) and *The Drowned World* (1962) portrayed the desolate landscapes of global disasters; later works would retain the images of physical catastrophe, but focused more on what Ballard called "inner space," the private responses of characters confronted by a world breaking down around them. Ballard is particularly interested in the impact on the human psyche of a machine-dominated world, and in novels such as *Crash* (1972) and *Concrete Island* (1974) he pursues modern man's love affair with the machine to violent and extreme conclusions. Critics have traced the source of Ballard's seeming obsession with violence and catastrophe to his childhood experiences in Shanghai, which formed the basis of his 1984 novel *Empire of the Sun*. That work brought him the Guardian Fiction Prize in 1984, and the James Tait Black Memorial Prize in 1985; subsequently the book was adapted for the screen by Tom Stoppard, and filmed by Steven Spielberg (1987). A second novel by Ballard was adapted for the screen: the movie *Crash* (1996) was written and directed by David Cronenberg.

Ballard's rather grim view of life in modern society seems to leave human beings as witnesses to their own destruction, passive figures who take refuge in fantasy or a brutal eroticism. Ballard repeatedly emphasizes how we have allowed ourselves to become enslaved by our own technological ingenuity. In "The Secret History of World War 3" (1988), Ballard shows how technology, in the form of mass communications, can shape our consciousness and define our reality. Despite the story's elements of the absurd, one need only recall the Gulf War of 1991 to recognize the truth behind Ballard's grotesque vision.

The Secret History of World War 3

Now that World War 3 has safely ended, I feel free to comment on two remarkable aspects of the whole terrifying affair. The first is that this long-dreaded nuclear confrontation, which was widely expected to erase all life from our planet, in fact lasted barely four minutes. This will surprise many of those reading the present document, but World War 3 took place on January 27, 1995, between 6:47 and 6:51 p.m. Eastern Standard Time. The entire duration of hostilities, from President

Reagan's formal declaration of war, to the launch of five sea-based nuclear missiles (three American and two Russian), to the first peace-feelers and the armistice agreed by the President and First Secretary Gorbachov, lasted no more than 245 seconds. World War 3 was over almost before anyone realised that it had begun.

The other extraordinary feature of World War 3 is that I am virtually the only person to know that it ever occurred. It may seem strange that a suburban paediatrician living in Arlington, a few miles west of Washington D.C., should alone be aware of this unique historical event. After all, the news of every downward step in the deepening political crisis, the ailing President's declaration of war and the following nuclear exchange, was openly broadcast on nationwide television. World War 3 was not a secret, but people's minds were addressed to more important matters. In their obsessive concern for the health of their political leadership, they were miraculously able to ignore a far greater threat to their own well-being.

Of course, strictly speaking, I was not the only person to have witnessed World War 3. A small number of senior military personnel in the Nato and Warsaw Pact high commands, as well as President Reagan, Secretary Gorbachov and their aides, and the submarine officers who decrypted the nuclear launch codes and sent the missiles on their way (into unpopulated areas of Alaska and eastern Siberia), were well aware that war had been declared, and a cease-fire agreed four minutes later. But I have yet to meet a member of the ordinary public who has heard of World War 3. Whenever I refer to the war people stare at me with incredulity. Several parents have withdrawn their children from the paediatric clinic, obviously concerned for my mental stability. Only yesterday one mother to whom I casually mentioned the war later telephoned my wife to express her anxieties. But Susan, like everyone else, has forgotten the war, even though I have played video-recordings to her of the ABC, NBC and CNN newscasts on January 27 which actually announce that World War 3 has begun.

■ ■ ■

That I alone happened to learn of the war I put down to the curious character of the Reagan third term. It is no exaggeration to say that the United States, and much of the western world, had deeply missed this amiable old actor who retired to California in 1989 after the inauguration of his luckless successor. The multiplication of the world's problems — the renewed energy crises, the second Iran/Iraq conflict, the destabilisation of the Soviet Union's Asiatic republics, the unnerving alliance in the USA between Islam and militant feminism — all prompted an intense nostalgia for the Reagan years. There was an immense affectionate memory of his gaffes and little incompetencies, his fondness (shared by those who elected him) for watching TV in his pyjamas rather than attending to more important matters, his confusion of reality with the half-remembered movies of his youth.

Tourists congregated in their hundreds outside the gates of the Reagans' retirement home in Santa Barbara, and occasionally the former President would totter out to pose on the porch. There, prompted by a still soignée Nancy, he would utter some amiable generality that brought tears to his listeners' eyes, and lifted both their hearts and stock markets around the world. As his successor's term in office drew to its unhappy close, the necessary constitutional amendment was swiftly passed through both Houses of Congress, with the express purpose of seeing that Reagan could enjoy his third term in the White House.

In February 1993, after the first uncontested Presidential election in the history of the United States, more than a million people turned out to cheer his inaugural drive through the streets of Washington, while the rest of the world watched on television. If the cathode eye could weep, it did so then.

Nonetheless, a few doubts remained, as the great political crises of the world stubbornly refused to be banished even by the aged President's ingratiating grin. The Iran/Iraq war threatened to embroil Turkey and Afghanistan. In defiance of the Kremlin, the Baltic republics of the USSR were forming armed militias. Yves Saint Laurent had designed the first chador for the power-dressing Islamicised feminists in the fashionable offices of Manhattan, London and Paris. Could even the Reagan presidency cope with a world so askew?

Along with my fellow-physicians who had watched the President on television, I seriously doubted it. At this time, in the summer of 1994, Ronald Reagan was a man of 83, showing all the signs of advancing senility. Like many old men, he enjoyed a few minutes each day of modest lucidity, during which he might utter some gnomic remark, and then lapse into a glassy twilight. His eyes were now too blurred to read the teleprompter, but his White House staff took advantage of the hearing aid he had always worn to insert a small microphone, so that he was able to recite his speeches by repeating like a child whatever he heard in his ear-piece. The pauses were edited out by the TV networks, but the hazards of remote control were revealed when the President, addressing the Catholic Mothers of America, startled the massed ranks of blue-rinsed ladies by suddenly repeating a studio engineer's aside: 'Shift your ass, I gotta take a leak.'

Watching this robotic figure with his eerie smiles and goofy grins, a few people began to ask if the President was brain-dead, or even alive at all. To reassure the nervous American public, unsettled by a falling stock market and by the news of armed insurrection in the Ukraine, the White House physicians began to release a series of regular reports on the President's health. A team of specialists at the Walter Reed Hospital assured the nation that he enjoyed the robust physique and mental alertness of a man fifteen years his junior. Precise details of Reagan's blood-pressure, his white and red cell counts, pulse and respiration were broadcast on TV and had an immediately calming effect. On the following day the world's stock markets showed a memorable lift, interest rates fell and Secretary Gorbachov was able to announce that the Ukrainian separatists had moderated their demands.

Taking advantage of the unsuspected political asset represented by the President's bodily functions, the White House staff decided to issue their medical bulletins on a weekly basis. Not only did Wall Street respond positively, but opinion polls showed a strong recovery by the Republican Party as a whole. By the time of the mid-term Congressional elections, the medical reports were issued daily, and successful Republican candidates swept to control of both House and Senate thanks to an eve-of-poll bulletin on the regularity of the Presidential bowels.

■ ■ ■

From then on the American public was treated to a continuous stream of information on the President's health. Successive newscasts throughout the day would carry updates on the side-effects of a slight chill or the circulatory benefits of a dip in the White House pool. I well remember watching the news on Christmas Eve as my wife prepared our evening meal, and noticing that details of the President's health occupied five of the six leading news items.

'So his blood sugar is a little down,' Susan remarked as she laid the festival table. 'Good news for Quaker Oats and Pepsi.'

'Really? Is there a connection, for heaven's sake?'

'Much more than you realise.' She sat beside me on the sofa, pepper-mill in hand. 'We'll have to wait for his latest urinalysis. It could be crucial.'

'Dear, what's happening on the Pakistan border could be crucial. Gorbachov has threatened a pre-emptive strike against the rebel enclaves. The US has treaty obligations, theoretically war could —'

'Sh . . .' Susan tapped my knee with the pepper-mill. 'They've just run an Eysenck Personality Inventory — the old boy's scored full marks on emotional resonance and ability to relate. Results corrected for age, whatever that means.'

'It means he's practically a basket case.' I was about to change channels, hoping for some news of the world's real troublespots, but a curious pattern had appeared along the bottom of the screen, some kind of Christmas decoration I assumed, a line of stylised holly leaves. The rhythmic wave stabbed softly from left to right, accompanied by the soothing and nostalgic strains of 'White Christmas.'

'Good God . . .' Susan whispered in awe. 'It's Ronnie's pulse. Did you hear the announcer? "Transmitted live from the Heart of the Presidency." '

■ ■ ■

This was only the beginning. During the next few weeks, thanks to the miracle of modern radio-telemetry, the nation's TV screens became a scoreboard registering every detail of the President's physical and mental functions. His brave, if tremulous heartbeat drew its trace along the lower edge of the screen, while above it newscasters expanded on his daily physical routines, on the 28 feet he had walked in the rose garden, the calorie count of his modest lunches, the results of his latest brain-scan, read-outs of his kidney, liver and lung function. In addition, there was a daunting sequence of personality and IQ tests, all designed to reassure the American public that the man at the helm of the free world was more than equal to the daunting tasks that faced him across the Oval Office desk.

For all practical purposes, as I tried to explain to Susan, the President was scarcely more than a corpse wired for sound. I and my colleagues at the paediatric clinic were well aware of the old man's ordeal in submitting to this battery of tests. However, the White House staff knew that the American public was almost mesmerised by the spectacle of the President's heart-beat. The trace now ran below all other programmes, accompanying sit-coms, basketball matches and old World War 2 movies. Uncannily, its quickening beat would sometimes match the audience's own emotional responses, indicating that the President himself was watching the same war films, including those in which he himself had appeared.

To complete the identification of President, audience and TV screen — a consummation of which his political advisers had dreamed for so long — the White House staff arranged for further layers of information to be transmitted. Soon a third of the nation's TV screens was occupied by print-outs of heartbeat, blood pressure and EEG readings.

Controversy briefly erupted when it became clear that delta waves predominated, confirming the long-held belief that the President was asleep for most of the day. However, the audiences were thrilled to know when Mr Reagan moved into REM sleep, the dream-time of the nation coinciding with that of its chief executive.

Untouched by this endless barrage of medical information, events in the real world continued down their perilous road. I bought every newspaper I could find, but their pages were dominated by graphic displays of the Reagan health bulletins and by expository articles outlining the significance of his liver enzyme functions and the slightest rise or fall in the concentration of the Presidential urine. Tucked away on the back pages I found a few brief references to civil war in the Asiatic republics of the Soviet Union, an attempted pro-Russian putsch in Pakistan, the Chinese invasion of Nepal, the mobilisation of Nato and Warsaw Pact reserves, the reinforcement of the US 5th and 7th Fleets.

But these ominous events, and the threat of a Third World War, had the ill luck to coincide with a slight down-turn in the President's health. First reported on January 20, this trivial cold caught by Reagan from a visiting grandchild drove all other news from the television screens. An army of reporters and film crews camped outside the White House, while a task force of specialists from the greatest research institutions in the land appeared in relays on every channel, interpreting the stream of medical data.

Like a hundred million Americans, Susan spent the next week sitting by the TV set, eyes following the print-out of the Reagan heartbeat.

'It's still only a cold,' I reassured her when I returned from the clinic on January 27. 'What's the latest from Pakistan? There's a rumour that the Soviets have dropped paratroops into Karachi. The Delta force is moving from Subik Bay . . .'

'Not now!' She waved me aside, turning up the volume as an anchorman began yet another bulletin.

'. . . here's an update on our report of two minutes ago. Good news on the President's CAT scan. There are no abnormal variations in the size or shape of the President's ventricles. Light rain is forecast for the D.C. area tonight, and the 8th Air Cavalry have exchanged fire with Soviet border patrols north of Kabul. We'll be back after the break with a report on the significance of that left temporal lobe spike . . .'

'For God's sake, there's no significance.' I took the remote control unit from Susan's clenched hand and began to hunt the channels. 'What about the Russian Baltic Fleet? The Kremlin is putting counter-pressure on Nato's northern flank. The US has to respond . . .'

By luck, I caught a leading network newscaster concluding a bulletin. He beamed confidently at the audience, his glamorous co-presenter smiling in anticipation.

'. . . as of 5:05 Eastern Standard Time we can report that Mr Reagan's inter-cranial pressure is satisfactory. All motor and cognitive functions are normal for a man of the President's age. Repeat, motor and cognitive functions are normal. Now, here's a newsflash that's just reached us. At 2:35 local time President Reagan completed a satisfactory bowel motion.' The newscaster turned to his co-presenter. 'Barbara, I believe you have similar good news on Nancy?'

'Thank you, Dan,' she cut in smoothly. 'Yes, just one hour later, at 3:35 local time, Nancy completed her very own bowel motion, her second for the day, so it's all happening in the First Family.' She glanced at a slip of paper pushed across her desk. 'The traffic in Pennsylvania Avenue is seizing up again, while F-16s of the 6th Fleet have shot down seven MiG 29s over the Bering Strait. The President's blood pressure is 100 over 60. The ECG records a slight left-hand tremor . . .'

'A tremor of the left hand . . .' Susan repeated, clenching her fists. 'Surely that's serious?'

I tapped the channel changer. 'It could be. Perhaps he's thinking about having to press the nuclear button. Or else —'

An even more frightening possibility had occurred to me. I plunged through the medley of competing news bulletins, hoping to distract Susan as I glanced at the evening sky over Washington. The Soviet deep-water fleet patrolled 400 miles from the eastern coast of the United States. Soon mushroom clouds could be rising above the Pentagon.

'. . . mild pituitary dysfunction is reported, and the President's physicians have expressed a modest level of concern. Repeat, a modest level of concern. The President convened the National Security Council some thirty minutes ago. SAC headquarters in Omaha, Nebraska, report all B-52 attack squadrons airborne. Now, I've just been handed a late bulletin from the White House Oncology Unit. A benign skin tumour was biopsied at 4:15 Washington time . . .'

'. . . the President's physicians have again expressed their concern over Mr Reagan's calcified arteries and hardened cardiac valves. Hurricane Clara is now expected to bypass Puerto Rico, and the President has invoked the Emergency War Powers Act. After the break we'll have more expert analysis of Mr Reagan's retrograde amnesia. Remember, this condition can point to suspected Korsakoff syndrome . . .'

'. . . psychomotor seizures, a distorted sense of time, colour changes and dizziness. Mr Reagan also reports an increased awareness of noxious odours. Other late news — blizzards cover the mid-west, and a state of war now exists between the United States and the Soviet Union. Stay tuned to this channel for a complete update on the President's brain metabolism . . .'

■ ■ ■

'We're at war,' I said to Susan, and put my arms around her shoulders. But she was pointing to the erratic heart trace on the screen. Had the President suffered a brain storm and launched an all-out nuclear attack on the Russians? Were the incessant medical bulletins a clever camouflage to shield a volatile TV audience from the consequences of a desperate response to a national emergency? It would take only minutes for the Russian missiles to reach Washington, and I stared at the placid winter sky. Holding Susan in my arms, I listened to the cacophony of medical bulletins until, some four minutes later, I heard:

'. . . the President's physicians report dilated pupils and convulsive tremor, but neurochemical support systems are functioning adequately. The President's brain metabolism reveals glucose production. Scattered snow-showers are forecast overnight, and a cessation of hostilities has been agreed between the US and the USSR. After the break — the latest expert comment on that attack of Presidential flatulence. And why Nancy's left eyelid needed a tuck . . .'

I switched off the set and sat back in the strange silence. A small helicopter was crossing the grey sky over Washington. Almost as an afterthought, I said to Susan: 'By the way, World War 3 has just ended.'

■ ■ ■

Of course, Susan had no idea that the war had ever begun, a common failure among the public at large, as I realised over the next few weeks. Most people had only a vague recollection of the unrest in the Middle East. The news that nuclear bombs had landed in the deserted mountains of Alaska and eastern Siberia was lost in the torrent of medical reports that covered President Reagan's recovery from his cold.

In the second week of February 1995 I watched him on television as he presided over an American Legion ceremony on the White House lawn. His aged, ivory face was set in its familiar amiable grin, his eyes unfocused as he stood supported by two aides, the ever-watchful First Lady standing in her steely way beside him. Somewhere beneath the bulky black overcoat the radio-telemetry sensors transmitted the live print-outs of pulse, respiration and blood pressure that we could see on our screens. I guessed that the President, too, had forgotten that he had recently launched the Third World War. After all, no one had been killed, and in the public's mind the only possible casualty of those perilous hours had been Mr Reagan himself as he struggled to survive his cold.

Meanwhile, the world was a safer place. The brief nuclear exchange had served its warning to the quarrelling factions around the planet. The secessionist movements in the Soviet Union had disbanded themselves, while elsewhere invading armies withdrew behind their frontiers. I could almost believe that World War 3 had been contrived by the Kremlin and the White House staff as a peacemaking device, and that the Reagan cold had been a diversionary trap into which the TV networks and newspapers had unwittingly plunged.

In tribute to the President's recuperative powers, the liner traces of his vital functions still notched their way across our TV screens. As he saluted the assembled veterans of the American Legion, I sensed the audience's collective pulse beating faster when the old actor's heart responded to the stirring sight of these marching men.

Then, among the Medal of Honour holders, I noticed a dishevelled young man in an ill-fitting uniform, out of step with his older companions. He pushed through the marching files as he drew a pistol from his tunic. There was a flurry of confusion while aides grappled with each other around the podium. The cameras swerved to catch the young man darting towards the President. Shots sounded above the wavering strains of the band. In the panic of uniformed men the President seemed to fall into the First Lady's arms and was swiftly borne away.

Searching the print-outs below the TV screen, I saw at once that the President's blood pressure had collapsed. The erratic pulse had levelled out into an unbroken horizontal line, and all respiratory function had ceased. It was only ten minutes later, as news was released of an unsuccessful assassination attempt, that the traces resumed their confident signatures.

Had the President died, perhaps for a second time? Had he, in a strict sense, ever lived during his third term of office? Will some animated spectre of himself, reconstituted from the medical print-outs that still parade across our TV screens, go on to yet further terms, unleashing Fourth and Fifth World Wars, whose secret histories will expire within the interstices of our television schedules, forever lost within the ultimate urinalysis, the last great biopsy in the sky?

Donald Barthelme

Born in Philadelphia, Donald Barthelme (1931–89) was educated in Texas. After graduating from the University of Houston, he worked for a time as a museum director, and also as an editor of *Location*, a journal concerned with art and literature; this interest in the visual arts, including the cinema, is reflected in all his writing. The title of his first collection of short stories, *Come Back, Dr. Caligari* (1964), alludes to an early German film, which employed expressionistic and surrealistic techniques; and Barthelme's extraordinary mixture and manipulation of styles at times seems to approximate film more closely than traditional literary modes. Rejecting literary convention as a means of conveying the writer's sense of absurdity or meaninglessness in life is itself a convention, one that Barthelme inherits from Rabelais, Sterne, and Joyce; but his more immediate literary antecedents are Poe and Kafka. Like them, he conveys a sense of purposeless evil underlying the surface of our lives; his stories are amusing and yet macabre, turning sense into non-sense, and disturbing our notions of reality. In his novel *Snow White* (1967), and such collections of stories as *City Life* (1971), *Great Days* (1979), and *Overnight to Many Distant Cities* (1983), he moves still further away from conventional methods of narration, sometimes combining typographical devices and pictures with his text, to create a dizzying series of surreal and cryptic images. "Report," from *Unspeakable Practices, Unnatural Acts* (1968), is not experimental in terms of technique; but by his adaptation and imitation of scientific jargon, Barthelme projects a bizarre picture of the human potential for self-destruction, in an age when technology seems to have deprived us of the capacity for natural feeling.

Report

Our group is against the war. But the war goes on. I was sent to Cleveland to talk to the engineers. The engineers were meeting in Cleveland. I was supposed to persuade them not to do what they are going to do. I took United's 4:45 from LaGuardia arriving in Cleveland at 6:13. Cleveland is dark blue at that hour. I went directly to the motel, where the engineers were meeting. Hundreds of engineers attended the Cleveland meeting. I noticed many fractures among the engineers, bandages, traction. I noticed what appeared to be fracture of the carpal scaphoid in six examples. I noticed numerous fractures of the humeral shaft, of the os calcis, of the pelvic girdle. I noticed a high incidence of clay-shoveller's fracture. I could not account for these fractures. The engineers were making calculations, taking measurements, sketching on the blackboard, drinking beer, throwing bread, buttonholing employers, hurling glasses into the fireplace. They were friendly.

They were friendly. They were full of love and information. The chief engineer wore shades. Patella in Monk's traction, clamshell fracture by the look of it. He was standing in a slum of beer bottles and microphone cable. "Have some of this chicken à la Isambard Kingdom Brunel the Great Ingineer," he said. "And declare who you are and what we can do for you. What is your line, distinguished guest?"

"Software," I said. "In every sense. I am here representing a small group of interested parties. We are interested in your thing, which seems to be functioning. In the midst of so much dysfunction, function is interesting. Other people's things don't seem to be working. The U.N.'s thing doesn't seem to be working. The democratic left's thing doesn't seem to be working. Buddha's thing—"

"Ask us anything about our thing, which seems to be working," the chief engineer said. "We will open our hearts and heads to you, Software Man, because we want to be understood and loved by the great lay public, and have our marvels appreciated by that public, for which we daily unsung produce tons of new marvels each more life-enhancing than the last. Ask us anything. Do you want to know about evaporated thin-film metallurgy? Monolithic and hybrid integrated-circuit processes? The algebra of inequalities? Optimization theory? Complex high-speed micro-miniature closed and open loop systems? Fixed variable mathematical cost searches? Epitaxial deposition of semi-conductor materials? Gross interfaced space gropes? We also have specialists in the cuckoo-flower, the doctorfish, and the dumdum bullet as these relate to aspects of today's expanding technology, and they do in the damnedest ways."

I spoke to him then about the war. I said the same things people always say when they speak against the war. I said that the war was wrong. I said that large countries should not burn down small countries. I said that the government had made a series of errors. I said that these errors once small and forgivable were now immense and unforgivable. I said that the government was attempting to conceal its original errors under layers of new errors. I said that the government was sick with error, giddy with it. I said that ten thousand of our soldiers had already been killed in pursuit of government's errors. I said that tens of thousands of the enemy's soldiers and civilians had been killed because of various errors, ours and theirs. I said that we are responsible for errors made in our name. I said that the government should not be allowed to make additional errors.

"Yes, yes," the chief engineer said, "there is doubtless much truth in what you say, but we can't possibly *lose* the war, can we? And stopping is losing, isn't it? The war regarded as a process, stopping regarded as an abort? We don't know *how* to lose a war. That skill is not among our skills. Our array smashes their array, that is what we know. That is the process. That is what is.

"But let's not have any more of this dispiriting downbeat counterproductive talk. I have a few new marvels here I'd like to discuss with you just briefly. A few new marvels that are just about ready to be gaped at by the admiring layman. Consider for instance the area of realtime online computer-controlled wish evaporation. Wish evaporation is going to be crucial in meeting the rising expectations of the world's peoples, which are as you know rising entirely too fast."

I noticed then distributed about the room a great many transverse fractures of the ulna. "The development of the pseudo-ruminant stomach for underdeveloped peoples," he went on, "is one of our interesting things you should be interested in. With the pseudo-ruminant stomach they can chew cuds, that is to say, eat grass. Blue is the most popular color worldwide and for that reason we are working with certain strains of your native Kentucky *Poa pratensis*, or bluegrass, as the staple input for the p/r stomach cycle, which would also give a shot in the arm to our balance-of-payments thing don't you know. . . . " I noticed about me then a great number of metatarsal fractures in banjo splints. "The kangaroo initiative . . . eight hundred thousand harvested last year . . . highest percentage of edible protein of any herbivore yet studied. . . . "

"Have new kangaroos been planted?"

The engineer looked at me.

"I intuit your hatred and jealousy of our thing," he said. "The ineffectual always hate our thing and speak of it as anti-human, which is not at all a meaningful way to speak of our thing. Nothing mechanical is alien to me," he said (amber spots making bursts of light in his shades), "because I am human, in a sense, and if I think it up, then 'it' is human too, whatever 'it' may be. Let me tell you, Software Man, we have been damned forbearing in the matter of this little war you declare yourself to be interested in. Function is the cry, and our thing is functioning like crazy. There are things we could do that we have not done. Steps we could take that we have not taken. These steps are, regarded in a certain light, the light of our enlightened self-interest, quite justifiable steps. We could, of course, get irritated. We could, of course, *lose patience*.

"We could, of course, release thousands upon thousands of self-powered crawling-along-the-ground lengths of titanium wire eighteen inches long with a diameter of .0005 centimetres (that is to say, invisible) which, scenting an enemy, climb up his trouser leg and wrap themselves around his neck. We have developed those. They are within our capabilities. We could, of course, release in the arena of the upper air our new improved pufferfish toxin which precipitates an identity crisis. No special technical problems there. That is almost laughably easy. We could, of course, place up to two million maggots in their rice within twenty-four hours. The maggots are ready, massed in secret staging areas in Alabama. We have hypodermic darts capable of piebalding the enemy's pigmentation. We have rots, blights, and rusts capable of attacking his alphabet. Those are dandies. We have a hut-shrinking chemical which penetrates the fibres of the bamboo, causing it, the hut, to strangle its occupants. This operates only after 10 P.M., when people are sleeping. Their mathematics are at the mercy of a suppurating surd we have invented. We have a family of fishes trained to attack their fishes. We have the deadly testicle-destroying telegram. The cable companies are cooperating. We have a green substance that, well, I'd rather not talk about. We have a secret word that, if pronounced, produces multiple fractures in all living things in an area the size of four football fields."

"That's why—"

"Yes. Some damned fool couldn't keep his mouth shut. The point is that the whole structure of enemy life is within our power to *rend, vitiate, devour*, and *crush*. But that's not the interesting thing."

"You recount these possibilities with uncommon relish."

"Yes I realize that there is too much relish here. But you must realize that these capabilities represent in and of themselves highly technical and complex and interesting problems and hurdles on which our boys have expended many thousands of hours of hard work and brilliance. And that the effects are often grossly exaggerated by irresponsible victims. And that the whole thing represents a fantastic series of triumphs for the multi-disciplined problem solving team concept."

"I appreciate that."

"We *could* unleash all this technology at once. You can imagine what would happen then. But that's not the interesting thing."

"What is the interesting thing?"

"The interesting thing is that we have a *moral sense*. It is on punched cards, perhaps the most advanced and sensitive moral sense the world has ever known."

"Because it is on punched cards?"

"It considers all considerations in endless and subtle detail," he said. "It even quibbles. With this great new moral tool, how can we go wrong?

I confidently predict that, although we *could* employ all this splendid new weaponry I've been telling you about, *we're not going to do it*."

"We're not going to do it?"

I took United's 5:44 from Cleveland arriving at Newark at 7:19. New Jersey is bright pink at that hour. Living things move about the surface of New Jersey at that hour molesting each other only in traditional ways. I made my report to the group. I stressed the friendliness of the engineers. I said, It's all right. I said, We have a moral sense. I said, *We're not going to do it*. They didn't believe me.

Clark Blaise

Associated in the 1960s with a group called the Montreal Story Teller, Clark Blaise has moved repeatedly between Canada and the United States. Born to Canadian parents in Fargo, North Dakota, in 1940, he grew up in Manitoba, on the urban American east coast, and in the rural South, and was educated in Ohio and Iowa. From 1966 to 1978 he lived in Montreal, then spent two years teaching at York University in Toronto, before returning to the US in 1980. He now lives in San Francisco. His several books, including the collection *Resident Alien* (1986), reflect this mobility, assert his French heritage and his American upbringing, and focus on the problems of alienation that in various ways beset modern men and women. *Lunar Attractions* (1979) won the *Books in Canada* First Novel award. His widely praised short story collection *A North American Education* (1973) expresses even by its title the continental range of his background; and the stories themselves, cast as personal narratives, draw readers into an intensely immediate world. The second-person narrative technique of "Eyes" enforces such a reaction, and the story's sombre tone—the watchfulness it suggests—skillfully links method with meaning. But the immediacy rises from the author's intention as well.

In an essay on the short story form—"To Begin, To Begin," the title a quotation from Donald Barthelme—Blaise asserts that theme is of secondary importance to the writer who is undergoing the process of writing a story. Narrative climax and the elegant contrivance of resolution, however important, are also of less moment than the mysteries of genesis. A good story, he says, is made by its first sentence and by the embellishments that the first paragraph gives it. The first sentence must imply its own opposite—"a good sensuous description of May sets up the possibility of a May disaster"; it must start the story neither too late nor too soon; it must disrupt and reorder the reader's sense of how things are; and it must have a rhythm all its own. The moment plot appears, in "the simple terrifying adverb: *Then,*" the characters start to realize the implications of the initial mysteries; such a moment "is the cracking of the perfect, smug egg of possibility." But what preceded it is what allowed it; in the beginning is the identity that the story seems later to acquire or reveal. And in realizing and appreciating this identity, readers engage themselves with the artist in the creation of the story's own truths.

Eyes

You jump into this business of a new country cautiously. First you choose a place where English is spoken, with doctors and bus lines at hand, and a supermarket in a *centre d'achats* not too far away. You ease yourself into the city, approaching by car or bus down a single artery, aiming yourself along the boulevard that begins small and tree-lined in your suburb but broadens into the canyoned aorta of the city five miles beyond. And by that first winter when you know the routes and bridges, the standard congestions reported from the helicopter on your favorite radio station, you start to think of moving. What's the good of a place like this when two of your neighbors have come from Texas and the French paper you've dutifully subscribed to arrives by mail two days late? These French are all around you, behind the counters at the shopping center, in a house or two on your block; why isn't your little boy learning French at least? Where's the nearest *maternelle*? Four miles away.

In the spring you move. You find an apartment on a small side street where the dogs outnumber children and the row houses resemble London's, divided equally between the rundown and remodeled. Your neighbors are the young personalities of French television who live on delivered chicken, or the old pensioners who shuffle down the summer sidewalks in pajamas and slippers in a state of endless recuperation. Your neighbors pay sixty a month for rent, or three hundred; you pay two-fifty for a two-bedroom flat where the walls have been replastered and new fixtures hung. The bugs *d'antan* remain, as well as the hulks of cars abandoned in the fire alley behind, where downtown drunks sleep in the summer night.

Then comes the night in early October when your child is coughing badly, and you sit with him in the darkened nursery, calm in the bubbling of a cold-steam vaporizer while your wife mends a dress in the room next door. And from the dark, silently, as you peer into the ill-lit fire alley, he comes. You cannot believe it at first, that a rheumy, pasty-faced Irishman in slate-gray jacket and rubber-soled shoes has come purposely to *your* small parking space, that he has been here before and he is not drunk (not now, at least, but you know him as a panhandler on the main boulevard a block away), that he brings with him a crate that he sets on end under your bedroom window and raises himself to your window ledge and hangs there nose-high at a pencil of light from the ill-fitting blinds. And there you are, straining with him from the uncurtained nursery, watching the man watching your wife, praying silently that she is sleeping under the blanket. The man is almost smiling, a leprechaun's face that sees what you cannot. You are about to lift the window and shout, but your wheezing child lies just under you; and what of your wife in the room next door? You could, perhaps, throw open the window and leap to the ground, tackle the man before he runs and smash his face into the bricks, beat him senseless then call the cops . . . Or better, find the camera, affix the flash, rap once at the window

maternelle = nursery school

and shoot when he turns. Do nothing and let him suffer. *He is at your mercy,* no one will ever again be so helpless—but what can you do? You know, somehow, he'll escape. If you hurt him, he can hurt you worse, later, viciously. He's been a regular at your window, he's watched the two of you when you prided yourself on being young and alone and masters of the city. He knows your child and the park he plays in, your wife and where she shops. He's a native of the place, a man who knows the city and maybe a dozen such windows, who knows the fire escapes and alleys and roofs, knows the habits of the city's heedless young.

And briefly you remember yourself, an adolescent in another country slithering through the mosquito-ridden grassy fields behind a housing development, peering into those houses where newlyweds had not yet put up drapes, how you could spend five hours in a motionless crouch for a myopic glimpse of a slender arm reaching from the dark to douse a light. Then you hear what the man cannot; the creaking of your bed in the far bedroom, the steps of your wife on her way to the bathroom, and you see her as you never have before: blond and tall and rangily built, a north-Europe princess from a constitutional monarchy, sensuous mouth and prominent teeth, pale, tennis-ball breasts cupped in her hands as she stands in the bathroom's light.

"How's Kit?" she asks. "I'd give him a kiss except that there's no blind in there," and she dashes back to bed, nude, and the man bounces twice on the window ledge.

"You coming?"

You find yourself creeping from the nursery, turning left at the hall and then running to the kitchen telephone; you dial the police, then hang up. How will you prepare your wife, not for what is happening, but for what has already taken place?

"It's stuffy in here," you shout back, "I think I'll open the window a bit." You take your time, you stand before the blind blocking his view if he's still looking, then bravely you part the curtains. He is gone, the crate remains upright. "Do we have any masking tape?" you ask, lifting the window a crack.

And now you know the city a little better. A place where millions come each summer to take pictures and walk around must have its voyeurs too. And that place in all great cities where rich and poor coexist is especially hard on the people in-between. It's health you've been seeking, not just beauty; a tough urban health that will save you money in the bargain, and when you hear of a place twice as large at half the rent, in a part of town free of Texans, English, and French, free of young actors and stewardesses who deposit their garbage in pizza boxes, you move again.

It is, for you, a city of Greeks. In the summer you move you attend a movie at the corner cinema. The posters advertise a war movie, in Greek, but the uniforms are unfamiliar. Both sides wear mustaches, both sides handle machine guns, both leave older women behind dressed in black. From the posters outside there is a promise of sex; blond women in slips, dark-eyed peasant girls. There will be rubble, executions against a wall. You can follow the story from the stills alone: mustached boy goes to war, embraces dark-eyed village girl. Black-draped mother and admiring young brother stand behind. Young soldier, mustache fuller, embraces blond prostitute on a tangled bed. Enter soldier, boy hides under sheets. Final shot, back in village. Mother in black; dark-eyed village girl in black. Young brother marching to the front.

You go in, pay your ninety cents, pay a nickel in the lobby for a wedge of *halvah*-like sweets. You understand nothing, you resent their laughter and you even resent the picture they're running. Now you know the Greek for "Coming Attractions," for this is a gangster movie at least thirty years old. The eternal Mediterranean gangster movie set in Athens instead of Naples or Marseilles, with smaller cars and narrower roads, uglier women and more sinister killers. After an hour the movie flatters you. No one knows you're not a Greek, that you don't belong in this theatre, or even this city. That, like the Greeks, you're hanging on.

Outside the theater the evening is warm and the wide sidewalks are clogged with Greeks who nod as you come out. Like the Ramblas in Barcelona, with children out past midnight and families walking back and forth for a long city block, the men filling the coffeehouses, the women left outside, chatting. Not a blond head on the sidewalk, not a blond head for miles. Greek music pours from the coffeehouses, flies stumble on the pastry, whole families munch their *torsades molles* as they walk. Dry goods are sold at midnight from the sidewalk, like New York fifty years ago. You're wandering happily, glad that you moved, you've rediscovered the innocence of starting over.

Then you come upon a scene directly from Spain. A slim blond girl in a floral top and white pleated skirt, tinted glasses, smoking, with bad skin, ignores a persistent young Greek in a shiny Salonika suit. "Whatsamatta?" he demands, slapping a ten-dollar bill on his open palm. And without looking back at him she drifts closer to the curb and a car makes a sudden squealing turn and lurches to a stop on the cross street. Three men are inside, the back door opens and not a word is exchanged

torsades molles = soft, twisted rolls

as she steps inside. How? What refinement of gesture did we immigrants miss? You turn to the Greek boy in sympathy, you know just how he feels, but he's already heading across the street, shouting something to his friends outside a barbecue stand. You have a pocketful of bills and a Mediterranean soul, and money this evening means a woman, and blond means whore and you spend it all on another blond with open pores; all this a block from your wife and tenement. And you hurry home.

Months later you know the place. You trust the Greeks in their stores, you fear their tempers at home. Eight bathrooms adjoin a central shaft, you hear the beatings of your son's friends, the thud of fist on bone after the slaps. Your child knows no French, but he plays cricket with Greeks and Jamaicans out in the alley behind Pascal's hardware. He brings home the oily tires from the Esso station, plays in the boxes behind the appliance store. You watch from a greasy back window, at last satisfied. None of his friends is like him, like you. He is becoming Greek, becoming Jamaican, becoming a part of this strange new land. His hair is nearly white; you can spot him a block away.

On Wednesdays the butcher quarters his meat. Calves arrive by refrigerator truck, still intact but for their split-open bellies and sawed-off hooves. The older of the three brothers skins the carcass with a small thin knife that seems all blade. A knife he could shave with. The hide rolls back in a continuous flap, the knife never pops the membrane over the fat.

Another brother serves. Like yours, his French is adequate. "*Twa lif d'hamburger*," you request, still watching the operation on the rickety sawhorse. Who could resist? It's a Levantine treat, the calf's stumpy legs high in the air, the hide draped over the edge and now in the sawdust, growing longer by the second.

The store is filling. The ladies shop on Wednesday, especially the old widows in black overcoats and scarves, shoes and stockings. Yellow, mangled fingernails. Wednesdays attract them with boxes in the window, and they call to the butcher as they enter, the brother answers, and the women dip their fingers in the boxes. The radio is loud overhead, music from the Greek station.

"Une et soixante, m'sieur. Du bacon, jambon?"

And you think, taking a few lamb chops but not their saltless bacon, how pleased you are to manage so well. It is a Byzantine moment with blood and widows and sides of dripping beef, contentment in a snowy slum at five below.

Twa lif = trois livres (3 pounds).

The older brother, having finished the skinning, straightens, curses, and puts away the tiny knife. A brother comes forward to pull the hide away, a perfect beginning for a gameroom rug. Then, bending low at the rear of the glistening carcass, the legs spread high and stubby, the butcher digs in his hands, ripping hard where the scrotum is, and pulls on what seems to be a strand of rubber, until it snaps. He puts a single glistening prize in his mouth, pulls again and offers the other to his brother, and they suck.

The butcher is singing now, drying his lips and wiping his chin, and still he's chewing. The old black-draped widows with the parchment faces are also chewing. On leaving, you check the boxes in the window. Staring out are the heads of pigs and lambs, some with the eyes lifted out and a red socket exposed. A few are loose and the box is slowly dissolving from the blood, and the ice beneath.

The women have gathered around the body; little pieces are offered to them from the head and entrails. The pigs' heads are pink, perhaps they've been boiled, and hairless. The eyes are strangely blue. You remove your gloves and touch the skin, you brush against the grainy ear. How the eye attracts you! How you would like to lift one out, press its smoothness against your tongue, then crush it in your mouth. And you cannot. Already your finger is numb and the head, it seems, has shifted under you. And the eye, in panic, grows white as your finger approaches. You would take that last half inch but for the certainty, in this world you have made for yourself, that the eye would blink and your neighbors would turn upon you.

PAUL BOWLES

New York-born Paul Bowles (1910–99) secured recognition for his contribution to film and the performing arts before winning acclaim as a writer. After a short period at the University of Virginia, he travelled to Europe, then studied music with the celebrated American composers Aaron Copeland and Virgil Thomson. Subsequently he entered upon a successful career as a composer of film scores, operas, and ballets, and wrote incidental music for such plays as Tennessee Williams's *Summer and Smoke*. In 1941 his musical accomplishments were rewarded with a Guggenheim Fellowship. While still a young man, Bowles left North America to travel extensively in Europe, Central America, India, and North Africa, and although his work frequently took him back to the United States, he and his wife (the writer Jane Bowles) eventually settled in Morocco. His fascination with the exotic bore fruit in travel essays as well as numerous translations from works in French, Arabic, Spanish, and Italian. He published several novels, including *The Sheltering Sky* (1949) and *Let It Come Down* (1952), and his *Collected Stories 1939–1976* appeared in 1979. *The Sheltering Sky* was made into a film in 1990, directed by Bernardo Bertolucci.

The unusual and exotic settings of Bowles's stories arise naturally from his easy familiarity with many foreign cultures, but they reflect also his dissatisfaction with Western life and manners. Some of his characters are Americans or Europeans who find themselves isolated or alienated in an environment that rejects the materialism and sophistication of the modern West. What they learn offers no consolation: they are met by hostility, even violence, from a way of life that spurns them. Bowles does not offer solutions; he seems to suggest that the search for values is ultimately futile. Despite the bleakness of his vision, however, he is a fine storyteller, with the ability to realize a scene in sharp physical detail while investing it with a sense of mystery. "Allal" (1976) is a transformation tale that blends reality and fantasy in a manner suggestive of the folk tale, dramatically portraying the violence latent in all forms of life. Its Gothic quality is reminiscent of Poe's tales, and it is worth noting that Bowles's first short story collection, *The Delicate Prey* (1950), was dedicated to his mother, "who first read me the stories of Poe."

Allal

He was born in the hotel where his mother worked. The hotel had only three dark rooms which gave on a courtyard behind the bar. Beyond was another smaller patio with many doors. This was where the servants lived, and where Allal spent his childhood.

The Greek who owned the hotel had sent Allal's mother away. He was indignant because she, a girl of fourteen, had dared to give birth while she was working for him. She would not say who the father was, and it angered him to reflect that he himself had not taken advantage of the situation while he had had the chance. He gave the girl three months' wages and told her to go home to Marrakech. Since the cook and his wife liked the girl and offered to let her live with them for a while, he agreed that she might stay on until the baby was big enough to travel. She remained in the back patio for a few months with the cook and his wife, and then one day she disappeared, leaving the baby behind. No one heard of her again.

As soon as Allal was old enough to carry things, they set him to work. It was not long before he could fetch a pail of water from the well behind the hotel. The cook and his wife were childless, so that he played alone.

When he was somewhat older he began to wander over the empty table-land outside. There was nothing else up here but the barracks, and they were enclosed by a high blind wall of red adobe. Everything else was below in the valley: the town, the gardens, and the river winding southward among the thousands of palm trees. He could sit on a point of rock far above and look down at the people walking in the alleys of the town. It was only later that he visited the place and saw what the inhabitants were like. Because he had been left behind by his mother they called him a son of sin, and laughed when they looked at him. It seemed to him that in this way they hoped to make him into a shadow, in order not to have to think of him as real and alive. He awaited with dread the time when he would have to go each morning to the town and work. For the moment he helped in the kitchen and served the officers from the barracks, along with the few motorists who passed through the region. He got small tips in the restaurant, and free food and lodging in a cell of the servants' quarters, but the Greek gave him no wages. Eventually he reached an age when the situation seemed shameful, and he went of his own accord to the town below and began to work, along with other boys of his age, helping to make the mud bricks people used for building their houses.

Living in the town was much as he had imagined it would be. For two years he stayed in a room behind a blacksmith's shop, leading a life without quarrels, and saving whatever money he did not have to spend to keep himself alive. Far from making any friends during this time, he formed a thorough hatred for the people of the town, who never allowed him to forget that he was a son of sin, and therefore not like others, but *meskhot*—damned. Then he found a small house, not much more than a hut, in the palm groves outside the town. The rent was low and no one lived nearby. He went to live there, where the only sound was the wind in the trees, and avoided the people of the town when he could.

One hot summer evening shortly after sunset he was walking under the arcades that faced the town's main square. A few paces ahead of him an old man in a white turban was trying to shift a heavy sack from one shoulder to the other. Suddenly it fell to the ground, and Allal stared as two dark forms flowed out of it and disappeared into the shadows. The old man pounced upon the sack and fastened the top of it, at the same time beginning to shout: Look out for the snakes! Help me find my snakes!

Many people turned quickly around and walked back the way they had come. Others stood at some distance, watching. A few called to the old man: Find your snakes fast and get them out of here! Why are they here? We don't want snakes in this town!

Hopping up and down in his anxiety, the old man turned to Allal. Watch this for me a minute, my son. He pointed at the sack lying on the earth at his feet, and snatching up a basket he had been carrying, went swiftly around the corner into an alley. Allal stood where he was. No one passed by.

It was not long before the old man returned, panting with triumph. When the onlookers in the square saw him again, they began to call out, this time to Allal: Show that berrani the way out of town! He has no right to carry those things in here. Out! Out!

Allal picked up the big sack and said to the old man: Come on.

They left the square and went through the alleys until they were at the edge of town. The old man looked up then, saw the palm trees black against the fading sky ahead, and turned to the boy beside him.

Come on, said Allal again, and he went to the left along the rough path that led to his house. The old man stood perplexed.

You can stay with me tonight, Allal told him.

And these? he said, pointing first at the sack and then at the basket. They have to be with me.

Allal grinned. They can come.

When they were sitting in the house Allal looked at the sack and the basket. I'm not like the rest of them here, he said.

It made him feel good to hear the words being spoken. He made a contemptuous gesture. Afraid to walk through the square because of a snake. You saw them.

The old man scratched his chin. Snakes are like people, he said. You have to get to know them. Then you can be their friends.

Allal hesitated before he asked: Do you ever let them out?

Always, the old man said with energy. It's bad for them to be inside like this. They've got to be healthy when they get to Taroudant, or the man there won't buy them.

He began a long story about his life as a hunter of snakes, explaining that each year he made a voyage to Taroudant to see a man who bought them for the Aissaoua snake-charmers in Marrakech. Allal made tea while he listened, and brought out a bowl of kif paste to eat with the tea. Later, when they were sitting comfortably in the midst of the pipesmoke, the old man chuckled. Allal turned to look at him.

Shall I let them out?

Fine!

But you must sit and keep quiet. Move the lamp nearer.

He untied the sack, shook it a bit, and returned to where he had been sitting. Then in silence, Allal watched the long bodies move cautiously out into the light. Among the cobras were others with markings so delicate and perfect that they seemed to have been designed and painted by an artist. One reddish-gold serpent, which coiled itself lazily in the middle of the floor, he found particularly beautiful. As he stared at it, he felt a great desire to own it and have it always with him.

The old man was talking. I've spent my whole life with snakes, he said. I could tell you some things about them. Did you know that if you give them majoun you can make them do what you want, and without saying a word? I swear by Allah!

Allal's face assumed a doubtful air. He did not question the truth of the other's statement, but rather the likelihood of his being able to put the knowledge to use. For it was at that moment that the idea of actually taking the snake first came into his head. He was thinking that whatever he was to do must be done quickly, for the old man would be leaving in the morning. Suddenly he felt a great impatience.

Put them away so I can cook dinner, he whispered. Then he sat admiring the ease with which the old man picked up each one by its head and slipped it into the sack. Once again he dropped two of the snakes into the basket, and one of these, Allal noted, was the red one. He imagined he could see the shining of its scales through the lid of the basket.

As he set to work preparing the meal Allal tried to think of other things. Then, since the snake remained in his mind in spite of everything, he began to devise a way of getting it. While he squatted over the fire in a corner, he mixed some kif paste in a bowl of milk and set it aside.

The old man continued to talk. That was good luck, getting the two snakes back like that, in the middle of the town. You can never be sure what people are going to do when they find out you're carrying snakes. Once in El Kelaa they took all of them and killed them, one after the other, in front of me. A year's work. I had to go back home and start all over again.

Even as they ate, Allal saw that his guest was growing sleepy. How will things happen? he wondered. There was no way of knowing beforehand precisely what he was going to do, and the prospect of having to handle the snake worried him. It could kill me, he thought.

Once they had eaten, drunk tea and smoked a few pipes of kif, the old man lay back on the floor and said he was going to sleep. Allal sprang up. In here! he told him, and led him to his own mat in an alcove. The old man lay down and swiftly fell asleep.

Several times during the next half hour Allal went to the alcove and peered in, but neither the body in its burnous nor the head in its turban had stirred.

First he got out his blanket, and after tying three of its corners together spread it on the floor with the fourth corner facing the basket. Then he set the bowl of milk and kif paste on the blanket. As he loosened the strap from the cover of the basket the old man coughed. Allal stood immobile, waiting to hear the cracked voice speak. A small breeze had sprung up, making the palm branches rasp one against the other, but there was no further sound from the alcove. He crept to the far side of the room and squatted by the wall, his gaze fixed on the basket.

Several times he thought he saw the cover move slightly, but each time he decided he had been mistaken. Then he caught his breath. The shadow along the base of the basket was moving. One of the creatures had crept out from the far side. It waited for a while before continuing into the light, but when it did, Allal breathed a prayer of thanks. It was the red and gold one.

When finally it decided to go to the bowl, it made a complete tour around the edge, looking in from all sides, before lowering its head toward the milk. Allal watched, fearful that the foreign flavor of the kif paste might repel it. The snake remained there without moving.

He waited a half hour or more. The snake stayed where it was, its head in the bowl. From time to time Allal glanced at the basket, to be certain that the second snake was still in it. The breeze went on, rubbing the palm branches together. When he decided it was time, he rose slowly, and keeping an eye on the basket where apparently the other snake still slept, he reached over and gathered together the three tied corners of the blanket. Then he lifted the fourth corner, so that both the snake and the bowl slid to the bottom of the improvised sack. The snake moved slightly, but he did not think it was angry. He knew exactly where he would hide it: between some rocks in the dry river bed.

Holding the blanket in front of him he opened the door and stepped out under the stars. It was not far up the road, to a group of high palms, and then to the left down into the oued. There was a space between the boulders where the bundle would be invisible. He pushed it in with care, and hurried back to the house. The old man was asleep.

There was no way of being sure that the other snake was still in the basket, so Allal picked up his burnous and went outside. He shut the door and lay down on the ground to sleep.

Before the sun was in the sky the old man was awake, lying in the alcove coughing. Allal jumped up, went inside, and began to make a fire in the mijmah. A minute later he heard the other exclaim: They're loose again! Out of the basket! Stay where you are and I'll find them.

It was not long before the old man grunted with satisfaction. I have the black one! he cried. Allal did not look up from the corner where he crouched, the old man came over, waving a cobra. Now I've got to find the other one.

He put the snake away and continued to search. When the fire was blazing, Allal turned and said: Do you want me to help you look for it?

No, No! Stay where you are.

Allal boiled the water and made the tea, and still the old man was crawling on his knees, lifting boxes and pushing sacks. His turban had slipped off and his face ran with sweat.

Come and have tea, Allal told him.

The old man did not seem to have heard him at first. Then he rose and went into the alcove, where he rewound his turban. When he came out he sat down with Allal, and they had breakfast.

Snakes are very clever, the old man said. They can get into places that don't exist. I've moved everything in this house.

After they had finished eating, they went outside and looked for the snake between the close-growing trunks of the palms near the house. When the old man was convinced that it was gone, he went sadly back in.

That was a good snake, he said at last. And now I'm going to Taroudant.

They said good-bye, and the old man took his sack and basket and started up the road toward the highway.

All day long as he worked, Allal thought of the snake, but it was not until sunset that he was able to go to the rocks in the oued and pull out the blanket. He carried it back to the house in a high state of excitement.

Before he untied the blanket, he filled a wide dish with milk and kif paste, and set it on the floor. He ate three spoonfuls of the paste himself and sat back to watch, drumming on the low wooden tea-table with his fingers. Everything happened just as he had hoped. The snake came slowly out of the blanket, and very soon had found the dish and was drinking the milk. As long as it drank he kept drumming; when it had finished and raised its head to look at him, he stopped, and it crawled back inside the blanket.

Later that evening he put down more milk, and drummed again on the table. After a time the snake's head appeared, and finally all of it, and the entire pattern of action was repeated.

That night and every night thereafter, Allal sat with the snake, while with infinite patience he sought to make it his friend. He never attempted to touch it, but soon he was able to summon it, keep it in front of him for as long as he pleased, merely by tapping on the table, and dismiss it at will. For the first week or so he used the kif paste; then he tried the routine without it. In the end the results were the same. After that he fed it only milk and eggs.

Then one evening as his friend lay gracefully coiled in front of him, he began to think of the old man, and formed an idea that put all other things out of his mind. There had not been any kif paste in the house for several weeks, and he decided to make some. He bought the ingredients the following day, and after work he prepared the paste. When it was done, he mixed a large amount of it in a bowl with milk and set it down for the snake. Then he himself ate four spoonfuls, washing them down with tea.

He quickly undressed, and moving the table so that he could reach it, stretched out naked on a mat near the door. This time he continued to tap on the table, even after the snake had finished drinking the milk. It lay still, observing him, as if it were in doubt that the familiar drumming came from the brown body in front of it.

Seeing that even after a long time it remained where it was, staring at him with its stony yellow eyes, Allal began to say to it over and over: Come here. He knew it could not hear his voice, but he believed it could feel his mind as he urged it. You can make them do what you want, without saying a word, the old man had told him.

Although the snake did not move, he went on repeating his command, for by now he knew it was going to come. And after another long wait, all at once it lowered its head and began to move toward him. It reached his hip and slid along his leg. Then it climbed up his leg and lay for a time across his chest. Its body was heavy and tepid, its scales wonderfully smooth. After a time it came to rest, coiled in the space between his head and his shoulders.

By this time the kif paste had completely taken over Allal's mind. He lay in a state of pure delight, feeling the snake's head against his own, without a thought save that he and the snake were together. The patterns forming and melting behind his eyelids seemed to be the same ones that covered the snake's back. Now and then in a huge frenzied movement they all swirled up and shattered into fragments which swiftly became one great yellow eye, split through the middle by the narrow vertical pupil that pulsed with his own heartbeat. Then the eye would recede, through shifting shadow and sunlight, until only the designs of the scales were left, swarming with renewed insistence as they merged and separated. At last the eye returned, so huge this time that it had no edge around it, its pupil dilated to form an aperture almost wide enough for him to enter. As he stared at the blackness within, he understood that he was being slowly propelled towards the opening. He put out his hands to touch the polished surface of the eye on each side, and as he did this he felt the pull from within. He slid through the crack and was swallowed by darkness.

On awakening Allal felt that he had returned from somewhere far away. He opened his eyes and saw, very close to him, what looked like the flank of an enormous beast, covered with coarse, stiff hair. There was a repeated vibration in the air, like distant thunder curling around the edges of the sky. He sighed, or imagined that he did, for his breath made no sound. Then he shifted his head a bit, to try and see beyond the mass of hair beside him. Next he saw the ear, and he knew he was looking at his own head from the outside. He had not expected this; he had hoped only that his friend would come in and share his mind with him. But it did not strike him as being at all strange; he merely said to himself that now he was seeing through the eyes of the snake, rather than through his own.

Now he understood why the serpent had been so wary of him: from here the boy was a monstrous creature, with all the bristles on his head and his breathing that vibrated inside him like a far-off storm.

He uncoiled himself and glided across the floor to the alcove. There was a break in the mud wall wide enough to let him out. When he had pushed himself through, he lay full length on the ground in the crystal moonlight, staring at the strangeness of the landscape, where shadows were not shadows.

He crawled around the side of the house and started up the road toward the town, rejoicing in the sense of freedom different from any he had ever imagined. There was no feeling of having a body, for he was perfectly contained in the skin that covered him. It was beautiful to caress the earth with the length of his belly as he moved along the silent road, smelling the sharp veins of wormwood in the wind. When the voice of the muezzin floated out over the countryside from the mosque, he could not hear it, or know that within the hour night would end.

On catching sight of a man ahead, he left the road and hid behind a rock until the danger had passed. But then as he approached the town there began to be more people, so that he let himself down into the seguia, the deep ditch that went along beside the road. Here the stones and clumps of dead plants impeded his progress. He was still struggling along the floor of the seguia, pushing himself around the rocks and through the dry tangles of matted stalks left by the water, when dawn began to break.

The coming of daylight made him anxious and unhappy. He clambered up the bank of the seguia and raised his head to examine the road. A man walking past saw him, stood quite still, and then turned and ran back. Allal did not wait; he wanted now to get home as fast as possible.

Once he felt the thud of a stone as it struck the ground somewhere behind him. Quickly he threw himself over the edge of the seguia and rolled squirming down the bank. He knew the terrain here: where the road crossed the oued, there were two culverts not far apart. A man stood at some distance ahead of him with a shovel, peering down into the seguia. Allal kept moving, aware that he would reach the first culvert before the man could get to him.

The floor of the tunnel under the road was ribbed with hard little waves of sand. The smell of the mountains was in the air that moved through. There were places in here where he could have hidden, but he kept moving, and soon reached the other end. Then he continued to the second culvert and went under the road in the other direction, emerging once again into the seguia. Behind him several men had gathered at the entrance to the first culvert. One of them was on his knees, his head and shoulders inside the opening.

He now set out for the house in a straight line across the open ground, keeping his eye on the clump of palm beside it. The sun had just come up, and the stones began to cast long bluish shadows. All at once a small boy appeared from behind some nearby palms, saw him, and opened his eyes and mouth wide with fear. He was so close that Allal went straight to him and bit him in the leg. The boy ran wildly towards the group of men in the seguia.

Allal hurried on to the house, looking back only as he reached the hole between the mud bricks. Several men were running among the trees toward him. Swiftly he glided through into the alcove. The brown body still lay near the door. But there was no time, and Allal needed time to get back to it, to lie close to its head and say: Come here.

As he stared out into the room at the body, there was a great pounding on the door. The boy was on his feet at the first blow, as if a spring had been released, and Allal saw with despair the expression of total terror in his face, and the eyes with no mind behind them. The boy stood panting, his fists clenched. The door opened and some of the men peered inside. Then with a roar the boy lowered his head and rushed through the doorway. One of the men reached out to seize him, but lost his balance and fell. An instant later all of them turned and began to run through the palm grove after the naked figure.

Even when, from time to time, they lost sight of him, they could hear the screams, and then they would see him, between the palm trunks, still running. Finally he stumbled and fell face downward. It was then that they caught him, bound him, and covered his nakedness, and took him away, to be sent one day soon to the hospital at Berrechid.

That afternoon the same group of men came to the house to carry out the search they had meant to make earlier. Allal lay in the alcove, dozing. When he awoke, they were already inside. He turned and crept to the hole. He saw the man waiting out there, a club in his hand.

The rage always had been in his heart; now it burst forth. As if his body were a whip, he sprang out into the room. The men nearest him were on their hands and knees, and Allal had the joy of pushing his fangs into two of them before a third severed his head with an axe.

MORLEY CALLAGHAN

Morley Callaghan (1903–90) was fiercely committed to a sense of artistic independence. The author of more than a dozen novels, many stories, and an important memoir of Paris in the 1920s, *That Summer in Paris* (1963), he enjoyed a reputation outside Canada before becoming a national literary figure. One of Ernest Hemingway's co-workers at *The Toronto Star*, he published in Ezra Pound's avant-garde magazine *exile*, as well as in *Transition, Scribner's, The New Yorker* and other journals. A gathering of his work appeared in 1959 under the title *Morley Callaghan's Stories*. Yet from the 1930s until Edmund Wilson rediscovered him in 1960—"a writer whose work may be mentioned without absurdity in association with Chekhov's and Turgenev's"—he was virtually unknown. With English critics responding warmly to his work in the 1970s, his fortunes altered.

Born and educated in Toronto, he won several Canadian literary prizes. Yet his style and literary intention were shaped less by the cultural milieu in Toronto than by what he refers to as his own "North American" consciousness: Hemingway, Scott Fitzgerald, and particularly Sherwood Anderson were his guides. He worked at paring from his style any words that might draw attention away from his protagonists; he was concerned with focusing on moral dilemmas and with presenting clearly the forces that turn ordinary events in ordinary lives into momentous drama. The result can more easily be termed parable than naturalism. If his stories are realistic, they are so only within their own terms; at their best they have the power of truth without the interference of petty detail, and the credibility that accompanies intense conviction. The impact of "Two Fishermen" (*Now That April's Here and other stories*, 1936) derives from the tension between deeply held moral convictions and the placid surface style. The story leads into a contemplation of the ways in which abstract principles—justice, for example—take real but imperfect forms.

Two Fishermen

The only reporter on the town paper, the *Examiner*, was Michael Foster, a tall long-legged, eager young fellow, who wanted to go to the city some day and work on an important newspaper.

The morning he went into Bagley's Hotel, he wasn't at all sure of himself. He went over to the desk and whispered to the proprietor, Ted Bagley, "Did he come here, Mr. Bagley?"

Bagley said slowly, "Two men came here from this morning's train. They're registered." He put his spatulate forefinger on the open book and said, "Two men. One of them's a drummer. This one here T. Woodley. I know because he was through this way last year and just a minute ago he walked across the road to Molson's hardware store. The other one . . . here's his name, K. Smith."

"Who's K. Smith?" Michael asked.

"I don't know. A mild, harmless-looking little guy."

"Did he look like the hangman, Mr. Bagley?"

"I couldn't say that, seeing as I never saw one. He was awfully polite and asked where he could get a boat so he could go fishing on the lake this evening, so I said likely down at Smollet's place by the powerhouse."

"Well, thanks. I guess if he was the hangman, he'd go over to the jail first," Michael said.

He went along the street, past the Baptist church to the old jail with the high brick fence around it. Two tall maple trees, with branches drooping low over the sidewalk, shaded one of the walls from the morning sunlight. Last night, behind those walls, three carpenters, working by lamplight, had nailed the timbers for the scaffold. In the morning, young Thomas Delaney, who had grown up in the town, was being hanged: he had killed old Matthew Rhinehart whom he had caught molesting his wife when she had been berrypicking in the hills behind town. There had been a struggle and Thomas Delaney had taken a bad beating before he had killed Rhinehart. Last night a crowd had gathered on the sidewalk by the lamppost, and while moths and smaller insects swarmed around the high blue carbon light, the crowd had thrown sticks and bottles and small stones at the out-of-town workmen in the jail yard. Billy Hilton, the town constable, had stood under the light with his head down, pretending not to notice anything. Thomas Delaney was only three years older than Michael Foster.

Michael went straight to the jail office, where Henry Steadman, the sheriff, a squat, heavy man, was sitting on the desk idly wetting his long moustaches with his tongue. "Hello, Michael, what do you want?" he asked.

"Hello, Mr. Steadman, the *Examiner* would like to know if the hangman arrived yet."

"Why ask me?"

"I thought he'd come here to test the gallows. Won't he?"

"My, you're a smart young fellow, Michael, thinking of that."

"Is he in there now, Mr. Steadman?"

"Don't ask me. I'm saying nothing. Say, Michael, do you think there's going to be trouble? You ought to know. Does anybody seem sore at me? I can't do nothing. You can see that."

"I don't think anybody blames you, Mr. Steadman. Look here, can't I see the hangman? Is his name K. Smith?"

"What does it matter to you, Michael? Be a sport, go on away and don't bother us any more."

"All right, Mr. Steadman," Michael said very competently, "just leave it to me."

Early that evening, when the sun was setting, Michael Foster walked south of the town on the dusty road leading to the powerhouse and Smollet's fishing pier. He knew that if Mr. K. Smith wanted to get a boat he would go down to the pier. Fine powdered road dust whitened Michael's shoes. Ahead of him he saw the power-plant, square and low, and the smooth lake water. Behind him the sun was hanging over the blue hills beyond the town and shining brilliantly on square patches of farm land. The air around the powerhouse smelt of steam.

Out of the jutting, tumbledown pier of rock and logs, Michael saw a little fellow without a hat, sitting down with his knees hunched up to his chin, a very small man with little gray baby curls on the back of his neck, who stared steadily far out over the water. In his hand he was holding a stick with a heavy fishing-line twined around it and a gleaming copper spoon bait, the hooks brightened with bits of feathers such as they used in the neighbourhood when trolling for lake trout. Apprehensively Michael walked out over the rocks toward the stranger and called, "Were you thinking of going fishing, mister?" Standing up, the man smiled. He had a large head, tapering down to a small chin, a birdlike neck and a very wistful smile. Puckering his mouth up, he said shyly to Michael, "Did you intend to go fishing?"

"That's what I came down here for. I was going to get a boat back at the boat-house there. How would you like if we went together?"

"I'd like it first rate," the shy little man said eagerly. "We could take turns rowing. Does that appeal to you?"

"Fine. Fine. You wait here and I'll go back to Smollet's place and ask for a row-boat and I'll row around here and get you."

"Thanks. Thanks very much," the mild little man said as he began to untie his line. He seemed very enthusiastic.

When Michael brought the boat around to the end of the old pier and invited the stranger to make himself comfortable so he could handle the line, the stranger protested comically that he ought to be allowed to row.

Pulling strongly at the oars, Michael was soon out in the deep water and the little man was letting his line out slowly. In one furtive glance, he had noticed that the man's hair, gray at the temples, was inclined to curl to his ears. The line was out full length. It was twisted around the little man's forefinger, which he let drag in the water. And then Michael looked full at him and smiled because he thought he seemed so meek and quizzical. "He's a nice little guy," Michael assured himself and he said, "I work on the town paper, the *Examiner*."

"Is it a good paper? Do you like the work?"

"Yes. But it's nothing like a first-class city paper and I don't expect to be working on it long. I want to get a reporter's job on a city paper. My name's Michael Foster."

"Mine's Smith. Just call me Smitty."

"I was wondering if you'd been over to the jail yet."

Up to this time the little man had been smiling with the charming ease of a small boy who finds himself free, but now he became furtive and disappointed. Hesitating, he said, "Yes, I was over there first thing this morning."

"Oh, I just knew you'd go there," Michael said. They were a bit afraid of each other. By this time they were far out on the water which had a mill-pond smoothness. The town seemed to get smaller, with white houses in rows and streets forming geometric patterns, just as the blue hills behind the town seemed to get larger at sundown.

Finally Michael said, "Do you know this Thomas Delaney that's dying in the morning?" He knew his voice was slow and resentful.

"No. I don't know anything about him. I never read about them. Aren't there any fish at all in this old lake? I'd like to catch some fish," he said rapidly. "I told my wife I'd bring her home some fish." Glancing at Michael, he was appealing, without speaking, that they should do nothing to spoil an evening's fishing.

The little man began to talk eagerly about fishing as he pulled out a small flask from his hip pocket. "Scotch," he said, chuckling with delight. "Here, take a swig." Michael drank from the flask and passed it back. Tilting his head back and saying, "Here's to you, Michael," the little man took a long pull at the flask. "The only time I take a drink," he said still chuckling, "is when I go on a fishing trip by myself. I usually go by myself," he added apologetically as if he wanted the young fellow to see how much he appreciated his company.

They had gone far out on the water but they had caught nothing. It began to get dark. "No fish tonight, I guess, Smitty," Michael said.

"It's a crying shame," Smitty said. "I looked forward to coming up here when I found out the place was on the lake. I wanted to get some fishing in. I promised my wife I'd bring her back some fish. She'd often like to go fishing with me, but of course, she can't because she can't travel around from place to place like I do. Whenever I get a call to go some place, I always look at the map to see if it's by a lake or on a river, then I take my lines and hooks along."

"If you took another job, you and your wife could probably go fishing together," Michael suggested.

"I don't know about that. We sometimes go fishing together anyway." He looked away, waiting for Michael to be repelled and insist that he ought to give up the job. And he wasn't ashamed as he looked down at the water, but he knew that Michael thought he ought to be ashamed. "Somebody's got to do my job. There's got to be a hangman," he said.

"I just meant that if it was such disagreeable work, Smitty."

The little man did not answer for a long time. Michael rowed steadily with sweeping, tireless strokes. Huddled at the end of the boat, Smitty suddenly looked up with a kind of melancholy hopelessness and said mildly, "The job hasn't been so disagreeable."

"Good God, man, you don't mean you like it?"

"Oh, no," he said, to be obliging, as if he knew what Michael expected him to say, "I mean you get used to it, that's all." But he looked down again at the water, knowing he ought to be ashamed of himself.

"Have you got any children?"

"I sure have. Five. The oldest boy is fourteen. It's funny, but they're all a lot bigger and taller than I am. Isn't that funny?"

They started a conversation about fishing rivers that ran into the lake farther north. They felt friendly again. The little man, who had an extraordinary gift for story-telling, made many quaint faces, puckered up his lips, screwed up his eyes and moved around restlessly as if he wanted to get up in the boat and stride around for the sake of more expression. Again he brought out the whiskey flask and Michael stopped rowing. Grinning, they toasted each other and said together, "Happy days." The boat remained motionless on the placid water. Far out, the sun's last rays gleamed on the water-line. And then it got dark and they could only see the town lights. It was time to turn around and pull for the shore. The little man tried to take the oars from Michael, who shook his head resolutely and insisted that he would prefer to have his friend catch a fish on the way back to the shore.

"It's too late now, and we may have scared all the fish away." Smitty laughed happily. "But we're having a grand time, aren't we?"

When they reached the old pier by the powerhouse, it was full night and they hadn't caught a single fish. As the boat bumped against the rocks Michael said, "You can get out here. I'll take the boat around to Smollet's."

"Won't you be coming my way?"

"Not just now. I'll probably talk with Smollet a while."

The little man got out of the boat and stood on the pier looking down at Michael. "I was thinking dawn would be the best time to catch some fish," he said. "At about five o'clock. I'll have an hour and a half to spare anyway. How would you like that?" He was speaking with so much eagerness that Michael found himself saying, "I could try. But if I'm not here at dawn, you go on without me."

"All right. I'll walk back to the hotel now."

"Good night, Smitty."

"Good night, Michael. We had a fine neighbourly time, didn't we?"

As Michael rowed the boat around to the boat-house, he hoped that Smitty wouldn't realize he didn't want to be seen walking back to town with him. And later, when he was going slowly along the dusty road in the dark and hearing all the crickets chirping in the ditches, he couldn't figure out why he felt so ashamed of himself.

At seven o'clock next morning Thomas Delaney was hanged in the town jail yard. There was hardly a breeze on that leaden gray morning and there were no small whitecaps out over the lake. It would have been a fine morning for fishing. Michael went down to the jail, for he thought it his duty as a newspaperman to have all the facts, but he was afraid he might get sick. He hardly spoke to all the men and women who were crowded under the maple trees by the jail wall. Everybody he knew was staring at the wall and muttering angrily. Two of Thomas Delaney's brothers, big, strapping fellows with bearded faces, were there on the sidewalk. Three automobiles were at the front of the jail.

Michael, the town newspaperman, was admitted into the courtyard by old Willie Mathews, one of the guards, who said that two newspapermen from the city were at the gallows on the other side of the building. "I guess you can go around there, too, if you want to," Mathews said, as he sat down slowly on the step. White-faced, and afraid, Michael sat down on the step with Mathews and they waited and said nothing.

At last the old fellow said, "Those people outside there are pretty sore, ain't they?"

"They're pretty sullen, all right. I saw two of Delaney's brothers there."

"I wish they'd go," Mathews said. "I don't want to see anything. I didn't even look at Delaney. I don't want to hear anything. I'm sick." He put his head back against the wall and closed his eyes.

The old fellow and Michael sat close together till a small procession came around the corner from the other side of the yard. First came Mr. Steadman, the sheriff, with his head down as though he were crying, then Dr. Parker, the physician, then two hard-looking young newspapermen from the city, walking with their hats on the backs of their heads, and behind them came the little hangman, erect, stepping out with military precision and carrying himself with a strange cocky dignity. He was dressed in a long black cutaway coat with gray striped trousers, a gates-ajar collar and narrow red tie, as if he alone felt the formal importance of the occasion. He walked with brusque precision till he saw Michael, who was standing up, staring at him with his mouth open.

The little hangman grinned and soon as the procession reached the doorstep, he shook hands with Michael. They were all looking at Michael. As though his work were over now, the hangman said eagerly to Michael, "I thought I'd see you here. You didn't get down to the pier at dawn?"

"No. I couldn't make it."

"That was tough, Michael. I looked for you," he said. "But never mind. I've got something for you." As they all went into the jail, Dr. Parker glanced angrily at Michael, then turned his back on him. In the office, where the doctor prepared to sign a certificate, Smitty was bending down over his fishing-basket which was in the corner. Then he pulled out two good-sized salmon-bellied trout, folded in a newspaper, and said, "I was saving these for you, Michael. I got four in an hour's fishing." Then he said, "I'll talk about that later, if you wait. We'll be busy here, and I've got to change my clothes."

Michael went out to the street with Dr. Parker and the two city newspapermen. Under his arm he was carrying the fish, folded in the newspaper. Outside, at the jail door, Michael thought that the doctor and the two newspapermen were standing a little apart from him. Then the small crowd, with their clothes all dust-soiled from the road, surged forward and the doctor said to them, "You might as well go home, boys. It's all over."

"Where's old Steadman?" somebody demanded. "We'll wait for the hangman," somebody else shouted.

The doctor walked away by himself. For a while Michael stood beside the two city newspapermen, and tried to look as nonchalant as they were looking, but he lost confidence in them when he smelled whiskey. They only talked to each other. Then they mingled with the crowd, and Michael stood alone. At last he could stand there no longer looking at all those people he knew so well, so he, too, moved out and joined the crowd.

When the sheriff came out with the hangman and two of the guards, they got half-way down to one of the automobiles before someone threw an old boot. Steadman ducked into one of the cars, as the boot hit him on the shoulder, and the two guards followed him. Those in the car must have thought at first that the hangman was with them for the car suddenly shot forward, leaving him alone on the sidewalk. The crowd threw small rocks and sticks, hooting at him as the automobile backed up slowly towards him. One small stone hit him on the head. Blood trickled from the side of his head as he looked around helplessly at all the angry people. He had the same expression on his face, Michael thought, as he had had last night when he had seemed ashamed and had looked down steadily at the water. Only now, he looked around wildly, looking for someone to help him as the crowd kept pelting him. Farther and farther Michael backed into the crowd and all the time he felt dreadfully ashamed as though he were betraying Smitty, who last night had had such a good neighbourly time with him. "It's different now, it's different," he kept thinking, as he held the fish in the newspaper tight under his arm. Smitty started to run toward the automobile but James Mortimer, a big fisherman, shot out his foot and tripped him and sent him sprawling on his face.

Mortimer, the big fisherman, looking for something to throw, said to Michael, "Sock him, sock him."

Michael shook his head and felt sick.

"What's the matter with you, Michael?"

"Nothing. I got nothing against him."

The big fisherman started pounding his fists up and down in the air. "He just doesn't mean anything to me at all," Michael said quickly. The fisherman, bending down, kicked a small rock loose from the road bed and heaved it at the hangman. Then he said, "What are you holding there, Michael, what's under your arm? Fish. Pitch them at him. Here, give them to me." Still in a fury, he snatched the fish, and threw them one at a time at the little man just as he was getting up from the road. The fish fell in the thick dust in front of him, sending up a little cloud. Smitty seemed to stare at the fish with his mouth hanging open, then he didn't even look at the crowd. That expression on Smitty's face as he saw the fish on the road made Michael hot with shame and he tried to get out of the crowd.

Smitty had his hands over his head, to shield his face as the crowd pelted him, yelling, "Sock the little rat. Throw the runt in the lake." The sheriff pulled him into the automobile. The car shot forward in a cloud of dust.

Peter Carey

Born in Bacchus Marsh, Victoria, in 1943, and now a resident of Sydney, Peter Carey is one of several contemporary stylists who have been refashioning short fiction in Australia. Like some of the others, he is a social iconoclast, working in fantasy. Elements of the fantastic are everywhere in his work, yet they do not provide escapist entertainment; paradoxically the fantastic serves instead to expose the ordinary cruelties that people tend to accept passively in their society. Writing in his introduction to *New Australian Short Stories* (1981), Craig Munro refers to Carey's "uncanny flair for significant settings and events." The significance derives from the associative resonances of his settings; the reader supplies it, recognizing the degree of overlap between the fictional exaggerations and ordinary life. The stories, Munro adds, "seem to fuse the past, present and future into super-real scenarios in which the gap between the observed and the imagined disappears."

Carey has published several novels and short story collections, including *The Fat Man in History* (1974) and *War Crimes* (1979), in which "'Do You Love Me?'" appeared. His novel *Bliss* was published in 1981 and subsequently filmed; another novel, *Oscar and Lucinda,* won the Booker Prize in 1988, and was made into a film directed by Gillian Armstrong in 1997. His most recent novel, *Jack Maggs* (1998), won the Miles Franklin Award for best Australian fiction.

The sardonic comedy of "'Do You Love Me?'" characterizes much of Carey's fiction. His stories amuse, but they also expose weaknesses in the fabric of society. Critical of those who accept the map-makers' version of events and also of those who emptily reject the map-makers, Carey shows that uncertainty can sometimes prove debilitating. Those who accept received standards as though they were universal truths and those who dispute such standards without having anything adequate to replace them alike empty the world of love—and therefore potentially of meaning.

"Do You Love Me?"

1. The Role of the Cartographers

Perhaps a few words about the role of the Cartographers in our present society are warranted.

To begin with one must understand the nature of the yearly census, a manifestation of our desire to know, always, exactly where we stand. The census, originally a count of the population, has gradually extended until it has become a total inventory of the contents of the nation, a mammoth task which is continuing all the time—no sooner has one census been announced than work on another begins.

The results of the census play an important part in our national life and have, for many years, been the pivot point for the yearly "Festival of the Corn" (an ancient festival, related to the wealth of the earth).

We have a passion for lists. And nowhere is this more clearly illustrated than in the Festival of the Corn which takes place in midsummer, the weather always being fine and warm. On the night of the festival, the householders move their goods and possessions, all furniture, electrical goods, clothing, rugs, kitchen utensils, bathrobes, slippers, cushions, lawnmowers, curtains, doorstops, heirlooms, cameras, and anything else that can be moved into the street so that the census officials may the more easily check the inventory of each household.

The Festival of the Corn is, however, much more than a clerical affair. And, the day over and the night come, the householders invite each other to view their possessions which they refer to, on this night, as gifts. It is like nothing more than a wedding feast—there is much cooking, all sorts of traditional dishes, fine wines, strong liquors, music is played loudly in quiet neighbourhoods, strangers copulate with strangers, men dance together, and maidens in yellow robes distribute small barley sugar corn-cobs to young and old alike.

And in all this the role of the Cartographers is perhaps the most important, for our people crave, more than anything else, to know the extent of the nation, to know, exactly, the shape of the coastline, to hear what land may have been lost to the sea, to know what has been reclaimed and what is still in doubt. If the Cartographers' report is good the Festival of the Corn will be a good festival. If the report is bad, one can always sense, for all the dancing and drinking, a feeling of nervousness and apprehension in the revellers, a certain desperation. In the year of a bad Cartographers' report there will always be fights and, occasionally, some property will be stolen as citizens attempt to compensate themselves for their sense of loss.

Because of the importance of their job the Cartographers have become an elite—well-paid, admired, envied, and having no small opinion of themselves. It is said by some that they are overproud, immoral, vain and foot-loose, and it is perhaps the last charge (by necessity true) that brings about the others. For the Cartographers spend their years travelling up and down the coast, along the great rivers, traversing great mountains and vast deserts. They travel in small parties of three, four, sometimes five, making their own time, working as they please, because eventually it is their own responsibility to see that their team's task is completed in time.

My father, a Cartographer himself, often told me stories about himself or his colleagues and the adventures they had in the wilderness.

There were other stories, however, that always remained in my mind and, as a child, caused me considerable anxiety. These were the stories of the nether regions and I doubt if they were known outside a very small circle of Cartographers and government officials. As a child in a house frequented by Cartographers, I often heard these tales which invariably made me cling closely to my mother's skirts.

It appears that for some time certain regions of the country had become less and less real and these regions were regarded fearfully even by the Cartographers, who prided themselves on their courage. The regions in question were invariably uninhabited, unused for agriculture or industry. There were certain sections of the Halverson Ranges, vast stretches of the Greater Desert, and long pieces of coastline which had begun to slowly disappear like the image on an improperly fixed photograph.

It was because of these nebulous areas that the Fischerscope was introduced. The Fischerscope is not unlike radar in its principle and is able to detect the presence of any object, no matter how dematerialized or insubstantial. In this way the Cartographers were still able to map the questionable parts of the nether regions. To have returned with blanks on the maps would have created such public anxiety that no one dared think what it might do to the stability of our society. I now have reason to believe that certain areas of the country disappeared so completely that even the Fischerscope could not detect them and the Cartographers, acting under political pressure, used old maps to fake-in the missing sections. If my theory is grounded in fact, and I am sure it is, it would explain my father's cynicism about the Festival of the Corn.

2. *The Archetypal Cartographer*

My father was in his fifties but he had kept himself in good shape. His skin was brown and his muscles still firm. He was a tall man with a thick head of grey hair, a slightly less grey moustache and a long aquiline nose. Sitting on a horse he looked as proud and cruel as Genghis Khan. Lying on the beach clad only in bathers and sunglasses he still managed to retain his authoritative air.

Beside him I always felt as if I had betrayed him. I was slightly built, more like my mother.

It was the day before the festival and we lay on the beach, my father, my mother, my girlfriend and I. As was usual in these circumstances my father addressed all his remarks to Karen. He never considered the members of his own family worth talking to. I always had the uncomfortable feeling that he was flirting with my girlfriends and I never knew what to do about it.

People were lying in groups up and down the beach. Near us a family of five were playing with a large beach ball.

"Look at those fools," my father said to Karen.

"Why are they fools?" Karen asked.

"They're fools," said my father. "They were born fools and they'll die fools. Tomorrow they'll dance in the streets and drink too much."

"So," said Karen triumphantly, in the manner of one who has become privy to secret information. "It will be a good Cartographers' report?"

My father roared with laughter.

Karen looked hurt and pouted. "Am I a fool?"

"No," my father said, "you're really quite splendid."

3. The Most Famous Festival

The festival, as it turned out, was the greatest disaster in living memory.

The Cartographers' report was excellent, the weather was fine, but somewhere something had gone wrong.

The news was confusing. The television said that, in spite of the good report, various items had been stolen very early in the night. Later there was a news flash to say that a large house had completely disappeared in Howie Street.

Later still we looked out the window to see a huge band of people carrying lighted torches. There was a lot of shouting. The same image, exactly, was on the television and a reporter was explaining that bands of vigilantes were out looking for thieves.

My father stood at the window, a martini in his hand, and watched the vigilantes set alight a house opposite.

My mother wanted to know what we should do.

"Come and watch the fools," my father said, "they're incredible."

4. The I.C.I. Incident

The next day the I.C.I. building disappeared in front of a crowd of two thousand people. It took two hours. The crowd stood silently as the great steel and glass structure slowly faded before them.

The staff who were evacuated looked pale and shaken. The caretaker who was amongst the last to leave looked almost translucent. In the days that followed he made some name for himself as a mystic, claiming that he had been able to see other worlds, layer upon layer, through the fabric of the here and now.

5. Behaviour When Confronted With Dematerialization

The anger of our people when confronted with acts of theft has always been legendary and was certainly highlighted by the incidents which occurred on the night of the festival.

But the fury exhibited on this famous night could not compare with the intensity of emotion displayed by those who witnessed the earliest scenes of dematerialization.

The silent crowd who watched the I.C.I. building erupted into hysteria when they realized that it had finally gone and wasn't likely to come back.

It was like some monstrous theft for which punishment must be meted out.

They stormed into the Shell building next door and smashed desks and ripped down office partitions. Reporters who attended the scene were rarely impartial observers, but one of the cooler headed members of the press remarked on the great number of weeping men and women who hurled typewriters from windows and scattered files through crowds of frightened office workers.

Five days later they displayed similar anger when the Shell building itself disappeared.

6. Behaviour of Those Dematerializing

The first reports of dematerializing people were not generally believed and were suppressed by the media. But these things were soon common knowledge and few families were untouched by them. Such incidents were obviously not all the same but in many victims there was a tendency to exhibit extreme aggression towards those around them. Murders and assaults committed by these unfortunates were not uncommon and in most cases they exhibited an almost unbelievable rage, as if they were the victims of a shocking betrayal.

My friend James Bray was once stopped in the street by a very beautiful woman who clawed and scratched his face and said: "You did this to me you bastard, you did this to me."

He had never seen her before but he confessed that, in some irrational way, he felt responsible and didn't defend himself. Fortunately she disappeared before she could do him much damage.

7. Some Theories That Arose at the Time

1. The world is merely a dream dreamt by god who is waking after a long sleep. When he is properly awake the world will disappear completely. When the world disappears we will disappear with it and be happy.
2. The world has become sensitive to light. In the same way that prolonged use of say penicillin can suddenly result in a dangerous allergy, prolonged exposure of the world to the sun has made it sensitive to light.

The advocates of this theory could be seen bustling through the city crowds in their long, hooded black robes.

3. The fact that the world is disappearing has been caused by the sloppy work of the Cartographers and census takers. Those who filled out their census forms incorrectly would lose those items they had neglected to describe. People overlooked in the census by impatient officials would also disappear. A strong pressure group demanded that a new census be taken quickly before matters got worse.

8. My Father's Theory

The world, according to my father, was exactly like the human body and had its own defence mechanisms with which it defended itself against anything that either threatened it or was unnecessary to it. The I.C.I. building and the I.C.I. company had obviously constituted some threat to the world or had simply been irrelevant. That's why it had disappeared and not because some damn fool god was waking up and rubbing his eyes.

"I don't believe in god," my father said. "Humanity is god. Humanity is the only god I know. If humanity doesn't need something it will disappear. People who are not loved will disappear. Everything that is not loved will disappear from the face of the earth. We only exist through the love of others and that's what it's all about."

9. A Contradiction

"Look at those fools," my father said, "they wouldn't know if they were up themselves."

10. An Unpleasant Scene

The world at this time was full of unpleasant and disturbing scenes. One that I recall vividly took place in the middle of the city on a hot, sultry Tuesday afternoon. It was about one-thirty and I was waiting for Karen by the post office when a man of forty or so ran past me. He was dematerializing rapidly. Everybody seemed to be deliberately looking the other way, which seemed to me to make him dematerialize faster. I stared at him hard, hoping that I could do something to keep him there until help arrived. I tried to love him, because I believed in my father's theory. I thought, I must love that man. But his face irritated me. It is not so easy to love a stranger and I'm ashamed to say that he had the small mouth and close-together eyes that I have always disliked in a person. I tried to love him but I'm afraid I failed.

While I watched he tried to hail taxi after taxi. But the taxi drivers were only too well aware of what was happening and had no wish to spend their time driving a passenger who, at any moment, might cease to exist. They looked the other way or put up their NOT FOR HIRE signs.

Finally he managed to way-lay a taxi at some traffic lights. By this time he was so insubstantial that I could see right through him. He was beginning to shout. A terrible thin noise, but penetrating nonetheless. He tried to open the cab door, but the driver had already locked it. I could hear the man's voice, high and piercing: "I want to go home." He repeated it over and over again. "I want to go home to my wife."

The taxi drove off when the lights changed. There was a lull in the traffic. People had fled the corner and left it deserted and it was I alone who saw the man finally disappear.

I felt sick.

Karen arrived five minutes later and found me pale and shaken. "Are you alright?" she said.

"Do you love me?" I said.

11. The Nether Regions

My father had an irritating way of explaining things to me I already understood, refusing to stop no matter how much I said "I know" or "You told me before."

Thus he expounded on the significance of the nether regions, adopting the tone of a lecturer speaking to a class of particularly backward children.

"As you know," he said, "the nether regions were amongst the first to disappear and this in itself is significant. These regions, I'm sure you know, are seldom visited by men and only then by people like me whose sole job is to make sure that they're still there. We had no use for these areas, these deserts, swamps, and coastlines which is why, of course, they disappeared. They were merely possessions of ours and if they had any use at all it was as symbols for our poets, writers and film makers. They were used as symbols of alienation, lovelessness, loneliness, uselessness and so on. Do you get what I mean?"

"Yes," I said, "I get what you mean."

"But do you?" My father insisted. "But do you really, I wonder." He examined me seriously, musing on the possibilities of my understanding him. "How old are you?"

"Twenty," I said.

"I knew, of course," he said. "Do you understand the significance of the nether regions?"

I sighed, a little too loudly and my father narrowed his eyes. Quickly

I said: "They are like everything else. They're like the cities. The cities are deserts where people are alone and lonely. They don't love one another."

"Don't love one another," intoned my father, also sighing. "We no longer love one another. When we realize that we need one another we will stop disappearing. This is a lesson to us. A hard lesson, but, I hope, an effective one."

My father continued to speak, but I watched him without listening. After a few minutes he stopped abruptly: "Are you listening to me?" he said. I was surprised to detect real concern in his voice. He looked at me questioningly. "I've always looked after you," he said, "ever since you were little."

12. *The Cartographers' Fall*

I don't know when it was that I noticed that my father had become depressed. It probably happened quite gradually without either my mother or me noticing it.

Even when I did become aware of it I attributed it to a woman. My father had a number of lovers and his moods usually reflected the success or failure of these relationships.

But I know now that he had heard already of Hurst and Jamov, the first two Cartographers to disappear. The news was suppressed for several weeks and then, somehow or other, leaked to the press. Certainly the Cartographers had enemies amongst the civil servants who regarded them as overproud and overpaid, and it was probably from one of these civil servants that the press heard the news.

When the news finally broke I understood my father's depression and felt sorry for him.

I didn't know how to help him. I wanted, badly, to make him happy. I had never ever been able to give him anything or do anything for him that he couldn't do better himself. Now I wanted to help him, to show him I understood.

I found him sitting in front of the television one night when I returned from my office and I sat quietly beside him. He seemed more kindly now and he placed his hand on my knee and patted it.

I sat there for a while, overcome with the new warmth of this relationship and then, unable to contain my emotion any more, I blurted out: "You could change your job."

My father stiffened and sat bolt upright. The pressure of his hand on my knee increased until I yelped with pain, and still he held on, hurting me terribly.

"You are a fool," he said, "you wouldn't know if you were up yourself."

Through the pain in my leg, I felt the intensity of my father's fear.

13. Why the World Needs Cartographers

My father woke me at 3 a.m. to tell me why the world needed Cartographers. He smelled of whisky and seemed, once again, to be very gentle.

"The world needs Cartographers," he said softly, "because if they didn't have Cartographers the fools wouldn't know where they were. They wouldn't know if they were up themselves if they didn't have a Cartographer to tell them what's happening. The world needs Cartographers," my father said, "it fucking well needs Cartographers."

14. One Final Scene

Let me describe a final scene to you. I am sitting on the sofa my father brought home when I was five years old. I am watching television. My father is sitting in a leather armchair that once belonged to his father and which has always been exclusively his. My mother is sitting in the dining alcove with her cards spread across the table, playing one more interminable game of patience.

I glance casually across at my father to see if he is doing anything more than stare into space, and notice, with a terrible shock, that he is showing the first signs of dematerializing.

"What are you staring at?" My father, in fact, has been staring at me.

"Nothing."

"Well, don't."

Nervously I return my eyes to the inanity of the television. I don't know what to do. Should I tell my father that he is dematerializing? If I don't tell him will he notice? I feel I should do something but I can feel, already, the anger in his voice. His anger is nothing new. But this is possibly the beginning of a tide of uncontrollable rage. If he knows he is dematerializing, he will think I don't love him. He will blame me. He will attack me. Old as he is, he is still considerably stronger than I am and he could hurt me badly. I stare determinedly at the television and feel my father's eyes on me.

I try to feel love for my father, I try very, very hard.

I attempt to remember how I felt about him when I was little, in the days when he was still occasionally tender towards me.

But it's no good.

Because I can only remember how he has hit me, hurt me, humiliated me and flirted with my girlfriends. I realize, with a flush of panic and guilt, that I don't love him. In spite of which I say: "I love you."

My mother looks up sharply from her cards and lets out a surprised cry.

I turn to my father. He has almost disappeared. I can see the leather of the chair through his stomach.

I don't know whether it is my unconvincing declaration of love or my mother's exclamation that makes my father laugh. For whatever reason, he begins to laugh uncontrollably: "You bloody fools," he gasps, "I wish you could see the looks on your bloody silly faces."

And then he is gone.

My mother looks across at me nervously, a card still in her hand. "Do you love me?" she asks.

ANGELA CARTER

Born and educated in England, Angela Carter (1940–92) began her writing career as a journalist. Her first novel, *Shadow Dance*, appeared in 1965, the year she graduated from the University of Bristol. Carter won early recognition: her second novel, *The Magic Toyshop*, was awarded the John Llewellyn Rhys Prize in 1967, and her third, *Several Perceptions*, brought her the Somerset Maugham Award in 1968. *Nights at the Circus* was joint winner of the James Tait Black Memorial Prize in 1985. Before her death from cancer at the age of 52, she produced work in many different genres: as a scriptwriter for radio, television, and the cinema; as a writer of children's books; as a poet and essayist; and, perhaps most notably, as a short story writer.

The elements of gothic violence, suspense, and fantasy, evident in much of Carter's writing, are at the forefront in such short story collections as *The Bloody Chamber* (1979) and *Black Venus* (1985). In many stories she is especially effective at blending myth and reality, or rather, at reinventing reality from a mythic perspective. She likes to play with motifs from traditional folk and fairy tales, turning them into bizarre reflections of the uncertainties and hidden terrors that beset human life. "The Company of Wolves," first published in 1977, brings together Carter's feminism, her fascination with European fairy tale, and her sly insistence on the power of female sexuality to assert itself over masculine violence. It is one of several stories by Carter that blend the tale of Little Red Riding Hood with dark and bloody legends of the werewolf, and that she adapted with Neil Jordan for his 1984 film *The Company of Wolves*.

The Company of Wolves

One beast and only one howls in the woods by night.

The wolf is carnivore incarnate and he's as cunning as he is ferocious; once he's had a taste of flesh then nothing else will do.

At night, the eyes of wolves shine like candle flames, yellowish, reddish, but that is because the pupils of their eyes fatten on darkness and catch the light from your lantern to flash it back to you—red for danger; if a wolf's eyes reflect only moonlight, then they gleam a cold and unnatural green, a mineral, a piercing colour. If the benighted traveller spies those luminous, terrible sequins stitched suddenly on the black thickets, then he knows he must run, if fear has not struck him stock-still.

But those eyes are all you will be able to glimpse of the forest assassins as they cluster invisibly round your smell of meat as you go through the wood unwisely late. They will be like shadows, they will be like wraiths, grey members of a congregation of nightmare; hark! his long, wavering howl . . . an aria of fear made audible.

The wolfsong is the sound of the rending you will suffer, in itself a murdering.

It is winter and cold weather. In this region of mountain and forest, there is now nothing for the wolves to eat. Goats and sheep are locked up in the byre, the deer departed for the remaining pasturage on the southern slopes—wolves grow lean and famished. There is so little flesh on them that you could count the starveling ribs through their pelts, if they gave you time before they pounced. Those slavering jaws; the lolling tongue; the rime of saliva on the grizzled chops—of all the teeming perils of the night and the forest, ghosts, hobgoblins, ogres that grill babies upon gridirons, witches that fatten their captives in cages for cannibal tables, the wolf is worst for he cannot listen to reason.

You are always in danger in the forest, where no people are. Step between the portals of the great pines where the shaggy branches tangle about you, trapping the unwary traveller in nets as if the vegetation itself were in a plot with the wolves who live there, as though the wicked trees go fishing on behalf of their friends—step between the gateposts of the forest with the greatest trepidation and infinite precautions, for if you stray from the path for one instant, the wolves will eat you. They are grey as famine, they are as unkind as plague.

The grave-eyed children of the sparse villages always carry knives with them when they go to tend the little flocks of goats that provide the homesteads with acrid milk and rank, maggoty cheese. Their knives are half as big as they are, the blades are sharpened daily.

But the wolves have ways of arriving at your own hearthside. We try and try but sometimes we cannot keep them out. There is no winter's night the cottager does not fear to see a lean, grey, famished snout questing under the door, and there was a woman once bitten in her own kitchen as she was straining the macaroni.

Fear and flee the wolf; for, worst of all, the wolf may be more than he seems.

There was a hunter once, near here, that trapped a wolf in a pit. This wolf had massacred the sheep and goats; eaten up a mad old man who used to live by himself in a hut halfway up the mountain and sing to Jesus all day; pounced on a girl looking after the sheep, but she made such a commotion that men came with rifles and scared him away and tried to track him to the forest but he was cunning and easily gave them the slip. So this hunter dug a pit and put a duck in it, for bait, all alive-oh; and he covered the pit with straw smeared with wolf dung. Quack,

quack! went the duck and a wolf came slinking out of the forest, a big one, a heavy one, he weighed as much as a grown man and the straw gave way beneath him—into the pit he tumbled. The hunter jumped down after him, slit his throat, cut off all his paws for a trophy.

And then no wolf at all lay in front of the hunter but the bloody trunk of a man, headless, footless, dying, dead.

A witch from up the valley once turned an entire wedding party into wolves because the groom had settled on another girl. She use to order them to visit her, at night, from spite, and they would sit and howl around her cottage for her, serenading her with their misery.

Not so very long ago, a young woman in our village married a man who vanished clean away on her wedding night. The bed was made with new sheets and the bride lay down in it; the groom said, he was going out to relieve himself, insisted on it, for the sake of decency, and she drew the coverlet up to her chin and lay there. And she waited and she waited and then she waited again—surely he's been gone a long time? Until she jumps up in bed and shrieks to hear a howling, coming on the wind from the forest.

That long-drawn, wavering howl has, for all its fearful resonance, some inherent sadness in it, as if the beasts would love to be less beastly if only they knew how and never cease to mourn their own condition. There is a vast melancholy in the canticles of the wolves, melancholy infinite as the forest, endless as these long nights of winter and yet that ghastly sadness, that mourning for their own, irremediable appetites, can never move the heart for not one phrase in it hints at the possibility of redemption; grace could not come to the wolf from its own despair, only through some external mediator, so that, sometimes, the beast will look as if he half welcomes the knife that dispatches him.

The young woman's brothers searched the outhouses and the haystacks but never found any remains so the sensible girl dried her eyes and found herself another husband not too shy to piss into a pot who spent the nights indoors. She gave him a pair of bonny babies and all went right as a trivet until, one freezing night, the night of the solstice, the hinge of the year when things do not fit together as well as they should, the longest night, her first good man came home again.

A great thump on the door announced him as she was stirring the soup for the father of her children and she knew him the moment she lifted the latch to him although it was years since she'd worn black for him and now he was in rags and his hair hung down his back and never saw a comb, alive with lice.

'Here I am again, missus,' he said. 'Get me my bowl of cabbage and be quick about it.'

Then her second husband came in with wood for the fire and when the first one saw she'd slept with another man and, worse, clapped his red eyes on her little children who'd crept into the kitchen to see what all the din was about, he shouted: 'I wish I were a wolf again, to teach this whore a lesson!' So a wolf he instantly became and tore off the eldest boy's left foot before he was chopped by the hatchet they used for chopping logs. But when the wolf lay bleeding and gasping its last, the pelt peeled off again and he was just as he had been, years ago, when he ran away from his marriage bed, so that she wept and her second husband beat her.

They say there's an ointment the Devil gives you that turns you into a wolf the minute you rub it on. Or, that he was born feet first and had a wolf for his father and his torso is a man's but his legs and genitals are a wolf's. And he has a wolf's heart.

Seven years is a werewolf's natural span but if you burn his human clothes you condemn him to wolfishness for the rest of his life, so old wives hereabouts think it some protection to throw a hat or an apron at the werewolf, as if clothes made the man. Yet by the eyes, those phosphorescent eyes, you know him in all his shapes; the eyes alone unchanged by metamorphosis.

Before he can become a wolf, the lycanthrope strips stark naked. If you spy a naked man among the pines, you must run as if the Devil were after you.

■ ■ ■

It is midwinter and the robin, the friend of man, sits on the handle of the gardener's spade and sings. It is the worst time in all the year for wolves but this strong-minded child insists she will go off through the wood. She is quite sure the wild beasts cannot harm her although, well-warned, she lays a carving knife in the basket her mother has packed with cheeses. There is a bottle of harsh liquor distilled from brambles; a batch of flat oatcakes baked on the hearthstone; a pot or two of jam. The girl will take these delicious gifts to a reclusive grandmother so old the burden of her years is crushing her to death. Granny lives two hours' trudge through the winter woods; the child wraps herself up in her thick shawl, draws it over her head. She steps into her stout wooden shoes; she is dressed and ready and it is Christmas Eve. The malign door of the solstice still swings upon its hinges but she has been too much loved ever to feel scared.

Children do not stay young for long in this savage country. There are no toys for them to play with so they work hard and grow wise but this one, so pretty and the youngest of her family, a little late-comer, had been indulged by her mother and the grandmother who'd knitted her the red shawl that, today, has the ominous if brilliant look of blood on snow. Her breasts have just begun to swell; her hair is like lint, so fair it hardly makes a shadow on her pale forehead; her cheeks are an emblematic scarlet and white and she has just started her woman's bleeding, the clock inside her that will strike, henceforward, once a month.

She stands and moves within the invisible pentacle of her own virginity. She is an unbroken egg; she is a sealed vessel; she has inside her a magic space the entrance to which is shut tight with a plug of membrane; she is a closed system; she does not know how to shiver. She has her knife and she is afraid of nothing.

Her father might forbid her, if he were home, but he is away in the forest, gathering wood, and her mother cannot deny her.

The forest closed upon her like a pair of jaws.

There is always something to look at in the forest, even in the middle of winter—the huddled mounds of birds, succumbed to the lethargy of the season, heaped on the creaking boughs and too forlorn to sing; the bright frills of the winter fungi on the blotched trunks of the trees; the cuneiform slots of rabbits and deer, the herringbone tracks of the birds, a hare as lean as a rasher of bacon streaking across the path where the thin sunlight dapples the russet brakes of last year's bracken.

When she heard the freezing howl of a distant wolf, her practised hand sprang to the handle of her knife, but she saw no sign of a wolf at all, nor of a naked man, neither, but then she heard a clattering among the brushwood and there sprang on to the path a fully clothed one, a very handsome young one, in the green coat and wideawake hat of a hunter, laden with carcasses of game birds. She had her hand on her knife at the first rustle of twigs but he laughed with a flash of white teeth when he saw her and made her a comic yet flattering little bow; she'd never seen such a fine fellow before, not among the rustic clowns of her native village. So on they went, through the thickening light of the afternoon.

Soon they were laughing and joking like old friends. When he offered to carry her basket, she gave it to him although her knife was in it because he told her his rifle would protect them. As the day darkened, it began to snow again; she felt the first flakes settle on her eyelashes but now there was only half a mile to go and there would be a fire, and hot tea, and a welcome, a warm one surely, for the dashing huntsman as well as for herself.

This young man had a remarkable object in his pocket. It was a compass. She looked at the little round glassface in the palm of his hand and watched the wavering needle with a vague wonder. He assured her this compass had taken him safely through the wood on his hunting trip because the needle always told him with perfect accuracy where the north was. She did not believe it; she knew she should never leave the path on the way through the wood or else she would be lost instantly. He laughed at her again; gleaming trails of spittle clung to his teeth. He said, if he plunged off the path into the forest that surrounded them, he would guarantee to arrive at her grandmother's house a good quarter of an hour before she did, plotting his way through the undergrowth with his compass, while she trudged the long way, along the winding path.

I don't believe you. Besides, aren't you afraid of the wolves?

He only tapped the gleaming butt of his rifle and grinned.

Is it a bet? he asked her. Shall we make a game of it? What will you give me if I get to your grandmother's house before you?

What would you like? she asked disingenuously.

A kiss.

Commonplaces of a rustic seduction; she lowered her eyes and blushed.

He went through the undergrowth and took her basket with him but she forgot to be afraid of the beasts, although now the moon was rising, for she wanted to dawdle on her way to make sure the handsome gentleman would win his wager.

Grandmother's house stood by itself a little way out of the village. The freshly falling snow blew in eddies about the kitchen garden and the young man stepped delicately up the snowy path to the door as if he were reluctant to get his feet wet, swinging his bundle of game and the girl's basket and humming a little tune to himself.

There is a faint trace of blood on his chin; he has been snacking on his catch.

He rapped upon the panels with his knuckles.

Aged and frail, granny is three-quarters succumbed to the mortality the ache in her bones promises her and almost ready to give in entirely. A boy came out from the village to build up her hearth for the night an hour ago and the kitchen crackles with busy firelight. She has her Bible for company, she is a pious old woman. She is propped up on several pillows in the bed set into the wall peasant-fashion, wrapped up in the patchwork quilt she made before she was married, more years ago than she cares to remember. Two china spaniels with liver-coloured blotches on their coats and black noses sit on either side of the fireplace. There is a bright rug of woven rags on the pantiles. The grandfather clock ticks away her eroding time.

We keep the wolves outside by living well.

He rapped upon the panels with his hairy knuckles.

It is your granddaughter, he mimicked in a high soprano.

Lift up the latch and walk in, my darling.

You can tell them by their eyes, eyes of a beast of prey, nocturnal, devastating eyes as red as a wound; you can hurl your Bible at him and your apron after, granny, you thought that was a sure prophylactic against these infernal vermin . . . now call on Christ and his mother and all the angels in heaven to protect you but it won't do you any good.

His feral muzzle is sharp as a knife; he drops his golden burden of gnawed pheasant on the table and puts down your dear girl's basket, too. Oh, my God, what have you done with her?

Off with his disguise, that coat of forest-coloured cloth, the hat with the feather tucked into the ribbon; his matted hair streams down his white shirt and she can see the lice moving in it. The sticks in the hearth shift and hiss; night and the forest has come into the kitchen with darkness tangled in its hair.

He strips off his shirt. His skin is the colour and texture of vellum. A crisp stripe of hair runs down his belly, his nipples are ripe and dark as poison fruit but he's so thin you could count the ribs under his skin if only he gave you the time. He strips off his trousers and she can see how hairy his legs are. His genitals, huge. Ah! huge.

The last thing the old lady saw in all this world was a young man, eyes like cinders, naked as a stone, approaching her bed.

The wolf is carnivore incarnate.

When he had finished with her, he licked his chops and quickly dressed himself again, until he was just as he had been when he came through her door. He burned the inedible hair in the fireplace and wrapped the bones up in a napkin that he hid away under the bed in the wooden chest in which he found a clean pair of sheets. These he carefully put on the bed instead of the tell-tale stained ones he stowed away in the laundry basket. He plumped up the pillows and shook out the patchwork quilt, he picked up the Bible from the floor, closed it and laid it on the table. All was as it had been before except that grandmother was gone. The sticks twitched in the grate, the clock ticked and the young man sat patiently, deceitfully beside the bed in granny's nightcap.

Rat-a-tap-tap.

Who's there, he quavers in granny's antique falsetto.

Only your granddaughter.

So she came in, bringing with her a flurry of snow that melted in tears on the tiles, and perhaps she was a little disappointed to see only her grandmother sitting beside the fire. But then he flung off the blanket and sprang to the door, pressing his back against it so that she could not get out again.

The girl looked round the room and saw there was not even the indentation of a head on the smooth cheek of the pillow and how, for the first time she'd seen it so, the Bible lay closed on the table. The tick of the clock cracked like a whip. She wanted her knife from her basket but she did not dare to reach for it because his eyes were fixed upon her—huge eyes that now seemed to shine with a unique, interior light, eyes the size of saucers, saucers full of Greek fire, diabolic phosphorescence.

What big eyes you have.

All the better to see you with.

No trace at all of the old woman except for a tuft of white hair that had caught in the bark of an unburned log. When the girl saw that, she knew she was in danger of death.

Where is my grandmother?

There's nobody here but we two, my darling.

Now a great howling rose up all around them, near, very near as close as the kitchen garden, the howling of a multitude of wolves; she knew the worst wolves are hairy on the inside and she shivered, in spite of the scarlet shawl she pulled more closely round herself as if it could protect her although it was as red as the blood she must spill.

Who has come to sing us carols, she said.

Those are the voices of my brothers, darling; I love the company of wolves. Look out of the window and you'll see them.

Snow half-caked the lattice and she opened it to look into the garden. It was a white night of moon and snow; the blizzard whirled round the gaunt, grey beasts who squatted on their haunches among the rows of winter cabbage, pointing their sharp snouts to the moon and howling as if their hearts would break. Ten wolves; twenty wolves—so many wolves she could not count them, howling in concert as if demented or deranged. Their eyes reflected the light from the kitchen and shone like a hundred candles.

It is very cold, poor things, she said; no wonder they howl so.

She closed the window on the wolves' threnody and took off her scarlet shawl, the colour of poppies, the colour of sacrifices, the colour of her menses, and, since her fear did her no good, she ceased to be afraid.

What shall I do with my shawl?

Throw it on the fire, dear one. You won't need it again.

She bundled up her shawl and threw it on the blaze, which instantly consumed it. Then she drew her blouse over her head; her small breasts gleamed as if the snow had invaded the room.

What shall I do with my blouse?

Into the fire with it, too, my pet.

The thin muslin went flaring up the chimney like a magic bird and now off came her skirt, her woollen stockings, her shoes, and on to the fire they went, too, and were gone for good. The firelight shone through the edges of her skin; now she was clothed only in her untouched integument of flesh. This dazzling, naked she combed out her hair with her fingers; her hair looked white as the snow outside. Then went directly to the man with red eyes in whose unkempt mane the lice moved; she stood up on tiptoe and unbuttoned the collar of his shirt.

What big arms you have.

All the better to hug you with.

Every wolf in the world now howled a prothalamion outside the window as she freely gave him the kiss she owed him.

What big teeth you have!

She saw how his jaw began to slaver and the room was full of the clamour of the forest's *Liebestod* but the wise child never flinched, even as he answered: All the better to eat you with.

The girl burst out laughing; she knew she was nobody's meat. She laughed at him full in the face, she ripped off his shirt for him and flung it into the fire, in the fiery wake of her own discarded clothing. The flames danced like dead souls on Walpurgisnacht and the old bones under the bed set up a terrible clattering but she did not pay them any heed.

Carnivore incarnate, only immaculate flesh appeases him.

She will lay his fearful head on her lap and she will pick out the lice from his pelt and perhaps she will put the lice into her mouth and eat them, as he will bid her, as she would do in a savage marriage ceremony.

The blizzard will die down.

The blizzard died down, leaving the mountains as randomly covered with snow as if a blind woman had thrown a sheet over them, the upper branches of the forest pines limed, creaking, swollen with the fall.

Snowlight, moonlight, a confusion of paw-prints.

All silent, all silent.

Midnight; and the clock strikes. It is Christmas day, the werewolves' birthday, the door of the solstice stands wide open; let them all sink through.

See! sweet and sound she sleeps in granny's bed, between the paws of the tender wolf.

George Clutesi

George Clutesi (1905–88), a member of the Tse-Shaht band of the Pacific coast, was one of Canada's foremost First Nations artists. A painter as well as a writer, he showed his work internationally; a twelve-metre mural, designed for the world's fair Expo 67, is now on display at Montreal's permanent "Man and His World" exhibition, and his own designs illustrate *Son of Raven, Son of Deer* (1967), from which "Ko-ishin-mit and the Shadow People" is taken. Contact with the "European" bureaucracies of the Canadian government—particularly in regard to Indian affairs—led Clutesi to become a teacher of Native culture, confident that the subject has significant meaning for Aboriginal and non-Aboriginal people alike.

"Ko-ishin-mit and the Shadow People," like all folk tales, emerges directly from a specific culture; though it can often be related to parallel stories from other cultures, it reflects its own society's structure, beliefs, superstitions, and values, and draws its particular language, its metaphors and analogies, from the local landscape. Primarily an oral art, the folk tale generally served a moral purpose and functioned as the didactic medium through which traditional values were handed from generation to generation. In his introduction to *Son of Raven, Son of Deer,* Clutesi notes that it was "Nan-is," the grandparent, who told such tales to the "ka-coots" (grandchildren), and that this pattern of behaviour not only gave the aged a respected position within society but also gave the young a sense of security. He criticizes such tales as "Henny Penny" and "Little Jack Horner," both for their implicit violence and for the gap between the child behaviour that society expects and approves, and the models hallowed by the stories themselves. The Indian stories, by contrast, assert the closeness between human beings and nature, focus on the interpenetration of mythic stories and moral truths, and give expression (in Clutesi's own words) to the "imaginative, romantic and resourceful" capacities of the Indian mind.

Ko-ishin-mit and the Shadow People

"Finders keepers—losers weepers."

Most of you, no doubt, have heard this old saying. To the non-Indian way of life it means that if anyone finds anything it is his to keep, while the one who has lost it may as well cry because it is lost to him, even though someone may have found it. This did not apply to the Indian way of life.

Ko-ishin-mit, the Son of Raven, was a very selfish and greedy person. He was always longing to own other people's possessions and coveted everything that was not his. Oh, he was greedy!

One fine day, early in the spring of the year, when the sun was shining and smiling with warmth, Ko-ishin-mit overheard a group of menfolk talking about a strange place where you could see everything you could think of lying about, with never a person in sight.

"What kind of things? Where is this place? How far is it from here?" Ko-ishin-mit demanded in a high state of excitement. He was hopping up and down and his voice became croaky as he kept asking where to find the place.

The menfolk ignored his frantic questions and the speaker, a grey-haired, wizened old man, kept on with his story.

"There are canoes," he told, "big ones and small ones, paddles, fishing gear, tools, all sorts of play things and food galore. Oh, there is lots and lots of food, and the food is always fresh, even though no one is ever seen in the place.

Ko-ishin-mit became more and more excited and his voice was raspy as he screamed, "Who owns all these things? Where? How can I find them?"

The storyteller continued with his tale. "It is said that this strange place is on a little isle around the point and across the bay. The secret is that one must get there by sundown, and one must leave before sunup. It is said, too, that the first person who finds this place may keep everything."

Ko-ishin-mit ran all the way home. "I must find this strange place first," he kept repeating to himself. "I must find the place first. I must. I must."

He flitted into his little house, and because he was out of breath he rasped and croaked, "Pash-hook, Pash-hook, Pash-hook, nah, my dear, get ready quickly. We are going out. Make some lunch. We may be gone all night," he croaked.

Pash-hook, the Daughter of Dsim-do the squirrel, scurried about. She did not need to be coaxed for she was always a fast and frisky little person. She never questioned her husband's wishes. Whatever her husband said had always been good enough for her and she was always eager to please him. So she hurried and she hurried.

Ko-ishin-mit grew more and more excited as he flitted here and hopped there inside his little house. He got out two paddles. He hopped down to the beach and pulled and tugged at his canoe until he had it to the water, a feat he had never before done alone.

Flitting back to the house he pressed and coaxed his little wife. "Hurry, hurry! Pash-hook, hurry! We must get there first. Hurry before we are too late. We must get there first. Oh, let us be first," he kept repeating, mostly to himself.

The sun was setting when they paddled into the bay of the little isle around the point. It was a beautiful little isle with small clumpy spreading spruce trees growing from mossy green hills. The little bay was ringed with white sandy beaches. The tide was out and the green sea-grass danced and waved at them to come ashore and rest awhile. This is what Pash-hook imagined as she eased her paddling and glided their little canoe towards the glistening beach. Pash-hook was the dreamer.

"Paddle harder! Paddle harder!" Ko-ishin-mit commanded his little wife.

Straight for the beach they glided. Ko-ishin-mit flitted out onto the wet sand. "Pull the canoe up," he ordered as he hopped up the beach looking about to see if there was anyone else there ahead of him. He could see long rows of beautiful canoes, big and small, pulled up well above the high-water mark. They all had pretty canoe mats covering them from the heat of the day and the cool of the night. There was no one in sight. Ko-ishin-mit was hopping up the beach. He did not wait to help his small wife with their canoe.

"I got here first!" he rasped as he hopped and flitted up to the neat row of houses on the grassy knoll that lay just below the spreading and clumpy spruce trees.

"I got here first!" the greedy Ko-ishin-mit croaked as he flitted swiftly to the biggest of the great houses. The huge door was shut and he pushed it open and hopped inside. He did not look back to see if his little wife Pash-hook was following. "I got here first," he chanted. Ko-ishin-mit, Son of Raven, was very, very greedy.

No one was to be seen. There was not a sound to be heard other than, "I got here first." Ko-ishin-mit's beady little black eyes grew even smaller in his greed to grab, grab, grab. "All is mine! All is mine!" his voice rasped out as he croaked, the way ravens do when they espy food.

"The whole village is mine. I got here first," he reasoned to himself. He hopped around the earthen floor of the great room. Big cedar boxes lined the walls. Ko-ishin-mit's greedy instinct told him that they would be full of dried and smoked food-stuffs. Indeed he did find smoked salmon, cured meats, oils, preserved fish eggs, dried herring roe, cured qwanis (camus bulbs), and dried berries.

"Everything, everything! All is mine. All is mine," he croaked as he flitted and hopped about opening boxes of oil, dried bulbs and fish-heads. Everything he saw he wanted. He wanted it all. His own drool spilled out of his mouth. He was very greedy.

Presently Pash-hook came into the great house. For the first time in her life she was not hurrying to do her husband's bidding. She did not scurry one little bit. Instead of helping her husband to carry out all the things and food-stuff down to their little canoe on the sandy beach, she slowly approached a small pile of embers that were still glowing on the centre hearth. There was no flame. The embers glowed warmly and invitingly. Pash-hook sat down and began to warm herself. She spread out her tiny hands. The embers still glowed warmly.

Ko-ishin-mit was so excited and so busy carrying out the food-stuff that he, for the first time in their married lives, forgot to make his wife do all the work.

"I shall never be hungry again. I shall never be hungry again," he kept repeating.

He worked hard packing, packing, packing, all he could lift and move down the long sloping beach. The tide was out and their little canoe was far down from the great houses. Pash-hook sat by the embers warming herself while Ko-ishin-mit worked at loading the canoe. At last the canoe was filled. It was so full there was hardly any room left for himself or for Pash-hook.

"One more trip. One more trip." How greedy Ko-ishin-mit was! He decided to put the last load where his wife would sit. He hopped up the high sloping beach and flitted into the now nearly empty cedar box and decided again he would put the very last load where Pash-hook would sit.

All of a sudden he remembered her. Pash-hook was still sitting by the fire warming herself at the embers.

"Come Pash-hook! Hurry! We must come back as fast as we can. We must take all. We must take all. We must come back before daylight returns. Hurry, hurry, Pash-hook!"

But Pash-hook still sat without moving, before the embers of the fire. Ko-ishin-mit lost his temper. He hopped to his wife's side demanding in his raspy voice, "What's the matter with you, woman? You have never disobeyed me like this before. Get up at once. We must go."

Pash-hook did not move. She did not speak, she did not look up at her husband.

Ko-ishin-mit was alarmed. He became very frightened.

"Get up, get up!" he croaked. In anger he grabbed Pash-hook by the shoulder and tried to pull her up. The harder he pulled the heavier she became. He could not budge the small little person. She felt like a rooted stone. Ko-ishin-mit was now trembling with fear. He hop-flitted out and down to his canoe and pushed and heaved trying to move it out to deeper water, but the harder he pulled and heaved the heavier the little canoe became.

"Something is wrong. Something is terribly wrong," he told himself. He tried to shout but only a weak croak came out. He flitted back to the great house and hopped inside. Pash-hook still sat by the embers of the fire.

Ko-ishin-mit noticed she was trying very hard to tell him something. He very gingerly approached her and bent his head towards her moving lips. Brave, gallant Pash-hook tried with all her might.

"There are strange people holding me down. I can't move," she whispered, almost out of breath. "Put back all you took," she entreated her husband.

Ko-ishin-mit flitted back to his canoe and once more tried to push it out into the stream. It would not move. He tried pulling it farther up onto the beach. It moved with hardly any effort at all. Trembling, Ko-ishin-mit grabbed the topmost bale and hauled it back to the great house. He worked very hard toting all the boxes and bales back to where he found them. When the last article had been returned to its own cedar box then only did Pash-hook stir.

"Heahh," she breathed, "I'm free," and shook herself and stood up. Her husband led her out and down the long, long beach to their canoe.

Pash-hook hopped in as her now very meek husband pushed the canoe into the stream. They both paddled with all their might and main until they were at a safe distance from the strange, strange place. When they at last stopped to rest Pash-hook spoke her first words since leaving the great house.

"Heahh, I'm free," she repeated. "There are people up there in the great house with the earthen floors. I'm sure of it. I felt hands, heavy hands, upon my shoulders holding me down. I'm certain that one of them sat on me because I felt so crushed down from above. I was very frightened. I couldn't speak. I couldn't tell you."

Ko-ishin-mit looked at his wife with great love. "Choo, choo, choo, all right, all right, Pash-hook, my mate. Don't be afraid any more. We shall never go to that isle again."

It is said that all things belong to someone. The old people say it is not wise to keep anything you find.

Around the point and across the bay
There is an Isle with clumpy spruce
That stands on mossy knolls
Green with salal.
The beaches are covered with sea-shells white
When the tide runs out sea-grasses wave and beckon you in.
The shadow people live there, it is said—
Shadow people one cannot see until the sun is up
To cast their shadows on the sands of the sea-shells white.

Alice Elliott Dark

The American writer Alice Elliott Dark's first collection of stories, *Naked to the Waist* (1991), quickly established her as a writer sensitive to the nuances of daily life. Dark, who was born in 1953, has published stories in *The New Yorker* and *Double Take*, and has been recognized by a grant from the National Endowment for the Arts. Her second collection, *In the Gloaming*, was published in 2000; the title story, included here, first appeared in *The New Yorker* in 1993, and was chosen by John Updike for inclusion in the anthology *The Best American Short Stories of the Century* (1999). The story was dramatized for television by HBO in 1997, directed by Christopher Reeve.

"In the Gloaming" offers a searching look at one of the closest of all bonds, that between a mother and her son, at the final moments of the son's life. The son has AIDS. Dark does not spare us the pain, emotional on the mother's side and primarily physical on the son's, as the latter slips towards death. What gives this story its special strength is that it shuns all sentimentality. Accompanying the description of events, largely relayed from the mother's point of view, there is an unflinching recognition of the approaching end, and an acceptance born of understanding and love.

In the Gloaming

Her son wanted to talk again, suddenly. During the days, he still brooded, scowling at the swimming pool from the vantage point of his wheelchair, where he sat covered with blankets despite the summer heat. In the evenings, though, Laird became more like his old self—his *old* old self, really. He became sweeter, the way he'd been as a child, before he began to cloak himself with layers of irony and clever remarks. He spoke with an openness that astonished her. No one she knew talked that way—no man, at least. After he was asleep, Janet would run through the conversations in her mind, and realize what it was she wished she had said. She knew she was generally considered sincere, but that had more to do with her being a good listener than with how she expressed herself. She found it hard work to keep up with him, but it was the work she had pined for all her life.

A month earlier, after a particularly long and grueling visit with a friend who'd come up on the train from New York, Laird had declared a new policy: no visitors, no telephone calls. She didn't blame him. People who hadn't seen him for a while were often shocked to tears by his appearance, and, rather than having them cheer him up, he felt obliged to comfort them. She'd overheard bits of some of those conversations. The final one was no worse than the others, but he was fed up. He had said more than once that he wasn't cut out to be the brave one, the one who would inspire everybody to walk away from a visit with him feeling uplifted, shaking their heads in wonder. He had liked being the most handsome and missed it very much; he was not a good victim. When he had had enough he went into a self-imposed retreat, complete with a wall of silence and other ascetic practices that kept him busy for several weeks.

Then he softened. Not only did he want to talk again; he wanted to talk to *her*.

It began the night they ate outside on the terrace for the first time all summer. Afterward, Martin—Laird's father—got up to make a telephone call, but Janet stayed in her wicker chair, resting before clearing the table. It was one of those moments when she felt nostalgic for cigarettes. On nights like this, when the air was completely still, she used to blow her famous smoke rings for the children, dutifully obeying their commands to blow one through another or three in a row, or to make big, ropy circles that expanded as they floated up to the heavens. She did exactly what they wanted, for as long as they wanted, sometimes going through a quarter of a pack before they allowed her to stop. Incredibly, neither Anne nor Laird became smokers. Just the opposite; they nagged at her to quit, and were pleased when she finally did. She wished they had been just a little bit sorry; it was a part of their childhood coming to an end, after all.

Out of habit, she took note of the first lightning bug, the first star. The lawn darkened, and the flowers that had sulked in the heat all day suddenly released their perfumes. She laid her head back on the rim of the chair and closed her eyes. Soon she was following Laird's breathing, and found herself picking up the vital rhythms, breathing along. It was so peaceful, being near him like this. How many mothers spend so much time with their thirty-three-year-old sons? she thought. She had as much of him now as she had had when he was an infant; more, in a way, because she had the memory of the intervening years as well, to round out her thoughts about him. When they sat quietly together she felt as close to him as she ever had. It was still him in there, inside the failing shell. *She still enjoyed him.*

"The gloaming," he said, suddenly.

She nodded dreamily, automatically, then sat up. She turned to him. "What?" Although she had heard.

"I remember when I was little you took me over to the picture window and told me that in Scotland this time of day was called the 'gloaming.' "

Her skin tingled. She cleared her throat, quietly, taking care not to make too much of an event of his talking again. "You thought I said 'gloomy.' "

He gave a smile, then looked at her searchingly. "I always thought it hurt you somehow that the day was over, but you said it was a beautiful time because for a few moments the purple light made the whole world look like the Scottish Highlands on a summer night."

"Yes. As if all the earth were covered with heather."

"I'm sorry I never saw Scotland," he said.

"You're a Scottish lad nonetheless," she said. "At least on my side." She remembered offering to take him to Scotland once, but Laird hadn't been interested. By then, he was in college and already sure of his own destinations, which had diverged so thoroughly from hers. "I'm amazed you remember that conversation. You couldn't have been more than seven."

"I've been remembering a lot lately."

"Have you?"

"Mostly about when I was very small. I suppose it comes from having you take care of me again. Sometimes, when I wake up and see your face, I feel I can remember you looking in on me when I was in my crib. I remember your dresses."

"Oh, no!" She laughed lightly.

"You always had the loveliest expressions," he said.

She was astonished, caught off guard. Then, she had a memory, too—of her leaning over Laird's crib and suddenly having a picture of looking up at her own mother. "I know what you mean," she said.

"You do, don't you?"

He looked at her in a close, intimate way that made her self-conscious. She caught herself swinging her leg nervously, like a pendulum, and stopped.

"Mom," he said. "There are still a few things I need to do. I have to write a will, for one thing."

Her heart went flat. In his presence she had always maintained that he would get well. She wasn't sure she could discuss the other possibility.

"Thank you," he said.

"For what?"

"For not saying that there's plenty of time for that, or some similar sentiment."

"The only reason I didn't say it was to avoid the cliché, not because I don't believe it."

"You believe there is plenty of time?"

She hesitated; he noticed, and leaned forward slightly. "I believe there is time," she said.

"Even if I were healthy, it would be a good idea."

"I suppose."

"I don't want to leave it until it's too late. You wouldn't want me to suddenly leave everything to the nurses, would you?"

She laughed, pleased to hear him joking again. "All right, all right, I'll call the lawyer."

"That would be great." There was a pause. "Is this still your favorite time of day, Mom?"

"Yes, I suppose it is," she said, "although I don't think in terms of favorites anymore."

"Never mind favorites, then. What else do you like?"

"What do you mean?" she asked.

"I mean exactly that."

"I don't know. I care about all the ordinary things. You know what I like."

"Name one thing."

"I feel silly"

"Please?"

"All right. I like my patch of lilies of the valley under the trees over there. Now can we change the subject?"

"Name one more thing."

"Why?"

"I want to get to know you."

"Oh, Laird, there's nothing to know."

"I don't believe that for a minute."

"But it's true. I'm average. The only extraordinary thing about me is my children."

"All right," he said. "Then let's talk about how you feel about me."

"Do you flirt with your nurses like this when I'm not around?"

"I don't dare. They've got me where they want me." He looked at her. "You're changing the subject."

She smoothed her skirt. "I know how you feel about church, but if you need to talk I'm sure the minister would be glad to come over. Or if you would rather have a doctor . . ."

He laughed.

"What?"

"That you still call psychiatrists 'doctors.' "

She shrugged.

"I don't need a professional, Ma." He laced his hands and pulled at them as he struggled for words.

"What can I do?" she asked.

He met her gaze. "You're where I come from. I need to know about you."

That night she lay awake, trying to think of how she could help, of what, aside from her time, she had to offer. She couldn't imagine.

■ ■ ■

She was anxious the next day when he was sullen again, but the next night, and on each succeeding night, the dusk worked its spell. She set dinner on the table outside, and afterward, when Martin had vanished into the maw of his study, she and Laird began to speak. The air around them seemed to crackle with the energy they were creating in their effort to know and be known. Were other people so close, she wondered. She never had been, not to anybody. Certainly she and Martin had never really connected, not soul to soul, and with her friends, no matter how loyal and reliable, she always had a sense of what she could do that would alienate them. Of course, her friends had the option of cutting her off, and Martin could always ask for a divorce, whereas Laird was a captive audience. Parents and children were all captive audiences to each other; in view of this, it was amazing how little comprehension there was of one another's stories. Everyone stopped paying attention so early on, thinking they had figured it all out. She recognized that she was as guilty of this as anyone. She was still surprised whenever she went over to her daughter's house and saw how neat she was; in her mind, Anne was still a sloppy teenager who threw sweaters into the corner of her closet and candy wrappers under her bed. It still surprised her that Laird wasn't interested in girls. He had been, hadn't he? She remembered lying awake listening for him to come home, hoping that he was smart enough to apply what he knew about the facts of life, to take precautions.

Now she had the chance to let go of these old notions. It wasn't that she liked everything about Laird—there was much that remained foreign to her—but she wanted to know about all of it. As she came to her senses every morning in the moment or two after she awoke, she found herself aching with love and gratitude, as if he were a small, perfect creature again and she could look forward to a day of watching him grow. Quickly, she became greedy for their evenings. She replaced her half-facetious, half-hopeful reading of the horoscope in the daily newspaper with a new habit of tracking the time the sun would set, and drew satisfaction from seeing it come earlier as the summer waned; it meant she didn't have to wait as long. She took to sleeping late, shortening the day even more. It was ridiculous, she knew. She was behaving like a girl with a crush, behaving absurdly. It was a feeling she had thought she'd never have again, and now here it was. She immersed herself in it, living her life for the twilight moment when his eyes would begin to glow, the signal that he was stirring into consciousness. Then her real day would begin.

"Dad ran off quickly," he said one night. She had been wondering when he would mention it.

"He had a phone call to make," she said automatically.

Laird looked directly into her eyes, his expression one of gentle reproach. He was letting her know he had caught her in the central lie of her life, which was that she understood Martin's obsession with his work. She averted her gaze. The truth was that she had never understood. Why couldn't he sit with her for half an hour after dinner, or, if not with her, why not with his dying son?

She turned sharply to look at Laird. The word "dying" had sounded so loudly in her mind that she wondered if she had spoken it, but he showed no reaction. She wished she hadn't even thought it. She tried to stick to good thoughts in his presence. When she couldn't, and he had a bad night afterward, she blamed herself, as her efficient memory dredged up all the books and magazine articles she had read emphasizing the effect of psychological factors on the course of the disease. She didn't entirely believe it, but she felt compelled to give the benefit of the doubt to every theory that might help. It couldn't do any harm to think positively. And if it gave him a few more months . . .

"I don't think Dad can stand to be around me."

"That's not true." It was true.

"Poor Dad. He's always been a hypochondriac—we have that in common. He must hate this."

"He just wants you to get well."

"If that's what he wants, I'm afraid I'm going to disappoint him again. At least this will be the last time I let him down."

He said this merrily, with the old, familiar light darting from his eyes. She allowed herself to be amused. He had always been fond of teasing, and held no subject sacred. As the de facto authority figure in the house—Martin hadn't been home enough to be the real disciplinarian—she had often been forced to reprimand Laird, but, in truth, she shared his sense of humor. She responded to it now by leaning over to cuff him on the arm. It was an automatic response, prompted by a burst of high spirits that took no notice of the circumstances. It was a mistake. Even through the thickness of his terrycloth robe, her knuckles knocked on bone. There was nothing left of him.

"It's his loss," she said, the shock of Laird's thinness making her serious again. It was the furthest she would go in criticizing Martin.

She had always felt it her duty to maintain a benign image of him for the children. He had become a character of her invention, with a whole range of postulated emotions whereby he missed them when he was away on a business trip and thought of them every few minutes when he had to work late. Some years earlier, when she was secretly seeing a doctor—a psychiatrist—she had finally admitted to herself that Martin was never going to be the lover she had dreamed of. He was an ambitious, competitive, self-absorbed man who probably should never have got married. It was such a relief to be able to face it that she wanted to share the news with her children, only to discover that they were dependent on the myth. They could hate his work, but they could not bring themselves to believe he had any choice in the matter. She had dropped the subject.

"Thank you, Ma. It's his loss in your case, too."

A throbbing began behind her eyes, angering her. The last thing she wanted to do was cry. There would be plenty of time for that. "It's not all his fault," she said when she had regained some measure of control. "I'm not very good at talking about myself. I was brought up not to."

"So was I," he said.

"Yes, I suppose you were."

"Luckily, I didn't pay any attention." He grinned.

"I hope not," she said, and meant it. "Can I get you anything?"

"A new immune system?"

She rolled her eyes, trying to disguise the way his joke had touched on her prayers. "Very funny. I was thinking more along the lines of an iced tea or an extra blanket."

"I'm fine. I'm getting tired, actually."

Her entire body went on the alert, and she searched his face anxiously for signs of deterioration. Her nerves darted and pricked whenever he wanted anything; her adrenaline rushed. The fight-or-flight response, she supposed. She had often wanted to flee, but had forced herself to stay, to fight with what few weapons she had. She responded to his needs, making sure there was a fresh, clean set of sheets ready when he was tired, food when he was hungry. It was what she could do.

"Shall I get a nurse?" She pushed her chair back from the table.

"O.K.," Laird said weakly. He stretched out his hand to her, and the incipient moonlight illuminated his skin so it shone like alabaster. His face had turned ashy. It was a sight that made her stomach drop. She ran for Maggie, and by the time they returned Laird's eyes were closed, his head lolling to one side. Automatically, Janet looked for a stirring in his chest. There it was: his shoulders expanded; he still breathed. Always, in the second before she saw movement, she became cold and clinical as she braced herself for the possibility of discovering that he was dead.

Maggie had her fingers on his wrist and was counting his pulse against the second hand on her watch, her lips moving. She laid his limp hand back on his lap. "Fast," she pronounced.

"I'm not surprised," Janet said, masking her fear with authority. "We had a long talk."

Maggie frowned. "Now I'll have to wake him up again for his meds."

"Yes, I suppose that's true. I forgot about that."

Janet wheeled him into his makeshift room downstairs and helped Maggie lift him into the rented hospital bed. Although he weighed almost nothing, it was really a job for two; his weight was dead weight. In front of Maggie, she was all brusque efficiency, except for the moment when her fingers strayed to touch Laird's pale cheek and she prayed she hadn't done any harm.

■ ■ ■

"Who's your favorite author?" he asked one night.

"Oh, there are so many," she said.

"Your real favorite."

She thought. "The truth is there are certain subjects I find attractive more than certain authors. I seem to read in cycles, to fulfill an emotional yearning."

"Such as?"

"Books about people who go off to live in Africa or Australia or the South Seas."

He laughed. "That's fairly self-explanatory. What else?"

"When I really hate life I enjoy books about real murders. 'True crime,' I think they're called now. They're very punishing."

"Is that what's so compelling about them? I could never figure it out. I just know that at certain times I loved the gore, even though I felt absolutely disgusted with myself for being interested in it."

"You need to think about when those times were. That will tell you a lot." She paused. "I don't like reading about sex."

"Big surprise!"

"No, no," she said. "It's not for the reason you think, or not only for that reason. You see me as a prude, I know, but remember, it's part of a mother's job to come across that way. Although perhaps I went a bit far . . ."

He shrugged amiably. "Water under the bridge. But go on about sex."

"I think it should be private. I always feel as though these writers are showing off when they describe a sex scene. They're not really trying to describe sex, but to demonstrate that they're not afraid to write about it. As if they're thumbing their noses at their mothers."

He made a moue.

Janet went on. "You don't think there's an element of that? I *do* question their motives, because I don't think sex can ever actually be portrayed—the sensations and the emotions are . . . beyond language. If you only describe the mechanics, the effect is either clinical or pornographic, and if you try to describe intimacy instead, you wind up with abstractions. The only sex you could describe fairly well is bad sex—and who wants to read about that, for God's sake, when everyone is having bad sex of their own?"

"Mother!" He was laughing helplessly, his arms hanging limply over the sides of his chair.

"I mean it. To me it's like reading about someone using the bathroom."

"Good grief!"

"Now who's the prude?"

"I never said I wasn't," he said. "Maybe we should change the subject."

She looked out across the land. The lights were on in other people's houses, giving the evening the look of early fall. The leaves were different, too, becoming droopy. The grass was dry, even with all the watering and tending from the gardener. The summer was nearly over.

"Maybe we shouldn't," she said. "I've been wondering. Was that side of life satisfying for you?"

"Ma, tell me you're not asking me about my sex life."

She took her napkin and folded it carefully, lining up the edges and running her fingers along the hems. She felt very calm, very pulled together and all of a piece, as if she'd finally got the knack of being a dignified woman. She threaded her fingers and laid her hands in her lap. "I'm asking about your love life," she said. "Did you love, and were you loved in return?"

"Yes."

"I'm glad."

"That was easy," he said.

"Oh, I've gotten very easy, in my old age."

"Does Dad know about this?" His eyes were twinkling wickedly.

"Don't be fresh," she said.

"You started it."

"Then I'm stopping it. Now."

He made a funny face, and then another, until she could no longer keep from smiling. His routine carried her back to memories of his childhood efforts to charm her: watercolors of her favorite vistas (unrecognizable without the captions), bouquets of violets self-consciously flung into her lap, chores performed without prompting. He had always gone too far, then backtracked to regain even footing. She had always allowed herself to be wooed.

Suddenly she realized: Laird had been the love of her life.

■ ■ ■

One night it rained hard. Janet decided to serve the meal in the kitchen, since Martin was out. They ate in silence; she was freed from the compulsion to keep up the steady stream of chatter that she used to affect when Laird hadn't talked at all; now she knew she could save her words for afterward. He ate nothing but comfort foods lately: mashed potatoes, vanilla ice cream, rice pudding. The days of his strict macrobiotic regime, and all the cooking classes she had taken in order to help him along with it, were past. His body was essentially a thing of the past, too; when he ate, he was feeding what was left of his mind. He seemed to want to recapture the cosseted feeling he'd had when he'd been sick as a child and she would serve him flat ginger ale, and toast soaked in cream, and play endless card games with him, using his blanket-covered legs as a table. In those days, too, there'd been a general sense of giving way to illness: then, he let himself go completely because he knew he would soon be better and active and have a million things expected of him again. Now he let himself go because he had fought long enough.

Finally, he pushed his bowl toward the middle of the table, signaling that he was finished. (His table manners had gone to pieces. Who cared?) She felt a light, jittery excitement, the same jazzy feeling she got when she was in a plane that was picking up speed on the runway. She arranged her fork and knife on the rim of her plate and pulled her chair in closer. "I had an odd dream last night," she said.

His eyes remained dull.

She waited uncertainly, thinking that perhaps she had started to talk too soon. "Would you like something else to eat?"

He shook his head. There was no will in his expression; his refusal was purely physical, a gesture coming from the satiation in his stomach. An animal walking away from its bowl, she thought.

To pass the time, she carried the dishes to the sink, gave them a good hot rinse, and put them in the dishwasher. She carried the ice cream to the counter, pulled a spoon from the drawer and scraped off a mouthful of the thick, creamy residue that stuck to the inside of the lid. She ate it without thinking, so the sudden sweetness caught her by surprise. All the while she kept track of Laird, but every time she thought she noticed signs of his readiness to talk and hurried back to the table, she found his face still blank.

She went to the window. The lawn had become a floodplain and was filled with broad pools; the branches of the evergreens sagged, and the sky was the same uniform grayish yellow it had been since morning. She saw him focus his gaze on the line where the treetops touched the heavens, and she understood. There was no lovely interlude on this rainy night, no heathered dusk. The gray landscape had taken the light out of him.

"I'm sorry" she said aloud, as if it were her fault.

He gave a tiny, helpless shrug.

She hovered for a few moments, hoping, but his face was slack, and she gave up. She felt utterly forsaken, too disappointed and agitated to sit with him and watch the rain. "It's all right," she said. "It's a good night to watch television."

She wheeled him to the den and left him with Maggie, then did not know what to do with herself. She had no contingency plan for this time. It was usually the one period of the day when she did not need the anesthesia of tennis games, bridge lessons, volunteer work, errands. She had not considered the present possibility. For some time, she hadn't given any thought to what Martin would call "the big picture." Her conversations with Laird had lulled her into inventing a parallel big picture of her own. She realized that a part of her had worked out a whole scenario: the summer evenings would blend into fall; then, gradually, the winter would arrive, heralding chats by the fire, Laird resting his feet on the pigskin ottoman in the den while she dutifully knitted her yearly Christmas sweaters for Anne's children.

She had allowed herself to imagine a future. That had been her mistake. This silent, endless evening was her punishment, a reminder of how things really were.

She did not know where to go in her own house, and ended up wandering through the rooms, propelled by a vague, hunted feeling. Several times, she turned around, expecting someone to be there, but, of course, no one ever was. She was quite alone. Eventually, she realized that she was imagining a person in order to give material properties to the source of her wounds. She was inventing a villain. There should be a villain, shouldn't there? There should be an enemy, a devil, an evil force that could be driven out. Her imagination had provided it with aspects of a corporeal presence so she could pretend, for a moment, that there was a real enemy hovering around her, someone she could have the police come and take away. But the enemy was part of Laird, and neither he nor she nor any of the doctors or experts or ministers could separate the two.

She went upstairs and took a shower. She barely paid attention to her own body anymore, and only noticed abstractly that the water was too hot, her skin turning pink. Afterward, she sat on the chaise longue in her bedroom and tried to read. She heard something; she leaned forward and cocked her head toward the sound. Was that Laird's voice? Suddenly she believed that he had begun to talk after all—she believed he was talking to Maggie. She dressed and went downstairs. He was alone in the den, alone with the television. He didn't hear or see her. She watched him take a drink from a cup, his hand shaking badly. It was a plastic cup with a straw poking through the lid, the kind used by small children while they are learning to drink. It was supposed to prevent accidents, but it couldn't stop his hands from trembling. He managed to spill the juice anyway.

■ ■ ■

Laird had always coveted the decadent pile of cashmere lap blankets she had collected over the years in the duty-free shops of the various British airports. Now he wore one around his shoulders, one over his knees. She remembered similar balmy nights when he would arrive home from soccer practice after dark, a towel slung around his neck.

"I suppose it has to be in the church," he said.

"I think it should," she said, "but it's up to you."

"I guess it's not the most timely moment to make a statement about my personal disbeliefs. But I'd like you to keep it from being too lugubrious. No lilies, for instance."

"God forbid."

"And have some decent music."

"Such as?"

"I had an idea, but now I can't remember."

He pressed his hands to his eyes. His fingers were so transparent that they looked as if he were holding them over a flashlight.

"Please buy a smashing dress, something mournful yet elegant."

"All right."

"And don't wait until the last minute."

She didn't reply.

■ ■ ■

Janet gave up on the idea of a rapprochement between Martin and Laird; she felt freer when she stopped hoping for it. Martin rarely came home for dinner anymore. Perhaps he was having an affair? It was a thought she'd never allowed herself to have before, but it didn't threaten her now. Good for him, she even decided, in her strongest, most magnanimous moments. Good for him if he's actually feeling bad and trying to do something to make himself feel better.

Anne was brave and chipper during her visits, yet when she walked back out to her car, she would wrap her arms around her ribs and shudder. "I don't know how you do it, Mom. Are you really all right?" she always asked, with genuine concern.

"Anne's become such a hopeless matron," Laird always said, with fond exasperation, when he and his mother were alone again later. Once, Janet began to tease him for finally coming to friendly terms with his sister, but she cut it short when she saw that he was blinking furiously.

They were exactly the children she had hoped to have: a companionable girl, a mischievous boy. It gave her great pleasure to see them together. She did not try to listen to their conversations but watched from a distance, usually from the kitchen as she prepared them a snack reminiscent of their childhood, like watermelon boats or lemonade. Then she would walk Anne to the car, their similar good shoes clacking across the gravel. They hugged, pressing each other's arms, and their brief embraces buoyed them up—forbearance and grace passing back and forth between them like a piece of shared clothing, designated for use by whoever needed it most. It was the kind of parting toward which she had aimed her whole life, a graceful, secure parting at the close of a peaceful afternoon. After Anne left, Janet always had a tranquil moment or two as she walked back to the house through the humid September air. Everything was so still. Occasionally there were the hums and clicks of a lawnmower or the shrieks of a band of children heading home from school. There were the insects and the birds. It was a straightforward, simple life she had chosen. She had tried never to ask for too much, and to be of use. Simplicity had been her hedge against bad luck. It had worked for so long. For a brief moment, as she stepped lightly up the single slate stair and through the door, her legs still harboring all their former vitality, she could pretend her luck was still holding.

Then she would glance out the window and there would be the heart-catching sight of Laird, who would never again drop by for a casual visit. Her chest would ache and flutter, a cave full of bats.

Perhaps she had asked for too much, after all.

■ ■ ■

"What did you want to be when you grew up?" Laird asked.

"I was expected to be a wife and mother. I accepted that. I wasn't a rebel."

"There must have been something else."

"No," she said. "Oh, I guess I had all the usual fantasies of the day, of being the next Amelia Earhart or Margaret Mead, but that was all they were—fantasies. I wasn't even close to being brave enough. Can you imagine me flying across the ocean on my own?" She laughed and looked over for his laughter, but he had fallen asleep.

■ ■ ■

A friend of Laird's had somehow got the mistaken information that Laird had died, so she and Martin received a condolence letter. There was a story about a time a few years back when the friend was with Laird on a bus in New York. They had been sitting behind two older women, waitresses who began to discuss their income taxes, trying to decide how much of their tip income to declare to sound realistic so they wouldn't attract an audit. Each woman offered up bits of folk wisdom on the subject, describing in detail her particular situation. During a lull in the conversation, Laird stood up.

"Excuse me, I couldn't help overhearing," he said, leaning over them. "May I have your names and addresses, please? I work for the IRS."

The entire bus fell silent as everyone watched to see what would happen next. Laird took a small notebook and pen from the inside pocket of his jacket. He faced his captive audience. "I'm part of a new IRS outreach program," he told the group. "For the next ten minutes I'll be taking confessions. Does anyone have anything he or she wants to tell me?"

Smiles. Soon the whole bus was talking, comparing notes—when they'd first realized he was kidding, and how scared they had been before they caught on. It was difficult to believe these were the same New Yorkers who were supposed to be so gruff and isolated.

"Laird was the most vital, funniest person I ever met," his friend wrote.

Now, in his wheelchair, he faced off against slow-moving flies, waving them away.

■ ■ ■

"The gloaming," Laird said.

Janet looked up from her knitting, startled. It was midafternoon, and the living room was filled with bright October sun. "Soon," she said.

He furrowed his brow. A little flash of confusion passed through his eyes, and she realized that for him it was already dark.

He tried to straighten his shawl, his hands shaking. She jumped up to help; then, when he pointed to the fireplace, she quickly laid the logs as she wondered what was wrong. Was he dehydrated? She thought she recalled that a dimming of vision was a sign of dehydration. She tried to remember what else she had read or heard, but even as she grasped for information, facts, her instincts kept interrupting with a deeper, more dreadful thought that vibrated through her, rattling her and making her gasp as she often did when remembering her mistakes, things she wished she hadn't said or done, wished she had the chance to do over. She knew what was wrong, and yet she kept turning away from the truth, her mind spinning in every other possible direction as she worked on the fire, only vaguely noticing how wildly she made the sparks fly as she pumped the old bellows.

Her work was mechanical—she had made hundreds of fires—and soon there was nothing left to do. She put the screen up and pushed him close, then leaned over to pull his flannel pajamas down to meet his socks, protecting his bare shins. The sun streamed in around him, making him appear trapped between bars of light. She resumed her knitting, with mechanical hands.

"The gloaming," he said again. It did sound somewhat like "gloomy," because his speech was slurred.

"When all the world is purple," she said, hearing herself sound falsely bright. She wasn't sure whether he wanted her to talk. It was some time since he had talked—not long, really, in other people's lives, perhaps two weeks—but she had gone on with their conversations, gradually expanding into the silence until she was telling him stories and he was listening. Sometimes, when his eyes closed, she trailed off and began to drift. There would be a pause that she didn't always realize she was making, but if it went on too long he would call out "Mom?" with an edge of panic in his voice, as if he were waking from a nightmare. Then she would resume, trying to create a seamless bridge between what she had been thinking and where she had left off.

"It was really your grandfather who gave me my love for the gloaming," she said. "Do you remember him talking about it?" She looked up politely, expectantly, as if Laird might offer her a conversational reply. He seemed to like hearing the sound of her voice, so she went on, her needles clicking. Afterward, she could never remember for sure at what point she had stopped talking and had floated off into a jumble of her own thoughts, afraid to move, afraid to look up, afraid to know at which exact moment she became alone. All she knew was that at a certain point the fire was in danger of dying out entirely, and when she got up to stir the embers she glanced at him in spite of herself and saw that his fingers were making knitting motions over his chest, the way people did as they were dying. She knew that if she went to get the nurse, Laird would be gone by the time she returned, so she went and stood behind him, leaning over to press her face against his, sliding her hands down his busy arms, helping him along with his fretful stitches until he finished this last piece of work.

■ ■ ■

Later, after the most pressing calls had been made and Laird's body had been taken away, Janet went up to his old room and lay down on one of the twin beds. She had changed the room into a guest room when he went off to college, replacing his things with guest room decor, thoughtful touches such as luggage racks at the foot of each bed, a writing desk stocked with paper and pens, heavy wooden hangers and shoe trees. She made an effort to remember the room as it had been when he was a little boy; she had chosen a train motif, then had to redecorate when Laird decided trains were silly. He had wanted it to look like a jungle, so she had hired an art student to paint a jungle mural on the walls. When he decided *that* was silly, he hadn't bothered her to do anything about it, but had simply marked time until he could move on.

Anne came over, offered to stay, but was relieved to be sent home to her children.

Presently, Martin came in. Janet was watching the trees turn to mere silhouettes against the darkening sky, fighting the urge to pick up a true-crime book, a debased urge. He lay down on the other bed.

"I'm sorry," he said.

"It's so wrong," she said angrily. She hadn't felt angry until that moment; she had saved it up for him. "A child shouldn't die before his parents. A young man shouldn't spend his early thirties wasting away talking to his mother. He should be out in the world. He shouldn't be thinking about me, or what I care about, or my opinions. He shouldn't have had to return my love to me—it was his to squander. Now I have it all back and I don't know what I'm supposed to do with it," she said.

She could hear Martin weeping in the darkness. He sobbed, and her anger veered away.

They were quiet for some time.

"Is there going to be a funeral?" Martin asked finally.

"Yes. We should start making the arrangements."

"I suppose he told you what he wanted."

"In general. He couldn't decide about the music."

She heard Martin roll onto his side, so that he was facing her across the narrow chasm between the beds. He was still in his office clothes. "I remember being very moved by the bagpipes at your father's funeral."

It was an awkward offering, to be sure, awkward and late, and seemed to come from someone on the periphery of her life who knew her only slightly. It didn't matter; it was perfectly right. Her heart rushed toward it.

"I think Laird would have liked that idea very much," she said.

It was the last moment of the gloaming, the last moment of the day her son died. In a breath, it would be night; the moon hovered behind the trees, already rising to claim the sky, and she told herself she might as well get on with it. She sat up and was running her toes across the bare floor, searching for her shoes, when Martin spoke again, in a tone she used to hear on those long-ago nights when he rarely got home until after the children were in bed and he relied on her to fill him in on what they'd done that day. It was the same curious, shy, deferential tone that had always made her feel as though all the frustrations and boredom and mistakes and rushes of feeling in her days as a mother did indeed add up to something of importance, and she decided that the next round of telephone calls could wait while she answered the question he asked her: "Please tell me—what else did my boy like?"

WILLIAM FAULKNER

The main body of the fiction of William Faulkner (1897–1962) stands as a memorial to the American South, the old South of rich plantation owners and poor white trash, of slavery and sudden violence: a region not without its glories, but suffering a progressive decay from within. Faulkner was born in Oxford, Mississippi, into a family whose roots reached back into the old South; and out of this background grew the fictional city of Jefferson in Yoknapatawpha County, the history of which forms the principal subject of Faulkner's work. After service in the Canadian Flying Corps during World War I and a period at the University of Mississippi, he turned to literature as a profession, publishing his first novel, *Soldiers' Pay,* in 1926. With *Sartoris* (1929) he began his re-creation and exploration of the South, which were to continue in such works as *The Sound and the Fury* (1929), *As I Lay Dying* (1930), *Light in August* (1932), *Absalom, Absalom!* (1936), and *Go Down, Moses* (1942). In these and other works, Faulkner chronicles the fortunes of the Sartorises and the Snopeses, the Compsons and the McCaslins, characters who recur throughout his writings, sometimes at the centre, at other times at the periphery of the action; and although the novels and stories do not form a continuous series, they are linked by common themes and preoccupations: the breakdown of social traditions, the strengths and weaknesses of the old Southern code, the strained and often bloody relations between black and white in the aftermath of slavery. "Dry September," from Faulkner's first collection of stories, *These Thirteen* (1931), is a powerful evocation of the frustration, bigotry, and passion pervading a society in which old fears and hatreds die hard.

Faulkner's achievement, however, extends beyond the dramatic creation of a Southern myth; in the moral problems and the racial tensions of his imaginary community in Mississippi, he has imaged sources of guilt and conflict that beset our larger society. In his address upon receiving the Nobel Prize for literature in 1950, Faulkner spoke of the role of the artist in terms applicable to himself, exhorting young writers to depict "the old verities and truths of the heart, the old universal truths lacking which any story is ephemeral and doomed—love and honour and pity and pride and compassion and sacrifice."

Dry September

Through the bloody September twilight, aftermath of sixty-two rainless days, it had gone like a fire in dry grass—the rumor, the story, whatever it was. Something about Miss Minnie Cooper and a Negro. Attacked, insulted, frightened: none of them, gathered in the barber shop on that Saturday evening where the ceiling fan stirred, without freshening it, the vitiated air, sending back upon them, in recurrent surges of stale pomade and lotion, their own stale breath and odors, knew exactly what had happened.

"Except it wasn't Will Mayes," a barber said. He was a man of middle age; a thin, sand-colored man with a mild face, who was shaving a client. "I know Will Mayes. He's a good nigger. And I know Miss Minnie Cooper, too."

"What do you know about her?" a second barber said.

"Who is she?" the client said. "A young girl?"

"No," the barber said. "She's about forty, I reckon. She aint married. That's why I dont believe—"

"Believe, hell!" a hulking youth in a sweat-stained silk shirt said. "Won't you take a white woman's word before a nigger's?"

"I dont believe Will Mayes did it," the barber said. "I know Will Mayes."

"Maybe you know who did it, then. Maybe you already got him out of town, you damn niggerlover."

"I dont believe anybody did anything. I dont believe anything happened. I leave it to you fellows if them ladies that get old without getting married dont have notions that a man cant—"

"Then you are a hell of a white man," the client said. He moved under the cloth. The youth had sprung to his feet.

"You dont?" he said. "Do you accuse a white woman of lying?"

The barber held the razor poised above the half-risen client. He did not look around.

"It's this durn weather," another said. "It's enough to make a man do anything. Even to her."

Nobody laughed. The barber said in his mild, stubborn tone, "I aint accusing nobody of nothing. I just know and you fellows know how a woman that never—"

"You damn niggerlover!" the youth said.

"Shut up, Butch," another said. "We'll get the facts in plenty of time to act."

"Who is? Who's getting them?" the youth said. "Facts, hell! I—"

"You're a fine white man," the client said. "Aint you?" In his frothy beard he looked like a desert rat in moving pictures. "You can tell them, Jack," he said to the youth. "If there aint any white men in this town you can count on me, even if I aint only a drummer and a stranger."

"That's right, boys," the barber said. "Find out the truth first. I know Will Mayes."

"Well, by God!" the youth shouted. "To think that a white man in this town—"

"Shut up, Butch," the second speaker said. "We got plenty of time."

The client sat up. He looked at the speaker. "Do you claim that anything excuses a nigger attacking a white woman? Do you mean to tell me you are a white man and you'll stand for it? You better go back North were you came from. The South dont want your kind here."

"North what?" the second said. "I was born and raised in this town."

"Well, by God!" the youth said. He looked about with a strained, baffled gaze, as if he was trying to remember what it was he wanted to say or to do. He drew his sleeve across his sweating face. "Damn if I'm going to let a white woman—"

"You tell them, Jack," the drummer said. "By God, if they—"

The screen door crashed open. A man stood in the floor, his feet apart and his heavy-set body poised easily. His white shirt was open at the throat; he wore a felt hat. His hot, bold glance swept the group. His name was McLendon. He had commanded troops at the front in France and had been decorated for valor.

"Well," he said, "are you going to sit there and let a black son rape a white woman on the streets of Jefferson?"

Butch sprang up again. The silk of his shirt clung flat to his heavy shoulders. At each armpit was a dark halfmoon. "That's what I been telling them! That's what I—"

"Did it really happen?" a third said. "This aint the first man scare she ever had, like Hawkshaw says. Wasn't there something about a man on the kitchen roof, watching her undress, about a year ago?"

"What?" the client said. "What's that?" The barber had been slowly forcing him back into the chair; he arrested himself reclining, his head lifted, the barber still pressing him down.

McLendon whirled on the third speaker. "Happen? What the hell difference does it make? Are you going to let the black sons get away with it until one really does it?"

"That's what I'm telling them!" Butch shouted. He cursed, long and steady, pointless.

"Here, here," a fourth said. "Not so loud. Dont talk so loud."

"Sure," McLendon said, "no talking necessary at all. I've done my talking. Who's with me?" He poised on the balls of his feet, roving his gaze.

The barber held the drummer's face down, the razor poised. "Find out the facts first, boys. I know Willy Mayes. It wasn't him. Let's get the sheriff and do this thing right."

McLendon whirled upon him furious, rigid face. The barber did not look away. They looked like men of different races. The other barbers had ceased also above their prone clients. "You mean to tell me," McLendon said, "that you'd take a nigger's word before a white woman's? Why, you damn niggerloving—"

The third speaker rose and grasped McLendon's arm; he too had been a soldier. "Now, now. Let's figure this thing out. Who knows anything about what really happened?"

"Figure out hell!" McLendon jerked his arm free. "All that're with me get up from there. The ones that aint—" He roved his gaze, dragging his sleeve across his face.

Three men rose. The drummer in the chair sat up. "Here," he said, jerking at the cloth about his neck; "get this rag off me. I'm with him. I dont live here, but by God, if our mothers and wives and sisters—" He smeared the cloth over his face and flung it to the floor. McLendon stood in the floor and cursed the others. Another rose and moved towards him. The remainder sat uncomfortable, not looking at one another, then one by one they rose and joined him.

The barber picked the cloth from the floor. He began to fold it neatly. "Boys, dont do that. Will Mayes never done it. I know."

"Come on," McLendon said. He whirled. From his hip pocket protruded the butt of a heavy automatic pistol. They went out. The screen door crashed behind them reverberant in the dead air.

The barber wiped the razor carefully and swiftly, and put it away and ran to the rear, and took his hat from the wall. "I'll be back as soon as I can," he said to the other barbers. "I cant let—" He went out, running. The two other barbers followed him to the door and caught it on the rebound, leaning out and looking up the street after him. The air was flat and dead. It had a metallic taste at the base of the tongue.

"What can he do?" the first said. The second one was saying "Jees Christ, Jees Christ" under his breath. "I'd just as lief be Will Mayes as Hawk, if he gets McLendon riled."

"Jees Christ, Jees Christ," the second whispered.

"You reckon he really done it to her?" the first said.

II

She was thirty-eight or thirty-nine. She lived in a small frame house with her invalid mother and a thin, sallow, unflagging aunt, where each morning between ten and eleven she would appear on the porch in a lace-trimmed boudoir cap, to sit swinging in the porch swing until noon. After dinner she lay down for a while, until the afternoon began to cool. Then, in one of the three or four new voile dresses which she had each summer, she would go downtown to spend the afternoon in the stores with the other ladies, where they would handle the goods and haggle over the prices in cold, immediate voices, without any intention of buying.

She was of comfortable people—not the best in Jefferson, but good people enough—and she was still on the slender side of ordinary-looking, with a bright, faintly haggard manner and dress. When she was young she had had a slender nervous body and a sort of hard vivacity which had enabled her for a time to ride upon the crest of the town's social life as exemplified by the high school party and church social period of her contemporaries while still children enough to be unclass-conscious.

She was the last to realize that she was losing ground; that those among whom she had been a little brighter and louder flame than any other were beginning to learn the pleasure of snobbery—male—and retaliation—female. That was when her face began to wear that bright, haggard look. She still carried it to parties on shadowy porticoes and summer lawns, like a mask or a flag, with that bafflement of furious repudiation of truth in her eyes. One evening at a party she heard a boy and two girls, all schoolmates, talking. She never accepted another invitation.

She watched the girls with whom she had grown up as they married and got homes and children, but no man ever called on her steadily until the children of the other girls had been calling her "aunty" for several years, the while their mothers told them in bright voices about how popular Aunt Minnie had been as a girl. Then the town began to see her driving on Sunday afternoons with the cashier in the bank. He was a widower of about forty—a high-colored man, smelling always faintly of the barber shop or of whisky. He owned the first automobile in town, a red runabout; Minnie had the first motoring bonnet and veil the town ever saw. Then the town began to say: "Poor Minnie." "But she is old enough to take care of herself," others said. That was when she began to ask her old schoolmates that their children call her "cousin" instead of "aunty."

It was twelve years now since she had been relegated into adultery by public opinion, and eight years since the cashier had gone to a Memphis bank, returning for one day each Christmas, which he spent at an annual bachelors' party at a hunting club on the river. From behind their curtains the neighbors would see the party pass, and during the over-the-way Christmas day visiting they would tell her about him, about how well he looked, and how they heard that he was prospering in the city, watching with bright, secret eyes her haggard, bright face. Usually, by that hour there would be the scent of whiskey on her breath. It was supplied her by a youth, a clerk at the soda fountain: "Sure; I buy it for the old gal. I reckon she's entitled to a little fun."

Her mother kept to her room altogether now; the gaunt aunt ran the house. Against that background Minnie's bright dresses, her idle and empty days, had a quality of furious unreality. She went out in the evenings only with women now, neighbors, to the moving pictures. Each afternoon she dressed in one of the new dresses and went downtown alone, where her young "cousins" were already strolling in the late afternoons with their delicate, silken heads and thin, awkward arms and conscious hips, clinging to one another or shrieking and giggling with paired boys in the soda fountain when she passed and went on along the serried store fronts, in the doors of which the sitting and lounging men did not even follow her with their eyes any more.

III

The barber went swiftly up the street where the sparse lights, insect-swirled, glared in rigid and violent suspension in the lifeless air. The day had died in a pall of dust; above the darkened square, shrouded by the spent dust, the sky was as clear as the inside of a brass bell. Below the east was a rumor of the twice-waxed moon.

When he overtook them McLendon and three others were getting into a car parked in an alley. McLendon stooped his thick head, peering out beneath the top, "Changed your mind, did you?" he said. "Damn good thing; by God, tomorrow when this town hears about how you talked tonight—"

"Now, now," the other ex-soldier said. "Hawkshaw's all right. Come on, Hawk; jump in."

"Will Mayes never done it, boys," the barber said. "If anybody done it. Why, you all know well as I do there aint any town where they got better niggers than us. And you know how a lady will kind of think things about men when there aint any reason to, and Miss Minnie anyway—"

"Sure, sure," the soldier said. "We're just going to talk to him a little; that's all."

"Talk hell!" Butch said. "When we're through with the—"

"Shut up, for God's sake!" the soldier said. "Do you want everybody in town—"

"Tell them, by God!" McLendon said. "Tell every one of the sons that'll let a white woman—"

"Let's go; let's go; here's the other car." The second car slid squealing out of a cloud of dust at the alley mouth. McLendon started his car and took the lead. Dust lay like a fog in the street. The street lights hung nimbused as in water. They drove out of town.

A rutted lane turned at right angles. Dust hung above it too, and above all the land. The dark bulk of the ice plant, where the Negro Mayes was night watchman, rose against the sky. "Better stop here, hadn't we?" the soldier said. McLendon did not reply. He hurled the car up and slammed to a stop, the headlights glaring on the blank wall.

"Listen here, boys," the barber said; "if he's here, dont that prove he never done it? Dont it? If it was him, he would run. Dont you see he would?" The second car came up and stopped. McLendon got down; Butch sprang down beside him. "Listen, boys," the barber said.

"Cut the lights off!" McLendon said. The breathless dark rushed down. There was no sound in it save their lungs as they sought air in the parched dust in which for two months they had lived; then the diminishing crunch of McLendon's and Butch's feet, and a moment later McLendon's voice:

"Will! . . . Will!"

Below the east the wan hemorrhage of the moon increased. It heaved above the ridge, silvering the air, the dust, so that they seemed to breathe, live, in a bowl of molten lead. There was no sound of night-bird nor insect, no sound save their breathing and a faint ticking of contracting metal about the cars. Where their bodies touched one another they seemed to sweat dryly, for no more moisture came. "Christ!" a voice said; "let's get out of here."

But they didn't move until vague noises began to grow out of the darkness ahead; then they got out and waited tensely in the breathless dark. There was another sound: a blow, a hissing expulsion of breath and McLendon cursing in undertone. They stood a moment longer, then they ran forward. They ran in a stumbling clump, as though they were fleeing something. "Kill him, kill the son," a voice whispered. McLendon flung them back.

"Not here," he said. "Get him into the car. Kill him, kill the black son!" the voice murmured. They dragged the Negro to the car. The barber had waited beside the car. He could feel himself sweating and he knew he was going to be sick at the stomach.

"What is it, captains?" the Negro said. "I aint done nothing. 'Fore God, Mr John." Someone produced handcuffs. They worked busily about the Negro as though he were a post, quiet, intent, getting in one another's way. He submitted to the handcuffs, looking swiftly and constantly from dim face to dim face. "Who's here, captains?" he said, leaning to peer into the faces until they could feel his breath and smell his sweaty reek. He spoke a name or two. "What you all say I done, Mr John?"

McLendon jerked the car door open. "Get in!" he said.

The Negro did not move. "What you all going to do with me, Mr John? I aint done nothing. White folks, captains, I aint done nothing: I swear 'fore God." He called another name.

"Get in!" McLendon said. He struck the Negro. The others expelled their breath in a dry hissing and struck him with random blows and he whirled and cursed them, and swept his manacled hands across their faces and slashed the barber upon the mouth, and the barber struck him also. "Get him in there," McLendon said. They pushed at him. He ceased struggling and got in and sat quietly as the others took their places. He sat between the barber and the soldier, drawing his limbs in so as not to touch them, his eyes going swiftly and constantly from face to face. Butch clung to the running board. The car moved on. The barber nursed his mouth with his handkerchief.

"What's the matter, Hawk?" the soldier said.

"Nothing," the barber said. They regained the highroad and turned away from town. The second car dropped back out of the dust. They went on, gaining speed; the final fringe of houses dropped behind.

"Goddamn, he stinks!" the soldier said.

"We'll fix that," the drummer in front beside McLendon said. On the running board Butch cursed into the hot rush of air. The barber leaned suddenly forward and touched McLendon's arm.

"Let me out, John," he said.

"Jump out, niggerlover," McLendon said without turning his head. He drove swiftly. Behind them the sourceless lights of the second car glared in the dust. Presently McLendon turned into a narrow road. It was rutted with disuse. It led back to an abandoned brick kiln—a series of reddish mounds and weed- and vine-choked vats without bottom. It had been used for pasture once, until one day the owner missed one of his mules. Although he prodded carefully in the vats with a long pole, he could not even find the bottom of them.

"John," the barber said.

"Jump out, then," McLendon said, hurling the car along the ruts. Beside the barber the Negro spoke:

"Mr Henry."

The barber sat forward. The narrow tunnel of the road rushed up and past. Their motion was like an extinct furnace blast: cooler, but utterly dead. The car bounded from rut to rut.

"Mr Henry," the Negro said.

The barber began to tug furiously at the door. "Look out, there!" the soldier said, but the barber had already kicked the door open and swung onto the running board. The soldier leaned across the Negro and grasped at him, but he had already jumped. The car went on without checking speed.

The impetus hurled him crashing through dust-sheathed weeds, into the ditch. Dust puffed about him, and in a thin, vicious crackling of sapless stems he lay choking and retching until the second car passed and died away. Then he rose and limped on until he reached the highroad and turned towards town, brushing at his clothes with his hands. The moon was higher, riding high and clear of the dust at last, and after a while the town began to glare beneath the dust. He went on, limping. Presently he heard cars and the glow of them grew in the dust until they passed. McLendon's car came last now. There were four people in it and Butch was not on the running board.

They went on; the dust swallowed them; the glare and the sound died away. The dust of them hung for a while, but soon the eternal dust absorbed it again. The barber climbed back onto the road and limped on toward town.

IV

As she dressed for supper on that Saturday evening, her own flesh felt like fever. Her hands trembled among the hooks and eyes, and her eyes had a feverish look, and her hair swirled crisp and crackling under the comb. While she was still dressing the friends called for her and sat while she donned her sheerest underthings and stockings and a new voile dress. "Do you feel strong enough to go out?" they said, their eyes bright too, with a dark glitter. "When you have had time to get over the shock, you must tell us what happened. What he said and did; everything."

In the leafed darkness, as they walked toward the square, she began to breathe deeply, something like a swimmer preparing to dive, until she ceased trembling, the four of them walking slowly because of the terrible heat and out of solicitude for her. But as they neared the square she began to tremble again, walking with her head up, her hands clenched at her sides, their voices about her murmurous, also with that feverish, glittering quality of their eyes.

They entered the square, she in the center of the group, fragile in her fresh dress. She was trembling worse. She walked slower and slower, as children eat ice cream, her head up and her eyes bright in the haggard banner of her lace, passing the hotel and the coatless drummers in chairs along the curb looking around at her. "That's the one: see? The one in pink in the middle." "Is that her? What did they do with the nigger? Did they—?" "Sure. He's all right." "All right, is he?" "Sure. He went on a little trip." Then the drug store, where even the young men lounging in the doorway tipped their hats and followed with their eyes the motion of her hips and legs when she passed.

They went on, passing the lifted hats of the gentlemen, the suddenly ceased voices, deferent, protective. "Do you see?" the friends said. Their voices sounded like long, hovering sighs of hissing exultation. "There's not a Negro on the square. Not one."

They reached the picture show. It was like a miniature fairyland with its lighted lobby and colored lithographs of life caught in its terrible and beautiful mutations. Her lips began to tingle. In the dark, when the picture began, it would be all right; she could hold back the laughing so it would not waste away so fast and so soon. So she hurried on before the turning faces, the undertones of low astonishment, and they took their accustomed places where she could see the aisle against the silver glare and the young men and girls coming in two and two against it.

The lights flicked away; the screen glowed silver, and soon life began to unfold, beautiful and passionate and sad, while still the young men and girls entered, scented and sibilant in the half dark, their paired backs in silhouette delicate and sleek, their slim, quick bodies awkward, divinely young, while beyond them the silver dream accumulated, inevitably on and on. She began to laugh. In trying to suppress it, it made more noise than ever; heads began to turn. Still laughing, her friends raised her and led her out, and she stood at the curb, laughing on a high, sustained note, until the taxi came up and they helped her in.

They removed the pink voile and the sheer underthings and the stockings, and put her to bed, and cracked ice for her temples, and sent for the doctor. He was hard to locate, so they ministered to her with hushed ejaculations, renewing the ice and fanning her. While the ice was fresh and cold she stopped laughing and lay still for a time, moaning only a little. But soon the laughing welled again and her voice rose screaming.

"Shhhhhhhhhhh Shhhhhhhhhhhhhhh!" they said, freshening the icepack, smoothing her hair, examining it for gray; "poor girl!" Then to one another: "Do you suppose anything really happened?" their eyes darkly aglitter, secret and passionate. "Shhhhhhhhhh! Poor girl! Poor Minnie!"

V

It was midnight when McLendon drove up to his neat new house. It was trim and fresh as a birdcage and almost as small, with its clean, green-and-white paint. He locked the car and mounted the porch and entered. His wife rose from a chair beside the reading lamp. McLendon stopped in the floor and stared at her until she looked down.

"Look at that clock," he said, lifting his arm, pointing. She stood before him, her face lowered, a magazine in her hands. Her face was pale, strained, and weary-looking. "Haven't I told you about sitting up like this, waiting to see when I come in?"

"John," she said. She laid the magazine down. Poised on the balls of his feet, he glared at her with his hot eyes, his sweating face.

"Didn't I tell you?" He went toward her. She looked up then. He caught her shoulder. She stood passive, looking at him.

"Dont, John. I couldn't sleep . . . The heat; something. Please, John. You're hurting me."

"Didn't I tell you? He released her and half struck, half flung her across the chair, and she lay there and watched him quietly as he left the room.

He went on through the house, ripping off his shirt, and on the dark, screened porch at the rear he stood and mopped his head and shoulders with the shirt and flung it away. He took the pistol from his hip and laid it on the table beside the bed, and sat on the bed and removed his shoes, and rose and slipped his trousers off. He was sweating again already, and he stooped and hunted furiously for the shirt. At last he found it and wiped his body again, and, with his body pressed against the dusty screen, he stood panting. There was no movement, no sound, not even an insect. The dark world seemed to lie stricken beneath the cold moon and the lidless stars.

Richard Ford

Born in Jackson, Mississippi, in 1944, and raised both there and in Arkansas, Richard Ford was educated at Michigan State University and the University of California at Irvine. A lecturer at various universities during the 1970s and 1980s, he has spent extended periods of time in Europe, Mississippi, and Montana. The author of numerous novels and collections of stories, he won the 1996 Pulitzer Prize for fiction for *Independence Day*, a novel about a man's efforts to come to terms with his loss of one son, his love for his surviving son, his divorce, and his newfound appreciation of what "independence" means. Other works include *The Sportswriter* (1986), *Wildlife* (1990), and *Women with Men* (1997).

"Great Falls," which first appeared in *Esquire*, was collected in *Rock Springs* (1987). When this volume first appeared, it was praised for its stylistic flair and eloquence, and for the way it engaged readers in what the *New York Times* reviewer called "the sad wisdom of art." Set in Montana and told in retrospect, "Great Falls" recounts a time in the narrator's youth when he abruptly had to come to terms with fear, death, separation, and the reasons why people make choices in life. The story's laconic idiom reinforces the indeterminacy of these reasons, and emphasizes at the same time that all choices have consequences, whatever the initial reasons were. The quiet is deceptive. Perhaps, on the surface, it suggests that objectivity will resolve the dilemmas of choice and change—yet by its close the story also reveals how "detachment" is an illusion in a world where the moral universe has gone awry.

Great Falls

This is not a happy story. I warn you.

My father was a man named Jack Russell, and when I was a young boy in my early teens, we lived with my mother in a house to the east of Great Falls, Montana, near the small town of Highwood and the Highwood Mountains and the Missouri River. It is a flat, treeless benchland there, all of it used for wheat farming, though my father was never a farmer, but was brought up near Tacoma, Washington, in a family that worked for Boeing.

He—my father—had been an Air Force sergeant and had taken his discharge in Great Falls. And instead of going home to Tacoma, where my mother wanted to go, he had taken a civilian's job with the Air Force, working on planes, which was what he liked to do. And he had rented the house out of town from a farmer who did not want it left standing empty.

The house itself is gone now—I have been to the spot. But the double row of Russian olive trees and two of the outbuildings are still standing in the milkweeds. It was a plain, two-story house with a porch on the front and no place for the cars. At the time, I rode the school bus to Great Falls every morning, and my father drove in while my mother stayed home.

My mother was a tall pretty woman, thin, with black hair and slightly sharp features that made her seem to smile when she wasn't smiling. She had grown up in Wallace, Idaho, and gone to college a year in Spokane, then moved out to the coast, which is where she met Jack Russell. She was two years older than he was, and married him, she said to me, because he was young and wonderful looking, and because she thought they could leave the sticks and see the world together—which I suppose they did for a while. That was the life she wanted, even before she knew much about wanting anything else or about the future.

When my father wasn't working on airplanes, he was going hunting or fishing, two things he could do as well as anyone. He had learned to fish, he said, in Iceland, and to hunt ducks up on the DEW line—stations he had visited in the Air Force. And during the time of this—it was 1960—he began to take me with him on what he called his "expeditions." I thought even then, with as little as I knew, that these were opportunities other boys would dream of having but probably never would. And I don't think that I was wrong in that.

It is a true thing that my father did not know limits. In the spring, when we would go east to the Judith River Basin and camp up on the banks, he would catch a hundred fish in a weekend, and sometimes more than that. It was all he did from morning until night, and it was never hard for him. He used yellow corn kernels stacked onto a #4 snelled hook, and he would rattle this rig-up along the bottom of a deep pool below a split-shot sinker, and catch fish. And most of the time, because he knew the Judith River and knew how to feel his bait down deep, he could catch fish of good size.

It was the same with ducks, the other thing he liked. When the northern birds were down, usually by mid-October, he would take me and we would build a cattail and wheat-straw blind on one of the tule ponds or sloughs he knew about down the Missouri, where the water was shallow enough to wade. We would set out his decoys to the leeward side of our blind, and he would sprinkle corn on a hunger-line from the decoys to where we were. In the evenings when he came home from the base, we would go and sit out in the blind until the roosting flights came and put down among the decoys—there was never calling involved. And after a while, sometimes it would be an hour and full dark, the ducks would find the corn, and the whole raft of them—sixty, sometimes—would swim in to us. At the moment he judged they were close enough, my father would say to me, "Shine, Jackie," and I would stand and shine a seal-beam car light out onto the pond, and he would stand up beside me and shoot all the ducks that were there, on the water if he could, but flying and getting up as well. He owned a Model 11 Remington with a long-tube magazine that would hold ten shells, and with that many, and shooting straight over the surface rather than down onto it, he could kill or wound thirty ducks in twenty seconds' time. I remember distinctly the report of that gun and the flash of it over the water into the dark air, one shot after another, not even so fast, but measured in a way to hit as many as he could.

What my father did with the ducks he killed, and the fish, too, was sell them. It was against the law then to sell wild game, and it is against the law now. And though he kept some for us, most he would take—his fish laid on ice, or his ducks still wet and bagged in the burlap corn sacks—down to the Great Northern Hotel, which was still open then on Second Street in Great Falls, and sell them to the Negro caterer who bought them for his wealthy customers and for the dining car passengers who came through. We would drive in my father's Plymouth to the back of the hotel—always this was after dark—to a concrete loading ramp and lighted door that were close enough to the yards that I could sometimes see passenger trains waiting at the station, their car lights yellow and warm inside, the passengers dressed in suits, all bound for someplace far away from Montana—Milwaukee or Chicago or New York City, unimaginable places to me, a boy fourteen years old, with my father in the cold dark selling illegal game.

The caterer was a tall, stooped-back man in a white jacket, who my father called "Professor Ducks" or "Professor Fish," and the Professor referred to my father as "Sarge." He paid a quarter per pound for trout, a dime for whitefish, a dollar for a mallard duck, two for a speckle or a blue goose, and four dollars for a Canada. I have been with my father when he took away a hundred dollars for fish he'd caught and, in the fall, more than that for ducks and geese. When he had sold game in that way, we would drive out 10th Avenue and stop at a bar called The Mermaid which was by the air base, and he would drink with some friends he knew there, and they would laugh about hunting and fishing while I played pinball and wasted money in the jukebox.

It was on such a night as this that the unhappy things came about. It was in late October. I remember the time because Halloween had not been yet, and in the windows of the houses that I passed every day on the bus to Great Falls, people had put pumpkin lanterns, and set scarecrows in their yards in chairs.

My father and I had been shooting ducks in a slough on the Smith River, upstream from where it enters on the Missouri. He had killed thirty ducks, and we'd driven them down to the Great Northern and sold them there, though my father had kept two back in his corn sack.

And when we had driven away, he suddenly said, "Jackie, let's us go back home tonight. Who cares about those hard-dicks at The Mermaid. I'll cook these ducks on the grill. We'll do something different tonight." He smiled at me in an odd way. This was not a thing he usually said, or the way he usually talked. He liked The Mermaid, and my mother—as far as I knew—didn't mind it if he went there.

"That sounds good," I said.

"We'll surprise your mother," he said. "We'll make her happy."

We drove out past the air base on Highway 87, past where there were planes taking off into the night. The darkness was dotted by the green and red beacons, and the tower light swept the sky and trapped planes as they disappeared over the flat landscape toward Canada or Alaska and the Pacific.

"Boy-oh-boy," my father said—just out of the dark. I looked at him and his eyes were narrow, and he seemed to be thinking about something. "You know, Jackie," he said, "your mother said something to me once I've never forgotten. She said, 'Nobody dies of a broken heart.' This was somewhat before you were born. We were living down in Texas and we'd had some big blow-up, and that was the idea she had. I don't know why." He shook his head.

He ran his hand under the seat, found a half-pint bottle of whiskey, and held it up to the lights of the car behind us to see what there was left of it. He unscrewed the cap and took a drink, then held the bottle out to me. "Have a drink, son," he said. "Something oughta be good in life." And I felt that something was wrong. Not because of the whiskey, which I had drunk before and he had reason to know about, but because of some sound in his voice, something I didn't recognize and did not know the importance of, though I was certain it was important.

I took a drink and gave the bottle back to him, holding the whiskey in my mouth until it stopped burning and I could swallow it a little at a time. When we turned out the road to Highwood, the lights of Great Falls sank below the horizon, and I could see the small white lights of farms, burning at wide distances in the dark.

"What do you worry about, Jackie," my father said. "Do you worry about girls? Do you worry about your future sex life? Is that some of it?" He glanced at me, then back at the road.

"I don't worry about that," I said.

"Well, what then?" my father said. "What else is there?"

"I worry if you're going to die before I do," I said, though I hated saying that, "or if Mother is. That worries me."

"It'd be a miracle if we didn't," my father said, with the half-pint held in the same hand he held the steering wheel. I had seen him drive that way before. "Things pass too fast in your life, Jackie. Don't worry about that. If I were you, I'd worry we might not." He smiled at me, and it was not the worried, nervous smile from before, but a smile that meant he was pleased. And I don't remember him ever smiling at me that way again.

We drove on out behind the town of Highwood and onto the flat field roads toward our house. I could see, out on the prairie, a moving light where the farmer who rented our house to us was disking his field for winter wheat. "He's waited too late with that business," my father said and took a drink, then threw the bottle right out the window. "He'll lose that," he said, "the cold'll kill it." I did not answer him, but what I thought was that my father knew nothing about farming, and if he was right it would be an accident. He knew about planes and hunting game, and that seemed all to me.

"I want to respect your privacy," he said then, for no reason at all that I understood. I am not even certain he said it, only that it is in my memory that way. I don't know what he was thinking of. Just words. But I said to him, I remember well, "It's all right. Thank you."

We did not go straight out the Geraldine Road to our house. Instead my father went down another mile and turned, went a mile and turned back again so that we came home from the other direction. "I want to stop and listen now," he said. "The geese should be in the stubble." We stopped and he cut the lights and engine, and we opened the car windows and listened. It was eight o'clock at night and it was getting colder, though it was dry. But I could hear nothing, just the sound of air moving lightly through the cut field, and not a goose sound. Though I could smell the whiskey on my father's breath and on mine, could hear the motor ticking, could hear him breathe, hear the sound we made sitting side by side on the car seat, our clothes, our feet, almost our hearts beating. And I could see out in the night the yellow lights of our house, shining through the olive trees south of us like a ship on the sea. "I hear them, by God," my father said, his head stuck out the window. "But they're high up. They won't stop here now, Jackie. They're high flyers, those boys. Long gone geese."

■ ■ ■

There was a car parked off the road, down the line of wind-break trees, beside a steel thresher the farmer had left there to rust. You could see moonlight off the taillight chrome. It was a Pontiac, a two-door hard-top.

My father said nothing about it and I didn't either, though I think now for different reasons.

The floodlight was on over the side door of our house and lights were on inside, upstairs and down. My mother had a pumpkin on the front porch, and the wind chime she had hung by the door was tinkling. My dog, Major, came out of the quonset shed and stood in the car lights when we drove up.

"Let's see what's happening here," my father said, opening the door and stepping out quickly. He looked at me inside the car, and his eyes were wide and his mouth drawn tight.

We walked in the side door and up the basement steps into the kitchen, and a man was standing there—a man I had never seen before, a young man with blond hair, who might've been twenty or twenty-five. He was tall and was wearing a short-sleeved shirt and beige slacks with pleats. He was on the other side of the breakfast table, his fingertips just touching the wooden tabletop. His blue eyes were on my father, who was dressed in hunting clothes.

"Hello," my father said.

"Hello," the young man said, and nothing else. And for some reason I looked at his arms, which were long and pale. They looked like a young man's arms, like my arms. His short sleeves had each been neatly rolled up, and I could see the bottom of a small green tattoo edging out from underneath. There was a glass of whiskey on the table, but no bottle.

"What's your name?" my father said, standing in the kitchen under the bright ceiling light. He sounded like he might be going to laugh.

"Woody," the young man said and cleared his throat. He looked at me, then he touched the glass of whiskey, just the rim of the glass. He wasn't nervous, I could tell that. He did not seem to be afraid of anything.

"Woody," my father said and looked at the glass of whiskey. He looked at me, then sighed and shook his head. "Where's Mrs. Russell, Woody? I guess you aren't robbing my house, are you?"

Woody smiled. "No," he said. "Upstairs. I think she went upstairs."

"Good," my father said, "that's a good place." And he walked straight out of the room, but came back and stood in the doorway. "Jackie, you and Woody step outside and wait on me. Just stay there and I'll come out." He looked at Woody then in a way I would not have liked him to look at me, a look that meant he was studying Woody. "I guess that's your car," he said.

"That Pontiac." Woody nodded.

"Okay. Right," my father said. Then he went out again and up the stairs. At that moment the phone started to ring in the living room, and I heard my mother say, "Who's that?" And my father say, "It's me. It's Jack." And I decided I wouldn't go answer the phone. Woody looked at me, and I understood he wasn't sure what to do. Run, maybe. But he didn't have run in him. Though I thought he would probably do what I said if I would say it.

"Let's just go outside," I said.

And he said, "All right."

Woody and I walked outside and stood in the light of the floodlamp above the side door. I had on my wool jacket, but Woody was cold and stood with his hands in his pockets, and his arms bare, moving from foot to foot. Inside, the phone was ringing again. Once I looked up and saw my mother come to the window and look down at Woody and me. Woody didn't look up or see her, but I did. I waved at her, and she waved back at me and smiled. She was wearing a powder-blue dress. In another minute the phone stopped ringing.

Woody took a cigarette out of his shirt pocket and lit it. Smoke shot through his nose into the cold air, and he sniffed, looked around the ground and threw his match on the gravel. His blond hair was combed backwards and neat on the sides, and I could smell his aftershave on him, a sweet, lemon smell. And for the first time I noticed his shoes. They were two-tones, black with white tops and black laces. They stuck out below his baggy pants and were long and polished and shiny, as if he had been planning on a big occasion. They looked like shoes some country singer would wear, or a salesman. He was handsome, but only like someone you would see beside you in a dime store and not notice again.

"I like it out here," Woody said, his head down, looking at his shoes. "Nothing to bother you. I bet you'd see Chicago if the world was flat. The Great Plains commence here."

"I don't know," I said.

Woody looked up at me, cupping his smoke with one hand. "Do you play football?"

"No," I said. I thought about asking him something about my mother. But I had no idea what it would be.

"I *have* been drinking," Woody said, "but I'm not drunk now."

The wind rose then, and from behind the house I could hear Major bark once from far away, and I could smell the irrigation ditch, hear it hiss in the field. It ran down from Highwood Creek to the Missouri, twenty miles away. It was nothing Woody knew about, nothing he could hear or smell. He knew nothing about anything that was here. I heard my father say the words, "That's a real joke," from inside the house, then the sound of a drawer being opened and shut, and a door closing. Then nothing else.

Woody turned and looked into the dark toward where the glow of Great Falls rose on the horizon, and we both could see the flashing lights of a plane lowering to land there.

"I once passed my brother in the Los Angeles airport and didn't even recognize him," Woody said, staring into the night. "He recognized *me,* though. He said, 'Hey, bro, are you mad at me, or what?' I wasn't mad at him. We both had to laugh."

Woody turned and looked at the house. His hands were still in his pockets, his cigarette clenched between his teeth, his arms taut. They were, I saw, bigger, stronger arms than I had thought. A vein went down the front of each of them. I wondered what Woody knew that I didn't. Not about my mother—I didn't know anything about that and didn't want to—but about a lot of things, about the life out in the dark, about coming out here, about airports, even about me. He and I were not so far apart in age, I knew that. But Woody was one thing, and I was another. And I wondered how I would ever get to be like him, since it didn't necessarily seem so bad a thing to be.

"Did you know your mother was married before?" Woody said.

"Yes," I said. "I knew that."

"It happens to all of them, now," he said. "They can't wait to get divorced."

"I guess so," I said.

Woody dropped his cigarette into the gravel and toed it out with his black-and-white shoe. He looked up at me and smiled the way he had inside the house, a smile that said he knew something he wouldn't tell, a smile to make you feel bad because you weren't Woody and never could be.

It was then that my father came out of the house. He still had on his plaid hunting coat and his wool cap, but his face was as white as snow, as white as I have ever seen a human being's face to be. It was odd. I had the feeling that he might've fallen inside, because he looked roughed up, as though he had hurt himself somehow.

My mother came out the door behind him and stood in the floodlight at the top of the steps. She was wearing the powder-blue dress I'd seen through the window, a dress I had never seen her wear before, though she was also wearing a car coat and carrying a suitcase. She looked at me and shook her head in a way that only I was supposed to notice, as if it was not a good idea to talk now.

My father had his hands in his pockets, and he walked right up to Woody. He did not even look at me. "What do you do for a living?" he said, and he was very close to Woody. His coat was close enough to touch Woody's shirt.

"I'm in the Air Force," Woody said. He looked at me and then at my father. He could tell my father was excited.

"Is this your day off, then?" my father said. He moved even closer to Woody, his hands still in his pockets. He pushed Woody with his chest, and Woody seemed willing to let my father push him.

"No," he said, shaking his head.

I looked at my mother. She was just standing, watching. It was as if someone had given her an order, and she was obeying it. She did not smile at me, though I thought she was thinking about me, which made me feel strange.

"What's the matter with you?" my father said into Woody's face, right into his face—his voice tight, as if it had gotten hard for him to talk. "Whatever in the world is the matter with you? Don't you understand something?" My father took a revolver pistol out of his coat and put it up under Woody's chin, into the soft pocket behind the bone, so that Woody's whole face rose, but his arms stayed at his sides, his hands open. "I don't know what to do with you," my father said. "I don't have any idea what to do with you. I just don't." Though I thought that what he wanted to do was hold Woody there just like that until something important took place, or until he could simply forget about all this.

My father pulled the hammer back on the pistol and raised it tighter under Woody's chin, breathing into Woody's face—my mother in the light with her suitcase, watching them, and me watching them. A half a minute must've gone by.

And then my mother said, "Jack, let's stop now. Let's just stop."

My father stared into Woody's face as if he wanted Woody to consider doing something—moving or turning around or anything on his own to stop this—that my father would then put a stop to. My father's eyes grew narrowed, and his teeth were gritted together, his lips snarling up to resemble a smile. "You're crazy, aren't you?" he said. "You're a goddamned crazy man. Are you in love with her, too? Are you, crazy man? Are you? Do you say you love her? Say you love her! Say you love her so I can blow your fucking brains in the sky."

"All right," Woody said. "No. It's all right."

"He doesn't love me, Jack. For God's sake," my mother said. She seemed so calm. She shook her head at me again. I do not think she thought my father would shoot Woody. And I don't think Woody thought so. Nobody did, I think, except my father himself. But I think he did, and was trying to find out how to.

My father turned suddenly and glared at my mother, his eyes shiny and moving, but with the gun still on Woody's skin. I think he was afraid, afraid he was doing this wrong and could mess all of it up and make matters worse without accomplishing anything.

"You're leaving," he yelled at her. "That's why you're packed. Get out. Go on."

"Jackie has to be at school in the morning," my mother said in just her normal voice. And without another word to any one of us, she walked out of the floodlamp light carrying her bag, turned the corner at the front porch steps and disappeared toward the olive trees that ran in rows back into the wheat.

My father looked back at me where I was standing in the gravel, as if he expected to see me go with my mother toward Woody's car. But I hadn't thought about that—though later I would. Later I would think I should have gone with her, and that things between them might've been different. But that isn't how it happened.

"You're sure you're going to get away now, aren't you, mister?" my father said into Woody's face. He was crazy himself, then. Anyone would've been. Everything must have seemed out of hand to him.

"I'd like to," Woody said. "I'd like to get away from here."

"And I'd like to think of some way to hurt you," my father said and blinked his eyes. "I feel helpless about it." We all heard the door to Woody's car close in the dark. "Do you think that I'm a fool?" my father said.

"No," Woody said. "I don't think that."

"Do you think you're important?"

"No," Woody said. "I'm not."

My father blinked again. He seemed to be becoming someone else at that moment, someone I didn't know. "Where are you from?"

And Woody closed his eyes. He breathed in, then out, a long sigh. It was as if this was somehow the hardest part, something he hadn't expected to be asked to say.

"Chicago," Woody said. "A suburb of there."

"Are your parents alive?" my father said, all the time with his blue magnum pistol pushed under Woody's chin.

"Yes," Woody said. "Yessir."

"That's too bad," my father said. "Too bad they have to know what you are. I'm sure you stopped meaning anything to them a long time ago. I'm sure they both wish you were dead. You didn't know that. But I know it. I can't help them out, though. Somebody else'll have to kill you. I don't want to have to think about you anymore. I guess that's it."

My father brought the gun down to his side and stood looking at Woody. He did not back away, just stood, waiting for what I don't know to happen. Woody stood a moment, then he cut his eyes at me uncomfortably. And I know that I looked down. That's all I could do. Though I remember wondering if Woody's heart was broken and what any of this meant to him. Not to me, or my mother, or my father. But to him, since he seemed to be the one left out somehow, the one who would be lonely soon, the one who had done something he would someday wish he hadn't and would have no one to tell him that it was all right, that they forgave him, that these things happen in the world.

Woody took a step back, looked at my father and at me again as if he intended to speak, then stepped aside and walked away toward the front of our house, where the wind chime made a noise in the new cold air.

My father looked at me, his big pistol in his hand. "Does this seem stupid to you?" he said. "All this? Yelling and threatening and going nuts? I wouldn't blame you if it did. You shouldn't even see this. I'm sorry. I don't know what to do now."

"It'll be all right," I said. And I walked out to the road. Woody's car started up behind the olive trees. I stood and watched it back out, its red taillights clouded by exhaust. I could see their two heads inside, with the headlights shining behind them. When they got into the road, Woody touched his brakes, and for a moment I could see that they were talking, their heads turned toward each other, nodding. Woody's head and my mother's. They sat that way for a few seconds, then drove slowly off. And I wondered what they had to say to each other, something important enough that they had to stop right at that moment and say it. Did she say, *I love you*? Did she say, *This is not what I expected to happen?* Did she say, *This is what I've wanted all along*? And did he say, *I'm sorry for all this*, or *I'm glad*, or *None of this matters to me*? These are not the kinds of things you can know if you were not there. And I was not there and did not want to be. It did not seem like I should be there. I heard the door slam when my father went inside, and I turned back from the road where I could still see their taillights disappearing, and went back into the house where I was to be alone with my father.

■ ■ ■

Things seldom end in one event. In the morning I went to school on the bus as usual, and my father drove in to the air base in his car. We had not said very much about all that had happened. Harsh words, in a sense, are all alike. You can make them up yourself and be right. I think we both believed that we were in a fog we couldn't see through yet, though in a while, maybe not even a long while, we would see lights and know something.

In my third-period class that day a messenger brought a note for me that said I was excused from school at noon, and I should meet my mother at a motel down 10th Avenue South—a place not so far from my school—and we would eat lunch together.

It was a gray day in Great Falls that day. The leaves were off the trees and the mountains to the east of town were obscured by a low sky. The night before had been cold and clear, but today it seemed as if it would rain. It was the beginning of winter in earnest. In a few days there would be snow everywhere.

The motel where my mother was staying was called the Tropicana, and was beside the city golf course. There was a neon parrot on the sign out front, and the cabins made a U shape behind a little white office building. Only a couple of cars were parked in front of cabins, and no car was in front of my mother's cabin. I wondered if Woody would be here, or if he was at the air base. I wondered if my father would see him there, and what they would say.

I walked back to cabin 9. The door was open, though a DO NOT DISTURB sign was hung on the knob outside. I looked through the screen and saw my mother sitting on the bed alone. The television was on, but she was looking at me. She was wearing the powder-blue dress she had had on the night before. She was smiling at me, and I liked the way she looked at that moment, through the screen, in shadows. Her features did not seem as sharp as they had before. She looked comfortable where she was, and I felt like we were going to get along, no matter what had happened, and that I wasn't mad at her—that I had never been mad at her.

She sat forward and turned the television off. "Come in, Jackie," she said, and I opened the screen door and came inside. "It's the height of grandeur in here, isn't it?" My mother looked around the room. Her suitcase was open on the floor by the bathroom door, which I could see through and out the window onto the golf course, where three men were playing under the milky sky. "Privacy can be a burden, sometimes," she said, and reached down and put on her high-heeled shoes. "I didn't sleep very well last night, did you?"

"No," I said, though I had slept all right. I wanted to ask her where Woody was, but it occurred to me at that moment that he was gone now and wouldn't be back, that she wasn't thinking in terms of him and didn't care where he was or ever would be.

"I'd like a nice compliment from you," she said. "Do you have one of those to spend?"

"Yes," I said. "I'm glad to see you."

"That's a nice one," she said and nodded. She had both her shoes on now. "Would you like to go have lunch? We can walk across the street to the cafeteria. You can get hot food."

"No," I said. "I'm not really hungry now."

"That's okay," she said and smiled at me again. And, as I said before, I liked the way she looked. She looked pretty in a way I didn't remember seeing her, as if something that had had a hold on her had let her go, and she could be different about things. Even about me.

"Sometimes, you know," she said, "I'll think about something I did. Just anything. Years ago in Idaho, or last week, even. And it's as if I'd read it. Like a story. Isn't that strange?"

"Yes," I said. And it did seem strange to me because I was certain then what the difference was between what had happened and what hadn't, and knew I always would be.

"Sometimes," she said, and she folded her hands in her lap and stared out the little side window of her cabin at the parking lot and the curving row of other cabins. "Sometimes I even have a moment when I completely forget what life's like. Just altogether." She smiled. "That's not so bad, finally. Maybe it's a disease I have. Do you think I'm just sick and I'll get well?"

"No. I don't know," I said. "Maybe. I hope so." I looked out the bathroom window and saw the three men walking down the golf course fairway carrying golf clubs.

"I'm not very good at sharing things right now," my mother said. "I'm sorry." She cleared her throat, and then she didn't say anything for almost a minute while I stood there. "I *will* answer anything you'd like me to answer, though. Just ask me anything, and I'll answer it the truth, whether I want to or not. Okay? I will. You don't even have to trust me. That's not a big issue with us. We're both grown-ups now."

And I said, "Were you ever married before?"

My mother looked at me strangely. Her eyes got small, and for a moment she looked the way I was used to seeing her—sharp-faced, her mouth set and taut. "No," she said. "Who told you that? That isn't true. I never was. Did Jack say that to you? Did your father say that? That's an awful thing to say. I haven't been that bad."

"He didn't say that," I said.

"Oh, of course he did," my mother said. "He doesn't know just to let things go when they're bad enough."

"I wanted to know that," I said. "I just thought about it. It doesn't matter."

"No, it doesn't," my mother said. "I could've been married eight times. I'm just sorry he said that to you. He's not generous sometimes."

"He didn't say that," I said. But I'd said it enough, and I didn't care if she believed me or didn't. It was true that trust was not a big issue between us then. And in any event, I know now that the whole truth of anything is an idea that stops existing finally.

"Is that all you want to know, then?" my mother said. She seemed mad, but not at me, I didn't think. Just at things in general. And I sympathized with her. "Your life's your own business, Jackie," she said.

"Sometimes it scares you to death it's so much your own business. You just want to run."

"I guess so," I said.

"I'd like a less domestic life, is all." She looked at me, but I didn't say anything. I didn't see what she meant by that, though I knew there was nothing I could say to change the way her life would be from then on. And I kept quiet.

In a while we walked across 10th Avenue and ate lunch in the cafeteria. When she paid for the meal I saw that she had my father's silver-dollar money clip in her purse and that there was money in it. And I understood that he had been to see her already that day, and no one cared if I knew it. We were all of us on our own in this.

When we walked out onto the street, it was colder and the wind was blowing. Car exhausts were visible and some drivers had their lights on, though it was only two o'clock in the afternoon. My mother had called a taxi, and we stood and waited for it. I didn't know where she was going, but I wasn't going with her.

"Your father won't let me come back," she said, standing on the curb. It was just a fact to her, not that she hoped I would talk to him or stand up for her or take her part. But I did wish then that I had never let her go the night before. Things can be fixed by staying; but to go out into the night and not come back hazards life, and everything can get out of hand.

My mother's taxi came. She kissed me and hugged me very hard, then got inside the cab in her powder-blue dress and high heels and her car coat. I smelled her perfume on my cheeks as I stood watching her. "I used to be afraid of more things than I am now," she said, looking up at me, and smiled. "I've got a knot in my stomach, of all things." And she closed the cab door, waved at me, and rode away.

■ ■ ■

I walked back toward my school. I thought I could take the bus home if I got there by three. I walked a long way down 10th Avenue to Second Street, beside the Missouri River, then over to town. I walked by the Great Northern Hotel, where my father had sold ducks and geese and fish of all kinds. There were no passenger trains in the yard and the loading dock looked small. Garbage cans were lined along the edge of it, and the door was closed and locked.

As I walked toward school I thought to myself that my life had turned suddenly, and that I might not know exactly how or which way for possibly a long time. Maybe, in fact, I might never know. It was a thing that happened to you—I knew that—and it had happened to me in this way now. And as I walked on up the cold street that afternoon in Great Falls, the questions I asked myself were these: why wouldn't my father let my mother come back? Why would Woody stand in the cold with me outside my house and risk being killed? Why would he say my mother had been married before, if she hadn't been? And my mother herself—why would she do what she did? In five years my father had gone off to Ely, Nevada, to ride out the oil strike there, and been killed by accident. And in the years since then I have seen my mother from time to time—in one place or another, with one man or other—and I can say, at least, that we know each other. But I have never known the answer to these questions, have never asked anyone their answers. Though possibly it—the answer—is simple: it is just low-life, some coldness in us all, some helplessness that causes us to misunderstand life when it is pure and plain, makes our existence seem like a border between two nothings, and makes us no more or less than animals who meet on the road—watchful, unforgiving, without patience or desire.

E.M. Forster

Edward Morgan Forster (1879–1970) was born into a London family connected with the group of wealthy Evangelicals known as the Clapham Sect. His upbringing and education (Tonbridge School and King's College, Cambridge) were solidly middle class; yet despite this background, Forster turned a critical and satirical eye on the snobbery and superficiality of English society. After leaving Cambridge in 1901, he travelled through Italy and Greece, and in the Mediterranean temperament he perceived qualities of passion and responsiveness very different from the coldness and reserve of the English character. In his novels *Where Angels Fear to Tread* (1905), *The Longest Journey* (1907), and *Howards End* (1910), he exposes middle-class illusions, and sets the deadening force of social convention against the liberating power of feeling, a conflict enacted on both the spiritual and the sexual level. This opposition between social pressures and individual feeling is often expressed as a clash between the rational faculties and the imagination, and it takes on a broader significance in *A Passage to India* (1924), in which two cultures meet but do not merge: the Englishman and the Indian are symbolically parted at the end of that novel, as if to emphasize how the Western mind has lost touch with the deeper springs of intuitive awareness and the sources of natural harmony.

These concerns also find expression in Forster's short stories, collected in *The Celestial Omnibus* (1911) and *The Eternal Moment* (1928), where he gives freer rein to allegorical and mythical tendencies. In "The Road from Colonus" *(The Celestial Omnibus)*, Forster juxtaposes the shallowness of contemporary English values with the spirit of life in an ancient land. The title alludes to the story of Oedipus, who, old and blind, was transfigured by his experience in the sacred grove at Colonus, and enabled to meet his death with pride and dignity.

The Road from Colonus

I

For no very intelligible reason, Mr Lucas had hurried ahead of his party. He was perhaps reaching the age at which independence becomes valuable, because it is so soon to be lost. Tired of attention and consideration, he liked breaking away from the younger members, to ride by himself, and to dismount unassisted. Perhaps he also relished that more subtle pleasure of being kept waiting for lunch, and of telling the others on their arrival that it was of no consequence.

So, with childish impatience, he battered the animal's sides with his heels, and made the muleteer bang it with a thick stick and prick it with a sharp one, and jolted down the hill sides through clumps of flowering shrubs and stretches of anemones and asphodel, till he heard the sound of running water, and came in sight of the group of plane trees where they were to have their meal.

Even in England those trees would have been remarkable, so huge were they, so interlaced, so magnificently clothed in quivering green. And here in Greece they were unique, the one cool spot in that hard brilliant landscape, already scorched by the heat of an April sun. In their midst was hidden a tiny Khan or country inn, a frail mud building with a broad wooden balcony in which sat an old woman spinning, while a small brown pig, eating orange peel, stood beside her. On the wet earth below squatted two children, playing some primaeval game with their fingers; and their mother, none too clean either, was messing with some rice inside. As Mrs Forman would have said, it was all very Greek, and the fastidious Mr Lucas felt thankful that they were bringing their own food with them, and should eat it in the open air.

Still, he was glad to be there—the muleteer had helped him off—and glad that Mrs Forman was not there to forestall his opinions—glad even that he should not see Ethel for quite half an hour. Ethel was his youngest daughter, still unmarried. She was unselfish and affectionate, and it was generally understood that she was to devote her life to her father, and be the comfort of his old age. Mrs Forman always referred to her as Antigone, and Mr Lucas tried to settle down to the role of Oedipus, which seemed the only one that public opinion allowed him.

He had this in common with Oedipus, that he was growing old. Even to himself it had become obvious. He had lost interest in other people's affairs, and seldom attended when they spoke to him. He was fond of talking himself but often forgot what he was going to say, and even when he succeeded, it seldom seemed worth the effort. His phrases and gestures had become stiff and set, his anecdotes, once so successful, fell flat, his silence was as meaningless as his speech. Yet he had led a healthy, active life, had worked steadily, made money, educated his children. There was nothing and no one to blame: he was simply growing old.

At the present moment, here he was in Greece, and one of the dreams of his life was realized. Forty years ago he had caught the fever of Hellenism, and all his life he had felt that could he but visit that land, he would not have lived in vain. But Athens had been dusty, Delphi wet, Thermopylae flat, and he had listened with amazement and cynicism to the rapturous exclamations of his companions. Greece was like England: it was a man who was growing old, and it made no difference whether that man looked at the Thames or the Eurotas. It was his last hope of contradicting that logic of experience, and it was failing.

Yet Greece had done something for him, though he did not know it. It had made him discontented, and there are stirrings of life in discontent. He knew that he was not the victim of continual ill-luck. Something great was wrong, and he was pitted against no mediocre or accidental enemy. For the last month a strange desire had possessed him to die fighting.

"Greece is the land for young people," he said to himself as he stood under the plane trees, "but I will enter into it, I will possess it. Leaves shall be green again, water shall be sweet, the sky shall be blue. They were so forty years ago, and I will win them back. I do mind being old, and I will pretend no longer."

He took two steps forward, and immediately cold waters were gurgling over his ankle.

"Where does the water come from?" he asked himself. "I do not even know that." He remembered that all the hill sides were dry; yet here the road was suddenly covered with flowing streams.

He stopped still in amazement, saying: "Water out of a tree—out of a hollow tree? I never saw nor thought of that before."

For the enormous plane that leant towards the Khan was hollow—it had been burnt out for charcoal—and from its living trunk there gushed an impetuous spring, coating the bark with fern and moss, and flowing over the mule track to create fertile meadows beyond. The simple country folk had paid to beauty and mystery such tribute as they could, for in the rind of the tree a shrine was cut, holding a lamp and a little picture of the Virgin, inheritor of the Naiad's and Dryad's joint abode.

"I never saw anything so marvelous before," said Mr Lucas. "I could even step inside the trunk and see where the water comes from."

For a moment he hesitated to violate the shrine. Then he remembered with a smile his own thought—"the place shall be mine; I will enter it and possess it"—and leapt almost aggressively on to a stone within.

The water pressed up steadily and noiselessly from the hollow roots and hidden crevices of the plane, forming a wonderful amber pool ere it spilt over the lip of bark on to the earth outside. Mr Lucas tasted it and it was sweet, and when he looked up the black funnel of the trunk he saw sky which was blue, and some leaves which were green; and he remembered, without smiling, another of his thoughts.

Others had been before him—indeed he had a curious sense of companionship. Little votive offerings to the presiding Power were fastened on to the bark—tiny arms and legs and eyes in tin, grotesque models of the brain or the heart—all tokens of some recovery of strength or wisdom or love. There was no such thing as the solitude of nature, for the sorrows and joys of humanity had pressed even into the bosom of a tree. He spread out his arms and steadied himself against the soft charred wood, and then slowly leant back, till his body was resting on the trunk behind. His eyes closed, and he had the strange feeling of one who is moving, yet at peace—the feeling of the swimmer, who, after long struggling with chopping seas, finds that after all the tide will sweep him to his goal.

So he lay motionless, conscious only of the stream below his feet, and that all things were a stream, in which he was moving.

He was aroused at last by a shock—the shock of an arrival perhaps, for when he opened his eyes, something unimagined, indefinable, had passed over all things, and made them intelligible and good.

There was meaning in the stoop of the old woman over her work, and in the quick motions of the little pig, and in her diminishing globe of wool. A young man came singing over the streams on a mule, and there was beauty in his pose and sincerity in his greeting. The sun made no accidental patterns upon the spreading roots of the trees, and there was intention in the nodding clumps of asphodel, and in the music of the water. To Mr Lucas, who, in a brief space of time, had discovered not only Greece, but England and all the world and life, there seemed nothing ludicrous in the desire to hang within the tree another votive offering—a little model of an entire man.

"Why, here's papa, playing at being Merlin."

All unnoticed they had arrived—Ethel, Mrs Forman, Mr Graham, and the English-speaking dragoman. Mr Lucas peered out at them suspiciously. They had suddenly become unfamiliar, and all that they did seemed strained and coarse.

"Allow me to give you a hand," said Mr Graham, a young man who was always polite to his elders.

Mr Lucas felt annoyed. "Thank you, I can manage perfectly well by myself," he replied. His foot slipped as he stepped out of the tree, and went into the spring.

"Oh papa, my papa!" said Ethel, "what are you doing? Thank goodness I have got a change for you on the mule."

She tended him carefully, giving him clean socks and dry boots, and then sat him down on the rug beside the lunch basket, while she went with the others to explore the grove.

They came back in ecstasies, in which Mr Lucas tried to join. But he found them intolerable. Their enthusiasm was superficial, commonplace, and spasmodic. They had no perception of the coherent beauty that was flowering around them. He tried at least to explain his feelings, and what he said was:

"I am altogether pleased with the appearance of this place. It impresses me very favourably. The trees are fine, remarkably fine for Greece, and there is something very poetic in the spring of clear running water. The people too seem kindly and civil. It is decidedly an attractive place."

Mrs Forman upbraided him for his tepid praise.

"Oh, it is a place in a thousand!" she cried, "I could live and die here! I really would stop if I had not to be back at Athens! It reminds me of the Colonus of Sophocles."

"Well *I* must stop," said Ethel. "I positively must."

"Yes, do! You and your father! Antigone and Oedipus. Of course you must stop at Colonus!"

Mr Lucas was almost breathless with excitement. When he stood within the tree, he had believed that his happiness would be independent of locality. But these few minutes' conversation had undeceived him. He no longer trusted himself to journey through the world, for old thoughts, old weariness might be waiting to rejoin him as soon as he left the shade of the planes, and the music of the virgin water. To sleep in the Khan with the gracious, kind-eyed people, to watch the bats flit about within the globe of shade, and see the moon turn the golden patterns into silver—one such night would place him beyond relapse, and confirm him for ever in the kingdom he had regained. But all his lips could say was: "I should be willing to put in a night here."

"You mean a week, papa! It would be sacrilege to put in less."

"A week then, a week," said his lips, irritated at being corrected, while his heart was leaping with joy. All through lunch he spoke to them no more, but watched the place he should know so well, and the people who would so soon be his companions and friends. The inmates of the Khan only consisted of an old woman, a middle-aged woman, a young man and two children, and to none of them had he spoken, yet he loved them as he loved everything that moved or breathed or existed beneath the benedictory shade of the planes.

"En route!" said the shrill voice of Mrs Forman. "Ethel! Mr Graham! The best of things must end."

"To-night," thought Mr Lucas, "they will light the little lamp by the shrine. And when we all sit together on the balcony, perhaps they will tell me which offerings they put up."

"I beg your pardon, Mr Lucas," said Graham, "but they want to fold up the rug you are sitting on."

Mr Lucas got up, saying to himself: "Ethel shall go to bed first, and then I will try to tell them about my offering too—for it is a thing I must do. I think they will understand if I am left with them alone."

Ethel touched him on the cheek. "Papa! I've called you three times. All the mules are here."

"Mules? What mules?"

"Our mules. We're all waiting. Oh, Mr Graham, do help my father on."

"I don't know what you're talking about, Ethel."

"My dearest papa, we must start. You know we have to get to Olympia tonight."

Mr Lucas in pompous, confident tones replied: "I always did wish, Ethel, that you had a better head for plans. You know perfectly well that we are putting in a week here. It is your own suggestion."

Ethel was startled into impoliteness. "What a perfectly ridiculous idea. You must have known I was joking. Of course I meant I wished we could."

"Ah! if we could only do what we wished!" sighed Mrs Forman, already seated on her mule.

"Surely," Ethel continued in calmer tones, "you didn't think I meant it."

"Most certainly I did. I have made all my plans on the supposition that we are stopping here, and it will be extremely inconvenient, indeed, impossible for me to start."

He delivered this remark with an air of great conviction, and Mrs Forman and Mr Graham had to turn away to hide their smiles.

"I am sorry I spoke so carelessly; it was wrong of me. But, you know, we can't break up our party, and even one night here would make us miss the boat at Patras."

Mrs Forman, in an aside, called Mr Graham's attention to the excellent way in which Ethel managed her father.

"I don't mind about the Patras boat. You said that we should stop here, and we are stopping."

It seemed as if the inhabitants of the Khan had divined in some mysterious way that the altercation touched them. The old woman stopped her spinning, while the young man and the two children stood behind Mr Lucas, as if supporting him.

Neither arguments nor entreaties moved him. He said little, but he was absolutely determined, because for the first time he saw his daily life aright. What need had he to return to England? Who would miss him? His friends were dead or cold. Ethel loved him in a way, but, as was right, she had other interests. His other children he seldom saw. He had only one other relative, his sister Julia, whom he both feared and hated. It was no effort to struggle. He would be a fool as well as a coward if he stirred from the place which brought him happiness and peace.

At last Ethel, to humour him, and not disinclined to air her modern Greek, went into the Khan with the astonished dragoman to look at the rooms. The woman inside received them with loud welcomes, and the young man, when no one was looking, began to lead Mr Lucas's mule to the stable.

"Drop it, you brigand!" shouted Graham, who always declared that foreigners could understand English if they chose. He was right, for the man obeyed, and they all stood waiting for Ethel's return.

She emerged at last, with close-gathered skirts, followed by the dragoman bearing the little pig, which he had bought at a bargain.

"My dear papa, I will do all I can for you, but stop in that Khan—no."

"Are there—fleas?" asked Mrs Forman.

Ethel intimated that "fleas" was not the word.

"Well, I am afraid that settles it," said Mrs Forman, "I know how particular Mr Lucas is."

"It does not settle it," said Mr Lucas. "Ethel, you go on. I do not want you. I don't know why I ever consulted you. I shall stop here alone."

"That is absolute nonsense," said Ethel, losing her temper. "How can you be left alone at your age? How would you get your meals or your bath? All your letters are waiting for you at Patras. You'll miss the boat. That means missing the London operas, and upsetting all your engagements for the month. And as if you could travel by yourself!"

"They might knife you," was Mr Graham's contribution.

The Greeks said nothing; but whenever Mr Lucas looked their way, they beckoned him towards the Khan. The children would even have drawn him by the coat, and the old woman on the balcony stopped her almost completed spinning, and fixed him with mysterious appealing eyes. As he fought, the issue assumed gigantic proportions, and he believed that he was not merely stopping because he had regained youth or seen beauty or found happiness, but because in that place and with those people a supreme event was awaiting him which would transfigure the face of the world. The moment was so tremendous that he abandoned words and arguments as useless, and rested on the strength of his mighty unrevealed allies: silent men, murmuring water, and whispering trees. For the whole place called with one voice, articulate to him, and his garrulous opponents became every minute more meaningless and absurd. Soon they would be tired and go chattering away into the sun, leaving him to the cool grove and the moonlight and the destiny he foresaw.

Mrs Forman and the dragoman had indeed already started, amid the piercing screams of the little pig, and the struggle might have gone on indefinitely if Ethel had not called in Mr Graham.

"Can you help me?" she whispered. "He is absolutely unmanageable."

"I'm no good at arguing—but if I could help you in any other way—" and he looked down complacently at his well-made figure.

Ethel hesitated. Then she said: "Help me in any way you can. After all, it is for his good that we do it."

"Then have his mule led up behind him."

So when Mr Lucas thought he had gained the day, he suddenly felt himself lifted off the ground, and sat sideways on the saddle, and at the same time the mule started off at a trot. He said nothing, for he had nothing to say, and even his face showed little emotion as he felt the shade pass and heard the sound of the water cease. Mr Graham was running at his side, hat in hand, apologizing.

"I know I had no business to do it, and I do beg your pardon awfully. But I do hope that some day you too will feel that I was—damn!"

A stone had caught him in the middle of the back. It was thrown by the little boy, who was pursuing them along the mule track. He was followed by his sister, also throwing stones.

Ethel screamed to the dragoman, who was some way ahead with Mrs Forman, but before he could rejoin them, another adversary appeared. It was the young Greek, who had cut them off in front, and now dashed down at Mr Lucas' bridle. Fortunately Graham was an expert boxer, and it did not take him a moment to beat down the youth's feeble defence, and to send him sprawling with a bleeding mouth into the asphodel. By this time the dragoman had arrived, the children, alarmed at the fate of their brother, had desisted, and the rescue party, if such it is to be considered, retired in disorder to the trees.

"Little devils!" said Graham, laughing with triumph. "That's the modern Greek all over. Your father meant money if he stopped, and they consider we were taking it out of their pocket."

"Oh, they are terrible—simple savages! I don't know how I shall ever thank you. You've saved my father."

"I only hope you didn't think me brutal."

"No," replied Ethel with a little sigh. "I admire strength."

Meanwhile the cavalcade reformed, and Mr Lucas, who, as Mrs Forman said, bore his disappointment wonderfully well, was put comfortably on to his mule. They hurried up the opposite hillside, fearful of another attack, and it was not until they had left the eventful place far behind that Ethel found an opportunity to speak to her father and ask his pardon for the way she had treated him.

"You seemed so different, dear father, and you quite frightened me. Now I feel that you are your old self again."

He did not answer, and she concluded that he was not unnaturally offended at her behaviour.

By one of those curious tricks of mountain scenery, the place they had left an hour before suddenly reappeared far below them. The Khan was hidden under the green dome, but in the open there still stood three figures, and through the pure air rose up a faint cry of defiance or farewell.

Mr Lucas stopped irresolutely, and let the reins fall from his hand. "Come, father dear," said Ethel gently.

He obeyed, and in another moment a spur of the hill hid the dangerous scene for ever.

II

It was breakfast time, but the gas was alight, owing to the fog. Mr Lucas was in the middle of an account of a bad night he had spent. Ethel, who was to be married in a few weeks, had her arms on the table, listening.

"First the door bell rang, then you came back from the theatre. Then the dog started, and after the dog the cat. And at three in the morning a young hooligan passed by singing. Oh yes: then there was the water gurgling in the pipe above my head."

"I think that was only the bath water running away," said Ethel, looking rather worn.

"Well, there's nothing I dislike more than running water. It's perfectly impossible to sleep in the house. I shall give it up. I shall give notice next quarter. I shall tell the landlord plainly, 'The reason I am giving up the house is this: it is perfectly impossible to sleep in it.' If he says—says—well, what has he got to say?"

"Some more toast, father?"

"Thank you, my dear." He took it, and there was an interval of peace.

But he soon recommenced. "I'm not going to submit to the practising next door as tamely as they think. I wrote and told them so—didn't I?"

"Yes," said Ethel, who had taken care that the letter should not reach. "I have seen the governess, and she has promised to arrange it differently. And Aunt Julia hates noise. It will sure to be all right."

Her aunt, being the only unattached member of the family, was coming to keep house for her father when she left him. The reference was not a happy one, and Mr Lucas commenced a series of half articulate sighs, which was only stopped by the arrival of the post.

"Oh, what a parcel!" cried Ethel. "For me! What can it be! Greek stamps. This is most exciting!"

It proved to be some asphodel bulbs, sent by Mrs Forman from Athens for planting in the conservatory.

"Doesn't it bring it all back! You remember the asphodels, father. And all wrapped up in Greek newspapers. I wonder if I can read them still. I used to be able to, you know."

She rattled on, hoping to conceal the laughter of the children next door—a favourite source of querulousness at breakfast time.

"Listen to me! 'A rural disaster.' Oh, I've hit on something sad. But never mind. 'Last Tuesday at Plataniste, in the province of Messenia, a shocking tragedy occurred. A large tree'—aren't I getting on well?—'blew down in the night and'—wait a minute—oh dear! 'crushed to death the five occupants of the little Khan there, who had apparently been sitting in the balcony. The bodies of Maria Rhomaides, the aged proprietress, and of her daughter, aged forty-six, were easily recognizable, whereas that of her grandson'—oh, the rest is really too horrid; I wish I had never tried it, and what's more I feel to have heard the name Plataniste before. We didn't stop there, did we, in the spring?"

"We had lunch," said Mr Lucas, with a faint expression of trouble on his vacant face. "Perhaps it was where the dragoman bought the pig."

"Of course," said Ethel in a nervous voice. "Where the dragoman bought the little pig. How terrible!"

"Very terrible!" said her father, whose attention was wandering to the noisy children next door. Ethel suddenly started to her feet with genuine interest.

"Good gracious!" she exclaimed. "This is an old paper. It happened not lately but in April—the night of Tuesday the eighteenth—and we—we must have been there in the afternoon."

"So we were," said Mr Lucas. She put her hand to her heart, scarcely able to speak.

"Father, dear father, I must say it: you wanted to stop there. All those people, those poor half savage people, tried to keep you, and they're dead. The whole place, it says, is in ruins, and even the stream has changed its course. Father, dear, if it had not been for me, and if Arthur had not helped me, you must have been killed."

Mr Lucas waved his hand irritably. "It is not a bit of good speaking to the governess, I shall write to the landlord and say, 'The reason I am giving up the house is this: the dog barks, the children next door are intolerable, and I cannot stand the noise of running water.' "

Ethel did not check his babbling. She was aghast at the narrowness of the escape, and for a long time kept silence. At last she said: "Such a marvelous deliverance does make one believe in Providence."

Mr Lucas, who was still composing his letter to the landlord, did not reply.

Mavis Gallant

Mavis Gallant was born in Montreal in 1922, and educated at schools both there and in New York. After an early career working for the National Film Board and as a reporter for the Montreal *Standard* newspaper, Gallant moved to Europe; she has lived in Paris since the early 1960s. A frequent contributor to *The New Yorker*, and a much-published novelist (e.g., *Green Water, Green Sky*, 1959) and essayist (e.g., *The Affair of Gabrielle Russier*, 1971; and *Paris Notebooks*, 1988), she remains best known for her many collections of short stories and novellas. These include *My Heart is Broken* (1964), *The Pegnitz Junction* (1973), *From the Fifteenth District* (1979), and a selection called *The Moslem Wife & Other Stories* (1994). Altogether her stories range through a variety of settings (Northern Ontario, Montreal, Paris, Switzerland, Spain, southern France, and postwar Germany), and they range in tone from the wryly comic to the deeply pessimistic. Sometimes they satirically expose an imperceptive bureaucracy. At other times they sympathetically reveal how a single character, whether accidentally or by deliberate choice, finds a way of dealing with the disparities between personal memory and official history.

"With a Capital T" first appeared in a special Gallant issue of *Canadian Fiction Magazine* in 1978; it was later collected in *Home Truths* (1981), a book in which several related stories feature the character Linnet Muir. This particular story draws on the writer's knowledge of journalism. With some asperity and much humour, it tells of an accommodation to what is often thought of as "real life." The central character, aware of the differences between how she sees the world and how the newspaper she works for represents it, learns that society places limits on what it is willing to accept as "Truth with a capital T." Characteristically, Gallant reveals this process of change through her handling of time; in the shifting patterns of verbal form—tense and modality, for example—she conveys the shifting nuances of both relationship and understanding.

With a Capital T

For Madeleine and Jean-Paul Lemieux

In wartime, in Montreal, I applied to work on a newspaper. Its name was *The Lantern*, and its motto, "My light shall shine," carried a Wesleyan ring of veracity and plain dealing. I chose it because I thought it was a place where I would be given a lot of different things to do. I said to the man who consented to see me, "But not the women's pages. Nothing like that." I was eighteen. He heard me out and suggested I come back at twenty-one, which was a soft way of getting rid of me. In the meantime I was to acquire experience; he did not say of what kind.

On the stroke of twenty-one I returned and told my story to a different person. I was immediately accepted; I had expected to be. I still believed, then, that most people meant what they said. I supposed that the man I had seen that first time had left a memorandum in the files: "To whom it may concern—Three years from this date, Miss Linnet Muir will join the editorial staff." But after I'd been working for a short time I heard one of the editors say, "If it hadn't been for the god-damned war we would never have hired even one of the god-damned women," and so I knew.

In the meantime I had acquired experience by getting married. I was no longer a Miss Muir, but a Mrs. Blanchard. My husband was overseas. I had longed for emancipation and independence, but I was learning that women's autonomy is like a small inheritance paid out a penny at a time. In a journal I kept I scrupulously noted everything that came into my head about this, and about God, and about politics. I took it for granted that our victory over Fascism would be followed by a sunburst of revolution—I thought that was what the war was about. I wondered if going to work for the capitalist press was entirely moral. "Whatever happens," I wrote, "it will be the Truth, nothing half-hearted, the Truth with a Capital T."

The first thing I had to do was write what goes under the pictures. There is no trick to it. You just repeat what the picture has told you like this:

"Boy eats bun as bear looks on."

The reason why anything has to go under the picture at all is that a reader might wonder, "Is that a bear looking on?" It looks like a bear, but that is not enough reason for saying so. Pasted across the back of the photo you have been given is a strip of paper on which you can read: "Saskatoon, Sask. 23 Nov. Boy eats bun as bear looks on." Whoever composed this knows two things more than you do—a place and a time.

You have a space to fill in which the words must come out even. The space may be tight; in that case, you can remove "as" and substitute a comma, though that makes the kind of terse statement to which your reader is apt to reply, "So what?" Most of the time, the Truth with a Capital T is a matter of elongation: "Blond boy eats small bun as large bear looks on."

"Blond boy eats buttered bun . . ." is livelier, but unscrupulous. You have been given no information about the butter. "Boy eats bun as hungry bear looks on," has the beginnings of a plot, but it may inspire your reader to protest: "That boy must be a mean sort of kid if he won't share his food with a starving creature." Child-lovers, though less prone to fits of anguish than animal-lovers, may he distressed by the word "hungry" for a different reason, believing "boy" subject to attack from "bear." You must not lose your head and type, "Blond bear eats large boy as hungry bun looks on," because your reader may notice, and write a letter saying, "Some of you guys around there think you're pretty smart, don't you?" while another will try to enrich your caption with, "Re your bun write-up, my wife has taken better pictures than that in the very area you mention."

At the back of your mind, because your mentors have placed it there, is an obstruction called "the policy factor." Your paper supports a political party. You try to discover what this party has had to say about buns and bears, how it intends to approach them in the future. Your editor, at golf with a member of parliament, will not want to have his game upset by: "It's not that I want to interfere but some of that bun stuff seems pretty negative to me." The young and vulnerable reporter would just as soon not pick up the phone to be told, "I'm ashamed of your defeatist attitude. Why, I knew your father! He must be spinning in his grave!" or, more effectively, "I'm telling you this for your own good—I think you're subversive without knowing it."

Negative, defeatist and subversive are three of the things you have been cautioned not to be. The others are seditious, obscene, obscure, ironic, intellectual and impulsive.

You gather up the photo and three pages of failed captions, and knock at the frosted glass of a senior door. You sit down and are given a view of boot soles. You say that the whole matter comes down to an ethical question concerning information and redundancy; unless "reader" is blotto, can't he see for himself that this is about a boy, a bun, and a bear?

Your senior person is in shirtsleeves, hands clasped behind his neck. He thinks this over, staring at the ceiling; swings his feet to the floor; reads your variations on the bear-and-bun theme; turns the photo upside-down. He tells you patiently, that it is not the business of "reader" to draw conclusions. Our subscribers are not dreamers or smart alecks; when they see a situation in a picture, they want that situation confirmed. He reminds you about negativism and obscuration; advises you to go sit in the library and acquire a sense of values by reading the back issues of *Life*.

The back numbers of *Life* are tatty and incomplete, owing to staff habits of tearing out whatever they wish to examine at leisure. A few captions, still intact, allow you to admire a contribution to pictorial journalism, the word "note":

"American flag flies over new post office. Note stars on flag."

"GI waves happily from captured Italian tank. Note helmet on head."

So, "Boy eats bun as bear looks on. Note fur on bear." All that can happen now will be a letter asking, "Are you sure it was a bun?"

■ ■ ■

From behind frosted-glass doors, as from a leaking intellectual bath, flow instructions about style, spelling, caution, libel, brevity, and something called "the ground rules." A few of these rules have been established for the convenience of the wives of senior persons and reflect their tastes and interests, their inhibitions and fears, their desire to see close friends' pictures when they open to the social page, their fragile attention span. Other rules demand that we pretend to be independent of British foreign policy and American commerce—otherwise our readers, discouraged, will give up caring who wins the war. (Soon after victory British foreign policy will cease to exist; as for American commerce, the first grumbling will be heard when a factory in Buffalo is suspected of having flooded the country with defective twelve-inch pie tins.) Ground rules maintain that you must not be flippant about the Crown—an umbrella term covering a number of high-class subjects, from the Royal Family to the nation's judicial system—or about our war effort or, indeed, our reasons for making any effort about anything. Religions, in particular those observed by decent Christians, are not up for debate. We may however, describe and denounce marginal sects whose puritanical learnings are even more dizzily slanted than our own. The Jehovah's Witnesses, banned as seditious, continue to issue inflammatory pamphlets about Jesus; patriotic outrage abounds over this. The children of Witnesses are beaten up in public schools for refusing to draw Easter bunnies. An education officer, interviewed, declares that the children's obstinate observance of the Second Commandment is helping Hitler. Everyone knows that the Easter bunny, along with God and Santa Claus, is on our side.

To argue a case for the children is defeatist; to advance reasons against their persecution is obscure. Besides, your version of the bunny conflict may be unreliable. Behind frosted-glass doors lurk male fears of female mischief. Women, having no inborn sense of history, are known to invent absurd stories. Celebrated newspaper hoaxes (perpetrated by men, as it happens) are described to you, examples of irresponsible writing that have brought down trusting editors. A few of these stories have been swimming, like old sea turtles, for years now, crawling ashore wherever British possessions are still tinted red on the map. "As the niece of the Governor-General rose from a deep curtsey, the Prince, with the boyish smile that has made him the darling of five continents, picked up a bronze bust of his grandmother and battered Lady Adeline to death" is one version of a perennial favorite.

Privately, you think you could do better. You will never get the chance. The umpires of ground rules are nervous and watchful behind those doors. Wartime security hangs heavy. So does the fear that the end of hostilities will see them turfed out to make way for war correspondents wearing nonchalant mustaches, battered caps, carelessly-knotted white scarves, raincoats with shoulder tabs, punctuating their accounts of Hunnish atrocities perceived at Claridges and the Savoy with "Roger!" and "Jolly-oh!" and "Over to you!"

Awaiting this dreadful invasion the umpires sit, in shirt-sleeves and braces, scribbling initials with thick blue pencils. "NDG" stands for "No Damned Good." (Clairvoyant, you will begin to write "NBF" in your journal meaning "No Bloody Future.") As a creeping, climbing wash of conflicting and contradictory instructions threatens to smother you, you discover the possibilities of the quiet, or lesser, hoax. Obeying every warning and precept, you will write, turn in, and get away with, "Dressed in shoes, stockings and hat appropriate to the season, Mrs. Horatio Bantam, the former Felicity Duck-pond, grasped the bottle of champagne in her white-gloved hand and sent it swinging against the end of HMCS *Makeweight* that was nearest the official party, after which, swaying slightly, she slid down the ways and headed for open waters."

■ ■ ■

As soon as I realized that I was paid about half the salary men were earning, I decided to do half the work. I had spent much of my adolescence as a resourceful truant, evolving the good escape dodges that would serve one way and another all my life. At *The Lantern* I used reliable school methods. I would knock on a glass door—a door that had nothing to do with me.

"Well, Blanchard, what do you want?"

"Oh, Mr. Watchmaster—it's just to tell you I'm going out to look something up."

"What for?"

"An assignment."

"Don't tell *me*. Tell Amstutz."

"He's organizing fire-drill in case of air-raids."

"Tell Cranach. He can tell Amstutz."

"Mr. Cranach has gone to stop the art department from striking."

"*Striking*? Don't those buggers know there's a war on? I'd like to see Accounting try that. What do they want now?"

"Conditions. They're asking for conditions. Is it all right if I go now, Mr. Watchmaster?"

"You know what we need around here, don't you? One German

regiment. Regiment? What am I saying? *Platoon*. That'd take the mickey out of 'em. Teach them something about hard work. Loving your country. Your duty. Give me one trained German sergeant. I'd lead him in. 'O.K.—you've been asking for this!' Ratatatat. You wouldn't hear any more guff about conditions. What's your assignment?"

"The Old Presbyterians. They've decided they're against killing people because of something God said to Moses."

"Seditious bastards. Put 'em in work camps, the whole damned lot. All right, Blanchard, carry on."

I would go home, wash my hair, listen to Billie Holiday records.

"Say, Blanchard, where the hell were you yesterday? Seventy-nine people were poisoned by ham sandwiches at a wedding party on Durocher Street. The sidewalk was like a morgue."

"Actually, I just happened to be in Mr. Watchmaster's office. But only for a minute."

"Watchmaster's got no right to ask you to do anything. One of these days I'm going to close in on him. I can't right now—there's a war on. The only good men we ever had in this country were killed in the last one. Look, next time Watchmaster gets you to run his errands, refer it to Cranach. Got that? All right, Blanchard, on your way."

■ ■ ■

No good dodge works forever.

"Oh, Mr. Watchmaster, I just wanted to tell you I'm going out for an hour or two. I have to look something up. Mr. Cranach's got his door locked, and Mr. Amstutz had to go home to see why his wife was crying."

"Christ, what an outfit. What do you have to look up?"

"What Mussolini did to the Red Cross dogs. It's for the 'Whither Italy?' supplement."

"You don't need to leave the building for that. You can get all you want by phone. You highbrows don't even know what a phone is. Drop around Advertising some time and I'll show you down-to-earth people using phones as working instruments. All you have to do is call the Red Cross, a veterinarian, an Italian priest, maybe an Italian restaurant, and a kennel. They'll tell you all you need to know. Remember what Churchill said about Mussolini, eh? That he was a fine Christian gentleman. If you want my opinion, whatever those dogs got they deserved."

■ ■ ■

Interviews were useful: you could get out and ride around in taxis and waste hours in hotel lobbies reading the new American magazines, which were increasingly difficult to find.

"I'm just checking something for *The Lantern*—do you mind?"

"Just so long as you don't mar the merchandise. I've only got five *Time*, three *Look*, four *Photoplay* and two *Ladies' Home*. Don't wander away with the *Esquire*. There's a war on."

Once I was sent to interview my own godmother. Nobody knew I knew her, and I didn't say. She was president of a committee that sent bundles to prisoners-of-war. The committee was launching an appeal for funds; that was the reason for the interview, I took down her name as if I had never heard it before: Miss Edna May Henderson. My parents had called her "Georgie," though I don't know why.

I had not seen my godmother since I was eight. My father had died, and I had been dragged away to be brought up in different cities. At eighteen, I had summoned her to a telephone: "It's Linnet," I said. "I'm here, in Montreal. I've come back to stay."

"Linnet," she said. "Good gracious me." Her chain-smoker's voice made me homesick, though it could not have been for a place—I was in it. Her voice, and her particular Montreal accent, were like the unexpected signatures that underwrite the past: If this much is true, you will tell yourself, then so is all the rest I have remembered.

She was too busy with her personal war drive to see me then, though she did ask for my phone number. She did not enquire where I had been since my father's death, or if I had anything here to come back to. It is true that she and my mother had quarrelled years before; still, it was Georgie who had once renounced in my name "the devil and all his works, the vain pomp and glory of the world, with all covetous desires of the same, and carnal desires of the flesh." She might have been curious to see the result of her bizarre undertaking, but a native canny Anglo-Montreal prudence held her still.

I was calling from a drugstore; I lived in one room of a cold-water flat in the east end. I said, "I'm completely on my own, and entirely self-supporting." That was so Georgie would understand I was not looking for help; at all events, for nothing material.

I realize now how irregular, how fishy even, this must have sounded. Everybody has a phone, she was probably thinking. What is the girl trying to hide?

"Nothing" would have been the answer. There seemed no way to connect. She asked me to call her again in about a month's time, but of course I never did.

■ ■ ■

My godmother spent most of her life in a block of granite designed to look like a fortress. Within the fortress were sprawling apartments, drawn to an Edwardian pattern of high ceilings, dark corridors, and enormous kitchens full of pipes. Churches and schools, banks and prisons, dwellings and railway stations were part of an imperial convallation that wound round the globe, designed to impress on the minds of indigenous populations that the builders had come to stay. In Georgie's redoubt, the doorman was shabby and lame; he limped beside me along a gloomy passage as far as the elevator, where only one of the sconce lights fixed to the panelling still worked. I had expected someone else to answer my ring, but it was Georgie who let me in, took my coat, and indicated with a brusque gesture, as if I did not know any English, the mat where I was to leave my wet snowboots. It had not occurred to me to bring shoes. Padding into her drawing room on stockinged feet, I saw the flash photograph her memory would file as further evidence of Muir incompetence; for I believe to this day that she recognized me at once. I was the final product, the last living specimen of a strain of people whose imprudence, lack of foresight, and refusal to take anything seriously had left one generation after another unprepared and stranded, obliged to build life from the ground up, fashioning new materials every time.

My godmother was tall, though not so tall as I remembered. Her face was wide and flat. Her eyes were small, deep-set, slightly tilted, as if two invisible thumbs were pulling at her temples. Her skin was as coarse and lined as a farm woman's; indifference to personal appearance of that kind used to be a matter of pride.

Her drawing room was white, and dingy and worn-looking. Curtains and armchairs needed attention, but that may have been on account of the war: it had been a good four years since anyone had bothered to paint or paper or have slipcovers made. The lamps were blue-and-white, and on this winter day already lighted. The room smelled of the metallic central heating of old apartment buildings, and of my godmother's Virginia cigarettes. We sat on worn white sofas, facing each other, with a table in between.

My godmother gave me Scotch in a heavy tumbler and pushed a dish of peanuts towards me, remarking in that harsh evocative voice, "Peanuts are harder to find than Scotch now."

Actually, Scotch was off the map for most people; it was a civilian casualty, expensive and rare.

We were alone except for a Yorkshire terrier, who lay on a chair in the senile sleep that is part of dying.

"I would like it if Minnie could hang on until the end of the war," Georgie said. "I'm sure she'd like the victory parades and the bands. But she's thirteen, so I don't know."

That was the way she and my parents and their friends had talked to each other. The duller, the more earnest, the more literal generation I stood for seemed to crowd the worn white room, and to darken it further.

I thought I had better tell her straightaway who I was, though I imagined she knew. I did not intend to be friendly beyond that, unless she smiled. And even there, the quality of the smile would matter. Some smiles are instruments of repression.

Telling my new name, explaining that I had married, that I was now working for a newspaper, gave an accounting only up to a point. A deserted continent stretched between us, cracked and fissured with bottomless pits over which Georgie stepped easily. How do you deal with life? her particular Canadian catechism asked. By ignoring its claims on feeling. Any curiosity she may have felt about such mysteries as coincidence and continuity (my father was said to have been the love of her life; I was said to resemble him) had been abandoned, like a game that was once the rage. She may have been unlucky with games, which would explain the committee work; it may be dull, but you can be fairly sure of the outcome. I often came across women like her, then, who had no sons or lovers or husbands to worry about, and who adopted the principle of the absent, endangered male. A difference between us was that, to me, the absence and danger had to be taken for granted; another was that what I thought of as men, Georgie referred to as "boys." The rest was beyond my reach. Being a poor judge of probabilities, she had expected my father to divorce. I was another woman's child, foolish and vulnerable because I had lost my dignity along with my boots; paid to take down her words in a notebook; working not for a lark but for a living, which was unforgivable even then within the shabby fortress. I might have said, "I am innocent," but she already knew that.

My godmother was dressed in a jaunty blue jacket with a double row of brass buttons, and a pleated skirt. I supposed this must be the costume she and her committee wore when they were packing soap and cigarettes and second-hand cheery novels for their boys over there in the coop. She told me the names of the committee women, and said, "Are you getting everything down all right?" People ask that who are not used to being interviewed. "They told me there'd be a picture," she complained. That explained the uniform.

"I'm sorry. He should be here now."

"Do you want me to spell those names for you?"

"No. I'm sure I have them."

"You're not writing much."

"I don't need to," I said. "Not as a rule."

"You must have quite a memory."

She seemed to be trying to recall where my knack of remembering came from, if it was inherited, wondering whether memory is of any use to anyone except to store up reasons for discord.

We gave up waiting for the photographer. I stood stork-like in the passage, pulling on a boot. Georgie leaned on the wall, and I saw that she was slightly tight.

"I have four godchildren," she said. "People chose me because I was an old maid, and they thought I had money to leave. Well, I haven't. There'll be nothing for the boys. All my godchildren were boys. I never liked girls."

She had probably been drinking for much of the day, on and off; and of course there was all the excitement of being interviewed, and the shock of seeing me: still, it was a poor thing to say. Supposing, just supposing, that Georgie had been all I had left? My parents had been perfectly indifferent to money—almost pathologically so, I sometimes thought. The careless debts they had left strewn behind and that I kept picking up and trying to settle were not owed in currency.

Why didn't I come straight out with that? Because you can't—not in that world. No one can have the last retort, not even when there is truth to it. Hints and reminders flutter to the ground in overheated winter rooms, lie stunned for a season, are reborn as everlasting grudges.

"Goodbye, Linnet," she said.

"Goodbye."

"Do you still *not* have a telephone?" No answer. "When will it come out?" She meant the interview.

"On Saturday."

"I'll be looking for it." On her face was a look I took to mean anxiety over the picture, and that I now see to have been mortal terror. I never met her again, not even by accident. The true account I wrote of her committee and its need for public generosity put us at a final remove from each other.

I did not forget her, but I forgot about her. Her life seemed silent and slow and choked with wrack, while mine moved all in a rush, dislodging every obstacle it encountered. Then mine slowed too; stopped flooding its banks. The noise of it abated and I could hear the past. She had died by then—thick-skinned, chain-smoking survivor of the regiment holding the fort.

I saw us in the decaying winter room, saw the lamps blazing coldly on the dark window panes; I heard our voices: "Peanuts are harder to find than Scotch now." "Do you send parcels to Asia, or just to Germany?"

What a dull girl she is, Georgie must have thought; for I see, now, that I was seamless, and as smooth as brass; that I gave her no opening.

When she died, the godsons mentioned in her will swarmed around for a while, but after a certain amount of scuffling with trustees they gave up all claim, which was more dignified for them than standing forlorn and hungry-looking before a cupboard containing nothing. Nobody spoke up for the one legacy the trustees would have relinquished: a dog named Minnie, who was by then the equivalent of one hundred and nineteen years old in human time, and who persisted so unreasonably in her right to outlive the rest of us that she had to be put down without mercy.

NADINE GORDIMER

A native of Springs, Transvaal, where she was born in 1923, Nadine Gordimer focuses almost exclusively in her work on the impact of South Africa on the individual consciousness. Though she has been a visiting lecturer at several American universities (Harvard, Princeton, Northwestern, Michigan, Columbia), and has lived for short periods in England, the world outside South Africa enters her fictional world only through the experience of exiles, émigrés, and foreign travellers. Yet the appeal of her work is not diminished by this restriction in locale. She is not a polemical writer, even though she does respond morally to such questions as justice and apartheid in her country. Writing should not, she observes in an interview with Alan Ross, be put at the service of a cause, although a cause may itself become a topic of a story. "I write about . . . private selves," she adds; but these, "even in the most private situations, . . . are what they are because . . . lives are regulated and . . . mores formed by the political situation. You see, in South Africa, society is the political situation. To paraphrase, one might say . . . politics is character."

This relation between society and individual behaviour is one that she has variously probed in many novels and volumes of short stories published since 1949. *A World of Strangers* (1958), for example, examines the inability of a young Englishman to reconcile his attraction to South Africa with his rejection of the racial divisions he finds there. *The Late Bourgeois World* (1966) presents the paralysis of will that affects one level of white society in the country—a world in which a clock ticking "afraid, alive, afraid, alive . . . " renders the moral tension in a single terse image. Gordimer's 1998 novel *The House Gun* exposes the uncertainties and contradictions of white liberalism in post-apartheid South Africa. In 1991 she won the Nobel Prize for literature.

"No Place Like," which originally appeared in *The Southern Review* and then was collected in *Livingstone's Companions* (1971), demonstrates the talent for trenchant observation to be found in all Gordimer's writing. Details of setting and style—the fragmentary phrases, the tone, the repetitiousness, and the point of view—all contribute to the story's effect. Momentary experiences are made into the arenas where the mind can discover or fail to discover significant meaning in life, and ideas about human behaviour and human potential are distilled into exact images and precisely rendered scenes.

No Place Like

The relief of being down, out, and on the ground after hours in the plane was brought up short for them by the airport building: dirty, full of up-ended chairs like a closed restaurant. *Transit? Transit?* Some of them started off on a stairway but were shooed back exasperatedly in a language they didn't understand. The African heat in the place had been cooped up for days and nights; somebody tried to open one of the windows but again there were remonstrations from the uniformed man and the girl in her white gloves and leopard-skin pillbox hat. The windows were sealed, anyway, for the air-conditioning that wasn't working; the offender shrugged. The spokesman that every group of travellers produces made himself responsible for a complaint; at the same time some of those sheep who can't resist a hole in a fence had found a glass door unlocked on the far side of the transit lounge—they were leaking to an open passage-way: grass, bougainvillea trained like standard roses, a road glimpsed there! But the uniformed man raced to round them up and a cleaner trailing his broom was summoned to bolt the door.

The woman in beige trousers had come very slowly across the tarmac, putting her feet down on this particular earth once more, and she was walking even more slowly round the dirty hall. Her coat dragged from the crook of her elbow, her shoulder was weighed by the strap of a bag that wouldn't zip over a package of duty-free European liquor, her bright silk shirt opened dark mouths of wet when she lifted her arms. Fellow-glances of indignance or the seasoned superiority of a sense of humour found no answer in her. As her pace brought her into the path of the black cleaner, the two faces matched perfect indifference: his, for whom the distance from which these people came had no existence because he had been nowhere outside the two miles he walked from his village to the airport; hers, for whom the distance had no existence because she had been everywhere and arrived back.

Another black man, struggling into a white jacket as he unlocked wooden shutters, opened the bar, and the businessmen with their hard-top briefcases moved over to the row of stools. Men who had got talking to unattached women—not much promise in that now; the last leg of the journey was ahead—carried them glasses of gaudy synthetic fruit juice. The Consul who had wanted to buy her a drink with dinner on the plane had found himself a girl in red boots with a small daughter in identical red boots. The child waddled away and flirtation took the form of the two of them hurrying after to scoop it up, laughing. There was a patient queue of ladies in cardigans waiting to get into the lavatories. She passed—once, twice, three times in her slow rounds—a woman who was stitching petit-point. The third time she made out that the subject was a spaniel dog with orange-and-black-streaked ears. Beside the needle-woman was a husband of a species as easily identifiable as the breed of dog—an American, because of the length of boot-lace, slotted through some emblem or badge, worn in place of a tie. He sighed and his wife looked up over her glasses as if he had made a threatening move.

The woman in the beige trousers got rid of her chit for Light Refreshment in an ashtray but she had still the plastic card that was her authority to board the plane again. She tried to put it in the pocket of the coat but she couldn't reach, so she had to hold the card in her teeth while she unharnessed herself from the shoulder-bag and the coat. She wedged the card into the bag beside the liquor packages, leaving it to protrude a little so that it would be easy to produce when the time came. But it slipped down inside the bag and she had to unpack the whole thing—the hairbrush full of her own hair, dead, shed; yesterday's newspaper from a foreign town; the book whose jacket tore on the bag's zip as it came out; wads of pink paper handkerchiefs, gloves for a cold climate, the quota of duty-free cigarettes, the Swiss pocket-knife that you couldn't buy back home, the wallet of travel documents. There at the bottom was the shiny card. Without it, you couldn't board the plane again. With it, you were committed to go on to the end of the journey, just as the passport bearing your name committed you to a certain identity and place. It was one of the nervous tics of travel to feel for the reassurance of that shiny card. She had wandered to the revolving stand of paperbacks and came back to make sure where she had put the card: yes, it was there. It was not a bit of paper; shiny plastic, you couldn't tear it up—indestructible, it looked, of course they use them over and over again. *Tropic of Capricorn, Kamasutra, Something of Value.* The stand revolved and brought round the same books, yet one turned it again in case there should be a book that had escaped notice, a book you'd been wanting to read all your life. If one were to find such a thing, here and now, on this last stage, this last stop . . . She felt strong hope, the excitation of weariness and tedium perhaps. They came round—*Something of Value, Kamasutra, Tropic of Capricorn.*

She went to the seat where she had left her things and loaded up again, the coat, the shoulder-bag bearing down. Somebody had fallen asleep, mouth open, bottom fly-button undone, an Austrian hat with plaited cord and feather cutting into his damp brow. How long had they been in this place? What time was it where she had left? (Some airports had a whole series of clockfaces showing what time it was everywhere.) Was it still yesterday, there?—Or tomorrow. And where she was going? She thought, I shall find out when I get there.

A pair of curio vendors had unpacked their wares in a corner. People stood about in a final agony of indecision: What would he do with a thing like that? Will she appreciate it, I mean? A woman repeated as she must have done in bazaars and shops and marketplaces all over the world, I've seen them for half the price . . . But this was the last stop of all, the last chance *to take back something*. How else stake a claim? The last place of all the other places of the world.

Bone bracelets lay in a collapsed spiral of overlapping circles. Elephant hair ones fell into the pattern of the Olympic symbol. There were the ivory paper-knives and the little pictures of palm trees, huts and dancers on black paper. The vendor, squatting in the posture that derives from the necessity of the legless beggar to sit that way and has become as much a mark of the street professional, in such towns as the one that must be somewhere behind the airport, as the hard-top briefcase was of the international businessman drinking beer at the bar, importuned her with the obligation to buy. To refuse was to upset the ordination of roles. He was there to sell "ivory" bracelets and "African" art; they—these people shut up for him in the building—had been brought there to buy. He had a right to be angry. But she shook her head, she shook her head, while he tried out his few words of German and French (*bon marché, billig*) as if it could only be a matter of finding the right cue to get her to play the part assigned to her. He seemed to threaten, in his own tongue, finally, his head in its white skullcap hunched between jutting knees. But she was looking again at the glass case full of tropical butterflies under the President's picture. The picture was vivid, and new; a general successful in coup only months ago, in full dress uniform, splendid as the dark one among the Magi. The butterflies, relic of some colonial conservationist society, were beginning to fall away from their pins in grey crumbs and gauzy fragments. But there was one big as a bat and brilliantly emblazoned as the general: something in the soil and air, in whatever existed out there—whatever "out there" there was—that caused nature and culture to imitate each other . . . ?

If it were possible to take a great butterfly. Not take back; just take. But she had the Swiss knife and the bottles, of course. The plastic card. It would see her onto the plane once more. Once the plastic card was handed over, nowhere to go but across the tarmac and up the stairway into the belly of the plane, no turning back past the air hostess in her leopard-skin pillbox, past the barrier. It wasn't allowed; against regulations. The plastic card would send her to the plane, the plane would arrive at the end of the journey, the Swiss knife would be handed over for a kiss, the bottles would be exchanged for an embrace—she was shaking her head at the curio vendor (he had actually got up from his knees and come after her, waving his pictures), *no thanks, no thanks.* But he wouldn't give up and she had to move away, to walk up and down once more in the hot, enclosed course dictated by people's feet, the upended chairs and tables, the little shored-up piles of hand-luggage.

The Consul was swinging the child in red boots by its hands, in an arc. It was half-whimpering, half-laughing, yelling to be let down, but the larger version of the same model, the mother, was laughing in a way to make her small breasts shake for the Consul, and to convey to everyone how marvelous such a distinguished man was with children.

There was a gritty crackle and then the announcement in careful, African-accented English, of the departure of the flight. A kind of concerted shuffle went up like a sigh: at last! The red-booted mother was telling her child it was silly to cry, the Consul was gathering their things together, the woman was winding the orange thread for her needlework rapidly round a spool, the sleepers woke and the beer-drinkers threw the last of their foreign small change on the bar counter. No queue outside the Ladies' now and the woman in the beige trousers knew there was plenty of time before the second call. She went in and, once more, unharnessed herself among the crumpled paper towels and spilt powder. She tipped all the liquid soap containers in turn until she found one that wasn't empty; she washed her hands thoroughly in hot and then cold water and put her wet palms on the back of her neck, under her hair. She went to one of the row of mirrors and looked at what she saw there a moment, and then took out from under the liquor bottles, the Swiss knife and the documents, the hairbrush. It was full of hair; a web of dead hairs that bound the bristles together so that they could not go through a head of live hair. She raked her fingers slowly through the bristles and was aware of a young Indian woman at the next mirror moving quickly and efficiently about an elaborate toilet. The Indian backcombed the black, smooth hair cut in Western style to hang on her shoulders, painted her eyes, shook her ringed hands dry rather than use the paper towels, sprayed French perfume while she extended her neck, repleated the green and silver sari that left bare a small roll of lavender-grey flesh between waist and *choli*.

This is the final call for all passengers.

The hair from the brush was no-colour, matted and coated with fluff. Twisted round the forefinger (like the orange thread for the spaniel's ears) it became a fibrous funnel, dusty and obscene. She didn't want the Indian girl to be confronted with it and hid it in her palm while she went over to the dustbin. But the Indian girl saw only herself, watching her reflection appraisingly as she turned and swept out.

The brush went easily through the living hair, now. Again and again, until it was quite smooth and fell, as if it had a memory, as if it were cloth that had been folded and ironed a certain way, along the lines in which it had been arranged by professional hands in another hemisphere. A latecomer rushed into one of the lavatories, sounded the flush and hurried out, plastic card in hand.

The woman in the beige trousers had put on lipstick and run a nail-file under her nails. Her bag was neatly packed. She dropped a coin in the saucer set out, like an offering for some humble household god, for the absent attendant. The African voice was urging all passengers to proceed immediately through Gate B. The voice had some difficulty with *l*'s, pronouncing them more like *r*'s; a pleasant, reasoning voice, asking only for everyone to present the boarding pass, avoid delay, come quietly.

She went into one of the lavatories marked "Western-type toilet" that bolted automatically as the door shut, a patent device ensuring privacy; there was no penny to pay. She had the coat and bag with her and arranged them, the coat folded and balanced on the bag, on the cleanest part of the floor. She thought what she remembered thinking so many times before: not much time, I'll have to hurry. That was what the plastic card was for—surely not for being left behind, never. She had it stuck in the neck of the shirt now, in the absence of a convenient pocket; it felt cool and wafer-stiff as she put it there but had quickly taken on the warmth of her body. Some tidy soul determined to keep up Western-type standards had closed the lid and she sat down as if on a bench—the heat and the weight of the paraphernalia she had been carrying about were suddenly exhausting. She thought she would smoke a cigarette; there was no time for that. But the need for a cigarette hollowed out a deep sigh within her and she got the pack carefully out of the pocket of her coat without disturbing the arrangement on the floor. All passengers delaying departure of the flight were urged to proceed immediately through Gate B. Some of the words were lost over the echoing intercommunication system and at times the only thing that could be made out was the repetition, Gate B, a vital fact from which all grammatical contexts could fall away without rendering the message unintelligible. Gate B. If you remembered, if you knew Gate B, the key to mastery of the whole procedure remained intact with you. Gate B was the converse of the open sesame; it would keep you, passing safely through it, in the known, familiar, and inescapable, safe from caves of treasure and shadow. *Immediately. Gate B. Gate B.*

She could sense from the different quality of the atmosphere outside the door, and the doors beyond it, that the hall was emptying now. They were trailing, humping along under their burdens—the petit-point, the child in red boots—to the gate where the girl in the leopard-skin pillbox collected their shiny cards.

She took hers out. She looked around the cell as one looks around for a place to set down a vase of flowers or a note that mustn't blow away. It would not flush down the outlet; plastic doesn't disintegrate in water. As she had idly noticed, before, it wouldn't easily tear up. She was not at all agitated; she was simply looking for somewhere to dispose of it, now. She heard the voice (was there a shade of hurt embarrassment in the rolling *r*-shaped *l*'s) appealing to the passenger who was holding up flight so-and-so to please . . . She noticed for the first time that there was actually a tiny window, with the sort of pane that tilts outwards from the bottom, just above the cistern. She stood on the seat-lid and tried to see out, just managing to post the shiny card like a letter through the slot.

Gate B, the voice offered, *Gate B*. But to pass through Gate B you had to have a card, without a card Gate B had no place in the procedure. She could not manage to see anything at all, straining precariously from up there, through the tiny window; there was no knowing at all where the card had fallen. But as she half-jumped, half-clambered down again, for a second the changed angle of her vision brought into sight something like a head—the top of a huge untidy palm tree, up in the sky, rearing perhaps between buildings or above shacks and muddy or dusty streets where there were donkeys, bicycles and barefoot people. She saw it only for that second but it was so very clear, she saw even that it was an old palm tree, the fronds rasping and sharpening against each other. And there was a crow—she was sure she had seen the black flap of a resident crow.

She sat down again. The cigarette had made a brown aureole round itself on the cistern. In the corner what she had thought was a date-pit was a dead cockroach. She flicked the dead cigarette butt at it. Heel-taps clattered into the outer room, an African voice said, Who is there? Please, are you there? She did not hold her breath or try to keep particularly still. There was no one there. All the lavatory doors were rattled in turn. There was a high-strung pause, as if the owner of the heels didn't know what to do next. Then the heels rang away again and the door of the Ladies' swung to with the heavy sound of fanned air.

There were bursts of commotion without, reaching her muffledly where she sat. The calm grew longer. Soon the intermittent commotion would cease; the jets must be breathing fire by now, the belts fastened and the cigarettes extinguished, although the air-conditioning wouldn't be working properly yet, on the ground, and they would be patiently sweating. They couldn't wait forever, when they were so nearly there. The plane would be beginning to trundle like a huge perambulator, it would be turning, winking, shuddering in summoned power.

Take off. It was perfectly still and quiet in the cell. She thought of the great butterfly; of the general with his beautiful markings of braid and medals. Take off.

So that was the sort of place it was: crows in old dusty palm trees, crows picking the carrion in open gutters, legless beggars threatening in an unknown tongue. Not Gate B, but some other gate. Suppose she were to climb out that window, would they ask her for her papers and put her in some other cell, at the general's pleasure? The general had no reason to trust anybody who did not take Gate B. No sound at all, now. The lavatories were given over to their own internal rumblings; the cistern gulped now and then. She was quite sure, at last, that flight so-and-so had followed its course; was gone. She lit another cigarette. She did not think at all about what to do next, not at all; if she had been inclined to think that, she would not have been sitting wherever it was she was. The butterfly, no doubt, was extinct and the general would dislike strangers; the explanations (everything has an explanation) would formulate themselves, in her absence, when the plane reached its destination. The duty-free liquor could be poured down the lavatory, but there remained the problem of the Swiss pocket-knife. And yet—through the forbidden doorway: grass, bougainvillea trained like standard roses, a road glimpsed there!

Kate Grenville

Praised for her comic and astute feminist novels—*Lilian's Story* (1985), *Dreamhouse* (1986), and *Joan Makes History* (1988)—Kate Grenville has also published a guidebook on how to write, and worked as a film editor and writer in Australia and England. *Lilian's Story* was adapted for the screen in 1995, directed by Jerzy Domaradzki. Born Catherine Elizabeth Gee in Sydney, New South Wales, in 1950, Grenville is a graduate of the University of Sydney and the University of Colorado.

In an interview for *Contemporary Authors* 118, she observes that she began writing in order to find out—and thereby express—what it was like to be a woman. Her concern was not to write sociology or social realism, she says, but to "dignify the dilemmas of contemporary women" and to "lay out contemporary sexual politics for examination and satire." Her work does not locate answers to these dilemmas or resolve the conflicts between men and women; rather it reveals the way language can mask or assert the feelings that variously underpin and undermine relationships. In *The Ideal of Perfection* (1999) Grenville continues her exploration of the pain and ambivalence of love, but with a stronger sense of the possibilities of happiness.

In "Slow Dissolve" (which appeared in *Bearded Ladies*, 1984), the cinematic method alluded to by the title hints at dissolution also, which in the story itself takes several forms. Here language is sometimes romantic, sometimes violent; it both disguises and declares power, and ultimately the story is about power.

Slow Dissolve

My name's gone from the label by the bell. Now there's just a neatly-typed C. Stone. I wonder how she likes it on her own. I can hear her coming down the inside stairs. A nice smile now.

—Caroline!

—Mirrie!

—Nice to see you!

—It's been so long!

I feel that my smile shows too many teeth. So does hers. We stare at each other's mouths for a moment.

—I kept meaning . . .

—Nearly phoned you . . .

—Absolutely flat out . . .

—Tried to call you . . .

And here we are. There was nothing to say when we shared this flat, and there's still nothing to say.

—Hope my things haven't been in your way.

—No, no, plenty of room.

—Good good I kept meaning.

—Cup of tea?

—Lovely thanks.

The smell of the kitchen is the same as ever. The ghosts of a thousand sausages still hang in the air. Greasy fluff clings to the leg of the stove as it always did. The gap in the lino is full of the same black crumbs.

Caroline is straight out of the pages of the glossy magazines. What London's best-dressed secretaries are wearing.

— You're looking good Caroline.

—Oh thanks but I'm a mess my hair's terrible today.

She still talks in a whine like a broken motor. Her sharp little cat-face only cracks its varnish to smile when absolutely necessary.

—That's a great dress, I say.

—Oh this old thing. Just an old thing for work.

Her eyes flicker over my collection from the jumble sales.

—You're looking good too.

Making the tea, she moves around the kitchen slowly as if drugged. There's a slow walk to the cupboard for the sugarbowl and she lifts it down slowly from the shelf. There's another slow walk back to the table with the sugar and a long consideration about where to put it. She hovers it down as cautiously as the helicopter containing the Queen. It might be dangerous to interrupt this trance but if I don't speak I'll break into a high-pitched cackle.

—Going away this summer?

—I don't really know.

She takes a teabag out of the box.

—I went away last summer.

After frowning thought she takes out another teabag.

—I went to Bermuda.

—That must have been good.

She closes the box carefully, as if small creatures are seething inside.

—It was all right.

The box is finally safe back on the shelf.

—Did you go there with someone?

—Yes, oh yes I went there with a fellow I knew here, see, he asked me to go, only we had a fight and then he came back here but I didn't want to so I stayed there.

After this she seems exhausted.

—But it must have been good being in Bermuda? Even without him?

The silence has set like old yolk.

—It was all right. Sun and . . . beaches. Beaches and . . . swimming and all that. I got a good tan.

She inspects a patch of arm.

—Gone now.

She scratches with a fingernail at the vanished tan.

—I was really brown. But it faded.

—You didn't meet anyone else?

—Well you see everyone there was like in a couple. Every man was with a woman and there weren't any free men. And it was really expensive. Eating cost a lot and even a Coke was nearly a pound.

She stares bleakly round the room.

—See, if I'd of found a man he could've taken me out to dinner and bought me drinks and that and I could've stayed at his hotel and it wouldn't have cost me hardly anything, he could've taken me out to dinner every night. I couldn't afford to eat hardly by myself, but all the men were with women, they'd brought them with them, see.

She stares at me until I nod, then goes on.

—Anyway just before I had to leave I found a man and it was all right then. He was kind of old but all right. But I only had a few days of that and then I had to go back home. But the last few days were okay it didn't cost me anything and I could move out of my hotel and all that and he could buy me dinner.

The kettle makes a stifled screaming noise and after staring at it for a moment she pours the water into the mugs. When she puts the kettle back on the stove it keens softly to itself.

—What about your boyfriend, I ask. Still seeing him?

—You mean Pete, well he and I broke up. He had a lot of money you know, quite well off really. But he was very mean with it. Never took me anywhere nice or anything.

She stirs her tea as if she plans to wear through the bottom of the mug with the spoon.

—I mean I don't expect people to spend a lot of money on me all the time or anything. But when they've got it, it seems mean I think. He had a good job and all that.

She shifts in the chair and smooths the skirt over her knees.

—And there was another girl of course. I knew about her all along, it was all right by me. But she was just out for what she could get. Clothes and fancy meals. Jewellery even. Then she just dumped him, must have got all she wanted.

She licks the spoon and holds its curve against her cheek as if warming herself.

—Makes you think doesn't it. Like you should be out for what you can get. I was with him two years, two years I spent on him.

The spoon must be cold and she flips it across the room towards the sink, where it skitters along the enamel and disappears down the back. She watches as if expecting to see it crawl back up.

—Two years. Nearly three really. And then we broke up and I'm back where I started.

Her lips pucker towards the steaming tea and for a moment she looks like an old woman with her teeth out. She sighs.

—Everything's so dear. I've got to get my hair done once a week and that's going on ten pounds right there. Then clothes, they get dearer all the time, but you've got to look nice, otherwise . . .

She glances at me but doesn't finish the sentence.

—And after two years.

She runs a hand down her shin, closely inspecting it. It's a fine shin, but the sell-by date is moving up fast and the goods will soon start to look a little shabby. With a sputter and pop she squeezes cream out of a bottle and smooths it into her hands.

—Want to get your things?

These two shabby coats, the boots that need mending, and the boxes of tired paints were hardly worth coming back for. The suitcase bulges when everything's packed in. I'm leaving her the broken pith helmet and the eiderdown that leaks feathers. She must get cold alone here at night.

The living-room is full of a faint twittering from the television, and ghostly shadows of colours move about on the screen. Caroline sits unblinking, staring at a huge mouthing face.

—I asked someone to meet me here at six, mind if I wait?

—Of course, fine.

She shifts in the chair so her body is receptively turned to me as if for a chat but her attention is now fixed on three women pointing at a wet floor.

—So what are you up to these days, Mirrie, she says. Still doing your drawings?

I remind myself that the only artist she knows by name is Leonardo da Vinski.

—Yes. Paintings actually.

—And what about . . . still by yourself?

She waits for my well-practised explanation of how much I like living on my own. Practice makes perfect, but it makes a nice change to surprise her.

—Actually there's a man I'm seeing quite a lot of.

Caroline sits forward in her chair.

—That's wonderful, she whispers. Wonderful.

Her eyes retreat to the television. I'm afraid she might suddenly crack the varnish and start to cry.

—It may not last, of course, I say. Who can tell?

She glances at me sharply. I see she's thinking there's already trouble.

—I mean, we just get on well. That's all.

Her attention on me is so great that I can see her inspecting first my right eye, then my left, for the truth. Her eyes are devouring my face.

—But I never believe in looking into the future.

Caroline nods and I hear myself rushing on.

—Just enjoy the moment, that's what I always say.

Caroline switches the television off and turns her full attention on me. I feel myself smiling brightly.

—Known him long?

—Three months.

She nods like a housewife sniffing a dubious grapefruit.

—What's he do?

— He's a designer.

—How old is he?

—Thirty-five.

—Sounds good. Planning to get married?

—We don't see the point of marriage. We don't believe a piece of paper makes any difference.

She nods but her smile doesn't seem quite convinced.

—Anyway, I've got my work.

She glances at my clothes again.

—Wouldn't it be easier if you got married?

One of my fingernails has just broken and I have to stop myself tearing at it.

—We just don't think it's necessary.

She glances out the window at the darkening sky.

—He been married before?

—Well yes. But it was a long time ago. And she was a bitch.

Caroline is rubbing a hand over and over the same patch of her knee. She's stopped watching me. Somehow she's got the wrong idea of all this.

Finally, in a voice that's a pitch too high, she says:

—Well that's wonderful Mirrie, I'm sure you'll be really happy, I certainly hope it all works out for you.

She snaps on the television again and switches from channel to channel. At last the doorbell rings.

—That'll be Allan now.

She glances at her watch and I can't avoid hearing what I know she's going to say, although I hurry out of the room.

—Bit late isn't he?

I run down the stairs two at a time. When I open the door, there he'll be, my lovely man. I open the door and Allan is staring at me as if he wants to break my nose.

—You gave me the wrong fucking address.

I start to apologize and put my hand on his shoulder but he pushes past me up the stairs. Up in the living-room, Caroline has turned off the television and is standing with welcoming smile. Allan barely glances at her.

—These your things?

He's already picked up my bag and is waiting for me by the door. Caroline is smiling, and keeps smiling as Allan goes heavily down the stairs.

—He's a real strong silent type isn't he, she says and giggles. Real strong and silent.

We can hear Allan get into his car and slam the door. He starts the engine with a gnashing sound and revs up so hard that the whole house seems to shake. When he gives a blast on the horn, the living-room is filled with the blare. Caroline and I stand staring at each other, listening to the noise echoing until at last it fades away.

Mark Helprin

Born in 1947 and educated at Harvard College and at Harvard's Center for Middle Eastern Studies, Mark Helprin served in the British Merchant Navy and in the Israeli Army and Air Force. His military experience has provided him with much material for his fiction; his first novel, *Refiner's Fire* (1977), is a picaresque narrative depicting the adventures of a young American caught up in Israel's conflict with its neighbours. Helprin is a frequent contributor to *The New Yorker,* and his stories, collected in *A Dove of the East* (1975) and *Ellis Island & other stories* (1981), have a breadth of subject and setting that reflects the diversity of his experience. *Ellis Island & other stories* won the 1982 National Jewish Book Award for fiction. More recent works of fiction include *A Soldier of the Great War* (1991) and *Memoir from Antproof Case* (1995).

Whether focusing on a Middle Eastern battlefield, mountain climbing in the Alps, or scullers racing on the River Charles in Boston, Helprin's writing is grounded in sharp, realistic detail born of careful observation. At the same time, his characters spring from a more romantic tradition; moved by a mixture of idealism and doubt, they have an awareness of inexplicable forces at work within themselves as well as in the external environment, and like classical heroes they struggle to make an assertion of self over the physical limits of their existence. These tensions are sometimes conveyed through an injection of fantasy (a prominent element of Helprin's 1983 novel *Winter's Tale*), which enables him to give his characters and situations an archetypal dimension. In "Letters from the *Samantha*" (*Ellis Island & other stories*), a story cast in traditional epistolary form, he has produced a variation on the theme of Coleridge's "Rime of the Ancient Mariner"; a ship's captain must try to maintain the orderly values of the civilized society he represents in the face of an unexpected and a threatening presence. As in the tales of Joseph Conrad, the shipboard setting becomes an arena of moral conflict in which the protagonist must make a crucial decision affecting others as well as himself.

Letters from the *Samantha*

These letters were recovered in good condition from the vault of the sunken *Samantha*, an iron-hulled sailing ship of one thousand tons, built in Scotland in 1879 and wrecked during the First World War in the Persian Gulf off Basra.

20 August, 1909, 20° 14′ 18″ S,
43° 51′ 57″ E
Off Madagascar

DEAR SIR:
Many years have passed since I joined the Green Star Line. You may note in your records and logs, if not, indeed, by memory, the complete absence of disciplinary action against me. During my command, the *Samantha* has been a trim ship on time. Though my subordinates sometimes complain, they are grateful, no doubt, for my firm rule and tidiness. It saves the ship in storms, keeps them healthy, and provides good training—even though they will be masters of steamships.

No other vessel of this line has been as punctual or well run. Even today we are a week ahead and our Madagascar wood will reach Alexandria early. Bound for London, the crew are happy, and though we sail the Mozambique Channel, they act as if we had just caught sight of Margate. There are no problems on this ship. But I must in conscience report an irregular incident for which I am ready to take full blame.

Half a day out of Androka, we came upon a sea so blue and casual that its waters seemed fit to drink. Though the wind was slight and we made poor time, we were elated by perfect climate and painter's colors, for off the starboard side Madagascar rose as green and tranquil as a well-watered palm, its mountains engraved by thrashing freshwater streams which beat down to the coast. A sweet up-welling breeze blew steadily from shore and confounded our square sails. Twenty minutes after noon, the lookout sighted a tornado on land. In the ship's glass I saw it, horrifying and enormous. Though at a great distance, its column appeared as thick as a massive tree on an islet in an atoll, and stretched at least 70 degrees upward from the horizon.

I have seen these pipes of windy fleece before. If there is sea nearby, they rush to it. So did this. When it became not red and black from soil and debris but silver and green from the water it drew, I began to tighten ship. Were the typhoon to have struck us directly, no preparation would have saved us. But what a shame to be swamped by high waves, or to be dismasted by beaten sea and wind. Hatches were battened as if for storm, minor sails furled, and the mainsail driven down half.

It moved back and forth over the sea in illegible patterning, as if tacking to changing winds. To our dismay, the distance narrowed. We were afraid, though every man on deck wanted to see it, to feel it, perhaps to ride its thick swirling waters a hundred times higher than our mast—higher than the peaks inland. I confess that I have wished to be completely taken up by such a thing, to be lifted into the clouds, arms and legs pinned in the stream. The attraction is much like that of phosphorescent seas, when glowing lights and smooth swell are dangerously magnetic even for hardened masters of good ships. I have wanted to surrender to plum-colored seas, to know what one might find there naked and alone. But I have not, and will not.

Finally, we began to run rough water. The column was so high that we bent our heads to see its height, and the sound was greater than any engine, causing masts and spars to resonate like cords. Waves broke over the prow. Wind pushed us on, and the curl of the sea rushed to fill the depression of the waters. No more than half a mile off the starboard bow, the column veered to the west, crossing our path to head for Africa as rapidly as an express. Within minutes, we could not even see it.

As it crossed our bows, I veered in the direction from which it had come. It seemed to communicate a decisiveness of course, and here I took opportunity to evade. In doing so we came close to land. This was dangerous not only for the presence of reefs and shoals but because of the scattered debris. Trees as tall as masts and much thicker, roots sucked clean, lay in puzzlement upon the surface. Brush and vines were everywhere. The water was reddish brown from earth which had fallen from the cone. We were meticulously careful in piloting through this fresh salad, as a good ram against a solid limb would have been the end. Our cargo is hardwoods, and would have sunk us like granite. I myself straddled the sprit stays, pushing aside small logs with a boat hook and calling out trim to the wheel.

Nearly clear, we came upon a clump of tangled vegetation. I could not believe my eyes, for floating upon it was a large monkey, bolt upright and dignified. I sighted him first, though the lookout called soon after. On impulse, I set trim for the wavy mat and, as we smashed into it, offered the monkey an end of the boat hook. When he seized it I was almost pulled in, for his weight is almost equal to mine. I observed that he had large teeth, which appeared both white and sharp. He came close, and then took to the lines until he sat high on the topgallant. As he passed, his foot cuffed my shoulder and I could smell him.

My ship is a clean ship. I regretted immediately my gesture with the hook. We do not need the mysterious defecations of such a creature, or the threat of him in the rigging at night. But we could not capture him to throw him back into the sea and, even had we collared him, might not have been able to get him overboard without danger to ourselves. We are now many miles off the coast. It is dark, and he sits high off the deck. The night watch is afraid and requests that I fell him with my rifle. They have seen his sharp teeth, which he displays with much screaming and gesticulating when they near him in the rigging. I think he is merely afraid, and I cannot bring myself to shoot him. I realize that no animals are allowed on board and have often had to enforce this rule when coming upon a parrot or cat hidden belowdecks where some captains do not go. But this creature we have today removed from the sea is like a man, and he has ridden the typhoon. Perhaps we will pass a headland and throw him overboard on a log. He must eventually descend for want of food. Then we will have our way. I will report further when the matter is resolved, and assure you that I regret this breach of regulations.

Yours & etc.,
SAMSON LOW
MASTER, S/V SAMANTHA

■ ■ ■

23 August, 1909, 10° 43′ 3″ S,
49° 5′ 27″ E
South of the Seychelles

DEAR SIR:
We have passed the Channel and are heading north-northeast, hoping to ride the summer monsoon. It is shamefully hot, though the breeze is less humid than usual. Today two men dropped from the heat but they resumed work by evening. Because we are on a homeward tack, morale is at its best, or rather would be were it not for that damned ape in the rigging. He has not come down, and we have left behind his island and its last headland. He will have to have descended by the time we breach passage between Ras Asir and Jazirat Abd al-Kuri. The mate has suggested that there we throw him into the sea on a raft, which the carpenter has already set about building. He has embarked upon this with my permission, since there is little else for him to do. It has been almost an overly serene voyage and the typhoon caused no damage.

The raft he designed is very clever and has become a popular subject of discussion. It is about six feet by three feet, constructed of spare pine dunnage we were about to cast away when the typhoon was sighted. On each side is an outrigger for stability in the swell. In the center is a box, in which is a seat. Flanking this box are several smaller ones for fruit, biscuit, and a bucket of fresh water, in case the creature should drift a long time on the sea. This probably will not be so; the currents off Ras Asir drive for the beach, and we have noted that dunnage is quickly thrown upon the strand. Nevertheless, the crew have added their own touch—a standard distress flag flying from a ten-foot switch. They do not know, but I will order it replaced by a banner of another color, so that a hapless ship will not endanger itself to rescue a speechless monkey.

The crew have divided into two factions—those who wish to have the monkey shot, and those who would wait for him to descend and then put him in his boat. I am with the latter, since I would be the huntsman, and have already mentioned my lack of enthusiasm for this. A delegation of the first faction protested. They claimed that the second faction comprised those who stayed on deck, that the creature endangered balance in the rigging, and that he produced an uncanny effect in his screeching and bellicose silhouettes, which from below are humorous but which at close range, they said, are disconcerting and terrifying.

Since I had not seen him for longer than a moment and wanted to verify their complaint, I went up. Though sixty years of age, I did not use the bosun's chair, and detest those masters who do. It is pharaonic, and smacks of days in my father's youth when he saw with his own eyes gentlemen in sedan chairs carried about the city. The sight of twenty men laboring to hoist a ship's rotund captain is simply Egyptian, and I will not have it. Seventy feet off the deck, a giddy height to which I have not ascended in years, I came even with the ape. The ship was passing a boisterous sea and had at least a twenty-degree roll, which flung the two of us from side to side like pendula.

I am not a naturalist, nor have we on board a book of zoology, so the most I can do is to describe him. He is almost my height (nearly five feet ten inches) and appears to be sturdily built. Feet and hands are human in appearance except that they have a bulbous, skew, arthritic look common to monkeys. He is muscular and covered with fine reddish-brown hair. One can see the whiteness of his tendons when he stretches an arm or leg. I have mentioned the sharp, dazzling white teeth, set in rows like a trap, canine and pointed. His face is curiously delicate, and covered with orange hair leading to a snow-white crown of fur. My breath nearly failed when I looked into his eyes, for they are a bright, penetrating blue.

At first, he began to scream and swing as if he would come at me. If he had, I would have fared badly. The sailors fear him, for there is no man on board with half his strength, no man on the sea with a tenth his agility in the ropes, and if there is a man with the glacierlike pinnacled teeth, then he must be in a Scandinavian or Eastern European circus, for there they are fond of such things. To my surprise, he stopped his pantomime and, with a gentle and quizzical tilt of his head, looked me straight in the eyes. I had been sure that as a man I could answer his gaze as if from infallibility, and I calmly looked back. But he had me. His eyes unset me, so that I nearly shook. From that moment, he has not threatened or bared his teeth, but merely rests near the top of the foremast. The crew have attributed his conversion to my special power. This is flattering, though not entirely, as it assumes my ability to commune with an ape. Little do they suspect that it is I and not the monkey who have been converted, although to what I do not know. I am still thoroughly ashamed of my indiscretion and the troubles arising from it. We will get him and put him adrift off Ras Asir.

This evening, the cook grilled up some beef. I had him thoroughly vent the galley and use a great many herbs. The aroma was maddening. I sat in near-hypnotic ease in a canvas chair on the quarterdeck, a glass of wine in hand, as the heat fell to a cool breeze. We are all sunburnt and have been working hard, as the ape silently watches, to trim regularly and catch the best winds. We are almost in the full swift of the monsoon, and shortly will ride it in all its speed. It was wonderful to sit on deck and smell the herb-laden meat. The sea itself must have been jealous. I had several men ready with cargo net and pikes, certain that he would come down. We stared up at him as if he were the horizon, waiting. He smelled the food and agitated back and forth. Though he fretted, he did not descend. Even when we ate we saw him shunting to and fro on a yardarm. We left a dish for him away from us but he did not venture to seize it. If he had, we would have seized him.

From his impatience, I predict that tomorrow he will surrender to his stomach. Then we will catch him and this problem will be solved. I truly regret such an irregularity, though it would be worthwhile if he could only tell us how far he was lifted inside the silvered cone, and what it was like.

Yours & etc.,
SAMSON LOW

■ ■ ■

25 August, 1909, 2° 13′ 10″ N,
51° 15′ 17″ E
Off Mogadishu

DEAR SIR:
Today he came down. After the last correspondence, it occurred to me that he might be vegetarian, and that though he was hungry, the meat had put him off. Therefore, I searched my memory for the most aromatic vegetable dish I know. In your service as a fourth officer, I called at Jaffa

port, in Palestine, in January of 1873. We went up to Sfat, a holy town high in the hills, full of Jews and Arabs, quiet and mystical. There were so many come into that freezing velvet dome of stars that all hostelries were full. I and several others paid a small sum for private lodging and board. At two in the morning, after we had returned from Mt. Jermak, the Arabs made a hot lively fire from bundles of dry cypress twigs, and in a great square pan heated local oil and herbs, in which they fried thick sections of potato. I have never eaten so well. Perhaps it was our hunger, the cold, the silence, being high in the mountains at Sfat, where air is like ether and all souls change. Today I made the cook follow that old receipt.

We had been in the monsoon for several hours, and the air was littered with silver sparks—apparitions of heat from a glittering afternoon. Though the sun was low, iron decks could not be tread. In the rigging, he appeared nearly finished, limp and slouching, an arm hanging without energy, his back bent. We put potatoes in a dish on the forecastle. He descended slowly, finally touching deck lightly and ambling to the bows like a spider, all limbs brushing the planks. He ate his fill, and we threw the net over him. We had expected a ferocious struggle, but his posture and expression were so peaceful that I ordered the net removed. Sailors stood ready with pikes, but he stayed in place. Then I approached him and extended my hand as if to a child.

In imitation, he put out his arm, looking much less fearsome. Without a show of teeth, in his tired state, crouched on all fours to half our heights, he was no more frightening than a hound. I led him to the stern and back again while the crew cheered and laughed. Then the mate took him, and then the entire hierarchy of the ship, down to the cabin boys, who are smaller than he and seemed to interest him the most. By dark, he had strolled with every member of the crew and was miraculously tame. But I remembered his teeth, and had him chained to his little boat.

He was comfortable there, surrounded by fruit and water (which he ate and drank methodically) and sitting on a throne of sorts, with half a dozen courtiers eager to look in his eyes and hold his obliging wrist. Mine is not the only London post in which he will be mentioned. Those who can write are describing him with great zeal. I have seen some of these letters. He has been portrayed as a "mad baboon," a "man-eating gorilla of horrible colors, muscled but as bright as a bird," a "pygmy man set down on the sea by miracle and typhoon," and as all manner of Latin names, each different from the others and incorrectly spelled.

Depending on the bend of the monsoon and whether it continues to run strongly, we will pass Ras Asir in three days. I thought of casting him off early but was implored to wait for the Cape. I relented, and in doing so was made to understand why those in command must stay by rules. I am sure, however, that my authority is not truly diminished, and when the ape is gone I will again tighten discipline.

I have already had the distress flag replaced by a green banner. It flies over the creature on his throne. Though in splendor, he is in chains and in three days' time will be on the sea once more.

Yours & etc.,
SAMSON LOW

■ ■ ■

28 August, 1909, 12° 4′ 39″ N,
50° 1′ 2″ E
North of Ras Asir

DEAR SIR:
A most alarming incident has occurred. I must report, though it is among the worst episodes of my command. This morning, I arose, expecting to put the ape over the side as we rounded Ras Asir at about eleven. (The winds have been consistently excellent and a northward breeze veering off the monsoon has propelled us as steadily as an engine.) Going out on deck, I discovered that his boat was nowhere to be seen. At first, I thought that the mate had already disposed of him, and was disappointed that we were far from the coast. Then, to my shock, I saw him sitting unmanacled atop the main cargo hatch.

I screamed at the mate, demanding to know what had happened to the throne (as it had come to be called). He replied that it had gone overboard during the twelve-to-four watch. I stormed below and got that watch out in a hurry. Though sleepy-eyed, they were terrified. I told them that if the guilty one did not come forth I would put them all in irons. My temper was short and I could have struck them down. Two young sailors, as frightened as if they were surrendering themselves to die, admitted that they had thrown it over. They said they did not want to see the ape put to drift.

They are in irons until we make Suez. Their names are Mulcahy and Esper, and their pay is docked until they are freed. As we rounded the Cape, cutting close in (for the waters there are deep), we could see that though the creature would have been immediately cast up on shore, the shore itself was barren and inhospitable, and surely he would have died there. My Admiralty chart does not detail the inland topography of this area and shows only a yellow tongue marked "Africa" thrusting into the Gulf of Aden.

I can throw him overboard now or later. I do not want to do it. I brought him on board in the first place. There is nothing with which to fashion another raft. We have tons of wood below, but not a cubic foot of it is lighter than water. The wind is good and we are making for the Bab al-Mandab, where we will pass late tomorrow afternoon—after that, the frustrating run up the Red Sea to the Canal.

The mate suggests that we sell him to the Egyptians. But I am reluctant to make port with this in mind, as it would be a victory for the two in chains and in the eyes of many others. And we are not animal traders. If he leaves us at sea the effects of his presence will be invalidated, we will touch land with discipline restored, and I will have the option of destroying these letters, though everything here has been entered in short form in the log. I have ordered him not to be fed, but they cast him scraps. I must get back my proper hold on the ship.

Yours & etc.,
SAMSON LOW

■ ■ ■

30 August 1909, 15° 49′ 30″ N,
41° 5′ 32″ E
Red Sea off Massawa

DEAR SIR:
I have been felled by an attack of headaches. Never before has this happened. There is pressure in my skull enough to burst it. I cannot keep my balance; my eyes roam and I am drunk with pain. For the weary tack up the Red Sea I have entrusted the mate with temporary command, retiring to my cabin with the excuse of heat prostration. I have been in the Red Sea time and again but have never felt apprehension that death would follow its heat. We have always managed. To the east, the mountains of the Hijaz are so dry and forbidding that I have seen sailors look away in fright.

The ape has begun to suffer from the heat. He is listless and ignored. His novelty has worn off (with the heat as it is) and no one pays him any attention. He will not go belowdecks but spends most of the day under the canvas sun shield, chewing slowly, though there is nothing in his mouth. It is hot there—the light so white and uncompromising it sears the eyes. I have freed his champions from irons and restored their pay. By this act I have won over the crew and caused the factions to disappear. No one thinks about the ape. But I dare not risk a recurrence of bad feeling and have decided to cast him into the sea. Where we found him, a strong seaward current would have carried him to the open ocean. Here, at least, he can make the shore, although it is the most barren coast on earth. But who would have thought he might survive the typhoon? He has been living beyond his time. To be picked up and whirled at incomprehensible speed, carried for miles above the earth where no man has ever been, and thrown into the sea is a death sentence. If he survived that, perhaps he can survive Arabian desert.

His expression is neither sad nor fierce. He looks like an old man, neutral to the world. In the last two days he has become the target of provocation and physical blows. I have ordered this stopped, but a sailor will sometimes throw a nail on a piece of wood at him. We shall soon be rid of him.

Yesterday we came alongside another British ship, the *Stonepool*, of the Dutch Express Line. On seeing the ape, they were envious. What is it, their captain asked, amazed at his coloring. I replied that he was a Madagascar ape we had fished from the sea, and I offered him to them, saying he was tame as a dog. At first, they wanted him. The crew cried out for his acceptance, but the captain demurred, shaking his head and looking into my eyes as if he were laughing at me. "Damn!" I said, and went below without even a salute at parting.

My head aches. I must stop. At first light tomorrow, I will toss him back.

Yours & etc.,
SAMSON LOW

■ ■ ■

3 September 1909
Suez

DEAR SIR:
The morning before last I went on deck at dawn. The ape was sitting on the main hatch, his eyes upon me from the moment I saw him. I walked over to him and extended my arm, which he would not take in his customary manner. I seized his wrist, which he withdrew. However, as he did this I laid hold of the other wrist, and pulled him off the hatch. He did not bare his teeth. He began to scream. Awakened by this, most of the crew stood in the companionways or on deck, silently observing.

He was hard to drag, but I towed him to the rail. When I took his other arm to hoist him over, he bared his teeth with a frightening shriek. Everyone was again terrified. The teeth must be six inches long.

He came at me with those teeth, and I could do nothing but throttle him. With my hands on his throat, his arms were free. He grasped my side. I felt the pads of his hands against my ribs. I had to tolerate that awful sensation to keep hold of his throat. No man aboard came close. He shrieked and moaned. His eyes reddened. My response was to tighten my hold, to end the horror. I gripped so hard that my own teeth were bared and I made sounds similar to his. He put his hands around my neck as if to strangle me back, but I had already taken the inside position and, despite his great strength, lessened the power of his grip merely by lifting my arms against his. Nevertheless he choked me. But I had a great head start. We held this position for long minutes, sweating, until his arms dropped and his body convulsed. In rage, I threw him by the neck into the sea, where he quickly sank.

Some of the crew have begun to talk about him as if he were about to be canonized. Others see him as evil. I assembled them as the coasts began to close on Suez and the top of the sea was white and still. I made my views clear, for in years of command in a life on the sea I have learned much. I felt confident of what I told them.

He is not a symbol. He stands neither for innocence nor for evil. There is no parable and no lesson in his coming and going. I was neither right nor wrong in bringing him aboard (though it was indeed incorrect) or in what I later did. We must get on with the ship's business. He does not stand for a man or men. He stands for nothing. He was an ape, simian and lean, half sensible. He came on board, and now he is gone.

Yours & etc.,
SAMSON LOW

Ernest Hemingway

Perhaps the most widely read and influential writer of his generation, Ernest Hemingway (1899–1961) embodied the vigour, the restlessness, and the despair of the twentieth century, in his life as well as his writings. The son of a physician, he was born in Oak Park, near Chicago, and spent his boyhood in Illinois and Michigan. After leaving school in 1917 and working briefly as a reporter for the *Kansas City Star,* he joined the Red Cross, and drove an ambulance on the Italian front until he was wounded. After the war, he became a reporter for *The Toronto Star,* in company with Morley Callaghan. Then Hemingway began to produce novels and stories about the waste and sterility that marked the postwar period, of which his friend Gertrude Stein remarked, "You are all a lost generation." *In Our Time* appeared in 1924, followed by *The Sun Also Rises* (1926), and *Men Without Women* (1927); in these works Hemingway revealed an originality of plot and a striking economy of style that quickly established him as a major writer. *A Farewell to Arms* (1929) was inspired by his war experiences in Italy; and *For Whom the Bell Tolls* (1940) grew out of the period he spent in Spain in 1937 during the Spanish Civil War. Between 1941 and 1945 he was a war correspondent in Europe and the Far East. His last major work was *The Old Man and the Sea* (1952), which brought him the Pulitzer Prize in 1953; and in 1954 he was awarded the Nobel Prize for literature. In his last years Hemingway suffered periods of illness and depression; while in Idaho in July 1961 he committed suicide with a shotgun.

Hemingway's life was filled with action and adventure. His preoccupation with the physical aspect of existence, particularly its violence, is reflected in most of his writing. Whether his subject is the horror of war, or the struggle between human beings and nature, Hemingway draws a picture of a world where the only certainties are pain, deprivation, or death. Whatever their hopes or ideals may have been, his characters learn that life is a futile ordeal; to counter this, they must develop a protective shell of toughness, or endure their fate with numb resignation. Even in "Hills Like White Elephants" (*Men Without Women*), a story far removed from the brutalities of war or the bullring, there is an undercurrent of emotional violence. The dialogue is terse and laconic; but Hemingway's spare style conveys hidden tensions with admirable understatement, hinting at the sterility and breakdown of a whole way of life.

Hills Like White Elephants

The hills across the valley of the Ebro were long and white. On this side there was no shade and no trees and the station was between two lines of rails in the sun. Close against the side of the station there was the warm shadow of the building and a curtain, made of strings of bamboo beads, hung across the open door into the bar, to keep out flies. The American and the girl with him sat at a table in the shade, outside the building. It was very hot and the express from Barcelona would come in forty minutes. It stopped at this junction for two minutes and went on to Madrid.

"What should we drink?" the girl asked. She had taken off her hat and put it on the table.

"It's pretty hot," the man said.

"Let's drink beer."

"Dos cervezas," the man said into the curtain.

"Big ones?" a woman asked from the doorway.

"Yes. Two big ones."

The woman brought two glasses of beer and two felt pads. She put the felt pads and the beer glasses on the table and looked at the man and the girl. The girl was looking off at the line of hills. They were white in the sun and the country was brown and dry.

"They look like white elephants," she said.

"I've never seen one," the man drank his beer.

"No, you wouldn't have."

"I might have," the man said. "Just because you say I wouldn't have doesn't prove anything."

The girl looked at the bead curtain. "They've painted something on it," she said. "What does it say?"

"Anis del Toro. It's a drink."

"Could we try it?"

The man called "Listen" through the curtain. The woman came out from the bar.

"Four reales."

"We want two Anis del Toro."

"With water?"

"Do you want it with water?"

"I don't know," the girl said. "Is it good with water?"

"It's all right."

"You want them with water?" asked the woman.

"Yes, with water."

"It tastes like licorice," the girl said and put the glass down.

"That's the way with everything."

"Yes," said the girl. "Everything tastes of licorice. Especially all the things you've waited so long for, like absinthe."

"Oh, cut it out."

"You started it," the girl said. "I was being amused. I was having a fine time."

"Well, let's try and have a fine time."

"All right. I was trying. I said the mountains looked like white elephants. Wasn't that bright?"

"That was bright."

"I wanted to try this new drink. That's all we do, isn't it—look at things and try new drinks?"

"I guess so."

The girl looked across at the hills.

"They're lovely hills," she said. "They don't really look like white elephants. I just meant the coloring of their skin through the trees."

"Should we have another drink?"

"All right."

The warm wind blew the bead curtain against the table.

"The beer's nice and cool," the man said.

"It's lovely," the girl said.

"It's really an awfully simple operation, Jig," the man said. "It's not really an operation at all."

The girl looked at the ground the table legs rested on.

"I know you wouldn't mind it, Jig. It's really not anything. It's just to let the air in."

The girl did not say anything.

"I'll go with you and I'll stay with you all the time. They just let the air in and then it's all perfectly natural."

"Then what will we do afterward?"

"We'll be fine afterward. Just like we were before."

"What makes you think so?"

"That's the only thing that bothers us. It's the only thing that's made us unhappy."

The girl looked at the bead curtain, put her hand out and took hold of two of the strings of beads.

"And you think then we'll be all right and be happy."

"I know we will. You don't have to be afraid. I've known lots of people that have done it."

"So have I," said the girl. "And afterward they were all so happy."

"Well," the man said, "if you don't want to you don't have to. I wouldn't have you do it if you didn't want to. But I know it's perfectly simple."

"And you really want to?"

"I think it's the best thing to do. But I don't want you to do it if you don't really want to."

"And if I do it you'll be happy and things will be like they were and you'll love me?"

"I love you now. You know I love you."

"I know. But if I do it, then it will be nice again if I say things are like white elephants, and you'll like it?"

"I'll love it. I love it now but I just can't think about it. You know how I get when I worry."

"If I do it you won't ever worry?"

"I won't worry about that because it's perfectly simple."

"Then I'll do it. Because I don't care about me."

"What do you mean?"

"I don't care about me."

"Well, I care about you."

"Oh yes. But I don't care about me. And I'll do it and then everything will be fine."

"I don't want you to do it if you feel that way."

The girl stood up and walked to the end of the station. Across, on the other side, were fields of grain and trees along the banks of the Ebro. Far away, beyond the river, were mountains. The shadow of a cloud moved across the field of grain and she saw the river through the trees.

"And we could have all this," she said. "And we could have everything and every day we make it more impossible."

"What did you say?"

"I said we could have everything."

"We can have everything."

"No, we can't."

"We can have the whole world."

"No, we can't."

"We can go everywhere."

"No, we can't. It isn't ours any more."

"It's ours."

"No, it isn't. And once they take it away, you never get it back."

"But they haven't taken it away."

"We'll wait and see."

"Come on back in the shade," he said. "You mustn't feel that way."

"I don't feel any way," the girl said. "I just know things."

"I don't want you to do anything that you don't want to do—"

"Nor that isn't good for me," she said. "I know. Could we have another beer?"

"All right. But you've got to realize—"

"I realize," the girl said. "Can't we maybe stop talking?"

They sat down at the table and the girl looked across at the hills on the dry side of the valley and the man looked at her and at the table.

"You've got to realize," he said, "that I don't want you to do it if you don't want to. I'm perfectly willing to go through with it if it means anything to you."

"Doesn't it mean anything to you? We could get along."

"Of course it does. But I don't want anybody but you. I don't want any one else. And I know it's perfectly simple."

"Yes, you know it's perfectly simple."

"It's all right for you to say that, but I do know it."

"Would you do something for me now?"

"I'd do anything for you."

"Would you please please please please please please please stop talking?"

He did not say anything but looked at the bags against the wall of the station. There were labels on them from all the hotels where they had spent nights.

"But I don't want you to," he said. "I don't care anything about it."

"I'll scream," the girl said.

The woman came out through the curtains with two glasses of beer and put them down on the damp felt pads. "The train comes in five minutes," she said.

"What did she say?" asked the girl.

"That the train is coming in five minutes."

The girl smiled brightly at the woman, to thank her.

"I'd better take the bags over to the other side of the station," the man said. She smiled at him.

"All right. Then come back and we'll finish the beer."

He picked up the two heavy bags and carried them around the station to the other tracks. He looked up the tracks but could not see the train. Coming back, he walked through the barroom, where people waiting for the train were drinking. He drank an Anis at the bar and looked at the people. They were all waiting reasonably for the train. He went out through the bead curtain. She was sitting at the table and smiled at him.

"Do you feel better?" he asked.

"I feel fine," she said. "There's nothing wrong with me. I feel fine."

Jack Hodgins

Jack Hodgins was born in 1938 in Merville, in northern Vancouver Island, where he lived until his 1956 departure to attend university in Vancouver. He later returned to the Island to teach in Nanaimo; subsequently he left to teach at the University of Ottawa, then returned once more, this time to teach creative writing at the University of Victoria. The Island community, where Hodgins's family were loggers for two generations, is still a rural one. His memories of this rural life—its anecdotal dialogues, its penchant for tall tales and grand gestures—give much of his writing its vigorous character, as in the story collections *Spit Delaney's Island* (1976) and *The Barclay Family Theatre* (1981) and in such novels as *The Invention of the World* (1977) and *Broken Ground* (1998). These narratives teem with incidents and individuals, and yet the exaggeration that gives them their comic quality also serves as a reminder of the chance dreams and stern realities that generate the exaggeration in the first place. It is a process of transformation. As the literary critic W.J. Keith observes, such points of transformation constitute the narrative heart of Hodgins's fiction; comedy, says Keith (in *The Canadian Forum*, 1981), is always teetering on the edge of something else—tragedy, perhaps, or a recognition of the sadness of the unattainable. It is this recognition that turns "his local backyard into an image of the whole creative universe."

In "Over Here," which first appeared in 1995 as a prize-winning story in *Prism International*, this setting is the stage for a competition between the crude politics of marginalization and the defensive strategies of private survival. The phrase "over here" implies the counterphrase "over there," and the existence of this implicit boundary line spells out how readily people will use "difference" to claim "superiority." Race, religion, family structure, appearance, wealth, language: any attribute, the story reveals, can serve as a weapon in the minds of those who are poor in spirit. Whether the boy who narrates the story has been trained to believe irrevocably in stereotypes, however, or has somehow, through his father, been freed from the town's biases, is more open to question.

Over Here

Will you take a look at this, my dad said. This here's how you and me will make our fortune.

He opened a jack-knife and ran a slit along the bark of a fallen tree.

He'd chopped down three of them. Chips flew. You had to hold up your arm to protect your eyes. The trees creaked and groaned as they tilted, then they fell with a swish. You could feel the thump through your feet. This was out in a back corner of the farm. Even the huckleberries were tall.

Now he cut a ring around the trunk. Using his fingers and the blade of the knife, he started to pry off strips of bark. Thin as leather, orange behind the grey. The inside was wet and yellow.

We'll lay these out on the barn roof to dry in the sun, he said. Then we'll sack 'em up and take them in to the depot.

The depot was where we took the beer bottles from Sunday morning ditches, and burlap sacks of sticky fir cones in summer.

What will they do with it? I said.

Here, smell. You like that?

He held the inside of a piece of bark to my face. A sharp sweet smell.

Tastes good too, he said, but I wouldn't go licking it, you'd spend the rest of the day on the run.

What is it?

They make stuff in bottles out of it, for people who'd be glad to run to the toilet for a change. It's cascara. Here—

He rooted around in his pocket and came up with another jack-knife like his own, and gave it to me. Cracked mother-of-pearl on one side, with four different blades folded along the length.

You can do this just as good as I can. Start on that one over there.

I had to press hard with the point to get it started. I used both hands and leaned my weight into it. He gave me a flat wide chisel for where the bark didn't want to come away. The knife blade was wet. I didn't lick.

It was like skinning something alive.

It was like being one of the Indians we'd learned about in school. The Blackfoot, the Iroquois. Burning missionaries at the stake, cutting out hearts, peeling off a living man's skin. Putting on parties where they gave away everything they owned. Miss Percy cooked a pot of fish-head soup. We sat under a tree and listened to her read from a book about a talking raven. You had to have courage to be an Indian. You had to he strong. Miss Percy had known an Indian who died in the recent War.

Any minute now a band of warbling braves would burst into this clearing and capture me. They would scalp my dad and drag me off to be a slave in their village. I'd have to fight with the dogs for food scraps thrown to the ground. Until one day I saved the tribe from extinction. Then they'd reward me by making me their chief.

You think there was ever an Indian village here?

Well now, my dad said. Have you seen pictures of Indian villages in this part of the world?

Wooden longhouses, I said, with totem poles out front.

Always along a beach. Do we live on a beach, can you tell me?

The beach is two miles away.

Well, do we live on a river filled with salmon then?

We don't even have a creek.

What kind of Indians would build a village on this here gravel pit here? They'd rather sit back and laugh at some idiot white man, breaking his neck to grow puny spuds and stunted hay from this goddam rocky soil.

My dad drank from the wide-mouth mason jar of cherry Freshie he'd kept in the shade. Then he leaned back against a standing tree and rolled a cigarette.

Do you think there were any wars? I said.

On our ranch, you mean?

It was never a farm, it was always a ranch, though we had only twelve acres left, most of it bush. One cow. Thirteen chickens. A pig.

Tribes slaughtering one another, I said. Battles.

Only if they wanted to make sure they never found each other, my dad said. Back in them days trees here were as thick as the hair on your head. Didn't that teacher tell you anything? Wars happen on plains—the Plains of Abraham weren't populated with Douglas firs.

We don't have any plains around here.

He set fire to the scraggly tobacco at the end of his cigarette.

That's my point. They'd have their battles out on the water maybe, in their longboats. Or down along the beach.

I guess I'll never find any arrowheads then, I said.

No Indian ever wanted this here place, said my dad. They were smarter'n that. It took a bureaucrat in Ottawa to decide this land should be opened up. Gave it to Great War vets like your fool grandfather, that didn't know nothing better than the rocks of Connemara.

Without their bark, the cascara trunks were as slick and pale as human flesh in the bath. The naked legs of giants.

■ ■ ■

There were no Indians at school. Some Indians lived on a Reserve twenty miles to the north, some lived ten miles to the south. They went to other schools. Miss Percy invited a woman from a Reserve to speak about their way of life. She told us how they smoked salmon. She told us about making oolichan grease. Once, when a raiding party was coming south they sent their women and children to safety up into the mountains, but when they went to get them afterwards they'd disappeared. Nobody ever found them. Nobody even found bones, or footprints. Today, the band was mostly well-to-do fishermen with a chief who didn't look like an Indian at all. She held up a picture for us to see.

Then one Indian came to school, but she didn't know that that was what she was.

And don't you ever tell her, said my dad.

Why not?

The Tremblays would have your hide. So would I. You could ruin that girl's life. They want her to have a chance to make something of herself.

A priest had driven up Wolf Lake Road on Tuesday and handed her over to the Tremblays, who lived across from us. On Wednesday she was sitting across the aisle from me in school.

As if raising five boys of their own isn't enough work for that poor woman, my dad said. The priest don't care how hard she works, they do what he tells them to do.

The Tremblays were the only Catholics in this part of the district and had to drive all the way in to town for church. My dad was scared that Mr. Tremblay might take it into his head to donate a corner of his property for a church out here in the bush. Right across the road from us, he imagined. Right smack in front of our kitchen window. Cars boiling up dust down the gravel road, parking all over the place, ruining our breakfast.

What did they tell her she was? I said.

Who know? A child of God, maybe. She's got five brothers now to tell her she's a Norwegian queen.

Nettie Tremblay. I watched her out of the corner of my eye across the aisle. You weren't supposed to stare. How could you not know something that was known by everyone else? I could change everything, if I wanted. A scrap of paper with the news scribbled on it. No name. Just knowing I could do this made me feel warm and generous towards her. I was protecting her. We all were. One word and her life would be blown apart.

She'd go nuts and pull out her hair. She wouldn't be able to stand it. She'd kill herself.

Except, why wouldn't she want to know?

If we knew something about Nettie Tremblay that she didn't know herself, this could be true of me as well. When I turned twenty-one maybe I would find out that I'd been an Indian brave all along. Grandson of a Huron chief, sent out to learn the ways of the white man before being called home to rule my people. I wouldn't fall apart when I heard. I'd have my own hut, my own animal skin robes. I would have my own slaves who did everything I told them to do. I'd be the richest man in the tribe.

■ ■ ■

On Saturdays my father cut down half a dozen trees and left me to peel cascara bark on my own. He'd thought of another way to get rich. Nettie Tremblay came across to watch. I offered her a share of my allowance if she'd fill the gunny sacks and help me lay out the bark on the root of the barn.

You like the smell of that? I said.

She nodded. It was a pleasant smell. Sometimes it was almost impossible not to lick the inside of the bark, except that you remembered what would happen.

I guess you've eaten bark before, I said.

No, she said. Why would I?

Do you like smoked fish better than beef? I said.

I don't know.

Her eyes went blank, as though she'd gone away inside. She must have been lying.

Do you like to eat berries? I said.

Sure, she said. She snatched huckleberries off a nearby bush and ate them.

Not like that, I said. You break off a whole branch, like this. Then you carry it around.

There was a war here once, I said. Right where we're standing. An Indian war. Seventy-six braves were slaughtered right here, their blood soaked into the earth. Some of them were skinned alive. Pieces of flesh were cut off and fed to the dogs. Had you heard about that? You could be standing right on top of a Kwakiutl skull.

She wasn't interested in my war. She carried slabs of bark to the gunny sack and stuffed them inside.

I wouldn't mind being an Indian, I said. *Hyas klahowyum nikt.*

I'd memorized some Chinook, since I didn't know which language I would need when the time came.

She made a face. I'm going to be a movie actress.

You can't be a movie actress.

Why not?

Because.

I can if I want. Why can't I?

Because. You don't look like a movie actress.

I will when I'm older.

No you won't. They'll make you go and be a servant to the nuns.

She blew a raspberry. Maybe I'll be a nun myself.

I bet you won't.

I bet I will.

I bet you'll have eighteen kids and some of them will die.

She dropped her armload of bark to the ground and started to leave.

They won't die, I said. I'll be a doctor by then and I'll save them.

Nettie Tremblay's skin was the dark red-brown of the soil around rotted stumps. Her hair was black as crows but it was not parted down the middle with two long braids at the back. Mrs. Tremblay hacked it off short and curled it. She didn't have the beauty of a Mohawk girl in a book. She was chubby. Her face was wide and quite flat, like the drunks outside the beer parlour of the Lorne Hotel.

■ ■ ■

Are there any Indians in our family? I asked my dad at the supper table. He was prying stubborn eggs off the frying pan.

Not so nobody'd notice, he said. Some figured Aunt Elsie's Frank for one but he turned out to be just another Italian.

He put my plate down in front of me. Fried potatoes with an egg broken over them. Boiled peas.

I mean in our veins, I said. Uncle Leo's pretty dark.

Uncle Leo was my mother's brother. Maybe my mother had had Indian blood in her veins. Maybe when she went off for a better life she'd gone to rejoin her tribe.

He pulled in his chair and started forking up his food. My dad ate fast, hardly noticing what he was doing. His left hand picked at the flaking paint on the table.

I'd like to be an Iroquois, I said. No, I'd like to be a Blackfoot and live in a teepee. Moving around. It'd be fun to shoot buffalo.

I'd rather be a Haida myself, my dad said. Then I could lie around carving sticks of wood while my slaves did all the work.

He could say things that made you wonder if he read your mind. He winked. The patch of bared table grew larger every day, like a continent expanding and changing shape, eating up the paint.

Maybe you'd rather be one of their whalers, I said. In a boat hollowed out of a log. Throwing spears.

I wouldn't like that at all, my dad said. I'd have to drag the whales back to shore and cut them up. Too much work.

He mopped the broken egg-yolk off his plate with a piece of bread.

Then I'd have to eat the blubber, he said. I guess I'll stay the way I am, ignorant and poor and white. At least I've got spuds on the table, and once in a while a chicken.

Maybe even beautiful Iroquois maidens had flat plain faces when they were young. Maybe Nettie Tremblay would be pretty when she grew up. She'd never be a movie actress but she might be beautiful enough to marry.

Our children would be half-breeds. Half Indian, half mongrel Irish. We'd go in search of her roots, and find out that she was a hereditary princess. The first thing I would do is order a raiding party to go off and capture a dozen slaves—white, brown, it didn't matter. My father would be amongst them. Maybe I'd pretend I'd never seen him before. My throat tightened when I thought of this. My father would give his life for me in a minute but I was an ungrateful son who would take my time about deciding what to do with him. After all, he'd had no business stealing me and bringing me up as his own.

■ ■ ■

The brothers kept an eye on her at school. Five wild Tremblays—Lucien, Paul, Rene, Pierre, Antoine. They'd kill you if you told.

They'd kill you even if you said something to someone else. You could never find out who else had been warned. Everyone, you guessed. Because anybody could see what she was. Anyone could blurt it out.

You couldn't take a chance. Even if you said, "Look at the squaw scratching her bum," it could be to someone who might tell her and you'd be to blame. Nettie Tremblay would go nuts and kill herself. And the brothers would rip off your head.

You'd never get off the school bus alive. And if you did, you'd never run fast enough to get home. And if you did, they'd climb in through your bedroom window and smother you with your pillow. After they'd pulled all your teeth, and cut off your dick. Paul Tremblay was sixteen, still in Grade Five, a hundred and seventy pounds. He could do that all himself, while the others sawed off your toes.

If you whispered for Nettie to lend an eraser, you could see Pierre trying to hear what you said.

If you looked too long at Nettie, you'd find Miss Percy glaring. She wasn't as scary as the Tremblay brothers but she folded her arms like a sentry on guard, her face clenched up like a fist. Paul Tremblay asked her to a movie once, but she laughed. So he rammed his elbow into Warner Hilton's nose. It was a blood bath. Miss Percy mopped it up.

There were no more lessons about life in an Indian village. No more stories about ravens. We learned about Incas and Mayans instead. They threw maidens into wells but never set foot on this island.

You couldn't even be mean, not without risking your life. When Neil Saunders made a face behind Nettie's back, the brothers dragged him into the woods and beat him up. Then they took off his clothes and left him behind a tree. They stuffed his pants and shirt down the toilet but passed his underpants around on a stick.

Nettie Tremblay didn't notice. She might have been the only person in class. She did her work. She ate her lunch. She smiled and nodded if you said a few words but she acted like someone who lived in a world with glass around it.

You'd think being so protected would make her proud. But she didn't stand with her gaze on the horizon, like an Iroquois princess waiting for the warriors to come home. She walked with her head tilted down, her eyes on the ground. She scuffed along with one pigeon-toed foot in front of the other. She wasn't like an Indian at all, not the Indians we'd read about in books. Not the Indians Miss Percy had told us about in her lessons on Our Proud Neighbours.

Nettie Tremblay didn't know how much trouble we went to, to keep her ignorant and safe, or she might have tried a little harder. After a while you wondered if she was worth it.

She was different on Saturdays, though. She talked a blue streak while she helped. She didn't want to be a movie star any more, she wanted to be a nurse. She'd be a nurse for a while and then a doctor, in a giant city hospital.

Her brothers didn't follow when she came across the road. It was because they trusted me, my dad said. The Tremblays knew what sort of people we were, over here.

■ ■ ■

One day she showed up at the bus shelter wearing glasses. Purple frames. Who ever heard of an Indian wearing glasses?

Why are you wearing those things?

So I can see, she said.

You could see before.

Doctor says I'm short-sighted, like Miss Percy.

She pushed them up with her thumb. She didn't have enough nose to keep them from sliding down.

Four eyes, they called her when we got to school, but not where her brothers could hear.

Goggle face.

Everyone wearing glasses was called something. It didn't count.

The next day she showed up at the bus shelter wearing lipstick as well as the glasses. She'd never worn lipstick before. No girl in our class wore lipstick, you had to be thirteen or fourteen for that. It didn't make her look pretty, it made her look dumb.

Does you mother know you painted your face? I said.

My mother's the one put it on.

She opened her lunch bag and showed me a lipstick tube next to her sandwiches. Maybe her mother wanted to make her feel better about wearing glasses.

War paint, I said.

It makes you look cheap, Eleanor Laitinen said. The Tremblay brothers weren't close enough to hear. They'd murder Eleanor if they'd heard her, even if she was a girl.

You better wipe it off before we get to school, I said. You don't want to look like a tramp.

Tramp was my dad's word for women who painted themselves up and smoked and swung their purses. My mother had not been a tramp, but she'd thought she was too good for us and went off to live somewhere else.

It didn't really make her look like a tramp. Tramps were supposed to be pretty, even if they looked cheap. She probably thought the lipstick made her look pretty but it didn't. She needed someone smarter than those brothers to protect her. She'd make a fool of herself.

I sat beside her on the bus. Her brothers sat at the back, but you could be sure they kept an eye open. You had to be careful they didn't hear. Lucien. Paul. Rene. Antoine. Pierre.

It doesn't suit you, I said. It doesn't look nice on you the way it does on some girls.

She looked out the window.

You're not old enough, I said.

She pulled in both her lips as though she might swallow them. This flattened her nose. She had to push her glasses up again.

You don't want people to laugh at you, I said, you're not like Shelley Price.

Shelley Price was fourteen, six grades ahead of us. She was blonde, and pretty. She was the first girl to wear nylon stockings to school.

Drop dead, she said. I'll do what I want. Go sit somewhere else.

I hated her. She didn't even know how lucky she was. I didn't *have* to feel sorry for her. Let them laugh, if she was going to be like that.

West Coast Indians aren't real Indians, I told my dad that night. Charlie Morris said they came from China on a raft.

That must've been some raft, my dad said. I'd like to see it.

I'd rather be an Algonquin, I said.

Good idea, my dad said. You'll be closer to Ottawa. You can dance for the Great White Father when he's in town. Tell him he's welcome to a night on the kitchen cot if he's ever short of funds in this neck of the woods.

■ ■ ■

The whole south slope of the barn roof was covered with bark. Slabs were nearly dry enough. Some had curled up, and cracked when I stomped on them. Their colour was a dark red now—dried blood. I thought of the little bottles, for people who couldn't go to the toilet without some help.

From the peak of the barn I could look out over the small green field. The pig's smelly pen was below. Our house had not been painted since some time before I was born. Flecks of white were stuck here and there on the weather-blackened boards. My dad was going to paint it one day soon.

When Nettie came across the field I said I didn't need her today.

You can go home. My dad didn't cut any trees.

She came up the ladder anyway.

You want me to go so you won't have to pay me, she said.

Maybe that's why she'd kept coming over. She wouldn't talk to me at school any more but she talked to me while we worked. Money.

Not true, I said.

She came up the roof on all fours, and sat on the peak beside me. She didn't wear lipstick on weekends, but she wore her glasses every day.

How rich will I be? she said.

I don't know. My dad never said how much they pay.

How do you know you'll get any of it?

He gives me an allowance.

Most of it's gonna be mine.

Not most.

You said fifty cents for every day I helped.

I didn't say that.

You did so.

You didn't help all day, you only helped for a couple of hours each time. When you got bored you went home.

He won't pay you anyway, she said. You won't get any allowance, he needs the money for groceries. Daddy says you're only a step away from the poorhouse over here.

Whaddaya mean by that?

Just look at this place, she said. Daddy says a man with one arm and a wooden leg could make better use of it than your father does.

You're lying, I said. My Dad's always been nice to Mr. Tremblay.

He says if you were Catholics the priests would take you away from your father and put you in a home.

That's dumb, I said.

They would.

Nobody's going to take me away from my dad.

You don't know everything. Maybe somebody will.

No.

Somebody could be coming to get you right now. You don't know everything.

Yeah? I know something.

What?

I know something you don't know, I said.

What?

Something about yourself.

What?

If I tell you, you have to promise you won't tell anyone else. You have to promise you won't tell anyone that I told you.

It was like standing on the edge of a cliff. She was at my mercy. She had always been at my mercy. One word and over she'd go. Nothing would be the same.

What is it? she said. I won't believe you anyhow. You lie.

I won't tell you then.

Tell me.

Promise?

Okay, I promise. What is it?

What do you think you are?

Whaddaya mean?

What kind of ancestors do you think you have? Do you think you're a Swede?

Don't be stupid, she said. She laughed.

The priest brought you here from somewhere. Didn't you ever ask?

She went away from behind her eyes again. She didn't deserve to know. I wouldn't tell her. She could be a Haida princess. She could be descended from Big Bear. She could be Sitting Bull's niece. But she didn't deserve to know. Let her think she was just an ordinary girl who looked silly in glasses and stupid wearing lipstick.

What do you think you know? she said.

Nothing.

You better tell me, you think you're so smart.

I don't.

She stood up and hit me across the head with a slab of bark.

Stupid! Stupid! Stupid! Stupid!

She hit me again and again. Then she scrambled down the roof and turned to go down the ladder. Stupid stupid stupid. She knows, doesn't she? I said to my dad. I bet she's known all along.

I suppose she must've, he said.

We were filling the burlap bags, for the trip to the depot in town. Nine sacks. First we'd broken the dried bark into smaller pieces.

And you knew she did too, I said.

I suppose I did.

So why'd you tell me not to tell her?

Everybody was told not to tell her. Do you think if they'd just asked everybody not to call her names they wouldn't? Did you hear anyone call her names?

No.

And why is that, do you think?

Because of the brothers.

The brothers aren't always there. The brothers wouldn't be in the girls' washroom, for instance. Do you think anyone ever called her things in the washroom?

I guess not.

I guess not, he said. Do you know why people would've called her names, if they had?

I don't know, I said. To make her cry? To make themselves feel better'n her?

I'll tell you why they didn't, he said. Because they were part of a conspiracy. They didn't have to call her names, they could feel superior just by being part of a plot to keep her from knowing the facts. Them Tremblays are not so dumb.

The gunny sacks leaned against one another with their tops gaping open. My dad began to tie them closed with binder twine.

Was anything said between you? he said.

No.

Then leave it up to her. Maybe she'll go to school in beaded moccasins one day and tell you to call her Laughing Squirrel.

It isn't fair, I said.

Maybe she'd agree with you there, he said.

What would they do if I wore animal skins to school and told them to call me Mighty Warrior?

They'd laugh in your face.

What would they say?

Worse than they'd ever say to Nettie Tremblay, I'll tell you that. Maybe they'd just tell you to your face what they say behind your back.

This was something new. My skin felt funny and cold.

What do they say behind my back?

Maybe there's more than one plot out there, I bet you never thought of that. Maybe there's a plot to keep you from finding out something too. Do you think there's something they could say about us, if they decided they didn't give a hoot for your feelings?

He winked. We're not so dumb either, is what he meant. We know who we are.

I don't know, I said.

You don't? Then they must have a better grip on their tongues than I thought.

Anyway, I said, it wouldn't be my fault.

He laughed. Poor thing, stuck with your old man. C'mon, let's get these buggers onto the truck.

I could have killed him. I could run off to look for my mother. It wasn't fair. I was the one who should have been related to Big Bear. I was the one who ought to be Sitting Bull's son. You can be sure I'd stand up and give them a fight. I'd chase the white people right off the land, I'd drive them into the sea. I'd make them all go back to Ireland where they'd have nothing to eat but rotted spuds and rain, where you could die just from being poor.

Witi Ihimaera

Witi Ihimaera was born in Gisborne, New Zealand, in 1944, and educated at Victoria University, Wellington, and at Auckland University, where (after having spent several years as a journalist, and as New Zealand's consul in New York) he now teaches. In his fiction—the stories of *Pounamu, Pounamu* (1972) and *The New Net Goes Fishing* (1977), and such novels as *Tangi* (1973), *Whanau* (1974), and *The Matriarch* (1986)—Ihimaera draws directly on his Maori heritage, his several tribal affiliations, and his observations of Maori experience in the modern city. In editing numerous anthologies of Maori writing, moreover, he has contributed directly and effectively to the renewal of respect for traditional Maori culture and to the recognition of the artistic achievements of contemporary writers. "Personally," he told a *Landfall* interviewer in 1991, "I like to think I'm on a luminous voyage."

His collection *Dear Miss Mansfield* (1989)—from which "The Washerwoman's Children" is taken—was written on the occasion of the centenary of Katherine Mansfield's birth in Wellington. Subtitled "A Tribute . . .," this volume collects a series of stories that parallel or "reread" several of Mansfield's stories. Ihimaera's versions bring to the foreground not just such issues as race and class relations, or marginalization, although these are important, but also an alternative world view. While his stories acknowledge Mansfield's insights into human behaviour and her literary skills, he also probes what her stories leave out. Hence Ihimaera introduces Maori characters into the social situations that Mansfield imagined, or he reinterprets incidents from a counter (generally Maori) perspective, or he pursues a Mansfield narrative into the future. "The Washerwoman's Children," for example, imagines the effect on Lil and Our Else of Kezia Burnell's small rebellion in "The Doll's House." It suggests that some people fly from the past but cannot forget it, that others remember it without clarity, that some continue through life with their biases intact, and that still others can actually learn from the opportunity they are given to change.

The Washerwoman's Children

Mrs Justice Fairfax-Lawson, sitting in the morning-room of her home at Calverley Park, Tunbridge Wells, received the morning post. Lying on the salver was a brown manila envelope from New Zealand bearing a crest that she had not seen for some fifty years. Despite her usual habit of opening the post before pouring her tea, this letter sat until Penny had cleared. Only then, with a self-directed criticism of 'Elspeth, you are being ridiculous,' did she lift her letter knife and open the envelope. Inside was a form letter, with blank spaces that had been filled in by hand, as follows:

45 Jackson Crescent
Wellington
New Zealand

Dear Elspeth,

Your name has been referred to the Karori Primary School Anniversary Committee by your sister, Lilian Bates.

The Committee, which has been actively working towards the centennial celebrations of the School, would like to extend to you a warm invitation to attend an Anniversary Dinner in the school hall on 10 August this year, at 7.30 p.m. Roll Call, by year, will be taken at 5 p.m. A photographer will record the happy event. The Committee hopes you will be able to come along.

Yours sincerely
(Mrs) Lena Holmes

The letter was perforated with a tear-off portion bearing the address of the committee and, 'I will be able/unable to attend: I attended Karori Primary School from . . . . to . . . . My registration fee of $20 is/is not enclosed.'

Mrs Justice Fairfax-Lawson was somewhat nonplussed. The use of her Christian name by a person whom she did not know, called Lena Holmes, irritated her. But most of all the letter brought memories of school days which she hoped had faded forever. Bearing in mind the time difference between England and New Zealand, she telephoned her sister in Wellington. 'Lilian, dear? *What* is going on?'

Given her initial reaction to the invitation, Mrs Justice Fairfax-Lawson was amused to find herself, three months later, sitting in the third row of the Business Class section of an Air New Zealand flight from Gatwick to Los Angeles en route for Auckland. Not only that, but no sooner had she seated herself than the purser, on the advice of the ground staff who had recognised her, invited her to take a seat in First Class. Her sense of gratification was only undercut by the fact that the passenger seated next to her, when told that she 'was in the judiciary,' assumed she was a typist or else the wife of a judge (she was not the sort to be mistaken for a mistress); silly pompous little man. Luckily there was a window seat vacant three rows ahead and Mrs Justice Fairfax-Lawson firmly invited her neighbour to take it. Once that was achieved she took up her Dorothy Sayers, but only briefly before setting it to one side and watching England sinking beneath her.

If anybody had been looking at Mrs Justice Fairfax-Lawson, they would have seen a slim and elegant woman of pleasant good looks and a fresh English rose complexion. They would certainly not have guessed from her appearance, or even any intonation of voice or physical mannerism, that she had actually been born and raised in New Zealand. There was not a shred of the Antipodean about her, nor any of the hallmarks of the Antipodean Woman Abroad — the tightly curled perm, twinset and pearls and bright magpie look which characterised all New Zealanders south of Balmoral. Instead, what any other passenger would have seen was exactly what Mrs Justice Fairfax-Lawson had become — a romantic Englishwoman, in her prime, knowing exactly where she is because she can remember quite clearly exactly how far she has travelled — and Mrs Justice Fairfax-Lawson had travelled a very long way indeed. Home Counties style had always meant so much to her that being taken for English was quite a compliment and logical enough. All the same, there was a sense of fairness in Mrs Justice Fairfax-Lawson which allowed her to accept that her country of birth would want to claim her — as it was prone to do, given her successes — as one of its very own. As a judge, Mrs Justice Fairfax-Lawson well knew that all *known* facts must be taken into account when any case came before the bench and, if she was trying herself for identification, she would have to weigh against the fact that although she was British by virtue of her marriage to the late Hon. Rupert Fairfax-Lawson, she had nevertheless maintained dual citizenship with the country of her birth. Much as she disliked the idea of balancing on both sides of the scales, Mrs Justice Fairfax-Lawson had to admit that giving up *anything* at all had always been difficult for her. Add to this that all her side of the family obstinately remained in New Zealand and that they were her *only* family (she and the Hon. Rupert Fairfax-Lawson being childless and not at all pleased with the Hon. Rupert Fairfax-Lawson's scurrilous nephews), and one realised the depth of her dilemma. She was as much a New Zealander because her family made her one. She could not escape them — and nor would she want to — because she loved them; yes, *loved* was not too strong a word And she did so with familial pride and devotion, particularly her elder sister Lilian, who had become a grandmother again. So it was a *fait accompli* really, with the gavel confirming the decision and dismissing the court.

Mrs Justice Fairfax-Lawson was about to resume her Dorothy Sayers, but by that time champagne and caviar were being served. Not long after that, dinner — either roast duck or lamb — was offered. Bearing in mind the long journey ahead, Mrs justice Fairfax-Lawson therefore decided to nap rather than to read. Eight hours later, after more champagne and more roast duck, her flight landed at Los Angeles. Shortly thereafter she was on her way again, with fourteen hours of flying time ahead and the vast expanse of the South Pacific below, bound for Auckland and thence Wellington, New Zealand.

Lilian Bates was waiting with her husband George at the Domestic Terminal. There was, at close inspection, a family resemblance to her younger sister Elspeth, but no one would ever have taken Lilian for anything but a New Zealander — at a pinch, an Australian perhaps — and that was where the likeness ended. Lilian's cheeks were ruddy, whereas her sister's were pallid, and Lilian's spontaneity expressed itself in its overeagerness and anxiousness, whereas Elspeth's was under control, *quite*. Apart from that, years of healthy living and appetite had turned Lilian's figure to pear-shaped, whereas Elspeth was still, as ever, a wishbone. Somewhere far back in their lives there had been a parting of the ways. In Elspeth's case it had been the winning of a major scholarship to Cambridge when she was nineteen. As for Lilian, her fate had been forever sealed when George Bates, then garage mechanic and now proprietor of Bates Towaway Trucks, admiring her lines, cast an eye over her, ran her round the block a couple of times, found her bodywork in good condition and pronounced, 'She'll do.'

'Now, George, don't forget,' Lilian told him. 'She likes to be called Elspeth. Not Elsie. Or Ellie. Or Else. Or anything but Elspeth.' She picked at his tie. 'The way you go on,' George replied, 'you'd think she was the bloody Queen of England.' Lilian grimaced as if she had never heard such words from his lips before. 'And keep your bloodys to your trucks, George — or save them up for when it's just us.' George rolled his eyes and Lilian tried to hug him around. 'Oh please, George, *do* behave. You know I haven't seen Elspeth for six years now. That's such a long time. She's my only sister after all and — Oh, there she is! Oh, George' — Lilian broke away from him and began to run toward the woman who had just come through the gate. George had always known that his wife was a real softie, but her abrupt emotional departure surprised him. *Why, they're as different as chalk to cheese,* he thought. He watched as Lilian flung her arms around her sister and wept on her shoulder — he hadn't realised that Lilian would be so affected. He felt a lump in his throat at the sight of these two middle-aged women embracing like this — Lilian, as always, so open with her emotions, and *Elspeth* as gracious as ever — you'd think she was waving from a bloody Rolls. He walked over to them. Elspeth said, 'Why, George!' in that cultured voice of hers and proffered a cheek for him to kiss. And Lilian stepped aside, saying, 'It's really her, George, she's really here,' as if he couldn't see that for himself.

Mrs Justice Fairfax-Lawson had planned to stay in New Zealand for three weeks but had not expected that her sister would want to make the most of it. She should have realised when they arrived at the house and were greeted by Lilian's two daughters and their three children — plus the new baby — that she would be kept busy. And it was understandable, she supposed, that Lilian would want to have dinner on the first evening for 'Just us and the family' — but when confronted with the cheery barbecue that evening and guests including the local mayor, she knew that life was not going to be that simple. Over that first week Lilian would alternate between expressions of 'Oh, you must still be jet-lagged, Elspeth. Why don't you go up to the bedroom and rest?' and frequent trips to answer the front doorbell with, 'Why, hello!' to yet more neighbours bearing yet more platefuls of lamingtons, pikelets or scones. Nor could the visits possibly be accidental, despite protestations that 'We just dropped by' — Oh no, these ladies in their cardies and pearls had just been to the local hairdressing salon, and once ensconced in Lilian's sitting-room with a cuppa, were there to *stay*. Even the innocent 'I'm just popping down to the shop, Elspeth. Why not come for a ride?' would turn into a virtual royal procession throughout the land. And at each house the hostess would be ready and waiting with 'Why, Lilian, do come in! And this is your sister, isn't it! Elspeth? Lilian has told us so much about you. You're just in time for a cuppa tea —' before opening the door wider and turning to others gathered inside '— isn't she, ladies!' These ladies knew that New Zealand hospitality was the best in the world, and they weren't going to let the side down — especially with such a famous person in their midst. And so the polite conversation would begin, with everybody minding their p's and q's and trying not to be too colonial — clinking the teacups ever so softly and not dropping one crumb of the lamingtons — until, with a little squeak of a cough, the hostess would turn to Mrs Justice Fairfax-Lawson and ask, 'So you live in England, do you?' Whereupon all tea-drinking would be suspended as Mrs Justice Fairfax-Lawson, as custom required, told them about life as it was lived by those whose Title and Reputation enabled an English Existence spread between an apartment in Westminster and a country home in Tunbridge Wells. On her part, Mrs Justice Fairfax-Lawson knew that *she,* too, couldn't let the side down — her side being her sister — and she rose to every occasion. For despite her caustic tongue, Mrs Justice Fairfax-Lawson would not have hurt her sister for anything in the world. And success was measured by the indrawn gasps of 'You don't *say*!', 'Listen to *that,* Millie!', 'How *interesting!*' and 'Do go on.' And if, near the end of the socialising, the hostess sighed, 'Oh, it sounds so different from life here,' then Mrs Justice Fairfax-Lawson knew also that form required her to offer generalities like 'But you are so lucky, New Zealand is such a paradise, it is so green, and your food is so delicious' — even if she didn't really mean it herself. Then Lilian would drive her sister home, and Mrs Justice Fairfax-Lawson would go up to her bedroom and have a lie-down and listen to Lilian's happy voice downstairs as she responded to telephone calls from the friends just visited — 'Oh yes, I'll tell her! Yes, we are all very proud of her! No, *really,* do you really think we are that alike?' Such things had always been important to Lilian.

However, when, at the beginning of the second week, Mrs Justice Fairfax-Lawson came across her photograph on page seven of the *Dominion* and read the accompanying article she became most displeased. It wasn't really the photograph, which was at the very *least* twenty years old — and while Mrs Justice Fairfax-Lawson was as vain as the next person, a photograph of that vintage could only draw unhappy comparisons with one's current estate — nor was it the article itself, which was succinct and to the point:

> *Mrs Justice Elspeth Fairfax-Lawson, M.B.E., (pictured right) returned last week for a private visit to New Zealand, her first in six years. Mrs Fairfax-Lawson recently retired from the U.K. judiciary following the death of her husband, the late Hon. Rupert Fairfax-Lawson, M.P. Born in Wellington in 1910, Mrs Fairfax-Lawson will be well known to New Zealanders as the founder and first chairperson of the Wellington Women's Co-operative. Educated at Cambridge, England, Mrs Fairfax-Lawson served in British Intelligence during the Second World War, where she met her husband. Following the war she began a private legal practice in London, Fairfax and Madden, and was invited to join the U.K. judiciary in 1962. Her M.B.E. was awarded by H.R.H. Queen Elizabeth II in 1970.*

The displeasure stemmed from the headline and last sentence of the text, to wit: FAMOUS NZER RETURNS FOR SCHOOL REUNION and 'Mrs Justice Fairfax-Lawson is a guest speaker at next week's Anniversary Dinner of the Karori Primary School, which she attended from 1915 to 1923.'

Mrs Justice Fairfax-Lawson was therefore *very* cross when she went down to breakfast that morning and, seeing this, Lilian said to George, 'You'd best leave us a minute, George dear.' To do her justice, Lilian was looking very contrite. She poured Elspeth a hot cuppa and, 'The photo's nice,' she said. But Elspeth could not be pacified so easily. 'How could you *do* this, Lilian. You *know* that my main reason for coming was to see you, and that I have only agreed to attend the school reunion because *you* want to go. I am going under sufferance, Lilian. You know how much I *hated* that school. The way the parents treated Mother and vilified Father was so unspeakable. Just because she had to take in washing and because father was a bankrupt.' Lilian bit her lip and, 'Yes, Elspeth,' she said. 'Can't you remember anything at all?' Elspeth continued. 'It wasn't Mother's fault that she had to send us to school in dresses made from bits given her by other people — other people's cast-offs and curtain material — but did the other children understand? No, they *didn't.*' Whenever Lilian was embarrassed, her face took on a silly shamefaced smile, and, 'You're quite right, Elspeth,' she said, her heart aching from the pain of the reprimand. *And a vivid picture flashed into her mind of Lena Logan sliding, gliding, dragging one foot, giggling behind her hand, shrilling, 'Is it true you're going to be a servant when you grow up, Lil Kelvey?' And taunting her again with 'Yah, yer father's in prison!' before running away giggling with the other girls.* 'We were *always* on the outside,' Elspeth said. 'They never invited us to play in any of their games, because we weren't good enough for them. And *now* I read in the newspaper that I am to be guest speaker —' Lilian folded her hands in her lap and looked down and, 'They only want you to say a few words,' she said. 'A few words?' Elspeth cried. 'That's more than they deserve. There was only one girl, just *one,* who ever showed us a kindness and —'

Lilian couldn't take any more. Her silly smile opened too wide and let the tears through. She tried to say something to Elspeth, gulped and instead patted Elspeth on the hand and kissed her right cheek. Then she stood up and left the table. Elspeth, still furious, sat there in the grip of her own recollections and how, it seemed, she had only managed to survive by holding on with a piece of Lil's skirt screwed up in her hand; holding on all day, *every* day, holding on so tight, so *tight.* And not saying a word to anybody but wanting to scream, just *scream,* with the loneliness and pain and awfulness of it all. Then Elspeth heard George and looked up into his disapproving face. 'You were too hard on her, Elspeth,' he said. 'Lilian may be the elder of the two of you but she's the one who suffers more. You should have a care for your sister. She thinks the bloody world of you.' And that only made Elspeth feel worse — about her petulance and, oh, at Lilian too for being such a *martyr* and running off like that! You'd think they were still children the way Lilian behaved — going off so bravely to sulk like that and make her feel so *mean.* Elspeth looked at George and sighed. He indicated the direction in which Lilian had gone.

'Lilian? Lilian,' Elspeth called. She heard Lilian reply, 'In here, dear,' and found her at a small card table in the lounge. Lilian had put on her reading glasses and was cutting the article about Elspeth out of the newspaper. 'What *are* you doing?' Elspeth asked. She came up behind Lilian and looked over Lilian's shoulder. On the card table was a large scrapbook. Elspeth recognised it instantly — it was the book their mother had begun when her daughters had both started school and filled year by year with school reports, handwritten memories, school magazine photographs, newspaper clippings: ELSPETH KELVEY IS DUX OF SCHOOL; LOCAL GIRL WINS CAMBRIDGE SCHOLARSHIP; MORE HONOURS FOR KELVEY; OUR ELSPETH TOPS CLASS AT CAMBRIDGE; ENGAGEMENT OF ELSPETH KELVEY TO SON OF LORD FAIRFAX-LAWSON — and other memorabilia. Elspeth gave a small cry and reached over to leaf through the pages: LOCAL PERSONALITY AWARDED M.B.E.; FAIRFAX-LAWSON RETIRES FROM U.K. JUDICIARY. 'It's mostly all about you,' Lilian said softly. 'I never did much myself except marry George and have my two girls. But oh, Mother was so proud of you, Else, love. You wouldn't believe the times she would go through this scrapbook. "Look at our Else," she used to say. "All those brains, where'd they come from!" ' The mood sweetened between the two sisters, and Elspeth reached over and put her hand in Lilian's. 'Anyway,' Lilian said, 'when Mother died I kept the scrapbook going. I don't know why really. It would have been a shame to just let it go, don't you think?' And suddenly Lilian started to weep again, saying, 'I'm so sorry, Else, I just didn't realise —' And Elspeth replied, 'Come, come, Lilian. Oh, Lilian, *do* stop' — because she had begun to recall how difficult it had all been for Mother and Lilian to keep her at school. 'Oh, *Lilian*!' she said, furious, because tears were so unseemly at their age.

Afterwards Elspeth told Lilian that she had better check with the Karori Centenary Committee how many words a 'few' constituted. They had a cuppa tea and laughed about the absurdity of two grown women losing control like that. 'There was never a jealous bone in your body, was there?' Elspeth asked her sister. 'A couple of times,' Lilian admitted. Elspeth smiled and turned away, intending to go up to her bedroom. Just as she went through the door, Lilian called to her. 'Oh, Elspeth,' she said. Elspeth turned and, 'Yes?' she asked. Lilian's attitude was resolute and firm. 'Although we may have been a washerwoman's children,' she said, 'we were never too proud' —which was just the sort of infuriating commonplace thing Lilian always liked to say.

And after all that, not to mention the effort that Elspeth had put into preparing a ten-minute address, Lilian came down with a bad flu on the very night of the dinner. 'You will get up this instant,' Elspeth ordered. 'Put on your pearls and come with me.' Her tone was similar to that she used when addressing felons from the Bench. Lilian nodded and tried but, 'Oh, Elsbed, I don'd thig I cad,' she said. 'You bedder go wib Geord. Geord? You go wib Elsbed to the didder.' Lilian reached for a handkerchief. George, taken by surprise, said, 'Go back to school? Not on your bloody life.' Then Elspeth interrupted him, saying, 'Lilian Kelvey, it is already after five. You are as strong as a horse and *never* get the flu. Get up at once.' But it was obvious that no command would work. 'Oh, by dose,' Lilian said, blowing on it. 'By hed,' she said, holding it. 'Elsbed, you should rig the cobbidee and ask theb to ged sobody to pig you ub.' And that was that — which explains how Mrs Justice Fairfax-Lawson was delivered, an hour late, by a nice but obviously awestruck Maori committee member called Mrs Maraki.

No sooner had Mrs Justice Fairfax-Lawson walked through the door of the crowded Assembly Hall than she saw a woman gasp and whisper behind her hand to her companion, and then *sliding, gliding, dragging one foot and shrilling* she came, calling, 'Elspeth! Yoo hoo, Elspeth!' And Mrs Justice Fairfax-Lawson reeled backward as if she had been hit, and reached out for Lil's hand and to hold a piece of Lil's skirt. 'Elspeth?' the woman laughed. 'You *must* remember me! I'm Lena Holmes! See?' She pointed rather superfluously at a small tag on her dress with her name and CHAIRMAN ANNIVERSARY COMMITTEE written on it. 'I used to be Lena Logan. Remember? Lil and I were in the same class. But you were much younger of course. Come along with me.' Proudly, Lena Holmes took Mrs Justice Fairfax-Lawson's arm and began to steer her possessively in the direction of other committee members. *Yah, yer father's in prison.* 'Cora? May I introduce Elspeth to you? But you know her of course. Weren't you in Mrs Fredericks' class together? Oh, you will have some stories to tell! And this is Peggy, Elspeth. Peggy used to be the horrid little girl who did ballet — oh, we hated her, didn't we! And you can remember Annabelle? Her aunt was the postmistress. Oh, you *must* remember Miss Leckey and that terrible hat she used to wear! *Oh yes, I remember. When Miss Leckey had no further use for it, she gave it to Mother. Lilian used to wear it.* 'We are so sorry, Elspeth, to hear that Lilian won't be able to come. What a shame. Never mind, you are in good hands now. We'll look after you, won't we ladies!' *Yes, you'll all run after me and make fun of me and sneer and laugh and wrinkle your noses as I pass and —*

'Are you all right, Elspeth?' The voice sounded so loud in her ear that Mrs Justice Fairfax-Lawson was startled. Lena Holmes was looking at her, concernedly. 'Oh. Yes,' Mrs Justice Fairfax-Lawson said. 'The trip. The strain.' Lena Holmes nodded. 'I do hope you aren't catching your sister's flu. There's a lot of it going around,' she said. 'But come along, we must get you tagged!' She laughed as she took Mrs Justice Fairfax-Lawson's hand. *Yah, yah, your mother washes clothes and your father's a jailbird.* 'There!' Lena Holmes cried as she branded Mrs Justice Fairfax-Lawson with a label, ELSIE KELVEY, so that everybody — *everybody* — could remember that awful little girl with cropped hair, remember ladies? That's her, over *there.*

Suddenly a hand bell began to ring. A middle-aged man who could *never* have been young was standing in the centre of the hall, swinging the bell to and fro. His face was red with mirth as the bell clanged and boomed and shattered the conversation. Lena Holmes put her hands to her ears and said, 'Oh, that Johnny Johnston! Isn't he a one?' One of the other men ran out to wrestle with 'Johnny' and the crowd watched and grinned with amusement — Wasn't this fun? That Johnny, he *never* changed, good old Johnny. And all of a sudden Johnny was running between people, trying to escape his friend, and the women gave little screams and the men pretended to scrimmage and then he was heading for Mrs Justice Fairfax-Lawson and the shock of recognition spread over his face as, pointing at her, he said, 'I know you! You're you're — ' *Yes. My name is Elsie. My sister is Lil. My mother washes your mother's clothes. You are a horrid boy.* But before he could say anything more he was tackled and down he went. And Lena Holmes, pretending to be a little girl, went over to the two men lying on the floor, wagged a little finger and said in a squeaky voice, 'Bad boys. Bad *boys.* I'm going to tell Mrs Fredericks on you!' What a laugh that caused — that Lena Logan, the same as ever. Then Lena Holmes laughed herself and clapped her hands, clap, clap, CLAP. 'Roll call, everybody! Roll call! Everybodeeee,' and she led the way to the English Room, where the group photograph was to be taken.

Mrs Justice Fairfax-Lawson closed her eyes and took a deep breath. *Pull yourself together,* she said to herself. The shock, the crowd, the smell of chalk, the bonhomie, all these people acting like children, pretending that school had been such fun and they were all friends. Whereas she had only had one friendly gesture made toward her. *Stop it, Elspeth.* For who was she to make such assumptions? *STOP IT.* Feeling better, Mrs Justice Fairfax-Lawson joined the others. She smiled at everybody and was as charming as they expected her to be. She laughed just like everybody else at the photographer's frantic attempts to arrange the 'children' according to height, and when she had to say CHEEEESE she did so as long as the rest did until the flashbulb popped But deep inside her the little girl she once was still cringed and sought for a piece of dress to hold on to.

The bell rang again, far away, to announce that dinner would soon be served. Well-wishers approached Mrs Justice Fairfax-Lawson to say,

'We are so looking forward to hearing you speak,' or, 'We are so delighted that you will be speaking on our behalf as fellow pupils of the school,' and she was so surprised, absolutely *overwhelmed,* by the warmth of it all. And she realised that the address she *was* going to give would be too pompous and too serious, for these returned pupils wished only for companionship and good memories and wonderful tributes to friends and school. And she heard Lilian's voice in her mind saying, We *were never too proud, Elspeth, never too proud.*

So that when, following the dinner in the hall, it was time for Mrs Justice Fairfax-Lawson to rise and speak, she had to pause and reconsider her words. The hall looked so gay and colourful, with streamers hanging from the ceiling and flowers arranged on the trestles and food — jellies, pavlovas, salads, lamingtons — sparkling on the tables. And there were all those ridiculous elderly people, sitting on forms, faces gazing up at hers in expectation. And it came to her just what she should say. 'Ladies and gentlemen,' she began. 'Boys and girls,' and everybody laughed. 'Like you all, I attended this school with my sister. There was once a little girl and her sisters who came to school one day and told us all about a wonderful gift — a doll's house.' To one side Elspeth heard Lena Holmes gasp with pleasure. 'Inside was a little lamp.' Mrs Justice Fairfax-Lawson paused at the memory. *You can come and see our doll's house if you want to, said Kezia. Come on. Nobody's looking.* 'I think that girl died some years ago but what she did stands as a shining symbol to all of us. Certainly it became a symbol for me.' The silence was such that a dropped pin could have been heard. 'Although my sister and I were the children of a washerwoman' — *There, it was out* — 'that girl showed us the little lamp. I have never forgotten that lamp, ever. Its flame has been a constant inspiration to me to always reach out — like that girl did — to others. To extend myself, become a better person and perhaps make the world a better place to live in. Were it not for that kindness, or similar kindnesses which I'm sure you all remember being done to you at this school, none of us would have become the people we are today. I would not have become the person I have.'

Mrs Justice Fairfax-Lawson had to pause again. *I seen the little lamp, she said softly.* She went to resume but somebody had begun to clap and very soon that person was followed by another and another, until the whole hall was on its feet and clapping at the memory of a school-friend, now gone, who had been so important in all their lives. And as they did so, Mrs Justice Fairfax-Lawson smiled a rare smile and thought to herself that what she had said was just the silly commonplace sort of thing that Lilian would have liked.

W.W. Jacobs

William Wymark Jacobs (1863–1943) was born and raised in Wapping, London, where his father was manager of a ships' wharf. Following his education at a private school in London and at Birkbeck College, he entered the civil service, and worked in the Savings Bank department from 1883 to 1899. During this period he began to submit stories and sketches to the popular magazines of the day, *Blackfriars, The Idler,* and *Strand Magazine*, with such success that by 1899 he was earning enough from his writing to enable him to give up his job and devote himself to full-time authorship. Between 1896 and 1926 Jacobs wrote more than 150 short stories, five novels, and several plays; but he spent the final seventeen years of his life in retirement, publishing almost nothing at all.

Jacobs is especially remembered for his humorous tales about seafaring men and dockyard workers, gathered in such collections as *Many Cargoes* (1896) and *Odd Craft* (1904); his settings are cheap lodging houses, ships' wharves, or dockside pubs where old sea dogs gather to swap yarns or spin tall tales. "The Monkey's Paw," from *The Lady of the Barge* (1902), is a somewhat macabre exception to Jacobs's usual light comedy, though it too has the flavour of the tall tale. He introduces the supernatural into a plain domestic setting with a clarity and an economy of style that lend the plot added force and authenticity, intensifying the horror of the outcome.

The Monkey's Paw

I

Without, the night was cold and wet, but in the small parlour of Laburnam Villa the blinds were drawn and the fire burned brightly. Father and son were at chess, the former, who possessed ideas about the game involving radical changes, putting his king into such sharp and unnecessary perils that it even provoked comment from the white-haired old lady knitting placidly by the fire.

"Hark at the wind," said Mr. White, who, having seen a fatal mistake after it was too late, was amiably desirous of preventing his son from seeing it.

"I'm listening," said the latter, grimly surveying the board as he stretched out his hand. "Check."

"I should hardly think that he'd come tonight," said his father, with his hand poised over the board.

"Mate," replied the son.

"That's the worst of living so far out," bawled Mr. White, with sudden and unlooked-for violence; "of all the beastly, slushy, out-of-the-way places to live in, this is the worse. Pathway's a bog, and the road's a torrent. I don't know what people are thinking about. I suppose because only two houses in the road are let, they think it doesn't matter."

"Never mind, dear," said his wife, soothingly; "perhaps you'll win the next one."

Mr. White looked up sharply, just in time to intercept a knowing glance between mother and son. The words died away on his lips, and he hid a guilty grin in his thin grey beard.

"There he is," said Herbert White, as the gate banged to loudly and heavy footsteps came toward the door.

The old man rose with hospitable haste, and opening the door, was heard condoling with the new arrival. The new arrival also condoled with himself, so that Mrs. White said, "Tut, tut!" and coughed gently as her husband entered the room, followed by a tall, burly man, beady of eye and rubicund of visage.

"Sergeant-Major Morris," he said, introducing him.

The sergeant-major shook hands, and taking the proffered seat by the fire, watched contentedly while his host got out whiskey and tumblers and stood a small copper kettle on the fire.

At the third glass his eyes got brighter, and he began to talk, the little family circle regarding with eager interest this visitor from distant parts, as he squared his broad shoulders in the chair and spoke of wild scenes and doughty deeds; of wars and plagues and strange peoples.

"Twenty-one years of it," said Mr. White, nodding at his wife and son. "When he went away he was a slip of youth in the warehouse. Now look at him."

"He don't look to have taken much harm," said Mrs. White, politely.

"I'd like to go to India myself," said the old man, "just to look round a bit, you know."

"Better where you are," said the sergeant-major, shaking his head. He put down the empty glass, and sighing softly, shook it again.

"I should like to see those old temples and fakirs and jugglers," said the old man. "What was that you started telling me the other day about a monkey's paw or something, Morris?"

"Nothing," said the soldier hastily. "Leastways nothing worth hearing."

"Monkey's paw?" said Mrs. White, curiously.

"Well, it's just a bit of what you might call magic, perhaps," said the sergeant-major, offhandedly.

His three listeners leaned forward eagerly. The visitor absent-mindedly put his empty glass to his lips and then set it down again. His host filled it for him.

"To look at," said the sergeant-major, fumbling in his pocket, "it's just an ordinary little paw, dried to a mummy."

He took something out of his pocket and proffered it. Mrs. White drew back with a grimace, but her son, taking it, examined it curiously.

"And what is there special about it?" inquired Mr. White as he took it from his son, and having examined it, placed it upon the table.

"It had a spell put on it by an old fakir," said the sergeant-major, "a very holy man. He wanted to show that fate ruled people's lives, and that those who interfered with it did so to their sorrow. He put a spell on it so that three separate men could each have three wishes from it."

His manner was so impressive that his hearers were conscious that their light laughter jarred somewhat.

"Well, why don't you have three, sir?" said Herbert White, cleverly.

The soldier regarded him in the way that middle age is wont to regard presumptuous youth. "I have," he said, quietly, and his blotchy face whitened.

"And did you really have the three wishes granted?" asked Mrs. White.

"I did," said the sergeant-major, and his glass tapped against his strong teeth.

"And has anybody else wished?" persisted the old lady.

"The first man had his three wishes. Yes," was the reply; "I don't know what the first two were, but the third was for death. That's how I got the paw."

His tones were so grave that a hush fell upon the group.

"If you've had your three wishes, it's no good to you now, then, Morris," said the old man at last. "What do you keep it for?"

The soldier shook his head. "Fancy, I suppose," he said, slowly. "I did have some idea of selling it, but I don't think I will. It has caused enough mischief already. Besides, people won't buy. They think it's a fairy tale, some of them, and those who do think anything of it want to try it first and pay me afterward."

"If you could have another three wishes," said the old man, eyeing him keenly, "would you have them?"

"I don't know," said the other. "I don't know."

He took the paw, and dangling it between his forefinger and thumb, suddenly threw it upon the fire. White, with a slight cry, stooped down and snatched it off.

"Better let it burn," said the soldier, solemnly.

"If you don't want it, Morris," said the other, "give it to me."

"I won't," said his friend, doggedly. "I threw it on the fire. If you keep it, don't blame me for what happens. Pitch it on the fire again like a sensible man."

The other shook his head and examined his new possession closely. "How do you do it?" he inquired.

"Hold it up in your right hand and wish aloud," said the sergeant-major, "but I warn you of the consequences."

"Sounds like the *Arabian Nights*," said Mrs. White, as she rose and began to set the supper. "Don't you think you might wish for four pairs of hands for me?"

Her husband drew the talisman from his pocket, and then all three burst into laughter as the sergeant-major, with a look of alarm on his face, caught him by the arm.

"If you must wish," he said, gruffly, "wish for something sensible."

Mr. White dropped it back in his pocket, and placing chairs, motioned his friend to the table. In the business of supper the talisman was partly forgotten, and afterward the three sat listening in an enthralled fashion to a second instalment of the soldier's adventures in India.

"If the tale about the monkey's paw is not more truthful than those he has been telling us," said Herbert, as the door closed behind their guest, just in time for him to catch the last train, "we shan't make much out of it."

"Did you give him anything for it, father?" inquired Mrs. White, regarding her husband closely.

"A trifle," said he, colouring slightly. "He didn't want it, but I made him take it. And he pressed me again to throw it away."

"Likely," said Herbert, with pretended horror. "Why, we're going to be rich, and famous and happy. Wish to be an emperor, father, to begin with; then you can't be henpecked."

He darted round the table, pursued by the maligned Mrs. White armed with an antimacassar.

Mr. White took the paw from his pocket and eyed it dubiously. "I don't know what to wish for, and that's a fact," he said, slowly. "It seems to me I've got all I want."

"If you only cleared the house, you'd be quite happy, wouldn't you?" said Herbert, with his hand on his shoulder. "Well, wish for two hundred pounds, then; that'll just do it."

His father, smiling shamefacedly at his own credulity, held up the talisman, as his son, with a solemn face, somewhat marred by a wink at his mother, sat down at the piano and struck a few impressive chords.

"I wish for two hundred pounds," said the old man distinctly.

A fine crash from the piano greeted the words, interrupted by a shuddering cry from the old man. His wife and son ran toward him.

"It moved," he cried, with a glance of disgust at the object as it lay on the floor. "As I wished, it twisted in my hand like a snake."

"Well, I don't see the money," said his son as he picked it up and placed it on the table, "and I bet I never shall."

"It must have been your fancy, father," said his wife, regarding him anxiously.

He shook his head. "Never mind, though; there's no harm done, but it gave me a shock all the same."

They sat down by the fire again while the two men finished their pipes. Outside, the wind was higher than ever, and the old man started nervously at the sound of a door banging upstairs. A silence unusual and depressing settled upon all three, which lasted until the old couple rose to retire for the night.

"I expect you'll find the cash tied up in a big bag in the middle of your bed," said Herbert, as he bade them good-night, "And something horrible squatting up on top the wardrobe watching you as you pocket your ill-gotten gains."

He sat alone in the darkness, gazing at the dying fire, and seeing faces in it. The last face was so horrible and so simian that he gazed at it in amazement. It got so vivid that, with a little uneasy laugh, he felt on the table for a glass containing a little water to throw over it. His hand grasped the monkey's paw, and with a little shiver he wiped his hand on his coat and went up to bed.

II

In the brightness of the wintry sun next morning as it streamed over the breakfast table he laughed at his fears. There was an air of prosaic wholesomeness about the room which it had lacked on the previous night, and the dirty, shrivelled little paw was pitched on the sideboard with a carelessness which betokened no great belief in its virtues.

"I suppose all old soldiers are the same," said Mrs. White. "The idea of our listening to such nonsense! How could wishes be granted in these days? And if they could, how could two hundred pounds hurt you, father?"

"Might drop on his head from the sky," said the frivolous Herbert.

"Morris said the things happened so naturally," said his father, "that you might if you so wished attribute it to coincidence."

"Well, don't break into the money before I come back," said Herbert as he rose from the table. "I'm afraid it'll turn you into a mean, avaricious man, and we shall have to disown you."

His mother laughed, and following him to the door, watched him down the road; and returning to the breakfast table, was very happy at the expense of her husband's credulity. All of which did not prevent her from scurrying to the door at the postman's knock, nor prevent her from referring somewhat shortly to retired sergeant-majors of bibulous habits when she found that the post brought a tailor's bill.

"Herbert will have some more of his funny remarks, I expect, when he comes home," she said, as they sat at dinner.

"I dare say," said Mr. White, pouring himself out some beer; "but for all that, the thing moved in my hand; that I'll swear to."

"You thought it did," said the old lady soothingly.

"I say it did," replied the other. "There was no thought about it; I have just—What's the matter?"

His wife made no reply. She was watching the mysterious movements of a man outside, who, peering in an undecided fashion at the house, appeared to be trying to make up his mind to enter. In mental connection with the two hundred pounds, she noticed that the stranger was well dressed, and wore a silk hat of glossy newness. Three times he paused at the gate, and then walked on again. The fourth time he stood with his hand upon it, and then with sudden resolution flung it open and walked up the path. Mrs. White at the same moment placed her hands behind her, and hurriedly unfastening the strings of her apron, put that useful article of apparel beneath the cushion of her chair.

She brought the stranger, who seemed ill at ease, into the room. He gazed at her furtively, and listened in a preoccupied fashion as the old lady apologized for the appearance of the room, and her husband's coat, a garment which he usually reserved for the garden. She then waited as patiently as her sex would permit, for him to broach his business, but he was at first strangely silent.

"I—was asked to call," he said at last, and stooped and picked a piece of cotton from his trousers. "I come from 'Maw and Meggins.' "

The old lady started. "Is anything the matter?" she asked, breathlessly. "Has anything happened to Herbert? What is it? What is it?"

Her husband interposed. "There, there, mother," he said, hastily. "Sit down, and don't jump to conclusions. You've not brought bad news, I'm sure, sir," and he eyed the other wistfully.

"I'm sorry—" began the visitor.

"Is he hurt?" demanded the mother, wildly.

The visitor bowed in assent. "Badly hurt," he said, quietly, "but he is not in any pain."

"Oh, thank God!" said the old woman, clasping her hands. "Thank God for that! Thank—"

She broke off suddenly as the sinister meaning of the assurance dawned upon her and she saw the awful confirmation of her fears in the other's perverted face. She caught her breath, and turning to her slower-witted husband, laid her trembling old hand upon his. There was a long silence.

"He was caught in the machinery," said the visitor at length in a low voice.

"Caught in the machinery," repeated Mr. White, in a dazed fashion, "yes."

He sat staring blankly out at the window, and taking his wife's hand between his own, pressed it as he had been wont to do in their old courting-days nearly forty years before.

"He was the only one left to us," he said, turning gently to the visitor. "It is hard."

The other coughed, and rising, walked slowly to the window. "The firm wished me to convey their sincere sympathy with you in your great loss," he said, without looking round. "I beg that you will understand I am only their servant and merely obeying orders."

There was no reply; the old woman's face was white, her eyes staring, and her breath inaudible; on the husband's face was a look such as his friend the sergeant might have carried into his first action.

"I was to say that Maw and Meggins disclaim all responsibility," continued the other. "They admit no liability at all, but in consideration of your son's services, they wish to present you with a certain sum as compensation."

Mr. White dropped his wife's hand, and rising to his feet, gazed with a look of horror at his visitor. His dry lips shaped the words, "How much?"

"Two hundred pounds," was the answer.

Unconscious of his wife's shriek, the old man smiled faintly, put out his hands like a sightless man, and dropped, a senseless heap, to the floor.

III

In the huge new cemetery, some two miles distant, the old people buried their dead, and came back to a house steeped in shadow and silence. It was all over so quickly that at first they could hardly realize it, and remained in a state of expectation as though of something else to happen—something else which was to lighten this load, too heavy for old hearts to bear.

But the days passed, and expectation gave place to resignation—the hopeless resignation of the old, sometimes miscalled apathy.

Sometimes they hardly exchanged a word, for now they had nothing to talk about, and their days were long to weariness.

It was about a week after that the old man, waking suddenly in the night, stretched out his hand and found himself alone. The room was in darkness, and the sound of subdued weeping came from the window. He raised himself in bed and listened.

"Come back," he said, tenderly. "You will be cold."

"It is colder for my son," said the old woman, and wept afresh.

The sound of her sobs died away on his ears. The bed was warm, and his eyes heavy with sleep. He dozed fitfully, and then slept until a sudden wild cry from his wife awoke him with a start.

"*The paw*!" she cried wildly. "The monkey's paw!"

He started up in alarm. "Where? Where is it? What's the matter?"

She came stumbling across the room toward him. "I want it," she said, quietly. "You've not destroyed it?"

"It's in the parlour, on the bracket," he replied, marvelling. "Why?"

She cried and laughed together, and bending over, kissed his cheek.

"I only just thought of it," she said, hysterically. "Why didn't I think of it before? Why didn't *you* think of it?"

"Think of what?" he questioned.

"The other two wishes," she replied, rapidly. "We've only had one."

"Was not that enough?" he demanded, fiercely.

"No," she cried, triumphantly; "we'll have one more. Go down and get it quickly, and wish our boy alive again."

The man sat up in bed and flung the bedclothes from his quaking limbs. "Good God, you are mad!" he cried, aghast.

"Get it," she panted; "get it quickly, and wish—Oh, my boy, my boy!"

Her husband struck a match and lit the candle. "Get back to bed," he said, unsteadily. "You don't know what you are saying."

"We had the first wish granted," said the old woman, feverishly; "why not the second?"

"A coincidence," stammered the old man.

"Go and get it and wish," cried his wife, quivering with excitement.

The old man turned and regarded her, and his voice shook. "He has been dead ten days, and besides he—I would not tell you else, but—I could only recognize him by his clothing. If he was too terrible for you to see then, how now?"

"Bring him back," cried the old woman, and dragged him toward the door. "Do you think I fear the child I have nursed?"

He went down in the darkness, and felt his way to the parlour, and then to the mantelpiece. The talisman was in its place, and a horrible fear that the unspoken wish might bring his mutilated son before him ere he could escape from the room seized upon him, and he caught his breath as he found that he had lost the direction of the door. His brow cold with sweat, he felt his way round the table, and groped along the wall until he found himself in the small passage with the unwholesome thing in his hand.

Even his wife's face seemed changed as he entered the room. It was white and expectant, and to his fears seemed to have an unnatural look upon it. He was afraid of her.

"Wish!" she cried, in a strong voice.

"It is foolish and wicked," he faltered.

"Wish!" repeated his wife.

He raised his hand. "I wish my son alive again."

The talisman fell to the floor, and he regarded it fearfully. Then he sank trembling into a chair as the old woman, with burning eyes, walked to the window and raised the blind.

He sat until he was chilled with the cold, glancing occasionally at the figure of the old woman peering through the window. The candle-end, which had burned below the rim of the china candlestick, was throwing pulsating shadows on the ceiling and walls, until, with a flicker larger than the rest, it expired. The old man, with an unspeakable sense of relief at the failure of the talisman, crept back to his bed, and a minute or two afterward the old woman came silently and apathetically beside him.

Neither spoke, but lay silently listening to the ticking of the clock. A stair creaked, and a squeaky mouse scurried noisily through the wall. The darkness was oppressive, and after lying for some time screwing up his courage, he took the box of matches, and striking one, went downstairs for a candle.

At the foot of the stairs the match went out, and he paused to strike another; and at the same moment a knock, so quiet and stealthy as to be scarcely audible, sounded on the front door.

The matches fell from his hand and spilled in the passage. He stood motionless, his breath suspended until the knock was repeated. Then he turned and fled swiftly back to his room, and closed the door behind him. A third knock sounded through the house.

"What's that?" cried the old woman, starting up.

"A rat," said the old man in shaking tones—"a rat. It passed me on the stairs."

His wife sat up in bed listening. A loud knock resounded through the house.

"It's Herbert!" she screamed. "It's Herbert!"

She ran to the door, but her husband was before her, and catching her by the arm, held her tightly.

"What are you going to do?" he whispered hoarsely.

"It's my boy; it's Herbert!" she cried, struggling mechanically. "I forgot it was two miles away. What are you holding me for? Let go. I must open the door."

"For God's sake don't let it in," cried the old man, trembling.

"You're afraid of your own son," she cried, struggling. "Let me go. I'm coming, Herbert; I'm coming."

There was another knock, and another. The old woman with a sudden wrench broke free and ran from the room. Her husband followed to the landing, and called after her appealingly as she hurried downstairs. He heard the chain rattle back and the bottom bolt drawn slowly and stiffly from the socket. Then the old woman's voice, strained and panting.

"The bolt," she cried, loudly. "Come down. I can't reach it."

But her husband was on his hands and knees groping wildly on the floor in search of the paw. If he could only find it before the thing outside got in. A perfect fusillade of knocks reverberated through the house, and he heard the scraping of a chair as his wife put it down in the passage against the door. He heard the creaking of the bolt as it came slowly back, and at the same moment he found the monkey's paw, and frantically breathed his third and last wish.

The knocking ceased suddenly, although the echoes of it were still in the house. He heard the chair drawn back, and the door opened. A cold wind rushed up the staircase, and a long loud wail of disappointment and misery from his wife gave him courage to run down to her side, and then to the gate beyond. The street lamp flickering opposite shone on a quiet and deserted road.

Mark Anthony Jarman

Mark Anthony Jarman, born in Edmonton, Alberta, in 1955, is a graduate of the University of Victoria and of the University of Iowa writing school. Published in numerous journals and anthologies in both Canada and the United States, Jarman frequently writes of cross-border experiences, as in his picaresque novel *Salvage King, Ya!* (1997), about an aging hockey player named Drinkwater, who is bounced from farm team to farm team as his skills (including his survival skills on and perhaps also off ice) slowly fall apart. Critics have suggested that Jarman's prose combines elements from both James Joyce and Jack Kerouac—including a lyrical sensuality and complex allusions to pop culture—and they have applauded the author for his humour, his "dizzying" exuberance, his "fierce" confrontation with reality, and his fondness for vivid physical detail.

Among Jarman's stories are the two collections *Dancing Nightly in the Tavern* (1984) and *New Orleans is Sinking* (1998); "California Cancer Journeys" appeared in the latter volume. Beginning at sea, on the ferry crossing from Victoria, British Columbia, to Port Angeles, Washington, the story opens in transition, and opens out into a meditation on suffering, relationship, and responsibility. Some of the allusions (Blondie, Nixon, the LA Crips, Tom Cruise, and the Sons of the Pioneers) are straightforward; others (the double helix of DNA, or Charon, the ferryboatman on the River Styx) convey more indirectly the author's reflections on life and death and the connection between them. The character of connection, moreover, is what finally matters to the narrator. He gathers together the fragments of his understanding, realizing in some rudimentary way that the "crossing" on which he has embarked leads not only to sadness but also to joy.

California Cancer Journeys

I dwindle . . . dynamite no more.
I ask for a natural death,
no teeth on the ground—Robert Lowell.

At sea, a whitewater ferry crossing, rocking our way to Port Angeles on the venerable M.V. *Coho.* The Customs man on the other side looks like my dead father. He drawls an order: "You bring us back some sunshine now."

We drive verdant Highway 101 for a day before sneaking up on Interstate 5 and its oceanless rain and speed blurring county after sandy county. Five heads, five brains, $500 in traveller's cheques: my brand new family entering that ordered thirteen-day hallucination that is the trip to Grandmother's house. Grandmother, Sharon's mother, possesses any number of amiable cancers. We want to visit. She is looking forward to our visit. Our job is to bring sunshine.

■ ■ ■

At the same moment, in an upstairs room of a half-finished farmhouse in Grande Prairie, my best friend Levi is trying to kill a brain tumour; perhaps this fabled presence in his skull looks like a softball, or perhaps an orchard tangle. Whatever: Levi has lost interest in metaphor. He's taking injections in the thigh. He shuns chemo. He travels to Hawaii instead. R & R. While we travel, Mr. Levi Dronyk's brain is on a parallel journey. We move and something in his head moves, shakes out tiny reticulate leaves. They cut out as much tumour as they could without making him a vegetable (My vegetable love should grow more slow). They couldn't yank all its tendrils without cutting his brain. Standing in my sunlit backyard Levi talks to me, he's still himself. He's lost some vocabulary but he's still Levi. How long will this last? The doctors don't like to tell you you're dead. They want you to obey them. Balance and release seems the name of this relentless new dream, disease the new Elizabethan masque.

■ ■ ■

A first trip for our children; Gabriel is six months, Kelly is two years, and Martin is four. They love dinosaurs and bloodthirsty pirates. They love their parents. We gaze out clear car windows; we take in America the beautiful while something hesitant tries to shut down in my friend's head. Eighteen years I have known Levi. Windows close, a humming human ailment creeping in a joyful conspiracy, an impractical joke blossoming with the same crazy energy he displayed in everything: softball, beat poetry, chickenskin music, union business, random city travel, wild letters and dubbed tapes mailed to friends in the mountains. Levi wanted us to know the new singers, the obscure voices with their implied eyes and lipsync violence, their homey versions of winter. Selling his share of the house and blowing the money on records. Levi plays with his one-year-old by my garage. I think, His children will not know him. His records will last longer. He has no estate. He wanted to play a shining horn, had the Motown moves down like stink; a good dancer, a sharp-dressed man with a hawk-like Slavic face, a good talker and romancer. Now Levi will be the guy that died years ago. The guy that stood squinting by my garage with his one-year-old. He'll be the guy that worked for the union, giving twenty years to a small TV station, to phantom voices and talk shows and electric lines zipping right through his head all day every day. Levi got zapped, he got a smoked brain as a dowry, a perk from the owners, like a poached smokehouse salmon. Inhaling the room, fuming, fusing, having the company air while having an affair with the woman at work: and then someone slashed the roof of his Mustang in the staff lot, the car he had to sell later, bankrupt, moving from town to town, prowling the boondocks of affordable real estate. Who orders a life wisely?

■ ■ ■

We try. Sharon and I have borrowed against the house and bought a new car, a white car from a country both our fathers fought against. We drive under the huge hydro towers, following the ordered lines of the American Aqueduct, the orchards, this translation of the banquet with bouquets, this demon demonstration of the demand for water, the inalienable right to take over. Los Angeles is thirsty for power, lights, action. California Republic is thirsty; its lines run off the globe, its big metal legs stride the world, a Colossus, a shaking tectonic hangover. As I drive staring at the wires that lead off the horizon, I wonder, Could you actually *run* atop this power line tightrope, run all the way to some East L.A. taco stand? Walk a wire to that lovely infestation of poseurs and confidence men and executive producers? Would it kill you if you're not careful, not articulate? Could you walk to Los Angeles' Crip frijoles or would it fry your brain first? Not unlike TV screens and TV monitors and wires raving all around you in a tiny editing-room.

■ ■ ■

At work Levi was surfing electrical waves, moving his waged brain through a web of invisible beams and hemlines, through bones and border crossings. We force our new car to leap through invisible interstate borders; my three young kids dazed, thirsty, their new blond heads swivelling, leaving home for the first time, miles to go before we weep. New miles go on the new car. That's all right: rack them up, rack up the miles.

At the other end of these thick wires they are jump-starting a tiny star in the concrete sidewalk, fixing a hole where the rain got in, where they worship the saucers and strangle hookers with their own bra. The quake drops sections of freeway. Hop-scotch. It's exciting to arrive at midnight, as if party to a moonlight escape.

■ ■ ■

Trying to remember the motive, the votive, the fine print, we go through the spiny and naked desert, through the non-woods to Grandmother's house. Breast cancer was her first wolf; bone cancer was next. Her hip. Then her ribs. At least it's not soft tissue. Soft tissue is without hope. Maybe she'll escape. The social contract has changed since our last visit. Now one brings a basket of shark cartilage, cranberry juice, hoping and making small talk: My what big teeth.

Yes well you know they're all using teeth whitener now, like Tom Cruise.

Oh is that so? one says.

Yes. He's into some cult. They all have personality problems. They have a distorted view of life.

But very distorted is what sells, very distorted is boffo box office.

Yes, that's true enough, I say. This is a nice house you have here, I say.

Hmmph. More like half a house, Gladys complains. (It's bigger than our place and she lives alone.) She painted over the "yella," transplanted small palm trees, she owns it outright, but it's not really her place. She's magic with succulents, blossoms, fruit trees. The avenues are lined with gold and guacamole, but she's depressed about everything.

"I just don't know what's going to come of this," she says. "I don't know what's at the other end of this now." She's from the treed hills of Pennsylvania. No-one here is like her and she's alone most of the year. The barrios are too close. Her oldest daughter, Sharon's big sister, died of a brain tumour. She died when Nixon was President. Her parents voted for George Wallace. I had never before met anyone who voted for Wallace.

"I'm in pretty bad shape. Where's the baby? How did this happen," she wonders. Mexican workers outside listen to a Spanish version of Blondie's *Call Me.* They drive in, work fast on the perfect grass, and get out. Diagonal stripes. The teenage Italian woman across the street bleaches her hair white as cocaine and favours leopardskin and leather. Everyone strives to be blond, to be dark, to be hip, to be ethnic, to be straight, to be crooked, to be something they saw in *Interview* magazine. No-one here votes for George Wallace. The pavement glitters. They've never heard of George Wallace. It's a house of straw in a storm, a stop, likely her last in this state. Neighbours pretend no-one else exists, avert their eyes when I try to say hi. Dying is not the in thing. Unless you're beautiful and famous. And how long will she exist? Can she escape this? Gladys has stopped going to the movies or walking at night. Gladys has stopped playing pipe-organ at the church. Soon she'll have to stop driving. Then the rented wheelchair: I can't get to the bathroom at night! Then: I can't get out of bed, I'm choking because I have to eat on my back. I have no garden; I'm going to drown in a teaspoon. This, you recall, is California. There is always that struggle to keep mobile, to unlearn the unclean past: The frightening sun of a polished asylum, the sum of every plane alive and reflecting its new sheen. Doubt not, though no-one will buy an older house, an old shoe or an old story unfolding under an old sun squeezing out too much light over the new house up the cul-de-sac from the giant power lines, the new house in the 24-hour white sun with grass green as paint and grieved with envy beside the spare brittle music of the desert.

■ ■ ■

In the back of my head I keep hearing the Sons of the Pioneers croon, "Water, cooool clear water." And perhaps this is how tumours begin: something as innocent as an irritating song; that piece of sand that leads to the pearl that leads to the heebie jeebies or the mulberry bush or the river worth gathering at. No-one lied to us: the wind rides in from the foggy salt ocean and splits in the scorched valley; the wind heads south and the wind heads north, riding madly in all directions at once. Sea and desert; here are spirited worlds meeting and stripping each other like sex. Birds panic in their guided skyway. Ladders grow into the leather trees, searching for what grows. Like a tumour in a good friend's head. A double helix ladder. The pickers used to be Chinese. They had to go.

■ ■ ■

Hikers find smashed earthenware in a cavern, broken crockery in a head. Anarchy in a tiny place. Or is sickness a normal state, and health unnatural? Someone slashed the roof of Levi's Mustang; the surgeon slashed the roof of Levi's haunted head.

■ ■ ■

My quiet father died last year in California on Valentine's Day. He had a heart attack while walking out for a copy of *The San Diego Union*. He made it back to the rented condo but my mother was at the pool above the sandy cliffs, waiting for him. Finally she knew she had to check. She told me later I was lucky not to hear the sounds he made on someone else's chesterfield. They lost him at the hospital. I'm beginning to associate California with death, with sounds I should not hear. He had been diagnosed with liver cancer but the heart stepped up first. The squeaky wheel gets the grease, greases *you*. People said we were lucky not to see him waste away. To nothing. My aunt in England wrote me: "One felt he was the sort of chap who would go on forever quite cheerfully. As in life he was considerate to the end and to me it seems he decided to unfold his wings and just fly away—thoughtful as ever."

At the Coroner's he lay in the sliding drawer. My mother kissed him goodbye for all of us.

On the highway we read air's long history, the grasses waiting to bend, willing to wilt, while cattle hang on steep hillsides with black stoic faces; and the white horse lingers, looking for just one tree's shelter. I don't know if my father flew away. The pressed grasses are written on, something in this country stolen or moved and something genuine and fine. The greasers stare at the ground, at the creosote, at the white horse. The Sons of the Pioneers keep singing of water, singing of cool water.

■ ■ ■

This is my three sons' first long trip. They seem so well behaved, benign (as opposed to malignant). We fall from motel beds and drive about three inches and Martin asks if we're looking for a motel yet.

Soon, I say, in about twelve hours.

Why? he asks. How come? How long is twelve hours?

I don't know.

He'll forget it after a while. I've forgotten so much. Like reservations. I walk into motel offices covered in baby spit-up and cranberry juice and demand a business discount. I'm in the business of raising blond kids; I'm in the business of going through the non-woods to or from Grandmother's house. I want my discount.

■ ■ ■

Take Jesus into your heart, they say. Take Jesus into your liver, they don't say. When they're older and my graphic heart or liver has burst will my children remember this earthquake country? This voodoo volcano country? The squashed valleys with such a hard light that all the year's colours have gone dull? Will my young wife become pregnant at my wake? Believe me: I know of this exact event. Remember me? mumbles the ghost bent under the stage in a leather jerkin. Ah forget it, he says after a while.

There is no shade, no cover, just saltwhite ground and greasewood scrub, rattlesnakes and Borax muletrain memories. Will my children remember falling between the motel bed and motel wall and screaming, trapped, not knowing where they are? I tried to soothe them. This stripped mezzotint country reminds me of Merle Haggard and the Strangers; Buck Owens and the Buckaroos. These clouds have never seen clover. I remember bits of these trips with my parents. The patched canvas tent and the moose bellowing in the river. The Lethe Motel & Bar-B-Q. The bobcats jumping on tourists and the backseat's play within the play. Will our children remember *us?* We know so little of where we pass: last week, last decade, last century. Think of the pobladores, the lost families in this series of valleys: Alvarado, Castro, Wolfskill, Pico, Duran, Pacifico, de la Guerra y Noriega. The irrigation squabbles, scalps lifted like weeds, night riders and vigilante lynchings, complicated slaughter in the blind canyon. Now: brief moon-flowers and insects and cement overpasses with cratered pale masses of swallow nests glued to their side, cells mutating like you know what. Waiting for the airport and the surveyors' ribbons and subdivisions and the all-night Mexican places. We see no people, see no rabble. Just the power lines; just the huge Möbius road. What used to seem an *escape.*

■ ■ ■

Who lives here other than kingsnakes and sidewinders and swallows and their aboriginal oatmeal nests? Where are they all hiding? The dusty questions as you roll blind and yawning through another squinting crossroads, rattle your fine city bones on another corduroy road, past adobe bungalows and hedgerows that have run out of talent.

Sharon says, "My mother is dying and she still has that ability to drive me crazy." Gladys sprays more chemicals at the spiders in her garage, eats fast food from Jack-In-The-Box. She points to the pastel houses: This is what we call a development. Will she be resurrected again? Or is this the last time? It's the last time. It's a development. She has been gathering in death for a decade, learning and turning dying into performance art. I do the dishes every night at 7.20. I am restless, spooked. My children are thrilled by this trip to see their dying grandmother. They bang and clang on her piano and break her sprinkler system and scatter rocks to meet the Mexican's lawnmower. At night, though, my children cry out from their sleeping-bags on the floor, afraid of her Victorian furniture piled high in their room. Their grandfather (divorced and remarried) flies in from Las Vegas to tell war stories, stories I like more than anyone. He apologizes for telling them, apologizes for the divorce.

■ ■ ■

Gladys' lungs slowly fill with fluid; there is a hole in her hipbone from radiation. She shuffles into the kitchen, zaps her frozen "entrée."

"There is a level," she says, "beyond which I won't allow myself to fall." That doesn't last long. That level is history. History is a bunkbed. Her ribs start killing her. Her doctor quits and the office is bedlam. After a fortnight of sunny chaos we have lost our heads, lost our sleep, lost our saintly intentions; Sharon and I just want to get the hell out, to escape California Republic, to stop drinking cranberry juice. Gladys wants to die and she cannot; she lives on, mourning doves mumbling from her steep backyard. She hallucinates, believes she is chasing chickens in Pennsylvania, is shopping for bargains at the mall, that she is going to have to sue. Levi wants to live and yet he dies. The message arrives from Grande Prairie thousands of miles to the north: He's dying, she says, he's checking out. News falls from the buzzing wire, Levi falls from the wire without learning the instrument. Mourning doves have such slim heads. This end has happened so fast I can't believe it. As students Levi and I hopped the ferry to Port Angeles to drink in The Salty Dawg, to thumb up to the glacier at Hurricane Ridge. Suddenly someone is coming to get my friend Levi in a pickup truck, crossing the northern steppes to pick up what's left of him, as if he is a bale of green hay or a dry cord of tamarack to be burned. Not even a purple hearse to Joshua Tree. Not even a drummer or a staggering New Orleans horn.

■ ■ ■

How to forget that urge to escape somehow? And escape exactly what? Escaping escape? The restless dishes at 7.20? The salt on the ground? The routine blossoms inside your skin and skull? The desert sand that should look different on Valentine's Day? Or is it the displays in all the Encinitas shop windows: those red shiny Valentine hearts everywhere like masks, like masks with lace teeth, and on this day of hearts my father has a heart attack. Going for the newspaper in the morning sunlight by the Pacific Ocean. I flew down and drove his rental car to the mortuary. I was sick of goatees then and I'm sick of them now.

■ ■ ■

Your lungs with fluid; but your heart with something other. Levi and Gladys and all those in that blind canyon, all those in that last place of scalps and complicated slaughter, have reasons to seek escape, to feel betrayed, reasons to hop in a vintage Mustang or Meteor Rocket and hit the highway. To lose their lost skin beneath the mercury-lit overpass and lingering Northern Lights. To unfold wings and be thought considerate. Escaping escape. Pennsylvania. England. Terra Nova. The rest of us zooming under the prefab trestles are faking it, copping an attitude. Three blond heads chatter like cheerful wrens in the cracker-strewn backseat. (My father never allowed food in his cherished Oldsmobile, the Delta 88 I smashed.) I'm not saying anything to the boys. I am holding a wheel like it's a chisel, but I'm not escaping. I have my father's face, my father's hands, my father's heart. Ocean at my back, I'm going for a morning paper: The noises. A beautiful sweet breeze, sun-hot tiles and tiny reticulate leaves rushing toward me.

THOMAS KING

Of Cherokee, German, and Greek background, Thomas King was born in Sacramento, California, in 1943. After teaching some years in the Native studies department at the University of Lethbridge, he returned to the United States, to teach American studies at the University of Minnesota. In the 1980s, King became a leading spokesman for Native writing in Canada, drawing attention to its quality and variety. As an anthologist and critic, he edited such works as *The Canadian Fiction Magazine*'s Native Fiction issue (no. 60, 1987), *"All My Relations": An Anthology of Contemporary Canadian Native Prose* (1990), and (with Cheryl Carver and Helen Hoy) *The Native in Literature* (1985). But it is as a storyteller in his own right—in short fiction, poetry, and three novels (among them, *Medicine River*, 1990, and *Truth and Bright Water*, 1999)— that he has attracted most attention. In all three genres, he brings oral forms to the written page, not only to convey the voices of his characters but also to heighten the reader's appreciation of the oral culture being written about. King's aim is not merely to entertain, but also to expose the ridiculousness of social biases and demonstrate the power that is invested in them. His satire reveals bombast and greed, and questions the entrenched priorities of bureaucratic institutions.

"Borders" appeared first in *Saturday Night* in 1991, and was collected in *One Good Story, That One* (1993). As with *Truth and Bright Water*, the "borderlines" in "Borders" express cultural differences, but not always the obvious ones. (In the novel, one of the characters, an artist, repaints some buildings in the town—the local church among them—using the colours of the natural landscape so successfully that these "European" structures actually seem to disappear from view; this accomplishment does not, however, prevent other characters from walking into and tripping over the structures that continue to exist and therefore to affect them.) As King's narratives show—using comedy to both satirize and celebrate—borders can become arbitrary when bureaucracies take them over, but always there are solutions. Characteristically using dialogue to advance his narrative, King modulates the voices in such a way as to shift the tone from farce to social critique. Trickery abounds. But ultimately the power to reconstruct events is given to the narrator-storyteller, reasserting the value of the artist in Aboriginal societies and the potential of art to undermine unexamined biases and to protect the vitality of belief.

Borders

When I was twelve, maybe thirteen, my mother announced that we were going to go to Salt Lake City to visit my sister who had left the reserve, moved across the line, and found a job. Laetitia had not left home with my mother's blessing, but over time my mother had come to be proud of the fact that Laetitia had done all of this on her own.

"She did real good," my mother would say.

Then there were the fine points to Laetitia's going. She had not, as my mother liked to tell Mrs. Manyfingers, gone floating after some man like a balloon on a string. She hadn't snuck out of the house, either, and gone to Vancouver or Edmonton or Toronto to chase rainbows down alleys. And she hadn't been pregnant.

"She did real good."

I was seven or eight when Laetitia left home. She was seventeen. Our father was from Rocky Boy on the American side.

"Dad's American," Laetitia told my mother, "so I can go and come as I please."

"Send us a postcard."

Laetitia packed her things, and we headed for the border. Just outside of Milk River, Laetitia told us to watch for the water tower.

"Over the next rise. It's the first thing you see."

"We got a water tower on the reserve," my mother said. "There's a big one in Lethbridge, too."

"You'll be able to see the tops of the flagpoles, too. That's where the border is."

When we got to Coutts, my mother stopped at the convenience store and bought her and Laetitia a cup of coffee. I got an Orange Crush.

"This is real lousy coffee."

"You're just angry because I want to see the world."

"It's the water. From here on down, they got lousy water."

"I can catch the bus from Sweetgrass. You don't have to lift a finger."

"You're going to have to buy your water in bottles if you want good coffee."

There was an old wooden building about a block away, with a tall sign in the yard that said "Museum." Most of the roof had been blown away. Mom told me to go and see when the place was open. There were boards over the windows and doors. You could tell that the place was closed, and I told Mom so, but she said to go and check anyway. Mom and Laetitia stayed by the car. Neither one of them moved. I sat down on the steps of the museum and watched them, and I don't know that they ever said anything to each other. Finally, Laetitia got her bag out of the trunk and gave Mom a hug.

I wandered back to the car. The wind had come up, and it blew Laetitia's hair across her face. Mom reached out and pulled the strands out of Laetitia's eyes, and Laetitia let her.

"You can still see the mountain from here," my mother told Laetitia in Blackfoot.

"Lots of mountains in Salt Lake," Laetitia told her in English.

"The place is closed," I said. "Just like I told you."

Laetitia tucked her hair into her jacket and dragged her bag down the road to the brick building with the American flag flapping on a pole. When she got to where the guards were waiting, she turned, put the bag down, and waved to us. We waved back. Then my mother turned the car around, and we came home.

We got postcards from Laetitia regular, and, if she wasn't spreading jelly on the truth, she was happy. She found a good job and rented an apartment with a pool.

"And she can't even swim," my mother told Mrs. Manyfingers.

Most of the postcards said we should come down and see the city, but whenever I mentioned this, my mother would stiffen up.

So I was surprised when she bought two new tires for the car and put on her blue dress with the green and yellow flowers. I had to dress up, too, for my mother did not want us crossing the border looking like Americans. We made sandwiches and put them in a big box with pop and potato chips and some apples and bananas and a big jar of water.

"But we can stop at one of those restaurants, too, right?"

"We maybe should take some blankets in case you get sleepy."

"But we can stop at one of those restaurants, too, right?"

The border was actually two towns, though neither one was big enough to amount to anything. Coutts was on the Canadian side and consisted of the convenience store and gas station, the museum that was closed and boarded up, and a motel. Sweetgrass was on the American side, but all you could see was an overpass that arched across the highway and disappeared into the prairies. Just hearing the names of these towns, you would expect that Sweetgrass, which is a nice name and sounds like it is related to other places such as Medicine Hat and Moose Jaw and Kicking Horse Pass, would be on the Canadian side, and that Coutts, which sounds abrupt and rude, would be on the American side. But this was not the case.

Between the two borders was a duty-free shop where you could buy cigarettes and liquor and flags. Stuff like that.

We left the reserve in the morning and drove until we got to Coutts.

"Last time we stopped here," my mother said, "you had an Orange Crush. You remember that?"

"Sure," I said. "That was when Laetitia took off."

"You want another Orange Crush?"

"That means we're not going to stop at a restaurant, right?"

My mother got a coffee at the convenience store, and we stood around and watched the prairies move in the sunlight. Then we climbed back in the car. My mother straightened the dress across her thighs, leaned against the wheel, and drove all the way to the border in first gear, slowly, as if she were trying to see through a bad storm or riding high on black ice.

The border guard was an old guy. As he walked to the car, he swayed from side to side, his feet set wide apart, the holster on his hip pitching up and down. He leaned into the window, looked into the back seat, and looked at my mother and me.

"Morning, ma'am."

"Good morning."

"Where you heading?"

"Salt Lake City."

"Purpose of your visit?"

"Visit my daughter."

"Citizenship?"

"Blackfoot," my mother told him.

"Ma'am?"

"Blackfoot," my mother repeated.

"Canadian?"

"Blackfoot."

It would have been easier if my mother had just said "Canadian" and been done with it, but I could see she wasn't going to do that. The guard wasn't angry or anything. He smiled and looked towards the building. Then he turned back and nodded.

"Morning, ma'am."

"Good morning."

"Any firearms or tobacco?"

"No."

"Citizenship?"

"Blackfoot."

He told us to sit in the car and wait, and we did. In about five minutes, another guard came out with the first man. They were talking as they came, both men swaying back and forth like two cowboys headed for a bar or a gunfight.

"Morning, ma'am."

"Good morning."

"Cecil tells me you and the boy are Blackfoot."

"That's right."

"Now, I know that we got Blackfeet on the American side and the Canadians got Blackfeet on their side. Just so we can keep our records straight, what side do you come from?"

I knew exactly what my mother was going to say, and I could have told them if they had asked me.

"Canadian side or American side?" asked the guard.

"Blackfoot side," she said.

It didn't take them long to lose their sense of humor, I can tell you that. The one guard stopped smiling altogether and told us to park our car at the side of the building and come in.

We sat on a wood bench for about an hour before anyone came over to talk to us. This time it was a woman. She had a gun, too.

"Hi," she said. "I'm Inspector Pratt. I understand there is a little misunderstanding."

"I'm going to visit my daughter in Salt Lake City," my mother told her. "We don't have any guns or beer."

"It's a legal technicality, that's all."

"My daughter's Blackfoot, too."

The woman opened a briefcase and took out a couple of forms and began to write on one of them. "Everyone who crosses our border has to declare their citizenship. Even Americans. It helps us keep track of the visitors we get from the various countries."

She went on like that for maybe fifteen minutes, and a lot of the stuff she told us was interesting.

"I can understand how you feel about having to tell us your citizenship, and here's what I'll do. You tell me, and I won't put it down on the form. No-one will know but you and me."

Her gun was silver. There were several chips in the wood handle and the name "Stella" was scratched into the metal butt.

We were in the border office for about four hours, and we talked to almost everyone there. One of the men bought me a Coke. My mother brought a couple of sandwiches in from the car. I offered part of mine to Stella, but she said she wasn't hungry.

I told Stella that we were Blackfoot and Canadian, but she said that that didn't count because I was a minor. In the end, she told us that if my mother didn't declare her citizenship, we would have to go back to where we came from. My mother stood up and thanked Stella for her time. Then we got back in the car and drove to the Canadian border, which was only about a hundred yards away.

I was disappointed. I hadn't seen Laetitia for a long time, and I had never been to Salt Lake City. When she was still at home, Laetitia would go on and on about Salt Lake City. She had never been there, but her boyfriend Lester Tallbull had spent a year in Salt Lake at a technical school.

"It's a great place," Lester would say. "Nothing but blondes in the whole state."

Whenever he said that, Laetitia would slug him on his shoulder hard enough to make him flinch. He had some brochures on Salt Lake and some maps, and every so often the two of them would spread them out on the table.

"That's the temple. It's right downtown. You got to have a pass to get in."

"Charlotte says anyone can go in and look around."

"When was Charlotte in Salt Lake? Just when the hell was Charlotte in Salt Lake?"

"Last year."

"This is Liberty Park. It's got a zoo. There's good skiing in the mountains."

"Got all the skiing we can use," my mother would say. "People come from all over the world to ski at Banff. Cardston's got a temple, if you like those kinds of things."

"Oh, this one is real big," Lester would say. "They got armed guards and everything."

"Not what Charlotte says."

"What does she know?"

Lester and Laetitia broke up, but I guess the idea of Salt Lake stuck in her mind.

■ ■ ■

The Canadian border guard was a young woman, and she seemed happy to see us. "Hi," she said. "You folks sure have a great day for a trip. Where are you coming from?"

"Standoff."

"Is that in Montana?"

"No."

"Where are you going?"

"Standoff."

The woman's name was Carol and I don't guess she was any older than Laetitia. "Wow, you both Canadians?"

"Blackfoot."

"Really? I have a friend I went to school with who is Blackfoot. Do you know Mike Harley?"

"No."

"He went to school in Lethbridge, but he's really from Browning."

It was a nice conversation and there were no cars behind us, so there was no rush.

"You're not bringing any liquor back, are you?"

"No."

"Any cigarettes or plants or stuff like that?"

"No."

"Citizenship?"

"Blackfoot."

"I know," said the woman, "and I'd be proud of being Blackfoot if I were Blackfoot. But you have to be American or Canadian."

■ ■ ■

When Laetitia and Lester broke up, Lester took his brochures and maps with him, so Laetitia wrote to someone in Salt Lake City, and about a month later, she got a big envelope of stuff. We sat at the table and opened up all the brochures, and Laetitia read each one out loud.

"Salt Lake City is the gateway to some of the world's most magnificent skiing.

"Salt Lake City is the home of one of the newest professional basketball franchises, the Utah Jazz.

"The Great Salt Lake is one of the natural wonders of the world."

It was kind of exciting seeing all those color brochures on the table and listening to Laetitia read all about how Salt Lake City was one of the best places in the entire world.

"That Salt Lake City place sounds too good to be true," my mother told her.

"It has everything."

"We got everything right here."

"It's boring here."

"People in Salt Lake City are probably sending away for brochures of Calgary and Lethbridge and Pincher Creek right now."

In the end, my mother would say that maybe Laetitia should go to Salt Lake City, and Laetitia would say that maybe she would.

■ ■ ■

We parked the car to the side of the building and Carol led us into a small room on the second floor. I found a comfortable spot on the couch and flipped through some back issues of *Saturday Night* and *Alberta Report*.

When I woke up, my mother was just coming out of another office. She didn't say a word to me. I followed her down the stairs and out to the car. I thought we were going home, but she turned the car around and drove back towards the American border, which made me think we were going to visit Laetitia in Salt Lake City after all. Instead she pulled into the parking lot of the duty-free store and stopped.

"We going to see Laetitia?"

"No."

"We going home?"

Pride is a good thing to have, you know. Laetitia had a lot of pride, and so did my mother. I figured that someday, I'd have it, too.

"So where are we going?"

Most of that day, we wandered around the duty-free store, which wasn't very large. The manager had a name tag with a tiny American flag on one side and a tiny Canadian flag on the other. His name was Mel. Towards evening, he began suggesting that we should be on our way. I told him we had nowhere to go, that neither the Americans nor the Canadians would let us in. He laughed at that and told us that we should buy something or leave.

The car was not very comfortable, but we did have all that food and it was April, so even if it did snow as it sometimes does on the prairies, we wouldn't freeze. The next morning my mother drove to the American border.

It was a different guard this time, but the questions were the same. We didn't spend as much time in the office as we had the day before. By noon, we were back at the Canadian border. By two we were back in the duty-free shop parking lot.

The second night in the car was not as much fun as the first, but my mother seemed in good spirits, and, all in all, it was as much an adventure as an inconvenience. There wasn't much food left and that was a problem, but we had lots of water as there was a faucet at the side of the duty-free shop.

■ ■ ■

One Sunday, Laetitia and I were watching television. Mom was over at Mrs. Manyfingers's. Right in the middle of the program, Laetitia turned off the set and said she was going to Salt Lake City, that life around here was too boring. I had wanted to see the rest of the program and really didn't care if Laetitia went to Salt Lake City or not. When Mom got home, I told her what Laetitia had said.

What surprised me was how angry Laetitia got when she found out that I had told Mom.

"You got a big mouth."

"That's what you said."

"What I said is none of your business."

"I didn't say anything."

"Well, I'm going for sure, now."

That weekend, Laetitia packed her bags, and we drove her to the border.

■ ■ ■

Mel turned out to be friendly. When he closed up for the night and found us still parked in the lot, he came over and asked us if our car was broken down or something. My mother thanked him for his concern and told him that we were fine, that things would get straightened out in the morning.

"You're kidding," said Mel. "You'd think they could handle the simple things."

"We got some apples and a banana," I said, "but we're all out of ham sandwiches."

"You know, you read about these things, but you just don't believe it. You just don't believe it."

"Hamburgers would be even better because they got more stuff for energy."

My mother slept in the back seat. I slept in the front because I was smaller and could lie under the steering wheel. Late that night, I heard my mother open the car door. I found her sitting on her blanket leaning against the bumper of the car.

"You see all those stars," she said. "When I was a little girl, my grandmother used to take me and my sisters out on the prairies and tell us stories about all the stars."

"Do you think Mel is going to bring us any hamburgers?"

"Every one of those stars has a story. You see that bunch of stars over there that look like a fish?"

"He didn't say no."

"Coyote went fishing, one day. That's how it all started." We sat out under the stars that night, and my mother told me all sorts of stories. She was serious about it, too. She'd tell them slow, repeating parts as she went, as if she expected me to remember each one.

Early the next morning, the television vans began to arrive, and guys in suits and women in dresses came trotting over to us, dragging microphones and cameras and lights behind them. One of the vans had a table set up with orange juice and sandwiches and fruit. It was for the crew, but when I told them we hadn't eaten for a while, a really skinny blonde woman told us we could eat as much as we wanted.

They mostly talked to my mother. Every so often one of the reporters would come over and ask me questions about how it felt to be an Indian without a country. I told them we had a nice house on the reserve and that my cousins had a couple of horses we rode when we went fishing. Some of the television people went over to the American border, and then they went to the Canadian border.

Around noon, a good-looking guy in a dark blue suit and an orange tie with little ducks on it drove up in a fancy car. He talked to my mother for a while, and, after they were done talking, my mother called me over, and we got into our car. Just as my mother started the engine, Mel came over and gave us a bag of peanut brittle and told us that justice was a damn hard thing to get, but that we shouldn't give up.

I would have preferred lemon drops, but it was nice of Mel anyway.

"Where are we going now?"

"Going to visit Laetitia."

The guard who came out to our car was all smiles. The television lights were so bright they hurt my eyes, and, if you tried to look through the windshield in certain directions, you couldn't see a thing.

"Morning, ma'am."

"Good morning."

"Where you heading?"

"Salt Lake City."

"Purpose of your visit?"

"Visit my daughter."

"Any tobacco, liquor, or firearms?"

"Don't smoke."

"Any plants or fruit?"

"Not any more."

"Citizenship?"

"Blackfoot."

The guard rocked back on his heels and jammed his thumbs into his gun belt. "Thank you," he said, his fingers patting the butt of the revolver. "Have a pleasant trip."

My mother rolled the car forward, and the television people had to scramble out of the way. They ran alongside the car as we pulled away from the border, and, when they couldn't run any farther, they stood in the middle of the highway and waved and waved and waved.

We got to Salt Lake City the next day. Laetitia was happy to see us, and, that first night, she took us out to a restaurant that made really good soups. The list of pies took up a whole page. I had cherry. Mom had chocolate. Laetitia said that she saw us on television the night before and, during the meal, she had us tell her the story over and over again.

Laetitia took us everywhere. We went to a fancy ski resort. We went to the temple. We got to go shopping in a couple of large malls, but they weren't as large as the one in Edmonton, and Mom said so.

After a week or so, I got bored and wasn't at all sad when my mother said we should be heading back home. Laetitia wanted us to stay longer, but Mom said no, that she had things to do back home and that, next time, Laetitia should come up and visit. Laetitia said she was thinking about moving back, and Mom told her to do as she pleased, and Laetitia said that she would.

On the way home, we stopped at the duty-free shop, and my mother gave Mel a green hat that said "Salt Lake" across the front. Mel was a funny guy. He took the hat and blew his nose and told my mother that she was an inspiration to us all. He gave us some more peanut brittle and came out into the parking lot and waved at us all the way to the Canadian border.

It was almost evening when we left Coutts. I watched the border through the rear window until all you could see were the tops of the flagpoles and the blue water tower, and then they rolled over a hill and disappeared.

HANIF KUREISHI

The son of a Pakistani father and a British mother, Hanif Kureishi has explored the ambiguous world of the non-white immigrant to Britain in a number of works and in different genres. He was born in Bromley, Kent, in 1954. After completing a BA at King's College, London, he worked in various capacities in the theatre, rising from scene-shifter and usher to become playwright-in-residence at the Royal Court Theatre, London, in 1981. His first play, *Soaking Up the Heat*, was produced in London in 1976, and was followed in 1980 by *The Mother Country*, which won him the Thames Television Playwright Award. While continuing to write drama, Kureishi produced work for radio, television, and the movies, and in 1985 he wrote the screenplay for *My Beautiful Laundrette*, a film directed by Stephen Frears that won great critical acclaim and brought Kureishi a number of prestigious awards, including Best Screenplay Award from the New York Film Critics Circle. The screenplay was also nominated for an Oscar. *My Beautiful Laundrette* offered a fresh and realistic insight into the lives of Asians living in England, a subject Kureishi turned to in his next screenplay, *Sammy and Rosie Get Laid* (1987), also directed by Frears, the story of a racially mixed marriage. Kureishi also gained notice for his novel *The Buddha of Suburbia* (1990), a study of South Asian immigrant life in London for which Kureishi received the Whitbread First Novel Award, and which was adapted for television as a mini-series in 1993. In 1991 Kureishi wrote and directed the film *London Kills Me*. His recent work includes the novel *Intimacy* (1998) and a collection of stories entitled *Midnight All Day* (1999).

"My Son the Fanatic," first published in 1997 in the short story collection *Love in a Blue Time*, picks up a recurring subject in Kureishi's writing, the conflict between the beliefs and traditions that immigrants bring from the "old country" and the values of the new culture that seeks to assimilate them. Here the son's Islamic fundamentalism is set in stark and painful contrast to the father's acceptance of Western attitudes. Kureishi, who has been accused of being "an apologist for the morally lax," seems sympathetic to the father, who clearly cares deeply for his son; yet the story's conclusion forces the reader to re-examine the father's value system more critically. Turned into a screenplay by Kureishi, the story was produced as a film in 1998, directed by Udayan Prasad.

My Son the Fanatic

Surreptitiously the father began going into his son's bedroom. He would sit there for hours, rousing himself only to seek clues. What bewildered him was that Ali was getting tidier. Instead of the usual tangle of clothes, books, cricket bats, video games, the room was becoming neat and ordered; spaces began appearing where before there had been only mess.

Initially Parvez had been pleased: his son was outgrowing his teenage attitudes. But one day, beside the dustbin, Parvez found a torn bag which contained not only old toys, but computer discs, video tapes, new books and fashionable clothes the boy had bought just a few months before. Also without explanation, Ali had parted from the English girlfriend who used to come often to the house. His old friends had stopped ringing.

For reasons he didn't himself understand, Parvez wasn't able to bring up the subject of Ali's unusual behaviour. He was aware that he had become slightly afraid of his son, who, alongside his silences, was developing a sharp tongue. One remark Parvez did make, 'You don't play your guitar any more,' elicited the mysterious but conclusive reply, 'There are more important things to be done.'

Yet Parvez felt his son's eccentricity as an injustice. He had always been aware of the pitfalls which other men's sons had fallen into in England. And so, for Ali, he had worked long hours and spent a lot of money paying for his education as an accountant. He had bought him good suits, all the books he required and a computer. And now the boy was throwing his possessions out!

The TV, video and sound system followed the guitar. Soon the room was practically bare. Even the unhappy walls bore marks where Ali's pictures had been removed.

Parvez couldn't sleep; he went more to the whisky bottle, even when he was at work. He realised it was imperative to discuss the matter with someone sympathetic.

Parvez had been a taxi driver for twenty years. Half that time he'd worked for the same firm. Like him, most of the other drivers were Punjabis. They preferred to work at night, the roads were clearer and the money better. They slept during the day, avoiding their wives. Together they led almost a boy's life in the cabbies' office, playing cards and practical jokes, exchanging lewd stories, eating together and discussing politics and their problems.

But Parvez had been unable to bring this subject up with his friends. He was too ashamed. And he was afraid, too, that they would blame him for the wrong turning his boy had taken, just as he had blamed other fathers whose sons had taken to running around with bad girls, truanting from school and joining gangs.

For years Parvez had boasted to the other men about how Ali excelled at cricket, swimming and football, and how attentive a scholar he was, getting straight 'A's in most subjects. Was it asking too much for Ali to get a good job now, marry the right girl and start a family? Once this happened, Parvez would be happy. His dreams of doing well in England would have come true. Where had he gone wrong?

But one night, sitting in the taxi office on busted chairs with his two closest friends watching a Sylvester Stallone film, he broke his silence.

'I can't understand it!' he burst out. 'Everything is going from his room. And I can't talk to him any more. We were not father and son—we were brothers! Where has he gone? Why is he torturing me!'

And Parvez put his head in his hands.

Even as he poured out his account the men shook their heads and gave one another knowing glances. From their grave looks Parvez realised they understood the situation.

'Tell me what is happening!' he demanded.

The reply was almost triumphant. They had guessed something was going wrong. Now it was clear. Ali was taking drugs and selling his possessions to pay for them. That was why his bedroom was emptying.

'What must I do then?'

Parvez's friends instructed him to watch Ali scrupulously and then be severe with him, before the boy went mad, overdosed or murdered someone.

Parvez staggered out into the early morning air, terrified they were right. His boy—the drug addict killer!

To his relief he found Bettina sitting in his car.

Usually the last customers of the night were local 'brasses' or prostitutes. The taxi drivers knew them well, often driving them to liaisons. At the end of the girls' shifts, the men would ferry them home, though sometimes the women would join them for a drinking session in the office. Occasionally the drivers would go with the girls. 'A ride in exchange for a ride,' it was called.

Bettina had known Parvez for three years. She lived outside the town and on the long drive home, where she sat not in the passenger seat but beside him, Parvez had talked to her about his life and hopes, just as she talked about hers. They saw each other most nights.

He could talk to her about things he'd never be able to discuss with his own wife. Bettina, in turn, always reported on her night's activities. He liked to know where she was and with whom. Once he had rescued her from a violent client, and since then they had come to care for one another.

Though Bettina had never met the boy, she heard about Ali continually. That late night, when he told Bettina that he suspected Ali was on drugs, she judged neither the boy nor his father, but became businesslike and told him what to watch for.

'It's all in the eyes,' she said. They might be bloodshot; the pupils might be dilated; he might look tired. He could be liable to sweats, or sudden mood changes. 'Okay?'

Parvez began his vigil gratefully. Now he knew what the problem might be, he felt better. And surely, he figured, things couldn't have gone too far? With Bettina's help he would soon sort it out.

He watched each mouthful the boy took. He sat beside him at every opportunity and looked into his eyes. When he could he took the boy's hand, checking his temperature. If the boy wasn't at home Parvez was active, looking under the carpet, in his drawers, behind the empty wardrobe, sniffing, inspecting, probing. He knew what to look for: Bettina had drawn pictures of capsules, syringes, pills, powders, rocks.

Every night she waited to hear news of what he'd witnessed.

After a few days of constant observation, Parvez was able to report that although the boy had given up sports, he seemed healthy, with clear eyes. He didn't, as his father expected, flinch guiltily from his gaze. In fact the boy's mood was alert and steady in this sense: as well as being sullen, he was very watchful. He returned his father's long looks with more than a hint of criticism, of reproach even, so much so that Parvez began to feel that it was he who was in the wrong, and not the boy!

'And there's nothing else physically different?' Bettina asked.

'No!' Parvez thought for a moment. 'But he is growing a beard.'

One night, after sitting with Bettina in an all-night coffee shop, Parvez came home particularly late. Reluctantly he and Bettina had abandoned their only explanation, the drug theory, for Parvez had found nothing resembling any drugs in Ali's room. Besides, Ali wasn't selling his belongings. He threw them out, gave them away or donated them to charity shops.

Standing in the hall, Parvez heard his boy's alarm clock go off. Parvez hurried into his bedroom where his wife was still awake, sewing in bed. He ordered her to sit down and keep quiet, though she had neither stood up nor said a word. From this post, and with her watching him curiously, he observed his son through the crack in the door.

The boy went into the bathroom to wash. When he returned to his room Parvez sprang across the hall and set his ear at Ali's door. A muttering sound came from within. Parvez was puzzled but relieved.

Once this clue had been established, Parvez watched him at other times. The boy was praying. Without fail, when he was at home, he prayed five times a day.

Parvez had grown up in Lahore where all the boys had been taught the Koran. To stop him falling asleep when he studied, the Moulvi had attached a piece of string to the ceiling and tied it to Parvez's hair, so that if his head fell forward, he would instantly awake. After this indignity Parvez had avoided all religions. Not that the other taxi drivers had more respect. In fact they made jokes about the local mullahs walking around with their caps and beards, thinking they could tell people how to live, while their eyes roved over the boys and girls in their care.

Parvez described to Bettina what he had discovered. He informed the men in the taxi office. The friends, who had been so curious before, now became oddly silent. They could hardly condemn the boy for his devotions.

Parvez decided to take a night off and go out with the boy. They could talk things over. He wanted to hear how things were going at college; he wanted to tell him stories about their family in Pakistan. More than anything he yearned to understand how Ali had discovered the 'spiritual dimension,' as Bettina described it.

To Parvez's surprise, the boy refused to accompany him. He claimed he had an appointment. Parvez had to insist that no appointment could be more important than that of a son with his father.

The next day, Parvez went immediately to the street where Bettina stood in the rain wearing high heels, a short skirt and a long mac on top, which she would open hopefully at passing cars.

'Get in, get in!' he said.

They drove out across the moors and parked at the spot where on better days, with a view unimpeded for many miles by nothing but wild deer and horses, they'd lie back, with their eyes half closed, saying 'This is the life.' This time Parvez was trembling. Bettina put her arms around him.

'What's happened?'

'I've just had the worst experience of my life.'

As Bettina rubbed his head Parvez told her that the previous evening he and Ali had gone to a restaurant. As they studied the menu, the waiter, whom Parvez knew, brought him his usual whisky and water. Parvez had been so nervous he had even prepared a question. He was going to ask Ali if he was worried about his imminent exams. But first, wanting to relax, he loosened his tie, crunched a popadom and took a long drink.

Before Parvez could speak, Ali made a face.

'Don't you know it's wrong to drink alcohol?' he said. 'He spoke to me very harshly,' Parvez told Bettina. 'I was about to castigate the boy for being insolent, but managed to control myself.'

He had explained patiently to Ali that for years he had worked more than ten hours a day, that he had few enjoyments or hobbies and never went on holiday. Surely it wasn't a crime to have a drink when he wanted one?

'But it is forbidden,' the boy said.

Parvez shrugged, 'I know.'

'And so is gambling, isn't it?'

'Yes. But surely we are only human?'

Each time Parvez took a drink, the boy winced, or made a fastidious face as an accompaniment. This made Parvez drink more quickly. The waiter, wanting to please his friend, brought another glass of whisky. Parvez knew he was getting drunk, but he couldn't stop himself. Ali had a horrible look on his face, full of disgust and censure. It was as if he hated his father.

Halfway through the meal Parvez suddenly lost his temper and threw a plate on the floor. He had felt like ripping the cloth from the table, but the waiters and other customers were staring at him. Yet he wouldn't stand for his own son telling him the difference between right and wrong. He knew he wasn't a bad man. He had a conscience. There were a few things of which he was ashamed, but on the whole he had lived a decent life.

'When have I had time to be wicked?' he asked Ali.

In a low monotonous voice the boy explained that Parvez had not, in fact, lived a good life. He had broken countless rules of the Koran.

'For instance?' Parvez demanded.

Ali hadn't needed time to think. As if he had been waiting for this moment, he asked his father if he didn't relish pork pies?

'Well . . . '

Parvez couldn't deny that he loved crispy bacon smothered with mushrooms and mustard and sandwiched between slices of fried bread. In fact he ate this for breakfast every morning.

Ali then reminded Parvez that he had ordered his own wife to cook pork sausages, saying to her, 'You're not in the village now, this is England. We have to fit in!'

Parvez was so annoyed and perplexed by this attack that he called for more drink.

'The problem is this,' the boy said. He leaned across the table. For the first time that night his eyes were alive. 'You are too implicated in Western civilisation.'

Parvez burped; he thought he was going to choke. 'Implicated!' he said. 'But we live here!'

'The Western materialists hate us,' Ali said. 'Papa, how can you love something which hates you?'

'What is the answer then?' Parvez said miserably. 'According to you.'

Ali addressed his father fluently, as if Parvez were a rowdy crowd that had to be quelled and convinced. The Law of Islam would rule the world; the skin of the infidel would burn off again and again; the Jews and Christers would be routed. The West was a sink of hypocrites, adulterers, homosexuals, drug takers and prostitutes.

As Ali talked, Parvez looked out of the window as if to check that they were still in London.

'My people have taken enough. If the persecution doesn't stop there will be *jihad*. I, and millions of others, will gladly give our lives for the cause.'

'But why, why?' Parvez said.

'For us the reward will be in paradise.'

'Paradise!'

Finally, as Parvez's eyes filled with tears, the boy urged him to mend his ways.

'How is that possible?' Parvez asked.

'Pray,' Ali said. 'Pray beside me.'

Parvez called for the bill and ushered his boy out of the restaurant as soon as he was able. He couldn't take any more. Ali sounded as if he'd swallowed someone else's voice.

On the way home the boy sat in the back of the taxi, as if he were a customer.

'What has made you like this?' Parvez asked him, afraid that somehow he was to blame for all this. 'Is there a particular event which has influenced you?'

'Living in this country.'

'But I love England,' Parvez said, watching his boy in the mirror. 'They let you do almost anything here.'

'That is the problem,' he replied.

For the first time in years Parvez couldn't see straight. He knocked the side of the car against a lorry, ripping off the wing mirror. They were lucky not to have been stopped by the police: Parvez would have lost his licence and therefore his job.

Getting out of the car back at the house, Parvez stumbled and fell in the road, scraping his hands and ripping his trousers. He managed to haul himself up. The boy didn't even offer him his hand.

Parvez told Bettina he was now willing to pray, if that was what the boy wanted, if that would dislodge the pitiless look from his eyes.

'But what I object to,' he said, 'is being told by my own son that I am going to hell!'

What finished Parvez off was that the boy had said he was giving up accountancy. When Parvez had asked why, Ali had said sarcastically that it was obvious.

'Western education cultivates an anti-religious attitude.'

And, according to Ali, in the world of accountants it was usual to meet women, drink alcohol and practise usury.

'But it's well-paid work,' Parvez argued. 'For years you've been preparing!'

Ali said he was going to begin to work in prisons, with poor Muslims who were struggling to maintain their purity in the face of corruption. Finally, at the end of the evening, as Ali was going to bed, he had asked his father why he didn't have a beard, or at least a moustache.

'I feel as if I've lost my son,' Parvez told Bettina. 'I can't bear to be looked at as if I'm a criminal. I've decided what to do.'

'What is it?'

'I'm going to tell him to pick up his prayer mat and get out of my house. It will be the hardest thing I've ever done, but tonight I'm going to do it.'

'But you mustn't give up on him,' said Bettina. 'Many young people fall into cults and superstitious groups. It doesn't mean they'll always feel the same way.'

She said Parvez had to stick by his boy, giving him support, until he came through.

Parvez was persuaded that she was right, even though he didn't feel like giving his son more love when he had hardly been thanked for all he had already given.

Nevertheless, Parvez tried to endure his son's looks and reproaches. He attempted to make conversation about his beliefs. But if Parvez ventured any criticism, Ali always had a brusque reply. On one occasion Ali accused Parvez of 'grovelling' to the whites; in contrast, he explained, he was not 'inferior'; there was more to the world than the West, though the West always thought it was best.

'How is it you know that?' Parvez said, 'seeing as you've never left England?'

Ali replied with a look of contempt.

One night, having ensured there was no alcohol on his breath, Parvez sat down at the kitchen table with Ali. He hoped Ali would compliment him on the beard he was growing but Ali didn't appear to notice.

The previous day Parvez had been telling Bettina that he thought people in the West sometimes felt inwardly empty and that people needed a philosophy to live by.

'Yes,' said Bettina. 'That's the answer. You must tell him what your philosophy of life is. Then he will understand that there are other beliefs.'

After some fatiguing consideration, Parvez was ready to begin. The boy watched him as if he expected nothing.

Haltingly Parvez said that people had to treat one another with respect, particularly children their parents. This did seem, for a moment, to affect the boy. Heartened, Parvez continued. In his view this life was all there was and when you died you rotted in the earth. 'Grass and flowers will grow out of me, but something of me will live on—'

'How?'

'In other people. I will continue—in you.' At this the boy appeared a little distressed. 'And your grandchildren,' Parvez added for good measure. 'But while I am here on earth I want to make the best of it. And I want you to, as well!'

'What d'you mean by "make the best of it"?' asked the boy.

'Well,' said Parvez. 'For a start . . . you should enjoy yourself. Yes. Enjoy yourself without hurting others.'

Ali said that enjoyment was a 'bottomless pit.'

'But I don't mean enjoyment like that!' said Parvez. 'I mean the beauty of living!'

'All over the world our people are oppressed,' was the boy's reply.

'I know,' Parvez replied, not entirely sure who 'our people' were, 'but still—life is for living!'

Ali said, 'Real morality has existed for hundreds of years. Around the world millions and millions of people share my beliefs. Are you saying you are right and they are all wrong?'

Ali looked at his father with such aggressive confidence that Parvez could say no more.

One evening Bettina was sitting in Parvez's car, after visiting a client, when they passed a boy on the street.

'That's my son,' Parvez said suddenly. They were on the other side of town, in a poor district, where there were two mosques.

Parvez set his face hard.

Bettina turned to watch him. 'Slow down then, slow down!' She said, 'He's good-looking. Reminds me of you. But with a more determined face. Please, can't we stop?'

'What for?'

'I'd like to talk to him.'

Parvez turned the cab round and stopped beside the boy.

'Coming home?' Parvez asked. 'It's quite a way.'

The sullen boy shrugged and got into the back seat. Bettina sat in the front. Parvez became aware of Bettina's short skirt, gaudy rings and ice-blue eyeshadow. He became conscious that the smell of her perfume, which he loved, filled the cab. He opened the window.

While Parvez drove as fast as he could, Bettina said gently to Ali, 'Where have you been?'

'The mosque,' he said.

'And how are you getting on at college? Are you working hard?'

'Who are you to ask me these questions?' he said, looking out of the window. Then they hit bad traffic and the car came to a standstill.

By now Bettina had inadvertently laid her hand on Parvez's shoulder. She said, 'Your father, who is a good man, is very worried about you. You know he loves you more than his own life.'

'You say he loves me,' the boy said.

'Yes!' said Bettina.

'Then why is he letting a woman like you touch him like that?'

If Bettina looked at the boy in anger, he looked back at her with twice as much cold fury.

She said, 'What kind of woman am I that deserves to be spoken to like that?'

'You know,' he said. 'Now let me out.'

'Never,' Parvez replied.

'Don't worry, I'm getting out,' Bettina said.

'No, don't!' said Parvez. But even as the car moved she opened the door, threw herself out and ran away across the road. Parvez shouted after her several times, but she had gone.

Parvez took Ali back to the house, saying nothing more to him. Ali went straight to his room. Parvez was unable to read the paper, watch television or even sit down. He kept pouring himself drinks.

At last he went upstairs and paced up and down outside Ali's room. When, finally, he opened the door, Ali was praying. The boy didn't even glance his way.

Parvez kicked him over. Then he dragged the boy up by his shirt and hit him. The boy fell back. Parvez hit him again. The boy's face was bloody. Parvez was panting. He knew that the boy was unreachable, but he struck him nonetheless. The boy neither covered himself nor retaliated; there was no fear in his eyes. He only said, through his split lip: 'So who's the fanatic now?'

Jhumpa Lahiri

Born in 1967 in London, Jhumpa Lahiri grew up in Rhode Island, but during her youth often vacationed in Calcutta, the birthplace of her parents. Lahiri received her formal education at Barnard College and at Boston University, where she obtained a master's degree in creative writing and a doctorate in Renaissance studies. She then went on to a fellowship at the Provincetown Fine Arts Work Center, at which point—with three stories appearing in *The New Yorker* in 1998, and others in *The Louisville Review* ("When Mr. Pirzada Came to Dine"), *Story Quarterly, Epoch, Salamander,* and elsewhere—her writing career took off. A collection of stories, *Interpreter of Maladies,* appeared in 1999, and Lahiri was selected by *The New Yorker* that year as one of the "20 best young fiction writers in America."

Many of her stories, she told an interviewer for *PIF Magazine* in 1999, derive from "going to India and [from] observing people" both there and in the United States. Asked if different audiences react in different ways to her stories, she replied that the reactions are similar but the concerns are not the same. An Indian audience asks "more questions that are based on issues of identity and representation," she observed, adding tangentially that non-Indian readers tend to connect, at least initially, more with issues of morality and relationship: the odysseys of youth and the like. "When Mr. Pirzada Came to Dine" looks back to the narrator's youth, and to the character of life in the home of an Asian immigrant family in the United States. Outside the home swirl the politics of foreignness—education, cultural difference, war. Inside, a different set of rituals evolves, one measured in confection and hospitality. The narrator negotiates her way between the two, engaging with the world that is becoming hers, while those who remain alienated from it, those whose sense of order is fundamentally rooted elsewhere, watch it from afar, distanced by uncertainty and a flickering television screen.

When Mr. Pirzada Came to Dine

In the autumn of 1971 a man used to come to our house, bearing confections in his pocket and hopes of ascertaining the life or death of his family. His name was Mr. Pirzada, and he came from Dacca, now the capital of Bangladesh, but then a part of Pakistan. That year Pakistan was engaged in civil war. The eastern frontier, where Dacca was located, was fighting for autonomy from the ruling regime in the west. In March, Dacca had been invaded, torched, and shelled by the Pakistani army. Teachers were dragged onto streets and shot, women dragged into barracks and raped. By the end of the summer, three hundred thousand people were said to have died. In Dacca Mr. Pirzada had a three-story home, a lectureship in botany at the university, a wife of twenty years, and seven daughters between the ages of six and sixteen whose names all began with the letter A. "Their mother's idea," he explained one day, producing from his wallet a black-and-white picture of seven girls at a picnic, their braids tied with ribbons, sitting cross-legged in a row, eating chicken curry off of banana leaves. "How am I to distinguish? Ayesha, Amira, Amina, Aziza, you see the difficulty."

Each week Mr. Pirzada wrote letters to his wife, and sent comic books to each of his seven daughters, but the postal system, along with most everything else in Dacca, had collapsed, and he had not heard word of them in over six months. Mr. Pirzada, meanwhile, was in America for the year, for he had been awarded a grant from the government of Pakistan to study the foliage of New England. In spring and summer he had gathered data in Vermont and Maine, and in autumn he moved to a university north of Boston, where we lived, to write a short book about his discoveries. The grant was a great honor, but when converted into dollars it was not generous. As a result, Mr. Pirzada lived in a room in a graduate dormitory, and did not own a proper stove or a television set of his own. And so he came to our house to eat dinner and watch the evening news.

At first I knew nothing of the reason for his visits. I was ten years old, and was not surprised that my parents, who were from India, and had a number of Indian acquaintances at the university, should ask Mr. Pirzada to share our meals. It was a small campus, with narrow brick walkways and white pillared buildings, located on the fringes of what seemed to be an even smaller town. The supermarket did not carry mustard oil, doctors did not make house calls, neighbors never dropped by without an invitation, and of these things, every so often, my parents complained. In search of compatriots, they used to trail their fingers, at the start of each new semester, through the columns of the university directory, circling surnames familiar to their part of the world. It was in this manner that they discovered Mr. Pirzada, and phoned him, and invited him to our home.

I have no memory of his first visit, or of his second or his third, but by the end of September I had grown so accustomed to Mr. Pirzada's presence in our living room that one evening, as I was dropping ice cubes into the water pitcher, I asked my mother to hand me a fourth glass from a cupboard still out of my reach. She was busy at the stove, presiding over a skillet of fried spinach with radishes, and could not hear me because of the drone of the exhaust fan and the fierce scrapes of her spatula. I turned to my father, who was leaning against the refrigerator, eating spiced cashews from a cupped fist.

"What is it, Lilia?"

"A glass for the Indian man."

"Mr. Pirzada won't be coming today. More importantly, Mr. Pirzada is no longer considered Indian," my father announced, brushing salt from the cashews out of his trim black beard. "Not since Partition. Our country was divided. 1947."

When I said I thought that was the date of India's independence from Britain, my father said, "That too. One moment we were free and then we were sliced up," he explained, drawing an X with his finger on the countertop, "like a pie. Hindus here, Muslims there. Dacca no longer belongs to us." He told me that during Partition Hindus and Muslims had set fire to each other's homes. For many, the idea of eating in the other's company was still unthinkable.

It made no sense to me. Mr. Pirzada and my parents spoke the same language, laughed at the same jokes, looked more or less the same. They ate pickled mangoes with their meals, ate rice every night for supper with their hands. Like my parents, Mr. Pirzada took off his shoes before entering a room, chewed fennel seeds after meals as a digestive, drank no alcohol, for dessert dipped austere biscuits into successive cups of tea. Nevertheless my father insisted that I understand the difference, and he led me to a map of the world taped to the wall over his desk. He seemed concerned that Mr. Pirzada might take offense if I accidentally referred to him as an Indian, though I could not really imagine Mr. Pirzada being offended by much of anything. "Mr. Pirzada is Bengali, but he is a Muslim," my father informed me. "Therefore he lives in East Pakistan, not India." His finger trailed across the Atlantic, through Europe, the Mediterranean, the Middle East, and finally to the sprawling orange diamond that my mother once told me resembled a woman wearing a sari with her left arm extended. Various cities had been circled with lines drawn between them to indicate my parents' travels, and the place of their birth, Calcutta, was signified by a small silver star. I had been there only once and had no memory of the trip. "As you see, Lilia, it is a different country, a different color," my father said. Pakistan was yellow, not orange. I noticed that there were two distinct parts to it, one much larger than the other, separated by an expanse of Indian territory; it was as if California and Connecticut constituted a nation apart from the U.S.

My father rapped his knuckles on top of my head. "You are, of course, aware of the current situation? Aware of East Pakistan's fight for sovereignty?"

I nodded, unaware of the situation.

We returned to the kitchen, where my mother was draining a pot of boiled rice into a colander. My father opened up the can on the counter and eyed me sharply over the frames of his glasses as he ate some more cashews. "What exactly do they teach you at school? Do you study history? Geography?"

"Lilia has plenty to learn at school," my mother said. "We live here now, she was born here." She seemed genuinely proud of the fact, as if it were a reflection of my character. In her estimation, I knew, I was assured a safe life, an easy life, a fine education, every opportunity. I would never have to eat rationed food, or obey curfews, or watch riots from my rooftop, or hide neighbors in water tanks to prevent them from being shot, as she and my father had. "Imagine having to place her in a decent school. Imagine her having to read during power failures by the light of kerosene lamps. Imagine the pressures, the tutors, the constant exams." She ran a hand through her hair, bobbed to a suitable length for her part-time job as a bank teller. "How can you possibly expect her to know about Partition? Put those nuts away."

"But what does she learn about the world?" My father rattled the cashew can in his hand. "What is she learning?"

We learned American history, of course, and American geography. That year, and every year, it seemed, we began by studying the Revolutionary War. We were taken in school buses on field trips to visit Plymouth Rock, and to walk the Freedom Trail, and to climb to the top of the Bunker Hill Monument. We made dioramas out of colored construction paper depicting George Washington crossing the choppy waters of the Delaware River, and we made puppets of King George wearing white tights and a black bow in his hair. During tests we were given blank maps of the thirteen colonies, and asked to fill in names, dates, capitals. I could do it with my eyes closed.

■ ■ ■

The next evening Mr. Pirzada arrived, as usual, at six o'clock. Though they were no longer strangers, upon first greeting each other, he and my father maintained the habit of shaking hands.

"Come in, sir. Lilia, Mr. Pirzada's coat, please."

He stepped into the foyer, impeccably suited and scarved, with a silk tie knotted at his collar. Each evening he appeared in ensembles of plums, olives, and chocolate browns. He was a compact man, and though his feet were perpetually splayed, and his belly slightly wide, he nevertheless maintained an efficient posture, as if balancing in either hand two suitcases of equal weight. His ears were insulated by tufts of graying hair that seemed to block out the unpleasant traffic of life. He had thickly lashed eyes shaded with a trace of camphor, a generous mustache that turned up playfully at the ends, and a mole shaped like a flattened raisin in the very center of his left cheek. On his head he wore a black fez made from the wool of Persian lambs, secured by bobby pins, without which I was never to see him. Though my father always offered to fetch him in our car, Mr. Pirzada preferred to walk from his dormitory to our neighborhood, a distance of about twenty minutes on foot, studying trees and shrubs on his way, and when he entered our house his knuckles were pink with the effects of crisp autumn air.

"Another refugee, I am afraid, on Indian territory."

"They are estimating nine million at the last count," my father said.

Mr. Pirzada handed me his coat, for it was my job to hang it on the rack at the bottom of the stairs. It was made of finely checkered gray-and-blue wool, with a striped lining and horn buttons, and carried in its weave the faint smell of limes. There were no recognizable tags inside, only a hand-stitched label with the phrase "Z. Sayeed, Suitors" embroidered on it in cursive with glossy black thread. On certain days a birch or maple leaf was tucked into a pocket. He unlaced his shoes and lined them against the baseboard; a golden paste clung to the toes and heels, the result of walking through our damp, unraked lawn. Relieved of his trappings, he grazed my throat with his short, restless fingers, the way a person feels for solidity behind a wall before driving in a nail. Then he followed my father to the living room, where the television was tuned to the local news. As soon as they were seated my mother appeared from the kitchen with a plate of mincemeat kebabs with coriander chutney. Mr. Pirzada popped one into his mouth.

"One can only hope," he said, reaching for another, "that Dacca's refugees are as heartily fed. Which reminds me." He reached into his suit pocket and gave me a small plastic egg filled with cinnamon hearts. "For the lady of the house," he said with an almost imperceptible splay-footed bow.

"Really, Mr. Pirzada," my mother protested. "Night after night. You spoil her."

"I only spoil children who are incapable of spoiling."

It was an awkward moment for me, one which I awaited in part with dread, in part with delight. I was charmed by the presence of Mr. Pirzada's rotund elegance, and flattered by the faint theatricality of his attentions, yet unsettled by the superb ease of his gestures, which made me feel, for an instant, like a stranger in my own home. It had become our ritual, and for several weeks, before we grew more comfortable with one another, it was the only time he spoke to me directly. I had no response, offered no comment, betrayed no visible reaction to the steady stream of honey-filled lozenges, the raspberry truffles, the slender rolls of sour pastilles. I could not even thank him, for once, when I did, for an especially spectacular peppermint lollipop wrapped in a spray of purple cellophane, he had demanded, "What is this thank-you? The lady at the bank thanks me, the cashier at the shop thanks me, the librarian thanks me when I return an overdue book, the overseas operator thanks me as she tries to connect me to Dacca and fails. If I am buried in this country I will be thanked, no doubt, at my funeral."

It was inappropriate, in my opinion, to consume the candy Mr. Pirzada gave me in a casual manner. I coveted each evening's treasure as I would a jewel, or a coin from a buried kingdom, and I would place it in a small keepsake box made of carved sandalwood beside my bed, in which, long ago in India, my father's mother used to store the ground areca nuts she ate after her morning bath. It was my only memento of a grandmother I had never known, and until Mr. Pirzada came to our lives I could find nothing to put inside it. Every so often before brushing my teeth and laying out my clothes for school the next day, I opened the lid of the box and ate one of his treats.

That night, like every night, we did not eat at the dining table, because it did not provide an unobstructed view of the television set. Instead we huddled around the coffee table, without conversing, our plates perched on the edges of our knees. From the kitchen my mother brought forth the succession of dishes: lentils with fried onions, green beans with coconut, fish cooked with raisins in a yogurt sauce. I followed with the water glasses, and the plate of lemon wedges, and the chili peppers, purchased on monthly trips to Chinatown and stored by the pound in the freezer, which they liked to snap open and crush into their food.

Before eating Mr. Pirzada always did a curious thing. He took out a plain silver watch without a band, which he kept in his breast pocket, held it briefly to one of his tufted ears, and wound it with three swift flicks of his thumb and forefinger. Unlike the watch on his wrist, the pocket watch, he had explained to me, was set to the local time in Dacca, eleven hours ahead. For the duration of the meal the watch rested on his folded paper napkin on the coffee table. He never seemed to consult it.

Now that I had learned Mr. Pirzada was not an Indian, I began to study him with extra care, to try to figure out what made him different. I decided that the pocket watch was one of those things. When I saw it that night, as he wound it and arranged it on the coffee table, an uneasiness possessed me; life, I realized, was being lived in Dacca first. I imagined Mr. Pirzada's daughters rising from sleep, tying ribbons in their hair, anticipating breakfast, preparing for school. Our meals, our actions, were only a shadow of what had already happened there, a lagging ghost of where Mr. Pirzada really belonged.

At six-thirty, which was when the national news began, my father raised the volume and adjusted the antennas. Usually I occupied myself with a book, but that night my father insisted that I pay attention. On the screen I saw tanks rolling through dusty streets, and fallen buildings, and forests of unfamiliar trees into which East Pakistani refugees had fled, seeking safety over the Indian border. I saw boats with fan-shaped sails floating on wide coffee-colored rivers, a barricaded university, newspaper offices burnt to the ground. I turned to look at Mr. Pirzada; the images flashed in miniature across his eyes. As he watched he had an immovable expression on his face, composed but alert, as if someone were giving him directions to an unknown destination.

During the commercial my mother went to the kitchen to get more rice, and my father and Mr. Pirzada deplored the policies of a general named Yahyah Khan. They discussed intrigues I did not know, a catastrophe I could not comprehend. "See, children your age, what they do to survive," my father said as he served me another piece of fish. But I could no longer eat. I could only steal glances at Mr. Pirzada, sitting beside me in his olive green jacket, calmly creating a well in his rice to make room for a second helping of lentils. He was not my notion of a man burdened by such grave concerns. I wondered if the reason he was always so smartly dressed was in preparation to endure with dignity whatever news assailed him, perhaps even to attend a funeral at a moment's notice. I wondered, too, what would happen if suddenly his seven daughters were to appear on television, smiling and waving and blowing kisses to Mr. Pirzada from a balcony. I imagined how relieved he would be. But this never happened.

That night when I placed the plastic egg filled with cinnamon hearts in the box beside my bed, I did not feel the ceremonious satisfaction I normally did. I tried not to think about Mr. Pirzada, in his lime-scented overcoat, connected to the unruly, sweltering world we had viewed a few hours ago in our bright, carpeted living room. And yet for several moments that was all I could think about. My stomach tightened as I worried whether his wife and seven daughters were now members of the drifting, clamoring crowd that had flashed at intervals on the screen. In an effort to banish the image I looked around my room, at the yellow canopied bed with matching flounced curtains, at framed class pictures mounted on white and violet papered walls, at the penciled inscriptions by the closet door where my father recorded my height on each of my birthdays. But the more I tried to distract myself, the more I began to convince myself that Mr. Pirzada's family was in all likelihood dead. Eventually I took a square of white chocolate out of the box, and unwrapped it, and then I did something I had never done before. I put the chocolate in my mouth, letting it soften until the last possible moment, and then as I chewed it slowly, I prayed that Mr. Pirzada's family was safe and sound. I had never prayed for anything before, had never been taught or told to, but I decided, given the circumstances, that it was something I should do. That night when I went to the bathroom I only pretended to brush my teeth, for I feared that I would somehow rinse the prayer out as well. I wet the brush and rearranged the tube of paste to prevent my parents from asking any questions, and fell asleep with sugar on my tongue.

■ ■ ■

No one at school talked about the war followed so faithfully in my living room. We continued to study the American Revolution, and learned about the injustices of taxation without representation, and memorized passages from the Declaration of Independence. During recess the boys would divide in two groups, chasing each other wildly around the swings and seesaws, Redcoats against the colonies. In the classroom our teacher, Mrs. Kenyon, pointed frequently to a map that emerged like a movie screen from the top of the chalkboard, charting the route of the *Mayflower*, or showing us the location of the Liberty Bell. Each week two members of the class gave a report on a particular aspect of the Revolution, and so one day I was sent to the school library with my friend Dora to learn about the surrender at Yorktown. Mrs. Kenyon handed us a slip of paper with the names of three books to look up in the card catalogue. We found them right away, and sat down at a low round table to read and take notes. But I could not concentrate. I returned to the blond-wood shelves, to a section I had noticed labeled "Asia." I saw books about China, India, Indonesia, Korea. Eventually I found a book titled *Pakistan: A Land and Its People*. I sat on a footstool and opened the book. The laminated jacket crackled in my grip. I began turning the pages, filled with photos of rivers and rice fields and men in military uniforms. There was a chapter about Dacca, and I began to read about its rainfall, and its jute production. I was studying a population chart when Dora appeared in the aisle.

"What are you doing back here? Mrs. Kenyon's in the library. She came to check up on us."

I slammed the book shut, too loudly. Mrs. Kenyon emerged, the aroma of her perfume filling up the tiny aisle, and lifted the book by the tip of its spine as if it were a hair clinging to my sweater. She glanced at the cover, then at me.

"Is this book a part of your report, Lilia?"

"No, Mrs. Kenyon."

"Then I see no reason to consult it," she said, replacing it in the slim gap on the shelf. "Do you?"

■ ■ ■

As weeks passed it grew more and more rare to see any footage from Dacca on the news. The report came after the first set of commercials, sometimes the second. The press had been censored, removed, restricted, rerouted. Some days, many days, only a death toll was announced, prefaced by a reiteration of the general situation. More poets were executed, more villages set ablaze. In spite of it all, night after night, my parents and Mr. Pirzada enjoyed long, leisurely meals. After the television was shut off, and the dishes washed and dried, they joked, and told stories, and dipped biscuits in their tea. When they tired of discussing political matters they discussed, instead, the progress of Mr. Pirzada's book about the deciduous trees of New England, and my father's nomination for tenure, and the peculiar eating habits of my mother's American coworkers at the bank. Eventually I was sent upstairs to do my homework, but through the carpet I heard them as they drank more tea, and listened to cassettes of Kishore Kumar, and played Scrabble on the coffee table, laughing and arguing long into the night about the spellings of English words. I wanted to join them, wanted, above all, to console Mr. Pirzada somehow. But apart from eating a piece of candy for the sake of his family and praying for their safety, there was nothing I could do. They played Scrabble until the eleven o'clock news, and then, sometime around midnight, Mr. Pirzada walked back to his dormitory. For this reason I never saw him leave, but each night as I drifted off to sleep I would hear them, anticipating the birth of a nation on the other side of the world.

■ ■ ■

One day in October Mr. Pirzada asked upon arrival, "What are these large orange vegetables on people's doorsteps? A type of squash?"

"Pumpkins," my mother replied. "Lilia, remind me to pick one up at the supermarket."

"And the purpose? It indicates what?"

"You make a jack-o'-lantern," I said, grinning ferociously. "Like this. To scare people away."

"I see," Mr. Pirzada said, grinning back. "Very useful."

The next day my mother bought a ten-pound pumpkin, fat and round, and placed it on the dining table. Before supper, while my father and Mr. Pirzada were watching the local news, she told me to decorate it with markers, but I wanted to carve it properly like others I had noticed in the neighborhood.

"Yes, let's carve it," Mr. Pirzada agreed, and rose from the sofa. "Hang the news tonight." Asking no questions, he walked into the kitchen, opened a drawer, and returned, bearing a long serrated knife. He glanced at me for approval. "Shall I?"

I nodded. For the first time we all gathered around the dining table, my mother, my father, Mr. Pirzada, and I. While the television aired unattended we covered the tabletop with newspapers. Mr. Pirzada draped his jacket over the chair behind him, removed a pair of opal cuff links, and rolled up the starched sleeves of his shirt.

"First go around the top, like this," I instructed, demonstrating with my index finger.

He made an initial incision and drew the knife around. When he had come full circle he lifted the cap by the stem; it loosened effortlessly, and Mr. Pirzada leaned over the pumpkin for a moment to inspect and inhale its contents. My mother gave him a long metal spoon with which he gutted the interior until the last bits of string and seeds were gone. My father, meanwhile, separated the seeds from the pulp and set them out to dry on a cookie sheet, so that we could roast them later on. I drew two triangles against the ridged surface for the eyes, which Mr. Pirzada dutifully carved, and crescents for eyebrows, and another triangle for the nose. The mouth was all that remained, and the teeth posed a challenge. I hesitated.

"Smile or frown?" I asked.

"You choose," Mr. Pirzada said.

As a compromise I drew a kind of grimace, straight across, neither mournful nor friendly. Mr. Pirzada began carving, without the least bit of intimidation, as if he had been carving jack-o'-lanterns his whole life. He had nearly finished when the national news began. The reporter mentioned Dacca, and we all turned to listen: An Indian official announced that unless the world helped to relieve the burden of East Pakistani refugees, India would have to go to war against Pakistan. The reporter's face dripped with sweat as he relayed the information. He did not wear a tie or a jacket, dressed instead as if he himself were about to take part in the battle. He shielded his scorched face as he hollered things to the cameraman. The knife slipped from Mr. Pirzada's hand and made a gash dipping toward the base of the pumpkin.

"Please forgive me." He raised a hand to one side of his face, as if someone had slapped him there. "I am—it is terrible. I will buy another. We will try again."

"Not at all, not at all," my father said. He took the knife from Mr. Pirzada, and carved around the gash, evening it out, dispensing altogether with the teeth I had drawn. What resulted was a disproportionately large hole the size of a lemon, so that our jack-o'-lantern wore an expression of placid astonishment, the eyebrows no longer fierce, floating in frozen surprise above a vacant, geometric gaze.

■ ■ ■

For Halloween I was a witch. Dora, my trick-or-treating partner, was a witch too. We wore black capes fashioned from dyed pillowcases and conical hats with wide cardboard brims. We shaded our faces green with a broken eye shadow that belonged to Dora's mother, and my mother gave us two burlap sacks that had once contained basmati rice, for collecting candy. That year our parents decided that we were old enough to roam the neighborhood unattended. Our plan was to walk from my house to Dora's, from where I was to call to say I had arrived safely, and then Dora's mother would drive me home. My father equipped us with flashlights, and I had to wear my watch and synchronize it with his. We were to return no later than nine o'clock.

When Mr. Pirzada arrived that evening he presented me with a box of chocolate-covered mints.

"In here," I told him, and opened up the burlap sack. "Trick or treat!"

"I understand that you don't really need my contribution this evening," he said, depositing the box. He gazed at my green face, and the hat secured by a string under my chin. Gingerly he lifted the hem of the cape, under which I was wearing a sweater and a zipped fleece jacket. "Will you be warm enough?"

I nodded, causing the hat to tip to one side.

He set it right. "Perhaps it is best to stand still."

The bottom of our staircase was lined with baskets of miniature candy, and when Mr. Pirzada removed his shoes he did not place them there as he normally did, but inside the closet instead. He began to unbutton his coat, and I waited to take it from him, but Dora called me from the bathroom to say that she needed my help drawing a mole on her chin. When we were finally ready my mother took a picture of us in front of the fireplace, and then I opened the front door to leave. Mr. Pirzada and my father, who had not gone into the living room yet, hovered in the foyer. Outside it was already dark. The air smelled of wet leaves, and our carved jack-o'-lantern flickered impressively against the shrubbery by the door. In the distance came the sounds of scampering feet, and the howls of the older boys who wore no costume at all other than a rubber mask, and the rustling apparel of the youngest children, some so young that they were carried from door to door in the arms of their parents.

"Don't go into any of the houses you don't know," my father warned.

Mr. Pirzada knit his brows together. "Is there any danger?"

"No, no," my mother assured him. "All the children will be out. It's a tradition."

"Perhaps I should accompany them?" Mr. Pirzada suggested. He looked suddenly tired and small, standing there in his splayed, stockinged feet, and his eyes contained a panic I had never seen before. In spite of the cold I began to sweat inside my pillowcase.

"Really, Mr. Pirzada," my mother said, "Lilia will be perfectly safe with her friend."

"But if it rains? If they lose their way?"

"Don't worry," I said. It was the first time I had uttered those words to Mr. Pirzada, two simple words I had tried but failed to tell him for weeks, had said only in my prayers. It shamed me now that I had said them for my own sake.

He placed one of his stocky fingers on my cheek, then pressed it to the back of his own hand, leaving a faint green smear. "If the lady insists," he conceded, and offered a small bow.

We left, stumbling slightly in our black pointy thrift-store shoes, and when we turned at the end of the driveway to wave good-bye, Mr. Pirzada was standing in the frame of the doorway, a short figure between my parents, waving back.

"Why did that man want to come with us?" Dora asked.

"His daughters are missing." As soon as I said it, I wished I had not. I felt that my saying it made it true, that Mr. Pirzada's daughters really were missing, and that he would never see them again.

"You mean they were kidnapped?" Dora continued. "From a park or something?"

"I didn't mean they were missing. I meant, he misses them. They live in a different country, and he hasn't seen them in a while, that's all."

We went from house to house, walking along pathways and pressing doorbells. Some people had switched off all their lights for effect, or strung rubber bats in their windows. At the McIntyres' a coffin was placed in front of the door, and Mr. McIntyre rose from it in silence, his face covered with chalk, and deposited a fistful of candy corns into our sacks. Several people told me that they had never seen an Indian witch before. Others performed the transaction without comment. As we paved our way with the parallel beams of our flashlights we saw eggs cracked in the middle of the road, and cars covered with shaving cream, and toilet paper garlanding the branches of trees. By the time we reached Dora's house our hands were chapped from carrying our bulging burlap bags, and our feet were sore and swollen. Her mother gave us bandages for our blisters and served us warm cider and caramel popcorn. She reminded me to call my parents to tell them I had arrived safely, and when I did I could hear the television in the background. My mother did not seem particularly relieved to hear from me. When I replaced the phone on the receiver it occurred to me that the television wasn't on at Dora's house at all. Her father was lying on the couch, reading a magazine, with a glass of wine on the coffee table, and there was saxophone music playing on the stereo.

After Dora and I had sorted through our plunder, and counted and sampled and traded until we were satisfied, her mother drove me back to my house. I thanked her for the ride, and she waited in the driveway until I made it to the door. In the glare of her headlights I saw that our pumpkin had been shattered, its thick shell strewn in chunks across the grass. I felt the sting of tears in my eyes, and a sudden pain in my throat, as if it had been stuffed with the sharp tiny pebbles that crunched with each step under my aching feet. I opened the door, expecting the three of them to be standing in the foyer, waiting to receive me, and to grieve for our ruined pumpkin, but there was no one. In the living room Mr. Pirzada, my father, and mother were sitting side by side on the sofa. The television was turned off, and Mr. Pirzada had his head in his hands.

What they heard that evening, and for many evenings after that, was that India and Pakistan were drawing closer and closer to war. Troops from both sides lined the border, and Dacca was insisting on nothing short of independence. The war was to be waged on East Pakistani soil. The United States was siding with West Pakistan, the Soviet Union with India and what was soon to be Bangladesh. War was declared officially on December 4, and twelve days later, the Pakistani army, weakened by having to fight three thousand miles from their source of supplies, surrendered in Dacca. All of these facts I know only now, for they are available to me in any history book, in any library. But then it remained, for the most part, a remote mystery with haphazard clues. What I remember during those twelve days of the war was that my father no longer asked me to watch the news with them, and that Mr. Pirzada stopped bringing me candy, and that my mother refused to serve anything other than boiled eggs with rice for dinner. I remember some nights helping my mother spread a sheet and blankets on the couch so that Mr. Pirzada could sleep there, and high-pitched voices hollering in the middle of the night when my parents called our relatives in Calcutta to learn more details about the situation. Most of all I remember the three of them operating during that time as if they were a single person, sharing a single meal, a single body, a single silence, and a single fear.

■ ■ ■

In January, Mr. Pirzada flew back to his three-story home in Dacca, to discover what was left of it. We did not see much of him in those final weeks of the year; he was busy finishing his manuscript, and we went to Philadelphia to spend Christmas with friends of my parents. Just as

I have no memory of his first visit, I have no memory of his last. My father drove him to the airport one afternoon while I was at school. For a long time we did not hear from him. Our evenings went on as usual, with dinners in front of the news. The only difference was that Mr. Pirzada and his extra watch were not there to accompany us. According to reports Dacca was repairing itself slowly, with a newly formed parliamentary government. The new leader, Sheikh Mujib Rahman, recently released from prison, asked countries for building materials to replace more than one million houses that had been destroyed in the war. Countless refugees returned from India, greeted, we learned, by unemployment and the threat of famine. Every now and then I studied the map above my father's desk and pictured Mr. Pirzada on that small patch of yellow, perspiring heavily, I imagined, in one of his suits, searching for his family. Of course, the map was outdated by then.

Finally, several months later, we received a card from Mr. Pirzada commemorating the Muslim New Year, along with a short letter. He was reunited, he wrote, with his wife and children. All were well, having survived the events of the past year at an estate belonging to his wife's grandparents in the mountains of Shillong. His seven daughters were a bit taller, he wrote, but otherwise they were the same, and he still could not keep their names in order. At the end of the letter he thanked us for our hospitality, adding that although he now understood the meaning of the words "thank you" they still were not adequate to express his gratitude. To celebrate the good news my mother prepared a special dinner that evening, and when we sat down to eat at the coffee table we toasted our water glasses, but I did not feel like celebrating. Though I had not seen him for months, it was only then that I felt Mr. Pirzada's absence. It was only then, raising my water glass in his name, that I knew what it meant to miss someone who was so many miles and hours away, just as he had missed his wife and daughters for so many months. He had no reason to return to us, and my parents predicted, correctly, that we would never see him again. Since January, each night before bed, I had continued to eat, for the sake of Mr. Pirzada's family, a piece of candy I had saved from Halloween. That night there was no need to. Eventually, I threw them away.

D.H. LAWRENCE

The son of a coal miner in Nottingham, David Herbert Lawrence (1885–1930) was brought up in a household very similar to that depicted in his novel *Sons and Lovers* (1913), in which the father's coarse sensuality struggled against the mother's finer sensibilities. With his mother's encouragement, Lawrence developed his literary abilities, and after a spell as a teacher in Croydon, near London, he made writing his full-time profession, producing a great many essays, poems, and short stories. His work, particularly his novels, often aroused controversy because of his frank treatment of sexual relations; two of his novels, *The Rainbow* (1915) and *Lady Chatterley's Lover* (1928), were declared obscene and banned in England for many years. Disgusted by the response of the press and public, Lawrence left England with his German wife in 1919, and travelled in various parts of the world for a number of years, chiefly in the United States and Mexico.

In much of his writing, Lawrence examines the tension between men and women as social creatures, hemmed in by conventions and "responsibilities," and as feeling creatures, part of a larger universe of instinctive response. "The Horse Dealer's Daughter" dramatizes this conflict through the relationship of Dr. Fergusson with Mabel Pervin. Initially both are creatures of habit and convention, cut off from true feeling and turned in upon themselves. Once relieved of their social roles, they respond to each other with almost brutal urgency, in a manner reflecting Lawrence's antiromantic ideas about love and sexual awareness. "Accept the sexual, physical being of yourself," he wrote, "and of every other creature. Don't be afraid of the physical functions. . . . Conquer the fear of sex, and restore the natural flow" ("The State of Funk").

The Horse Dealer's Daughter

"Well, Mabel, and what are you going to do with yourself?" asked Joe, with foolish flippancy. He felt quite safe himself. Without listening for an answer, he turned aside, worked a grain of tobacco to the tip of his tongue, and spat it out. He did not care about anything, since he felt safe himself.

The three brothers and the sister sat round the desolate breakfast table, attempting some sort of desultory consultation. The morning's post had given the final tap to the family fortune, and all was over. The dreary dining-room itself, with its heavy mahogany furniture, looked as if it were waiting to be done away with.

But the consultation amounted to nothing. There was a strange air of ineffectuality about the three men, as they sprawled at table, smoking and reflecting vaguely on their own condition. The girl was alone, a rather short, sullen-looking young woman of twenty-seven. She did not share the same life as her brothers. She would have been good-looking, save for the impressive fixity of her face, "bulldog," as her brothers called it.

There was a confused tramping of horses' feet outside. The three men all sprawled round in their chairs to watch. Beyond the dark holly bushes that separated the strip of lawn from the high-road, they could see a cavalcade of shire horses swinging out of their own yard, being taken for exercise. This was the last time. These were the last horses that would go through their hands. The young men watched with critical, callous look. They were all frightened at the collapse of their lives, and the sense of disaster in which they were involved left them no inner freedom.

Yet they were three fine, well-set fellows enough. Joe, the eldest, was a man of thirty-three, broad and handsome in a hot, flushed way. His face was red, he twisted his black moustache over a thick finger, his eyes were shallow and restless. He had a sensual way of uncovering his teeth when he laughed, and his bearing was stupid. Now he watched the horses with a glazed look of helplessness in his eyes, a certain stupor of downfall.

The great draught-horses swung past. They were tied head to tail, four of them, and they heaved along to where a lane branched off from the high-road, planting their great hoofs floutingly in the fine black mud, swinging their great rounded haunches sumptuously, and trotting a few sudden steps as they were led into the lane, round the corner. Every movement showed a massive, slumbrous strength, and a stupidity which held them in subjection. The groom at the head looked back, jerking the leading rope. And the cavalcade moved out of sight up the lane, the tail of the last horse, bobbed up tight and stiff, held out taut from the swinging great haunches as they rocked behind the hedges in a motion-like sleep.

Joe watched with glazed hopeless eyes. The horses were almost like his own body to him. He felt he was done for now. Luckily he was engaged to a woman as old as himself, and therefore her father, who was steward of a neighbouring estate, would provide him with a job. He would marry and go into harness. His life was over, he would be a subject animal now.

He turned uneasily aside, the retreating steps of the horses echoing in his ears. Then, with foolish restlessness, he reached for the scraps of bacon-rind from the plates, and making a faint whistling sound, flung them to the terrier that lay against the fender. He watched the dog swallow them, and waited till the creature looked into his eyes. Then a faint grin came on his face, and in a high, foolish voice he said:

"You won't get much more bacon, shall you, you little b——?"

The dog faintly and dismally wagged its tail, then lowered its haunches, circled round, and lay down again.

There was another helpless silence at the table. Joe sprawled uneasily in his seat, not willing to go till the family conclave was dissolved. Fred Henry, the second brother, was erect, clean-limbed, alert. He had watched the passing of the horses with more *sang-froid*. If he was an animal, like Joe, he was an animal which controls, not one which is controlled. He was master of any horse, and he carried himself with a well-tempered air of mastery. But he was not master of the situations of life. He pushed his coarse brown moustache upwards, off his lip, and glanced irritably at his sister, who sat impassive and inscrutable.

"You'll go and stop with Lucy for a bit, shan't you?" he asked. The girl did not answer.

"I don't see what else you can do," persisted Fred Henry.

"Go as a skivvy," Joe interpolated laconically.

The girl did not move a muscle.

"If I was her, I should go in for training for a nurse," said Malcolm, the youngest of them all. He was the baby of the family, a young man of twenty-two, with a fresh, jaunty *museau*.

But Mabel did not take any notice of him. They had talked at her and round her for so many years, that she hardly heard them at all.

The marble clock on the mantelpiece softly chimed the half-hour, the dog rose uneasily from the hearthrug and looked at the party at the breakfast table. But still they sat on in ineffectual conclave.

"Oh, all right," said Joe suddenly, apropos of nothing. "I'll get a move on."

He pushed back his chair, straddled his knees with a downward jerk, to get them free, in horsey fashion, and went to the fire. Still he did not go out of the room; he was curious to know what the others would do or say. He began to charge his pipe, looking down at the dog and saying in a high, affected voice:

"Going wi' me? Going wi' me are ter? Tha'rt goin' further than tha counts on just now, dost hear?"

The dog faintly wagged its tail, the man stuck out his jaw and covered his pipe with his hands, and puffed intently, losing himself in the tobacco, looking down all the while at the dog with an absent brown eye. The dog looked up at him in mournful distrust. Joe stood with his knees stuck out, in real horsey fashion.

skivvy = cleaning woman.
museau = snout, face.
are ter = are you.

"Have you had a letter from Lucy?" Fred Henry asked of his sister.

"Last week," came the neutral reply.

"And what does she say?"

There was no answer.

"Does she *ask* you to go and stop there?" persisted Fred Henry.

"She says I can if I like."

"Well, then, you'd better. Tell her you'll come on Monday."

This was received in silence.

"That's what you'll do then, is it?" said Fred Henry, in some exasperation.

But she made no answer. There was a silence of futility and irritation in the room. Malcolm grinned fatuously.

"You'll have to make up your mind between now and next Wednesday," said Joe loudly, "or else find yourself lodgings on the kerbstone."

The face of the young woman darkened, but she sat on immutable.

"Here's Jack Fergusson!" exclaimed Malcolm, who was looking aimlessly out of the window.

"Where?" exclaimed Joe, loudly.

"Just gone past."

"Coming in?"

Malcolm craned his neck to see the gate.

"Yes," he said.

There was a silence. Mabel sat on like one condemned, at the head of the table. Then a whistle was heard from the kitchen. The dog got up and barked sharply. Joe opened the door and shouted:

"Come on."

After a moment a young man entered. He was muffled up in overcoat and a purple woollen scarf, and his tweed cap, which he did not remove, was pulled down on his head. He was of medium height, his face was rather long and pale, his eyes looked tired.

"Hello, Jack! Well, Jack!" exclaimed Malcolm and Joe. Fred Henry merely said, "Jack."

"What's doing?" asked the newcomer, evidently addressing Fred Henry.

"Same. We've got to be out by Wednesday. Got a cold?"

"I have—got it bad, too."

"Why don't you stop in?"

"*Me* stop in? When I can't stand on my legs, perhaps I shall have a chance." The young man spoke huskily. He had a slight Scotch accent.

"It's a knock-out, isn't it," said Joe, boisterously, "if a doctor goes round croaking with a cold. Looks bad for the patients, doesn't it?"

The young doctor looked at him slowly.

"Anything the matter with *you*, then?" he asked sarcastically.

"Not as I know of. Damn your eyes, I hope not. Why?"

"I thought you were very concerned about the patients, wondered if you might be one yourself."

"Damn it, no, I've never been patient to no flaming doctor, and hope I never shall be," returned Joe.

At this point Mabel rose from the table, and they all seemed to become aware of her existence. She began putting the dishes together. The young doctor looked at her, but did not address her. He had not greeted her. She went out of the room with the tray, her face impassive and unchanged.

"When are you off then, all of you?" asked the doctor.

"I'm catching the eleven-forty," replied Malcolm. "Are you goin' down wi' th' trap, Joe?"

"Yes, I've told you I'm going down wi' th' trap, haven't I?"

"We'd better be getting her in then. So long, Jack, if I don't see you before I go," said Malcolm, shaking hands.

He went out, followed by Joe, who seemed to have his tail between his legs.

"Well, this is the devil's own," exclaimed the doctor, when he was left alone with Fred Henry. "Going before Wednesday, are you?"

"That's the orders," replied the other.

"Where, to Northampton?"

"That's it."

"The devil!" exclaimed Fergusson, with quiet chagrin.

And there was silence between the two.

"All settled up, are you?" asked Fergusson.

"About."

There was another pause.

"Well, I shall miss yer, Freddy, boy," said the young doctor.

"And I shall miss thee, Jack," returned the other.

"Miss you like hell," mused the doctor.

Fred Henry turned aside. There was nothing to say. Mabel came in again, to finish clearing the table.

"What are *you* going to do, then, Miss Pervin?" asked Fergusson. "Going to your sister's, are you?"

Mabel looked at him with her steady, dangerous eyes, that always made him uncomfortable, unsettling his superficial ease.

"No," she said.

"Well, what in the name of fortune *are* you going to do? Say what you mean to do," cried Fred Henry, with futile intensity.

But she only averted her head, and continued her work. She folded the white table-cloth, and put on the chenille cloth.

"The sulkiest bitch that ever trod!" muttered her brother.

But she finished her task with perfectly impassive face, the young doctor watching her interestedly all the while. Then she went out.

Fred Henry stared after her, clenching his lips, his blue eyes fixing in sharp antagonism, as he made a grimace of sour exasperation.

"You could bray her into bits, and that's all you'd get out of her," he said, in a small, narrowed tone.

The doctor smiled faintly.

"What's she *going* to do, then?" he asked.

"Strike me if *I* know!" returned the other.

There was a pause. Then the doctor stirred.

"I'll be seeing you to-night, shall I?" he said to his friend.

"Ay—where's it to be? Are we going over to Jessdale?"

"I don't know. I've got such a cold on me. I'll come round to the 'Moon and Stars,' anyway."

"Let Lizzie and May miss their night for once, eh?"

"That's it—if I feel as I do now."

"All's one—"

The two young men went through the passage and down to the back door together. The house was large, but it was servantless now, and desolate. At the back was a small bricked house-yard, and beyond that a big square, gravelled fine and red, and having stables on two sides. Sloping, dank, winter-dark fields stretched away on the open sides.

But the stables were empty. Joseph Pervin, the father of the family, had been a man of no education, who had become a fairly large horse dealer. The stables had been full of horses, there was a great turmoil and come-and-go of horses and of dealers and grooms. Then the kitchen was full of servants. But of late things had declined. The old man had married a second time, to retrieve his fortunes. Now he was dead and everything was gone to the dogs, there was nothing but debt and threatening.

For months, Mabel had been servantless in the big house, keeping the home together in penury for her ineffectual brothers. She had kept house for ten years. But previously it was with unstinted means. Then, however brutal and coarse everything was, the sense of money had kept her proud, confident. The men might be foulmouthed, the women in the kitchen might have bad reputations, her brothers might have illegitimate children. But so long as there was money, the girl felt herself established, and brutally proud, reserved.

No company came to the house, save dealers and coarse men. Mabel had no associates of her own sex, after her sister went away. But she did not mind. She went regularly to church, she attended to her father.

And she lived in the memory of her mother, who had died when she was fourteen, and whom she had loved. She had loved her father, too, in a different way, depending upon him, and feeling secure in him, until at the age of fifty-four he married again. And then she had set hard against him. Now he had died and left them all hopelessly in debt.

She had suffered badly during the period of poverty. Nothing, however, could shake the curious sullen, animal pride that dominated each member of the family. Now, for Mabel, the end had come. Still she would not cast about her. She would follow her own way just the same. She would always hold the keys of her own situation. Mindless and persistent, she endured from day to day. Why should she think? Why should she answer anybody? It was enough that this was the end, and there was no way out. She need not pass any more darkly along the main street of the small town, avoiding every eye. She need not demean herself any more, going into the shops and buying the cheapest food. This was at an end. She thought of nobody, not even of herself. Mindless and persistent, she seemed in a sort of ecstasy to be coming nearer to her fulfilment, her own glorification, approaching her dead mother, who was glorified.

In the afternoon she took a little bag, with shears and sponge and a small scrubbing brush, and went out. It was a grey, wintry day, with saddened, dark green fields and an atmosphere blackened by the smoke of foundries not far off. She went quickly, darkly along the causeway, heeding nobody, through the town to the churchyard.

There she always felt secure, as if no one could see her, although as a matter of fact she was exposed to the stare of every one who passed along under the churchyard wall. Nevertheless, once under the shadow of the great looming church, among the graves, she felt immune from the world, reserved within the thick churchyard wall as in another country.

Carefully she clipped the grass from the grave, and arranged the pinky white, small chrysanthemums in the tin cross. When this was done, she took an empty jar from a neighbouring grave, brought water, and carefully, most scrupulously sponged the marble headstone and the coping-stone.

It gave her sincere satisfaction to do this. She felt in immediate contact with the world of her mother. She took minute pains, went through the park in a state bordering on pure happiness, as if in performing this task she came into a subtle, intimate connection with her mother. For the life she followed here in the world was far less real than the world of death she inherited from her mother.

The doctor's house was just by the church. Fergusson, being a mere hired assistant, was slave to the country-side. As he hurried now to attend to the outpatients in the surgery, glancing across the graveyard with his quick eye, he saw the girl at her task at the grave. She seemed so intent and remote, it was like looking into another world. Some mystical element was touched in him. He slowed down as he walked, watching her as if spell-bound.

She lifted her eyes, feeling him looking. Their eyes met. And each looked away again at once, each feeling, in some way, found out by the other. He lifted his cap and passed on down the road. There remained distinct in his consciousness, like a vision, the memory of her face, lifted from the tombstone in the churchyard, and looking at him with slow, large, portentous eyes. It *was* portentous, her face. It seemed to mesmerize him. There was a heavy power in her eyes which laid hold of his whole being, as if he had drunk some powerful drug. He had been feeling weak and done before. Now the life came back into him, he felt delivered from his own fretted, daily self.

He finished his duties at the surgery as quickly as might be, hastily filling up the bottles of the waiting people with cheap drugs. Then, in perpetual haste, he set off again to visit several cases in another part of his round, before teatime. At all times he preferred to walk if he could, but particularly when he was not well. He fancied the motion restored him.

The afternoon was falling. It was grey, deadened, and wintry, with a slow, moist, heavy coldness sinking in and deadening all the faculties. But why should he think or notice? He hastily climbed the hill and turned across the dark green fields, following the black cindertrack. In the distance, across a shallow dip in the country, the small town was clustered like smouldering ash, a tower, a spire, a heap of low, raw, extinct houses. And on the nearest fringe of the town, sloping into the dip, was Oldmeadow, the Pervins' house. He could see the stables and the outbuildings distinctly, as they lay towards him on the slope. Well, he would not go there many more times! Another resource would be lost to him, another place gone: the only company he cared for in the alien, ugly little town he was losing. Nothing but work, drudgery, constant hastening from dwelling to dwelling among the colliers and the iron-workers. It wore him out, but at the same time he had a craving for it. It was a stimulant to him to be in the homes of the working people, moving, as it were, through the innermost body of their life. His nerves were excited and gratified. He could come so near, into the very lives of the rough, inarticulate, powerfully emotional men and women. He grumbled, he said he hated the hellish hole. But as a matter of fact it excited him, the contact with the rough, strongly-feeling people was a stimulant applied direct to his nerves.

Below Oldmeadow, in the green, shallow, soddened hollow of fields, lay a square, deep pond. Roving across the landscape, the doctor's quick eye detected a figure in black passing through the gate of the field, down towards the pond. He looked again. It would be Mabel Pervin. His mind suddenly became alive and attentive.

Why was she going down there? He pulled up on the path on the slope above, and stood staring. He could just make sure of the small black figure moving in the hollow of the failing day. He seemed to see her in the midst of such obscurity, that he was like a clairvoyant, seeing rather with the mind's eye than with ordinary sight. Yet he could see her positively enough, whilst he kept his eye attentive. He felt, if he looked away from her, in the thick, ugly falling dusk, he would lose her altogether.

He followed her minutely as she moved, direct and intent, like something transmitted rather than stirring in voluntary activity, straight down the field towards the pond. There she stood on the bank for a moment. She never raised her head. Then she waded slowly into the water.

He stood motionless as the small black figure walked slowly and deliberately towards the centre of the pond, very slowly, gradually moving deeper into the motionless water, and still moving forward as the water got up to her breast. Then he could see her no more in the dusk of the dead afternoon.

"There!" he exclaimed. "Would you believe it?"

And he hastened straight down, running over the wet, soddened fields, pushing through the hedges, down into the depression of callous wintry obscurity. It took him several minutes to come to the pond. He stood on the bank, breathing heavily. He could see nothing. His eyes seemed to penetrate the dead water. Yes, perhaps that was the dark shadow of her black clothing beneath the surface of the water.

He slowly ventured into the pond. The bottom was deep, soft clay, he sank in, and the water clasped dead cold round his legs. As he stirred he could smell the cold, rotten clay that fouled up into the water. It was objectionable in his lungs. Still, repelled and yet not heeding, he moved deeper into the pond. The cold water rose over his thighs, over his loins, upon his abdomen. The lower part of his body was all sunk in the hideous cold element. And the bottom was so deeply soft and uncertain, he was afraid of pitching with his mouth underneath. He could not swim, and was afraid.

He crouched a little, spreading his hands under the water and moving them round, trying to feel for her. The dead cold pond swayed upon his chest. He moved again, a little deeper, and again, with his hands underneath, he felt all around under the water. And he touched her clothing. But it evaded his fingers. He made a desperate effort to grasp it.

And so doing he lost his balance and went under, horribly, suffocating in the foul earthy water, struggling madly for a few moments. At last, after what seemed an eternity, he got his footing, rose again into the air and looked around. He gasped, and knew he was in the world. Then he looked at the water. She had risen near him. He grasped her clothing, and drawing her nearer, turned to take his way to land again.

He went very slowly, carefully, absorbed in the slow progress. He rose higher, climbing out of the pond. The water was now only about his legs; he was thankful, full of relief to be out of the clutches of the pond. He lifted her and staggered on to the bank, out of the horror of wet, grey clay.

He laid her down on the bank. She was quite unconscious and running with water. He made the water come from her mouth, he worked to restore her. He did not have to work very long before he could feel the breathing begin again in her; she was breathing naturally. He worked a little longer. He could feel her live beneath his hands; she was coming back. He wiped her face, wrapped her in his overcoat, looked round into the dim, dark grey world, then lifted her and staggered down the bank and across the fields.

It seemed an unthinkably long way, and his burden so heavy he felt he would never get to the house. But at last he was in the stable-yard, and then in the house-yard. He opened the door and went into the house. In the kitchen he laid her down on the hearthrug, and called. The house was empty. But the fire was burning in the grate.

Then again he kneeled to attend to her. She was breathing regularly, her eyes were wide open and as if conscious, but there seemed something missing in her look. She was conscious in herself, but unconscious of her surroundings.

He ran upstairs, took blankets from a bed, and put them before the fire to warm. Then he removed her saturated, earthy-smelling clothing, rubbed her dry with a towel, and wrapped her naked in the blankets. Then he went into the dining-room, to look for spirits. There was a little whisky. He drank a gulp himself, and put some into her mouth.

The effect was instantaneous. She looked full into his face, as if she had been seeing him for some time, and yet had only just become conscious of him.

"Dr. Fergusson?" she said.

"What?" he answered.

He was divesting himself of his coat, intending to find some dry clothing upstairs. He could not bear the smell of the dead, clayey water, and he was mortally afraid for his own health.

"What did I do?" she asked.

"Walked into the pond," he replied. He had begun to shudder like one sick, and could hardly attend to her. Her eyes remained full on him, he seemed to be going dark in his mind, looking back at her helplessly. The shuddering became quieter in him, his life came back to him, dark and unknowing, but strong again.

"Was I out of my mind?" she asked, while her eyes were fixed on him all the time.

"Maybe, for the moment," he replied. He felt quiet, because his strength had come back. The strange fretful strain had left him.

"Am I out of my mind now?" she asked.

"Are you?" he reflected a moment. "No," he answered truthfully, "I don't see that you are." He turned his face aside. He was afraid now, because he felt dazed, and felt dimly that her power was stronger than his, in this issue. And she continued to look at him fixedly all the time. "Can you tell me where I shall find some dry things to put on?" he asked.

"Did you dive into the pond for me?" she asked.

"No," he answered. "I walked in. But I went in overhead as well."

There was silence for a moment. He hesitated. He very much wanted to go upstairs to get into dry clothing. But there was another desire in him. And she seemed to hold him. His will seemed to have gone to sleep, and left him, standing there slack before her. But he felt warm inside himself. He did not shudder at all, though his clothes were sodden on him.

"Why did you?" she asked.

"Because I didn't want you to do such a foolish thing," he said.

"It wasn't foolish," she said, still gazing at him as she lay on the floor, with a sofa cushion under her head. "It was the right thing to do. *I* knew best, then."

"I'll go and shift these wet things," he said. But still he had not the power to move out of her presence, until she sent him. It was as if she had the life of his body in her hands, and he could not extricate himself. Or perhaps he did not want to.

Suddenly she sat up. Then she became aware of her own immediate condition. She felt the blankets about her, she knew her own limbs. For a moment it seemed as if her reason were going. She looked round, with wild eye, as if seeking something. He stood still with fear. She saw her clothing lying scattered.

"Who undressed me?" she asked, her eyes resting full and inevitable on his face.

"I did," he replied, "to bring you round."

For some moments she sat and gazed at him awfully, her lips parted.

"Do you love me, then?" she asked.

He only stood and stared at her, fascinated. His soul seemed to melt. She shuffled forward on her knees, and put her arms round him, round his legs, as he stood there, pressing her breasts against his knees and thighs, clutching him with strange, convulsive certainty, pressing his thighs against her, drawing him to her face, her throat, as she looked up at him with flaring, humble eyes of transfiguration, triumphant in first possession.

"You love me," she murmured, in strange transport, yearning and triumphant and confident. "You love me. I know you love me, I know."

And she was passionately kissing his knees, through the wet clothing, passionately and indiscriminately kissing his knees, his legs, as if unaware of everything.

He looked down at the tangled wet hair, the wild, bare, animal shoulders. He was amazed, bewildered, and afraid. He had never thought of loving her. He had never wanted to love her. When he rescued her and restored her, he was a doctor, and she was a patient. He had had no single personal thought of her. Nay, this introduction of the personal element was very distasteful to him, a violation of his professional honour. It was horrible to have her there embracing his knees. It was horrible. He revolted from it, violently. And yet—and yet—he had not the power to break away.

She looked at him again, with the same supplication of powerful love, and that same transcendent, frightening light of triumph. In view of the delicate flame which seemed to come from her face like a light, he was powerless. And yet he had never intended to love her. He had never intended. And something stubborn in him could not give way.

"You love me," she repeated, in a murmur of deep, rhapsodic assurance. "You love me."

Her hands were drawing him, drawing him down to her. He was afraid, even a little horrified. For he had, really, no intention of loving her. Yet her hands were drawing him towards her. He put out his hand quickly to steady himself, and grasped her bare shoulder. A flame seemed to burn the hand that grasped her soft shoulder. He had no intention of loving her: his whole will was against his yielding. It was horrible. And yet wonderful was the touch of her shoulders, beautiful the shining of her face. Was she perhaps mad? He had a horror of yielding to her. Yet something in him ached also.

He had been staring away at the door, away from her. But his hand remained on her shoulder. She had gone suddenly very still. He looked down at her. Her eyes were now wide with fear, with doubt, the light was dying from her face, a shadow of terrible greyness was returning. He could not bear the touch of her eyes' question upon him, and the look of death behind the question.

With an inward groan he gave way, and let his heart yield towards her. A sudden gentle smile came on his face. And her eyes, which never left his face, slowly, slowly filled with tears. He watched the strange water rise in her eyes, like some slow fountain coming up. And his heart seemed to burn and melt away in his breast.

He could not bear to look at her any more. He dropped on his knees and caught her head with his arms and pressed her face against his throat. She was very still. His heart, which seemed to have broken, was burning with a kind of agony in his breast. And he felt her slow, hot tears wetting his throat. But he could not move.

He felt the hot tears wet his neck and the hollows of his neck, and he remained motionless, suspended through one of man's eternities. Only now it had become indispensable to him to have her face pressed close to him; he could never let her go again. He could never let her head go away from the close clutch of his arm. He wanted to remain like that for ever, with his heart hurting him in a pain that was also life to him. Without knowing, he was looking down on her damp, soft brown hair.

Then, as it were suddenly, he smelt the horrid stagnant smell of that water. And at the same moment she drew away from him and looked at him. Her eyes were wistful and unfathomable. He was afraid of them, and he fell to kissing her, not knowing what he was doing. He wanted her eyes not to have that terrible, wistful, unfathomable look.

When she turned her face to him again, a faint delicate flush was glowing, and there was again dawning that terrible shining of joy in her eyes, which really terrified him, and yet which he now wanted to see, because he feared the look of doubt still more.

"You love me?" she said, rather faltering.

"Yes." The word cost him a painful effort. Not because it wasn't true. But because it was too newly true, the *saying* seemed to tear open again his newly-torn heart. And he hardly wanted it to be true, even now.

She lifted her face to him, and he bent forward and kissed her on the mouth, gently, with the one kiss that is an eternal pledge. And as he kissed her his heart strained again in his breast. He never intended to love her. But now it was over. He had crossed over the gulf to her, and all that he had left behind had shrivelled and become void.

After the kiss, her eyes again slowly filled with tears. She sat still, away from him, with her face drooped aside, and her hands folded in her lap. The tears fell very slowly. There was complete silence. He too sat there motionless and silent on the hearthrug. The strange pain of his heart that was broken seemed to consume him. That he should love her? That this was love! That he should be ripped open in this way! Him, a doctor! How they would all jeer if they knew! It was agony to him to think they might know.

In the curious naked pain of the thought he looked again to her. She was sitting there drooped into a muse. He saw a tear fall, and his heart flared hot. He saw for the first time that one of her shoulders was quite uncovered, one arm bare, he could see one of her small breasts; dimly, because it had become almost dark in the room.

"Why are you crying?" he asked, in an altered voice.

She looked up at him, and behind her tears the consciousness of her situation for the first time brought a dark look of shame to her eyes.

"I'm not crying, really," she said, watching him, half frightened. He reached his hand, and softly closed it on her bare arm.

"I love you! I love you!" he said in a soft, low vibrating voice, unlike himself.

She shrank, and dropped her head. The soft, penetrating grip of his hand on her arm distressed her. She looked up at him.

"I want to go," she said. "I want to go and get you some dry things."

"Why?" he said. "I'm all right."

"But I want to go," she said. "And I want you to change your things."

He released her arm, and she wrapped herself in the blanket, looking at him rather frightened. And still she did not rise.

"Kiss me," she said wistfully.

He kissed her, but briefly, half in anger.

Then, after a second, she rose nervously, all mixed up in the blanket. He watched her in her confusion, as she tried to extricate herself and wrap herself up so that she could walk. He watched her relentlessly, as she knew. And as she went, the blanket trailing, and as he saw a glimpse of her feet and her white leg, he tried to remember her as she was when he had wrapped her in the blanket. But then he didn't want to remember, because she had been nothing to him then, and his nature revolted from remembering her as she was when she was nothing to him.

A tumbling, muffled noise from within the dark house startled him. Then he heard her voice:—"There are clothes." He rose and went to the foot of the stairs, and gathered up the garments she had thrown down. Then he came back to the fire, to rub himself down and dress. He grinned at his own appearance when he had finished.

The fire was sinking, so he put on coal. The house was now quite dark, save for the light of a street-lamp that shone in faintly from beyond the holly trees. He lit the gas with matches he found on the mantelpiece. Then he emptied the pockets of his own clothes, and threw all his wet things in a heap into the scullery. After which he gathered up her sodden clothes, gently, and put them in a separate heap on the coppertop in the scullery.

It was six o'clock on the clock. His own watch had stopped. He ought to go back to the surgery. He waited, and still she did not come down. So he went to the foot of the stairs and called:

"I shall have to go."

Almost immediately he heard her coming down. She had on her best dress of black voile, and her hair was tidy, but still damp. She looked at him—and in spite of herself, smiled.

"I don't like you in those clothes," she said.

"Do I look a sight?" he answered.

They were shy of one another.

"I'll make you some tea," she said.

"No, I must go."

"Must you?" And she looked at him again with the wide, strained doubtful eyes. And again, from the pain of his breast, he knew how he loved her. He went and bent to kiss her, gently, passionately, with his heart's painful kiss.

"And my hair smells so horrible," she murmured in distraction. "And I'm so awful, I'm so awful! Oh, no, I'm too awful." And she broke into bitter, heart-broken sobbing. "You can't want to love me, I'm horrible."

"Don't be silly, don't be silly," he said, trying to comfort her, kissing her, holding her in his arms. "I want you, I want to marry you, we're going to be married, quickly, quickly—tomorrow if I can."

But she only sobbed terribly, and cried:

"I feel awful. I feel awful. I feel I'm horrible to you."

"No, I want you, I want you," was all he answered, blindly, with that terrible intonation which frightened her almost more than her horror lest he should *not* want her.

Ursula K. Le Guin

Ursula K(roeber) Le Guin was born in 1929 and raised in Berkeley, California. Her father, Alfred Kroeber, was an anthropologist who passed on to his daughter an inexhaustible interest in the exploration of alternative cultures. Her mother, Theodora Kroeber, was the successful author of a study of the last Yahi Indian and his adoption by white society (*Ishi in Two Worlds,* 1961). In 1953 Ursula married the historian Charles Alfred Le Guin. Her first ambitions were academic: after receiving her bachelor's degree from Radcliffe in 1951 and obtaining a master's at Columbia in 1952, she taught languages at Mercer University and the University of Idaho. Strongly encouraged by her parents, she began her writing career in her teens with stories and poems, but it was not until she published in science fiction magazines that she began to win popular notice. Her first novels, *Rocannon's World* and *Planet of Exile,* both published in 1966, began a long series of works in which Le Guin explored new worlds born in her imagination, settings where her love of magic and fantasy could have free play. Her creativity and originality have brought her many awards, notably the Nebula and Hugo awards for *The Left Hand of Darkness* (1969) and *The Dispossessed: An Ambiguous Utopia* (1974). Le Guin has also won acclaim as a writer of books for children and young adults, and has published many essays and reviews in journals as different as *Yale Review* and *Playboy.*

Perhaps her most substantial work is the tetrology *Earthsea,* which begins with *A Wizard of Earthsea* (1968), and ends with *Tehanu: The Last Book of Earthsea* (1990). Here she develops a favourite theme, the need to recognize the universe holistically, as a system in tenuous equilibrium; her characters, whether human or alien, must learn to come to terms with the forces within them or externally opposing them. Good and evil play out in Le Guin's works as they do in more mainstream writing, but with a larger backdrop. "If you take seriously the science fiction premise," she has said, "you are furnished with an inexhaustible supply of absolutely beautiful and complex metaphors for our present situation, for who and where we are now."

"The First Contact with the Gorgonids," first published in 1991 and reprinted in Le Guin's collection *A Fisherman of the Inland Sea* (1994), takes an ironic look at "our present situation" by bringing space creatures into contact with a particularly obnoxious representative of our species, and reminding us that we may have more to fear from our own kind than from alien visitors.

The First Contact with the Gorgonids

Mrs. Jerry Debree, the heroine of Grong Crossing, liked to look pretty. It was important to Jerry in his business contacts, of course, and also it made her feel more confident and kind of happy to know that her cellophane was recent and her eyelashes really well glued on and that the highlighter blush was bringing out her cheekbones like the nice girl at the counter had said. But it was beginning to be hard to feel fresh and look pretty as this desert kept getting hotter and hotter and redder and redder until it looked, really, almost like what she had always thought the Bad Place would look like, only not so many people. In fact none.

"Could we have passed it, do you think?" she ventured at last, and received without surprise the exasperation she had safety-valved from him: "How the fuck could we have *passed* it when we haven't *passed* one fucking *thing* except those fucking *bushes* for ninety miles? *Christ* you're dumb."

Jerry's language was a pity. And sometimes it made it so hard to talk to him. She had had the least little tiny sort of feeling, woman's intuition maybe, that the men that had told him how to get to Grong Crossing were teasing him, having a little joke. He had been talking so loud in the hotel bar about how disappointed he had been with the Corroboree after flying all the way out from Adelaide to see it. He kept comparing it to the Indian dance they had seen at Taos. Actually he had been very bored and restless at Taos and they had had to leave in the middle so he could have a drink and she never had got to see the people with the masks come, but now he talked about how they really knew how to put on a native show in the U.S.A. He said a few scruffy abos jumping around weren't going to give tourists from the real world anything to write home about. The Aussies ought to visit Disney World and find out how to do the real thing, he said.

She agreed with that; she loved Disney World. It was the only thing in Florida, where they had to live now that Jerry was ACEO, that she liked much. One of the Australian men at the bar had seen Disneyland and agreed that it was amazing, or maybe he meant amusing; what he said was amizing. He seemed to be a nice man. Bruce, he said his name was, and his friend's name was Bruce too. "Common sort of name here," he said, only he said nime, but he meant name, she was quite sure. When Jerry went on complaining about the Corroboree, the first Bruce said, "Well, mite, you might go out to Grong Crossing, if you really want to see the real thing—right, Bruce?"

At first the other Bruce didn't seem to know what he meant, and that was when her woman's intuition woke up. But pretty soon both Bruces were talking away about this place, Grong Crossing, way out in "the bush," where they were certain to meet real abos really living in the desert. "Near Alice Springs," Jerry said knowledgeably, but it wasn't, they said; it was still farther west from here. They gave directions so precisely that it was clear they knew what they were talking about. "Few hours' drive, that's all," Bruce said, "but y'see most tourists want to keep on the beaten path. This is a bit more on the inside track."

"Bang-up shows," said Bruce. "Nightly Corroborees."

"Hotel any better than this dump?" Jerry asked, and they laughed. No hotel, they explained. "It's like a safari, see—tents under the stars. Never rines," said Bruce.

"Marvelous food, though," Bruce said. "Fresh kangaroo chops. Kangaroo hunts daily, see. Witchetty grubs along with the drinks before dinner. Roughing it in luxury, I'd call it; right, Bruce?"

"Absolutely," said Bruce.

"Friendly, are they, these abos?" Jerry asked.

"Oh, salt of the earth. Treat you like kings. Think white men are sort of gods, y'know," Bruce said. Jerry nodded.

So Jerry wrote down all the directions, and here they were driving and driving in the old station wagon that was all there was to rent in the small town they'd been at for the Corroboree, and by now you only knew the road was a road because it was perfectly straight forever. Jerry had been in a good humor at first. "This'll be something to shove up that bastard Thiel's ass," he said. His friend Thiel was always going to places like Tibet and having wonderful adventures and showing videos of himself with yaks. Jerry had bought a very expensive camcorder for this trip, and now he said, "Going to shoot me some abos. Show that fucking Thiel and his musk-oxes!" But as the morning went on and the road went on and the desert went on—did they call it "the bush" because there was one little thorny bush once a mile or so?—he got hotter and hotter and redder and redder, just like the desert. And she began to feel depressed and like her mascara was caking.

She was wondering if after another forty miles (four was her lucky number) she could say, "Maybe we ought to turn back?" for the first time, when he said, "There!"

There was something ahead, all right.

"There hasn't been any sign," she said, dubious. "They didn't say anything about a hill, did they?"

"Hell, that's no hill, that's a rock—what do they call it—some big fucking red rock—"

"Ayers Rock?" She had read the Welcome to Down Under flyer in the hotel in Adelaide while Jerry was at the plastics conference. "But that's in the middle of Australia, isn't it?"

"So where the fuck do you think we are? In the middle of Australia! What do you think this is, fucking East Germany?" He was shouting, and he speeded up. The terribly straight road shot them straight at the hill, or rock, or whatever it was. It *wasn't* Ayers Rock, she *knew* that, but there wasn't any use irritating Jerry, especially when he started shouting.

It was reddish, and shaped kind of like a huge VW bug, only lumpier; and there were certainly people all around it, and at first she was very glad to see them. Their utter isolation—they hadn't seen another car or farm or anything for two hours—had scared her. Then as they got closer she thought the people looked rather funny. Funnier than the ones at the Corroboree even. "I guess they're natives," she said aloud.

"What the shit did you expect, Frenchmen?" Jerry said, but he said it like a joke, and she laughed. But—"Oh! goodness!" she said involuntarily, getting her first clear sight of one of the natives.

"Big fellows, huh," he said. "Bushmen, they call 'em."

That didn't seem right, but she was still getting over the shock of seeing that tall, thin, black-and-white, weird person. It had been just standing looking at the car, only she couldn't see its eyes. Heavy brows and thick, hairy eyebrows hid them. Black, ropy hair hung over half its face and stuck out from behind its ears.

"Are they—are they painted?" she asked weakly.

"They always paint 'emselves up like that." His contempt for her ignorance was reassuring.

"They almost don't look human," she said, very softly so as not to hurt their feelings, if they spoke English, since Jerry had stopped the car and flung the doors open and was rummaging out the video camera.

"Hold this!"

She held it. Five or six of the tall black-and-white people had sort of turned their way, but they all seemed to be busy with something at the foot of the hill or rock or whatever it was. There were some things that might be tents. Nobody came to welcome them or anything, but she was actually just as glad they didn't.

"Hold this! Oh for Chrissake what did you do with the—All right, just give it here."

"Jerry, I wonder if we should ask them," she said.

"Ask who what?" he growled, having trouble with the cassette thing.

"The people here—if it's all right to photograph. Remember at Taos they said that when the—"

"For fuck sake you don't need fucking *permission* to photograph a bunch of *natives!* God! Did you ever *look* at the fucking *National Geographic?* Shit! *Permission!*"

It really wasn't any use when he started shouting. And the people didn't seem to be interested in what he was doing. Although it was quite hard to be sure what direction they were actually looking.

"Aren't you going to get out of the fucking *car?*"

"It's so hot," she said.

He didn't really mind it when she was afraid of getting too hot or sunburned or anything, because he liked being stronger and tougher. She probably could even have said that she was afraid of the natives, because he liked to be braver than her, too; but sometimes he got angry when she was afraid, like the time he made her eat that poisonous fish, or a fish that might or might not be poisonous, in Japan, because she said she was afraid to, and she threw up and embarrassed everybody. So she just sat in the car and kept the engine on and the air-conditioning on, although the window on her side was open.

Jerry had his camera up on his shoulder now and was panning the scene—the faraway hot red horizon, the queer rock-hill-thing with shiny places in it like glass, the black, burned-looking ground around it, and the people swarming all over. There were forty or fifty of them at least. It only dawned on her now that if they were wearing any clothes at all, she didn't know which was clothes and which was skin, because they were so strange-shaped, and painted or colored all in stripes and spots of white on black, not like zebras but more complicated, more like skeleton suits but not exactly. And they must be eight feet tall, but their arms were short, almost like kangaroos'. And their hair was like black ropes standing up all over their heads. It was embarrassing to look at people without clothes on, but you couldn't really see anything like *that*. In fact she couldn't tell, actually, if they were men or women.

They were all busy with their work or ceremony or whatever it was. Some of them were handling some things like big, thin, golden leaves, others were doing something with cords or wires. They didn't seem to be talking, but there was all the time in the air a soft, drumming, droning, rising and falling, deep sound, like cats purring or voices far away.

Jerry started walking towards them.

"Be careful," she said faintly. He paid no attention, of course.

They paid no attention to him either, as far as she could see, and he kept filming, swinging the camera around. When he got right up close to a couple of them, they turned towards him. She couldn't see their eyes at all, but what happened was their *hair* sort of stood up and bent towards Jerry—each thick, black rope about a foot long moving around and bending down exactly as if it were peering at him. At that, her own hair tried to stand up, and the blast of the air conditioner ran like ice down her sweaty arms. She got out of the car and called his name.

He kept filming.

She went towards him as fast as she could on the cindery, stony soil in her high-heeled sandals.

"Jerry, come back. I think—"

"Shut up!" he yelled so savagely that she stopped short for a moment. But she could see the hair better now, and she could see that it did have eyes, and mouths too, with little red tongues darting out.

"Jerry, come back," she said. "They're not natives, they're Space Aliens. That's their saucer." She knew from the *Sun* that there had been sightings down here in Australia.

"Shut the fuck up," he said. "Hey, big fella, give me a little action, huh? Don't just stand there. Dancee-dancee, OK?" His eye was glued to the camera.

"Jerry," she said, her voice sticking in her throat, as one of the Space Aliens pointed with its little weak-looking arm and hand at the car. Jerry shoved the camera right up close to its head, and at that it put its hand over the lens. That made Jerry mad, of course, and he yelled, "Get the fuck off that!" And he actually looked at the Space Alien, not through the camera but face to face. "Oh, gee," he said.

And his hand went to his hip. He always carried a gun, because it was an American's right to bear arms and there were so many drug addicts these days. He had smuggled it through the airport inspection the way he knew how. Nobody was going to disarm *him.*

She saw perfectly clearly what happened. The Space Alien opened its eyes.

There were eyes under the dark, shaggy brows; they had been kept closed till now. Now they were open and looked once straight at Jerry, and he turned to stone. He just stood there, one hand on the camera and one reaching for his gun, motionless.

Several more Space Aliens had gathered round. They all had their eyes shut, except for the ones at the ends of their hair. Those glittered and shone, and the little red tongues flickered in and out, and the humming, droning sound was much louder. Many of the hair-snakes writhed to look at her. Her knees buckled and her heart thudded in her throat, but she had to get to Jerry.

She passed right between two huge Space Aliens and reached him and patted him—"Jerry, wake up!" she said. He was just like stone, paralyzed. "Oh," she said, and tears ran down her face, "Oh, what should I do, what can I do?" She looked around in despair at the tall, thin, black-and-white faces looming above her, white teeth showing, eyes tight shut, hairs staring and stirring and murmuring. The murmur was soft, almost like music, not angry, soothing. She watched two tall Space Aliens pick up Jerry quite gently, as if he were a tiny little boy—a stiff one—and carry him carefully to the car.

They poked him into the back seat lengthwise, but he didn't fit. She ran to help. She let down the back seat so there was room for him in the back. The Space Aliens arranged him and tucked the video camera in beside him, then straightened up, their hairs looking down at her with little twinkly eyes. They hummed softly, and pointed with their childish arms back down the road.

"Yes," she said. "Thank you. Good-bye!"

They hummed.

She got in and closed the window and turned the car around there on a wide place in the road—and there *was* a signpost, Grong Crossing, although she didn't see any crossroad.

She drove back, carefully at first because she was shaky, then faster and faster because she should get Jerry to the doctor, of course, but also because she loved driving on long straight roads very fast, like this. Jerry never let her drive except in town.

The paralysis was total and permanent, which would have been terrible, except that she could afford full-time, round-the-clock, first-class care for poor Jerry, because of the really good deals she made with the TV people and then with the rights people for the video. First it was shown all over the world as "Space Aliens Land in Australian Outback," but then it became part of real science and history as "Grong Crossing, South Australia: The First Contact With the Gorgonids." In the voice-over they told how it was her, Annie Laurie Debree, who had been the first human to talk with our friends from Outer Space, even before they sent the ambassadors to Canberra and Reykjavik. There was only one good shot of her on the film, and Jerry had been sort of shaking, and her highlighter was kind of streaked, but that was all right. She was the heroine.

David Wong Louie

Born in Rockville Centre, New York, in 1954, David Wong Louie was educated at Vassar College and the University of Iowa. For a time he worked in advertising in New York, then became a teacher of creative writing at the University of California, Berkeley. From 1988 to 1992 he taught at Vassar College, then he moved to the University of California, Los Angeles. Louie's work has appeared in a number of periodicals and anthologies, and one of his short stories was selected for inclusion in the collection *The Best American Short Stories of 1989*. His first collection of stories, *Pangs of Love, and Other Stories* (1991), was well received and brought him several awards, including the *Los Angeles Times* Art Seidenbaum Award for first fiction. He has also received fellowships from the National Endowment for the Arts and the California Arts Council.

Louie's work examines the world of the Asian American, dramatizing the experience of alienation, newness, otherness that typifies the immigrant state. "The Movers," one of the stories gathered in *The Pangs of Love,* depicts the refashioning of identity that may accompany a change in external circumstance. The protagonist is almost literally refashioned by his move to a new place, losing his old self as he is abandoned by his girlfriend, and assuming some of the characteristics of the former owner of his new house. The first-person point of view helps us to experience the protagonist's confusion as he tries to reconcile memories of his former life with the new world that is pressing in on his consciousness.

The Movers

A week earlier we had left our old jobs, friends, and habits, and had driven across the state so we could start over fresh. Now we were in the place we had just rented, waiting for the Salvation Army to deliver our furniture. I was sitting on the edge of the kitchen sink fidgeting with the twin spigots, both running cold, when Suzy came right out and said we were out of love. She had this way of talking when she was mad: her lips scarcely moved, and she would point her hip at you and pat it as if it were a dog about to pounce. "We've made a mistake," she said. "We don't love each other anymore."

What could I do in that situation? Tell her she's wrong? That she's loved? I told her her news was no news to me, that her very thoughts had been incubating in my head, but I managed to keep them to myself. I wanted to believe that as long as we kept our mouths shut and let the negative thoughts that popped into our brains die there, there was hope for us. I told her this. She slapped her hip black and blue. Then, in menacing detail, she catalogued all that was wrong with me. She surveyed our common history, touching on incidents I thought were at worst benign, some even happy, that she now cited as reasons for her discontent.

Minutes into her testimony—by then I had already heard enough—someone knocked at the front door, and I gladly left the kitchen, thinking it was the furniture, anxious to catch my breath. A small kid was standing there. "Collect," he said.

"What?"

"Collect."

"They moved," I said, finally catching on.

"Collect," repeated the boy. We went on this way for a few more rounds. The kid was a tangle of woollies. Snot was frozen on his face. "Can't you see," I said, "you've never seen me before?" I heard Suzy coming to the door. "Send it back. We won't be needing the furniture anymore," she was saying before she saw I was talking to a kid. "Collect," he said the moment he laid eyes on her. "You're making a mistake," I told him.

"Ha!" Suzy said, brushing the boy aside as if he were a swinging gate. "*You're* the mistake." She ran out to the car. When she slipped on a patch of ice and almost fell, my heart stopped. But she quickly regained her balance, and so did I, and while the kid held back the storm door, I peppered her with insults, mostly names of barnyard animals, each leaving my lips with the ease of habit. All my screaming did little to mitigate my rage, so I cocked my middle finger and waved goodbye as she drove off in our car.

The kid stuck his mittened hand in my gut. "Collect," he said one last time. I reached into my pocket and brought out a crumpled dollar bill. I promised him more if he'd go. Then I apologized for the scene he had witnessed. "She's not always so difficult," I said as he left me.

■ ■ ■

I waited alone for the furniture. The manager at the store had promised delivery at three. By my watch it was already past four.

In the empty living room I sat on the floor near a window that faced the street. Cool air whistled through the cracked panes. Snow clouds darkened the sky. Beneath me the cold of the linoleum seeped through my pants; I felt as if I were sitting on a block of ice.

I got up and took down a set of bamboo blinds left by the previous tenants. As I unrolled the blinds, each slat clicked against the polished floor like beetles underfoot. I stretched out on this mat, hands dug deep in my pea jacket, and pretended I was dead, lying in a morgue in China. This succeeded where obscene gesture had failed. I felt transported, dead in a foreign land where the language of Suzy wasn't spoken. Who would understand our petty complaints there? Who could translate our squabbles and make them palatable to another tongue? No, I was a dead man, and all I had to do was shut my eyes and listen for the Salvation Army to come.

In time, I fell asleep and when I woke my legs were filled with sand. They were open in a V to the corner of the room reserved for Suzy's loom—there, she said, the northern exposure was perfect for selecting colors of thread. I scanned the adjacent wall where the fireplace stood. Above the mantelpiece there was a large opening of exposed lath, perhaps the work of a shotgun blast, over which Suzy's tapestry was to hang, hiding the blemishes of our domesticity.

Then I returned to the morgue. A heat vent nearby started to hiss, blowing damp, refrigerated air against my cheek. I needed to have the gas turned on, but I couldn't call because I didn't have a phone yet and I couldn't go because Suzy took the car. No phone, no heat, no car. No electricity at least for another day. I was out of love. And, even worse, I had no modern conveniences.

I had almost dozed off again when someone knocked at the front door. I got to my knees and peeked out the window but saw no truck on the street.

I heard the storm door pulled back, the lock turned in a single, sensuous click. Although a wall separated the vestibule from the living room, still I crawled quickly into Suzy's corner, where my hands came to rest on mounds of dirt that someone had swept up and left there.

"You're crazy, George," a girl whispered.

"Nobody's here," said her companion. "You heard me knock."

The door was shut and the lock secured.

She said, "I still think this is crazy."

My visitors ran upstairs, their footsteps echoing throughout the empty house. I remained frozen in place, afraid I might be discovered. Even though my pulse thumped loudly in my ears, I was still able to hear every word that passed between them.

"But where's the bed?" she asked.

"My parents just took everything out," said the boy. "Just be glad nobody's moved in yet."

She said, "We're trespassing, you know."

"Phyllis," he said, "I opened the door with my own key. How's that trespassing? Can't you be more spontaneous?"

I crept to the foot of the staircase.

"Here, smoke this gizmo," the boy said. "Who's going to hassle us? This is my house."

"But you don't live here anymore."

"Don't be so picky. Nobody lives here. This is open territory, like outer space. Now hold your breath."

The heavy scent of marijuana rolled down the stairs.

"Slow down, George. You're strangling me," she said. "Shut the door, at least."

I guessed by their voices they were in their teens. My watch said it was four-thirty and according to the wall, where trees earlier had been shadowed, the sun had set. The furniture probably wasn't going to show.

Someone shut the door upstairs. I could no longer hear them. And so, I reasoned, they couldn't hear me. I climbed the stairs.

I peered through the old-fashioned keyhole in the door of the room Suzy and I had designated as our bedroom. Inside, the light was as gray as a low-contrast photo. Still I saw plenty through my sharpshooter's squint: with his jeans knotted at his knees, his jacket half off, his arms free of his sweater, which was still looped around his neck, the boy thrashed about between the girl's skinny, naked legs. Her arms were extended out to her sides, each hand clutching a piece of clothing. At once, my intruders looked like a spirited heap of laundry and an exotic form of torture. But when their taut young bodies touched who could mistake the sounds of the wondrous suction of love, like water slapping up the sides of a tub? My intruders improvised with a bamboo blind. I wondered, if she were here—I didn't think of Suzy by name; names are for parents to give and strangers to learn—would we also make a mattress of bamboo, or would we dutifully wait for our bed's arrival? And even then, would we spontaneously fall onto our new used mattress where countless others had slept and loved, or would we wait longer still for our sheets due COD from UPS?

"What's that noise?" The girl pushed up on her elbows.

I heard the noise too. Another set of knocks at the front door. Sharp and urgent, a bare fist, I thought. The boy sat back on his heels and threaded his arms through the sleeves of his sweater. He scanned the room and then finally said, "Relax. It's the dumb paperboy. He collects on Fridays." The boy pushed the girl down onto her back. Her white hands disappeared inside his sweater. She lifted her knees. He rooted for her lips. She shook her head.

■ ■ ■

"My name is Grey," said the silhouette at the front door. His voice was full, confident, mature. He said, "I believe you know my daughter Phyllis. Our children are schoolmates."

With his back to the streetlight—or was it the moonlight?—my visitor didn't have a face. I couldn't see the scar that might've slashed his cheek in two or the desolate hole that once was home to a missing eye. All I was certain of was the silhouette's general shape—rounder and squatter than my own—and his voice, not just its sound, but the way it looked as it billowed in the chilled night air in fat, legible puffs like the speech of comic-strip characters.

"I didn't mean to barge in," he said, "but I tried calling, and the girl said your line had been temporarily disconnected." His presence sent the temperature of the house plunging. "Have you seen my daughter?" he asked.

I thought of my intruders up in the bedroom. Pictured the tiny figure of this man's daughter, her white knees, bare and strangely luminous, two moons in the gray light of the room, reaching for the ceiling—or, more ambitiously, straining for the heavens—as they cradled the boy.

"I can assure you," I began, "your daughter's safe with my boy." Those last two words, "my boy," thudded in my ears. I was astonished by my daring, and certain, despite my thirty years, that my voice lacked the easy authority of a parent. Without question, my "my boy" had just made its maiden voyage from my lips. So I took a precautionary step back into the dark house where age could best be discerned by a careful touch of my skin.

"Phyllis has to come home right away," the silhouette said. "My wife and I—it's our anniversary, and she has it in her head the kids should come to the restaurant with us." He sounded like a man who fretted over what his children dreamed at night. He said, "I asked her, 'Where were those kids when we got married?' But what's the use? When she gets something locked in her skull, you might as well be talking to a snail. You know how things go a little sour when kids come on the scene."

"Sure I do," I said. But what did I know? I took another step back from the door. I imagined having a man-to-man talk with the silhouette one night. And after a few beers he would say, "I'll get this eye fixed. Put in a fake one like that Sammy Davis, Jr. The ladies like that sort of thing. Makes a man mysterious, and gets the woman feeling sorry for you. I tell you, my wife can keep the kids. She can take them for burgers the rest of her days. You and me, we'll go out, we'll make a great team."

"That's right," I'd say. "Fathers have to stick together." And we'd shake hands like men.

He said, "Would you call Phyllis for me?"

"If she shows up," I said, "I'll send her straight home." The silhouette's shoulders rose and fell. "She's not here? Look, I'm sorry I've troubled you. Please ask her to call home. But your phone, it's out of order."

I reassured him I'd send her right home.

"Thanks," he said, "thanks." The silhouette extended his hand toward the storm door, but when I didn't make a move to offer him mine he clumsily stuffed his back into his pocket. Then he switched subjects and advised me to work things out with the phone company. "Drive a person mad being cut off from the outside like that," he said.

"I'll have it fixed first thing in the morning."

"Good. Now how about your lights? No juice, is there?" He cleared his throat. "Through our children, you can say we're friends. Phyllis has told me about your money troubles. Let me know how I can help."

"That's kind of you," I said, "but I'm okay. I'm just trying to conserve energy." I started to laugh but he didn't follow my lead. "Forget about me and Phyllis. Go have a nice dinner, and wish Mrs. Grey a happy anniversary for me."

I watched the silhouette step into the night. I was almost rid of him when his body was suddenly cut in half by a set of oncoming headlights.

It was the Salvation Army truck. The driver honked at the silhouette, who stopped to talk to a man hanging out the open passenger window of the truck's cab. The silhouette then turned and came halfway up the front walk toward the house. He stopped and called, "Are you expecting some used furniture?"

"Me?" I said indignantly. "What does a man like me need from the Salvation Army?"

"That's what I thought," said the silhouette. "But something's odd. They have the correct address on their invoice but the name's all wrong. I'll just send them on their way."

"Wait. Let me." I almost stepped out of the house, but thought better of it. "You've done enough already. Mrs. Grey's probably wondering where you are."

He stood there as still as a tree stump and stared in my direction.

"Mrs. Grey," I said, and finally he left, shrugging his shoulders at the truck as he passed.

■ ■ ■

"You got a Suzy Tree here?" the guy in the passenger window asked. Half a fat, unlighted cigar tugged at the corner of his mouth. He had on an old felt baseball cap, its bill tipped so low on his brow that his face seemed to start at his nose.

"That's us," I said.

The cap leaped from the cab. "Who's your boyfriend?" he asked as he pumped past me on his stumpy legs. "He almost chased us away."

"I should've let him," I said, watching the cap unlock and then disappear into the truck's dark trailer. "You're over two hours late."

"The snow," the cap said. "It's the damn snow."

"What snow? It's not snowing."

"Of course no snow," he said. "I'm talking about the idea of snow. People do things different when they're living with the idea of snow."

I didn't try to answer him. All I knew was if Suzy were here, this guy would be apologizing for their tardiness; he'd be almost too polite. I said, "Let's say I don't want this stuff anymore."

"Can't do," said a deep voice behind me. I turned and saw the driver, a man a head taller than the cap. He was wearing gloves with the tips cut away, exposing sausage-thick fingers that scissored what must've been the other half of his partner's cigar. "We only unload," he said. "If you don't want the merchandise, call the office and they'll send the pickup crew over."

I didn't care for these two men, but they certainly could work. At first, I thought it was an illusion of their cigars and stubble and utilitarian jumpsuits that gave me this impression. But in no time they had the vestibule filled with a gigantic tangle of wood, steel, Formica, and foam.

"It's a wrap," the driver announced as he carried in an armchair and lowered it on top of the heap.

"What do you mean?" I said. "Where's the bed?"

"What does that mean, where's the bed?"

Now that we were in the house, I could no longer see their faces. My guests had turned into shadows in the vestibule where there were no clean edges, no distinct boundaries.

"You say you got a bed coming?"

"No, I just said that so you'd stay a little longer."

"Hey, he's a pretty funny fellow," said the cap. "I better get me a chair so I don't fall over from laughing."

"Drop it," the driver said. "Let's get moving before I starve to death. You see anything left in the truck?"

"Nothing I'd put my back on," said the cap.

His partner chuckled.

"There was something rolled up and standing in a corner."

"Sounds like one of our mattresses all right." The driver clapped his big hands. "Let's get it and get going." They moved for the door.

"Hold it," I said. "I'll carry it in." This was one of Suzy's ideas. She wanted us to bring the bed into our new home, a variant of the bride-over-the-threshold ritual. I had opposed such a scheme from the start. And this she interpreted as proof that I didn't want to live with her. So she pointed her hip at me. Then the paperboy came.

"Can't do. Totally against regulations," the driver said.

"This is no time for amateurs," said the cap.

I clenched my fists. I could feel the muscles in my neck coiling into snakes. A sudden rush of heat thawed the tip of my nose. My breath turned quick and shallow.

But who was I mad at—the movers? Suzy?

I said in the voice of reasonable men, "Let me do the mattress. I'll make it worth your while."

■ ■ ■

The mattress was damp and musty. In all likelihood it had labored in a dank basement for years under piles of *National Geographics* and cracked clay flowerpots. I dragged it out into the night air. It seemed to sigh as it folded in half across my shoulder.

By the time I reached the house, I was in a sweat from the struggle the mattress had put up. I propped it against the wall but it slowly slithered to the floor as if it were filled with heavy syrup. "This isn't the one we bought," I said.

"We only unload," the driver said. "You don't want, call the office."

"Look, feel this. This is Jell-O. Would you want to sleep on this?"

"Sorry, bub," said the driver, chomping moistly on his cigar, "you're not my type."

The cap danced in carrying the box springs. He was whistling an inane tune. "You have to admire the work of a professional," he said as he let the load slide off his back. "Hey, what's the matter here?"

"He doesn't want the mattress."

"What's the matter? It's too firm for you?"

They chuckled.

"Forget it," I said. "Just leave me alone."

"Love to. But first we need Miss Tree to sign this invoice." The driver's heavy fingers tapped a clipboard he had magically produced out of the night air.

"I'll sign," I said, reaching for his pen.

"Can't do. We need the lady's signature. Company policy, see: 'Accept only the signature of the party named on the invoice.' "

The cap struck a match against a table leg and held the flame over the clipboard so I could see their silly rule. On the same match they lighted the cigars. With each puff l saw their faces, like gruesome orange masks. I could tell the driver from the cap by the relative height of the burning nib at the tip of his cigar.

"If I sign, you can go."

"I see we're dealing with a devious individual," the taller nib said. "You want us to break Army policy. Joey, should we give him an opportunity to deceive us?"

The shorter nib bobbed up and down.

"Okay then, what's your relationship to Miss Tree? You Mr. Tree?"

I told them no.

"Her brother?"

"No."

"I know you're not her father."

"How can you be so sure I'm not?"

"You don't sound like anyone's father," said the shorter nib, and instantly I touched my throat and thought back to the silhouette.

"Face it," the taller nib said, "no self-respecting father would let his kid near this kind of crap."

"For your information," I said, "I have a sixteen-year-old son."

"Sure you do. And my father's Smokey the Bear."

"That's not so hard to believe."

The shorter nib came at me, puffing wildly, but then suddenly stopped.

"Leave him," said his partner. "Tell me," he continued, "are you Miss Tree's sweetheart?"

I had to chew that one over. "You could've asked her yourself if you showed up when you were supposed to."

"S-s-shit," the taller nib hissed. "We're wasting our time. Let's move this stuff out of here."

"I thought you only unloaded," I said.

"We load, bub, when it's our mistake."

"So you admit you're wrong."

"Sure we're wrong. We'll take the rap for everything wrong in this town, in this state, on this planet. So what?"

The orange nibs floated through the vestibule burning smoky orange loops onto the black canvas while the hands and boots of the movers untangled the furniture pile.

"I paid for this junk," I said. "It's legally mine."

"Not till Miss Tree signs."

"Gentlemen," I said, wondering where that word had come from, "if you don't stop I'll be forced to call the police."

The shorter nib said, "Hey, you suppose we get overtime for this?"

I backed away to make good on my threat. I heard the tear and creak of furniture in distress. I heard the movers' steamy breaths, the *clomp clomp clomp* of their boots. Then I turned my back to the vestibule, and immediately, involuntarily, I threw my arms out in front of me. I saw nothing. My eyes were useless. In the dark the hands are what count. My fingers combed the air for the phone's smooth shell, solid and sleek, but I soon realized my movements lacked purpose. I was, of course, phoneless. But I continued on, simultaneously hoping for and dreading collisions.

There are no directions in the dark. All one has is memory and I had no memories of that house. I took recklessly long strides away from the vestibule, as if I were trying to outstep the darkness, as one steps over puddles. I waved my arms like a drowning man, groping for anything solid. I heard the nibs curse and grunt. They could've been singing "Whistle While You Work" and I wouldn't have been surprised. But what spooked me was the peculiar way their voices seemed to come at me from every angle, even though I hadn't veered from my original course.

A brief eternity later, finally, a collision. Two walls, one on either side of me—a narrow hallway. Here I moved with confidence. Each hand pressed flush against the walls, my fingertips tracing the cracks they found there as a palm reader follows a lifeline to its end. I stepped easily now, content inside that enclosed space, when without warning the walls gave way to air, and my arms spread open like the bellows of an accordion. My hands once again swatted at nothing. My legs turned wooden, my body froze, but my mind traveled on, back to Suzy and dark rooms where we once lay, where I extended my arms and at the ends of my fingertips I'd find her. It took a few moments, but soon I realized my flailing hands were moving in a distinct pattern. She was within reach. My hands had molded her from air.

Then I heard fresh footsteps. Not the dull thuds of the movers' boots, not my own because I still hadn't budged, but bright steps—a child's, perhaps, tentative in their approach.

"I'll sign," said a female voice.

I turned in time to see a match struck. Through the sulfurous smoke I saw illuminated by the fragile flame a most implausible trio—the bovine faces of the movers sandwiching Suzy's likeness.

"Where you been hiding?" asked the cap.

She answered by blowing out the flame. "Where do I sign?"

"Smart. She blows out the light and then wants to know where to sign. Sign in the dark, lady." The cap struck another match. The trio reappeared. The lambent flame washed over her close-set eyes, her fringed forehead, her brown lips, giving substance to the voice that said, "Where?"

"Right there, Miss Tree," the driver said. She signed and then blew out the flame.

The nibs bobbed toward the door. "Enjoy the bed," the shorter nib said, and they were gone.

"Thank you," I said to the darkened room. "You've been a great help." I moved in the direction where I believed I saw her last.

Those tentative footsteps suddenly took life. Quick, whispery steps, louder and then fading, the way an echo loses energy. They were somewhere behind me, and when I turned, they were behind me again. I spun around once more and saw the door opening.

"Go home," I said. "Your father wants you."

She was momentarily silhouetted in the doorway. She briefly looked in my general direction.

"Tell him I sent you home," I said as she left me, with a slam of the door.

I realized my hands were clutching the front of my shirt. Beneath it my ribs felt loose; my heart needed massage; in my stomach a little man was trying to punch his way out.

Before I knew which foot to move first, I heard a voice from above: "Hey, mister, I want you to have this key."

"Who's that?"

"You don't need my name. I used to live here."

"It's you," I said. "You're the one." I could tell he was on the stairs. "Please, strike a match." All I wanted was to see his face, to see myself there as I had seen Suzy in the girl's face.

"I don't have a match," he said. "I don't smoke. But, mister, here's the key."

I heard the metal clatter on the floor. Did he expect me to catch it? "Why didn't you leave with the girl?" I said.

"We meant no harm," he said. "Just taking a look around the old place." The stairs creaked under his weight as he started his descent. "You get the key?"

"Why did she leave you?"

"I'm coming down now," he said. "I don't want any trouble."

"You should go after her. Tell her you're sorry you did what you did. Tell her you love her, if that's what it takes."

"She's at dinner with her folks. You met her dad."

"He's not a very happy man," I said. "You give him so much to worry about."

"*Me?* You lied to him. Man, that was great. I swear, you really messed with his head." The boy stepped onto the floor.

"That was my mistake. I shouldn't have done such a thing. And don't get carried away. I didn't do it to impress you."

"Okay, mister, don't get hot." He pushed aside some furniture, clearing a path to the door. "Stay back now," he warned. "I'm leaving now."

"Wait. Give me a hand upstairs with the bed." I felt his body close to mine. I could reach out and turn his hand away from the door. But how long could I keep him? What did I have to say to a boy his age? I'd tell him about Suzy, then what? We could count snowflakes, if it snowed, and in the first light of the new day, I might see all we had in common. Surely there would be something—the slant of our eyes, the breadth of our noses, the cut of our hair, and, should Suzy appear, our mutual love for the same woman.

"Pick up the key," I said. "I want you to have it. Come back with the girl anytime."

"I'm gone, mister."

"No, not yet."

"I'm late." He turned the doorknob. I cupped my hand over his. How warm it felt.

"Where are you going? Maybe I'll come along."

He opened the door. An icy wind struck our faces. "I have to go eat dinner. That's all." He stepped outside. I didn't try to stop him. I asked if he had gloves, a hat, a scarf. I told him zip up tight. "Don't run if it starts to snow," I said.

"I'm okay, mister." With his back to me he looked up at the low sky. He took a step and made a half-turn toward the house. "Thanks for the visit," he said. "I think you'll like it here."

Katherine Mansfield

Born Kathleen Mansfield Beauchamp, the third of five children in a prosperous New Zealand family, Katherine Mansfield (1888–1923) grew up in Wellington, was educated at Queen's College (London), and returned only briefly to New Zealand before finally settling in Europe in 1908. In England she lived what was then considered a bohemian life, one marked by its love of theatre, its urbanity, and its shifting liaisons. On the edge of several famous literary circles—Bloomsbury, Garsington, and the milieu of D.H. and Frieda Lawrence, for example—she published stories in *The New Age, Rhythm, Adelphi,* and several other periodicals. A deft satirist in her early sketches (*In a German Pension,* 1911), she drew most attention for the later stories she collected in *Bliss* (1920) and *The Garden Party* (1922). Her sharp, spare style contrasted strongly with conventional forms of storytelling; she strove to break away from plotted narrative and to evoke through image and cadence the pressures, perspectives, and insights of particular frames of mind. For her, beauty was evanescent, order a fond dream; isolation at once fed and desolated the creative imagination. In a contemporary review, the poet Walter de la Mare wrote of her work: "The pitch of mind is invariably emotional, the poise lyrical. Nonetheless that mind is absolutely tranquil and attentive in its intellectual grasp of the matter in hand. And through all, Miss Mansfield's personality, whatever its disguises, haunts her work just as its customary inmate may haunt a vacant room, its genius a place." More recent critics have attempted to come to terms with how and why this process happens, finding her work variously confessional, political, and technically innovative.

One of the places that haunted her was New Zealand. It was—as "The Doll's House" (*The Dove's Nest,* 1923) suggests—something of a bittersweet memory. She rejected what she saw as New Zealand's provincialism, yet was attracted to its natural beauty—a double perspective clearly shown in "The Doll's House." It is a story about children, but it is an oblique one; it is not about childlike harmony. It is a story that animates instead the chance moments of insight and the codified techniques of social violence that strafe the child's world. As some of her other stories show, they strafe the adult's world as well. But the kind of order Mansfield could craft in prose always eluded her in life. In 1923 she died in France, of tuberculosis, at the Gurdjieff Institute for the Harmonious Development of Man.

The Doll's House

When dear old Mrs. Hay went back to town after staying with the Burnells she sent the children a doll's house. It was so big that the carter and Pat carried it into the courtyard, and there it stayed, propped up on two wooden boxes beside the feed-room. No harm could come to it; it was summer. And perhaps the smell of paint would have gone off by the time it had to be taken in. For, really, the smell of paint coming from that doll's house ("Sweet of old Mrs. Hay, of course; most sweet and generous!")—but the smell of paint was quite enough to make anyone seriously ill, in Aunt Beryl's opinion. Even before the sacking was taken off. And when it was. . . .

There stood the doll's house, a dark, oily, spinach green, picked out with bright yellow. Its two solid little chimneys, glued on to the roof, were painted red and white, and the door, gleaming with yellow varnish, was like a little slab of toffee. Four windows, real windows, were divided into panes by a broad streak of green. There was actually a tiny porch, too, painted yellow, with big lumps of congealed paint hanging along the edge.

But perfect, perfect little house! Who could possibly mind the smell. It was part of the joy, part of the newness.

"Open it quickly, someone!"

The hook at the side was stuck fast. Pat prised it open with his penknife, and the whole house front swung back, and—there you were, gazing at one and the same moment into the drawing-room and dining-room, the kitchen and two bedrooms. That is the way for a house to open! Why don't all houses open like that? How much more exciting than peering through the slit of a door into a mean little hall with a hat-stand and two umbrellas! That is—isn't it?—what you long to know about a house when you put your hand on the knocker. Perhaps it is the way God opens houses at the dead of night when He is taking a quiet turn with an angel. . . .

"Oh-oh!" The Burnell children sounded as though they were in despair. It was too marvellous; it was too much for them. They had never seen anything like it in their lives. All the rooms were papered. There were pictures on the walls, painted on the paper, with gold frames complete. Red carpet covered all the floors except the kitchen; red plush chairs in the drawing-room, green in the dining-room; tables, beds with real bedclothes, a cradle, a stove, a dresser with tiny plates and one big jug. But what Kezia liked more than anything, what she liked frightfully, was the lamp. It stood in the middle of the dining-room table, an exquisite little amber lamp with a white globe. It was even filled all ready for lighting, though, of course, you couldn't light it. But there was something inside that looked like oil and moved when you shook it.

The father and mother dolls, who sprawled very still as though they had fainted in the drawing-room, and their two little children asleep upstairs, were really too big for the doll's house. They didn't look as though they belonged. But the lamp was perfect. It seemed to smile at Kezia, to say "I live here." The lamp was real.

■ ■ ■

The Burnell children could hardly walk to school fast enough the next morning. They burned to tell everybody, to describe, to—well—to boast about their doll's house before the schoolbell rang.

"I'm to tell," said Isabel, "because I'm the eldest. And you two can join in after. But I'm to tell first."

There was nothing to answer. Isabel was bossy, but she was always right, and Lottie and Kezia knew too well the powers that went with being eldest. They brushed through the thick buttercups at the road edge and said nothing.

"And I'm to choose who's to come and see it first. Mother said I might."

For it had been arranged that while the doll's house stood in the courtyard they might ask the girls at school, two at a time, to come and look. Not to stay to tea, of course, or to come traipsing through the house. But just to stand quietly in the courtyard while Isabel pointed out the beauties, and Lottie and Kezia looked pleased. . . .

But hurry as they might, by the time they had reached the tarred palings of the boys' playground the bell had begun to jangle. They only just had time to whip off their hats and fall into line before the roll was called. Never mind. Isabel tried to make up for it by looking very important and mysterious and by whispering behind her hand to the girls near her, "Got something to tell you at playtime."

Playtime came and Isabel was surrounded. The girls of her class nearly fought to put their arms round her, to walk away with her, to beam flatteringly, to be her special friend. She held quite a court under the huge pine trees at the side of the playground. Nudging, giggling together, the little girls pressed up close. And the only two who stayed outside the ring were the two who were always outside, the little Kelveys. They knew better than to come anywhere near the Burnells.

For the fact was, the school the Burnell children went to was not at all the kind of place their parents would have chosen if there had been any choice. But there was none. It was the only school for miles. And the consequence was all the children of the neighbourhood, the Judge's little girls, the doctor's daughters, the storekeeper's children, the milkman's, were forced to mix together. Not to speak of there being an equal number of rude, rough little boys as well. But the line had to be drawn somewhere. It was drawn at the Kelveys. Many of the children, including the Burnells, were not allowed even to speak to them. They walked past the Kelveys with their heads in the air, and as they set the fashion in all matters of behaviour, the Kelveys were shunned by everybody.

Even the teacher had a special voice for them, and a special smile for the other children when Lil Kelvey came up to her desk with a bunch of dreadfully common-looking flowers.

They were the daughters of a spry, hard-working little washerwoman, who went about from house to house by the day. This was awful enough. But where was Mr. Kelvey? Nobody knew for certain. But everybody said he was in prison. So they were the daughters of a washerwoman and a gaolbird. Very nice company for other people's children! And they looked it. Why Mrs. Kelvey made them so conspicuous was hard to understand. The truth was they were dressed in "bits" given to her by the people for whom she worked. Lil, for instance, who was a stout, plain child, with big freckles, came to school in a dress made from a green art-serge tablecloth of the Burnells', with red plush sleeves from the Logans' curtains. Her hat, perched on top of her high forehead, was a grown-up woman's hat, once the property of Miss Lecky, the post-mistress. It was turned up at the back and trimmed with a large scarlet quill. What a little guy she looked! It was impossible not to laugh. And her little sister, our Else, wore a long white dress, rather like a nightgown, and a pair of little boy's boots. But whatever our Else wore she would have looked strange. She was a tiny wishbone of a child, with cropped hair and enormous solemn eyes—a little white owl. Nobody had ever seen her smile; she scarcely ever spoke. She went through life holding on to Lil, with a piece of Lil's skirt screwed up in her hand. Where Lil went, our Else followed. In the playground, on the road going to and from school, there was Lil marching in front and our Else holding on behind. Only when she wanted anything, or when she was out of breath, our Else gave Lil a tug, a twitch, and Lil stopped and turned around. The Kelveys never failed to understand each other.

Now they hovered at the edge; you couldn't stop them listening. When the little girls turned round and sneered, Lil, as usual, gave her silly, shamefaced smile, but our Else only looked.

And Isabel's voice, so very proud, went on telling. The carpet made a great sensation, but so did the beds with real bedclothes, and the stove with an oven door.

When she finished Kezia broke in. "You've forgotten the lamp, Isabel."

"Oh yes," said Isabel, "and there's a teeny little lamp, all made of yellow glass, with a white globe that stands on the dining-room table. You couldn't tell it from a real one."

"The lamp's best of all," cried Kezia. She thought Isabel wasn't making half enough of the little lamp. But nobody paid any attention. Isabel was choosing the two who were to come back with them that afternoon and see it. She chose Emmie Cole and Lena Logan. But when the others knew they were all to have a chance, they couldn't be nice enough to Isabel. One by one they put their arms round Isabel's waist and walked her off. They had something to whisper to her, a secret. "Isabel's *my* friend."

Only the little Kelveys moved away forgotten; there was nothing more for them to hear.

■ ■ ■

Days passed, and as more children saw the doll's house, the fame of it spread. It became the one subject, the rage. The one question was, "Have you seen Burnells' doll's house? Oh, ain't it lovely!" "Haven't you seen it? Oh, I say!"

Even the dinner hour was given up to talking about it. The little girls sat under the pines eating their thick mutton sandwiches and big slabs of johnny cake spread with butter. While always, as near as they could get, sat the Kelveys, our Else holding on to Lil, listening too, while they chewed their jam sandwiches out of a newspaper soaked with large red blobs.

"Mother," said Kezia, "can't I ask the Kelveys just once?"

"Certainly not, Kezia."

"But why not?"

"Run away, Kezia; you know quite well why not."

At last everybody had seen it except them. On that day the subject rather flagged. It was the dinner hour. The children stood together under the pine trees, and suddenly, as they looked at the Kelveys eating out of their paper, always by themselves, always listening, they wanted to be horrid to them. Emmie Cole started the whisper.

"Lil Kelvey's going to be a servant when she grows up."

"O-oh, how awful!" said Isabel Burnell, and she made eyes at Emmie.

Emmie swallowed in a very meaning way and nodded to Isabel as she'd seen her mother do on those occasions.

"It's true—it's true—it's true," she said.

Then Lena Logan's little eyes snapped. "Shall I ask her?" she whispered.

"Bet you don't," said Jessie May.

"Pooh, I'm not frightened," said Lena. Suddenly she gave a little squeal and danced in front of the other girls. "Watch! Watch me! Watch me now!" said Lena. And sliding, gliding, dragging one foot, giggling behind her hand, Lena went over to the Kelveys.

Lil looked up from her dinner. She wrapped the rest quickly away. Our Else stopped chewing. What was coming now?

"Is it true you're going to be a servant when you grow up, Lil Kelvey?" shrilled Lena.

Dead silence. But instead of answering, Lil only gave her silly, shamefaced smile. She didn't seem to mind the question at all. What a sell for Lena! The girls began to titter.

Lena couldn't stand that. She put her hands on her hips; she shot forward. "Yah, yer father's in prison!" she hissed spitefully.

This was such a marvellous thing to have said that the little girls rushed away in a body, deeply, deeply excited, wild with joy. Some one found a long rope, and they began skipping. And never did they skip so high, run in and out so fast, or do such daring things as on that morning.

In the afternoon Pat called for the Burnell children with the buggy and they drove home. There were visitors. Isabel and Lottie, who liked visitors, went upstairs to change their pinafores. But Kezia thieved out at the back. Nobody was about; she began to swing on the big white gates of the courtyard. Presently, looking along the road, she saw two little dots. They grew bigger, they were coming towards her. Now she could see that one was in front and one close behind. Now she could see that they were the Kelveys. Kezia stopped swinging. She slipped off the gate as if she was going to run away. Then she hesitated. The Kelveys came nearer, and beside them walked their shadows, very long, stretching right across the road with their heads in the buttercups. Kezia clambered back on the gate; she had made up her mind; she swung out.

"Hullo," she said to the passing Kelveys.

They were so astounded that they stopped. Lil gave her silly smile. Our Else stared.

"You can come and see our doll's house if you want to," said Kezia, and she dragged one toe on the ground. But at that Lil turned red and shook her head quickly.

"Why not?" asked Kezia.

Lil gasped, then she said, "Your ma told our ma you wasn't to speak to us."

"Oh, well," said Kezia. She didn't know what to reply. "It doesn't matter. You can come and see our doll's house all the same. Come on. Nobody's looking."

But Lil shook her head still harder.

"Don't you want to?" asked Kezia.

Suddenly there was a twitch, a tug at Lil's skirt. She turned round. Our Else was looking at her with big, imploring eyes; she was frowning; she wanted to go. For a moment Lil looked at our Else very doubtfully. But then our Else twitched her skirt again. She started forward. Kezia led the way. Like two little stray cats they followed across the courtyard to where the doll's house stood.

"There it is," said Kezia.

There was a pause. Lil breathed loudly, almost snorted; our Else was still as stone.

"I'll open it for you," said Kezia kindly. She undid the hook and they looked inside.

"There's the drawing-room and the dining-room, and that's the—"

"Kezia!"

Oh, what a start they gave!

"Kezia!"

It was Aunt Beryl's voice. They turned round. At the back door stood Aunt Beryl, staring as if she couldn't believe what she saw.

"How dare you ask the little Kelveys into the courtyard!" said her cold, furious voice. "You know as well as I do, you're not allowed to talk to them. Run away, children, run away at once. And don't come back again," said Aunt Beryl. And she stepped into the yard and shooed them out as if they were chickens.

"Off you go immediately!" she called, cold and proud.

They did not need telling twice. Burning with shame, shrinking together, Lil huddling along like her mother, our Else dazed, somehow they crossed the big courtyard and squeezed through the white gate.

"Wicked, disobedient little girl!" said Aunt Beryl bitterly to Kezia, and she slammed the doll's house to.

The afternoon had been awful. A letter had come from Willie Brent, a terrifying, threatening letter, saying if she did not meet him that evening in Pulman's Bush, he'd come to the front door and ask the reason why! But now that she had frightened those little rats of Kelveys and given Kezia a good scolding, her heart felt lighter. That ghastly pressure was gone. She went back to the house humming.

When the Kelveys were well out of sight of Burnells', they sat down to rest on a big red drainpipe by the side of the road. Lil's cheeks were still burning; she took off the hat with the quill and held it on her knee. Dreamily they looked over the hay paddocks, past the creek, to the group of wattles where Logan's cows stood waiting to be milked. What were their thoughts?

Presently our Else nudged up close to her sister. But now she had forgotten the cross lady. She put out a finger and stroked her sister's quill; she smiled her rare smile.

"I seen the little lamp," she said softly.

Then both were silent once more.

Rohinton Mistry

Born in 1952 to a Parsi family in Bombay, Rohinton Mistry emigrated to Canada in 1975, and worked in a Toronto bank. His writing career began in 1983, with a short story contributed to a literary competition, and two years later he gave up his banking job to write full time. Following a brief sojourn in California, Mistry returned to Canada, and now lives in Brampton, Ontario. Twice winner of the Commonwealth Writers' Prize—for *Such a Long Journey* (1991) and *A Fine Balance* (1996)—the author shortly established himself as one of Canada's leading contemporary novelists, a deft storyteller and creator of character, and a keen observer of political and social behaviour in both India and Canada. For these books, Mistry was also honoured with the Governor General's Award (1991) and the Giller Prize (1996).

"Swimming Lessons" is the concluding story in Mistry's collection *Tales from Firozsha Baag* (1987), a finalist for the Governor General's Award for fiction. The other stories are set in Firozsha Baag (an apartment complex in Bombay recalled by the narrator), and trace the interconnected lives of the various individuals who live there. "Swimming Lessons," in contrast, records the efforts of the narrator to accommodate himself to the unfamiliar culture he encounters in Canada, and his concerns about explaining to his parents in India his sense of difference and dislocation. By immersing himself in a new culture, he has begun to lose touch with the rituals and traditions that had previously shaped his life. In this context, the swimming lessons suggest, however, that he is also learning to adapt to his new environment.

Swimming Lessons

The old man's wheelchair is audible today as he creaks by in the hallway: on some days it's just a smooth whirr. Maybe the way he slumps in it, or the way his weight rests has something to do with it. Down to the lobby he goes, and sits there most of the time, talking to people on their way out or in. That's where he first spoke to me a few days ago. I was waiting for the elevator, back from Eaton's with my new pair of swimming-trunks.

"Hullo," he said. I nodded, smiled.

"Beautiful summer day we've got."

"Yes," I said, "it's lovely outside."

He shifted the wheelchair to face me squarely. "How old do you think I am?"

I looked at him blankly, and he said, "Go on, take a guess."

I understood the game; he seemed about seventy-five although the hair was still black, so I said, "Sixty-five?" He made a sound between a chuckle and a wheeze: "I'll be seventy-seven next month." Close enough.

I've heard him ask that question several times since, and everyone plays by the rules. Their faked guesses range from sixty to seventy. They pick a lower number when he's more depressed than usual. He reminds me of Grandpa as he sits on the sofa in the lobby, staring out vacantly at the parking lot. Only difference is, he sits with the stillness of stroke victims, while Grandpa's Parkinson's disease would bounce his thighs and legs and arms all over the place. When he could no longer hold the *Bombay Samachar* steady enough to read, Grandpa took to sitting on the veranda and staring emptily at the traffic passing outside Firozsha Baag. Or waving to anyone who went by in the compound: Rustomji, Nariman Hansotia in his 1932 Mercedes-Benz, the fat ayah Jaakaylee with her shopping-bag, the *kuchrawalli* with her basket and long bamboo broom.

The Portuguese woman across the hall has told me a little about the old man. She is the communicator for the apartment building. To gather and disseminate information, she takes the liberty of unabashedly throwing open her door when newsworthy events transpire. Not for Portuguese Woman the furtive peerings from thin cracks or spyholes. She reminds me of a character in a movie, *Barefoot In The Park* I think it was, who left empty beer cans by the landing for anyone passing to stumble and give her the signal. But PW does not need beer cans. The gutang-khutang of the elevator opening and closing is enough.

The old man's daughter looks after him. He was living alone till his stroke, which coincided with his youngest daughter's divorce in Vancouver. She returned to him and they moved into this low-rise in Don Mills. PW says the daughter talks to no one in the building but takes good care of her father.

Mummy used to take good care of Grandpa, too, till things became complicated and he was moved to the Parsi General Hospital. Parkinsonism and osteoporosis laid him low. The doctor explained that Grandpa's hip did not break because he fell, but he fell because the hip, gradually growing brittle, snapped on that fatal day. That's what osteoporosis does, hollows out the bones and turns effect into cause. It has an unusually high incidence in the Parsi community, he said, but did not say why. Just one of those mysterious things. We are the chosen people where osteoporosis is concerned. And divorce. The Parsi community has the highest divorce rate in India. It also claims to be the most westernized community in India. Which is the result of the other? Confusion again, of cause and effect.

The hip was put in traction. Single-handed, Mummy struggled valiantly with bedpans and dressings for bedsores which soon appeared like grim spectres on his back. *Mamaiji*, bent double with her weak back, could give no assistance. My help would be enlisted to roll him over on his side while Mummy changed the dressing. But after three months, the doctor pronounced a patch upon Grandpa's lungs, and the male ward of Parsi General swallowed him up. There was no money for a private nursing home. I went to see him once, at Mummy's insistence. She used to say that the blessings of an old person were the most valuable and potent of all, they would last my whole life long. The ward had rows and rows of beds; the din was enormous, the smells nauseating, and it was just as well that Grandpa passed most of his time in a less than conscious state.

But I should have gone to see him more often. Whenever Grandpa went out, while he still could in the days before parkinsonism, he would bring back pink and white sugar-coated almonds for Percy and me. Every time I remember Grandpa, I remember that; and then I think: I should have gone to see him more often. That's what I also thought when our telephone-owning neighbour, esteemed by all for that reason, sent his son to tell us the hospital had phoned that Grandpa died an hour ago.

■ ■ ■

The postman rang the doorbell the way he always did, long and continuous; Mother went to open it, wanting to give him a piece of her mind but thought better of it, she did not want to risk the vengeance of postmen, it was so easy for them to destroy letters; workers nowadays thought no end of themselves, strutting around like peacocks, ever since all this Shiv Sena agitation about Maharashtra for Maharashtrians, threatening strikes and Bombay bundh *all the time, with no respect for the public; bus drivers and conductors were the worst, behaving as if they owned the buses and were doing favours to commuters, pulling the bell before you were in the bus, the driver purposely braking and moving with big jerks to make the standees lose their balance, the conductor so rude if you did not have the right change.*

But when she saw the airmail envelope with a Canadian stamp her face lit up, she said wait to the postman, and went in for a fifty paisa piece, a little baksheesh *for you, she told him, then shut the door and kissed the envelope, went in running, saying my son has written, my son has sent a letter, and Father looked up from the newspaper and said, don't get too excited, first read it, you know what kind of letters he writes, a few lines of empty words, I'm fine, hope you are all right, your loving son—that kind of writing I don't call letter-writing.*

Then Mother opened the envelope and took out one small page and began to read silently, and the joy brought to her face by the letter's arrival began to ebb; Father saw it happening and knew he was right, he said read aloud, let me also hear what our son is writing this time, so Mother read: My dear Mummy and Daddy, Last winter was terrible, we had record-breaking low temperatures all through February and March, and the first official day of spring was colder than the first official day of winter had been, but it's getting warmer now. Looks like it will be a nice warm summer. You asked about my new apartment. It's small, but not bad at all. This is just a quick note to let you know I'm fine, so you won't worry about me. Hope everything is okay at home.

After Mother put it back in the envelope, Father said everything about his life is locked in silence and secrecy, I still don't understand why he bothered to visit us last year if he had nothing to say; every letter of his has been a quick note so we won't worry—what does he think we worry about, his health, in that country everyone eats well whether they work or not, he should be worrying about us with all the black market and rationing, has he forgotten already how he used to go to the ration-shop and wait in line every week; and what kind of apartment description is that, not bad at all; and if it is a Canadian weather report I need from him, I can go with Nariman Hansotia from A Block to the Cawasji Framji Memorial Library and read all about it, there they get newspapers from all over the world.

■ ■ ■

The sun is hot today. Two women are sunbathing on the stretch of patchy lawn at the periphery of the parking lot. I can see them clearly from my kitchen. They're wearing bikinis and I'd love to take a closer look. But I have no binoculars. Nor do I have a car to saunter out to and pretend to look under the hood. They're both luscious and gleaming. From time to time they smear lotion over their skin, on the bellies, on the inside of the thighs, on the shoulders. Then one of them gets the other to undo the string of her top and spread some there. She lies on her stomach with the straps undone. I wait. I pray that the heat and haze make her forget, when it's time to turn over, that the straps are undone.

But the sun is not hot enough to work this magic for me. When it's time to come in, she flips over, deftly holding up the cups, and reties the top. They arise, pick up towels, lotions and magazines, and return to the building.

This is my chance to see them closer. I race down the stairs to the lobby. The old man says hullo. "Down again?"

"My mailbox," I mumble.

"It's Saturday," he chortles. For some reason he finds it extremely funny. My eye is on the door leading in from the parking lot.

Through the glass panel I see them approaching. I hurry to the elevator and wait. In the dimly lit lobby I can see their eyes are having trouble adjusting after the bright sun. They don't seem as attractive as they did from the kitchen window. The elevator arrives and I hold it open, inviting them in with what I think is a gallant flourish. Under the fluorescent glare in the elevator I see their wrinkled skin, aging hands, sagging bottoms, varicose veins. The lustrous trick of sun and lotion and distance has ended.

I step out and they continue to the third floor. I have Monday night to look forward to, my first swimming lesson. The high school behind the apartment building is offering, among its usual assortment of macramé and ceramics and pottery classes, a class for non-swimming adults.

The woman at the registration desk is quite friendly. She even gives me the opening to satisfy the compulsion I have about explaining my non-swimming status.

"Are you from India?" she asks. I nod. "I hope you don't mind my asking, but I was curious because an Indian couple, husband and wife, also registered a few minutes ago. Is swimming not encouraged in India?"

"On the contrary," I say. "Most Indians swim like fish. I'm an exception to the rule. My house was five minutes walking distance from Chaupatty beach in Bombay. It's one of the most beautiful beaches in Bombay, or was, before the filth took over. Anyway, even though we lived so close to it, I never learned to swim. It's just one of those things. "

"Well," says the woman, "that happens sometimes. Take me, for instance, I never learned to ride a bicycle. It was the mounting that used to scare me, I was afraid of falling." People have lined up behind me. "It's been very nice talking to you," she says, "hope you enjoy the course."

The art of swimming had been trapped between the devil and the deep blue sea. The devil was money, always scarce, and kept the private swimming clubs out of reach; the deep blue sea of Chaupatty beach was grey and murky with garbage, too filthy to swim in. Every so often we would muster our courage and Mummy would take me there to try and teach me. But a few minutes of paddling was all we could endure. Sooner or later something would float up against our legs or thighs or waists, depending on how deep we'd gone in, and we'd be revulsed and stride out to the sand.

Water imagery in my life is recurring. Chaupatty beach, now the high-school swimming pool. The universal symbol of life and regeneration did nothing but frustrate me. Perhaps the swimming pool will overturn that failure.

When images and symbols abound in this manner, sprawling or rolling across the page without guile or artifice, one is prone to say, how obvious, how skilless; symbols, after all, should be still and gentle as dewdrops, tiny, yet shining with a world of meaning. But what happens when, on the page of life itself, one encounters the ever-moving, all-engirdling sprawl of the filthy sea? Dewdrops and oceans both have their rightful places; Nariman Hansotia certainly knew that when he told his stories to the boys of Firozsha Baag.

The sea of Chaupatty was fated to endure the finales of life's everyday functions. It seemed that the dirtier it became, the more crowds it attracted: street urchins and beggars and beachcombers, looking through the junk that washed up. (Or was it the crowds that made it dirtier?—another instance of cause and effect blurring and evading identification.)

Too many religious festivals also used the sea as repository for their finales. Its use should have been rationed, like rice and kerosene. On Ganesh Chaturthi, clay idols of the god Ganesh, adorned with garlands and all manner of finery, were carried in processions to the accompaniment of drums and a variety of wind instruments. The music got more frenzied the closer the procession got to Chaupatty and to the moment of immersion.

Then there was Coconut Day, which was never as popular as Ganesh Chaturthi. From a bystander's viewpoint, coconuts chucked into the sea do not provide as much of a spectacle. We used the sea, too, to deposit the leftovers from Parsi religious ceremonies, things such as flowers, or the ashes of the sacred sandalwood fire, which just could not be dumped with the regular garbage but had to be entrusted to the care of Avan Yazad, the guardian of the sea. And things which were of no use but which no one had the heart to destroy were also given to Avan Yazad. Such as old photographs.

After Grandpa died, some of his things were flung out to sea. It was high tide; we always checked the newspaper when going to perform these disposals; an ebb would mean a long walk in squelchy sand before finding water. Most of the things were probably washed up on shore. But we tried to throw them as far out as possible, then waited a few minutes; if they did not float back right away we would pretend they were in the permanent safekeeping of Avan Yazad, which was a comforting thought. I can't remember everything we sent out to sea, but his brush and comb were in the parcel, his *kusti*, and some Kemadrin pills, which he used to take to keep the parkinsonism under control.

Our paddling sessions stopped for lack of enthusiasm on my part. Mummy wasn't too keen either, because of the filth. But my main concern was the little guttersnipes, like naked fish with little buoyant penises, taunting me with their skills, swimming underwater and emerging unexpectedly all around me, or pretending to masturbate—I think they were too young to achieve ejaculation. It was embarrassing. When I look back, I'm surprised that Mummy and I kept going as long as we did.

I examine the swimming-trunks I bought last week. Surf King, says the label, Made in Canada-Fabriqué Au Canada. I've been learning bits and pieces of French from bilingual labels at the supermarket too. These trunks are extremely sleek and streamlined hipsters, the distance from waistband to pouch tip the barest minimum. I wonder how everything will stay in place, not that I'm boastful about my endowments. I try them on, and feel that the tip of my member lingers perilously close to the exit. Too close, in fact, to conceal the exigencies of my swimming lesson fantasy: a gorgeous woman in the class for non-swimmers, at whose sight I will be instantly aroused, and she, spying the shape of my desire, will look me straight in the eye with her intentions; she will come home with me, to taste the pleasures of my delectable Asian brown body whose strangeness has intrigued her and unleashed uncontrollable surges of passion inside her throughout the duration of the swimming lesson.

I drop the Eaton's bag and wrapper in the garbage can. The swimming-trunks cost fifteen dollars, same as the fee for the ten weekly lessons. The garbage bag is almost full. I tie it up and take it outside. There is a medicinal smell in the hallway; the old man must have just returned to his apartment.

PW opens her door and says, "Two ladies from the third floor were lying in the sun this morning. In bikinis."

"That's nice," I say, and walk to the incinerator chute. She reminds me of Najamai in Firozsha Baag, except that Najamai employed a bit more subtlety while going about her life's chosen work.

PW withdraws and shuts her door.

■ ■ ■

Mother had to reply because Father said he did not want to write to his son till his son had something sensible to write to him, his questions had been ignored long enough, and if he wanted to keep his life a secret, fine, he would get no letters from his father.

But after Mother started the letter he went and looked over her shoulder, telling her what to ask him, because if they kept on writing the same questions, maybe he would understand how interested they were in knowing about things over there; Father said go on, ask him what his work is at the insurance company, tell him to take some courses at night school, that's how everyone moves ahead over there, tell him not to be discouraged if his job is just clerical right now; hard work will get him ahead, remind him he is a Zoroastrian: manashni, gavashni, kunashni, *better write the translation also: good thoughts, good words, good deeds—he must have forgotten what it means, and tell him to say prayers and do* kusti *at least twice a day.*

Writing it all down sadly, Mother did not believe he wore his sudra *and* kusti *anymore, she would be very surprised if he remembered any of the prayers; when she had asked him if he needed new* sudras *he said not to take any trouble because the Zoroastrian Society of Ontario imported them from Bombay for their members, and this sounded like a story he was making up, but she was leaving it in the hands of God, ten thousand miles away there was nothing she could do but write a letter and hope for the best.*

Then she sealed it, and Father wrote the address on it as usual because his writing was much neater than hers, handwriting was important in the address and she did not want the postman in Canada to make any mistake; she took it to the post office herself, it was impossible to trust anyone to mail it ever since the postage rates went up because people just tore off the stamps for their own use and threw away the letter, the only safe way was to hand it over the counter and make the clerk cancel the stamps before your own eyes.

■ ■ ■

Berthe, the building superintendent, is yelling at her son in the parking lot. He tinkers away with his van. This happens every fine-weathered Sunday. It must be the van that Berthe dislikes because I've seen mother and son together in other quite amicable situations.

Berthe is a big Yugoslavian with high cheekbones. Her nationality, was disclosed to me by PW. Berthe speaks a very rough-hewn English, I've overheard her in the lobby scolding tenants for late rents and leaving dirty lint screens in the dryers. It's exciting to listen to her, her words fall like rocks and boulders, and one can never tell where or how the next few will drop. But her Slavic yells at her son are a different matter, the words fly swift and true, well-aimed missiles that never miss. Finally, the son slams down the hood in disgust, wipes his hands on a rag, accompanies mother Berthe inside.

Berthe's husband has a job in a factory. But he loses several days of work every month when he succumbs to the booze, a word Berthe uses often in her Slavic tirades on those days, the only one I can understand, as it clunks down heavily out of the tight-flying formation of Yugoslavian sentences. He lolls around in the lobby, submitting passively to his wife's tongue-lashings. The bags under his bloodshot eyes, his stringy moustache, stubbled chin, dirty hair are so vulnerable to the poison-laden barbs (poison works the same way in any language) emanating from deep within the powerful watermelon bosom. No one's presence can embarrass or dignify her into silence.

No one except the old man who arrives now. "Good morning," he says, and Berthe turns, stops yelling, and smiles. Her husband rises, positions the wheelchair at the favourite angle. The lobby will be peaceful as long as the old man is there.

■ ■ ■

It was hopeless. My first swimming lesson. The water terrified me. When did that happen, I wonder, I used to love splashing at Chaupatty, carried about by the waves. And this was only a swimming pool. Where did all that terror come from? I'm trying to remember.

Armed with my Surf King I enter the high school and go to the pool area. A sheet with instructions for the new class is pinned to the bulletin board. All students must shower and then assemble at eight by the shallow end. As I enter the showers three young boys, probably from a previous class, emerge. One of them holds his nose. The second begins to hum, under his breath: Paki Paki, smell like curry. The third says to the first two: pretty soon all the water's going to taste of curry. They leave.

It's a mixed class, but the gorgeous woman of my fantasy is missing. I have to settle for another, in a pink one-piece suit, with brown hair and a bit of a stomach. She must be about thirty-five. Plain-looking.

The instructor is called Ron. He gives us a pep talk, sensing some nervousness in the group. We're finally all in the water, in the shallow end. He demonstrates floating on the back, then asks for a volunteer. The pink one-piece suit wades forward. He supports her, tells her to lean back and let her head drop in the water.

She does very well. And as we all regard her floating body, I see what was not visible outside the pool: her bush, curly bits of it, straying out at the pink Spandex V. Tongues of water lapping against her delta, as if caressing it teasingly, make the brown hair come alive in a most tantalizing manner. The crests and troughs of little waves, set off by the movement of our bodies in a circle around her, dutifully irrigate her; the curls alternately wave free inside the crest, then adhere to her wet thighs, beached by the inevitable trough. I could watch this forever, and I wish the floating demonstration would never end.

Next we are shown how to grasp the rail and paddle, face down in the water. Between practising floating and paddling, the hour is almost gone. I have been trying to observe the pink one-piece suit, getting glimpses of her straying pubic hair from various angles. Finally, Ron wants a volunteer for the last demonstration, and I go forward. To my horror he leads the class to the deep end. Fifteen feet of water. It is so blue, and I can see the bottom. He picks up a metal hoop attached to a long wooden stick. He wants me to grasp the hoop, jump in the water, and paddle, while he guides me by the stick. Perfectly safe, he tells me. A demonstration of how paddling propels the body.

It's too late to back out; besides, I'm so terrified I couldn't find the words to do so even if I wanted to. Everything he says I do as if in a trance. I don't remember the moment of jumping. The next thing I know is, I'm swallowing water and floundering, hanging on to the hoop for dear life. Ron draws me to the rails and helps me out. The class applauds.

We disperse and one thought is on my mind: what if I'd lost my grip? Fifteen feet of water under me. I shudder and take deep breaths. This is it. I'm not coming next week. This instructor is an irresponsible person. Or he does not value the lives of non-white immigrants. I remember the three teenagers. Maybe the swimming pool is the hangout of some racist group, bent on eliminating all non-white swimmers, to keep their waters pure and their white sisters unogled.

The elevator takes me upstairs. Then gutang-khutang. PW opens her door as I turn the corridor of medicinal smells. "Berthe was screaming loudly at her husband tonight," she tells me.

"Good for her," I say, and she frowns indignantly at me.

■ ■ ■

The old man is in the lobby. He's wearing thick wool gloves. He wants to know how the swimming was, must have seen me leaving with my towel yesterday. Not bad, I say.

"I used to swim a lot. Very good for the circulation." He wheezes. "My feet are cold all the time. Cold as ice. Hands too."

Summer is winding down, so I say stupidly, "Yes, it's not so warm any more."

The thought of the next swimming lesson sickens me. But as I comb through the memories of that terrifying Monday, I come upon the straying curls of brown pubic hair. Inexorably drawn by them, I decide to go.

It's a mistake, of course. This time I'm scared even to venture in the shallow end. When everyone has entered the water and I'm the only one outside, I feel a little foolish and slide in.

Instructor Ron says we should start by reviewing the floating technique. I'm in no hurry. I watch the pink one-piece pull the swim-suit down around her cheeks and flip back to achieve perfect flotation. And then reap disappointment. The pink Spandex triangle is perfectly streamlined today, nothing strays, not a trace of fuzz, not one filament, not even a sign of post-depilation irritation. Like the airbrushed parts of glamour magazine models. The barrenness of her impeccably packaged apex is a betrayal. Now she is shorn like the other women in the class. Why did she have to do it?

The weight of this disappointment makes the water less manageable, more lung-penetrating. With trepidation, I float and paddle my way through the remainder of the hour, jerking my head out every two seconds and breathing deeply, to continually shore up a supply of precious, precious air without, at the same time, seeming too anxious and losing my dignity.

I don't attend the remaining classes. After I've missed three, Ron the instructor telephones. I tell him I've had the flu and am still feeling poorly, but I'll try to be there the following week.

He does not call again. My Surf King is relegated to an unused drawer. Total losses: one fantasy plus thirty dollars. And no watery rebirth. The swimming pool, like Chaupatty beach, has produced a stillbirth. But there is a difference. Water means regeneration only if it is pure and cleansing. Chaupatty was filthy, the pool was not. Failure to swim through filth must mean something other than failure of rebirth—failure of symbolic death? Does that equal success of symbolic life? death of a symbolic failure? death of a symbol? What is the equation?

■ ■ ■

The postman did not bring a letter but a parcel, he was smiling because he knew that every time something came from Canada his baksheesh *was guaranteed, and this time because it was a parcel Mother gave him a whole rupee, she was quite excited, there were so many stickers on it besides the stamps, one for Small Parcel, another Printed Papers, a red sticker saying Insured; she showed it to Father, and opened it, then put both hands on her cheeks, not able to speak because the surprise and happiness was so great, tears came to her eyes and she could not stop smiling, till Father became impatient to know and finally got up and came to the table.*

When he saw it he was surprised and happy too, he began to grin, then hugged Mother saying our son is a writer, and we didn't even know it, he never told us a thing, here we are thinking he is still clerking away at the insurance company, and he has written a book of stories, all these years in school and college he kept his talent hidden, making us think he was just like one of the boys in the Baag, shouting and playing the fool in the compound, and now what a surprise; then Father opened the book and began reading it, heading back to the easy chair, and Mother so excited, still holding his arm, walked with him, saying it was not fair him reading it first, she wanted to read it too, and they agreed that he would read the first story, then give it to her so she could also read it, and they would take turns in that manner.

Mother removed the staples from the padded envelope in which he had mailed the book, and threw them away, then straightened the folded edges of the envelope and put it away safely with the other envelopes and letters she had collected since he left.

■ ■ ■

The leaves are beginning to fall. The only ones I can identify are maple. The days are dwindling like the leaves. I've started a habit of taking long walks every evening. The old man is in the lobby when I leave, he waves as I go by. By the time I'm back, the lobby is usually empty.

Today I was woken up by a grating sound outside that made my flesh crawl. I went to the window and saw Berthe raking the leaves in the parking lot. Not in the expanse of patchy lawn on the periphery, but in the parking lot proper. She was raking the black tarred surface. I went back to bed and dragged a pillow over my head, not releasing it till noon.

When I return from my walk in the evening, PW, summoned by the elevator's gutang-khutang, says, "Berthe filled six big black garbage bags with leaves today."

"Six bags!" I say. "Wow!"

■ ■ ■

Since the weather turned cold, Berthe's son does not tinker with his van on Sundays under my window. I'm able to sleep late.

Around eleven, there's a commotion outside. I reach out and switch on the clock radio. It's a sunny day, the window curtains are bright. I get up, curious, and see a black Olds Ninety-Eight in the parking lot, by the entrance to the building. The old man is in his wheelchair, bundled up, with a scarf wound several times round his neck as though to immobilize it, like a surgical collar. His daughter and another man, the car-owner, are helping him from the wheelchair into the front seat, encouraging him with words like: that's it, easy does it, attaboy. From the open door of the lobby, Berthe is shouting encouragement too, but hers is confined to one word: yah, repeated at different levels of pitch and volume, with variations on vowel-length. The stranger could be the old man's son, he has the same jet black hair and piercing eyes.

Maybe the old man is not well, it's an emergency. But I quickly scrap that thought—this isn't Bombay, an ambulance would have arrived. They're probably taking him out for a ride. If he is his son, where has he been all this time, I wonder.

The old man finally settles in the front seat, the wheelchair goes in the trunk, and they're off. The one I think is the son looks up and catches me at the window before I can move away, so I wave, and he waves back.

In the afternoon I take down a load of clothes to the laundry room. Both machines have completed their cycles, the clothes inside are waiting to be transferred to dryers. Should I remove them and place them on top of a dryer, or wait? I decide to wait. After a few minutes, two women arrive, they are in bathrobes, and smoking. It takes me a while to realize that these are the two disappointments who were sunbathing in bikinis last summer.

"You didn't have to wait, you could have removed the clothes and carried on, dear," says one. She has a Scottish accent. It's one of the few I've learned to identify. Like maple leaves.

"Well," I say, "some people might not like strangers touching their clothes."

"You're not a stranger, dear," she says, "you live in this building, we've seen you before."

"Besides, your hands are clean," the other one pipes in. "You can touch my things any time you like."

Horny old cow. I wonder what they've got on under their bathrobes. Not much, I find, as they bend over to place their clothes in the dryers.

"See you soon," they say, and exit, leaving me behind in an erotic wake of smoke and perfume and deep images of cleavages. I start the washers and depart, and when I come back later, the dryers are empty.

PW tells me, "The old man's son took him out for a drive today. He has a big beautiful black car."

I see my chance, and shoot back: "Olds Ninety-Eight."

"What?"

"The car," I explain, "it's an Oldsmobile Ninety-Eight."

She does not like this at all, my giving her information. She is visibly nettled, and retreats with a sour face.

■ ■ ■

Mother and Father read the first five stories, and she was very sad after reading some of them, she said he must be so unhappy there, all his stories are about Bombay, he remembers every little thing about his childhood, he is thinking about it all the time even though he is ten thousand miles away, my poor son, I think he misses his home and us and everything he left behind, because if he likes it over there why would he not write stories about that, there must be so many new ideas that his new life could give him.

But Father did not agree with this, he said it did not mean that he was unhappy, all writers worked in the same way, they used their memories and experiences and made stories out of them, changing some things, adding some, imagining some, all writers were very good at remembering details of their lives.

Mother said, how can you be sure that he is remembering because he is a writer, or whether he started to write because he is unhappy and thinks of his past, and wants to save it all by making stories of it; and Father said that is not a sensible question, anyway, it is now my turn to read the next story.

■ ■ ■

The first snow has fallen, and the air is crisp. It's not very deep, about two inches, just right to go for a walk in. I've been told that immigrants from hot countries always enjoy the snow the first year, maybe for a couple of years more, then inevitably the dread sets in, and the approach of winter gets them fretting and moping. On the other hand, if it hadn't been for my conversation with the woman at the swimming registration desk, they might now be saying that India is a nation of non-swimmers.

Berthe is outside, shovelling the snow off the walkway in the parking lot. She has a heavy, wide pusher which she wields expertly.

The old radiators in the apartment alarm me incessantly. They continue to broadcast a series of variations on death throes, and go from hot to cold and cold to hot at will, there's no controlling their temperature. I speak to Berthe about it in the lobby. The old man is there too, his chin seems to have sunk deeper into his chest, and his face is a yellowish grey.

"Nothing, not to worry about anything," says Berthe, dropping rough-hewn chunks of language around me. "Radiator no work, you tell me. You feel cold, you come to me, I keep you warm," and she opens her arms wide, laughing. I step back, and she advances, her breasts preceding her like the gallant prows of two ice-breakers. She looks at the old man to see if he is appreciating the act: "You no feel scared, I keep you safe and warm."

But the old man is staring outside, at the flakes of falling snow. What thoughts is he thinking as he watches them? Of childhood days, perhaps, and snowmen with hats and pipes, and snowball fights, and white Christmases, and Christmas trees? What will I think of, old in this country, when I sit and watch the snow come down? For me, it is already too late for snowmen and snowball fights, and all I will have is thoughts about childhood thoughts and dreams, built around snowscapes and winter wonderlands on the Christmas cards so popular in Bombay; my snowmen and snowball fights and Christmas trees are in the pages of Enid Blyton's books, dispersed amidst the adventures of the Famous Five, and the Five Find-Outers, and the Secret Seven. My snowflakes are even less forgettable than the old man's, for they never melt.

■ ■ ■

It finally happened. The heat went. Not the usual intermittent coming and going, but out completely. Stone cold. The radiators are like ice. And so is everything else. There's no hot water. Naturally. It's the hot water that goes through the rads and heats them. Or is it the other way around? Is there no hot water because the rads have stopped circulating it? I don't care, I'm too cold to sort out the cause and effect relationship. Maybe there is no connection at all.

I dress quickly, put on my winter jacket, and go down to the lobby. The elevator is not working because the power is out, so I take the stairs. Several people are gathered, and Berthe has announced that she has telephoned the office, they are sending a man. I go back up the stairs. It's only one floor, the elevator is just a bad habit. Back in Firozsha Baag they were broken most of the time. The stairway enters the corridor outside the old man's apartment, and I think of his cold feet and hands. Poor man, it must be horrible for him without heat.

As I walk down the long hallway, I feel there's something different but can't pin it down. I look at the carpet, the ceiling, the wallpaper: it all seems the same. Maybe it's the freezing cold that imparts a feeling of difference.

PW opens her door: "The old man had another stroke yesterday. They took him to the hospital."

The medicinal smell. That's it. It's not in the hallway any more.

■ ■ ■

In the stories that he'd read so far Father said that all the Parsi families were poor or middle-class, but that was okay; nor did he mind that the seeds for the stories were picked from the sufferings of their own lives; but there should also have been something positive about Parsis, there was so much to be proud of: the great Tatas and their contribution to the steel industry, or Sir Dinshaw Petit in the textile industry who made Bombay the Manchester of the East, or Dadabhai Naoroji in the freedom movement, where he was the first to use the word swaraj, *and the first to be elected to the British Parliament where he carried on his campaign; he should have found some way to bring some of these wonderful facts into his stories, what would people reading these stories think, those who did not know about Parsis—that the whole community was full of cranky, bigoted people; and in reality it was the richest, most advanced and philanthropic community in India, and he did not need to tell his own son that Parsis had a reputation for being generous and family-oriented. And he could have written something also about the historic background, how Parsis came to India from Persia because of Islamic persecution in the seventh century, and were the descendants of Cyrus the Great and the magnificent Persian Empire. He could have made a story of all this, couldn't he?*

Mother said what she liked best was his remembering everything so well, how beautifully he wrote about it all, even the sad things, and though he changed some of it, and used his imagination, there was truth in it.

My hope is, Father said, that there will be some story based on his Canadian experience, that way we will know something about our son's life there, if not through his letters then in his stories; so far they are all about Parsis and Bombay, and the one with a little bit about Toronto, where a man perches on top of the toilet, is shameful and disgusting, although it is funny at times and did make me laugh, I have to admit, but where does he get such an imagination from, what is the point of such a fantasy; and Mother said that she would also enjoy some stories about Toronto and the people there; it puzzles me, she said, why he writes nothing about it, especially since you say that writers use their own experience to make stories out of.

Then Father said this is true, but he is probably not using his Toronto experience because it is too early; what do you mean, too early, asked Mother and Father explained it takes a writer about ten years time after an experience before he is able to use it in his writing, it takes that long to be absorbed internally and understood, thought out and thought about, over and over again, he haunts it and it haunts him if it is valuable enough, till the writer is comfortable with it to be able to use it as he wants; but this is only one theory I read somewhere, it may or may not be true.

That means, said Mother, that his childhood in Bombay and our home here is the most valuable thing in his life just now, because he is able to remember it all to write about it, and you were so bitterly saying he is forgetting where he came from; and that may be true, said Father, but that is not what the theory means, according to the theory he is writing of these things because they are far enough in the past for him to deal with objectively, he is able to achieve what critics call artistic distance, without emotions interfering; and what do you mean emotions, said Mother, you are saying he does not feel anything for his characters, how can he write so beautifully about so many sad things without any feelings in his heart?

But before Father could explain more, about beauty and emotion and inspiration and imagination, Mother took the book and said it was her turn now and too much theory she did not want to listen to, it was confusing and did not make as much sense as reading the stories, she would read them her way and Father could read them his.

■ ■ ■

My books on the windowsill have been damaged. Ice has been forming on the inside ledge, which I did not notice, and melting when the sun shines in. I spread them in a corner of the living-room to dry out.

The winter drags on. Berthe wields her snow pusher as expertly as ever, but there are signs of weariness in her performance. Neither husband nor son is ever seen outside with a shovel. Or anywhere else, for that matter. It occurs to me that the son's van is missing, too.

The medicinal smell is in the hall again. I sniff happily and look forward to seeing the old man in the lobby. I go downstairs and peer into the mailbox, see the blue and magenta of an Indian aerogramme with Don Mills, Ontario, Canada in Father's flawless hand through the slot.

I pocket the letter and enter the main lobby. The old man is there, but not in his usual place. He is not looking out through the glass door. His wheelchair is facing a bare wall where the wallpaper is torn in places. As though he is not interested in the outside world any more, having finished with all that, and now it's time to see inside. What does he see inside, I wonder? I go up to him and say hullo. He says hullo without raising his sunken chin. After a few seconds his grey countenance faces me. "How old do you think I am?" His eyes are dull and glazed; he is looking even further inside than I first presumed.

"Well, let's see, you're probably close to sixty-four."

"I'll be seventy-eight next August." But he does not chuckle or wheeze. Instead, he continues softly, "I wish my feet did not feel so cold all the time. And my hands." He lets his chin fall again.

In the elevator I start opening the aerogramme, a tricky business because a crooked tear means lost words. Absorbed in this while emerging, I don't notice PW occupying the centre of the hallway, arms folded across her chest: "They had a big fight. Both of them have left."

I don't immediately understand her agitation. "What . . . who?"

"Berthe. Husband and son both left her. Now she is all alone."

Her tone and stance suggest that we should not be standing here talking but do something to bring Berthe's family back. "That's very sad," I say, and go in. I picture father and son in the van, driving away, driving across the snow-covered country, in the dead of winter, away from wife and mother; away to where? how far will they go? Not son's van nor father's booze can take them far enough. And the further they go, the more they'll remember, they can take it from me.

■ ■ ■

All the stories were read by Father and Mother, and they were sorry when the book was finished, they felt they had come to know their son better now, yet there was much more to know, they wished there were many more stories; and this is what they mean, said Father, when they say that the whole story can never be told, the whole truth can never be known; what do you mean, they say, asked Mother, who they, and Father said writers, poets, philosophers. I don't care what they say, said Mother, my son will write as much or as little as he wants to, and if I can read it I will be happy.

The last story they liked the best of all because it had the most in it about Canada, and now they felt they knew at least a little bit, even if it was a very little bit, about his day-to-day life in his apartment; and Father said if he continues to write about such things he will become popular because I am sure they are interested there in reading about life through the eyes of an immigrant, it provides a different viewpoint; the only danger is if he changes and becomes so much like them that he will write like one of them and lose the important difference.

■ ■ ■

The bathroom needs cleaning. I open a new can of Ajax and scour the tub. Sloshing with mug from bucket was standard bathing procedure in the bathrooms of Firozsha Baag, so my preference now is always for a shower. I've never used the tub as yet; besides, it would be too much like Chaupatty or the swimming pool, wallowing in my own dirt. Still, it must be cleaned.

When I've finished, I prepare for a shower. But the clean gleaming tub and the nearness of the vernal equinox give me the urge to do something different today. I find the drain plug in the bathroom cabinet, and run the bath.

I've spoken so often to the old man, but I don't know his name. I should have asked him the last time I saw him, when his wheelchair was facing the bare wall because he had seen all there was to see outside and it was time to see what was inside. Well, tomorrow. Or better yet, I can look it up in the directory in the lobby. Why didn't I think of that before? It will only have an initial and a last name, but then I can surprise him with: hullo Mr Wilson, or whatever it is.

The bath is full. Water imagery is recurring in my life: Chaupatty beach, swimming pool, bathtub. I step in and immerse myself up to the neck. It feels good. The hot water loses its opacity when the chlorine, or whatever it is, has cleared. My hair is still dry. I close my eyes, hold my breath, and dunk my head. Fighting the panic, I stay under and count to thirty. I come out, clear my lungs and breathe deeply.

I do it again. This time I open my eyes under water, and stare blindly without seeing, it takes all my will to keep the lids from closing. Then I am slowly able to discern the underwater objects. The drain plug looks different, slightly distorted; there is a hair trapped between the hole and the plug, it waves and dances with the movement of the water. I come up, refresh my lungs, examine quickly the overwater world of the washroom, and go in again. I do it several times, over and over. The world outside the water I have seen a lot of, it is now time to see what is inside.

The spring session for adult non-swimmers will begin in a few days at the high school. I must not forget the registration date.

■ ■ ■

The dwindled days of winter are now all but forgotten; they have grown and attained a respectable span. I resume my evening walks, it's spring, and a vigorous thaw is on. The snowbanks are melting, the sound of water on its gushing, gurgling journey to the drains is beautiful. I plan to buy a book of trees, so I can identify more than the maple as they begin to bloom.

When I return to the building, I wipe my feet energetically on the mat because some people are entering behind me, and I want to set a good example. Then I go to the board with its little plastic letters and numbers. The old man's apartment is the one on the corner by the stairway, that makes it number 201. I run down the list, come to 201, but there are no little white plastic letters beside it. Just the empty black rectangle with holes where the letters would be squeezed in. That's strange. Well, I can introduce myself to him, then ask his name.

However, the lobby is empty. I take the elevator, exit at the second floor, wait for the gutang-khutang. It does not come: the door closes noiselessly, smoothly. Berthe has been at work, or has made sure someone else has. PW's cue has been lubricated out of existence.

But she must have the ears of a cockroach. She is waiting for me. I whistle my way down the corridor. She fixes me with an accusing look. She waits till I stop whistling, then says: "You know the old man died last night."

I cease groping for my key. She turns to go and I take a step towards her, my hand still in my trouser pocket. "Did you know his name?" I ask, but she leaves without answering.

■ ■ ■

Then Mother said, the part I like best in the last story is about Grandpa, where he wonders if Grandpa's spirit is really watching him and blessing him, because you know I really told him that, I told him helping an old suffering person who is near death is the most blessed thing to do, because that person will ever after watch over you from heaven, I told him this when he was disgusted with Grandpa's urine-bottle and would not touch it, would not hand it to him even when I was not at home.

Are you sure, said Father, that you really told him this, or you believe you told him because you like the sound of it, you said yourself the other day that he changes and adds and alters things in the stories but he writes it all so beautifully that it seems true, so how can you be sure; this sounds like another theory, said Mother, but I don't care, he says I told him and I believe now I told him, so even if I did not tell him then it does not matter now.

Don't you see, said Father, that you are confusing fiction with facts, fiction does not create facts, fiction can come from facts, it can grow out of facts by compounding, transposing, augmenting, diminishing, or altering them in any way; but you must not confuse cause and effect, you must not confuse what really happened with what the story says happened, you must not loose your grasp on reality, that way madness lies.

Then Mother stopped listening because, as she told Father so often, she was not very fond of theories, and she took out her writing pad and started a letter to her son; Father looked over her shoulder, telling her to say how proud they were of him and were waiting for his next book, he also said, leave a little space for me at the end, I want to write a few lines when I put the address on the envelope.

Alice Munro

For the settings of her prose fiction, Alice Munro has relied primarily on the small towns and rural landscapes of Western Ontario, where she was born in 1931. Although she started publishing short stories in such journals as *Queen's Quarterly, Tamarack Review,* and *The Canadian Forum* in the 1950s, her first book appeared only in 1968, when a collection of fifteen stories was published under the title *Dance of the Happy Shades* and immediately won critical acclaim. Like the novel that followed in 1971, *Lives of Girls and Women*—and stories in such subsequent collections as *Something I've Been Meaning to Tell You* (1974), *Who Do You Think You Are?* (1978), *The Moons of Jupiter* (1982), and *Friend of My Youth* (1990)—her fiction explores tensions between the orderly and the uncontrollable in modern life, particularly as they affect women. The orderly manifests itself in conventions of various kinds: the moral and social structure of small-town society, the dimensions of family life, the roles accorded men and women by tradition and inertia.

Munro's dramatization of these social realities brings her characters up against the knowledge of the limits that such order imposes on them. They rebel, or they surrender, or they question their ability to escape themselves—to escape the identities that the conventions have inevitably helped create. When the father in one of her stories ("Boys and Girls"), for example, dismisses his daughter's intentional rebellion with the phrase "she's only a girl," he dismisses implicitly her capacities for intelligence and independent judgment; moreover, the girl has become so pressured by family expectations that she acknowledges "maybe it was true."

In several later stories, such as "The Children Stay" (*The New Yorker,* 1997; collected in *The Love of a Good Woman,* 1998), Munro suggests that "truth" or "the real story" can never be found. Characters who enquire into the past find more questions—a series of stories-within-stories—rather than answers. Or, as with "The Children Stay," they probe the consequences of particular choices that some characters made in the past and now refuse to regret (even when they realize that the choices might have been "wrong"). Set not in Western Ontario but on Vancouver Island, "The Children Stay" draws on the love story of Orpheus and Eurydice to comment ironically on contemporary life. It negotiates the disputed territories of translation and accommodation, finding that *what one understands* and *where one lives* are matters more perceptual than material, informed both by desire and by pain.

The Children Stay

Thirty years ago, a family was spending a holiday together on the east coast of Vancouver Island. A young father and mother, their two small daughters, and an older couple, the husband's parents.

What perfect weather. Every morning, every morning it's like this, the first pure sunlight falling through the high branches, burning away the mist over the still water of Georgia Strait. The tide out, a great empty stretch of sand still damp but easy to walk on, like cement in its very last stage of drying. The tide is actually less far out; every morning, the pavilion of sand is shrinking, but it still seems ample enough. The changes in the tide are a matter of great interest to the grandfather, not so much to anyone else.

Pauline, the young mother, doesn't really like the beach as well as she likes the road that runs behind the cottages for a mile or so north till it stops at the bank of the little river that runs into the sea.

If it wasn't for the tide, it would be hard to remember that this is the sea. You look across the water to the mountains on the mainland, the ranges that are the western wall of the continent of North America. These humps and peaks coming clear now through the mist and glimpsed here and there through the trees, by Pauline as she pushes her daughter's stroller along the road, are also of interest to the grandfather. And to his son Brian, who is Pauline's husband. The two men are continually trying to decide which is what. Which of these shapes are actual continental mountains and which are improbable heights of the islands that ride in front of the shore? It's hard to sort things out when the array is so complicated and parts of it shift their distance in the day's changing light.

But there is a map, set up under glass, between the cottages and the beach. You can stand there looking at the map, then looking at what's in front of you, looking back at the map again, until you get things sorted out. The grandfather and Brian do this every day, usually getting into an argument—though you'd think there would not be much room for disagreement with the map right there. Brian chooses to see the map as inexact. But his father will not hear a word of criticism about any aspect of this place, which was his choice for the holiday. The map, like the accommodation and the weather, is perfect.

Brian's mother won't look at the map. She says it boggles her mind. The men laugh at her, they accept that her mind is boggled. Her husband believes that this is because she is a female. Brian believes that it's because she's his mother. Her concern is always about whether anybody is hungry yet, or thirsty, whether the children have their sun hats on and have been rubbed with protective lotion. And what is the strange bite on Caitlin's arm that doesn't look like the bite of a mosquito? She makes her husband wear a floppy cotton hat and thinks that Brian should wear one too—she reminds him of how sick he got from the sun, that summer they went to the Okanagan, when he was a child. Sometimes Brian says to her, "Oh, dry up, Mother." His tone is mostly affectionate, but his father may ask him if that's the way he thinks he can talk to his mother nowadays.

"She doesn't mind," says Brian.

"How do you know?" says his father.

"Oh for Pete's sake," says his mother.

■ ■ ■

Pauline slides out of bed as soon as she's awake every morning, slides out of reach of Brian's long, sleepily searching arms and legs. What wakes her are the first squeaks and mutters of the baby, Mara, in the children's room, then the creak of the crib as Mara—sixteen months old now, getting to the end of babyhood—pulls herself up to stand hanging on to the railing. She continues her soft amiable talk as Pauline lifts her out—Caitlin, nearly five, shifting about but not waking, in her nearby bed—and as she is carried into the kitchen to be changed, on the floor. Then she is settled into her stroller, with a biscuit and a bottle of apple juice, while Pauline gets into her sundress and sandals, goes to the bathroom, combs out her hair—all as quickly and quietly as possible. They leave the cottage; they head past some other cottages for the bumpy unpaved road that is still mostly in deep morning shadow, the floor of a tunnel under fir and cedar trees.

The grandfather, also an early riser, sees them from the porch of his cottage, and Pauline sees him. But all that is necessary is a wave. He and Pauline never have much to say to each other (though sometimes there's an affinity they feel, in the midst of some long-drawn-out antics of Brian's or some apologetic but insistent fuss made by the grandmother; there's an awareness of not looking at each other, lest their look should reveal a bleakness that would discredit others).

On this holiday Pauline steals time to be by herself—being with Mara is still almost the same thing as being by herself. Early morning walks, the late-morning hour when she washes and hangs out the diapers. She could have had another hour or so in the afternoons, while Mara is napping. But Brian has fixed up a shelter on the beach, and he carries the playpen down every day, so that Mara can nap there and Pauline won't have to absent herself. He says his parents may be offended if she's always sneaking off. He agrees though that she does need some time to go over her lines for the play she's going to be in, back in Victoria, this September.

Pauline is not an actress. This is an amateur production, but she is not even an amateur actress. She didn't try out for the role, though it happened that she had already read the play. *Eurydice* by Jean Anouilh. But then, Pauline has read all sorts of things.

She was asked if she would like to be in this play by a man she met at a barbecue, in June. The people at the barbecue were mostly teachers and their wives or husbands—it was held at the house of the principal of the high school where Brian teaches. The woman who taught French was a widow—she had brought her grown son who was staying for the summer with her and working as a night clerk in a downtown hotel. She told everybody that he had got a job teaching at a college in western Washington State and would be going there in the fall.

Jeffrey Toom was his name. "Without the *B*," he said, as if the staleness of the joke wounded him. It was a different name from his mother's, because she had been widowed twice, and he was the son of her first husband. About the job he said, "No guarantee it'll last, it's a one-year appointment."

What was he going to teach?

"Dram-ah," he said, drawing the word out in a mocking way.

He spoke of his present job disparagingly, as well.

"It's a pretty sordid place," he said. "Maybe you heard—a hooker was killed there last winter. And then we get the usual losers checking in to OD or bump themselves off."

People did not quite know what to make of this way of talking and drifted away from him. Except for Pauline.

"I'm thinking about putting on a play," he said. "Would you like to be in it?" He asked her if she had ever heard of a play called *Eurydice*.

Pauline said, "You mean Anouilh's?" and he was unflatteringly surprised. He immediately said he didn't know if it would ever work out. "I just thought it might be interesting to see if you could do something different here in the land of Noël Coward."

Pauline did not remember when there had been a play by Noël Coward put on in Victoria, though she supposed there had been several. She said, "We saw *The Duchess of Malfi* last winter at the college. And the little theater did *A Resounding Tinkle*, but we didn't see it."

"Yeah. Well," he said, flushing. She had thought he was older than she was, at least as old as Brian (who was thirty, though people were apt to say he didn't act it), but as soon as he started talking to her, in this offhand, dismissive way, never quite meeting her eyes, she suspected that he was younger than he'd like to appear. Now with that flush she was sure of it.

As it turned out, he was a year younger than she was. Twenty-five.

She said that she couldn't be Eurydice; she couldn't act. But Brian came over to see what the conversation was about and said at once that she must try it.

"She just needs a kick in the behind," Brian said to Jeffrey. "She's like a little mule, it's hard to get her started. No, seriously, she's too self-effacing, I tell her that all the time. She's very smart. She's actually a lot smarter than I am."

At that Jeffrey did look directly into Pauline's eyes—impertinently and searchingly—and she was the one who was flushing.

He had chosen her immediately as his Eurydice because of the way she looked. But it was not because she was beautiful. "I'd never put a beautiful girl in that part," he said. "I don't know if I'd ever put a beautiful girl on stage in anything. It's too much. It's distracting."

So what did he mean about the way she looked? He said it was her hair, which was long and dark and rather bushy (not in style at that time), and her pale skin ("Stay out of the sun this summer") and most of all her eyebrows.

"I never liked them," said Pauline, not quite sincerely. Her eyebrows were level, dark, luxuriant. They dominated her face. Like her hair, they were not in style. But if she had really disliked them, wouldn't she have plucked them?

Jeffrey seemed not to have heard her. "They give you a sulky look and that's disturbing," he said. "Also your jaw's a little heavy and that's sort of Greek. It would be better in a movie where I could get you close up. The routine thing for Eurydice would be a girl who looked ethereal. I don't want ethereal."

As she walked Mara along the road, Pauline did work at the lines. There was a speech at the end that was giving her trouble. She bumped the stroller along and repeated to herself, " 'You are terrible, you know, you are terrible like the angels. You think everybody's going forward, as brave and bright as you are—oh, don't look at me, please, darling, don't look at me—perhaps I'm not what you wish I was, but I'm here, and I'm warm, I'm kind, and I love you. I'll give you all the happiness I can. Don't look at me. Don't look. Let me live.' "

She had left something out. " 'Perhaps I'm not what you wish I was, but you feel me here, don't you? I'm warm and I'm kind—' "

She had told Jeffrey that she thought the play was beautiful.

He said, "Really?" What she'd said didn't please or surprise him—he seemed to feel it was predictable, superfluous. He would never describe a play in that way. He spoke of it more as a hurdle to be got over. Also a challenge to be flung at various enemies. At the academic snots—as he called them—who had done *The Duchess of Malfi*. And at the social twits—as he called them—in the little theater. He saw himself as an outsider heaving his weight against these people, putting on his play—he called it his—in the teeth of their contempt and opposition. In the beginning Pauline thought that this must be all in his imagination and that it was more likely these people knew nothing about him. Then something would happen that could be, but might not be, a coincidence. Repairs had to be done on the church hall where the play was to be performed, making it unobtainable. There was an unexpected increase in the cost of printing advertising posters. She found herself seeing it his way. If you were going to be around him much, you almost had to see it his way—arguing was dangerous and exhausting.

"Sons of bitches," said Jeffrey between his teeth, but with some satisfaction. "I'm not surprised."

The rehearsals were held upstairs in an old building on Fisgard Street. Sunday afternoon was the only time that everybody could get there, though there were fragmentary rehearsals during the week. The retired harbor pilot who played Monsieur Henri was able to attend every rehearsal, and got to have an irritating familiarity with everybody else's lines. But the hairdresser—who had experience only with Gilbert and Sullivan but now found herself playing Eurydice's mother—could not leave her shop for long at any other time. The bus driver who played her lover had his daily employment as well, and so had the waiter who played Orphée (he was the only one of them who hoped to be a real actor). Pauline had to depend on sometimes undependable high-school babysitters—for the first six weeks of the summer Brian was busy teaching summer school—and Jeffrey himself had to be at his hotel job by eight o'clock in the evenings. But on Sunday afternoons they were all there. While other people swam at Thetis Lake, or thronged Beacon Hill Park to walk under the trees and feed the ducks, or drove far out of town to the Pacific beaches, Jeffrey and his crew labored in the dusty high-ceilinged room on Fisgard Street. The windows were rounded at the top as in some plain and dignified church, and propped open in the heat with whatever objects could be found—ledger books from the 1920s belonging to the hat shop that had once operated downstairs, or pieces of wood left over from the picture frames made by the artist whose canvases were now stacked against one wall and apparently abandoned. The glass was grimy, but outside the sunlight bounced off the sidewalks, the empty gravelled parking lots, the low stuccoed buildings, with what seemed a special Sunday brightness. Hardly anybody moved through these downtown streets. Nothing was open except the occasional hole-in-the-wall coffee shop or fly-specked convenience store.

Pauline was the one who went out at the break to get soft drinks and coffee. She was the one who had the least to say about the play and the way it was going—even though she was the only one who had read it before—because she alone had never done any acting. So it seemed proper for her to volunteer. She enjoyed her short walk in the empty streets—she felt as if she had become an urban person, someone detached and solitary, who lived in the glare of an important dream. Sometimes she thought of Brian at home, working in the garden and keeping an eye on the children. Or perhaps he had taken them to Dallas Road—she recalled a promise—to sail boats on the pond. That life seemed ragged and tedious compared to what went on in the rehearsal room—the hours of effort, the concentration, the sharp exchanges, the sweating and tension. Even the taste of the coffee, its scalding bitterness, and the fact that it was chosen by nearly everybody in preference to a fresher-tasting and maybe more healthful drink out of the cooler seemed satisfying to her. And she liked the look of the shop-windows. This was not one of the dolled-up streets near the harbor—it was a street of shoe- and bicycle-repair shops, discount linen and fabric stores, of clothes and furniture that had been so long in the windows that they looked secondhand even if they weren't. On some windows sheets of golden plastic as frail and crinkled as old cellophane were stretched inside the glass to protect the merchandise from the sun. All these enterprises had been left behind just for this one day, but they had a look of being fixed in time as much as cave paintings or relics under sand.

■ ■ ■

When she said that she had to go away for the two-week holiday Jeffrey looked thunderstruck, as if he had never imagined that things like holidays could come into her life. Then he turned grim and slightly satirical, as if this was just another blow that he might have expected. Pauline explained that she would miss only the one Sunday—the one in the middle of the two weeks—because she and Brian were driving up the island on a Monday and coming back on a Sunday morning. She promised to get back in time for rehearsal. Privately she wondered how she would do this—it always took so much longer than you expected to pack up and get away. She wondered if she could possibly come back by herself, on the morning bus. That would probably be too much to ask for. She didn't mention it.

She couldn't ask him if it was only the play he was thinking about, only her absence from a rehearsal that caused the thundercloud. At the moment, it very likely was. When he spoke to her at rehearsals there was never any suggestion that he ever spoke to her in any other way. The only difference in his treatment of her was that perhaps he expected less of her, of her acting, than he did of the others. And that would be understandable to anybody. She was the only one chosen out of the blue, for the way she looked—the others had all shown up at the audition he had advertised on the signs put up in cafés and bookstores around town. From her he appeared to want an immobility or awkwardness that he didn't want from the rest of them. Perhaps it was because, in the latter part of the play, she was supposed to be a person who had already died.

Yet she thought they all knew, the rest of the cast all knew, what was going on, in spite of Jeffrey's offhand and abrupt and none too civil ways. They knew that after every one of them had straggled off home, he would walk across the room and bolt the staircase door. (At first Pauline had pretended to leave with the rest and had even got into her car and circled the block, but later such a trick had come to seem insulting, not just to herself and Jeffrey, but to the others whom she was sure would never betray her, bound as they all were under the temporary but potent spell of the play.)

Jeffrey crossed the room and bolted the door. Every time, this was like a new decision, which he had to make. Until it was done, she wouldn't look at him. The sound of the bolt being pushed into place, the ominous or fatalistic sound of the metal hitting metal, gave her a localized shock of capitulation. But she didn't make a move, she waited for him to come back to her with the whole story of the afternoon's labor draining out of his face, the expression of matter-of-fact and customary disappointment cleared away, replaced by the live energy she always found surprising.

■ ■ ■

"So. Tell us what this play of yours is about," Brian's father said. "Is it one of those ones where they take their clothes off on the stage?"

"Now don't tease her," said Brian's mother.

Brian and Pauline had put the children to bed and walked over to his parents' cottage for an evening drink. The sunset was behind them, behind the forests of Vancouver Island, but the mountains in front of them, all clear now and hard-cut against the sky, shone in its pink light. Some high inland mountains were capped with pink summer snow.

"Nobody takes their clothes off, Dad," said Brian in his booming schoolroom voice. "You know why? Because they haven't got any clothes on in the first place. It's the latest style. They're going to put on a bare-naked *Hamlet* next. Bare-naked *Romeo and Juliet*. Boy, that balcony scene where Romeo is climbing up the trellis and he gets stuck in the rosebushes—"

"Oh, Brian," said his mother.

"The story of Orpheus and Eurydice is that Eurydice died," Pauline said. "And Orpheus goes down to the underworld to try to get her back. And his wish is granted, but only if he promises not to look at her. Not to look back at her. She's walking behind him—"

"Twelve paces," said Brian. "As is only right."

"It's a Greek story, but it's set in modern times," said Pauline. "At least this version is. More or less modern. Orpheus is a musician travelling around with his father—they're both musicians—and Eurydice is an actress. This is in France."

"Translated?" Brian's father said.

"No," said Brian. "But don't worry, it's not in French. It was written in Transylvanian."

"It's so hard to make sense of anything," Brian's mother said with a worried laugh. "It's so hard, with Brian around."

"It's in English," Pauline said.

"And you're what's-her-name?"

She said, "I'm Eurydice."

"He get you back okay?"

"No," she said. "He looks back at me, and then I have to stay dead."

"Oh, an unhappy ending," Brian's mother said.

"You're so gorgeous?" said Brian's father skeptically. "He can't stop himself from looking back?"

"It's not that," said Pauline. But at this point she felt that something had been achieved by her father-in-law, he had done what he meant to do, which was the same thing that he nearly always meant to do, in any conversation she had with him. And that was to break through the structure of some explanation he had asked her for, and she had unwillingly but patiently given, and, with a seemingly negligent kick, knock it into rubble. He had been dangerous to her for a long time in this way, but he wasn't particularly so tonight.

But Brian did not know that. Brian was still figuring out how to come to her rescue.

"Pauline is gorgeous," Brian said.

"Yes indeed," said his mother.

"Maybe if she'd go to the hairdresser," his father said. But Pauline's long hair was such an old objection of his that it had become a family joke. Even Pauline laughed. She said, "I can't afford to till we get the veranda roof fixed." And Brian laughed boisterously, full of relief that she was able to take all this as a joke. It was what he had always told her to do.

"Just kid him back," he said. "It's the only way to handle him."

"Yeah, well, if you'd got yourselves a decent house," said his father. But this like Pauline's hair was such a familiar sore point that it couldn't rouse anybody. Brian and Pauline had bought a handsome house in bad repair on a street in Victoria where old mansions were being turned into ill-used apartment buildings. The house, the street, the messy old Garry oaks, the fact that no basement had been blasted out under the house, were all a horror to Brian's father. Brian usually agreed with him and tried to go him one further. If his father pointed at the house next door all crisscrossed with black fire escapes, and asked what kind of neighbors they had, Brian said, "Really poor people, Dad. Drug addicts." And when his father wanted to know how it was heated, he'd said, "Coal furnace. Hardly any of them left these days, you can get coal really cheap. Of course it's dirty and it kind of stinks."

So what his father said now about a decent house might be some kind of peace signal. Or could be taken so.

Brian was an only son. He was a math teacher. His father was a civil engineer and part owner of a contracting company. If he had hoped that he would have a son who was an engineer and might come into the company, there was never any mention of it. Pauline had asked Brian whether he thought the carping about their house and her hair and the books she read might be a cover for this larger disappointment, but Brian had said, "Nope. In our family we complain about just whatever we want to complain about. We ain't subtle, ma'am."

Pauline still wondered, when she heard his mother talking about how teachers ought to be the most honored people in the world and they did not get half the credit they deserved and that she didn't know how Brian managed it, day after day. Then his father might say, "That's right," or, "I sure wouldn't want to do it, I can tell you that. They couldn't pay me to do it."

"Don't worry Dad," Brian would say. "They wouldn't pay you much."

Brian in his everyday life was a much more dramatic person than Jeffrey. He dominated his classes by keeping up a parade of jokes and antics, extending the role that he had always played, Pauline believed, with his mother and father. He acted dumb, he bounced back from pretended humiliations, he traded insults. He was a bully in a good cause—a chivvying cheerful indestructible bully.

"Your boy has certainly made his mark with us," the principal said to Pauline. "He has not just survived, which is something in itself. He has made his mark."

Your boy.

Brian called his students boneheads. His tone was affectionate, fatalistic. He said that his father was the King of the Philistines, a pure and natural barbarian. And that his mother was a dishrag, good-natured and worn out. But however he dismissed such people, he could not be long without them. He took his students on camping trips. And he could not imagine a summer without this shared holiday. He was mortally afraid, every year, that Pauline would refuse to go along. Or that, having agreed to go, she was going to be miserable, take offense at something his father said, complain about how much time she had to spend with his mother, sulk because there was no way they could do anything by themselves. She might decide to spend all day in their own cottage, reading and pretending to have a sunburn.

All those things had happened, on previous holidays. But this year she was easing up. He told her he could see that, and he was grateful to her.

"I know it's an effort," he said. "It's different for me. They're my parents and I'm used to not taking them seriously."

Pauline came from a family that took things so seriously that her parents had got a divorce. Her mother was now dead. She had a distant, though cordial, relationship with her father and her two much older sisters. She said that they had nothing in common. She knew Brian could not understand how that could be a reason. She saw what comfort it gave him, this year, to see things going so well. She had thought it was laziness or cowardice that kept him from breaking the arrangement, but now she saw that it was something far more positive. He needed to have his wife and his parents and his children bound together like this, he needed to involve Pauline in his life with his parents and to bring his parents to some recognition of her—though the recognition, from his father, would always be muffled and contrary, and from his mother too profuse, too easily come by, to mean much. Also he wanted Pauline to be connected, he wanted the children to be connected, to his own childhood—he wanted these holidays to be linked to holidays of his childhood with their lucky or unlucky weather, car troubles or driving records, boating scares, bee stings, marathon Monopoly games, to all the things that he told his mother he was bored to death hearing about. He wanted pictures from this summer to be taken, and fitted into his mother's album, a continuation of all the other pictures that he groaned at the mention of.

The only time they could talk to each other was in bed, late at night. But they did talk then, more than was usual with them at home, where Brian was so tired that often he fell immediately asleep. And in ordinary daylight it was often hard to talk to him because of his jokes. She could see the joke brightening his eyes (his coloring was very like hers—dark hair and pale skin and gray eyes, but her eyes were cloudy and his were light, like clear water over stones). She could see it pulling at the corners of his mouth, as he foraged among your words to catch a pun or the start of a rhyme—anything that could take the conversation away, into absurdity. His whole body, tall and loosely joined together and still almost as skinny as a teenager's, twitched with comic propensity. Before she married him, Pauline had a friend named Gracie, a rather grumpy-looking girl, subversive about men. Brian had thought her a girl whose spirits needed a boost, and so he made even more than the usual effort. And Gracie said to Pauline, "How can you stand the nonstop show?"

"That's not the real Brian," Pauline had said. "He's different when we're alone." But looking back, she wondered how true that had ever been. Had she said it simply to defend her choice, as you did when you had made up your mind to get married?

So talking in the dark had something to do with the fact that she could not see his face. And that he knew she couldn't see his face.

But even with the window open on the unfamiliar darkness and stillness of the night, he teased a little. He had to speak of Jeffrey as Monsieur le Directeur, which made the play or the fact that it was a French play slightly ridiculous. Or perhaps it was Jeffrey himself, Jeffrey's seriousness about the play, that had to be called in question.

Pauline didn't care. It was such a pleasure and a relief to her to mention Jeffrey's name.

Most of the time she didn't mention him; she circled around that pleasure. She described all the others, instead. The hairdresser and the harbor pilot and the waiter and the old man who claimed to have once acted on the radio. He played Orphée's father and gave Jeffrey the most trouble, because he had the stubbornest notions of his own, about acting.

The middle-aged impresario Monsieur Dulac was played by a twenty-four-year-old travel agent. And Mathias, who was Eurydice's former boyfriend, presumably around her own age, was played by the manager of a shoe store, who was married and a father of children.

Brian wanted to know why Monsieur le Directeur hadn't cast these two the other way round.

"That's the way he does things," Pauline said. "What he sees in us is something only he can see."

For instance, she said, the waiter was a clumsy Orphée.

"He's only nineteen, he's so shy Jeffrey has to keep at him. He tells him not to act like he's making love to his grandmother. He has to tell him what to do. *Keep your arms around her a little longer, stroke her here a little.* I don't know how it's going to work—I just have to trust Jeffrey, that he knows what he's doing."

" 'Stroke her here a little'?" said Brian. "Maybe I should come around and keep an eye on these rehearsals."

When she had started to quote Jeffrey Pauline had felt a giving-way in her womb or the bottom of her stomach, a shock that had travelled oddly upwards and hit her vocal cords. She had to cover up this quaking by growling in a way that was supposed to be an imitation (though Jeffrey never growled or ranted or carried on in any theatrical way at all).

"But there's a point about him being so innocent," she said hurriedly. "Being not so physical. Being awkward." And she began to talk about Orphée in the play, not the waiter. Orphée has a problem with love or reality. Orphée will not put up with anything less than perfection. He wants a love that is outside of ordinary life. He wants a perfect Eurydice.

"Eurydice is more realistic. She's carried on with Mathias and with Monsieur Dulac. She's been around her mother and her mother's lover. She knows what people are like. But she loves Orphée. She loves him better in a way than he loves her. She loves him better because she's not such a fool. She loves him like a human person."

"But she's slept with those other guys," Brian said.

"Well with Mr. Dulac she had to, she couldn't get out of it. She didn't want to, but probably after a while she enjoyed it, because after a certain point she couldn't help enjoying it."

So Orphée is at fault, Pauline said decidedly. He looks at Eurydice on purpose, to kill her and get rid of her because she is not perfect. Because of him she has to die a second time.

Brian, on his back and with his eyes wide open (she knew that because of the tone of his voice) said, "But doesn't he die too?"

"Yes. He chooses to."

"So then they're together?"

"Yes. Like Romeo and Juliet. *Orphée is with Eurydice at last.* That's what Monsieur Henri says. That's the last line of the play. That's the end." Pauline rolled over onto her side and touched her cheek to Brian's shoulder—not to start anything but to emphasize what she said next. "It's a beautiful play in one way, but in another it's so silly. And it isn't really like *Romeo and Juliet* because it isn't bad luck or circumstances. It's on purpose. So they don't have to go on with life and get married and have kids and buy an old house and fix it up and—"

"And have affairs," said Brian. "After all, they're French."

Then he said, "Be like my parents."

Pauline laughed. "Do they have affairs? I can imagine."

"Oh sure," said Brian. "I meant their life.

"Logically I can see killing yourself so you won't turn into your parents," Brian said. "I just don't believe anybody would do it."

"Everybody has choices," Pauline said dreamily. "Her mother and his father are both despicable in a way, but Orphée and Eurydice don't have to be like them. They're not corrupt. Just because she's slept with those men doesn't mean she's corrupt. She wasn't in love then. She hadn't met Orphée. There's one speech where he tells her that everything she's done is sticking to her, and it's disgusting. Lies she's told him. The other men. It's all sticking to her forever. And then of course Monsieur Henri plays up to that. He tells Orphée that he'll be just as bad and that one day he'll walk down the street with Eurydice and he'll look like a man with a dog he's trying to lose."

To her surprise, Brian laughed.

"No," she said. "That's what's stupid. It's not inevitable. It's not inevitable at all."

They went on speculating, and comfortably arguing, in a way that was not usual, but not altogether unfamiliar to them. They had done this before, at long intervals in their married life—talked half the night about God or fear of death or how children should be educated or whether money was important. At last they admitted to being too tired to make sense any longer, and arranged themselves in a comradely position and went to sleep.

■ ■ ■

Finally a rainy day. Brian and his parents were driving into Campbell River to get groceries, and gin, and to take Brian's father's car to a garage, to see about a problem that had developed on the drive up from Nanaimo. This was a very slight problem, but there was the matter of the new-car warranty's being in effect at present, so Brian's father wanted to get it seen to as soon as possible. Brian had to go along, with his car, just in case his father's car had to be left in the garage. Pauline said that she had to stay home because of Mara's nap.

She persuaded Caitlin to lie down too—allowing her to take her music box to bed with her if she played it very softly. Then Pauline spread the script on the kitchen table and drank coffee and went over the scene in which Orphée says that it's intolerable, at last, to stay in two skins, two envelopes with their own blood and oxygen sealed up in their solitude, and Eurydice tells him to be quiet.

"Don't talk. Don't think. Just let your hand wander, let it be happy on its own."

Your hand is my happiness, says Eurydice. Accept that. Accept your happiness.

Of course he says he cannot.

Caitlin called out frequently to ask what time it was. She turned up the sound of the music box. Pauline hurried to the bedroom door and hissed at her to turn it down, not to wake Mara.

"If you play it like that again I'll take it away from you. Okay?"

But Mara was already rustling around in her crib, and in the next few minutes there were sounds of soft, encouraging conversation from Caitlin, designed to get her sister wide awake. Also of the music being quickly turned up and then down. Then of Mara rattling the crib railing, pulling herself up, throwing her bottle out onto the floor, and starting the bird cries that would grow more and more desolate until they brought her mother.

"I didn't wake her," Caitlin said. "She was awake all by herself. It's not raining anymore. Can we go down to the beach?"

She was right. It wasn't raining. Pauline changed Mara, told Caitlin to get her bathing suit on and find her sand pail. She got into her own bathing suit and put her shorts over it, in case the rest of the family arrived home while she was down there. ("Dad doesn't like the way some women just go right out of their cottages in their bathing suits," Brian's mother had said to her. "I guess he and I just grew up in other times.") She picked up the script to take it along, then laid it down. She was afraid that she would get too absorbed in it and take her eyes off the children for a moment too long.

The thoughts that came to her, of Jeffrey, were not really thoughts at all—they were more like alterations in her body. This could happen when she was sitting on the beach (trying to stay in the half shade of a bush and so preserve her pallor, as Jeffrey had ordered) or when she was wringing out diapers or when she and Brian were visiting his parents. In the middle of Monopoly games, Scrabble games, card games. She went right on talking, listening, working, keeping track of the children, while some memory of her secret life disturbed her like a radiant explosion. Then a warm weight settled, reassurance filling up all her hollows. But it didn't last, this comfort leaked away, and she was like a miser whose windfall has vanished and who is convinced such luck can never strike again. Longing buckled her up and drove her to the discipline of counting days. Sometimes she even cut the days into fractions to figure out more exactly how much time had gone.

She thought of going into Campbell River, making some excuse, so that she could get to a phone booth and call him. The cottages had no phones—the only public phone was in the hall of the lodge. But she did not have the number of the hotel where Jeffrey worked. And besides that, she could never get away to Campbell River in the evening. She was afraid that if she called him at home in the daytime his mother the French teacher might answer. He said his mother hardly ever left the house in the summer. Just once, she had taken the ferry to Vancouver for the day. Jeffrey had phoned Pauline to ask her to come over. Brian was teaching, and Caitlin was at her play group.

Pauline said, "I can't. I have Mara."

Jeffrey said, "Who? Oh. Sorry." Then "Couldn't you bring her along?"

She said no.

"Why not? Couldn't you bring some things for her to play with?"

No, said Pauline. "I couldn't," she said. "I just couldn't." It seemed too dangerous to her, to trundle her baby along on such a guilty expedition. To a house where cleaning fluids would not be bestowed on high shelves, and all pills and cough syrups and cigarettes and buttons put safely out of reach. And even if she escaped poisoning or choking, Mara might be storing up time bombs—memories of a strange house where she was strangely disregarded, of a closed door, noises on the other side of it.

"I just wanted you," Jeffrey said. "I just wanted you in my bed."

She said again, weakly, "No."

Those words of his kept coming back to her. *I wanted you in my bed.* A half-joking urgency in his voice but also a determination, a practicality, as if "in my bed" meant something more, the bed he spoke of taking on larger, less material dimensions.

Had she made a great mistake with that refusal? With that reminder of how fenced in she was, in what anybody would call her real life?

■ ■ ■

The beach was nearly empty—people had got used to its being a rainy day. The sand was too heavy for Caitlin to make a castle or dig an irrigation system—projects she would only undertake with her father, anyway, because she sensed that his interest in them was wholehearted, and Pauline's was not. She wandered a bit forlornly at the edge of the water. She probably missed the presence of other children, the nameless instant friends and occasional stone-throwing water-kicking enemies, the shrieking and splashing and falling about. A boy a little bigger than she was and apparently all by himself stood knee-deep in the water farther down the beach. If these two could get together it might be all right; the whole beach experience might be retrieved. Pauline couldn't tell whether Caitlin was now making little splashy runs into the water for his benefit or whether he was watching her with interest or scorn.

Mara didn't need company, at least for now. She stumbled towards the water, felt it touch her feet and changed her mind, stopped, looked around, and spotted Pauline. "Paw. Paw," she said, in happy recognition. "Paw" was what she said for "Pauline," instead of "Mother" or "Mommy." Looking around overbalanced her—she sat down half on the sand and half in the water, made a squawk of surprise that turned to an announcement, then by some determined ungraceful maneuvers that involved putting her weight on her hands, she rose to her feet, wavering and triumphant. She had been walking for half a year, but getting around on the sand was still a challenge. Now she came back towards Pauline, making some reasonable, casual remarks in her own language.

"Sand," said Pauline, holding up a clot of it. "Look. Mara. Sand."

Mara corrected her, calling it something else—it sounded like "whap." Her thick diaper under her plastic pants and her terry-cloth playsuit gave her a fat bottom, and that, along with her plump cheeks and shoulders and her sidelong important expression, made her look like a roguish matron.

Pauline became aware of someone calling her name. It had been called two or three times, but because the voice was unfamiliar she had not recognized it. She stood up and waved. It was the woman who worked in the store at the lodge. She was leaning over the balcony and calling, "Mrs. Keating. Mrs. Keating? Telephone, Mrs. Keating."

Pauline hoisted Mara onto her hip and summoned Caitlin. She and the little boy were aware of each other now—they were both picking up stones from the bottom and flinging them out into the water. At first she didn't hear Pauline, or pretended not to.

"Store," called Pauline. "Caitlin. Store." When she was sure Caitlin would follow—it was the word "store" that had done it, the reminder of the tiny store in the lodge where you could buy ice cream and candy and cigarettes and mixer—she began the trek across the sand and up the flight of wooden steps above the sand and the salal bushes. Halfway up she stopped, said, "Mara, you weigh a ton," and shifted the baby to her other hip. Caitlin banged a stick against the railing.

"Can I have a Fudgsicle? Mother? Can I?"

"We'll see."

"Can I please have a Fudgsicle?"

"Wait."

The public phone was beside a bulletin board on the other side of the main hall and across from the door to the dining room. A bingo game had been set up in there, because of the rain.

"Hope he's still hanging on," the woman who worked in the store called out. She was unseen now behind her counter.

Pauline, still holding Mara, picked up the dangling receiver and said breathlessly, "Hello?" She was expecting to hear Brian telling her about some delay in Campbell River or asking her what it was she had wanted him to get at the drugstore. It was just the one thing—calamine lotion—so he had not written it down.

"Pauline," said Jeffrey. "It's me."

Mara was bumping and scrambling against Pauline's side, anxious to get down. Caitlin came along the hall and went into the store, leaving wet sandy footprints. Pauline said, "Just a minute, just a minute." She let Mara slide down and hurried to close the door that led to the steps. She did not remember telling Jeffrey the name of this place, though she had told him roughly where it was. She heard the woman in the store speaking to Caitlin in a sharper voice than she would use to children whose parents were beside them.

"Did you forget to put your feet under the tap?"

"I'm here," said Jeffrey. "I didn't get along well without you. I didn't get along at all."

Mara made for the dining room, as if the male voice calling out "Under the *N*—" was a direct invitation to her.

"Here. Where?" said Pauline.

She read the signs that were tacked up on the bulletin board beside the phone.

NO PERSON UNDER FOURTEEN YEARS OF AGE NOT ACCOMPANIED BY ADULT ALLOWED IN BOATS OR CANOES.

FISHING DERBY.

BAKE AND CRAFT SALE, ST. BARTHOLOMEW'S CHURCH.

YOUR LIFE IS IN YOUR HANDS. PALMS AND CARDS READ. REASONABLE AND ACCURATE. CALL CLAIRE.

"In a motel. In Campbell River."

■ ■ ■

Pauline knew where she was before she opened her eyes. Nothing surprised her. She had slept but not deeply enough to let go of anything.

She had waited for Brian in the parking area of the lodge, with the children, and had asked him for the keys. She had told him in front of his parents that there was something else she needed, from Campbell River. He asked, What was it? And did she have any money?

"Just something," she said, so he would think that it was tampons or birth control supplies, that she didn't want to mention. "Sure."

"Okay but you'll have to put some gas in," he said.

Later she had to speak to him on the phone. Jeffrey said she had to do it.

"Because he won't take it from me. He'll think I kidnapped you or something. He won't believe it."

But the strangest thing of all the things that day was that Brian did seem, immediately, to believe it. Standing where she had stood not so long before, in the public hallway of the lodge—the bingo game over now but people going past, she could hear them, people on their way out of the dining room after dinner—he said, "Oh. Oh. Oh. Okay" in a voice that would have to be quickly controlled, but that seemed to draw on a supply of fatalism or foreknowledge that went far beyond that necessity.

As if he had known all along, all along, what could happen with her.

"Okay," he said. "What about the car?"

He said something else, something impossible, and hung up, and she came out of the phone booth beside some gas pumps in Campbell River.

"That was quick," Jeffrey said. "Easier than you expected."

Pauline said, "I don't know."

"He may have known it subconsciously. People do know."

She shook her head, to tell him not to say any more, and he said, "Sorry." They walked along the street not touching or talking.

■ ■ ■

They'd had to go out to find a phone booth because there was no phone in the motel room. Now in the early morning looking around at leisure—the first real leisure or freedom she'd had since she came into that room—Pauline saw that there wasn't much of anything in it. Just a junk dresser, the bed without a headboard, an armless upholstered chair, on the window a venetian blind with a broken slat and curtain of orange plastic that was supposed to look like net and that didn't have to be hemmed, just sliced off at the bottom. There was a noisy air conditioner—Jeffrey had turned it off in the night and left the door open on the chain, since the window was sealed. The door was shut now. He must have got up in the night and shut it.

This was all she had. Her connection with the cottage where Brian lay asleep or not asleep was broken, also her connection with the house that had been an expression of her life with Brian, of the way they wanted to live. She had no furniture anymore. She had cut herself off from all the large solid acquisitions like the washer and dryer and the oak table and the refinished wardrobe and the chandelier that was a copy of the one in a painting by Vermeer. And just as much from those things that were particularly hers—the pressed-glass tumblers that she had been collecting and the prayer rug which was of course not authentic, but beautiful. Especially from those things. Even her books, she might have lost. Even her clothes. The skirt and blouse and sandals she had put on for the trip to Campbell River might well be all she had now to her name. She would never go back to lay claim to anything. If Brian got in touch with her to ask what was to be done with things, she would tell him to do what he liked—throw everything into garbage bags and take it to the dump, if that was what he liked. (In fact she knew that he would probably pack up a trunk, which he did, sending on, scrupulously, not only her winter coat and boots but things like the waist cincher she had worn at her wedding and never since, with the prayer rug draped over the top of everything like a final statement of his generosity, either natural or calculated.)

She believed that she would never again care about what sort of rooms she lived in or what sort of clothes she put on. She would not be looking for that sort of help to give anybody an idea of who she was, what she was like. Not even to give herself an idea. What she had done would be enough, it would be the whole thing.

What she was doing would be what she had heard about and read about. It was what Anna Karenina had done and what Madame Bovary had wanted to do. It was what a teacher at Brian's school had done, with the school secretary. He had run off with her. That was what it was called. Running off with. Taking off with. It was spoken of disparagingly, humorously, enviously. It was adultery taken one step further. The people who did it had almost certainly been having an affair already, committing adultery for quite some time before they became desperate or courageous enough to take this step. Once in a long while a couple might claim their love was unconsummated and technically pure, but these people would be thought of—if anybody believed them—as being not only very serious and high-minded but almost devastatingly foolhardy, almost in a class with those who took a chance and gave up everything to go and work in some poor and dangerous country.

The others, the adulterers, were seen as irresponsible, immature, selfish, or even cruel. Also lucky. They were lucky because the sex they had been having in parked cars or the long grass or in each other's sullied marriage beds or most likely in motels like this one must surely have been splendid. Otherwise they would never have got such a yearning for each other's company at all costs or such a faith that their shared future would be altogether better and different in kind from what they had in the past.

Different in kind. That was what Pauline must believe now—that there was this major difference in lives or in marriages or unions between people. That some of them had a necessity, a fatefulness, about them that others did not have. Of course she would have said the same thing a year ago. People did say that, they seemed to believe that, and to believe that their own cases were all of the first, the special kind, even when anybody could see that they were not and that these people did not know what they were talking about. Pauline would not have known what she was talking about.

■ ■ ■

It was too warm in the room. Jeffrey's body was too warm. Conviction and contentiousness seemed to radiate from it, even in sleep. His torso was thicker than Brian's; he was pudgier around the waist. More flesh on the bones, yet not so slack to the touch. Not so good-looking in general—she was sure most people would say that. And not so fastidious. Brian in bed smelled of nothing. Jeffrey's skin, every time she'd been with him, had had a baked-in, slightly oily or nutty smell. He didn't wash last night—but then, neither did she. There wasn't time. Did he even have a toothbrush with him? She didn't. But she had not known she was staying.

When she met Jeffrey here it was still in the back of her mind that she had to concoct some colossal lie to serve her when she got home. And she—they—had to hurry. When Jeffrey said to her that he had decided that they must stay together, that she would come with him to Washington State, that they would have to drop the play because things would be too difficult for them in Victoria, she had looked at him just in the blank way you'd look at somebody the moment that an earthquake started. She was ready to tell him all the reasons why this was not possible, she still thought she was going to tell him that, but her life was coming adrift in that moment. To go back would be like tying a sack over her head.

All she said was "Are you sure?"

He said, "Sure." He said sincerely, "I'll never leave you."

That did not seem the sort of thing that he would say. Then she realized he was quoting—maybe ironically—from the play. It was what Orphée says to Eurydice within a few moments of their first meeting in the station buffet.

So her life was falling forwards; she was becoming one of those people who ran away. A woman who shockingly and incomprehensibly gave everything up. For love, observers would say wryly. Meaning, for sex. None of this would happen if it wasn't for sex.

And yet what's the great difference there? It's not such a variable procedure, in spite of what you're told. Skins, motions, contact, results. Pauline isn't a woman from whom it's difficult to get results. Brian got them. Probably anybody would, who wasn't wildly inept or morally disgusting.

But nothing's the same, really. With Brian—especially with Brian, to whom she has dedicated a selfish sort of goodwill, with whom she's lived in married complicity—there can never be this stripping away, the inevitable flight, the feelings she doesn't have to strive for but only to give in to like breathing or dying. That she believes can only come when the skin is on Jeffrey, the motions made by Jeffrey, and the weight that bears down on her has Jeffrey's heart in it, also his habits, thoughts, peculiarities, his ambition and loneliness (that for all she knows may have mostly to do with his youth).

For all she knows. There's a lot she doesn't know. She hardly knows anything about what he likes to eat or what music he likes to listen to or what role his mother plays in his life (no doubt a mysterious but important one, like the role of Brian's parents). One thing she's pretty sure of—whatever preferences or prohibitions he has will be definite.

She slides out from under Jeffrey's hand and from under the top steel which has a harsh smell of bleach, she slips down to the floor where the bedspread is lying and wraps herself quickly in that rag of greenish-yellow chenille. She doesn't want him to open his eyes and see her from behind and note the droop of her buttocks. He's seen her naked before, but generally in a more forgiving moment.

She rinses her mouth and washes herself, using the bar of soap that is about the size of two thin squares of chocolate and firm as stone. She's hard-used between the legs, swollen and stinking. Urinating takes an effort, and it seems she's constipated. Last night when they went out and got hamburgers she found she could not eat. Presumably she'll learn to do all these things again, they'll resume their natural importance in her life. At the moment it's as if she can't quite spare the attention.

She has some money in her purse. She has to go out and buy a toothbrush, toothpaste, deodorant, shampoo. Also vaginal jelly. Last night they used condoms the first two times but nothing the third time.

She didn't bring her watch and Jeffrey doesn't wear one. There's no clock in the room, of course. She thinks it's early—there's still an early look to the light in spite of the heat. The stores probably won't be open, but there'll be someplace where she can get coffee.

Jeffrey has turned onto his other side. She must have wakened him, just for a moment.

They'll have a bedroom. A kitchen, an address. He'll go to work. She'll go to the Laundromat. Maybe she'll go to work too. Selling things, waiting on tables, tutoring students. She knows French and Latin—do they teach French and Latin in American high schools? Can you get a job if you're not an American? Jeffrey isn't.

She leaves him the key. She'll have to wake him to get back in. There's nothing to write a note with, or on.

It is early. The motel is on the highway at the north end of town, beside the bridge. There's no traffic yet. She scuffs along under the cottonwood trees for quite a while before a vehicle of any kind rumbles over the bridge—though the traffic on it shook their bed regularly late into the night.

Something is coming now. A truck. But not just a truck—there's a large bleak fact coming at her. And it has not arrived out of nowhere—it's been waiting, cruelly nudging at her ever since she woke up, or even all night.

Caitlin and Mara.

Last night on the phone, after speaking in such a flat and controlled and almost agreeable voice—as if he prided himself on not being shocked, not objecting or pleading—Brian cracked open. He said with contempt and fury and no concern for whoever might hear him, "Well then—what about the kids?"

The receiver began to shake against Pauline's ear.

She said, "We'll talk—" but he did not seem to hear her.

"The children," he said, in this same shivering and vindictive voice. Changing the word "kids" to "children" was like slamming a board down on her—a heavy, formal, righteous threat.

"The children stay," Brian said. "Pauline. Did you hear me?"

"No," said Pauline. "Yes. I heard you but—"

"All right. You heard me. Remember. The children stay."

It was all he could do. To make her see what she was doing, what she was ending, and to punish her if she did so. Nobody would blame him. There might be finagling, there might be bargaining, there would certainly be humbling of herself, but there it was like a round cold stone in her gullet, like a cannonball. And it would remain there unless she changed her mind entirely. The children stay.

Their car—hers and Brian's—was still sitting in the motel parking lot. Brian would have to ask his father or his mother to drive him up here today to get it. She had the keys in her purse. There were spare keys—

he would surely bring them. She unlocked the car door and threw her keys on the seat and locked the door on the inside and shut it.

Now she couldn't go back. She couldn't get into the car and drive back and say that she'd been insane. If she did that he would forgive her, but he'd never get over it and neither would she. They'd go on, though, as people did.

She walked out of the parking lot, she walked along the sidewalk, into town.

The weight of Mara on her hip, yesterday. The sight of Caitlin's footprints on the floor.

Paw. Paw.

She doesn't need the keys to get back to them, she doesn't need the car. She could beg a ride on the highway. Give in, give in, get back to them any way at all, how can she not do that?

A sack over her head.

A fluid choice, the choice of fantasy, is poured out on the ground and instantly hardens; it has taken its undeniable shape.

■ ■ ■

This is acute pain. It will become chronic. Chronic means that it will be permanent but perhaps not constant. It may also mean that you won't die of it. You won't get free of it, but you won't die of it. You won't feel it every minute, but you won't spend many days without it. And you'll learn some tricks to dull it or banish it, trying not to end up destroying what you incurred this pain to get. It isn't his fault. He's still an innocent or a savage, who doesn't know there's a pain so durable in the world. Say to yourself, You lose them anyway. They grow up. For a mother there's always waiting this private slightly ridiculous desolation. They'll forget this time, in one way or another they'll disown you. Or hang around till you don't know what to do about them, the way Brian has.

And still, what pain. To carry along and get used to until it's only the past she's grieving for and not any possible present.

■ ■ ■

Her children have grown up. They don't hate her. For going away or staying away. They don't forgive her, either. Perhaps they wouldn't have forgiven her anyway, but it would have been for something different.

Caitlin remembers a little about the summer at the lodge, Mara nothing. One day Caitlin mentions it to Pauline, calling it "that place Grandma and Grandpa stayed at."

"The place we were at when you went away," she says. "Only we didn't know till later you went away with Orphée."

Pauline says, "It wasn't Orphée."

"It wasn't Orphée? Dad used to say it was. He'd say, 'And then your mother ran away with Orphée.' "

"Then he was joking," says Pauline.

"I always thought it was Orphée. It was somebody else then."

"It was somebody else connected with the play. That I lived with for a while."

"Not Orphée."

"No. Never him."

V.S. NAIPAUL

A Trinidadian born in 1932 who emigrated to England in 1950, an Oxonian, a novelist, a reporter, and the winner of such prestigious awards as the Hawthornden and Booker prizes, Vidiadhar Surajprasad Naipaul is a man of extraordinary talent and complex motivations. Profoundly influenced by both his Indian and West Indian heritages, he yet finds India and Trinidad to be constraining environments; and in his travel books (among them, *The Middle Passage,* 1962; *An Area of Darkness,* 1964; and *India,* 1991) he shrewdly observes the details of life in the two societies and broods over his own sense of alienation from them. From one vantage point, such "exile" can be seen as a reflection of the Caribbean predicament; that of societies founded by exiles and historically uncertain of their allegiances and identities: the acute consciousness of being alive and alone, the laconic acceptance of the fugitive joys and persistent sadness of life, the alternately grim and wry rendering of a society that cannot locate or cannot believe in a sustaining code of values. Naipaul's characteristically tragicomic tone catches at exactly this ambivalence.

The most lighthearted of his works are early books—the sketches of *Miguel Street* (1959) and the novel *The Mystic Masseur* (1957). But the vein of dislocating irony that occurs even here has grown larger with each succeeding work: *A House for Mr. Biswas* (1961), an inventive portrait of Trinidad domestic crises and individual pride; *A Flag on the Island* (1967), from which "My Aunt Gold Teeth" is taken; *The Mimic Men* (1967), about middle-class drive and human emptiness; *In a Free State* (1971), a collection of stories and journal entries that explores the dimensions of freedom in the mind and the modern world. Reading the present in a way that recognizes the hand of history in shaping it constitutes for him a kind of psychological burden, which his writing addresses but refuses to pretend to resolve. Accompanying this intellectual development is an increasing stylistic skill. Naipaul's incisive portraits, his intelligent understanding of human behaviour, and his powers of rendering intense awareness have made him one of the most accomplished and controversial prose writers to have emerged thus far from the nations of the Caribbean.

My Aunt Gold Teeth

I never knew her real name and it is quite likely that she did have one, though I never heard her called anything but Gold Teeth. She did, indeed, have gold teeth. She had sixteen of them. She had married early and she had married well, and shortly after her marriage she exchanged her perfectly sound teeth for gold ones, to announce to the world that her husband was a man of substance.

Even without her gold teeth my aunt would have been noticeable. She was short, scarcely five foot, and she was very fat. If you saw her in silhouette you would have found it difficult to know whether she was facing you or whether she was looking sideways.

She ate little and prayed much. Her family being Hindu, and her husband being a pundit, she, too, was an orthodox Hindu. Of Hinduism she knew little apart from the ceremonies and the taboos, and this was enough for her. Gold Teeth saw God as a Power, and religious ritual as a means of harnessing that Power for great practical good, her good.

I may have given the impression that Gold Teeth prayed because she wanted to be less fat. The fact was that Gold Teeth had no children and she was almost forty. It was her childlessness, not her fat, that oppressed her, and she prayed for the curse to be removed. She was willing to try any means—any ritual, any prayer—in order to trap and channel the supernatural Power.

And so it was that she began to indulge in surreptitious Christian practices.

She was living at the time in a country village called Cunupia, in County Caroni. Here the Canadian Mission had long waged war against the Indian heathen, and saved many. But Gold Teeth stood firm. The Minister of Cunupia expended his Presbyterian piety on her; so did the headmaster of the Mission school. But all in vain. At no time was Gold Teeth persuaded even to think about being converted. The idea horrified her. Her father had been in his day one of the best-known Hindu pundits, and even now her husband's fame as a pundit, as a man who could read and write Sanskrit, had spread far beyond Cunupia. She was in no doubt whatsoever the Hindus were the best people in the world, and that Hinduism was a superior religion. She was willing to select, modify and incorporate alien eccentricities into her worship; but to abjure her own faith—never!

Presbyterianism was not the only danger the good Hindu had to face in Cunupia. Besides, of course, the ever-present threat of open Muslim aggression, the Catholics were to be reckoned with. Their pamphlets were everywhere and it was hard to avoid them. In them Gold Teeth read of novenas and rosaries, of squads of saints and angels. These were things she understood and could even sympathize with, and they encouraged her to seek further. She read of the mysteries and the miracles, of penances and indulgences. Her scepticism sagged, and yielded to a quickening, if reluctant, enthusiasm.

One morning she took the train for the County town of Chaguanas, three miles, two stations and twenty minutes away. The Church of St Philip and St James in Chaguanas stands imposingly at the end of the Caroni Savannah Road, and although Gold Teeth knew Chaguanas well, all she knew of the church was that it had a clock, at which she had glanced on her way to the railway station nearby. She had hitherto been far more interested in the drab ochre-washed edifice opposite, which was the police station.

She carried herself into the churchyard, awed by her own temerity, feeling like an explorer in a land of cannibals. To her relief, the church was empty. It was not as terrifying as she had expected. In the gilt and images and the resplendent cloths she found much that reminded her of her Hindu temple. Her eyes caught a discreet sign: CANDLES TWO CENTS EACH. She undid the knot in the end of her veil, where she kept her money, took out three cents, popped them into the box, picked up a candle and muttered a prayer in Hindustani. A brief moment of elation gave way to a sense of guilt, and she was suddenly anxious to get away from the church as fast as her weight would let her.

She took a bus home, and hid the candle in her chest of drawers. She had half feared that her husband's Brahminical flair for clairvoyance would have uncovered the reason for her trip to Chaguanas. When after four days, which she spent in an ecstasy of prayer, her husband had mentioned nothing, Gold Teeth thought it safe to burn the candle. She burned it secretly at night, before her Hindu images, and sent up, as she thought, prayers of double efficacy.

Every day her religious schizophrenia grew, and presently she began wearing a crucifix. Neither her husband nor her neighbours knew she did so. The chain was lost in the billows of fat around her neck, and the crucifix was itself buried in the valley of her gargantuan breasts. Later she acquired two holy pictures, one of the Virgin Mary, the other of the crucifixion, and took care to conceal them from her husband. The prayers she offered to these Christian things filled her with new hope and buoyancy. She became an addict of Christianity.

Then her husband, Ramprasad, fell ill.

Ramprasad's sudden, unaccountable illness alarmed Gold Teeth. It was, she knew, no ordinary illness, and she knew too, that her religious transgression was the cause. The District Medical Officer at Chaguanas said it was diabetes, but Gold Teeth knew better. To be on the safe side, though, she used the insulin he prescribed and, to be even safer, she consulted Ganesh Pundit, the masseur with mystic leanings, celebrated as a faith-healer.

Ganesh came all the way from Fuente Grove to Cunupia. He came in great humility, anxious to serve Gold Teeth's husband, for Gold Teeth's husband was a Brahmin among Brahmins, a *Panday*, a man who knew all five Vedas; while he, Ganesh, was a mere *Chaubay* and knew only four.

With spotless white *koortah*, his *dhoti* cannily tied, and a tasselled green scarf as a concession to elegance, Ganesh exuded the confidence of the professional mystic. He looked at the sick man, observed his pallor, sniffed the air. "This man," he said, "is bewitched. Seven spirits are upon him."

He was telling Gold Teeth nothing she didn't know. She had known from the first that there were spirits in the affair, but she was glad that Ganesh had ascertained their number.

"But you mustn't worry," Ganesh added. "We will 'tie' the house—in spiritual bonds—and no spirit will be able to come in."

Then, without being asked, Gold Teeth brought out a blanket, folded it, placed it on the floor and invited Ganesh to sit on it. Next she brought him a brass jar of fresh water, a mango leaf and a plate full of burning charcoal.

"Bring me some ghee," Ganesh said, and after Gold Teeth had done so, he set to work. Muttering continuously in Hindustani he sprinkled the water from the brass jar around him with the mango leaf. Then he melted the ghee in the fire and the charcoal hissed so sharply that Gold Teeth could not make out his words. Presently he rose and said, "You must put some of the ash of this fire on your husband's forehead, but if he doesn't want you to do that, mix it with his food. You must keep the water in this jar and place it every night before your front door."

Gold Teeth pulled her veil over her forehead.

Ganesh coughed. "That," he said, rearranging his scarf, "is all. There is nothing more I can do. God will do the rest."

He refused payment for his services. It was enough honour, he said, for a man as humble as he was to serve Pundit Ramprasad, and she, Gold Teeth, had been singled out by fate to be the spouse of such a worthy man. Gold Teeth received the impression that Ganesh spoke from a first-hand knowledge of fate and its designs, and her heart, buried deep down under inches of mortal, flabby flesh, sank a little.

"Baba," she said hesitantly, "revered Father, I have something to say to you." But she couldn't say anything more and Ganesh, seeing this, filled his eyes with charity and love.

"What is it, my child?"

"I have done a great wrong, Baba."

"What sort of wrong?" he asked, and his tone indicated that Gold Teeth could do no wrong.

"I have prayed to Christian things."

koortah = long shirt.
dhoti = loincloth.

And to Gold Teeth's surprise, Ganesh chuckled benevolently. "And do you think God minds, daughter? There is only one God and different people pray to Him in different ways. It doesn't matter how you pray, but God is pleased if you pray at all."

"So it is not because of me that my husband has fallen ill?"

"No, to be sure, daughter."

In his professional capacity Ganesh was consulted by people of many faiths, and with the licence of the mystic he had exploited the commodiousness of Hinduism, and made room for all beliefs. In this way he had many clients, as he called them, many satisfied clients.

Henceforward Gold Teeth not only pasted Ramprasad's pale forehead with the sacred ash Ganesh had prescribed, but mixed substantial amounts with his food. Ramprasad's appetite, enormous even in sickness, diminished; and he shortly entered into a visible and alarming decline that mystified his wife.

She fed him more ash than before, and when it was exhausted and Ramprasad perilously macerated, she fell back on the Hindu wife's last resort. She took her husband home to her mother. That venerable lady, my grandmother, lived with us in Port-of-Spain.

Ramprasad was tall and skeletal, and his face was grey. The virile voice that had expounded a thousand theological points and recited a hundred *puranas* was now a wavering whisper. We cooped him up in a room called, oddly, "the pantry." It had never been used as a pantry and one can only assume that the architect had so designated it some forty years before. It was a tiny room. If you wished to enter the pantry you were compelled, as soon as you opened the door, to climb on to the bed: it fitted the room to a miracle. The lower half of the walls were concrete, the upper close lattice-work; there were no windows.

My grandmother had her doubts about the suitability of the room for a sick man. She was worried about the lattice-work. It let in air and light, and Ramprasad was not going to die from these things if she could help it. With cardboard, oil-cloth and canvas she made the lattice-work air-proof and light-proof.

And, sure enough, within a week Ramprasad's appetite returned, insatiable and insistent as before. My grandmother claimed all the credit for this, though Gold Teeth knew that the ash she had fed him had not been without effect. Then she realized with horror that she had ignored a very important thing. The house in Cunupia had been tied and no spirits could enter, but the house in the city had been given no such

puranas = Hindu scriptures.

protection and any spirit could come and go as it chose. The problem was pressing.

Ganesh was out of the question. By giving his services free he had made it impossible for Gold Teeth to call him in again. But thinking in this way of Ganesh, she remembered his words: "It doesn't matter how you pray, but God is pleased if you pray at all."

Why not, then, bring Christianity into play again?

She didn't want to take any chances this time. She decided to tell Ramprasad.

He was propped up in bed, and eating. When Gold Teeth opened the door he stopped eating and blinked at the unwonted light. Gold Teeth, stepping into the doorway and filling it, shadowed the room once more and he went on eating. She placed the palms of her hands on the bed. It creaked.

"Man," she said.

Ramprasad continued to eat.

"Man," she said in English, "I thinking about going to the church to pray. You never know, and it better to be on the safe side. After all, the house ain't tied—"

"I don't want you to pray in no church," he whispered, in English too.

Gold Teeth did the only thing she could do. She began to cry.

Three days in succession she asked his permission to go to church, and his opposition weakened in the face of her tears. He was now, besides, too weak to oppose anything. Although his appetite had returned, he was still very ill and very weak, and every day his condition became worse.

On the fourth day he said to Gold Teeth, "Well, pray to Jesus and go to church, if it will put your mind at rest."

And Gold Teeth straight away set about putting her mind at rest. Every morning she took the trolley-bus to the Holy Rosary Church, to offer worship in her private way. Then she was emboldened to bring a crucifix and pictures of the Virgin and the Messiah into the house. We were all somewhat worried by this, but Gold Teeth's religious nature was well known to us; her husband was a learned pundit and when all was said and done this was an emergency, a matter of life and death. So we could do nothing but look on. Incense and camphor and ghee burned now before the likeness of Krishna and Shiva as well as Mary and Jesus. Gold Teeth revealed an appetite for prayer that equalled her husband's for food, and we marvelled at both, if only because neither prayer nor food seemed to be of any use to Ramprasad.

One evening, shortly after bell and gong and conch-shell had announced that Gold Teeth's official devotions were almost over, a sudden chorus of lamentation burst over the house, and I was summoned to the room reserved for prayer. "Come quickly, something dreadful has happened to your aunt."

The prayer-room, still heavy with fumes of incense, presented an extraordinary sight. Before the Hindu shrine, flat on her face, Gold Teeth lay prostrate, rigid as a sack of flour. I had only seen Gold Teeth standing or sitting, and the aspect of Gold Teeth prostrate, so novel and so grotesque, was disturbing.

My grandmother, an alarmist by nature, bent down and put her ear to the upper half of the body on the floor. "I don't seem to hear her heart," she said.

We were all somewhat terrified. We tried to lift Gold Teeth but she seemed as heavy as lead. Then, slowly, the body quivered. The flesh beneath the clothes rippled, then billowed, and the children in the room sharpened their shrieks. Instinctively we all stood back from the body and waited to see what was going to happen. Gold Teeth's hand began to pound the floor and at the same time she began to gurgle.

My grandmother had grasped the situation. "She's got the spirit," she said.

At the word "spirit," the children shrieked louder, and my grandmother slapped them into silence.

The gurgling resolved itself into words pronounced with a lingering ghastly quaver. "Hail Mary, Hare Ram," Gold Teeth said, "the snakes are after me. Everywhere snakes. Seven snakes. Rama! Rama! Full of grace. Seven spirits leaving Cunupia by the four-o'clock train for Port-of-Spain."

My grandmother and my mother listened eagerly, their faces lit up with pride. I was rather ashamed at the exhibition, and annoyed with Gold Teeth for putting me into a fright. I moved towards the door.

"Who is that going away? Who is the young *caffar*, the unbeliever?" the voice asked abruptly.

"Come back quickly, boy," my grandmother whispered. "Come back and ask her pardon."

I did as I was told.

"It is all right, son," Gold Teeth replied, "you don't know. You are young."

Then the spirit appeared to leave her. She wrenched herself up to a sitting position and wondered why we were all there. For the rest of that evening she behaved as if nothing had happened, and she pretended she didn't notice that everyone was looking at her and treating her with unusual respect.

"I have always said it, and I will say it again," my grandmother said, "that these Christians are very religious people. That is why I encouraged Gold Teeth to pray to Christian things."

■ ■ ■

Ramprasad died early next morning and we had the announcement on the radio after the local news at one o'clock. Ramprasad's death was the only one announced and so, although it came between commercials, it made some impression. We buried him that afternoon in Mucurapo Cemetery.

As soon as we got back my grandmother said, "I have always said it, and I will say it again: I don't like these Christian things. Ramprasad would have got better if only you, Gold Teeth, had listened to me and not gone running after these Christian things."

Gold Teeth sobbed her assent; and her body squabbered and shook as she confessed the whole story of her trafficking with Christianity. We listened in astonishment and shame. We didn't know that a good Hindu, and a member of our family, could sink so low. Gold Teeth beat her breast and pulled ineffectually at her long hair and begged to be forgiven. "It is all my fault," she cried. "My own fault, Ma. I fell in a moment of weakness. Then I just couldn't stop."

My grandmother's shame turned to pity. "It's all right, Gold Teeth. Perhaps it was this you needed to bring you back to your senses."

That evening Gold Teeth ritually destroyed every reminder of Christianity in the house.

"You have only yourself to blame," my grandmother said, "if you have no children now to look after you."

JOYCE CAROL OATES

Joyce Carol Oates was born in New York in 1938 and educated at Syracuse University and the University of Wisconsin. After a period in Canada, teaching English at the University of Windsor, she took up a post at Princeton. Her work has received wide critical acclaim, and brought her many awards, including a Guggenheim Fellowship in 1967 and an O. Henry Special Award for Continuing Achievement in 1970. She is a prolific novelist as well as the author of several volumes of poetry and literary criticism (including commentaries on Emily Brontë, H.P. Lovecraft, and R.L. Stevenson), and has had two plays produced on the New York stage. In addition to these successes, her short stories have appeared in many journals and anthologies, and have been published in numerous collections, among them *The Assignation* (1988) and *The Collector of Hearts* (1998).

In her preoccupation with violence, emotional disturbance, and familial conflict, Oates has been likened to Faulkner; and there is undoubtedly a dark, sometimes melodramatic, quality to her writing that recalls the Gothic element in Faulkner's books; her novel *Wonderland* (1971), for example, opens with the shotgun slaying of five people. Many of her characters are ordinary people who, confronted by the apparent senselessness of life, are driven to extremes by fear or frustration; or they are stunned, like Sister Irene in "In the Region of Ice" (*The Wheel of Love*, 1970), by an awareness of human helplessness and isolation. In an exchange of letters with the American writer Joe David Bellamy, Oates wrote: "I believe that the storm of emotion constitutes our human tragedy, if anything does. It's our constant battle with nature (Nature), trying to subdue chaos outside and inside ourselves, occasionally winning small victories, then being swept along by some cataclysmic event of our own making. I feel an enormous sympathy with people who've gone under, who haven't won even the smallest victories. . . . "

In the Region of Ice

Sister Irene was a tall, deft woman in her early thirties. What one could see of her face made a striking impression—serious, hard gray eyes, a long slender nose, a face waxen with thought. Seen at the right time, from the right angle, she was almost handsome. In her past teaching positions she had drawn a little upon the fact of her being young and brilliant and also a nun, but she was beginning to grow out of that.

This was a new university and an entirely new world. She had heard—of course it was true—that the Jesuit administration of this school had hired her at the last moment to save money and to head off the appointment of a man of dubious religious commitment. She had prayed for the necessary energy to get her through this first semester.

She had no trouble with teaching itself; once she stood before a classroom she felt herself capable of anything. It was the world immediately outside the classroom that confused and alarmed her, though she let none of this show—the cynicism of her colleagues, the indifference of many of the students, and above all, the looks she got that told her nothing much would be expected of her because she was a nun. This took energy, strength. At times she had the idea that she was on trial and that the excuses she made to herself about her discomfort were only the common excuses made by guilty people. But in front of a class she had no time to worry about herself or the conflicts in her mind. She became, once and for all, a figure existing only for the benefit of others, an instrument by which facts were communicated.

About two weeks after the semester began, Sister Irene noticed a new student in her class. He was slight and fair-haired, and his face was blank, but not blank by accident, blank on purpose, suppressed and restricted into a dumbness that looked hysterical. She was prepared for him before he raised his hand, and when she saw his arm jerk, as if he had at last lost control of it, she nodded to him without hesitation.

"Sister, how can this be reconciled with Shakespeare's vision in *Hamlet*? How can these opposing views be in the same mind?"

Students glanced at him, mildly surprised. He did not belong in the class, and this was mysterious, but his manner was urgent and blind.

"There is no need to reconcile opposing views," Sister Irene said, leaning forward against the podium. "In one play Shakespeare suggests one vision, in another play another; the plays are not simultaneous creations, and even if they were, we never demand a logical—"

"We must demand a logical consistency," the young man said. "The idea of education is itself predicated upon consistency, order, sanity—"

He had interrupted her, and she hardened her face against him—for his sake, not her own, since she did not really care. But he noticed nothing. "Please see me after class," she said.

After class the young man hurried up to her.

"Sister Irene, I hope you didn't mind my visiting today. I'd heard some things, interesting things," he said. He stared at her, and something in her face allowed him to smile. "I . . . could we talk in your office? Do you have time?"

They walked down to her office. Sister Irene sat at her desk, and the young man sat facing her; for a moment they were self-conscious and silent.

"Well, I suppose you know—I'm a Jew," he said.

Sister Irene stared at him. "Yes?" she said.

"What am I doing at a Catholic university, huh?" He grinned. "That's what you want to know."

She made a vague movement of her hand to show that she had no thoughts on this, nothing at all, but he seemed not to catch it. He was sitting on the edge of the straight-backed chair. She saw that he was young but did not really look young. There were harsh lines on either side of his mouth, as if he had misused that youthful mouth somehow. His skin was almost as pale as hers, his eyes were dark and not quite in focus. He looked at her and through her and around her, as his voice surrounded them both. His voice was a little shrill at times.

"Listen, I did the right thing today—visiting your class! God, what a lucky accident it was; some jerk mentioned you, said you were a good teacher—I thought, what a laugh! These people know about good teachers here? But yes, listen, yes, I'm not kidding—you are good. I mean that."

Sister Irene frowned. "I don't quite understand what all this means."

He smiled and waved aside her formality, as if he knew better. "Listen, I got my B.A. at Columbia, then I came back here to this crappy city. I mean, I did it on purpose, I wanted to come back. I wanted to. I have my reasons for doing things. I'm on a three-thousand-dollar fellowship," he said, and waited for that to impress her. "You know, I could have gone almost anywhere with that fellowship, and I came back home here—my home's in the city—and enrolled here. This was last year. This is my second year. I'm working on a thesis, I mean I was, my master's thesis—but the hell with that. What I want to ask you is this: Can I enroll in your class, is it too late? We have to get special permission if we're late."

Sister Irene felt something nudging her, some uneasiness in him that was pleading with her not to be offended by his abrupt, familiar manner. He seemed to be promising another self, a better self, as if his fair, childish, almost cherubic face were doing tricks to distract her from what his words said.

"Are you in English studies?" she asked.

"I was in history. Listen," he said, and his mouth did something odd, drawing itself down into a smile that made the lines about it deepen like knives, "listen, they kicked me out."

He sat back, watching her. He crossed his legs. He took out a package of cigarettes and offered her one. Sister Irene shook her head, staring at his hands. They were small and stubby and might have belonged to a ten-year-old, and the nails were a strange near-violet color. It took him awhile to extract a cigarette.

"Yeah, kicked me out. What do you think of that?"

"I don't understand."

"My master's thesis was coming along beautifully, and then this bastard—I mean, excuse me, this professor, I won't pollute your office with his name—he started making criticisms, he said some things were unacceptable, he—" The boy leaned forward and hunched his narrow shoulders in a parody of secrecy. "We had an argument. I told him some frank things, things only a broad-minded person could hear about himself. That takes courage, right? He didn't have it! He kicked me out of the master's program, so now I'm coming into English. Literature is greater than history; European history is one big pile of garbage. Sky-high. Filth and rotting corpses, right? Aristotle says that poetry is higher than history; he's right; in your class today I suddenly realized that this is my field, Shakespeare, only Shakespeare is—"

Sister Irene guessed that he was going to say that only Shakespeare was equal to him, and she caught the moment of recognition and hesitation, the half-raised arm, the keen, frowning forehead, the narrowed eyes; then he thought better of it and did not end the sentence. "The students in your class are mainly negligible, I can tell you that. You're new here, and I've been here a year—I would have finished my studies last year but my father got sick, he was hospitalized, I couldn't take exams and it was a mess—but I'll make it through English in one year or drop dead. I can do it, I can do anything. I'll take six courses at once—" He broke off, breathless. Sister Irene tried to smile. "All right then, it's settled? You'll let me in? Have I missed anything so far?"

He had no idea of the rudeness of his question. Sister Irene, feeling suddenly exhausted, said, "I'll give you a syllabus of the course."

"Fine! Wonderful!"

He got to his feet eagerly. He looked through the schedule, muttering to himself, making favourable noises. It struck Sister Irene that she was making a mistake to let him in. There were these moments when one had to make an intelligent decision. . . . But she was sympathetic with him, yes. She was sympathetic with something about him.

She found out his name the next day: Allen Weinstein.

■ ■ ■

After this she came to her Shakespeare class with a sense of excitement. It became clear to her at once that Weinstein was the most intelligent student in the class. Until he had enrolled, she had not understood what was lacking, a mind that could appreciate her own. Within a week his jagged, protean mind had alienated the other students, and though he sat in the center of the class, he seemed totally alone, encased by a miniature world of his own. When he spoke of the "frenetic humanism of the High Renaissance," Sister Irene dreaded the raised eyebrows and mocking smiles of the other students, who no longer bothered to look at Weinstein. She wanted to defend him, but she never did, because there was something rude and dismal about his knowledge; he used it like a weapon, talking passionately of Nietzsche and Goethe and Freud until Sister Irene would be forced to close the discussion.

In meditation, alone, she often thought of him. When she tried to talk about him to a young nun, Sister Carlotta, everything sounded gross. "But no, he's an excellent student," she insisted. "I'm very grateful to have him in class. It's just that . . . he thinks ideas are real." Sister Carlotta, who loved literature also, had been forced to teach grade-school arithmetic for the last four years. That might have been why she said, a little sharply, "You don't think ideas are real?"

Sister Irene acquiesced with a smile, but of course she did not think so: only reality is real.

When Weinstein did not show up for class on the day the first paper was due, Sister Irene's heart sank, and the sensation was somehow a familiar one. She began her lecture and kept waiting for the door to open and for him to hurry noisily back to his seat, grinning an apology toward her—but nothing happened.

If she had been deceived by him, she made herself think angrily, it was as a teacher and not as a woman. He had promised her nothing.

Weinstein appeared the next day near the steps of the liberal arts building. She heard someone running behind her, a breathless exclamation: "Sister Irene!" She turned and saw him, panting and grinning in embarrassment. He wore a dark-blue suit with a necktie, and he looked, despite his childish face, like a little old man; there was something oddly precarious and fragile about him. "Sister Irene, I owe you an apology, right?" He raised his eyebrows and smiled a sad, forlorn, yet irritatingly conspiratorial smile. "The first paper—not in on time, and I know what your rules are. . . . You won't accept late papers, I know—that's good discipline, I'll do that when I teach too. But, unavoidably, I was unable to come to school yesterday. There are many—many—" He gulped for breath, and Sister Irene had the startling sense of seeing the real Weinstein stare out at her, a terrified prisoner behind the confident voice. "There are many complications in family life. Perhaps you are unaware—I mean—"

She did not like him, but she felt this sympathy, something tugging and nagging at her the way her parents had competed for her love so many years before. They had been whining, weak people, and out of their wet need for affection, the girl she had been (her name was Yvonne) had emerged stronger than either of them, contemptuous of tears because she had seen so many. But Weinstein was different; he was not simply weak—perhaps he was not weak at all—but his strength was confused and hysterical. She felt her customary rigidity as a teacher begin to falter. "You may turn your paper in today if you have it," she said, frowning.

Weinstein's mouth jerked into an incredulous grin. "Wonderful! Marvelous!" he said. "You are very understanding, Sister Irene, I must say. I must say . . . I didn't expect, really . . . " He was fumbling in a shabby old briefcase for the paper. Sister Irene waited. She was prepared for another of his excuses, certain that he did not have the paper, when he suddenly straightened up and handed her something. "Here! I took the liberty of writing thirty pages instead of just fifteen," he said. He was obviously quite excited; his cheeks were mottled pink and white. "You may disagree violently with my interpretation—I expect you to, in fact I'm counting on it—but let me warn you, I have the exact proof, right here in the play itself!" He was thumping at a book, his voice growing louder and shriller. Sister Irene, startled, wanted to put her hand over his mouth and soothe him.

"Look," he said breathlessly, "may I talk with you? I have a class now I hate, I loathe, I can't bear to sit through! Can I talk with you instead?"

Because she was nervous, she stared at the title page of the paper: " 'Erotic Melodies in *Romeo and Juliet*' by Allen Weinstein, Jr."

"All right?" he said. "Can we walk around here? Is it all right? I've been anxious to talk with you about some things you said in class."

She was reluctant, but he seemed not to notice. They walked slowly along the shaded campus paths. Weinstein did all the talking, of course, and Sister Irene recognized nothing in his cascade of words that she had mentioned in class. "The humanist must be committed to the totality of life," he said passionately. "This is the failing one finds everywhere in the academic world! I found it in New York and I found it here and I'm no ingénue, I don't go around with my mouth hanging open—I'm experienced, look, I've been to Europe, I've lived in Rome! I went everywhere in Europe except Germany, I don't talk about Germany . . . Sister Irene, think of the significant men in the last century, the men who've changed the world! Jews, right? Marx, Freud, Einstein! Not that I believe Marx, Marx is a madman . . . and Freud, no, my sympathies are with spiritual humanism. I believe that the Jewish race is the exclusive . . . the exclusive, what's the word, the exclusive means by which humanism will be extended. . . . Humanism begins by excluding the Jew, and now," he said with a high, surprised laugh, "the Jew will perfect it. After the Nazis, only the Jew is authorized to understand humanism, its limitations and its possibilities. So, I say that the humanist is committed to life in its totality and not just to his profession! The religious person is totally religious, he is his religion! What else? I recognize in you a humanist and a religious person—"

But he did not seem to be talking to her or even looking at her.

"Here, read this," he said. "I wrote it last night." It was a long free-verse poem, typed on a typewriter whose ribbon was worn out.

"There's this trouble with my father, a wonderful man, a lovely man, but his health—his strength is fading, do you see? What must it be to him to see his son growing up? I mean, I'm a man now, he's getting old, weak, his health is bad—it's hell, right? I sympathize with him. I'd do anything for him, I'd cut open my veins, anything for a father—right? That's why I wasn't in school yesterday," he said, and his voice dropped for the last sentence, as if he had been dragged back to earth by a fact.

Sister Irene tried to read the poem, then pretended to read it. A jumble of words dealing with "life" and "death" and "darkness" and "love."

"What do you think?" Weinstein said nervously, trying to read it over her shoulder and crowding against her.

"It's very . . . passionate," Sister Irene said.

This was the right comment; he took the poem back from her in silence, his face flushed with excitement. "Here, at this school, I have few people to talk with. I haven't shown anyone else that poem." He looked at her with his dark, intense eyes, and Sister Irene felt them focus upon her. She was terrified at what he was trying to do—he was trying to force her into a human relationship.

"Thank you for your paper," she said, turning away.

When he came the next day, ten minutes late, he was haughty and disdainful. He had nothing to say and sat with his arms folded. Sister Irene took back with her to the convent a feeling of betrayal and confusion. She had been hurt. It was absurd, and yet— She spent too much time thinking about him, as if he were somehow a kind of crystallization of her own loneliness; but she had no right to think so much of him. She did not want to think of him or of her loneliness. But Weinstein did so much more than think of his predicament: he embodied it, he acted it out, and that was perhaps why he fascinated her. It was as if he were doing a dance for her, a dance of shame and agony and delight, and so long as he did it, she was safe. She felt embarrassment for him, but also anxiety; she wanted to protect him. When the dean of the graduate school questioned her about Weinstein's work, she insisted that he was an "excellent" student, though she knew the dean had not wanted to hear that.

She prayed for guidance, she spent hours on her devotions, she was closer to her vocation than she had been for some years. Life at the convent became tinged with unreality, a misty distortion that took its tone from the glowering skies of the city at night, identical smokestacks ranged against the clouds and giving to the sky the excrement of the populated and successful earth. This city was not her city, this world was not her world. She felt no pride in knowing this, it was a fact. The little convent was not like an island in the center of this noisy world, but rather a kind of hole or crevice the world did not bother with, something of no interest. The convent's rhythm of life had nothing to do with the world's rhythm, it did not violate or alarm it in any way. Sister Irene tried to draw together the fragments of her life and synthesize them somehow in her vocation as a nun: she was a nun, she was recognized as a nun and had given herself happily to that life, she had a name, a place, she had dedicated her superior intelligence to the Church, she worked without pay and without expecting gratitude, she had given up pride, she did not think of herself but only of her work and her vocation, she did not think of anything external to these, she saturated herself daily in the knowledge that she was involved in the mystery of Christianity.

A daily terror attended this knowledge, however, for she sensed herself being drawn by that student, that Jewish boy, into a relationship she was not ready for. She wanted to cry out in fear that she was being forced into the role of Christian, and what did that mean? What could her studies tell her? What could the other nuns tell her? She was alone, no one could help; he was making her into a Christian, and to her that was a mystery, a thing of terror, something others slipped on the way they slipped on their clothes, casually and thoughtlessly, but to her a magnificent and terrifying wonder.

For days she carried Weinstein's paper, marked A, around with her; he did not come to class. One day she checked with the graduate office and was told that Weinstein had called in to say his father was ill and that he would not be able to attend classes for a while. "He's strange, I remember him," the secretary said. "He missed all his exams last spring and made a lot of trouble. He was in and out of here every day."

So there was no more of Weinstein for a while, and Sister Irene stopped expecting him to hurry into class. Then, one morning, she found a letter from him in her mailbox.

He had printed it in black ink, very carefully, as if he had not trusted handwriting. The return address was in bold letters that, like his voice, tried to grab onto her: Birchcrest Manor. Somewhere north of the city. "Dear Sister Irene," the block letters said, "I am doing well here and have time for reading and relaxing. The Manor is delightful. My doctor here is an excellent, intelligent man who has time for me, unlike my former doctor. If you have time, you might drop in on my father, who worries about me too much, I think, and explain to him what my condition is. He doesn't seem to understand. I feel about this new life the way that boy, what's his name, in *Measure for Measure*, feels about the prospects of a different life; you remember what he says to his sister when she visits him in prison, how he is looking forward to an escape into another world. Perhaps you could *explain* this to my father and he would stop worrying." The letter ended with the father's name and address, in letters that were just a little too big. Sister Irene, walking slowly down the corridor as she read the letter, felt her eyes cloud over with tears. She was cold with fear, it was something she had never experienced before. She knew what Weinstein was trying to tell her, and the desperation of his attempt made it all the more pathetic; he did not deserve this, why did God allow him to suffer so?

She read through Claudio's speech to his sister, in *Measure for Measure*:

Ay but to die, and go we know not where;
To lie in cold obstruction and to rot;
This sensible warm motion to become
A kneaded clod; and the delighted spirit
To bathe in fiery floods, or to reside
In thrilling region of thick-ribbed ice,
To be imprison'd in the viewless winds
And blown with restless violence round about
The pendent world; or to be worse than worst
Of those that lawless and incertain thought
Imagines howling! 'Tis too horrible!
The weariest and most loathed worldly life
That age, ache, penury, and imprisonment
Can lay on nature is a paradise
To what we fear of death.

Sister Irene called the father's number that day. "Allen Weinstein residence, who may I say is calling?" a woman said, bored. "May I speak to Mr. Weinstein? It's urgent—about his son," Sister Irene said. There was a pause at the other end. "You want to talk to his mother, maybe?" the woman said. "His mother? Yes, his mother, then. Please. It's very important."

She talked with this strange, unsuspected woman, a disembodied voice that suggested absolutely no face, and insisted upon going over that afternoon. The woman was nervous, but Sister Irene, who was a university professor, after all, knew enough to hide her own nervousness. She kept waiting for the woman to say, "Yes, Allen has mentioned you . . . " but nothing happened.

She persuaded Sister Carlotta to ride over with her. This urgency of hers was something they were all amazed by. They hadn't suspected that the set of her gray eyes could change to this blurred, distracted alarm, this sense of mission that seemed to have come to her from nowhere. Sister Irene drove across the city in the late afternoon traffic, with the high whining noises from residential streets where trees were being sawed down in pieces. She understood now the secret, sweet wildness that Christ must have felt, giving himself for man, dying for the billions of men who would never know of him and never understand the sacrifice. For the first time she approached the realization of that great act. In her troubled mind the city traffic was jumbled and yet oddly coherent, an image of the world that was always out of joint with what was happening in it, its inner history struggling with its external spectacle. This sacrifice of Christ's, so mysterious and legendary now, almost lost in time—it was that by which Christ transcended both God and man at one moment, more than man because of his fate to do what no other man could do, and more than God because no god could suffer as he did. She felt a flicker of something close to madness.

She drove nervously, uncertainly, afraid of missing the street and afraid of finding it too, for while one part of her rushed forward to confront these people who had betrayed their son, another part of her would have liked nothing so much as to be waiting as usual for the summons to dinner, safe in her room. . . . When she found the street and turned onto it, she was in a state of breathless excitement. Here lawns were bright green and marred with only a few leaves, magically clean, and the houses were enormous and pompous, a mixture of styles: ranch houses, colonial houses, French country houses, white-bricked wonders with curving glass and clumps of birch trees somehow encircled by white concrete. Sister Irene stared as if she had blundered into another world. This was a kind of heaven, and she was too shabby for it.

The Weinsteins' house was the strangest one of all: it looked like a small Alpine lodge, with an inverted V-shaped front entrance. Sister Irene drove up the black-topped driveway and let the car slow to a stop; she told Sister Carlotta she would not be long.

At the door she was met by Weinstein's mother, a small nervous woman with hands like her son's. "Come in, come in," the woman said. She had once been beautiful, that was clear, but now in missing beauty she was not handsome or even attractive but looked ruined and perplexed, the misshapen swelling of her white-blond professionally set hair like a cap lifting up from her surprised face. "He'll be right in. Allen?" she called, "our visitor is here." They went into the living room. There was a grand piano at one end and an organ at the other. In between were scatterings of brilliant modern furniture in conversational groups, and several puffed-up white rugs on the polished floor. Sister Irene could not stop shivering.

"Professor, it's so strange, but let me say when the phone rang I had a feeling—I had a feeling," the woman said, with damp eyes. Sister Irene sat, and the woman hovered about her. "Should I call you Professor? We don't . . . you know . . . we don't understand the technicalities that go with—Allen, my son, wanted to go here to the Catholic school; I told my husband why not? Why fight? It's the thing these days, they do anything they want for knowledge. And he had to come home, you know. He couldn't take care of himself. New York, that was the beginning of the trouble. . . . Should I call you Professor?"

"You can call me Sister Irene."

"Sister Irene?" the woman said, touching her throat in awe, as if something intimate and unexpected had happened.

Then Weinstein's father appeared, hurrying. He took long, impatient strides. Sister Irene stared at him and in that instant doubted everything—he was in his fifties, a tall, sharply handsome man, heavy but not fat, holding his shoulders back with what looked like an effort, but holding them back just the same. He wore a dark suit and his face was flushed, as if he had run a long distance.

"Now," he said, coming to Sister Irene and with a precise wave of his hand motioning his wife off, "now, let's straighten this out. A lot of confusion over that kid, eh?" He pulled a chair over, scraping it across a rug and pulling one corner over, so that its brown underside was exposed. "I came home early just for this, Libby phoned me. Sister, you got a letter from him, right?"

The wife looked at Sister Irene over her husband's head as if trying somehow to coach her, knowing that this man was so loud and impatient that no one could remember anything in his presence.

"A letter—yes—today—"

"He says what in it? You got the letter, eh? Can I see it?"

She gave it to him and wanted to explain, but he silenced her with a flick of his hand. He read through the letter so quickly that Sister Irene thought perhaps he was trying to impress her with his skill at reading.

"So?" he said, raising his eyes, smiling, "so what is this? He's happy out there, he says. He doesn't communicate with us any more, but he writes to you and says he's happy—what's that? I mean, what the hell is that?"

"But he isn't happy. He wants to come home," Sister Irene said. It was so important that she make him understand that she could not trust her voice; goaded by this man, it might suddenly turn shrill, as his son's did. "Someone must read their letters before they're mailed, so he tried to tell me something by making an allusion to—"

"What?"

"—an allusion to a play, so that I would know. He may be thinking suicide, he must be very unhappy—"

She ran out of breath. Weinstein's mother had begun to cry, but the father was shaking his head jerkily back and forth. "Forgive me, Sister, but it's a lot of crap, he needs the hospital, he needs help—right? It costs me fifty a day out there, and they've got the best place in the state, I figure it's worth it. He needs help, that kid, what do I care if he's unhappy? He's unbalanced!" he said angrily. "You want us to get him out again? We argued with the judge for two hours to get him in, an acquaintance of mine. Look, he can't control himself—he was smashing things here, he was hysterical. They need help, lady, and you do something about it fast! You do something! We made up our minds to do something and we did it! This letter—what the hell is this letter? He never talked like that to us!"

"But he means the opposite of what he says—"

"Then he's crazy! I'm the first to admit it." He was perspiring, and his face had darkened. "I've got no pride left this late. He's a little bastard, you want to know? He calls me names, he's filthy, got a filthy mouth—that's being smart, huh? They give him a big scholarship for his filthy mouth? I went to college too, and I got out and knew something, and I for Christ's sake did something with it; my wife is an intelligent woman, a learned woman, would you guess she does book reviews for the little newspaper out here? Intelligent isn't crazy—crazy isn't intelligent. Maybe for you at the school he writes nice papers and gets an A, but out here, around the house, he can't control himself, and we got him committed!"

"But—"

"We're fixing him up, don't worry about it!" He turned to his wife, "Libby, get out of here, I mean it. I'm sorry, but get out of here, you're making a fool of yourself, go stand in the kitchen or something, you and the goddamn maid can cry on each other's shoulders. That one in the kitchen is nuts too, they're all nuts. Sister," he said, his voice lowering, "I thank you immensely for coming out here. This is wonderful, your interest in my son. And I see he admires you—that letter there. But what about that letter? If he did want to get out, which I don't admit—he was willing to be committed, in the end he said okay himself—if he wanted out I wouldn't do it. Why? So what if he wants to come back? The next day he wants something else, what then? He's a sick kid, and I'm the first to admit it."

Sister Irene felt that sickness spread to her. She stood. The room was so big it seemed it must be a public place; there had been nothing personal or private about their conversation. Weinstein's mother was standing by the fireplace, sobbing. The father jumped to his feet and wiped his forehead in a gesture that was meant to help Sister Irene on her way out. "God, what a day," he said, his eyes snatching at hers for understanding, "you know—one of those days all day long? Sister, I thank you a lot. There should be more people in the world who care about others, like you. I mean that."

On the way back to the convent, the man's words returned to her, and she could not get control of them; she could not even feel anger. She had been pressed down, forced back, what could she do? Weinstein might have been watching her somehow from a barred window, and he surely would have understood. The strange idea she had had on the way over, something about understanding Christ, came back to her now and sickened her. But the sickness was small. It could be contained.

About a month after her visit to his father, Weinstein himself showed up. He was dressed in a suit as before, even the necktie was the same. He came right into her office as if he had been pushed and could not stop.

"Sister," he said, and shook her hand. He must have seen fear in her because he smiled ironically. "Look, I'm released. I'm let out of the nut house. Can I sit down?"

He sat. Sister Irene was breathing quickly, as if in the presence of an enemy who does not know he is an enemy.

"So, they finally let me out. I heard what you did. You talked with him, that was all I wanted. You're the only one who gave a damn. Because you're a humanist and a religious person, you respect . . . the individual. Listen," he said, whispering, "it was hell out there! Hell Birchcrest Manor! All fixed up with fancy chairs and *Life* magazines lying around—and what do they do to you? They locked me up, they gave me shock treatments! Shock treatments, how do you like that, it's discredited by everybody now—they're crazy out there themselves, sadists. They locked me up, they gave me hypodermic shots, they didn't treat me like a human being! Do you know what that is," Weinstein demanded savagely, "not to be treated like a human being? They made me an animal—for fifty dollars a day! Dirty filthy swine! Now I'm an outpatient because I stopped swearing at them. I found somebody's bobby pin, and when I wanted to scream I pressed it under my fingernail and it stopped me—the screaming went inside and not out—so they gave me good reports, those sick bastards. Now I'm an outpatient and I can walk along the street and breathe in the same filthy exhaust from the buses like all you normal people! Christ," he said, and threw himself back against the chair.

Sister Irene stared at him. She wanted to take his hand, to make some gesture that would close the aching distance between them. "Mr. Weinstein—"

"Call me Allen!" he said sharply.

"I'm very sorry—I'm terribly sorry—"

"My own parents committed me, but of course they didn't know what it was like. It was hell," he said thickly, "and there isn't any hell except what other people do to you. The psychiatrist out there, the main shrink, he hates Jews too, some of us were positive of that, and he's got a bigger nose than I do, a real beak." He made a noise of disgust. "A dirty bastard, a sick, dirty, pathetic bastard—all of them. Anyway, I'm getting out of here, and I came to ask you a favor."

"What do you mean."

"I'm getting out. I'm leaving. I'm going up to Canada and lose myself. I'll get a job, I'll forget everything. I'll kill myself maybe—what's the difference? Look, can you lend me some money?"

"Money?"

"Just a little! I have to get to the border, I'm going to take a bus."

"But I don't have any money—"

"No money?" He stared at her. "You mean—you don't have any? Sure you have some!"

She stared at him as if he had asked her to do something obscene. Everything was splotched and uncertain before her eyes.

"You must . . . you must go back," she said, "you're making a —"

"I'll pay it back. Look, I'll pay it back, can you go to where you live or something and get it? I'm in a hurry. My friends are sons of bitches: one of them pretended he didn't see me yesterday—I stood right in the middle of the sidewalk and yelled at him, I called him some appropriate names! So he didn't see me, huh? You're the only one who understands me, you understand me like a poet, you—"

"I can't help you, I'm sorry—I . . ."

He looked to one side of her and flashed his gaze back, as if he could control it. He seemed to be trying to clear his vision.

"You have the soul of a poet," he whispered, "you're the only one. Everybody else is rotten! Can't you lend me some money, ten dollars maybe? I have three thousand in the bank, and I can't touch it! They take everything away from me, they make me into an animal. . . . You know I'm not an animal, don't you. Don't you?"

"Of course," Sister Irene whispered.

"You could get money. Help me. Give me your hand or something, touch me, help me—please. . . . " He reached for her hand and she drew back. He stared at her and his face seemed about to crumble, like a child's. "I want something from you, but I don't know what—I want something!" he cried. "Something real! I want you to look at me like I was a human being, is that too much to ask? I have a brain, I'm alive, I'm suffering—what does that mean? Does that mean nothing? I want something real and not this phoney Christian love garbage—it's all in the books, it isn't personal—I want something real—look. . . . "

He tried to take her hand again, and this time she jerked away. She got to her feet. "Mr. Weinstein," she said, "please—"

"You! You nun!" he said scornfully, his mouth twisted into a mock grin. "You nun! There's nothing under that ugly outfit, right? And you're not particularly smart even though you think you are; my father has more brains in his foot than you—"

He got to his feet and kicked the chair.

"You bitch!" he cried.

She shrank back against her desk as if she thought he might hit her, but he only ran out of the office.

■ ■ ■

Weinstein: the name was to become disembodied from the figure, as time went on. The semester passed, the autumn drizzle turned into snow. Sister Irene rode to school in the morning and left in the afternoon, four days a week, anonymous in her black winter cloak, quiet and stunned. University teaching was an anonymous task, each day dissociated from the rest, with no necessary sense of unity among the teachers: they came and went separately and might for a year just miss a colleague who left his office five minutes before they arrived, and it did not matter.

She heard of Weinstein's death, his suicide by drowning, from the English Department secretary, a handsome white-haired woman who kept a transistor radio on her desk. Sister Irene was not surprised; she had been thinking of him as dead for months. "They identified him by some special television way they have now," the secretary said. "They're shipping the body back. It was up in Quebec. . . . "

Sister Irene could feel a part of herself drifting off, lured by the plains of white snow to the north, the quiet, the emptiness, the sweep of the Great Lakes up to the silence of Canada. But she called that part of herself back. She could only be one person in her lifetime. That was the ugly truth, she thought, that she could not really regret Weinstein's suffering and death; she had only one life and had already given it to someone else. He had come too late to her. Fifteen years ago, perhaps, but not now.

She was only one person, she thought, walking down the corridor in a dream. Was she safe in this single person, or was she trapped? She had only one identity. She could make only one choice. What she had done or hadn't done was the result of that choice, and how was she guilty? If she could have felt guilt, she thought, she might at least have been able to feel something.

FLANNERY O'CONNOR

Born in 1925 in Savannah, Georgia, Mary Flannery O'Connor suffered for much of her life from disseminated lupus, a rare blood disease from which she died in 1964. During her short life, she won numerous honours for her several novels and story collections, including the National Book Award for *The Complete Short Stories* (1972). Her best-known works include *Wise Blood* (1952), *A Good Man Is Hard to Find* (1955), *The Violent Bear It Away* (1960), and *Everything That Rises Must Converge* (1965). O'Connor's fiction frequently addresses the theme of violence in modern life, questioning the efficacy of religion as a way of overcoming evil. Paradoxically O'Connor, who was deeply committed to Roman Catholicism, has been called a theological writer, one who places ultimate faith in the power of Christian redemption. In her writing she is preoccupied with the issues of sin and grace, but she finds no easy solutions to the riddle of human nature.

"A Good Man Is Hard to Find" (the title is an ironic echo of an old popular song) exemplifies O'Connor's bleak perception of the dark side of the human soul. In the escaped convict known as "The Misfit" she presents an evil not explicable in rational terms, a violence that bursts through conventional forms of order, behaviour, and religious faith. By their own lights, the grandmother and her family are "good people," but they are guided by petty and selfish desires that draw them into the sphere of forces beyond understanding or control. What begins as domestic comedy turns, by a grotesque accident, into an event of profound horror that challenges the notion of a purposeful universe.

A Good Man Is Hard to Find

The grandmother didn't want to go to Florida. She wanted to visit some of her connections in east Tennessee and she was seizing at every chance to change Bailey's mind. Bailey was the son she lived with, her only boy. He was sitting on the edge of his chair at the table, bent over the orange sports section of the *Journal*. "Now look here, Bailey," she said, "see here, read this," and she stood with one hand on her thin hip and the other rattling the newspaper at his bald head. "Here this fellow that calls himself The Misfit is aloose from the Federal Pen and headed toward Florida and you read here what it says he did to these people. Just you read it. I wouldn't take my children in any direction with a criminal like that aloose in it. I couldn't answer to my conscience if I did."

Bailey didn't look up from his reading so she wheeled around then and faced the children's mother, a young woman in slacks, whose face was as broad and innocent as a cabbage and was tied around with a green head-kerchief that had two points on the top like rabbit's ears.

She was sitting on the sofa, feeding the baby his apricots out of a jar. "The children have been to Florida before," the old lady said. "You all ought to take them somewhere else for a change so they would see different parts of the world and be broad. They never have been to east Tennessee."

The children's mother didn't seem to hear her but the eight-year-old boy, John Wesley, a stocky child with glasses, said, "If you don't want to go to Florida, why dontcha stay at home?" He and the little girl, June Star, were reading the funny papers on the floor.

"She wouldn't stay at home to be queen for a day," June Star said without raising her yellow head.

"Yes and what would you do if this fellow, The Misfit, caught you?" the grandmother asked.

"I'd smack his face," John Wesley said.

"She wouldn't stay at home for a million bucks," June Star said. "Afraid she'd miss something. She has to go everywhere we go."

"All right, Miss," the grandmother said. "Just remember that the next time you want me to curl your hair."

June Star said her hair was naturally curly.

The next morning the grandmother was the first one in the car, ready to go. She had her big black valise that looked like the head of a hippopotamus in one corner, and underneath it she was hiding a basket with Pitty Sing, the cat, in it. She didn't intend for the cat to be left alone in the house for three days because he would miss her too much and she was afraid he might brush against one of the gas burners and accidentally asphyxiate himself. Her son, Bailey, didn't like to arrive at a motel with a cat.

She sat in the middle of the back seat with John Wesley and June Star on either side of her. Bailey and the children's mother and the baby sat in front and they left Atlanta at eight forty-five with the mileage on the car at 55890. The grandmother wrote this down because she thought it would be interesting to say how many miles they had been when they got back. It took them twenty minutes to reach the outskirts of the city.

The old lady settled herself comfortably, removing her white cotton gloves and putting them up with her purse on the shelf in front of the back window. The children's mother still had on slacks and still had her head tied up in a green kerchief, but the grandmother had on a navy blue straw sailor hat with a bunch of white violets on the brim and a navy blue dress with a small white dot in the print. Her collars and cuffs were white organdy trimmed with lace and at her neckline she had pinned a purple spray of cloth violets containing a sachet. In case of an accident, anyone seeing her dead on the highway would know at once that she was a lady.

She said she thought it was going to be a good day for driving, neither too hot nor too cold, and she cautioned Bailey that the speed limit was fifty-five miles an hour and that the patrolmen hid themselves behind billboards and small clumps of trees and sped out after you before you had a chance to slow down. She pointed out interesting details of the scenery: Stone Mountain; the blue granite that in some places came up to both sides of the highway; the brilliant red clay banks slightly streaked with purple; and the various crops that made rows of green lace-work on the ground. The trees were full of silver-white sunlight and the meanest of them sparkled. The children were reading comic magazines and their mother had gone back to sleep.

"Let's go through Georgia fast so we won't have to look at it much," John Wesley said.

"If I were a little boy," said the grandmother, "I wouldn't talk about my native state that way. Tennessee has the mountains and Georgia has the hills."

"Tennessee is just a hillbilly dumping ground," John Wesley said, "and Georgia is a lousy state too."

"You said it," June Star said.

"In my time," said the grandmother, folding her thin veined fingers, "children were more respectful of their native states and their parents and everything else. People did right then. Oh look at the cute little pickaninny!" she said and pointed to a Negro child standing in the door of a shack. "Wouldn't that make a picture, now?" she asked and they all turned and looked at the little Negro out of the back window. He waved.

"He didn't have any britches on," June Star said.

"He probably didn't have any," the grandmother explained. "Little niggers in the country don't have things like we do. If I could paint, I'd paint that picture," she said.

The children exchanged comic books.

The grandmother offered to hold the baby and the children's mother passed him over the front seat to her. She set him on her knee and bounced him and told him about the things they were passing. She rolled her eyes and screwed up her mouth and stuck her leathery thin face into his smooth bland one. Occasionally he gave her a faraway smile. They passed a large cotton field with five or six graves fenced in the middle of it, like a small island. "Look at the graveyard!" the grandmother said, pointing it out. "That was the old family burying ground. That belonged to the plantation."

"Where's the plantation?" John Wesley asked.

"Gone With the Wind," said the grandmother. "Ha. Ha."

When the children finished all the comic books they had brought, they opened the lunch and ate it. The grandmother ate a peanut butter sandwich and an olive and would not let the children throw the box and the paper napkins out the window. When there was nothing else to do they played a game by choosing a cloud and making the other two guess what shape it suggested. John Wesley took one the shape of a cow and June Star guessed a cow and John Wesley said, no, an automobile, and June Star said he didn't play fair, and they began to slap each other over the grandmother.

The grandmother said she would tell them a story if they would keep quiet. When she told a story, she rolled her eyes and waved her head and was very dramatic. She said once when she was a maiden lady she had been courted by a Mr. Edgar Atkins Teagarden from Jasper, Georgia. She said he was a very good-looking man and a gentleman and that he brought her a watermelon every Saturday afternoon with his initials cut in it, E. A. T. Well, one Saturday, she said, Mr. Teagarden brought the watermelon and there was nobody at home and he left it on the front porch and returned in his buggy to Jasper, but she never got the watermelon, she said, because a nigger boy ate it when he saw the initials, E. A. T.! This story tickled John Wesley's funny bone and he giggled and giggled but June Star didn't think it was any good. She said she wouldn't marry a man that just brought her a watermelon on Saturday. The grandmother said she would have done well to marry Mr. Teagarden because he was a gentleman and had bought Coca-Cola stock when it first came out and that he had died only a few years ago, a very wealthy man.

They stopped at The Tower for barbecued sandwiches. The Tower was a part stucco and part wood filling station and dance hall set in a clearing outside of Timothy. A fat man named Red Sammy Butts ran it and there were signs stuck here and there on the building and for miles up and down the highway saying, TRY RED SAMMY'S FAMOUS BARBECUE. NONE LIKE FAMOUS RED SAMMY'S! RED SAM! THE FAT BOY WITH THE HAPPY LAUGH. A VETERAN! RED SAMMY'S YOUR MAN!

Red Sammy was lying on the bare ground outside The Tower with his head under a truck while a gray monkey about a foot high, chained to a small chinaberry tree, chattered nearby. The monkey sprang back into the tree and got on the highest limb as soon as he saw the children jump out of the car and run toward him.

Inside, The Tower was a long dark room with a counter at one end and tables at the other and dancing space in the middle. They all sat down at a board table next to the nickelodeon and Red Sam's wife, a tall burnt-brown woman with hair and eyes lighter than her skin, came and took their order. The children's mother put a dime in the machine and played "The Tennessee Waltz," and the grandmother said that tune always made her want to dance. She asked Bailey if he would like to dance but he only glared at her. He didn't have a naturally sunny disposition like she did and trips made him nervous. The grandmother's brown eyes were very bright. She swayed her head from side to side and pretended she was dancing in her chair. June Star said play something she could tap to so the children's mother put in another dime and played a fast number and June Star stepped out onto the dance floor and did her tap routine.

"Ain't she cute?" Red Sam's wife said, leaning over the counter. "Would you like to come be my little girl?"

"No I certainly wouldn't," June Star said. "I wouldn't live in a broken-down place like this for a million bucks!" and she ran back to the table.

"Ain't she cute?" the woman repeated, stretching her mouth politely.

"Aren't you ashamed?" hissed the grandmother.

Red Sam came in and told his wife to quit lounging on the counter and hurry up with these people's order. His khaki trousers reached just to his hip bones and his stomach hung over them like a sack of meal swaying under his shirt. He came over and sat down at a table nearby and let out a combination sigh and yodel. "You can't win," he said. "You can't win," and he wiped his sweating red face off with a gray handkerchief. "These days you don't know who to trust," he said. "Ain't that the truth?"

"People are certainly not nice like they used to be," said the grandmother.

"Two fellers come in here last week," Red Sammy said, "driving a Chrysler. It was a old beat-up car but it was a good one and these boys looked all right to me. Said they worked at the mill and you know I let them fellers charge the gas they bought? Now why did I do that?"

"Because you're a good man!" the grandmother said at once.

"Yes'm, I suppose so," Red Sam said as if he were struck with this answer.

His wife brought the orders, carrying the five plates all at once without a tray, two in each hand and one balanced on her arm. "It isn't a soul in this green world of God's that you can trust," she said. "And I don't count nobody out of that, not nobody," she repeated, looking at Red Sammy.

"Did you read about that criminal, The Misfit, that's escaped?" asked the grandmother.

"I wouldn't be a bit surprised if he didn't attact this place right here," said the woman. "If he hears about it being here, I wouldn't be none surprised to see him. If he hears it's two cent in the cash register, I wouldn't be a tall surprised if he . . . "

"That'll do," Red Sam said. "Go bring these people their Co'-Colas," and the woman went off to get the rest of the order.

"A good man is hard to find," Red Sammy said. "Everything is getting terrible. I remember the day you could go off and leave your screen door unlatched. Not no more."

He and the grandmother discussed better times. The old lady said that in her opinion Europe was entirely to blame for the way things were now. She said the way Europe acted you would think we were made of money and Red Sam said it was no use talking about it, she was exactly right. The children ran outside into the white sunlight and looked at the monkey in the lacy chinaberry tree. He was busy catching fleas on himself and biting each one carefully between his teeth as if it were a delicacy.

They drove off again into the hot afternoon. The grandmother took cat naps and woke up every few minutes with her own snoring. Outside of Toombsboro she woke up and recalled an old plantation that she had visited in this neighbourhood once when she was a young lady. She said the house had six white columns across the front and that there was an avenue of oaks leading up to it and two little wooden trellis arbors on either side in front where you sat down with your suitor after a stroll in the garden. She recalled exactly which road to turn off to get to it. She knew that Bailey would not be willing to lose any time looking at an old house, but the more she talked about it, the more she wanted to see it once again and find out if the little twin arbors were still standing. "There was a secret panel in this house," she said craftily, not telling the truth but wishing that she were, "and the story went that all the family silver was hidden in it when Sherman came through but it was never found . . ."

"Hey!" John Wesley said. "Let's go see it! We'll find it! We'll poke all the woodwork and find it! Who lives there? Where do you turn off at? Hey Pop, can't we turn off there?"

"We never have seen a house with a secret panel!" June Star shrieked. "Let's go to the house with the secret panel! Hey Pop, can't we go see the house with the secret panel!"

"It's not far from here, I know," the grandmother said. "It wouldn't take over twenty minutes."

Bailey was looking straight ahead. His jaw was as rigid as a horseshoe. "No," he said.

The children began to yell and scream that they wanted to see the house with the secret panel. John Wesley kicked the back of the front seat and June Star hung over her mother's shoulder and whined desperately into her ear that they never had any fun even on their vacation, that they could never do what THEY wanted to do. The baby began to scream and John Wesley kicked the back of the seat so hard that his father could feel the blows in his kidney.

"All right!" he shouted and drew the car to a stop at the side of the road. "Will you all shut up? Will you all just shut up for one second? If you don't shut up, we won't go anywhere."

"It would be very educational for them," the grandmother murmured.

"All right," Bailey said, "but get this: this is the only time we're going to stop for anything like this. This is the one and only time."

"The dirt road that you have to turn down is about a mile back," the grandmother directed. "I marked it when we passed."

"A dirt road," Bailey groaned.

After they had turned and were headed toward the dirt road, the grandmother recalled other points about the house, the beautiful glass over the front doorway and the candle-lamp in the hall. John Wesley said that the secret panel was probably in the fireplace.

"You can't go inside this house," Bailey said. "You don't know who lives there."

"While you all talk to the people in front, I'll run around behind and get in a window," John Wesley suggested.

"We'll all stay in the car," his mother said.

They turned onto the dirt road and the car raced roughly along in a swirl of pink dust. The grandmother recalled the times when there were no paved roads and thirty miles was a day's journey. The dirt road was hilly and there were sudden washes in it and sharp curves on dangerous embankments. All at once they would be on a hill, looking down over the blue tops of trees for miles around, then the next minute, they would be in a red depression with the dust-coated trees looking down on them.

"This place had better turn up in a minute," Bailey said, "or I'm going to turn around."

The road looked as if no one had traveled on it in months.

"It's not much farther," the grandmother said and just as she said it, a horrible thought came to her. The thought was so embarrassing that she turned red in the face and her eyes dilated and her feet jumped up, upsetting her valise in the corner. The instant the valise moved, the newspaper top she had over the basket under it rose with a snarl and Pitty Sing, the cat, sprang onto Bailey's shoulder.

The children were thrown to the floor and their mother, clutching the baby, was thrown out the door onto the ground; the old lady was thrown into the front seat. The car turned over once and landed right-side-up in a gulch off the side of the road. Bailey remained in the driver's seat with the cat—gray-striped with a broad white face and an orange nose—clinging to his neck like a caterpillar.

As soon as the children saw they could move their arms and legs, they scrambled out of the car, shouting, "We've had an ACCIDENT!" The grandmother was curled up under the dashboard, hoping she was injured so that Bailey's wrath would not come down on her all at once. The horrible thought she had had before the accident was that the house she had remembered so vividly was not in Georgia but in Tennessee.

Bailey removed the cat from his neck with both hands and flung it out the window against the side of a pine tree. Then he got out of the car and started looking for the children's mother. She was sitting against the side of the red gutted ditch, holding the screaming baby, but she only had a cut down her face and a broken shoulder. "We've had an ACCIDENT!" the children screamed in a frenzy of delight.

"But nobody's killed," June Star said with disappointment as the grandmother limped out of the car, her hat still pinned to her head but the broken front brim standing up at a jaunty angle and the violet spray hanging off the side. They all sat down in the ditch, except the children, to recover from the shock. They were all shaking.

"Maybe a car will come along," said the children's mother hoarsely.

"I believe I have injured an organ," said the grandmother pressing her side, but no one answered her. Bailey's teeth were clattering. He had on a yellow sport shirt with bright blue parrots designed in it and his face was as yellow as the shirt. The grandmother decided that she would not mention that the house was in Tennessee.

The road was about ten feet above and they could see only the tops of the trees on the other side of it. Behind the ditch they were sitting in there were more woods, tall and dark and deep. In a few minutes they saw a car some distance away on top of a hill, coming slowly as if the occupants were watching them. The grandmother stood up and waved both arms dramatically to attract their attention. The car continued to come on slowly, disappeared around a bend and appeared again, moving even slower, on top of the hill they had gone over. It was a big black battered hearse-like automobile. There were three men in it.

It came to a stop just over them and for some minutes, the driver looked down with a steady expressionless gaze to where they were sitting, and didn't speak. Then he turned his head and muttered something to the other two and they got out. One was a fat boy in black trousers and a red sweat shirt with a silver stallion embossed on the front of it. He moved around on the right side of them and stood staring, his mouth partly open in a kind of loose grin. The other had on khaki pants and a blue striped coat and a gray hat pulled down very low, hiding most of his face. He came around slowly on the left side. Neither spoke.

The driver got out of the car and stood by the side of it, looking down at them. He was an older man than the other two. His hair was just beginning to gray and he wore silver-rimmed spectacles that gave him a scholarly look. He had a long creased face and didn't have on any shirt or undershirt. He had on blue jeans that were too tight for him and was holding a black hat and a gun. The two boys also had guns.

"We've had an ACCIDENT!" the children screamed.

The grandmother had the peculiar feeling that the bespectacled man was someone she knew. His face was as familiar to her as if she had known him all her life but she could not recall who he was. He moved away from the car and began to come down the embankment, placing his feet carefully so that he wouldn't slip. He had on tan and white shoes and no socks, and his ankles were red and thin. "Good afternoon," he said. "I see you all had you a little spill."

"We turned over twice!" said the grandmother.

"Oncet," he corrected. "We seen it happen. Try their car and see will it run, Hiram," he said quietly to the boy with the gray hat.

"What you got that gun for?" John Wesley asked. "Whatcha gonna do with that gun?"

"Lady," the man said to the children's mother, "would you mind calling them children to sit down by you? Children make me nervous. I want all you all to sit down right together there where you're at."

"What are you telling US what to do for?" June Star asked.

Behind them the line of woods gaped like a dark open mouth. "Come here," said their mother.

"Look here now," Bailey began suddenly, "we're in a predicament! We're in . . . "

The grandmother shrieked. She scrambled to her feet and stood staring. "You're The Misfit!" she said. "I recognized you at once!"

"Yes'm," the man said, smiling slightly as if he were pleased in spite of himself to be known, "but it would have been better for all of you, lady, if you hadn't of reckernized me."

Bailey turned his head sharply and said something to his mother that shocked even the children. The old lady began to cry and The Misfit reddened.

"Lady," he said, "don't you get upset. Sometimes a man says things he don't mean. I don't reckon he meant to talk to you thataway."

"You wouldn't shoot a lady, would you?" the grandmother said and removed a clean handkerchief from her cuff and began to slap at her eyes with it.

The Misfit pointed the toe of his shoe into the ground and made a little hole and then covered it up again. "I would hate to have to," he said.

"Listen," the grandmother almost screamed, "I know you're a good man. You don't look a bit like you have common blood. I know you must come from nice people!"

"Yes mam," he said, "finest people in the world." When he smiled he showed a row of strong white teeth. "God never made a finer woman than my mother and my daddy's heart was pure gold," he said. The boy with the red sweat shirt had come around behind them and was standing with his gun at his hip. The Misfit squatted down on the ground. "Watch them children, Bobby Lee," he said. "You know they make me nervous." He looked at the six of them huddled together in front of him and he seemed to be embarrassed as if he couldn't think of anything to say. "Ain't a cloud in the sky," he remarked, looking up at it. "Don't see no sun but don't see no cloud neither."

"Yes, it's a beautiful day," said the grandmother. "Listen," she said, "you shouldn't call yourself The Misfit because I know you're a good man at heart. I can just look at you and tell."

"Hush!" Bailey yelled. "Hush! Everybody shut up and let me handle this!" He was squatting in the position of a runner about to sprint forward but he didn't move.

"I pre-chate that, lady," The Misfit said and drew a little circle in the ground with the butt of his gun.

"It'll take a half a hour to fix this here car," Hiram called, looking over the raised hood of it.

"Well, first you and Bobby Lee get him and that little boy to step over yonder with you," The Misfit said, pointing to Bailey and John Wesley. "The boys want to ast you something," he said to Bailey. "Would you mind stepping back in them woods there with them?"

"Listen," Bailey began, "we're in a terrible predicament! Nobody realizes what this is," and his voice cracked. His eyes were as blue and intense as the parrots in his shirt and he remained perfectly still.

The grandmother reached up to adjust her hat brim as if she were going to the woods with him but it came off in her hand. She stood staring at it and after a second she let it fall on the ground. Hiram pulled Bailey up by the arm as if he were assisting an old man. John Wesley caught hold of his father's hand and Bobby Lee followed. They went off toward the woods and just as they reached the dark edge, Bailey turned and supporting himself against a gray naked pine trunk, he shouted, "I'll be back in a minute, Mamma, wait on me!"

"Come back this instant!" his mother shrilled but they all disappeared into the woods.

"Bailey Boy!" the grandmother called in a tragic voice but she found she was looking at The Misfit squatting on the ground in front of her. "I just know you're a good man," she said desperately, "You're not a bit common!"

"Nome, I ain't a good man," The Misfit said after a second as if he had considered her statement carefully, "but I ain't the worst in the world neither. My daddy said I was a different breed of dog from my brothers and sisters. 'You know,' Daddy said, 'it's some that can live their whole life out without asking about it and it's others has to know why it is, and this boy is one of the latters. He's going to be into everything!' " He put on his black hat and looked up suddenly and then away deep into the woods as if he were embarrassed again. "I'm sorry I don't have on a shirt before you ladies," he said, hunching his shoulders slightly. "We buried our clothes that we had on when we escaped and we're just making do until we can get better. We borrowed these from some folks we met," he explained.

"That's perfectly all right," the grandmother said. "Maybe Bailey has an extra shirt in his suitcase."

"I'll look and see terrectly," The Misfit said.

"Where are they taking him?" the children's mother screamed.

"Daddy was a card himself," The Misfit said. "You couldn't put anything over on him. He never got in trouble with the Authorities though. Just had the knack of handling them."

"You could be honest too if you'd only try," said the grandmother. "Think how wonderful it would be to settle down and live a comfortable life and not have to think about somebody chasing you all the time."

The Misfit kept scratching in the ground with the butt of his gun as if he were thinking about it. "Yes'm, somebody is always after you," he murmured.

The grandmother noticed how thin his shoulder blades were just behind his hat because she was standing up looking down at him. "Do you ever pray?" she asked.

He shook his head. All she saw was the black hat wiggle between his shoulder blades. "Nome," he said.

There was a pistol shot from the woods, followed closely by another. Then silence. The old lady's head jerked around. She could hear the wind move through the tree tops like a long satisfied insuck of breath. "Bailey Boy!" she called.

"I was a gospel singer for a while," The Misfit said. "I been most everything. Been in the arm service, both land and sea, at home and abroad, been twict married, been an undertaker, been with the railroads, plowed Mother Earth, been in a tornado, seen a man burnt alive oncet," and he looked up at the children's mother and the little girl who were sitting close together, their faces white and their eyes glassy; "I even seen a woman flogged," he said.

"Pray, pray," the grandmother began, "pray, pray . . . "

"I never was a bad boy that I remember of," The Misfit said in an almost dreamy voice, "but somewheres along the line I done something wrong and got sent to the penitentiary. I was buried alive," and he looked up and held her attention to him by a steady stare.

"That's when you should have started to pray," she said. "What did you do to get sent to the penitentiary that first time?"

"Turn to the right, it was a wall," The Misfit said, looking up again at the cloudless sky. "Turn to the left, it was a wall. Look up it was a ceiling, look down it was a floor. I forget what I done, lady. I set there and set there, trying to remember what it was I done and I ain't recalled it to this day. Oncet in a while, I would think it was coming to me, but it never come."

"Maybe they put you in by mistake," the old lady said vaguely.

"Nome," he said. "It wasn't no mistake. They had the papers on me."

"You must have stolen something," she said.

The Misfit sneered slightly. "Nobody had nothing I wanted," he said. "It was a head-doctor at the penitentiary said what I had done was kill my daddy but I known that for a lie. My daddy died in nineteen ought nineteen of the epidemic flu and I never had a thing to do with it. He was buried in the Mount Hopewell Baptist churchyard and you can go there and see for yourself."

"If you would pray," the old lady said, "Jesus would help you."

"That's right," The Misfit said.

"Well then, why don't you pray?" she asked trembling with delight suddenly.

"I don't want no hep," he said. "I'm doing all right by myself."

Bobby Lee and Hiram came ambling back from the woods. Bobby Lee was dragging a yellow shirt with bright blue parrots in it.

"Thow me that shirt, Bobby Lee," The Misfit said. The shirt came flying at him and landed on his shoulder and he put it on. The grandmother couldn't name what the shirt reminded her of. "No, lady," The Misfit said while he was buttoning it up, "I found out the crime don't matter. You can do one thing or you can do another, kill a man or take a tire off his car, because sooner or later you're going to forget what it was you done and just be punished for it."

The children's mother had begun to make heaving noises as if she couldn't get her breath. "Lady," he asked, "would you and that little girl like to step off yonder with Bobby Lee and Hiram and join your husband?"

"Yes, thank you," the mother said faintly. Her left arm dangled helplessly and she was holding the baby, who had gone to sleep, in the other. "Hep that lady up, Hiram," The Misfit said as she struggled to climb out of the ditch, "and Bobby Lee, you hold onto that little girl's hand."

"I don't want to hold hands with him," June Star said. "He reminds me of a pig."

The fat boy blushed and laughed and caught her by the arm and pulled her off into the woods after Hiram and her mother.

Alone with The Misfit, the grandmother found that she had lost her voice. There was not a cloud in the sky nor any sun. There was nothing around her but woods. She wanted to tell him that he must pray. She opened and closed her mouth several times before anything came out. Finally she found herself saying, "Jesus. Jesus," meaning, Jesus will help you, but the way she was saying it, it sounded as if she might be cursing.

"Yes'm," The Misfit said as if he agreed. "Jesus thown everything off balance. It was the same case with Him as with me except He hadn't committed any crime and they could prove I had committed one because they had the papers on me. Of course," he said, "they never shown me my papers. That's why I sign myself now. I said long ago, you get you a signature and sign everything you do and keep a copy of it. Then you'll know what you done and you can hold up the crime to the punishment and see do they match and in the end you'll have something to prove you ain't been treated right. I call myself The Misfit," he said, "because I can't make what all I done wrong fit what all I gone through in punishment."

There was a piercing scream from the woods, followed closely by a pistol report. "Does it seem right to you, lady, that one is punished a heap and another ain't punished at all?"

"Jesus!" the old lady cried. "You've got good blood! I know you wouldn't shoot a lady! I know you come from nice people! Pray! Jesus, you ought not to shoot a lady. I'll give you all the money I've got!"

"Lady," The Misfit said, looking beyond her far into the woods, "there never was a body that give the undertaker a tip."

There were two more pistol reports and the grandmother raised her head like a parched old turkey hen crying for water and called, "Bailey Boy, Bailey Boy!" as if her heart would break.

"Jesus was the only One that ever raised the dead," The Misfit continued, "and He shouldn't have done it. He thown everything off balance. If He did what He said, then it's nothing for you to do but thow away everything and follow Him, and if He didn't, then it's nothing for you to do but enjoy the few minutes you got left the best way you can—by killing somebody or burning down his house or doing some other meanness to him. No pleasure but meanness," he said and his voice had become almost a snarl.

"Maybe He didn't raise the dead," the old lady mumbled, not knowing what she was saying and feeling so dizzy that she sank down in the ditch with her legs twisted under her.

"I wasn't there so I can't say He didn't," The Misfit said. "I wisht I had of been there," he said, hitting the ground with his fist. "It ain't right I wasn't there because if I had of been there I would of known. Listen lady," he said in a high voice, "if I had of been there I would of known and I wouldn't be like I am now." His voice seemed about to crack and the grandmother's head cleared for an instant. She saw the man's face twisted close to her own as if he were going to cry and she murmured, "Why you're one of my babies. You're one of my own children!" She reached out and touched him on the shoulder. The Misfit sprang back as if a snake had bitten him and shot her three times through the chest. Then he put his gun down on the ground and took off his glasses and began to clean them.

Hiram and Bobby Lee returned from the woods and stood over the ditch, looking down at the grandmother who half sat and half lay in a puddle of blood with her legs crossed under her like a child's and her face smiling up at the cloudless sky.

Without his glasses, The Misfit's eyes were red-rimmed and pale and defenseless-looking. "Take her off and thow her where you thown the others," he said, picking up the cat that was rubbing itself against his leg.

"She was a talker, wasn't she?" Bobby Lee said, sliding down the ditch with a yodel.

"She would of been a good woman," The Misfit said, "if it had been somebody there to shoot her every minute of her life."

"Some fun!" Bobby Lee said.

"Shut up, Bobby Lee," The Misfit said. "It's no real pleasure in life."

Katherine Anne Porter

Katherine Anne Porter (1890–1980) was born in Texas, and her formal education was limited to girls' schools in the South; but she learned much from her own reading, and early formed the desire to be a writer. Her first collection of short stories, *Flowering Judas and other stories* (1930; augmented edition, 1935), won immediate critical praise for her smooth, spare prose, and for the psychological insights of such stories as "He." The success of *Flowering Judas and other stories* brought her a Guggenheim Fellowship, which enabled her to travel; and her subsequent voyage to Europe in 1931 provided the material for her longest work, the novel *Ship of Fools* (1962). The many awards and distinctions conferred upon her include a Pulitzer Prize, which she received in 1966.

In her introduction in the 1940 edition of *Flowering Judas and other stories,* Porter describes how she sought "to understand the logic of this majestic and terrible failure of the life of man in the Western world"; and to a greater or lesser extent, this concern is reflected in all her work. She dramatizes the human struggle for contact and communication in the face of all the fears, prejudices, and frustrations that alienate people from each other. Like the protagonist in her long story "The Leaning Tower" (1944), many of her characters confront a society in the process of disintegration, or experience "an infernal desolation of the spirit, and chill and the knowledge of death. . . . " Porter's stories reflect her sense of the confusion that characterizes human life; she investigates "self-betrayal and self-deception—the way that all human beings deceive themselves about the way they operate. . . . Everyone takes his stance, asserts his own rights and feelings, mistaking the motives of others, and his own . . . " (*Paris Review* interview, 1963). In "He," Mrs. Whipple succeeds for a while in shutting away the truth about her feelings for her son; but the author passes no harsh judgment on her self-delusion and insincerity, and portrays with compassion the dawning horror of her final recognition of failure.

He

Life was very hard for the Whipples. It was hard to feed all the hungry mouths, it was hard to keep the children in flannels during the winter, short as it was. "God knows what would become of us if we lived north," they would say; keeping them decently clean was hard. "It looks like our luck won't never let up on us," said Mr Whipple, but Mrs Whipple was all for taking what was sent and calling it good, anyhow when the neighbours were in earshot. "Don't ever let a soul hear us complain," she kept saying to her husband. She couldn't stand to be pitied. "No, not if it comes to it that we have to live in a wagon and pick cotton around the country," she said, "nobody's going to get a chance to look down on us."

Mrs Whipple loved her second son, the simple-minded one, better than she loved the other two children put together. She was for ever saying so, and when she talked with certain of her neighbours, she would even throw in her husband and her mother for good measure.

"You needn't keep on saying it around," said Mr Whipple, "you'll make people think nobody else has any feelings about Him but you."

"It's natural for a mother," Mrs Whipple would remind him. "You know yourself it's more natural for a mother to be that way. People don't expect so much of fathers, some way."

This didn't keep the neighbours from talking plainly among themselves. "A Lord's pure mercy if He should die," they said. "It's the sins of the fathers," they agreed among themselves. "There's bad blood and bad doings somewhere, you can bet on that." This behind the Whipples' backs. To their faces everybody said, "He's not so bad off. He'll be all right yet. Look how He grows!"

Mrs Whipple hated to talk about it, she tried to keep her mind off it, but every time anybody set foot in the house, the subject always came up, and she had to talk about Him first, before she could get on to anything else. It seemed to ease her mind. "I wouldn't have anything happen to Him for all the world, but it just looks like I can't keep Him out of mischief. He's so strong and active. He's always into everything; He was like that since He could walk. It's actually funny sometimes the way He can do anything; it's laughable to see Him up to His tricks. Emly has more accidents; I'm for every tying up her bruises, and Adna can't fall a foot without cracking a bone. But He can do anything and not get a scratch. The preacher said such a nice thing once when he was here. He said, and I'll remember it to my dying day, 'The innocent walk with God—that's why He don't get hurt.' " Whenever Mrs Whipple repeated these words, she always felt a warm pool spread in her breast, and the tears would fill her eyes, and then she could talk about something else.

He did grow and He never got hurt. A plank blew off the chicken house and struck Him on the head and He never seemed to know it. He had learned a few words, and after this He forgot them. He didn't whine for food as the other children did, but waited until it was given Him; He ate squatting in the corner, smacking and mumbling. Rolls of fat covered Him like an overcoat, and He could carry twice as much wood and water as Adna. Emly had a cold in the head most of the time—"she takes that after me," said Mrs Whipple—so in bad weather they gave her the extra blanket off His cot. He never seemed to mind the cold.

Just the same, Mrs Whipple's life was a torment for fear something might happen to Him. He climbed the peach trees much better than Adna and went skittering along the branches like a monkey, just a regular monkey. "Oh, Mrs Whipple, you hadn't ought to let Him do that. He'll lose His balance sometime. He can't rightly know what He's doing."

Mrs Whipple almost screamed out at the neighbour. "He *does* know what He's doing! He's as able as any other child! Come down out of there, you!" When He finally reached the ground she could hardly keep her hands off Him for acting like that before people, a grin all over His face and her worried sick about Him all the time.

"It's the neighbours," said Mrs Whipple to her husband. "Oh, I do mortally wish they would keep out of our business. I can't afford to let Him do anything for fear they'll come nosing around about it. Look at the bees, now. Adna can't handle them, they sting him so. I haven't got time to do everything, and now I don't dare let Him. But if He gets a sting He don't really mind."

"It's just because He ain't got sense enough to be scared of anything," said Mr Whipple.

"You ought to be ashamed of yourself," said Mrs Whipple, "talking that way about your own child. Who's to take up for Him if we don't, I'd like to know? He sees a lot that goes on, He listens to things all the time. And anything I tell Him to do He does it. Don't never let anybody hear you say such things. They'd think you favoured the other children over Him."

"Well, now I don't, and you know it, and what's the use of getting all worked up about it? You always think the worst of everything. Just let Him alone, He'll get along somehow. He gets plenty to eat and wear, don't He?" Mr Whipple suddenly felt tired out. "Anyhow, it can't be helped now."

Mrs Whipple felt tired too; she complained in a tired voice: "What's done can't never be undone, I know that good as anybody; but He's my child, and I'm not going to have people say anything. I get sick of people coming around saying things all the time."

In the early autumn Mrs Whipple got a letter from her brother saying he and his wife and two children were coming over for a little visit next Sunday week. "Put the big pot in the little one," he wrote at the end. Mrs Whipple read this part out loud twice, she was so pleased. Her brother was a great one for saying funny things. "We'll just show him that's no joke," she said, "we'll just butcher one of the sucking pigs."

"It's a waste and I don't hold with waste the way we are now," said Mr Whipple. "That pig'll be worth money by Christmas."

"It's a shame and a pity we can't have a decent meal's vittles once in a while when my own family comes to see us," said Mrs Whipple. "I'd hate for his wife to go back and say there wasn't a thing in the house to eat. My God, it's better than buying up a great chance of meat in town. There's where you'd spend the money!"

"All right, do it yourself then," said Mr Whipple. "Christamighty, no wonder we can't get ahead!"

The question was how to get the little pig away from his ma, a great fighter, worse than a Jersey cow. Adna wouldn't try it: "That sow'd rip my insides out all over the pen." "All right, old fraidy," said Mrs Whipple, "*He's* not scared. Watch *Him* do it." And she laughed as though it was all a good joke and gave Him a little push towards the pen. He sneaked up and snatched the pig right away from the teat and galloped back and was over the fence with the sow raging at His heels. The little black squirming thing was screeching like a baby in a tantrum, stiffening its back and stretching its mouth to the ears. Mrs Whipple took the pig with her face stiff and sliced its throat with one stroke. When He saw the blood He gave a great jolting breath and ran away. "But He'll forget and eat plenty, just the same," thought Mrs Whipple. Whenever she was thinking, her lips moved, making words. "He'd eat it all if I didn't stop Him. He'd eat up every mouthful from the other two if I'd let Him."

She felt badly about it. He was ten years old now and a third again as large as Adna, who was going on fourteen. "It's a shame, a shame," she kept saying under her breath, "and Adna with so much brains!"

She kept on feeling badly about all sorts of things. In the first place it was the man's work to butcher; the sight of the pig scraped pink and naked made her sick. He was too fat and soft and pitiful-looking. It was simply a shame the way things had to happen. By the time she had finished it up, she almost wished her brother would stay at home.

Early on Sunday morning Mrs Whipple dropped everything to get Him all cleaned up. In an hour He was dirty again, with crawling under fences after an opossum, and straddling along the rafters of the barn looking for eggs in the hayloft. "My lord, look at you now after all my trying! And here's Adna and Emly staying so quiet. I get tired trying to keep you decent. Get off that shirt and put on another; people will say I don't half dress you!" And she boxed Him on the ears, hard. He blinked and blinked and rubbed His head, and His face hurt Mrs Whipple's feelings. Her knees began to tremble, she had to sit down while she buttoned His shirt. "I'm just all gone before the day starts."

The brother came with his plump healthy wife and two great roaring hungry boys. They had a grand dinner, with the pig roasted to a crackling in the middle of the table, full of dressing, a pickled peach in his mouth and plenty of gravy for the sweet potatoes.

"This looks like prosperity all right," said the brother; "you're going to have to roll me home like I was a barrel when I'm done."

Everybody laughed out loud; it was fine to hear them laughing all at once around the table. Mrs Whipple felt warm and good about it. "Oh, we've got six more of these; I say it's a little as we can do when you come to see us so seldom."

He wouldn't come into the dining-room and Mrs Whipple passed it off very well. "He's timider than my other two," she said. "He'll just have to get used to you. There isn't everybody He'll make up with, you know how it is with some children, even cousins." Nobody said anything out of the way.

"Just like my Alfy here," said the brother's wife. "I sometimes got to lick him to make him shake hands with his own grandmammy."

So that was over, and Mrs Whipple loaded up a big plate for Him first, before everybody. "I always say He ain't to be slighted, no matter who else goes without," she said, and carried it to Him herself.

"He can chin Himself on the top of the door," said Emly, helping along.

"That's fine. He's getting along fine," said the brother.

They went away after supper. Mrs Whipple rounded up the dishes, sent the children to bed, and sat down and unlaced her shoes. "You see?" she said to Mr Whipple. "That the way my whole family is. Nice and considerate about everything. No out-of-the-mouth remarks—they *have* got refinement. I get awfully sick of people's remarks. Wasn't that pig good?"

Mr Whipple said, "Yes, we're out three hundred pounds of pork, that's all. It's easy to be polite when you come to eat. Who knows what they had in their minds all along?"

"Yes, that's like you," said Mrs Whipple. "I don't expect anything else from you. You'll be telling me next that my own brother will be saying around that we made Him eat in the kitchen! Oh, my God!" She rocked her head in her hands, a hard pain started in the very middle of her forehead. "Now it's all spoiled, and everything was so nice and easy. All right, you don't like them and you never did—all right, they'll not come here again soon, never you mind! But they *can't* say He wasn't dressed every lick as good as Adna—oh, honest, sometimes I wish I was dead!"

"I wish you'd let up," said Mr Whipple. "It's bad enough as it is."

■ ■ ■

It was a hard winter. It seemed to Mrs Whipple that they hadn't ever known anything but hard times, and now to cap it all a winter like this. The crops were about half of what they had a right to expect; after the cotton was in it didn't do much more than cover the grocery bill. They swapped off one of the plough horses, and got cheated, for the new one died of the heaves. Mrs Whipple kept thinking all the time it was terrible to have a man you couldn't depend on not to get cheated. They cut down on everything, but Mrs Whipple kept saying there are things you can't cut down on, and they cost money. It took a lot of warm clothes for Adna and Emly, who walked four miles to school during the three-months session. "He sets around the fire a lot. He won't need so much," said Mr Whipple. "That's so," said Mrs Whipple, "and when He does the outdoor chores He can wear your tarpaulin coat. I can't do no better, that's all."

In February He was taken sick, and lay curled up under His blanket looking very blue in the face and acting as if He would choke. Mr and Mrs Whipple did everything they could for Him for two days, and then they were scared and sent for the doctor. The doctor told them they must keep Him warm and give Him plenty of milk and eggs. "He isn't as stout as He looks, I'm afraid," said the doctor. "You've got to watch them when they're like that. You must put more cover on Him, too."

"I just took off His big blanket to wash," said Mrs Whipple, ashamed. "I can't stand dirt."

"Well, you'd better put it back on the minute it's dry," said the doctor, "or He'll have pneumonia."

Mr and Mrs Whipple took a blanket off their own bed and put His cot in by the fire. "They can't say we didn't do everything for Him," she said, "even to sleeping cold ourselves on His account."

When the winter broke He seemed to be well again, but He walked as if His feet hurt Him. He was able to run a cotton planter during the season.

"I got it all fixed up with Jim Ferguson about breeding the cow next time," said Mr Whipple. "I'll pasture the bull this summer and give Jim some fodder in the autumn. That's better than paying out money when you haven't got it."

"I hope you didn't say such a thing before Jim Ferguson," said Mrs Whipple. "You oughtn't to let him know we're so down as all that."

"Godamighty, that ain't saying we're down! A man has got to look ahead sometimes. *He* can lead the bull over today. I need Adna on the place."

At first Mrs Whipple felt easy in her mind about sending Him for the bull. Adna was too jumpy and couldn't be trusted. You've got to be steady around animals. After He was gone she started thinking, and after a while she could hardly bear it any longer. She stood in the lane and watched for Him. It was nearly three miles to go and a hot day, but He oughtn't to be so long about it. She shaded her eyes and stared until coloured bubbles floated in her eyeballs. It was just like everything else in life, she must always worry and never know a moment's peace about anything. After a long time she saw Him turn into the side lane, limping. He came on very slowly, leading the big hulk of an animal by a ring in the nose, twirling a little stick in His hand, never looking back or sideways, but coming on like a sleepwalker with His eyes half shut.

Mrs Whipple was scared sick of bulls; she had heard awful stories about how they followed on quietly enough, and then suddenly pitched on with a bellow and pawed and gored a body to pieces. Any second now that black monster would come down on Him. My God. He'd never have sense enough to run.

She mustn't make a sound nor a move; she mustn't get the bull started. The bull heaved his head aside and horned the air at a fly. Her voice burst out of her in a shriek, and she screamed at Him to come on, for God's sake. He didn't seem to hear her clamour, but kept on twirling His switch and limping on, and the bull lumbered along behind him as gently as a calf. Mrs Whipple stopped calling and ran towards the house, praying under her breath: "Lord, don't let anything happen to Him. Lord, you *know* people will say we oughtn't to have sent Him. You *know* they'll say we didn't take care of Him. Oh, get Him home, safe home, safe home, and I'll look out for Him better! Amen."

She watched from the window while He led the beast in and tied him up in the barn. It was no use trying to keep up. Mrs Whipple couldn't bear another thing. She sat down and rocked and cried with her apron over her head.

From year to year the Whipples were growing poorer and poorer. The place just seemed to run down of itself, no matter how hard they worked. "We're losing our hold," said Mrs Whipple. "Why can't we do like other people and watch for our best chances? They'll be calling us poor white trash next."

"When I get to be sixteen I'm going to leave," said Adna. "I'm going to get a job in Powell's grocery store. There's money in that. No more farm for me."

"I'm going to be a school teacher," said Emly. "But I've got to finish the eighth grade, anyhow. Then I can live in town. I don't see any chances here."

"Emly takes after my family," said Mrs Whipple. "Ambitious every last one of them, and they don't take second place for anybody."

When autumn came Emly got a chance to wait at table in the railroad eating-house in the town near by, and it seemed such a shame not to take it when the wages were good and she could get her food too, that Mrs Whipple decided to let her take it, and not bother with school until the next session. "You've got plenty of time," she said. "You're young and smart as a whip."

With Adna gone too, Mr Whipple tried to run the farm with just Him to help. He seemed to get along fine, doing His work and part of Adna's without noticing it. They did well enough until Christmas time, when one morning He slipped on the ice coming up from the barn. Instead of getting up He thrashed round and round, and when Mr Whipple got to Him, He was having some sort of fit.

They brought Him inside and tried to make Him sit up, but He blubbered and rolled, so they put Him to bed and Mr Whipple rode to town for the doctor. All the way there and back he worried about where the money was to come from: it sure did look like he had about all the troubles he could carry.

From then on He stayed in bed. His legs swelled up double their size, and the fits kept coming back. After four months the doctor said, "It's no use, I think you'd better put Him in the County Home for treatment right away. I'll see about it for you. He'll have good care there and be off your hands."

"We don't begrudge Him any care, and I won't let Him out of my sight," said Mrs Whipple. "I won't have it said I sent my sick child off among strangers."

"I know how you feel," said the doctor. "You can't tell me anything about that, Mrs Whipple. I've got a boy of my own. But you'd better listen to me. I can't do anything more for Him, that's the truth."

Mr and Mrs Whipple talked it over a long time that night after they went to bed. "It's just charity," said Mrs Whipple, "that's what we've come to, charity! I certainly never looked for this."

"We pay taxes to help support the place just like everybody else," said Mr Whipple, "and I don't call that taking charity. I think it would be fine to have Him where He'd get the best of everything . . . and besides, I can't keep up with these doctor's bills any longer."

"Maybe that's why the doctor wants us to send Him—he's scared he won't get his money," said Mrs Whipple.

"Don't talk like that," said Mr Whipple, feeling pretty sick, "or we won't be able to send Him."

"Oh, but we won't keep Him there long," said Mrs Whipple. "Soon's He's better we'll bring Him right back home."

"The doctor has told you, and told you time and again, He can't ever get better, and you might as well stop talking," said Mr Whipple.

"Doctors don't know everything," said Mrs Whipple, feeling almost happy. "But anyhow, in the summer Emly can come home for a vacation, and Adna can get down for Sundays: we'll all work together and get on our feet again, and the children will feel they've got a place to come to."

All at once she saw it full summer again, with the garden going fine, and new white roller shades up all over the house, and Adna and Emly home, so full of life; all of them happy together. Oh, it could happen, things would ease up on them.

They didn't talk before Him much, but they never knew just how much He understood. Finally the doctor set the day and a neighbour who owned a double-seated carryall offered to drive them over. The hospital would have sent an ambulance, but Mrs Whipple couldn't stand to see Him going away looking so sick as all that. They wrapped Him in blankets, and the neighbour and Mr. Whipple lifted Him into the back seat of the carryall beside Mrs Whipple, who had on her black shirtwaist. She couldn't stand to go looking like charity.

"You'll be all right, I guess I'll stay behind," said Mr Whipple. "It don't look like everybody ought to leave the place at once."

"Besides, it ain't as if He was going to stay for ever," said Mrs Whipple to the neighbour. "This is only for a little while."

They started away, Mrs Whipple holding to the edges of the blankets to keep Him from sagging sideways. He sat there blinking and blinking. He worked His hands out and began rubbing His nose with his knuckles, and then with the end of the blanket. Mrs Whipple couldn't believe what she saw; He was scrubbing away big tears that rolled out of the corners of His eyes. He snivelled and made a gulping noise. Mrs Whipple kept saying, "Oh, honey, you don't feel so bad, do you? You don't feel so bad, do you?" for He seemed to be accusing her of something. Maybe He remembered that time she boxed His ears; maybe He had been scared that day with the bull; maybe He had slept cold and couldn't tell her about it; maybe He knew they were sending Him away for good and all because they were too poor to keep Him.

Whatever it was, Mrs Whipple couldn't bear to think of it. She began to cry, frightfully, and wrapped her arms tightly round him. His head rolled on her shoulder: she had loved Him as much as she possibly could; there were Adna and Emly who had to be thought of too, there was nothing she could do to make up to Him for His life. Oh, what a mortal pity He was ever born.

They came in sight of the hospital, with the neighbour driving very fast, not daring to look behind him.

E. Annie Proulx

E(dna) Annie Proulx traces her family heritage back to 1635, when her mother's ancestors arrived in Connecticut. She herself was born in Norwich, Connecticut, in 1935, the eldest of five daughters. After obtaining her BA in history at the University of Vermont in 1969, she attended Sir George Williams University (now called Concordia) in Montreal, taking an MA degree in 1973 and passing her doctoral orals in 1975. At that point she turned to freelance journalism, and to support her family she wrote articles on a wide range of subjects, from canoeing and mountain lions to lettuces and African beadwork. In this period she produced a number of commissioned "how-to" books, such as *Sweet & Hard Cider: Making It, Using It, and Enjoying It* (written with L. Nichols, 1980) and *The Fine Art of Salad Gardening* (1983). At the same time, she began to produce short stories, two or three a year, and in 1988 these were collected and published as *Heart Songs and Other Stories*. In 1989 she took up the writing of fiction full-time, a step made easier by grants from the National Endowment for the Arts in 1991 and the Guggenheim Foundation in 1992. Proulx's first novel, *Postcards*, was published in 1992 to warm critical acclaim, and won the PEN/Faulkner Award for Fiction. This success was rapidly followed by *The Shipping News* (1993), a novel set in Newfoundland, which brought Proulx the Irish Times International Prize in 1993, and the Pulitzer Prize in 1994. Proulx's third novel, *Accordion Crimes* (1996), a series of linked stories about the fate of a musical instrument passed from one owner to another, is a study of the immigrant experience in America.

Proulx loves the outdoors, and setting plays an important part in all her fictional writings. Many of her characters are born into the hard climate of northern New England, the rugged landscape of Newfoundland, or the rolling rangelands of Wyoming, and seem to draw strength from hostile weather and rough seas. "The Half-Skinned Steer" is set in wintry cattle country in Wyoming (where the writer now lives), and derives much of its force from Proulx's ability to capture the sweeping empty landscape blurred by snow that draws the protagonist on to his fate. First published in *The Atlantic Monthly* in 1997, then in Proulx's collection *Close Range: Wyoming Stories* (2000), the story is loosely based on an old Icelandic folk tale, "Þorgeir's Bull," several versions of which the writer heard in Canada. "In these tales, " explains Proulx, "the bull haunts Þorgeir's descendants for nine generations." Here folk tale and realism blend in a chilling narrative about the protagonist's gradual awakening to his own impending death.

The Half-Skinned Steer

In the long unfurling of his life, from tight-wound kid hustler in a wool suit riding the train out of Cheyenne to geriatric limper in this spooled-out year, Mero had kicked down thoughts of the place where he began, a so-called ranch on strange ground at the south hinge of the Big Horns. He'd got himself out of there in 1936, had gone to a war and come back, married and married again (and again), made money in boilers and air-duct cleaning and smart investments, retired, got into local politics and out again without scandal, never circled back to see the old man and Rollo bankrupt and ruined because he knew they were.

They called it a ranch and it had been, but one day the old man said it was impossible to run cows in such tough country where they fell off cliffs, disappeared into sinkholes, gave up large numbers of calves to marauding lions, where hay couldn't grow but leafy spurge and Canada thistle throve, and the wind packed enough sand to scour windshields opaque. The old man wangled a job delivering mail, but looked guilty fumbling bills into his neighbors' mailboxes.

Mero and Rollo saw the mail route as a defection from the work of the ranch, work that fell on them. The breeding herd was down to eighty-two and a cow wasn't worth more than fifteen dollars, but they kept mending fence, whittling ears and scorching hides, hauling cows out of mudholes and hunting lions in the hope that sooner or later the old man would move to Ten Sleep with his woman and his bottle and they could, as had their grandmother Olive when Jacob Corn disappointed her, pull the place taut. That bird didn't fly and Mero wound up sixty years later as an octogenarian vegetarian widower pumping an Exercycle in the living room of a colonial house in Woolfoot, Massachusetts.

One of those damp mornings the nail-driving telephone voice of a woman said she was Louise, Tick's wife, and summoned him back to Wyoming. He didn't know who she was, who Tick was, until she said, Tick Corn, your brother Rollo's son, and that Rollo had passed on, killed by a waspy emu though prostate cancer was waiting its chance. Yes, she said, you bet Rollo still owned the ranch. Half of it anyway. Me and Tick, she said, we been pretty much running it the last ten years.

An emu? Did he hear right?

Yes, she said. Well, of course you didn't know. You heard of Down Under Wyoming?

He had not. And thought, what kind of name was Tick? He recalled the bloated grey insects pulled off the dogs. This tick probably thought he was going to get the whole damn ranch and bloat up on it. He said, what the hell was this about an emu? Were they all crazy out there?

That's what the ranch was now, she said, Down Under Wyoming. Rollo'd sold the place way back when to the Girl Scouts, but one of the girls was dragged off by a lion and the G.S.A. sold out to the Banner ranch next door who ran cattle on it for a few years, then unloaded it on a rich Australian businessman who started Down Under Wyoming but it was too much long-distance work and he'd had bad luck with his manager, a feller from Idaho with a pawnshop rodeo buckle, so he'd looked up Rollo and offered to swap him a half-interest if he'd run the place. That was back in 1978. The place had done real well. Course we're not open now, she said, it's winter and there's no tourists. Poor Rollo was helping Tick move the emus to another building when one of them turned on a dime and come right for him with its big razor claws. Emus is bad for claws.

I know, he said. He watched the nature programs on television.

She shouted as though the telephone lines were down all across the country, Tick got your number off the computer. Rollo always said he was going to get in touch. He wanted you to see how things turned out. He tried to fight it off with his cane but it laid him open from belly to breakfast.

Maybe, he thought, things hadn't finished turning out. Impatient with this game he said he would be at the funeral. No point talking about flights and meeting him at the airport, he told her, he didn't fly, a bad experience years ago with hail, the plane had looked like a waffle iron when it landed. He intended to drive. Of course he knew how far it was. Had a damn fine car, Cadillac, always drove Cadillacs, Gislaved tires, interstate highways, excellent driver, never had an accident in his life knock on wood, four days, he would be there by Saturday afternoon. He heard the amazement in her voice, knew she was plotting his age, figuring he had to be eighty-three, a year or so older than Rollo, figuring he must be dotting around on a cane too, drooling the tiny days away, she was probably touching her own faded hair. He flexed his muscular arms, bent his knees, thought he could dodge an emu. He would see his brother dropped in a red Wyoming hole. That event could jerk him back; the dazzled rope of lightning against the cloud is not the downward bolt, but the compelled upstroke through the heated ether.

■ ■ ■

He had pulled away at the sudden point when it seemed the old man's girlfriend—now he couldn't remember her name—had jumped the track, Rollo goggling at her bloody bitten fingers, nails chewed to the quick, neck veins like wires, the outer forearms shaded with hairs, and the cigarette glowing, smoke curling up, making her wink her bulged mustang eyes, a teller of tales of hard deeds and mayhem. The old man's hair was falling out, Mero was twenty-three and Rollo twenty and she played them all like a deck of cards. If you admired horses you'd go for her with her arched neck and horsy buttocks, so high and haunchy you'd want to clap her on the rear. The wind bellowed around the house, driving crystals of snow through the cracks of the warped log door and all of them in the kitchen seemed charged with some intensity of purpose. She'd balanced that broad butt on the edge of the dog food chest, looking at the old man and Rollo, now and then rolling her glossy eyes over at Mero, square teeth nipping a rim of nail, sucking the welling blood, drawing on her cigarette.

The old man drank his Everclear stirred with a peeled willow stick for the bitter taste. The image of him came sharp in Mero's mind as he stood at the hall closet contemplating his hats; should he bring one for the funeral? The old man had had the damnedest curl to his hat brim, a tight roll on the right where his doffing or donning hand gripped it and a wavering downslope on the left like a shed roof. You could recognize him two miles away. He wore it at the table listening to the woman's stories about Tin Head, steadily emptying his glass until he was nine-times-nine drunk, his gangstery face loosening, the crushed rodeo nose and scar-crossed eyebrows, the stub ear dissolving as he drank. Now he must be dead fifty years or more, buried in the mailman sweater.

■ ■ ■

The girlfriend started a story, yeah, there was this guy named Tin Head down around Dubois when my dad was a kid. Had a little ranch, some horses, cows, kids, a wife. But there was something funny about him. He had a metal plate in his head from falling down some cement steps.

Plenty of guys has them, said Rollo in a challenging way.

She shook her head. Not like his. His was made out of galvy and it eat at his brain.

The old man held up the bottle of Everclear, raised his eyebrows at her: Well, darlin?

She nodded, took the glass from him and knocked it back in one swallow. Oh, that's not gonna slow *me* down, she said.

Mero expected her to neigh.

So what then, said Rollo, picking at the horse shit under his boot heel. What about Tin Head and his galvanized skull-plate?

I heard it this way, she said. She held out her glass for another shot of Everclear and the old man poured it and she went on.

■ ■ ■

Mero had thrashed all that ancient night, dreamed of horse breeding or hoarse breathing, whether the act of sex or bloody, cut-throat gasps he didn't know. The next morning he woke up drenched in stinking sweat, looked at the ceiling and said aloud, it could go on like this for some time. He meant cows and weather as much as anything, and what might be his chances two or three states over in any direction. In Woolfoot, riding the Exercycle, he thought the truth was somewhat different: he'd wanted a woman of his own without scrounging the old man's leftovers.

What he wanted to know now, tires spanking the tar-filled road cracks and potholes, funeral homburg sliding on the back-seat, was if Rollo had got the girlfriend away from the old man, thrown a saddle on her and ridden off into the sunset?

■ ■ ■

The interstate, crippled by orange pylons, forced traffic into single lanes, broke his expectation of making good time. His Cadillac, boxed between semis with hissing air brakes, snuffled huge rear tires, framed a looming Peterbilt in the back window. His thoughts clogged as if a comb working through his mind had stuck against a snarl. When the traffic eased and he tried to cover some ground the highway patrol pulled him over. The cop, a pimpled, mustached specimen with mismatched eyes, asked his name, where he was going. For the minute he couldn't think what he was doing there. The cop's tongue dapped at the scraggy mustache while he scribbled.

Funeral, he said suddenly. Going to my brother's funeral.

Well you take it easy, Gramps, or they'll be doing one for you.

You're a little polecat, aren't you, he said, staring at the ticket, at the pathetic handwriting, but the mustache was a mile gone, peeling through the traffic as Mero had peeled out of the ranch road that long time ago, squinting through the abraded windshield. He might have made a more graceful exit but urgency had struck him as a blow on the humerus sends a ringing jolt up the arm. He believed it was the horse-haunched woman leaning against the chest and Rollo fixed on her, the old man swilling Everclear and not noticing or, if noticing, not caring, that had worked in him like a key in an ignition. She had long grey-streaked braids, Rollo could use them for reins.

■ ■ ■

Yah, she said, in her low and convincing liar's voice. I'll tell you, on Tin Head's ranch things went wrong. Chickens changed color overnight, calves was born with three legs, his kids was piebald and his wife always crying for blue dishes. Tin Head never finished nothing he started, quit halfway through a job every time. Even his pants was half-buttoned so his wienie hung out. He was a mess with the galvy plate eating at his brain and his ranch and his family was a mess. But, she said. They had to eat, didn't they, just like anybody else?

I hope they eat pies better than the ones you make, said Rollo, who didn't like the mouthful of pits that came with the chokecherries.

■ ■ ■

His interest in women began a few days after the old man had said, take this guy up and show him them Indan drawrings, jerking his head at the stranger. Mero had been eleven or twelve at the time, no older. They rode along the creek and put up a pair of mallards who flew downstream and then suddenly reappeared, pursued by a goshawk who struck the drake with a sound like a handclap. The duck tumbled through the trees and into deadfall trash and the hawk shot as swiftly away as it had come.

They climbed through the stony landscape, limestone beds eroded by wind into fantastic furniture, stale gnawed bread-crusts, tumbled bones, stacks of dirty folded blankets, bleached crab claws and dog teeth. He tethered the horses in the shade of a stand of limber pine and led the anthropologist up through the stiff-branched mountain mahogany to the overhang. Above them reared corroded cliffs brilliant with orange lichen, pitted with holes and ledges darkened by millennia of raptor feces.

The anthropologist moved back and forth scrutinizing the stone gallery of red and black drawings: bison skulls, a line of mountain sheep, warriors carrying lances, a turkey stepping into a snare; a stick man upside-down dead and falling, red ochre hands, violent figures with rakes on their heads that he said were feather headdresses, a great red bear dancing forward on its hind legs, concentric circles and crosses and latticework. He copied the drawings in his notebook, saying rubba-dubba a few times.

That's the sun, said the anthropologist who resembled an unfinished drawing himself, pointing at an archery target, ramming his pencil into the air as though tapping gnats. That's an atlatl and that's a dragonfly. There we go. You know what this is; and he touched a cloven oval, rubbing the cleft with his dusty fingers. He got down on his hands and knees, pointed out more, a few dozen.

A horseshoe?

A horseshoe! The anthropologist laughed. No boy, it's a vulva. That's what all of these are. You don't know what that is, do you? You go to school on Monday and look it up in the dictionary.

It's a symbol, he said. You know what a symbol is?

Yes, said Mero, who had seen them clapped together in the high school marching band. The anthropologist laughed and told him he had a great future, gave him a dollar for showing him the place. Listen, kid, the Indians did it just like anybody else, he said.

He had looked the word up in the school dictionary, slammed the book closed in embarrassment, but the image was fixed for him (with the brassy background sound of a military march), blunt ochre tracing on stone, and no fleshy examples ever conquered his belief in the subterranean stony structure of female genitalia, the pubic bone a proof, except for the old man's girlfriend whom he imagined down on all fours, entered from behind and whinnying like a mare, a thing not of geology but flesh.

■ ■ ■

Thursday night, balked by detours and construction, he was on the outskirts of Des Moines and no farther. In the cinderblock motel room he set the alarm but his own stertorous breathing woke him before it rang. He was up at five-fifteen, eyes aflame, peering through the vinyl drapes at his snow-hazed car flashing blue under the motel sign SLEEP SLEEP. In the bathroom he mixed the packet of instant motel coffee and drank it black without ersatz sugar or chemical cream. He wanted the caffeine. The roots of his mind felt withered and punky.

A cold morning, light snow slanting down: he unlocked the Cadillac, started it and curved into the vein of traffic, all semis, double- and triple-trailers. In the headlights' red glare he missed the westbound ramp and got into torn-up muddy streets, swung right and right again, using the motel's SLEEP sign as a landmark, but he was on the wrong side of the interstate and the sign belonged to a different motel.

Another mudholed lane took him into a traffic circle of commuters sucking coffee from insulated cups, pastries sliding on dashboards. Halfway around the hoop he spied the interstate entrance ramp, veered for it, collided with a panel truck emblazoned STOP SMOKING! HYPNOSIS THAT WORKS!, was rammed from behind by a stretch limo, the limo in its turn rear-ended by a yawning hydroblast operator in a company pickup.

He saw little of this, pressed into his seat by the air bag, his mouth full of a rubbery, dusty taste, eyeglasses cutting into his nose. His first thought was to blame Iowa and those who lived in it. There were a few round spots of blood on his shirt cuff.

A star-spangled Band-Aid over his nose, he watched his crumpled car, pouring dark fluids onto the highway, towed away behind a wrecker. A taxi took him, his suitcase, the homburg funeral hat, in the other direction to Posse Motors where lax salesmen drifted like disorbited satellites and where he bought a secondhand Cadillac, black like the wreck, but three years older and the upholstery not cream leather but sun-faded velour. He had the good tires from the wreck brought over and mounted. He could do that if he liked, buy cars like packs of cigarettes and smoke them up. He didn't care for the way it handled out on the highway, throwing itself abruptly aside when he twitched the wheel and he guessed it might have a bent frame. Damn, he'd buy another for the return trip. He could do what he wanted.

He was half an hour past Kearney, Nebraska, when the full moon rose, an absurd visage balanced in his rearview mirror, above it a curled wig of a cloud, filamented edges like platinum hairs. He felt his swollen nose, palped his chin, tender from the stun of the air bag. Before he slept that night he swallowed a glass of hot tap water enlivened with whiskey, crawled into the damp bed. He had eaten nothing all day yet his stomach coiled at the thought of road food.

He dreamed that he was in the ranch house but all the furniture had been removed from the rooms and in the yard troops in dirty white uniforms fought. The concussive reports of huge guns were breaking the window glass and forcing the floorboards apart so that he had to walk on the joists and below the disintegrating floors he saw galvanized tubs filled with dark, coagulated fluid.

On Saturday morning, with four hundred miles in front of him, he swallowed a few bites of scorched eggs, potatoes painted with canned *salsa verde*, a cup of yellow coffee, left no tip, got on the road. The food was not what he wanted. His breakfast habit was two glasses of mineral water, six cloves of garlic, a pear. The sky to the west hulked sullen, behind him smears of tinselly orange shot through with blinding streaks. The thick rim of sun bulged against the horizon.

He crossed the state line, hit Cheyenne for the second time in sixty years. There was neon, traffic and concrete, but he knew the place, a railroad town that had been up and down. That other time he had been painfully hungry, had gone into the restaurant in the Union Pacific station although he was not used to restaurants and ordered a steak, but when the woman brought it and he cut into the meat the blood spread across the white plate and he couldn't help it, he saw the beast, mouth agape in mute bawling, saw the comic aspects of his revulsion as well, a cattleman gone wrong.

Now he parked in front of a phone booth, locked the car although he stood only seven feet away, and telephoned the number Tick's wife had given him. The ruined car had had a phone. Her voice roared out of the earpiece.

We didn't hear so we wondered if you changed your mind.

No, he said, I'll be there late this afternoon. I'm in Cheyenne now.

The wind's blowing pretty hard. They're saying it could maybe snow. In the mountains. Her voice sounded doubtful.

I'll keep an eye on it, he said.

He was out of town and running north in a few minutes.

The country poured open on each side, reduced the Cadillac to a finger-snap. Nothing had changed, not a goddamn thing, the empty pale place and its roaring wind, the distant antelope as tiny as mice, landforms shaped true to the past. He felt himself slip back, the calm of eighty-three years sheeted off him like water, replaced by a young man's scalding anger at a fool world and the fools in it. What a damn hard time it had been to hit the road. You don't know what it was like, he told his ex-wives until they said they did know, he'd pounded it into their ears two hundred times, the poor youth on the street holding up a sign asking for work, and the job with the furnace man, *yatata yatata ya*. Thirty miles out of Cheyenne he saw the first billboard, DOWN UNDER WYOMING, *Western Fun the Western Way*, over a blown-up photograph of kangaroos hopping through the sagebrush and a blond child grinning in a manic imitation of pleasure. A diagonal banner warned, *Open May 31*.

■ ■ ■

So what, Rollo had said to the old man's girlfriend, what about that Mr. Tin Head? Looking at her, not just her face, but up and down, eyes moving over her like an iron over a shirt and the old man in his mailman's sweater and lopsided hat tasting his Everclear and not noticing or not caring, getting up every now and then to lurch onto the porch and water the weeds. When he left the room the tension ebbed and they were only ordinary people to whom nothing happened. Rollo looked away from the woman, leaned down to scratch the dog's ears, saying, Snarleyow Snapper, and the woman brought a dish to the sink and ran water on it, yawning. When the old man came back to his chair, the Everclear like sweet oil in his glass, glances resharpened and inflections of voice again carried complex messages.

Well well, she said, tossing her braids back, every year Tin Head butchers one of his steers, and that's what they'd eat all winter long, boiled, fried, smoked, fricasseed, burned and raw. So one time he's out there by the barn and he hits the steer a good one with the axe and it drops stun down. He ties up the back legs, hoists it up and sticks it, shoves the tub under to catch the blood. When it's bled out pretty good he lets it down and starts skinning it, starts with the head, cuts back of the poll down past the eye to the nose, peels the hide back. He don't cut the head off but keeps on skinning, dewclaws to hock up the inside of the thigh and then to the cod and down the middle of the belly to brisket to tail. Now he's ready to start siding, working that tough old skin off. But siding is hard work—(the old man nodded)—and he gets the hide off about halfway and starts thinking about dinner. So he leaves the steer half-skinned there on the ground and he goes into the kitchen, but first he cuts out the tongue which is his favorite dish all cooked up and eat cold with Mrs. Tin Head's mustard in a forget-me-not teacup. Sets it on the ground and goes in to dinner. Dinner is chicken and dumplings, one of them changed-color chickens started out white and ended up blue, yessir, blue as your old daddy's eyes.

She was a total liar. The old man's eyes were murk brown.

■ ■ ■

Onto the high plains sifted the fine snow, delicately clouding the air, a rare dust, beautiful, he thought, silk gauze, but there was muscle in the wind rocking the heavy car, a great pulsing artery of the jet stream swooping down from the sky to touch the earth. Plumes of smoke rose hundreds of feet into the air, elegant fountains and twisting snow devils, shapes of veiled Arab women and ghost riders dissolving in white fume. The snow snakes writhing across the asphalt straightened into rods. He was driving in a rushing river of cold whiteout foam. He could see nothing, trod on the brake, the wind buffeting the car, a bitter, hard-flung dust hissing over metal and glass. The car shuddered. And as suddenly as it had risen the wind dropped and the road was clear; he could see a long, empty mile.

How do you know when there's enough of anything? What trips the lever that snaps up the STOP sign? What electrical currents fizz and crackle in the brain to shape the decision to quit a place? He had listened to her damn story and the dice had rolled. For years he believed he had left without hard reason and suffered for it. But he'd learned from television nature programs that it had been time for him to find his own territory and his own woman. How many women were out there! He had married three or four of them and sampled plenty.

■ ■ ■

With the lapping subtlety of incoming tide the shape of the ranch began to gather in his mind; he could recall the intimate fences he'd made, taut wire and perfect corners, the draws and rock outcrops, the watercourse valley steepening, cliffs like bones with shreds of meat on them rising and rising, and the stream plunging suddenly underground, disappearing into subterranean darkness of blind fish, shooting out of the mountain ten miles west on a neighbor's place, but leaving their ranch some badland red country as dry as a cracker, steep canyons with high caves suited to lions. He and Rollo had shot two early in that winter close to the overhang with the painted vulvas. There were good caves up there from a lion's point of view.

■ ■ ■

He traveled against curdled sky. In the last sixty miles the snow began again. He climbed out of Buffalo. Pallid flakes as distant from each other as galaxies flew past, then more and in ten minutes he was crawling at twenty miles an hour, the windshield wipers thumping like a stick dragged down the stairs.

The light was falling out of the day when he reached the pass, the blunt mountains lost in snow, the greasy hairpin turns ahead. He drove slowly and steadily in a low gear; he had not forgotten how to drive a winter mountain. But the wind was up again, rocking and slapping the car, blotting out all but whipping snow and he was sweating with the anxiety of keeping to the road, dizzy with the altitude. Twelve more miles, sliding and buffeted, before he reached Ten Sleep where streetlights glowed in revolving circles like Van Gogh's sun. There had not been electricity when he left the place. In those days there were seventeen black, lightless miles between the town and the ranch, and now the long arch of years compressed into that distance. His headlights picked up a sign: 20 MILES TO DOWN UNDER WYOMING. Emus and bison leered above the letters.

He turned onto the snowy road marked with a single set of tracks, faint but still discernible, the heater fan whirring, the radio silent, all beyond the headlights blurred. Yet everything was as it had been, the shape of the road achingly familiar, sentinel rocks looming as they had in his youth. There was an eerie dream quality in seeing the deserted Farrier place leaning east as it had leaned sixty years ago, the Banner ranch gate, where the companionable tracks he had been following turned off, the gate ghostly in the snow but still flying its wrought iron flag, unmarked by the injuries of weather, and the taut five-strand fences and dim shifting forms of cattle. Next would come the road to their ranch, a left-hand turn just over the crest of a rise. He was running now on the unmarked road through great darkness.

■ ■ ■

Winking at Rollo the girlfriend said, yes, she had said, yes sir, Tin Head eats half his dinner and then he has to take a little nap. After a while he wakes up again and goes outside stretching his arms and yawning, says, guess I'll finish skinning out that steer. But the steer ain't there. It's gone. Only the tongue, laying on the ground all covered with dirt and straw, and the tub of blood and the dog licking at it.

It was her voice that drew you in, that low, twangy voice, wouldn't matter if she was saying the alphabet, what you heard was the rustle of hay. She could make you smell the smoke from an unlit fire.

■ ■ ■

How could he not recognize the turnoff to the ranch? It was so clear and sharp in his mind: the dusty crimp of the corner, the low section where the snow drifted, the run where willows slapped the side of the truck. He went a mile, watching for it, but the turn didn't come up, then watched for the Bob Kitchen place two miles beyond, but the distance unrolled and there was nothing. He made a three-point turn and backtracked. Rollo must have given up the old entrance road, for it wasn't there. The Kitchen place was gone to fire or wind. If he didn't find the turn it was no great loss; back to Ten Sleep and scout a motel. But he hated to quit when he was close enough to spit, hated to retrace black miles on a bad night when he was maybe twenty minutes away from the ranch.

He drove very slowly, following his tracks, and the ranch entrance appeared on the right although the gate was gone and the sign down. That was why he'd missed it, that and a clump of sagebrush that obscured the gap.

He turned in, feeling a little triumph. But the road under the snow was rough and got rougher until he was bucking along over boulders and slanted rock and knew wherever he was it was not right.

He couldn't turn around on the narrow track and began backing gingerly, the window down, craning his stiff neck, staring into the redness cast by the taillights. The car's right rear tire rolled up over a boulder, slid and sank into a quaggy hole. The tires spun in the snow, but he got no purchase.

I'll sit here, he said aloud. I'll sit here until it's light and then walk down to the Banner place and ask for a cup of coffee. I'll be cold but I won't freeze to death. It played like a joke the way he imagined it with Bob Banner opening the door and saying, why, it's Mero, come on in and have some java and a hot biscuit, before he remembered that Bob Banner would have to be 120 years old to play that role. He was maybe three miles from Banner's gate, and the Banner ranch house was another seven miles beyond the gate. Say a ten-mile hike at altitude in a snowstorm. On the other hand he had half a tank of gas. He could run the car for a while, then turn it off, start it again all through the night. It was bad luck, but that's all. The trick was patience.

He dozed half an hour in the wind-rocked car, woke shivering and cramped. He wanted to lie down. He thought perhaps he could put a flat rock under the goddamn tire. Never say die, he said, feeling around the passenger-side floor for the flashlight in his emergency bag, then remembering the wrecked car towed away, the flares and car phone and AAA card and flashlight and matches and candle and Power Bars and bottle of water still in it, and probably now in the damn tow-driver's damn wife's car. He might get a good enough look anyway in the snow-reflected light. He put on his gloves and the heavy overcoat, got out and locked the car, sidled around to the rear, bent down. The taillights lit the snow beneath the rear of the car like a fresh bloodstain. There was a cradle-sized depression eaten out by the spinning tire. Two or three flat ones might get him out, or small round ones, he was not going to insist on the perfect stone. The wind tore at him, the snow was certainly drifting up. He began to shuffle on the road, feeling with his feet for rocks he could move, the car's even throbbing promising motion and escape. The wind was sharp and his ears ached. His wool cap was in the damn emergency bag.

■ ■ ■

My lord, she continued, Tin Head is just startled to pieces when he don't see that steer. He thinks somebody, some neighbor don't like him, plenty of them, come and stole it. He looks around for tire marks or footprints but there's nothing except old cow tracks. He puts his hand up to his eyes and stares away. Nothing in the north, the south, the east, but way over there in the west on the side of the mountain he sees something moving stiff and slow, stumbling along. It looks raw and it's got something bunchy and wet hanging down over its hindquarters. Yah, it was the steer, never making no sound. And just then it stops and it looks back. And all that distance Tin Head can see the raw meat of the head and the shoulder muscles and the empty mouth without no tongue open wide and its red eyes glaring at him, pure teetotal hate like arrows coming at him, and he knows he is done for and all of his kids and their kids is done for, and that his wife is done for and that every one of her blue dishes has got to break, and the dog that licked the blood is done for, and the house where they lived has to blow away or burn up and every fly or mouse in it.

There was a silence and she added, that's it. And it all went against him, too.

That's it? said Rollo. That's all there is to it?

■ ■ ■

Yet he knew he was on the ranch, he felt it and he knew this road, too. It was not the main ranch road but some lower entrance he could not quite recollect that cut in below the river. Now he remembered that the main entrance gate was on a side road that branched off well before the Banner place. He found a good stone, another, wondering which track this could be; the map of the ranch in his memory was not as bright now, but scuffed and obliterated as though trodden. The remembered gates collapsed, fences wavered, while the badland features swelled into massive prominence. The cliffs bulged into the sky, lions snarled, the river corkscrewed through a stone hole at a tremendous rate and boulders cascaded from the heights. Beyond the barbwire something moved.

He grasped the car door handle. It was locked. Inside, by the dashboard glow, he could see the gleam of the keys in the ignition where he'd left them to keep the car running. It was almost funny. He picked up a big two-handed rock and smashed it on the driver's-side window, slipped his arm in through the hole, into the delicious warmth of the car, a contortionist's reach, twisting behind the steering wheel and down, and had he not kept limber with exercise and nut cutlets and green leafy vegetables he never could have reached the keys. His fingers grazed and then grasped the keys and he had them. This is how they sort the men out from the boys, he said aloud. As his fingers closed on the keys he glanced at the passenger door. The lock button stood high. And even had it been locked as well, why had he strained to reach the keys when he had only to lift the lock button on the driver's side? Cursing, he pulled out the rubber floor mats and arranged them over the stones, stumbled around the car once more. He was dizzy, tremendously thirsty and hungry, opened his mouth to snowflakes. He had eaten nothing for two days but the burned eggs that morning. He could eat a dozen burned eggs now.

The snow roared through the broken window. He put the car in reverse and slowly trod the gas. The car lurched and steadied in the track and once more he was twisting his neck, backing in the red glare, twenty feet, thirty, but slipping and spinning; there was too much snow. He was backing up an incline that had seemed level on the way in but showed itself now as a remorselessly long hill studded with rocks and deep in snow. His incoming tracks twisted like rope. He forced out another twenty feet spinning the tires until they smoked, and the rear wheels slewed sideways off the track and into a two-foot ditch, the engine died and that was it. It was almost a relief to have reached this point where the celestial fingernails were poised to nip his thread. He dismissed the ten-mile distance to the Banner place: it might not be that far, or maybe they had pulled the ranch closer to the main road. A truck might come by. Shoes slipping, coat buttoned awry, he might find the mythical Grand Hotel in the sagebrush.

■ ■ ■

On the main road his tire tracks showed as a faint pattern in the pearly apricot light from the risen moon, winking behind roiling clouds of snow. His blurred shadow strengthened whenever the wind eased. Then the violent country showed itself, the cliffs rearing at the moon, the snow smoking off the prairie like steam, the white flank of the ranch slashed with fence cuts, the sagebrush glittering and along the creek black tangles of willow bunched like dead hair. There were cattle in the field beside the road, their plumed breaths catching the moony glow like comic strip dialogue balloons.

He walked against the wind, his shoes filled with snow, feeling as easy to tear as a man cut from paper. As he walked he noticed one from the herd inside the fence was keeping pace with him. He walked more slowly and the animal lagged. He stopped and turned. It stopped as well, huffing vapor, regarding him, a strip of snow on its back like a linen runner. It tossed its head and in the howling, wintry light he saw he'd been wrong again, that the half-skinned steer's red eye had been watching for him all this time.

Russell Smith

Born in South Africa in 1963, Russell Smith grew up in Halifax, Nova Scotia, becoming a Canadian citizen in 1972. He was educated at Queen's University in Kingston, Ontario, and at the universities of Poitiers and Paris in France. Well known in the 1990s as a Toronto "lifestyle" journalist—specializing in fashion and the character of urban chic—Smith also established a name as a lucid commentator on connections between urban life, music, and noise, as in a documentary he wrote for the CBC radio program *Ideas.*

His fictions—two novels, *How Insensitive* (1994) and *Noise* (1998), and the stories of *Young Men* (1999), from which "Responsibility" is taken—reveal a talent for comic writing. In an interview in *Cultcha* (May 1999), Smith affirms the influence of Kingsley Amis and Evelyn Waugh upon his work, and stresses the importance of style as a means of conveying the "real" qualities of the contemporary urban and suburban landscape. He is especially effective at rendering the arch exchanges that pass for conversation in some contemporary milieux, and at revealing the desperations that underlie these exchanges. In a world where appearance means everything, his stories implicitly ask, what becomes of fear, love, desire, understanding, commitment? Are they out of date? "Responsibility" probes two generations' desire to affirm their own definitions of value, and makes clear how the mother and son each want the recognition of the other, perhaps even seek validation from the other, even as they know they are growing apart. Ironically, it is in part their differences that link them, and their similarities that force them to separate.

Responsibility

"Perhaps you don't value it now, but as you get older money becomes more important," said his mother. She was sitting in the breakfast nook with her tea, looking out at the bird feeder. James too was looking out at the garden, standing at the sliding doors. Anyone who talked in the kitchen did so while looking at the garden.

"I'm sure that's true, but you see, believe it or not, I'm hoping to make money from my writing, eventually. I know that seems ridiculous to you and Dad." He waited for her to contradict him. "Some people actually make a great deal of money from what I . . . the kind of writing I'm trying to do. I'm talking to some people about a documentary, about my music column, it could be a book, it could . . ." He clenched his jaw shut. He felt helpless. "It could be the kind of book that would sell outside this little . . . anyway. Yes, it's a bigger risk, yes, but actually it could pay off very well, if you do something successful. So actually I'm being *more* ambitious than you and Dad were."

"I guess it's just the risk I worry about."

It was no longer surprising that this conversation came up, even that it came up on the Sunday afternoons of his visits, that it came up just as simultaneous relief and tension about the trip back to the city were growing with a mental hum, ripening in him, in his nervous and circulatory systems like some slowly developing and ultimately convulsive disease, just as they were all about to begin the bargaining about which parent in which car would drive him to the bus station and dump him in its stained limbo air and promise of metamorphosis, this was so familiar it was no longer surprising; what was surprising was how unfailingly and deeply it seared him with a fine painful clear sense of abandonment, as would some long penetrating parental angioscopic device, every time, and made him think, every time, that perhaps now, this time, was the time it would all come out, it would come clear exactly what it was about what he did that so disappointed her, and why her disappointment so irritated—no, worse, let's be honest—so hurt him. He said quickly, "And you worry about my lifestyle, that I'm not married and—"

"I don't care that you're not married, if you're happy."

"Yes you do. Don't pretend you don't. Of course you do. You'd like me to be married and have kids and a minivan and come over on Sundays and talk about eavestroughing with Dad."

"*I* don't think you could *handle* kids," said his mother with the restrained tone of someone producing an ace.

"No, I couldn't," said James.

She was silent for a moment. Then she said, "But when you do have children, you'll want to be able to provide for them, and I think you should think of that now."

He turned to her and said gently, "Mom, what would you say if I told you I might never have children? Do you think there's something wrong with that?"

She was silent again. She twirled a strand of hair around a finger, which meant that she was agitated. She would never sit down for so long in mid-morning unless she was upset. The tea in her cup was getting cold.

"You think that's somehow morally wrong, not to have children, don't you?" said James. He felt merciless; he felt this was the time to get it all out.

"No," she said quickly, "not at all. It's you I'm thinking of. I just think that you would be happier with children. Having children . . . it takes you out of yourself. You would stop chasing after every girl you met and—"

"What if I don't want to stop chasing after every girl I meet? You seem to feel that I have to at a certain point, because everybody does. Why? What if it makes me happy?"

"It won't make you happy forever."

"Will children?"

She was silent again. "Look, all I know is that all this tension in your life, all that awful time you had with Alison and that girl in the city when they wouldn't speak to each other and—"

"Yes," said James, "I know, go on."

"All that wouldn't happen if you had a family. You wouldn't have time for it. And all I know is that when you have a child, that's the most important thing. If your child is happy, then you're happy, it's as simple as that. And you're—what is it that Joanne Winterson always said? You're only as happy as your most unhappy child. It's true." She took quick sips at her tea, which by now was surely cold.

"Sounds terrific." He puffed out his cheeks. "Just remind me again why this is a better system?"

"Oh, don't be so snooty. You're so *arrogant*."

"What? Sorry. I'm not following you."

"Yes you are. You know exactly what I mean. You're so condescending."

James turned back to the garden. "I have no idea what you're talking about." But he did. He made an effort to make an effort to think about trying to be nicer. He said, "I don't mean to be nasty about anyone's choices. As long as you *make* choices."

"What about Jennifer? Doesn't she want children?"

James took a deep breath. "Well, not right now she doesn't. She's trying to get her own career going, she's in the same boat as me. We have more . . ." He stopped himself. He said, "She's just too busy, and she doesn't have the money or the stability in her life for it. She doesn't want kids right now."

"Well, she's over thirty now. She doesn't have much time left."

"So maybe she won't. Maybe she won't have time. I'm not sure, because we haven't talked about it a lot, but I think that right now at least she isn't too worried about it. She's thinking about herself, about her career. Like me."

"*Oh!* But . . ." His mother leaned over the table to pour more tea. She spilled the tea and said, "*Bother.*" She was frowning and biting her lip; she really was agitated and maybe about to cry. He wasn't sure what it was all about and he got agitated too. He handed her a cloth. At least they were getting somewhere.

"But what?" He sat down at the table.

She wiped the table with furious speed. "What she wants, what you want," she said, shaking her head. "You people—it's always what *you* want. You just think you can play around and have fun forever."

"Yes. Perhaps we do. What should we do instead?" His heart was beating fast.

She didn't answer.

"What is it, exactly, Mom, that upsets you? That I don't have enough responsibilities in life? Is that it?"

There was a long silence and then she said in a faint voice, "Yes."

"I have too much fun. I don't have enough to tie me down."

"James, if your father and I had felt like you," she said urgently, looking at him, "then you wouldn't even *be* here!"

"Right." James rubbed his face with his hands. "The logic of this is growing too much for me." He sighed. "Mom. You don't understand what I'm . . . Look at it this way. Imagine you had never had me. Or Kurt. Then you wouldn't, you wouldn't feel a responsibility to us, right? Because we wouldn't—"

"I can't imagine that," she said in a higher voice, her indignant voice. "Lucky for you, I couldn't imagine that."

"That's my point, Mom. That you're not imagining what I'm—"

"You think," she said rapidly, "that you can just live this student life forever, have no—"

"Why not? Why can't I—"

"But it's not all fun. At a certain point you have to pay the piper. At a certain point you just have to stop fooling around and accept your responsibilities."

James looked at her. She was fidgeting with a doily. "What responsibilities? My family responsibilities?"

"Yes."

"Mom, this is what I'm trying to get at. Think about it. If I don't have a wife or kids then who do I have a responsibility to?"

There was a long silence. She was fingering the doily on the tray that held the salt and pepper shakers and the bowl of sugar and the tiny antique silver spoons from the ancestral Germany that was unknown to them all, moving her eyes from the doily out to the bird feeder where there were no birds and back again.

"What is it?" he said more gently. "Is it that you think I have a responsibility to Jennifer, or maybe to you?"

"No, no, not to me, certainly."

"Is it just that you feel I have a responsibility to *have* kids? So that I can feel a responsibility to them? This is what I mean about logical—"

"No, no, I'm not saying that. I'm not saying you *have* to."

He waited. She did not go on. "I don't have to."

"No."

"Okay, so what—why—"

"I don't know." Her voice sounded weak now. "I'm not sure. I'm not sure—I don't know what I mean." She played with the doily.

James thought about this. He looked at the doily, which she had inherited from her mother who had crocheted in it Portage la Prairie, a place he had never been, and wondered for some reason how old she had been when it had been crocheted. He had a black-and-white picture of his mother in a rather Chanel-like tweed suit, leaning against the hood of a large American car, against an unblemished sky and a flat wheaty horizon of laughably pure rural nowhere. He wondered how old she had been in that photograph; probably younger, yes, much younger than him. "Are you saying, Mom, maybe that . . . maybe it's just that you, when you were young, I mean younger, you felt you didn't . . ." He stopped himself. He wanted to say, *You didn't have a choice.*

"Oh, we didn't even think about it. Everyone had children. It was all—it was what we wanted."

"Right." He paused. He had to go very carefully here. "But have you ever thought about how, about how things might have . . . about what you might have done if you hadn't"— he took a deep breath— "had me and Kurt."

She stood up abruptly and stood in the window, while James thought, She never does that, never takes a moment to stare at the garden without a vacuum cleaner or a duster in her hand. Her arms were folded and her shoulders hunched. She said, "You sound as if you *want* me to think about that."

"No." He didn't know what she was getting at, but the safe answer was no. "No, no. I just, I'm thinking of me, in my case—"

"If I hadn't got married? Is that what you mean?"

"I don't know. Was it impossible to get married and not have children? Not that I'm saying that's what you should—"

"Well, I suppose it wasn't impossible. But I wanted children. Your dad wanted children. And, you know, Jamie"—she gave a small laugh— "I was very flattered, you know, that Hans wanted to marry me. He was, I knew he was going to be very successful. You didn't turn down opportunity, in those days."

James laughed, too. As the refrigerator began to hum unevenly, he became aware of a cloud of worry too vague to describe, forming over his head. "It meant your problems were solved."

"Sure. And he wanted children too, you know, it wasn't just my idea."

"Yes. Okay. But what, I guess I mean to ask, what if you hadn't got married?"

"I suppose I would have had to get some kind of job."

James asked slowly, "Did you want . . . to do that?"

"No. I suppose not." She paused. "I don't know."

He held himself very still. Her voice had gone small as she had said it. His worry buzzed and shifted overhead. He didn't know what was approaching them here, but it was something grey and tight. He thought of the bus station, its cigarette air.

"I guess you don't respect at all what I did," she said in a wavering voice. "Bringing you two boys up."

"Of course I do, Mom. Of course I do. I know how much work it is, how hard—"

"No you don't."

It was James's turn to be silent.

She said, in a voice that fluttered and broke, "There was a time when people thought it was valuable, to run a house and sew and clean and cook for two boys and a man, and educate the boys, the way I read to you—"

"Mom," said James, agitated, "of course I value that. Of course I respect—"

"No you don't. You don't think it meant—it's not important to you. You think if it's not some big career it's not difficult and it's, it's some kind of cop-out."

"No," said James.

"I've heard you say it. When you found out Alison had a child you said it was a cop-out."

James opened his mouth and closed it. It was true, not only that he had said it, but that he believed it. It was a cop-out.

"The work of about twenty-two years. A cop-out."

He looked at the doily, her moving hands.

"And you're not the only one," she said quietly. "I can tell people laugh at me. The younger wives at Dad's firm."

James went cold. "No they don't. They wouldn't."

"They think we're ridiculous, me and Joanne and . . . all of my friends. I can tell. And maybe they're right."

"Oh, Mom, don't be—"

"You know, Jamie, I was thinking about this last week. I was trying to remember all the jobs I've had in my life. All the paying jobs." She counted on her fingers. "I used to babysit, as a teenager. I must have earned less than a dollar an hour. And I was in a nursing course when I met Dad, but I worked in an office in the summers. So that was two summers, about four months' total. And then I worked at the kindergarten, where you and Kurt went, for about two years, part-time, for a little extra cash, when we were just starting out."

James listened to the anxious fridge.

"So," she said, "I counted it all up. All the money I've ever earned. Myself. And I figured it came to a total of about three thousand five hundred dollars. In my whole life. That's all I've ever earned myself. I never thought about it, until now. I guess, I guess that's all the young women see. The other things we did, what we did, it's not important to anyone any more. I guess."

The refrigerator grunted, shuddered and stopped humming. The kitchen was silent.

He said as gently as he could, "Yes it is, Mom. I don't think the money's important. I do think it was a disappointing choice for Alison, because she had her music, and her . . ." He trailed off. He did not want to imply that his mother had had nothing else to do. But it was true. "She gave up her music. But you, there were fewer opportunities at that—"

"And I didn't have anything I could have done? Is that what you mean? And Alison shouldn't have done the most important thing in the world?" She balled her little hand into a fist and made to punch his shoulder, but of course she didn't. "You're all so selfish." Her voice wavered again.

"What?" said James, alarmed. "Who is? Alison?"

"It's just that . . . you're all so arrogant about everything. It's just not very . . . it's not very *nice*." Her voice cracked and he realized she was in tears.

He stood behind her and put a hand on her shoulder. His worry was gone, and in its place he had a pure, liquid anguish, a sense that the air itself was sad, over the silent garden, that forces were moving all around him like invisible rain. He said, "What isn't nice, Mom? Tell me."

"I can't explain it. It's just that . . ." She sniffled. "Nice people . . ." She paused and coughed. Then she said, loud and cracking, as if in physical distress, *"Nice people don't do things for themselves."*

She was really sobbing.

He felt as if the floor of his stomach had opened, and there was darkness below it.

He patted her shoulder. She sobbed and shook. There was nothing else to do but pat her shoulder. He looked around the immaculate kitchen, the slate-tiled floor, the island and the overhead wrought-iron pot hooks she had campaigned so hard to have his father put in. The sandy wall, the pristine counters. The pot lids were stacked in the pot-lid rack; the utensils hung from hooks over the island. "I'm sorry, Mom," he said. "*You're* nice."

He tried a laugh and she giggled, too, a sniffling giggle as if she was embarrassed, and wiped her eyes and blew her nose. He exhaled in relief, for if she was blowing her nose already, the whole thing was okay. He glanced at his watch: there was a bus back to the city at 3:15.

He put his arm around her shoulder and they looked at the empty garden, the wrought-iron chairs. He wondered what she was going to do that afternoon, after he got back on his bus. His dad had had to go into the office. And Kurt was gone, probably gone for good now, even when he got back from Whistler he would be looking for a job in the city. James wondered for a second if he should stay, maybe take her out to the craft shops. He thought of the drive through the industrial park, the deserted highways, the hot little shops. He thought of the hand-made towel racks and calico quilts and apple dolls they would look at. The photo frames in amusing shapes. If they drove out of town, they would have to stop and buy corn and squash, for it was that time, which would go into soups and preserves and pie fillings which only his dad would eat.

He stared at the garden. There were no birds at the bird feeder. The house was dead quiet; the whole neighbourhood was silent as a tomb. And he knew then that he wasn't nice, he wasn't a nice person, because all he wanted to do was get out, get the hell out of there.

Audrey Thomas

Born Audrey Callahan in Binghamton, New York, in 1935, Audrey Thomas was educated in the United States, Scotland, and Canada. Interrupting her formal education to spend two years in Ghana, she returned in 1966 to British Columbia, where she now lives. Her first collection of stories, *Ten Green Bottles,* appeared in 1967, and was rapidly followed by several novels, novellas, plays, and other story collections. Among her recent books are *Real Mothers* (1981), *Intertidal Life* (1984), *The Wild Blue Yonder* (1990), and *Graven Images* (1993). *Coming Down from Wa* (1995) deals with a young man returning to Africa to uncover the secrets of the past; *Isobel Gunn* (1999) traces in fictional form the life of a real Orkney woman who, masquerading as a man, joined the Hudson's Bay Company's exploits in nineteenth-century Canada, and who subsequently bewails the loss of a son. The "lost child" is a recurrent motif in Thomas's writing. Her fictions deal with the difficult relations between men and women, relations that often distinguish men's ostensible objectivity from women's intense, visceral response to sex, children, and death.

"The More Little Mummy in the World" (from *Ladies & Escorts,* 1977) not only documents the break-up of a relationship but also reconstructs in the text the psychological fragmentation that follows. The Mexican setting and the fragments of haltingly translated (or sometimes untranslated) Spanish speech intensify the female narrator's sense of alienation. The external world reads like a projection of her own turmoil. But out of this contact with uncertainty there emerges a sharp sense of the independence she has so painfully won. Preoccupied with death, the woman slowly converts her feelings of personal inadequacy and dependence into an outwardly directed, liberating anger.

The More Little Mummy in the World

Oscar A. Lempe
Denver, Color *U.S. 14-V-1876*
23-XI-1958

Guanauato, Gto.
Recuerdo de Su Esposa
Chijas
Pepetuidad

Recuerdo = in memory of his wife/daughters

Louis Montgomery Allen Sr.
New York City *Dec. 6-1887*
Feb. 12-1957

Guanauato, Gto.
Perpetuidad

Handprints on this one—of whom? *Su esposa? Su hermosa?* A passing, naughty, unrelated child?

Elisabeth Carnes Allen, D.A.R.

She wandered through the cemetery looking at every stone, imagining the people, what had brought them there, what the town had been like nearly a hundred years before. The lure of what riches? The silver mines perhaps.

Everywhere there were flowers stuck in tins—Mobil Oil tins, paint tins, tomatoes, green chillies:

Chiles Jalapenos, En Escapbeche

She took out her pocket dictionary.

The wind blowing through the cypress trees rattled the tins like bones.

To My Beloved Wife
Maria Concepcion Buchnan

Although there had been a long line-up to see the mummies there were very few people in the Pantheon itself. A young couple with their arms around one another, laughing, exchanging kisses, some old women in black, a gardener. And the dead of course, the multitude of dead stacked six or seven high. The soft brown hills beyond and El Pipla, the boy hero, alone on a hill above the Jardin de la Union, his arm upraised.

Ayer (yesterday). *Hoy* (today).
Mañana

Su hermosa = his mistress (i.e. his 'beautiful')
En Escapbeche = in vinegar and oil

Mother

Lily Mast McBride *Born Sept. 19-1882*
Died July 22-1926

A pretty blue-grey stone, this one, beautifully incised.

It was very peaceful here with the wreaths, the plastic flowers and the real—gladioli, lilies—the white ones she saw everywhere here, Easter lilies back home—geraniums, carnations. The flowers dead too of course, or dying, sucking up the last dregs of rusty water from the tins. Still, she liked this place better than the churches with their bleeding Christs, their oppressive smell of hot wax, their plaster damned pleading to her for one last chance at salvation.

Some stones were casually propped against still-occupied cabinets. (They couldn't be called tombs and she couldn't think of a better word than "cabinet"—cabin, verb, to confine in a small space, cramp). She turned one over.

Naci Inocente! . . .
Muerto Ignorante
Freyre Jose E.
V-7-1925
Perpetuidad

So much for *perpetuidad*!

She had been thinking of failures and of suicides and had gone to mass on Palm Sunday in the hopes of finding something positive—if only for a second, if only for an instant, if only, even, an aura or a whiff of hope for her salvation.

Buenos dias. Adios.

She straightened a tin of gladioli which had fallen over in the wind.

Outside the Parroquia women and men were braiding palms into elaborate patterns. She bought a small crucifix and went in, covering her head, but the Mass was a disappointment. She stood up. She sat down. She prayed. The priest was way way way up in the chancel. Little bells rang. There was no pageantry, no music, nothing to draw her spirit up and away from the deep well of despair into which it seemed to have fallen. Over the words of the priest a poem of Yeats' kept running through her mind:

Naci = born innocent/died ignorant

That is no country for old men
The young in one another's arms
Fish/flesh/and fowl commend
all summer long
Whatever is begotten, born or dies

They had been going to come down here together. Had maps, dreams, destinations. Even a tape:

Siento molestarle!
No es ninguna molestia!
Salud!

How much too much please thank you don't mention it.

Instead he took her out (at her request) the night before she left. To a Greek restaurant (again at her request). She drank a lot of wine, and crumbling a bit of bread between her fingers, told him it was she all along whom he really loved.

"Do you think so?" he said and smiled at her over his wine glass. Then in an offhand manner he asked her if she'd ever been in any of the other Greek restaurants along the street, places where you just walked in and took whatever was going, places where the Greeks themselves went, cheaper places than this. (And he, who never went into a restaurant alone, whom had he lingered with in a small café full of the smell of lamb and garlic and the whine of recorded music. Who? Don't ask, or, as he would have put it, "why humiliate yourself?") He had always been Machiavellian; had always known how to put her in her place.

Once they had been at the house of his best friend and contemporary, Peter:

"I was coming in on the bus from the island," her lover said, "toward sunset—a beautiful evening. Suddenly I looked up and there was this incredible cloud formation—incredible! I said to the fellow next to me, without really thinking about it, you know, 'My God, that looks just like the Mushroom Cloud!' I saw the guy look at me and give a little frown and then I realized with a start that he was younger, younger than the Bomb—that he didn't even know what I was talking about. The only mushroom cloud he knew was psilocybin!"

Siento = I'm sorry to bother you/You're not bothering me/hello.

Peter had laughed appreciatively. He was 35.

"It's true. People talk about the generation gap—as a metaphor I mean—but it seems to me there's a real gap—I almost see it as a physical space—between those born before or during the War and those born after it."

"Yes. There's a point at which Rachel and I just can't communicate; we were born into two different worlds." He had turned to her. "When I talk about Marlene Dietrich I don't know if you even know who I mean."

She was immediately defensive. He had wanted her to be, had set her up.

"Of course I know who Marlene Dietrich is."

"Ah yes—you know her name. But is your Marlene Dietrich the same as mine—I doubt it." Peter nodded and began singing "Lili Marlene." Her lover sat back and lit his pipe.

That night at the Greek restaurant he had given her a handsome present—a shoulderbag with three sections, or pouches, like a saddlebag.

"Now you will have three places to put all your clutter," he said, "instead of just one." ("It's not that she doesn't have a place for everything," he said once, at a party, "it's that she has several places." He was very tidy and they fought about the missing cap to the toothpaste.)

Buenos dias. Adios. No comprendo.

In one place there were freshly-dug graves, four in a row, an accident perhaps. This in a courtyard which led to a view of the city. Bougainvillaea had been splashed against the walls, the original purple and the scarlet, blood-coloured. In the distance she could hear the sound of children's voices.

Estoy esperando un paquete.
Lo tiene usted aqui?

When he came to get her at the hospital he was very brusque and efficient, annoyed that she was still in bed and crying. His sons were in the car—they were going camping. Yet still she wanted to buy him gifts—an onyx chess set, a heavy silver ring, a blanket for his bed. Things of beauty and whimsy, things that would make him think of her, remember her and want her.

Estoy = I'm waiting for a parcel/Have you got it here?

Donde este? Where is?

He had told her there was nothing wrong, that maybe she should see a shrink. The gifts would only embarrass him. When she began to cry at the bus station, he kissed her quickly on the forehead and then walked away. She hated him; no, she loved him.

She had read in the guidebook that if the rent was not kept up on the crypts (yes, that was the word she had been searching for), the bodies were removed after five years and the bones thrown into a common bone-house to make room for new arrivals. But the region was very dry and some of the bodies would be mummified. When they were, they were put into the museum. Directly outside the cemetery were souvenir stands—skeletons, on horseback or playing fiddles or dancing, with springy arms and legs. Postcards of the mummies, earthenware, bone letter-openers and crochet hooks (human bone?). There were mummies of pale beige toffee with raisin eyes. These were wrapped in red or yellow cellophane. As she approached a man had offered her two large ones in one packet, "*Momias Matrimonias,*" and laughed at her discomfort. Now she was trying to get up enough courage to go into the mummy museum itself.

Death and disease were accepted here. Death was even made fun of, made into toffee to chew or chocolate to lick or tiny plaster figures to decorate, along with gilded pictures of miraculous virgins, the windows and mirrors of buses and cars. She knew now that almost certainly, whenever she saw a street musician, either he was blind or lame or leprous or there was a terribly deformed creature, just out of sight, on behalf of whom he was playing his music.

Her operation had been therapeutic and therefore covered by her insurance. No back streets or borrowed money—things were easier now.

Ayer (yesterday). *Hoy* (today).
Mañana

This was a very strange town to walk around in and easy to get lost. The main road ran underneath the town in places, reappearing above ground several hundred yards beyond. It was really a stone-arched tunnel and rather frightening. And there were six or seven main squares, not just one. She had already, in spite of her map, been lost several times. The

Momias Matrimonias = "married" mummies

night before, wandering steep alleys full of wrought-iron balconies, she had stumbled upon a strange religious ceremony in one of the smaller lamplit squares. There were bleachers set out and many of the people were already seated, men, women and children, facing an old church. The church bell began to ring and then a priest appeared high up on the church steps, intoning Hail Marys and Our Fathers. And she understood a bit of it, the history of the week leading up to the arrest of Jesus. Below the steps stood men in purple sackcloth and black hoods, very mediaeval and frightening. A lifesized statue of Christ (looking not unlike the "Jesu Christo Superstare" she had seen in Mexico City) was brought out of the church by more hooded men, carried down the steep steps and put on a flower-decked platform. There was a rope around his neck and it hung down his back, binding his hands behind him. A child-angel and one of the masked men climbed up and sat on either side of him. Torches were lit and as the rest of the masked men shouldered their burden the crowd gave a deep moan of pity and anticipation. The statue had real hair and jointed, movable arms. He terrified her, for he hovered somewhere in a strange space between icon and the living god. The wind blew his hair across his gentle, accepting face. His gown was purple like the garments of the men but his was of velvet, not hemp. A workman beat a drum and the entire affair—Christ, angel, masked men, flowers, scaffolding, torches, priest—began to move. A young boy followed behind, playing a simple pipe and the procession slowly moved out from the small square into the larger one beyond. Behind came small children, some on tricycles, the women in black, the men, balloon sellers, a thin brown pariah dog. The bowed, bound figure of Christ rode above them all. It was amateurish in a way but very powerful; she hid herself in the crowd.

> *Por que?* Why? *No se.* I don't know.
> *Perdone.*

It was as though once she had decided she didn't want it he had washed his hands of the whole affair.

"Ruth Barnes"

Just a small stone marker with a dried-up geranium obscuring the date. Presumably to be buried in this small courtyard was more expensive than to be deposited on the shelves. The wind blowing rattled the tins like bones.

Perdone = sorry

If he were here he would have struck up a friendship with the gardener, would try out the little Spanish he knew and supplement it with laughter and broad gestures. His energy was one of the first things that had excited her. And his keen intelligence, his learning, the whole sum of his life experience. He had been married (twice), had children (one as old as her youngest sister), had suffered and taken chances.

"I find it impossible to live alone," he had said to her the first night, "and yet somehow I always seem to fuck it up—my relationships with women." He showed her pictures of his sons and took her home to bed.

Dispenseme. Excuse me.
Muchas gracias.

Everywhere down here men followed her and tried to feel her up—a woman alone deserved to be treated that way. Then they gave their paycheques to their mothers and went to mass on Sundays.

Hail Mary Full of Grace Blessed is
The Fruit of Thy Womb Jesus

On the train from Nuevo Laredo she had met a middle-aged man who lived in San Miguel. He said the happiest day of his life was the day when they nailed his wife's coffin shut. Federales came on the train looking for contraband. They wore their revolvers tucked in the back of their pants, Pancho Villa style.

"Watch for the Mordida," the American said.

She shook her head.

" 'The Bite.' To force someone to give you a bribe. It's a game between the Federales and the people coming back."

Was that what she had done by getting pregnant? Put the bite on him?

The boy-hero stood unconcerned on the distant hill, his arm upraised forever. Her first day in the town she had followed the crude signs and climbed steep stairs and back alleys until she reached the top of that hill. She had taken some bread and fruit with her and sat in a little summer house just below the enormous figure, eating slices of pineapple and writing in her journal. The boy had set fire to the granary in which the Royalists had barricaded themselves. At his feet it said, in Spanish,

"There are still other castles to burn."

She felt quite happy there, after her climb, the whole town at her feet. But in the evening, at a band concert in the Jardin de la Union, she sat on a wrought-iron bench and longed to have him with her, next to her, observing, commenting, loving. Canaries mocked her from the laurel trees around the square.

Where is? *No comprendo.*

She retraced her steps, back through the main courtyard with all its stacked and silent dead, back through the black iron gate with its simple cross on top. There were very few people in line now so there was no reason not to wait.

He had been quite calm when she told him. Just said, "Well, what do you want to do about it?" He left it entirely up to her. Had she wanted him to be otherwise? Had she wanted to bear his child? She wanted to be a writer, a poet—had he not encouraged her, sung her praises? In Chapultapec Park in Mexico City she sat on the grass one Sunday and watched the fathers spoil their children. They were immaculate—it was the mothers, of course, who saw to that. There were funny animal heads on the trash cans in the children's playground. The children laughed and squealed when they stuck their little heads in.

She paid her five pesos and went into the mummy museum.

In Chapultapec Park she had sat on the grass and wept. She wanted to be six years old in a white dress and riding on her father's shoulders, her small hands tugging at his curly hair. She wanted to be held and to be forgiven. She wanted a red balloon.

Her mother was at home making a delicious Sunday dinner.

Ayer (yesterday). *Hoy* (today).
Mañana.

The mummy museum was really a long artificially-lit corridor with the mummies displayed in glass cases along one side. The corridor was hot and very crowded, so that for a moment she experienced a wave of claustrophobia and almost turned around and ran.

Some of the names and dates on the stones had simply been scrawled in the wet plaster.

Aristo Perez
Manuel Torres M.
Maria de los Angeles Rodriguez

So there were the mummies, in glass cases like curios—which of course they were. Most were without clothes, jaundice-coloured and hideously wrinkled. A few had on mouldy shoes and there was one man who had on a complete suit of tattered black clothes. Very few had hair and this surprised her. Was it just an old wives' tale that the hair would keep on growing?

He read her, one night, from John Donne's "Funerale"

Whoever comes to shroud me,
  do not harme
Nor question much
That subtile wreathe of hair,
  which crowns my arme:

and from "A Feaver"

Oh doe not die, for I shall hate
  All women so, when thou art gone,
That thee I shall not celebrate,
  When I remember, thou wast one.

She got up and cut off a lock of her hair and gave it to him; he kissed her neck and put the lock in the back of his grandfather's gold watch.

Donde este? Where is?

The mummies' faces were full of anger and terror. Shrinkage had pulled their mouths open and their hands were clutched across their empty bellies. Her Spanish was not quick enough to understand everything the guides were saying, but there were abnormalities and tumours and other curious things being pointed out as they moved along. The mummies were tall or short, male and female, the men's papery genitals still visible, the women's wrinkled breasts.

She wrote him letter after letter and tore them all up.

Quiero comprar una postal. I wish to buy a postcard.

As she crossed the street to his car and his waiting sons, she stumbled, still drugged and swollen-eyed, against the curb, and turned her ankle. Suddenly she had to sit down on the grass and put her head between her knees. She knew the boys, his sons, were watching her. What had he said to them? Why had he brought them to the hospital? What was he trying to say?

People with limps, people with no legs, blind people, lepers, pariah dogs. The country swarmed with outcasts and with cripples. The tourists bought silver rings and onyx chess sets and turned their heads away. After all, it was not their problem. Charity begins. . . .

"They hate us," the American man had said. "They want our money but they hate us. They would prefer if we just mailed it down."

Almost at the end of the corridor was a display case full of child mummies—some in christening gowns and bonnets, some naked or wrapped in tiny shrouds. In front of the smallest of these a cardboard sign was propped. She pushed closer, in order to read it, then tugged at the guide's elbow.

"Please. *Por favor.* What does the sign say? *Que quiere decir?"*

"La Momia Mas Pequena del mundo." He smiled at her, showing perfect teeth.

"Si. Si. In English. *Habla Usted Inglis?"*

"Ah. Inglis."

He smiled again.

"The more little mummy in the world."

It sat there, no bigger than the rubber babies she had played with as a child.

Where were the parents? Why had these children been removed to this terrible glass limbo? She looked at la momia mas Pequena but it refused to answer.

The American had asked her to come and spend a few days with him in San Miguel.

She pushed her way through the tourists and out the exit door. The sun struck her like a slap. She half-ran, half-walked toward the souvenir stands, rummaged quickly through the cards until she found the one she was looking for, the one she knew was certain to be there.

Back at the apartment he had said, "D'you think you could rustle us up some dinner—we'd like to get away before dark." The boys were looking at her curiously. She went into the bedroom and began to pack, tears running down her face, the little plastic hospital bracelet still locked around her wrist.

Go. Come. Are you ready?
Don't forget.

She fumbled in her bag for the change purse, then headed back down the hill. Tonight, drinking her cho-ko-la-tay in that little restaurant near the Plazuela where she had seen the Christ, she would get out the card and address it.

"Having a wonderful time," she would write.

"Wish you were here."

John Updike

A product of the Middle America that gives him much of his material, John Updike was born in Shillington, Pennsylvania, in 1932, and educated at Harvard and the Ruskin School of Drawing and Fine Art in Oxford, England. After a spell on the staff of *The New Yorker* from 1955 to 1957, Updike became a freelance writer and journalist, developing a professionalism in his craft ("I would write ads for deodorant or labels for catsup bottles if I had to") which has led at times to a greater concern for surface than for substance, and earned him the charge of superficiality from some critics. Author of numerous novels, short stories, and essays, he writes best (and most frequently) about domestic life, drawing the relationship between husbands and wives, parents and children, with a detailed vividness born of close observation; indeed, many of his stories have an autobiographical basis, and his novel *The Centaur* (1963) focuses on a character modelled after his father. His later work deals increasingly with the domestic crises and emotional traumas accompanying middle age, without any loss of the wit and eloquence characteristic of all his writing. In 1981 his achievement was rewarded with a Pulitzer Prize for his novel *Rabbit is Rich,* and the study of this title character was continued in *Rabbit at Rest* (1990). Numerous other fictions and collections appeared in the 1980s and 1990s, including essays (*More Matter,* 1999), stories (*The Afterlife,* 1994), novels (*The Witches of Eastwick,* 1984, and *Brazil,* 1994), and an anthology of the American stories he considers the best of the twentieth century (1999).

Updike has summarized his major preoccupations as follows: "Domestic fierceness within the middle class, sex and death as riddles for the thinking animal, social existence as sacrifice, unexpected pleasures and rewards, corruption as a kind of evolution. . . . " Sex and death undoubtedly occupy the centre of his imagination, sometimes to morbid excess; *Couples* (1968) at times runs perilously close to refined pornography in its portrait of boredom and sexual decadence in suburban Massachusetts. But Updike is no pornographer; in his fiction he repeatedly shows the deadness of sex without love, and the frailty of domestic love in a society devoid of faith or purpose. In "Giving Blood" (*The Music School,* 1966) he depicts the strains of marriage with compassionate irony, and indicates how the selfish sensuality of contemporary human beings has blinded them to the ancient mystery of love, a mystery we can now apprehend only fleetingly.

Giving Blood

The Maples had been married now nine years, which is almost too long.

"Goddammit, goddammit," Richard said to Joan, as they drove into Boston to give blood, "I drive this road five days a week and now I'm driving it again. It's like a nightmare. I'm exhausted. I'm emotionally, mentally, physically exhausted, and she isn't even an aunt of mine. She isn't even an aunt of *yours*."

"She's a sort of cousin," Joan said.

"Well hell, every goddam body in New England is some sort of cousin of yours; must I spent the rest of my life trying to save them *all*?"

"Hush," Joan said. "She might die. I'm ashamed of you. Really ashamed."

It cut. His voice for the moment took on an apologetic pallor. "Well I'd be my usual goddam saintly self if I'd had any sort of sleep last night. Five days a week I bump out of bed and stagger out the door past the milkman and on the one day of the week when I don't even have to truck the blasphemous little brats to Sunday school you make an appointment to have me drained dry thirty miles away."

"Well it wasn't *me*," Joan said, "who had to stay till two o'clock doing the Twist with Marlene Brossman."

"We weren't doing the Twist. We were gliding around very chastely to 'Hits of the Forties.' And don't think I was so oblivious I didn't see you snoogling behind the piano with Harry Saxon."

"We weren't behind the piano, we were on the bench. And he was just talking to me because he felt sorry for me. Everybody there felt sorry for me; you could have at *least* let somebody else dance *once* with Marlene, if only for show."

"Show, show," Richard said. "That's your mentality exactly."

"Why, the poor Matthews or whatever they are looked absolutely horrified."

"Matthiessons," he said. "And that's another thing. Why are idiots like that being invited these days? If there's anything I hate, it's women who keep putting one hand on their pearls and taking a deep breath. I thought she had something stuck in her throat."

"They're a perfectly pleasant, decent young couple. The thing you resent about their coming is that their being there shows us what we've become."

"If you're so attracted," he said, "to little fat men like Harry Saxon, why didn't you marry one?"

"My," Joan said calmly, and gazed out the window away from him, at the scudding gasoline stations. "You honestly *are* hateful. It's not just a pose."

"Pose, show, my Lord, who are you performing for? If it isn't Harry Saxon, it's Freddie Vetter—all these dwarves. Every time I looked over at you last night it was like some pale Queen of the Dew surrounded by a ring of mushrooms."

"You're too absurd," she said. Her hand, distinctly thirtyish, dry and green-veined and rasped by detergents, stubbed out her cigarette in the dashboard ashtray. "You're not subtle. You think you can match me up with another man so you can swirl off with Marlene with a free conscience."

Her reading his strategy so correctly made his face burn; he felt again the tingle of Mrs. Brossman's hair as he pressed his cheek against hers and in this damp privacy inhaled the perfume behind her ear. "You're right," he said. "But I want to get you a man your own size; I'm very loyal that way."

"Let's not talk," she said.

His hope, of turning the truth into a joke, was rebuked. Any implication of permission was blocked. "It's that *smug*ness," he explained, speaking levelly, as if about a phenomenon of which they were both disinterested students. "It's your smugness that is really intolerable. Your stupidity I don't mind. Your sexlessness I've learned to live with. But that wonderfully smug, New England—I suppose we needed it to get the country founded, but in the Age of Anxiety it really does gall."

He had been looking over at her, and unexpectedly she turned and looked at him, with a startled but uncannily crystalline expression, as if her face had been in an instant rendered in tinted porcelain, even to the eyelashes.

"I asked you not to talk," she said. "Now you've said things that I'll always remember."

Plunged fathoms deep into the wrong, his face suffocated with warmth, he concentrated on the highway and sullenly steered. Though they were moving at sixty in the sparse Saturday traffic, he had travelled this road so often its distances were all translated into time, so that they seemed to him to be moving as slowly as a minute hand from one digit to the next. It would have been strategic and dignified of him to keep the silence; but he could not resist believing that just one more pinch of syllables would restore the fine balance which with each wordless mile slipped increasingly awry. He asked, "How did Bean seem to you?" Bean was their baby. They had left her last night, to go to the party, with a fever of 102.

Joan wrestled with her vow to say nothing, but guilt proved stronger than spite. She said, "Cooler. Her nose is a river."

"Sweetie," Richard blurted, "will they hurt me?" The curious fact was that he had never given blood before. Asthmatic and underweight, he had been 4-F, and at college and now at the office he had, less through his own determination than through the diffidence of the solicitors, evaded pledging blood. It was one of those tests of courage so trivial that no one had ever thought to make him face up to it.

■ ■ ■

Spring comes carefully to Boston. Speckled crusts of ice lingered around the parking meters, and the air, grayly stalemated between seasons, tinted the buildings along Longwood Avenue with a drab and homogeneous majesty. As they walked up the drive to the hospital entrance, Richard nervously wondered aloud if they would see the King of Arabia.

"He's in a separate wing," Joan said. "With four wives."

"Only four? What an ascetic." And he made bold to tap his wife's shoulder. It was not clear if, under the thickness of her winter coat, she felt it.

At the desk, they were directed down a long corridor floored with cigar-coloured linoleum. Up and down, right and left it went, in the secretive, disjointed way peculiar to hospitals that have been built annex by annex. Richard seemed to himself Hansel orphaned with Gretel; birds ate the bread crumbs behind them, and at last they timidly knocked on the witch's door, which said BLOOD DONATION CENTER. A young man in white opened the door a crack. Over his shoulder Richard glimpsed—horrors!—a pair of dismembered female legs stripped of their shoes and laid parallel on a bed. Glints of needles and bottles pricked his eyes. Without widening the crack, the young man passed out to them two long forms. In sitting side by side on the waiting bench, remembering their middle initials and childhood diseases, Mr. and Mrs. Maple were newly defined to themselves. He fought down that urge to giggle and clown and lie that threatened him whenever he was asked—like a lawyer appointed by the court to plead a hopeless case—to present, as it were, his statistics to eternity. It seemed to mitigate his case slightly that a few of these statistics (present address, date of marriage) were shared by the hurt soul scratching beside him, with his own pen. He looked over her shoulder. "I never knew you had whooping cough."

"My mother says. I don't remember it."

A pan crashed to a distant floor. An elevator chuckled remotely. A woman, a middle-aged woman top-heavy with rouge and fur, stepped out of the blood door and wobbled a moment on legs that looked familiar. They had been restored to their shoes. The heels of these shoes clicked firmly as, having raked the Maples with a defiant blue glance, she turned, and disappeared around a bend in the corridor. The young man appeared in the doorway holding a pair of surgical tongs. His noticeably recent haircut made him seem an apprentice barber. He clicked his tongs and smiled. "Shall I do you together?"

"Sure." It put Richard on his mettle that this callow fellow, to whom apparently they were to entrust their liquid essence, was so clearly younger than they. But when Richard stood, his indignation melted and his legs felt diluted under him. And the extraction of the blood sample from his middle finger seemed the nastiest and most needlessly prolonged physical involvement with another human being he had ever experienced. There is a touch that good dentists, mechanics, and barbers have, and this intern did not have it; he fumbled and in compensation was too rough. Again and again, an atrociously clumsy vampire, he tugged and twisted the purpling finger in vain. The tiny glass capillary tube remained transparent.

"He doesn't like to bleed, does he?" the intern asked Joan. As relaxed as a nurse, she sat in a chair next to a table of scintillating equipment.

"I don't think his blood moves much," she said, "until after midnight."

This stab at a joke made Richard in his extremity of fright laugh loudly, and the laugh at last seemed to jar the panicked coagulant. Red seeped upward in the thirsty little tube, as in a sudden thermometer.

The intern grunted in relief. As he smeared the samples on the analysis box, he explained idly, "What we ought to have down here is a pan of warm water. You just came in out of the cold. If you put your hand in hot water for a minute, the blood just pops out."

"A pretty thought," Richard said.

But the intern had already written him off as a clowner and continued calmly to Joan, "All we'd need would be a baby hot plate for about six dollars, then we could make our own coffee too. This way, when we get a donor who needs the coffee afterwards, we have to send up for it while we keep his head between his knees. Do you think you'll be needing coffee?"

"*No,*" Richard interrupted, jealous of their rapport.

The intern told Joan, "You're O."

"I know," she said.

"And he's A positive."

"Why that's very good, Dick!" she called to him.

"Am I rare?" he asked.

The boy turned and explained. "O positive and A positive are the most common types." Something in the patient tilt of his closecropped head as its lateral sheen mixed with the lazily bright midmorning air of the room sharply reminded Richard of the days years ago when he had tended a battery of teletype machines in a room much this size. By now, ten o'clock, the yards of copy that began pouring through the machines at five and that lay in great crimped heaps on the floor when he arrived at seven would have been harvested and sorted and pasted together and turned in, and there was nothing to do but keep up with the staccato appearance of the later news and to think about simple things like coffee. It came back to him, how pleasant and secure those hours had been when, king of his own corner, he was young and newly responsible.

The intern asked, "Who wants to be first?"

"Let me," Joan said. "He's never done it before."

"Her full name is Joan of Arc," Richard explained, angered at this betrayal, so unimpeachably selfless and smug.

The intern, threatened in his element, fixed his puzzled eyes on the floor between them and said, "Take off your shoes and each get on a bed." He added, "Please," and all three laughed, one after the other, the intern last.

The beds were at right angles to one another along two walls. Joan lay down and from her husband's angle of vision was novelly foreshortened. He had never before seen her quite this way, the combed crown of her hair so poignant, her bared arm so silver and long, her stocking feet toed in so childishly and docilely. There were no pillows on the beds, and lying flat made him feel tipped head down; the illusion of floating encouraged his hope that this unreal adventure would soon dissolve in the manner of a dream. "You OK?"

"Are you?" Her voice came softly from the tucked-under wealth of her hair. From the straightness of the parting it seemed her mother had brushed it. He watched a long needle sink into the flat of her arm and a piece of moist cotton clumsily swab the spot. He had imagined their blood would be drained into cans or bottles, but the intern, whose breathing was now the only sound within the room, brought to Joan's side what looked like a miniature plastic knapsack, all coiled and tied. His body cloaked his actions. When he stepped away, a plastic cord had been grafted, a transparent vine, to the flattened crook of Joan's extended arm, where the skin was translucent and the veins were faint blue tributaries shallowly buried. It was a tender, vulnerable place where in courting days she had liked being stroked. Now, without visible transition, the pale tendril planted there went dark red. Richard wanted to cry out.

The instant readiness of her blood to leave her body pierced him like a physical pang. Though he had not so much as blinked, its initial leap had been too quick for his eye. He had expected some visible sign of flow, but from the mere appearance of it the tiny looped hose might be pouring blood *into* her body or might be a curved line added, irrelevant as a mustache, to a finished canvas. The fixed position of his head gave what he saw a certain flatness.

And now the intern turned to him, and there was the tiny felt prick of the novocain needle, and then the coarse, half-felt intrusion of something resembling a medium-weight nail. Twice the boy mistakenly probed for the vein and the third time taped the successful graft fast with adhesive tape. All the while, Richard's mind moved aloofly among the constellations of the stained cracked ceiling. What was being done to him did not bear contemplating. When the intern moved away to hum and tinkle among his instruments, Joan craned her neck to show her husband her face and, upside down in his vision, grotesquely smiled.

It was not many minutes that they lay there at right angles together, but the time passed as something beyond the walls, as something mixed with the faraway clatter of pans and the approach and retreat of footsteps and the opening and closing of unseen doors. Here, conscious of a pointed painless pulse in the inner hinge of his arm but incurious as to what it looked like, he floated and imagined how his soul would float free when all his blood was underneath the bed. His blood and Joan's merged on the floor, and together their spirits glided from crack to crack, from star to star on the ceiling. Once she cleared her throat, and the sound make an abrasion like the rasp of a pebble loosened by a cliff-climber's boot.

■ ■ ■

The door opened. Richard turned his head and saw an old man, bald and sallow, enter and settle in a chair. He was one of those old men who hold within an institution an ill-defined but consecrated place. The young doctor seemed to know him, and the two talked, softly, as if not to disturb the mystical union of the couple sacrificially bedded together. They talked of persons and events that meant nothing—of Iris, of Dr. Greenstein, of Ward D, again of Iris, who had given the old man an undeserved scolding, of the shameful lack of a hot plate to make coffee on, of the rumored black bodyguards who kept watch with scimitars by the bed of the glaucomatous king. Through Richard's tranced ignorance these topics passed as clouds of impression, iridescent, massy—Dr. Greenstein with a pointed nose and almond eyes the color of ivy, Iris eighty feet tall and hurling sterilized thunderbolts of wrath. As in some theologies the proliferant deities are said to exist as ripples upon the featureless ground of Godhead, so these inconstant images lightly overlay his continuous awareness of Joan's blood, like his own, ebbing. Linked to a common loss, they were chastely conjoined; the thesis developed upon him that the hoses attached to them somewhere out of sight met. Testing this belief, he glanced down and saw that indeed the plastic vine taped to the flattened crook of his arm was the same dark red as hers. He stared at the ceiling to disperse a sensation of faintness.

Abruptly the young intern left off his desultory conversation and moved to Joan's side. There was a chirp of clips. When he moved away, she was revealed holding her naked arm upright, pressing a piece of cotton against it with the other hand. Without pausing, the intern came to Richard's side, and the birdsong of the clips repeated, nearer. "Look at that," he said to his elderly friend. "I started him two minutes later than her and he's finished at the same time."

"Was it a race?" Richard asked.

Clumsily firm, the boy fitted Richard's fingers to a pad and lifted his arm for him. "Hold it there for five minutes," he said.

"What'll happen if I don't?"

"You'll mess up your shirt." To the old man he said, "I had a woman in here the other day, she was all set to leave when all of a sudden, pow!—all over the front of this beautiful linen dress. She was going to Symphony."

"Then they try to sue the hospital for the cleaning bill," the old man muttered.

"Why was I slower than him?" Joan asked. Her upright arm wavered, as if vexed or weakened.

"The woman generally is," the boy told her. "Nine times out of ten, the man is faster. Their hearts are so much stronger."

"Is that really so?"

"Sure it's so," Richard told her. "Don't argue with medical science."

"Woman up in Ward C," the old man said, "they saved her life for her out of an auto accident and now I hear she's suing because they didn't find her dental plate."

Under such patter, the five minutes eroded. Richard's upheld arm began to ache. It seemed that he and Joan were caught together in a classroom where they would never be recognized, or in a charade that would never be guessed, the correct answer being Two Silver Birches in a Meadow.

"You can sit up now if you want," the intern told them. "But don't let go of the venipuncture."

They sat up on their beds, legs dangling heavily. Joan asked him, "Do you feel dizzy?"

"With my powerful heart? Don't be presumptuous."

"Do you think he'll need coffee?" the intern asked her. "I'll have to send up for it now."

The old man shifted forward in his chair, preparing to heave to his feet.

"I do *not* want any *coffee*"—Richard said it so loud he saw himself transposed, another Iris, into the firmament of the old man's aggrieved gossip. *Some dizzy bastard down in the blood room, I get up to get him some coffee and he damn near bit my head off.* To demonstrate simultaneously his essential good humor and his total presence of mind, Richard gestured toward the blood they had given—two square plastic sacks filled solidly fat—and declared, "Back where I come from in West Virginia sometimes you pick a tick off a dog that looks like that."

The men looked at him amazed. Had he not quite said what he meant to say? Or had they never seen anybody from West Virginia before?

Joan pointed at the blood, too. "Is that us? Those little doll pillows?"

"Maybe we should take one home to Bean," Richard suggested.

The intern did not seem convinced that this was a joke. "Your blood will be credited to Mrs. Henryson's account," he stated stiffly.

Joan asked him, "Do you know anything about her? When is she—when is her operation scheduled?"

"I think for tomorrow. The only thing on the tab this after is an open heart at two; that'll take about sixteen pints."

"Oh . . . " Joan was shaken. "Sixteen . . . that's a full person, isn't it?

"More," the intern answered, with the regal handwave that bestows largess and dismisses compliments.

"Could we visit her?" Richard asked, for Joan's benefit. ("Really ashamed," she had said; it had cut.) He was confident of the refusal.

"Well, you can ask at the desk, but usually before a major one like this it's just the nearest of kin. I guess you're safe now." He meant their punctures. Richard's arm bore a small raised bruise; the intern covered it with one of those ample, salmon, unhesitatingly adhesive bandages that only hospitals have. That was their specialty, Richard thought—packaging. They wrap the human mess for final delivery. Sixteen doll's pillows, uniformly dark and snug, marching into an open heart: the vision momentarily satisfied his hunger for cosmic order.

He rolled down his sleeve and slid off the bed. It startled him to realize, in the instant before his feet touched the floor, that three pairs of eyes were fixed upon him, fascinated and apprehensive and eager for scandal. He stood and towered above them. He hopped on one foot to slip into one loafer, and then on this foot to slip into the other loafer. Then he did the little shuffle-tap, shuffle-tap step that was all that remained to him of dancing lessons he had taken at the age of seven, driving twelve miles each Saturday into Morgantown. He made a small bow toward his wife, smiled at the old man, and said to the intern, "All my life people have been expecting me to faint. I have no idea why. I never faint."

His coat and overcoat felt a shade queer, a bit slithery and light, but as he walked down the length of the corridor, space seemed to adjust snugly around him. At his side, Joan kept an inquisitive and chastened silence. They pushed through the great glass doors. A famished sun was nibbling through the overcast. Above and behind them, the King of Arabia lay in a drugged dream of dunes and Mrs. Henryson upon her sickbed received like the comatose mother of twins their identical gifts of blood. Richard hugged his wife's padded shoulders and as they walked along leaning on each other whispered, "Hey, I love you. Love love *love* you."

■ ■ ■

Romance is, simply, the strange, the untried. It was unusual for the Maples to be driving together at eleven in the morning. Almost always it was dark when they shared a car. The oval of her face was bright in the corner of his eye. She was watching him, alert to take the wheel if he suddenly lost consciousness. He felt tender toward her in the eggshell light, and curious toward himself, wondering how far beneath his brain the black pit did lie. He felt no different; but then the quality of consciousness perhaps did not bear introspection. Something certainly had been taken from him; he was less himself by a pint and it was not impossible that like a trapeze artist saved by a net he was sustained in the world of light and reflection by a single layer of interwoven cells. Yet the earth, with its signals and buildings and cars and bricks, continued like a pedal note.

Boston behind them, he asked, "Where should we eat?"

"Should we eat?"

"Please, yes. Let me take you to lunch. Just like a secretary."

"I do feel sort of illicit. As if I've stolen something."

"You too? But what did we steal?"

"I don't know. The morning? Do you think Eve knows enough to feed them?" Eve was their sitter, a little sandy girl from down the street who would, in exactly a year, Richard calculated, be painfully lovely. They lasted three years on the average, sitters; you got them in the tenth grade and escorted them into their bloom and then, with graduation, like commuters who had reached their stop, they dropped out of sight, into nursing school or marriage. And the train went on, and took on other passengers, and itself became older and longer. The Maples had four children: Judith, Richard Jr., poor oversized, angel-faced John, and Bean.

"She'll manage. What would you like? All that talk about coffee has made me frantic for some."

"At the Pancake House beyond 128 they give you coffee before you even ask."

"Pancakes? Now? Aren't you gay? Do you think we'll throw up?"

"Do you feel like throwing up?"

"No, not really. I feel sort of insubstantial and gentle, but it's probably psychosomatic. I don't really understand this business of giving something away and still somehow having it. What is it—the spleen?"

"I don't know. Are the splenetic man and the sanguine man the same?"

"God. I've totally forgotten the humors. What are the others—phlegm and choler?'

"Bile and black bile are in there somewhere."

"One thing about you, Joan. You're educated. New England women are educated."

"Sexless as we are."

"That's right; drain me dry and then put me on the rack." But there was no wrath in his words; indeed, he had reminded her of their earlier conversation so that, in much this way, his words might be revived, diluted, and erased. It seemed to work. The restaurant where they served only pancakes was empty and quiet this early. A bashfulness possessed them both; it had become a date between two people who have little as yet in common but who are nevertheless sufficiently intimate to accept the fact without chatter. Touched by the stain her blueberry pancakes left on her teeth, he held a match to her cigarette and said, "Gee, I loved you back in the blood room."

"I wonder why."

"You were so brave."

"So were you."

"But I'm supposed to be. I'm paid to be. It's the price of having a penis."

"Shh."

"Hey. I didn't mean that about your being sexless."

The waitress refilled their coffee cups and gave them the check.

"And I promise never never to do the Twist, the cha-cha, or the schottische with Marlene Brossman."

"Don't be silly. I don't care."

This amounted to permission, but perversely irritated him. That smugness; why didn't she *fight*? Trying to regain their peace, scrambling uphill, he picked up their check and with an effort of acting, the pretense being that they were out on a date and he was a raw dumb suitor, said handsomely, "I'll pay."

But on looking into his wallet he saw only a single worn dollar there. He didn't know why this should make him so angry, except the fact somehow that it was only *one*. "Goddammit," he said. "Look at that." He waved it in her face. "I work like a bastard all week for you and those insatiable brats and at the end of it what do I have? One goddam crummy wrinkled dollar."

Her hands dropped to the pocketbook beside her on the seat, but her gaze stayed with him, her face having retreated, or advanced, into that porcelain shell of uncanny composure. "We'll both pay," Joan said.

Guy Vanderhaeghe

Born in Esterhazy, Saskatchewan, in 1951, Guy Vanderhaeghe now lives in Saskatoon. A contributor to numerous journals, he won the Governor General's Award for fiction for his first book, the short story collection *Man Descending* (1982). Two novels—*My Present Age* (1984) and *Homesick* (1989)—continued his fictional commentary on living the moral life in the face of private and public pressure to yield or compromise. Other works followed, including more stories (*Things As They Are?* 1992), a play (*I Had a Job I Liked. Once,* 1992), and the prize-winning novel *The Englishman's Boy* (1996). This extraordinary novel juxtaposes two stories: a historical narrative of the Cypress Hills massacre (which begins by following a troop of men north across the Medicine Line), and a twentieth-century narrative about a young Canadian who heads south to Hollywood to become a screenwriter, and who is asked to uncover (and then to falsify) the "real story" of a cowboy who might have taken part in that earlier escapade.

Violent in subject and raw in language, "Cages" (from *Man Descending*) depicts how economics, class, intelligence, age, rivalry, desire (for power, for freedom, for love), and responsibility all enclose human beings. The central character, an adolescent on the verge (he thinks) of breaking away, finds himself ultimately as constrained as any other ordinary person. The story stops short of judging or interpreting the protagonist's circumstances; they invite neither pity nor despair—they just are. The condition of being alive, it seems, imposes both connection and conflict; it allows people to aspire and dream, but it also requires them to learn to endure.

Cages

Here it is, 1967, the Big Birthday. Centennial Year they call it. The whole country is giving itself a pat on the back. Holy shit, boys, we made it.

I made it too for seventeen years, a spotless life, as they say, and for presents I get, in my senior year of high school, my graduating year for chrissakes, a six-month suspended sentence for obstructing a police officer, and my very own personal social worker.

The thing is I don't *need* this social worker woman. She can't tell me anything I haven't already figured out for myself. Take last Wednesday, Miss Krawchuk, who looks like the old widow chicken on the Bugs Bunny Show, the one who's hot to trot for Foghorn Leghorn, says to me: "You know, Billy, your father loves you just as much as he does Gene. He doesn't have a favourite."

Now I can get bullshit at the poolroom any time I want it—and without having to keep an appointment. Maybe Pop *loves* me as much as he does Gene, but Gene is still his favourite kid. Everybody has a favourite kid. I knew that much already when I was only eight and Gene was nine. I figured it out right after Gene almost blinded me.

Picture this. There the two of us were in the basement. It was Christmas holidays and the old man had kicked us downstairs to huck darts at this board he'd give us for a present. Somehow, I must've had horseshoes up my ass, I'd beat Gene six games straight. And was he pissed off! He never loses to me at nothing ever. And me being in such a real unique situation, I was giving him the needle-rooney.

"What's that now?" I said. "Is that six or seven what I won?"

"Luck," Gene said, and he sounded like somebody was slowly strangling him. "Luck. Luck. Luck." He could hardly get it out.

And that's when I put the capper on it. I tossed a bull's-eye. "Read 'er and weep," I told him. That's what the old man says whenever he goes out at rummy. It's his needle-rooney. "Read 'er and weep."

That did it. The straw what broke the frigging camel's back. All I saw was his arm blur when he let fly at me. I didn't even have time to *think* about ducking. Bingo. Dead centre in the forehead, right in the middle of the old noggin he drills me with a dart. And there it stuck. Until it loosened a bit. Then it sagged down real slow between my eyes, hung for a second, slid off of my nose, and dropped at my feet. I hollered bloody blue murder, you better believe it.

For once, Pop didn't show that little bastard any mercy. He took after him from room to room whaling him with this extension cord across the ass, the back of the legs, the shoulders. Really hard. Gene, naturally, was screaming and blubbering and carrying on like it was a goddamn axe murder or something. He'd try to get under a bed, or behind a dresser or something, and get stuck halfway. Then old Gene would really catch it. He didn't know whether to plough forward, back up, shit, or go blind. And all the time the old man was lacing him left and right and saying in this sad, tired voice: "You're the oldest. Don't you know no better? You could of took his eye out, you crazy little bugger."

But that was only justice. He wasn't all that mad at Gene. Me he was mad at. If that makes any sense. Although I have to admit he didn't lay a hand on me. But yell? Christ, can that man yell. Especially at me. Somehow I'm the one that drives him squirrelly.

"Don't you *never, never* tease him again!" he bellowed and his neck started to swell. When the old man gets mad you can see it swell, honest. "You know he can't keep a hold of himself. One day you'll drive him so goddamn goofy with that yap of yours he'll do something terrible! Something he'll regret for the rest of his life. And it'll all be your fault!" The old man had to stop there and slow down or a vein would've exploded in his brain, or his arsehole popped inside out, or something, "So smarten up," he said, a little quieter, finally, "or you'll be the death of me and all my loved ones."

So there you are. I never pretended the world was fair, and I never bitched because it wasn't. But I do resent the hell out of being forced to listen to some dried-up old broad who gets paid by the government to tell me it is. Fuck her. She never lived in the Simpson household with my old man waiting around for Gene to do that *terrible* thing. It spoils the atmosphere. Makes a person edgy, you know?

Of course, Gene has done a fair number of *bad things* while everybody was waiting around for him to do the one great big *terrible thing*; and he's done them in a fair number of places. That's because the old man is a miner, and for a while there he was always telling some foreman to go piss up a rope. So we moved around a lot. That's why the Simpson household has a real history. But Gene's is the best of all. In Elliot Lake he failed grade three; in Bombertown he got picked up for shoplifting; in Flin Flon he broke some snotty kid's nose and got sent home from school. And every grade he goes higher, it gets a little worse. Last year, when we were both in grade eleven, I'm sure the old man was positive Gene was finally going to pull off the *terrible thing* he's been worrying about as long as I can remember.

It's crazy. Lots of times when I think about it, I figure I don't get on with the old man because I treat him nice. That I try too hard to make him like me. I'm not the way Gene is, I respect Pop. He slogs it out, shift after shift, on a shitty job he hates. Really hates. In fact, he told me once he would have liked to have been a farmer. Which only goes to show you how crazy going down that hole day after day makes you. Since we moved to Saskatchewan I've seen lots of farmers, and if you ask me, being one doesn't have much to recommend it.

But getting back to that business of being nice to Dad. Last year I started waiting up for him to come home from the afternoon shift. The one that runs from four p.m. in the afternoon until midnight. It wasn't half bad. Most nights I'd fall asleep on the chesterfield with the TV playing after Mom went to bed. Though lots of times I'd do my best to make it past the national news to wait for Earl Cameron and his collection of screwballs. Those guys kill me. They're always yapping off because somebody or something rattled their chain. Most of those characters with all the answers couldn't pour piss out of a rubber boot if they read the instructions printed on the sole. They remind me of Gene; he's got all the answers too. But still, quite a few of them are what you'd call witty. Which Gene is in his own way too.

But most times, as I say, I'd doze off. Let me give you a sample evening. About twelve-thirty the lights of his half-ton would come shooting into the living-room, bouncing off the walls, scooting along the ceiling when he wheeled into the driveway like a madman. It was the lights flashing in my eyes that woke me up most nights, and if that didn't do it there was always his grand entrance. When the old man comes into the house, from the sound of it you'd think he never heard of door knobs. I swear sometimes I'm sure he's taking a battering-ram to the back door. Then he thunks his lunch bucket on the kitchen counter and bowls his hard hat into the landing. This is because he always comes home from work mad. Never once in his life has a shift ever gone right for that man. Never. They could pack his pockets with diamonds and send him home two hours early and he'd still bitch. So every night was pretty much the same. He had a mad on. Like in my sample night.

He flicked on the living-room light and tramped over to his orange recliner with the bottle of Boh. "If you want to ruin your eyes, do it on school-books, not on watching TV in the goddamn dark. It's up to somebody in this outfit to make something of themselves."

"I was sleeping."

"You ought to sleep in bed." *Keerash*! He weighs two hundred and forty-four pounds and he never sits down in a chair. He falls into it. "Who's that? Gary Cooper?" he asked. He figures any movie star on the late show taller than Mickey Rooney is Cooper. He doesn't half believe you when you tell him they aren't.

"Cary Grant."

"What?"

"Cary Grant. Not Gary Cooper. Cary Grant."

"Oh." There he sat in his recliner, big meaty shoulders sagging, belly propped up on his belt buckle like a pregnant pup's. Eyes red and sore, hair all mussed up, the top of his beer bottle peeking out of his fist like a little brown nipple. He has cuts all over those hands of his, barked knuckles and raspberries that never heal because the salt in the potash ore keeps them open, eats right down to the bone sometimes.

"How'd it go tonight?"

"Usual shit. We had a breakdown." He paused. "Where's your brother? In bed?"

"Out."

"Out? Out? *Out*? What kind of goddamn answer is that? Out where?"

I shrugged.

"Has he got his homework done?" That's the kind of question I get asked. *Has your brother got his homework done?*

"How the hell would I know?"

"I don't know why you don't help him with his school-work," the old man said, peeved as usual.

"You mean do it for him."

"Did I say that? Huh? I said help him. Didn't I say that?" he griped, getting his shit in a knot.

He thinks it's that easy. Just screw the top off old Gene and pour it in. No problem. Like an oil change.

"He's got to be around to help," I said.

That reminded him. He jumped out of the chair and gawked up and down the deserted street. "It's almost one o'clock. On a school night. I'll kick his ass." He sat down and watched the screen for a while and sucked on his barley sandwich.

Finally, he made a stab at acting civilized. "So how's baseball going?"

"What?"

"Baseball. For chrissakes clean out your ears. How's it going?"

"I quit last year. Remember?"

"Oh yeah." He didn't say nothing at first. Then he said: "You shouldn't have. You wasn't a bad catcher."

"The worst. No bat and no arm—just a flipper. They stole me blind."

"But you had the head," said the old man. And the way he said it made him sound like he was pissed at me for mean-mouthing myself. That surprised me. I felt kind of good about that. "You had the head," he repeated, shaking his own. "I never told you but Al came up to me at work and said you were smart back there behind the plate. He said he wished Gene had your head."

I can't say that surprised me. Gene is one of those cases of a million-dollar body carrying around a ten-cent head. He's a natural. Flop out his glove and, smack, the ball sticks. He's like Mickey Mantle. You know those stop-action photos where they caught Mickey with his eyes glommed onto the bat, watching the ball jump off the lumber? That's Gene. And he runs like a Negro, steals bases like Maury Wills for chrissake.

But stupid and conceited? You wouldn't believe the half of it. Give him the sign to bunt to move a runner and he acts as if you're asking him to bare his ass in public. Not him. He's a big shot. He swings for the fence. Nothing less. And old Gene is always in the game, if you know what I mean? I don't know what happens when he gets on base, maybe he starts thinking of the hair pie in the stands admiring him or something, but he always dozes off at the wheel. Once he even started to comb his hair at first base. Here it is, a 3 and 2 count with two men out, and my brother forgets to run on the pitch because he's combing his hair. I could have died. Really I could have. The guy is such an embarrassment sometimes.

"He can have my head," I said to Pop. "If I get his girls."

That made the old man wince. He's sure that Gene is going to knock up one of those seat-covers he takes out and make him a premature grandpa.

"You pay attention to school. There's plenty of time later for girls." And up he jumped again and stuck his nose against the window looking for Gene again. Mom has to wash the picture window once a week; he spots it all up with nose grease looking for Gene.

"I don't know why your mother lets him out of the house," he said. "Doesn't she have any control over that boy?"

That's what he does, blames everybody but himself. Oh hell, maybe nobody's to blame. Maybe Gene is just Gene, and there's nothing to be done about it.

"I don't know what she's supposed to do. You couldn't keep him in if you parked a tank in the driveway and strung barbed wire around the lot."

Of course that was the wrong thing to say. I usually say it.

"Go to bed!" he yelled at me. "You're no better than your brother. I don't see you in bed neither. What'd I do, raise alley cats or kids? Why can't you two keep hours like human beings!"

And then the door banged and we knew the happy wanderer was home. Gene makes almost as much noise as the old man does when he comes in. It's beneath his dignity to sneak in like me.

Dad hoisted himself out of the chair and steamed off for the kitchen. He can move pretty quick for a big guy when he wants to. Me, I was in hot pursuit. I don't like to miss much.

Old Gene was hammered, and grinning from ass-hole to ear-lobes. The boy's got a great smile. Even when he grins at old ladies my mother's age you can tell they like it.

"Come here and blow in my face," said my father.

"Go on with you," said Gene. All of a sudden the smile was gone and he was irritated. He pushed past Pop, took the milk out of the fridge and started to drink out of the container.

"Use a glass."

Gene burped. He's a slob.

"You stink of beer," said the old man. "Who buys beer for a kid your age?"

"I ain't drunk," said Gene.

"Not much. Your eyes look like two piss-holes in the snow."

"Sure, sure," said Gene. He lounged, he swivelled over to me and lifted my Players out of my shirt pocket. "I'll pay you back tomorrow," he said, taking out a smoke. I heard that one before.

"I don't want to lose my temper," said Dad, being patient with him as usual, "so don't push your luck, sunshine." The two of them eyeballed it, hard. Finally Gene backed down, looked away and fiddled with his matches. "I don't ride that son of a bitch of a cage up and down for my health. I do it for you two," Dad said. "But I swear to God, Gene, if you blow this year of school there'll be a pair of new work boots for you on the back step, come July 1. Both of you know my rules. Go to school, work, or pack up. I'm not having bums put their feet under my table."

"I ain't scared of work," said Gene. "Anyways, school's a pain in the ass."

"Well, you climb in the cage at midnight with three hours of sleep and see if *that* ain't a pain in the ass. Out there nobody says, please do this, please do that. It ain't school out there, it's life."

"Ah, I wouldn't go to the mine. The mine sucks."

"Just what the hell do you think you'd do?"

"He'd open up shop as a brain surgeon," I said. Of course, Gene took a slap at me and grabbed at my shirt. He's a tough guy. He wasn't really mad, but he likes to prevent uppityness.

"You go to bed!" the old man hollered. "You ain't helping matters!"

So off I went. I could hear them wrangling away even after I closed my door. You'd wonder how my mother does it, but she sleeps through it all. I think she's just so goddamn tired of the three of us she's gone permanently deaf to the sound of our voices. She just don't hear us any more.

The last thing I heard before I dropped off was Pop saying: "I've rode that cage all my life, and take it from me, there wasn't a day I didn't wish I'd gone to school and could sit in an office in a clean white shirt." Sometimes he can't remember what he wants to be, a farmer or a pencil-pusher.

The cage. He's always going on about the cage. It's what the men at the mine call the elevator car they ride down the shaft. They call it that because it's all heavy reinforced-steel mesh. The old man has this cage on the brain. Ever since we were little kids he's been threatening us with it. *Make something of yourself,* he'd warn us, *or you'll end up like your old man, a monkey in the cage!* Or: *What's this, Gene? Failed arithmetic? Just remember, dunces don't end up in the corner. Hell no, they end up in the cage! Look at me!* My old man really hates that cage and the mine. He figures it's the worst thing you can threaten anybody with.

I was in the cage, once. A few years ago, when I was fourteen, the company decided they'd open the mine up for tours. It was likely the brainstorm of some public relations tit sitting in head office in Chicago. In my book it was kind of like taking people into the slaughterhouse to prove you're kind to the cows. Anyway, Pop offered to take us on one of his days off. As usual, he was about four years behind schedule. When we were maybe eleven we might have been nuts about the idea, but just then it didn't thrill us too badly. Gene, who is about as subtle as a bag of hammers, said flat out he wasn't interested. I could see right away the old man was hurt by that. It isn't often he plays the buddy to his boys, and he probably had the idea he could whiz us about the machines and stuff. Impress the hell out of us. So it was up to me to slobber and grin like some kind of half-wit over the idea, to perk him up, see? Everybody suffers when the old man gets into one of his moods.

Of course, like always when I get sucked into this good-turn business, I shaft myself. I'd sort of forgotten how much I don't like tight places and being closed in. When we were younger, Gene used to make me go berserk by holding me under the covers, or stuffing a pillow in my face, or locking me in the garage whenever he got the chance. The jerk.

To start with, they packed us in the cage with twelve other people, which didn't help matters any. Right away my chest got tight and I felt like I couldn't breathe. Then the old cables started groaning and grinding and this fine red dust like chili powder sprinkled down through the mesh and dusted our hard hats with the word GUEST stencilled on them. It was rust. Kind of makes you think.

"Here we go," said Pop.

We went. It was like all of a sudden the floor fell away from under my boots. That cage just dropped in the shaft like a stone down a well. It rattled and creaked and banged. The bare light bulb in the roof started to flicker, and all the faces around me started to dance and shake up and down in the dark. A wind twisted up my pant-legs and I could hear the cables squeak and squeal. It made me think of big fat fucking rats.

"She needs new brake shoes," said this guy beside me and he laughed. He couldn't fool me. He was scared shitless too, in his own way.

"It's not the fall that kills you," his neighbour replied. "It's the sudden stop." There's a couple of horses' patoots in every crowd.

We seemed to drop forever. Everybody got quieter and quieter. They even stopped shuffling and coughing. Down. Down. Down. Then the cage started to slow, I felt a pressure build in my knees and my crotch and my ears. The wire box started to shiver and clatter and shake. *Bang!* We stopped. The cage bobbed a little up and down like a yo-yo on the end of a string. Not much though, just enough to make you queasy.

"Last stop, Hooterville!' said the guide, who thought he was funny, and threw back the door. Straight ahead I could see a low-roofed big open space with tunnels running from it into the ore. Every once in a while I could see the light from a miner's helmet jump around in the blackness of one of those tunnels like a firefly flitting in the night.

First thing I thought was: *What if I get lost? What if I lose the group? There's miles and miles and miles of tunnel under here.* I caught a whiff of the air. It didn't smell like air up top. It smelled used. You could taste the salt. *I'm suffocating,* I thought. *I can't breathe this shit.*

I hadn't much liked the cage but this was worse. When I was in the shaft I knew there was a patch of sky over my head with a few stars in it and clouds and stuff. But all of a sudden I realized how deep we were. How we were sort of like worms crawling in the guts of some dead animal. Over us were billions, no, trillions, of tons of rock and dirt and mud pressing down. I could imagine it caving in and falling on me, crushing my chest, squeezing the air out slowly, dust fine as flour trickling into my eyes and nostrils, or mud plugging my mouth so I couldn't even scream. And then just lying there in the dark, my legs and arms pinned so I couldn't even twitch them. For a long time maybe. Crazy, lunatic stuff was what I started to think right on the spot.

My old man gave me a nudge to get out. We were the last.

"No," I said quickly and hooked my fingers in the mesh.

"We get out here," said the old man. He hadn't caught on yet.

"No, I can't," I whispered. He must have read the look on my face then. I think he knew he couldn't have pried me off that mesh with a gooseneck and winch.

Fred, the cage operator, lifted his eyebrows at Pop. "What's up, Jack?"

"The kid's sick," said Pop. "We'll take her up. He don't feel right." My old man was awful embarrassed.

Fred said, "I wondered when it'd happen. Taking kids and women down the hole."

"Shut your own goddamn hole," said the old man. "He's got the flu. He was up all last night."

Fred looked what you'd call sceptical.

"Last time I take you any place nice," the old man said under his breath.

■ ■ ■

The last day of school has always got to be some big deal. By nine o'clock all the dipsticks are roaring their cars up and down main street with their goofy broads hanging out their windows yelling, and trying to impress on one another how drunk they are.

Dad sent me to look for Gene because he didn't come home for supper at six. I found him in the poolroom playing dollar-a-hand poker pool.

"Hey, little brother," he waved to me from across the smoky poolroom, "come on here and I'll let you hold my cards!" I went over. He grinned to the goofs he was playing with. "You watch out now, boys," he said, "my little brother always brings me luck. Not that I need it," he explained to me, winking.

Yeah, I always brought him luck. *I* kept track of the game. *I* figured out what order to take the balls down. *I* reminded him not to put somebody else out and to play the next guy safe instead of slamming off some cornball shot. When *I* did all that Gene won—because I brought him luck. Yeah.

Gene handed me his cards. "You wouldn't believe these two," he said to me out of the corner of his mouth, "genuine plough jockeys. These boys couldn't find their ass in the dark with both hands. I'm fifteen dollars to the good."

I admit they didn't look too swift. The biggest one, who was *big*, was wearing an out-of-town team jacket, a Massey-Ferguson cap, and shit-kicker wellingtons. He was maybe twenty-one, but his skin hadn't cleared up yet by no means. His pan looked like all-dressed pizza, heavy on the cheese. His friend was a dinky little guy with his hair designed into a duck's ass. The kind of guy who hates the Beatles. About two feet of a dirty comb was sticking out of his ass pocket.

Gene broke the rack and the nine went down. His shot.

"Dad's looking for you. He wants to know if you passed," I said.

"You could've told him."

"Well, I didn't."

"Lemme see the cards." I showed him. He had a pair of treys, a six, a seven, and a lady. Right away he stopped to pocket the three. I got a teacher who always talks about thought processes. Gene doesn't have them.

"Look at the table," I said. "Six first and you can come around up her." I pointed.

"No coaching," said Pizza Face. I could see this one was a poor loser.

Gene shifted his stance and potted the six.

"What now?" he asked.

"The queen, and don't forget to put pants on her." I paused. "Pop figured you were going to make it. He really did, Gene."

"So tough titty. I didn't. Who the hell cares? He had your suck card to slobber over, didn't he?" He drilled the lady in the side pocket. No backspin. He'd hooked himself on the three. "Fuck."

"The old man is on graveyard shift. You better go home and face the music before he goes to work. It'll be worse in the morning when he needs sleep," I warned him.

"Screw him."

I could see Gene eyeballing the four. He didn't have any four in his hand, so I called him over and showed him his cards. "You can't shoot the four. It's not in your hand."

"Just watch me." He winked. "I've been doing it all night. It's all pitch and no catch with these prizes." Gene strolled back to the table and coolly stroked down the four. He had shape for the three which slid in the top pocket like shit through a goose. He cashed in on the seven. "That's it, boys," he said. "That's all she wrote."

I was real nervous. I tried to bury the hand in the deck but the guy with the runny face stopped me. He was getting tired of losing, I guess. Gene doesn't even cheat smart. You got to let them win once in a while.

"Gimme them cards," he said. He started counting the cards off against the balls, flipping down the boards on the felt. "Three." He nodded. "Six, seven, queen. I guess you got them all," he said slowly, with a look on his face like he was pissing ground glass.

That's when Duck Ass chirped up. "Hey, Marvin," he said, "that guy shot the four. He shot the four."

"Nah," said Gene.

Marvin studied on this for a second, walked over to the table and pulled the four ball out of the pocket. Just like little Jack Horner lifting the plum out of the pie. "Yeah," he said. "You shot the four."

"Jeez," said Gene, "I guess I did. Honest mistake. Look, here's a dollar for each of you." He took two bills out of his shirt pocket. "You got to pay for your mistakes is what I was always taught."

"I bet you he's been cheating all along," said Duck Ass.

"My brother don't cheat," I said.

"I want all my money back," said Marvin. Quite loud. Loud enough that some heads turned and a couple of tables stopped playing. There was what you would call a big peanut gallery, it being the beginning of vacation and the place full of junior high kids and stags.

"You can kiss my ass, bozo," said Gene. "Like my brother here said, I never cheated nobody in my life."

"You give us our money back," threatened Marvin, "or I'll pull your head off, you skinny little prick."

Guys were starting to drift towards us, curious. The manager, Fat Bert, was easing his guts out from behind the cash register.

"Give them their money, Gene," I said, "and let's get out of here."

"No."

Well, that was that. You can't change his mind. I took a look at old Marvin. As I said before, Marvin was *big*. But what was worse was that he had this real determined look people who aren't too bright get when they finally dib on to the fact they've been hosed and somebody has been laughing up his sleeve at them. They don't like it too hot, believe me.

"Step outside, shit-head," said Marvin.

"Fight," somebody said encouragingly. A real clump of ringsiders was starting to gather. "Fight." Bert came hustling up, bumping his way through the kids with his bay window. "Outside, you guys. I don't want nothing broke in here. Get out or I'll call the cops."

Believe me, was I tense. Real tense. I know Gene pretty well and I was sure that he had looked at old Marvin's muscles trying to bust out everywhere. Any second I figured he was going to even the odds by pasting old Marv in the puss with his pool cue, or at least sucker-punching him.

But Gene is full of surprises. All of a sudden he turned peacemaker. He laid down his pool cue (which I didn't figure was too wise) and said: "You want to fight over this?" He held up the four ball. "Over this? An honest mistake?"

"Sure I do," said Marvin. "You're fucking right I do, cheater."

"Cheater, cheater," said Duck Ass. I was looking him over real good because I figured if something started in there I'd get him to tangle with.

Gene shrugged and even kind of sighed, like the hero does in the movies when he has been forced into a corner and has to do something that is against his better nature. He tossed up the four ball once, looked at it, and then reached behind him and shoved it back into the pocket. "All right," he said, slouching a little and jamming his hands into his jacket pockets. "Let's go, sport."

That started the stampede. "Fight! Fight!" The younger kids, the ones thirteen and fourteen, were really excited; the mob kind of swept Marvin and Gene out the door, across the street and into the OK Economy parking lot where most beefs get settled. There's lots of dancing-room there. A nice big ring.

Marvin settled in real quick. He tugged the brim of his Massey-Ferguson special a couple of times, got his dukes up and started to hop around like he'd stepped right out of the pages of *Ring* magazine. He looked pretty stupid, especially when Gene just looked at him, and kept his hands rammed in his jacket pockets. Marvin kind of clomped from foot to foot for a bit and he said: "Get 'em up."

"You get first punch," said Gene.

"What?" said Marv. He was so surprised his yap fell open.

"If I hit you first," said Gene, "you'll charge me with assault. I know your kind."

Marvin stopped clomping. I suspect it took too much co-ordination for him to clomp and think at the same time. "Oh no," he said, "I ain't falling for that. If I hit *you* first, you'll charge *me* with assault." No flies on Marvin. "*You* get the first punch."

"Fight. Come on, fight," said some ass-hole, real disgusted with all the talk and no action.

"Oh no," said Gene. "I ain't hitting *you* first."

Marvin brought his hands down. "Come on, come on, let fly."

"You're sure?" asked Gene.

"Give her your best shot," said Marvin. "You couldn't hurt a fly, you scrawny shit. Quit stalling. Get this show on the road."

Gene uncorked on him. It looked like a real pansy punch. His right arm whipped out of his jacket pocket, stiff at the elbow like a girl's when she slaps. It didn't look like it had nothing behind it, sort of like Gene had smacked him kind of contemptuous in the mouth with the flat of his hand. That's how it looked. It *sounded* like he'd hit him in the mouth with a ball-peen hammer. Honest to God, you could hear the teeth crunch when they broke.

Big Marvin dropped on his knees like he'd been shot in the back of the neck. His hands flew up to his face and the blood just ran through his fingers and into his cuffs. It looked blue under the parking-lot lights. There was an awful lot of it.

"Get up, you dick licker," said Gene.

Marvin pushed off his knees with a crazy kind of grunt that might have been a sob. I couldn't tell. He came up under Gene's arms, swept him off his feet and dangled him in the air, crushing his ribs in a bear hug.

"Waauugh!" said Gene. I started looking around right smartly for something to hit the galoot with before he popped my brother like a pimple.

But then Gene lifted his fist high above Marvin's head and brought it down on his skull, hard as he could. It made a sound like he was banging coconuts together. Marvin sagged a little at the knees and staggered. *Chunk! Chunk!* Gene hit him two more times and Marvin toppled over backwards. My brother landed on top of him and right away started pasting him left and right. Everybody was screaming encouragement. There was no invitation to the dick licker to get up this time. Gene was still clobbering him when I saw the cherry popping on the cop car two blocks away. I dragged him off Marvin.

"Cops," I said, yanking at his sleeve. Gene was trying to get one last kick at Marvin. "Come on, fucker," he was yelling. "Fight now!"

"Jesus," I said, looking at Gene's jacket and shirt, "you stupid bugger, you're all over blood." It was smeared all over him. Marvin tried to get up. He only made it to his hands and knees. There he stayed, drooling blood and saliva on the asphalt. The crowd started to edge away as the cop car bounced up over the curb and gave a long, low whine out of its siren.

I took off my windbreaker and gave it to Gene. He pulled off his jacket and threw it down. "Get the fuck out of here," I said. "Beat it."

"I took the wheels off his little red wagon," said Gene. "It don't pull so good now." His hands were shaking and so was his voice. He hadn't had half enough yet. "I remember that other guy," he said. "Where's his friend?"

I gave him a shove. "Get going." Gene slid into the crowd that was slipping quickly away. Then I remembered his hockey jacket. It was wet with blood. It also had flashes with his name and number on it. It wouldn't take no Sherlock Holmes cop to figure out who'd beat on Marvin. I picked it up and hugged it to my belly. Right away I felt something hard in the pocket. Hard and round. I started to walk away. I heard a car door slam. I knew what was in that pocket. The controversial four ball old Gene had palmed when he pretended to put it back. He likes to win.

I must have been walking too fast or with a guilty hunch to my shoulders, because I heard the cop call, "Hey you, the kid with the hair." Me, I'm kind of a hippy for this place, I guess. Lots of people mention my hair.

I ran. I scooted round the corner of the supermarket and let that pool ball fly as hard as I could, way down the alley. I never rifled a shot like that in my life. If coach Al had seen me trigger that baby he'd have strapped me into a belly pad himself. Of course, a jacket don't fly for shit. The bull came storming around the corner just as I give it the heave-ho. I was kind of caught with shit on my face, if you know what I mean?

■ ■ ■

Now a guy with half a brain could have talked his way out of that without too much trouble. Even a cop understands how somebody would try to help his brother. They don't hold it too much against you. And I couldn't really protect Gene. That geek Marvin would have flapped his trap if I hadn't. And it wasn't as if I hadn't done old Gene *some* good. After all, they never found out about that pool ball. The judge would have pinned Gene's ears back for him if he'd known he was going around thwacking people with a hunk of shatter-proof plastic. So Gene came out smelling like a rose, same suspended sentence as me, and a reputation for having hands of stone.

But at a time like that you get the nuttiest ideas ever. I watched them load Marvin in a squad car to drive him to the hospital while I sat in the back seat of another. And I thought to myself: *I'll play along with this. Let the old man come down to the cop shop over me for once. Me he takes for granted. Let him worry about Billy for a change. It wouldn't hurt him.*

So I never said one word about not being the guy who bopped Marvin. It was kind of fun in a crazy way, making like a hard case. At the station I was real rude and lippy. Particularly to a sergeant who was a grade A dink if I ever saw one. It was only when they took my shoelaces and belt that I started to get nervous.

"Ain't you going to call my old man?" I asked.

The ass-hole sergeant gave me a real smile. "In the morning," he said. "All in good time."

"In the morning?" And then I said like a dope: "Where am I going to sleep?"

"Show young Mr. Simpson where he's going to sleep," said the sergeant. He smiled again. It looked like a ripple on a slop pail. The constable who he was ordering around like he was his own personal slave took me down into the basement of the station. Down there it smelled of stale piss and old puke. I kind of gagged. I got a weak stomach.

Boy, was I nervous. I saw where he was taking me. There were four cells. They weren't even made out of bars, just metal strips riveted into a cross hatch you couldn't stick your hand through. They were all empty.

"Your choice," said the corporal. He was real humorous too, like his boss.

"You don't have to put me in one of them, sir," I said. "I won't run away."

"That's what all the criminals say." He opened the door. "Entrezvous."

I was getting my old crazy feeling really bad. Really bad. I felt kind of dizzy. "I got this thing," I said, "about being locked up. It's torture."

"Get in."

"No—please," I said. "I'll sit upstairs. I won't bother anybody."

"You think you've got a choice? You don't have a choice. Move your ass."

I was getting ready to cry. I could feel it. I was going to bawl in front of a cop. "I didn't do it," I said. "I never beat him up. Swear to Jesus I didn't."

"I'm counting three," he said, "and then I'm applying the boots to your backside."

It all came out. Just like that. *"It was my fucking ass-hole brother, Gene!"* I screamed. The only thing I could think of was, if they put me in there I'll be off my head by morning. I really will. *"I didn't do nothing! I never do nothing! You can't put me in there for him!"*

■ ■ ■

They called my old man. I guess I gave a real convincing performance. Not that I'm proud of it. I actually got sick on the spot from nerves. I just couldn't hold it down.

Pop had to sign for me and promise to bring Gene down in the morning. It was about twelve-thirty when everything got cleared up. He'd missed his shift and his ride in the cage.

When we got in the car he didn't start it. We just sat there with the windows rolled down. It was a beautiful night and there were lots of stars swimming in the sky. This town is small enough that street-lights and neon don't interfere with the stars. It's the only thing I like about this place. There's plenty of sky and lots of air to breathe.

"Your brother wasn't enough," he said. "You I trusted."

"I only tried to help him."

"You goddamn snitch." He needed somebody to take it out on, so he belted me. Right on the snout with the back of his hand. It started to bleed. I didn't try to stop it. I just let it drip on those goddamn furry seat-covers that he thinks are the cat's ass. "They were going to put me in this place, this cage, for him, for that useless shit!" I yelled. I'd started to cry. "No more, Pop. He failed! He failed on top of it all! So is he going to work? You got the boots ready on the back step? Huh? Is he going down in the fucking cage?"

"Neither one of you is going down in the cage. Not him, not you," he said.

"Nah, I didn't think so," I said, finally wiping at my face with the back of my hand. "I didn't think so."

"I don't have to answer to you," he said. "You just can't get inside his head. You were always the smart one. I didn't have to worry about you. You always knew what to do. But Gene . . . " He pressed his forehead against the steering-wheel, hard. "Billy, I see him doing all sorts of stuff. Stuff you can't imagine. I see it until it makes me sick." He looked at me. His face was yellow under the street-light, yellow like a lemon. "I try so hard with him. But he's got no sense. He just does things. He could have killed that other boy. He wouldn't even think of that, you know." All of a sudden the old man's face got all crumpled and creased like paper when you ball it up. "What's going to happen to him?" he said, louder than he had to. "What's going to happen to Eugene?" It was sad. It really was.

I can never stay mad at my old man. Maybe because we're so much alike, even though he can't see it for looking the other way. Our minds work alike. I'm a chip off the old block. Don't ever doubt it.

"Nothing."

"Billy," he said, "you mean it?"

I knew what he was thinking. "Yes," I said. "I'll do my best."

KURT VONNEGUT

The writings of Kurt Vonnegut (b. 1922) are characterized by a Swiftian sense of despair at the extremes of human folly. His books are about the horrors of war, the dehumanization of modern men and women, the loss of humane values in a society dedicated to technological progress. Though these are now fashionable subjects, Vonnegut's insights derive from personal experience. After serving in the US infantry during World War II, and witnessing the fire-bombing of Dresden as a prisoner of war, he became a police reporter in Chicago; then he entered the field of public relations, working for the General Electric Company until 1950, when he devoted himself full time to writing. Such a background provided him with ample material for his satire.

Gifted with a Kafka-esque sense of the absurd, Vonnegut works through a mixture of fantasy and realism to depict the deep springs of irrationality that govern human conduct; and he shows how the intellectual genius of modern science has been perverted to base and violent ends by the moral stupidity of the masses and their leaders. A prominent feature of his work is his interest in science fiction, which provides him with images of an automated and impersonal universe, where the individual is of less and less significance. Vonnegut's first novel, *Player Piano* (1952), depicts a United States in which government is conducted by computer, and people are of value only as consumers; the futility of human endeavour is set in an even bleaker perspective in *The Sirens of Titan* (1959), which presents human history as subject to control by the inhabitants of a distant planet. Vonnegut's vision is not totally pessimistic; his stories often include at least one character who, aware of the surrounding madness, seeks to restore a measure of sanity; thus the brilliant professor in "Report on the Barnhouse Effect" (1950; *Welcome to the Monkey House,* 1968) and his protégé, the narrator, are determined to turn their amazing discovery to good uses, much to the chagrin of their fellow citizens. But in the novel *Slaughterhouse Five* (1969) Vonnegut is less hopeful, for in his treatment of the Dresden bombing, he suggests that individual effort is powerless to alleviate the misery and suffering of the human condition. The elements of fantasy and science fiction continue to appear in subsequent works like *Hocus Pocus* (1990) and *Timequake* (1997), alongside his satire of Western materialism and political corruption.

Report on the Barnhouse Effect

Let me begin by saying that I don't know any more about where Professor Arthur Barnhouse is hiding than anyone else does. Save for one short, enigmatic message left in my mail box on Christmas Eve, I have not heard from him since his disappearance a year and a half ago.

What's more, readers of this article will be disappointed if they expect to learn how *they* can bring about the so-called "Barnhouse

Effect." If I were able and willing to give away that secret, I would certainly be something more important than a psychology instructor.

I have been urged to write this report because I did research under the professor's direction and because I was the first to learn of his astonishing discovery. But while I was his student I was never entrusted with knowledge of how the mental forces could be released and directed. He was unwilling to trust anyone with that information.

I would like to point out that the term "Barnhouse Effect" is a creation of the popular press, and was never used by Professor Barnhouse. The name he chose for the phenomenon was *"dynamopsychism,"* or *force of the mind.*

I cannot believe that there is a civilized person yet to be convinced that such a force exists, what with its destructive effects on display in every national capital. I think humanity has always had an inkling that this sort of force does exist. It has been common knowledge that some people are luckier than others with inanimate objects like dice. What Professor Barnhouse did was to show that such "luck" was a measurable force, which in his case could be enormous.

By my calculations, the professor was about fifty-five times more powerful than a Nagasaki-type atomic bomb at the time he went into hiding. He was not bluffing when, on the eve of "Operation Brainstorm," he told General Honus Barker: "Sitting here at the dinner table, I'm pretty sure I can flatten anything on earth—from Joe Louis to the Great Wall of China."

There is an understandable tendency to look upon Professor Barnhouse as a supernatural visitation. The First Church of Barnhouse in Los Angeles has a congregation numbering in the thousands. He is godlike in neither appearance nor intellect. The man who disarms the world is single, shorter than the average American male, stout, and averse to exercise. His IQ is 143, which is good but certainly not sensational. He is quite mortal, about to celebrate his fortieth birthday, and in good health. If he is alone now, the isolation won't bother him too much. He was quiet and shy when I knew him, and seemed to find more companionship in books and music than in his associations at the college.

Neither he nor his powers fall outside the sphere of Nature. His dynamopsychic radiations are subject to many known physical laws that apply in the field of radio. Hardly a person has not now heard the snarl of "Barnhouse static" on his home receiver. Contrary to what one might expect, the radiations are affected by sunspots and variations in the ionosphere.

However, his radiations differ from ordinary broadcast waves in several important ways. Their total energy can be brought to bear on any single point the professor chooses, and that energy is undiminished by distance. As a weapon, then, dynamopsychism has an impressive advantage over bacteria and atomic bombs, beyond the fact that it costs nothing to use: it enables the professor to single out critical individuals and objects instead of slaughtering whole populations in the process of maintaining international equilibrium.

As General Honus Barker told the House Military Affairs Committee: "Until someone finds Barnhouse, there is no defense against the Barnhouse Effect." Efforts to "jam" or block the radiations have failed. Premier Slezak could have saved himself the fantastic expense of his "Barnhouseproof" shelter. Despite the shelter's twelve-foot-thick lead armor, the premier has been floored twice while in it.

There is talk of screening the population for men potentially as powerful dynamopsychically as the professor. Senator Warren Foust demanded funds for this purpose last month, with the passionate declaration: "He who rules the Barnhouse Effect rules the world!" Commissar Kropotnik said much the same thing, so another costly armaments race, with a new twist, has begun.

This race at least has its comical aspects. The world's best gamblers are being coddled by governments like so many nuclear physicists. There may be several hundred persons with dynamopsychic talent on earth, myself included, but, without knowledge of the professor's technique, they can never be anything but dice-table despots. With the secret, it would probably take them ten years to become dangerous weapons. It took the professor that long. He who rules the Barnhouse Effect is Barnhouse and will be for some time.

Popularly, the "Age of Barnhouse" is said to have begun a year and a half ago, on the day of Operation Brainstorm. That was when dynamopsychism became significant politically. Actually, the phenomenon was discovered in May, 1942, shortly after the professor turned down a direct commission in the Army and enlisted as an artillery private. Like X-rays and vulcanized rubber, dynamopsychism was discovered by accident.

■ ■ ■

From time to time Private Barnhouse was invited to take part in games of chance by his barrack mates. He knew nothing about the games, and usually begged off. But one evening, out of social grace, he agreed to shoot craps. It was a terrible or wonderful thing that he played, depending upon whether or not you like the world as it now is.

"Shoot sevens, Pop," someone said.

So "Pop" shot sevens—ten in a row to bankrupt the barracks. He retired to his bunk and, as a mathematical exercise, calculated the odds against his feat on the back of a laundry slip. His chances of doing it, he found, were one in almost ten million! Bewildered, he borrowed a pair of dice from the man in the bunk next to his. He tried to roll sevens again, but got only the usual assortment of numbers. He lay back for a moment, then resumed his toying with the dice. He rolled ten more sevens in a row.

He might have dismissed the phenomenon with a low whistle. But the professor instead mulled over the circumstances surrounding his two lucky streaks. There was one single factor in common: on both occasions, *the same thought train had flashed through his mind just before he threw the dice.* It was that thought train which aligned the professor's brain cells into what has since become the most powerful weapon on earth.

■ ■ ■

The soldier in the next bunk gave dynamopsychism its first token of respect. In an understatement certain to bring wry smiles to the faces of the world's dejected demagogues, the soldier said, "You're hotter'n a two-dollar pistol, Pop." Professor Barnhouse was all of that. The dice that did his bidding weighed but a few grams, so the forces involved were minute; but the unmistakable fact that there were such forces was earth-shaking.

Professional caution kept him from revealing his discovery immediately. He wanted more facts and a body of theory to go with them. Later, when the atomic bomb was dropped on Hiroshima, it was fear that made him hold his peace. At no time were his experiments, as Premier Slezak called them, "a bourgeois plot to shackle the true democracies of the world." The professor didn't know where they were leading.

In time, he came to recognize another startling feature of dynamopsychism: *its strength increased with use.* Within six months, he was able to govern dice thrown by men the length of a barracks distant. By the time of his discharge in 1945, he could knock bricks loose from chimneys three miles away.

Charges that Professor Barnhouse could have won the last war in a minute, but did not care to do so, are perfectly senseless. When the war ended, he had the range and power of a 37-millimeter cannon, perhaps—certainly no more. His dynamopsychic powers graduated from the small arms class only after his discharge and return to Wyandotte College.

I enrolled in the Wyandotte Graduate School two years after the professor had rejoined the faculty. By chance, he was assigned as my thesis adviser. I was unhappy about the assignment, for the professor was, in the eyes of both colleagues and students, a somewhat ridiculous figure. He missed classes or had lapses of memory during lectures. When I arrived, in fact, his shortcomings had passed from the ridiculous to the intolerable.

"We're assigning you to Barnhouse as a sort of temporary thing," the dean of social studies told me. He looked apologetic and perplexed. "Brilliant man, Barnhouse, I guess. Difficult to know since his return, perhaps, but his work before the war brought a great deal of credit to our little school."

When I reported to the professor's laboratory for the first time, what I saw was more distressing than the gossip. Every surface in the room was covered with dust; books and apparatus had not been disturbed for months. The professor sat napping at his desk when I entered. The only signs of recent activity were three overflowing ash trays, a pair of scissors, and a morning paper with several items clipped from its front page.

As he raised his head to look at me, I saw that his eyes were clouded with fatigue. "Hi," he said, "just can't seem to get my sleeping done at night." He lighted a cigarette, his hands trembling slightly. "You the young man I'm supposed to help with a thesis?"

"Yes, sir," I said. In minutes he converted my misgivings to alarm.

"You an overseas veteran?" he asked.

"Yes, sir."

"Not much left over there, is there?" He frowned. "Enjoy the last war?"

"No, sir."

"Look like another war to you?"

"Kind of, sir."

"What can be done about it?"

I shrugged. "Looks pretty hopeless."

He peered at me intently. "Know anything about international law, the UN and all that?"

"Only what I pick up from the papers."

"Same here," he sighed. He showed me a fat scrapbook packed with newspaper clippings. "Never used to pay any attention to international politics. Now I study them the way I used to study rats in mazes. Everybody tells me the same thing—'Looks hopeless.' "

"Nothing short of a miracle—" I began.

"Believe in magic?" he asked sharply. The professor fished two dice from his vest pocket. "I will try to roll twos," he said. He rolled twos three times in a row. "One chance in about 47,000 of that happening. There's a miracle for you." He beamed for an instant, then brought the interview to an end, remarking that he had a class which had begun ten minutes ago.

He was not quick to take me into his confidence, and he said no more about his trick with the dice. I assumed they were loaded, and forgot about them. He set me the task of watching male rats cross electrified metal strips to get to food for female rats—an experiment that had been done to everyone's satisfaction in the 1930s. As though the pointlessness of my work were not bad enough, the professor annoyed me further with irrelevant questions. His favorites were: "Think we should have dropped the atomic bomb on Hiroshima?" and "Think every new piece of scientific information is a good thing for humanity?"

■ ■ ■

However, I did not feel put upon for long. "Give those poor animals a holiday," he said one morning, after I had been with him only a month. "I wish you'd help me look into a more interesting problem—namely, my sanity."

I returned the rats to their cages.

"What you must do is simple," he said, speaking softly. "Watch the inkwell on my desk. If you see nothing happen to it, say so, and I'll go quietly—relieved, I might add—to the nearest sanitarium."

I nodded uncertainly.

He locked the laboratory door and drew the blinds, so that we were in twilight for a moment. "I'm odd, I know," he said. "It's fear of myself that's made me odd."

"I've found you somewhat eccentric, perhaps, but certainly not—"

"If nothing happens to that inkwell, 'crazy as a bedbug' is the only description of me that will do," he interrupted, turning on the overhead lights. His eyes narrowed. "To give you an idea of how crazy, I'll tell you what's been running through my mind when I should have been sleeping. I think maybe I can save the world. I think maybe I can make every nation a *have* nation, and do away with war for good. I think maybe I can clear roads through jungles, irrigate deserts, build dams overnight."

"Yes, sir."

"Watch the inkwell!"

Dutifully and fearfully I watched. A high-pitched humming seemed to come from the inkwell; then it began to vibrate alarmingly, and finally to bound about the top of the desk, making two noisy circuits. It stopped, hummed again, glowed red, then popped in splinters with a blue-green flash.

Perhaps my hair stood on end. The professor laughed gently. "Magnets?" I managed to say at last.

"Wish to Heaven it were magnets," he murmured. It was then that he told me of dynamopsychism. He knew only that there was such a force; he could not explain it. "It's me and me alone—and it's awful."

"I'd say it was amazing and wonderful!" I cried.

"If all I could do was make inkwells dance, I'd be tickled silly with the whole business." He shrugged disconsolately. "But I'm no toy, my boy. If you like, we can drive around the neighborhood, and I'll show you what I mean." He told me about pulverized boulders, shattered oaks and abandoned farm buildings demolished within a fifty-mile radius of the campus. "Did every bit of it sitting right here, just thinking—not even thinking hard."

He scratched his head nervously. "I have never dared to concentrate as hard as I can for fear of the damage I might do. I'm to the point where a mere whim is a blockbuster." There was a depressing pause. "Up until a few days ago, I've thought it best to keep my secret for fear of what use it might be put to," he continued. "Now I realize that I haven't any more right to it than a man has a right to own an atomic bomb."

He fumbled through a heap of papers. "This says about all that needs to be said, I think." He handed me a draft of a letter to the Secretary of State.

Dear Sir:

I have discovered a new force which costs nothing to use, and which is probably more important than atomic energy. I should like to see it used most effectively in the cause of peace, and am, therefore, requesting your advice as to how this might best be done.

Yours truly,
A. Barnhouse.

"I have no idea what will happen next," said the professor.

■ ■ ■

There followed three months of perpetual nightmare, wherein the nation's political and military great came at all hours to watch the professor's trick with fascination.

We were quartered in an old mansion near Charlottesville, Virginia, to which we had been whisked five days after the letter was mailed.

Surrounded by barbed wire and twenty guards, we were labeled "Project Wishing Well," and were classified as Top Secret.

For companionship we had General Honus Barker and the State Department's William K. Cuthrell. For the professor's talk of peace-through-plenty they had indulgent smiles and much discourse on practical measures and realistic thinking. So treated, the professor, who had at first been almost meek, progressed in a matter of weeks towards stubbornness.

He had agreed to reveal the thought train by means of which he aligned his mind into a dynamopsychic transmitter. But, under Cuthrell's and Barker's nagging to do so, he began to hedge. At first he declared that the information could be passed on simply by word of mouth. Later he said that it would have to be written up in a long report. Finally, at dinner one night, just after General Barker had read the secret orders for Operation Brainstorm, the professor announced, "The report may take as long as five years to write." He looked fiercely at the general. "Maybe twenty."

The dismay occasioned by this flat announcement was offset somewhat by the exciting anticipation of Operation Brainstorm. The general was in a holiday mood. "The target ships are on their way to the Caroline Islands at this very moment," he declared ecstatically. "One hundred and twenty of them! At the same time, ten V-2s are being readied for firing in New Mexico, and fifty radio-controlled jet bombers are being equipped for a mock attack on the Aleutians. Just think of it!" Happily he reviewed his orders. "At exactly 1100 hours next Wednesday, I will give you the order to *concentrate*; and you, professor, will think as hard as you can about sinking the target ships, destroying the V-2s before they hit the ground, and knocking down the bombers before they reach the Aleutians! Think you can handle it?"

The professor turned gray and closed his eyes. "As I told you before, my friend, I don't know what I can do." He added bitterly, "As for this Operation Brainstorm, I was never consulted about it, and it strikes me as childish and insanely expensive."

General Barker bridled. "Sir," he said, "your field is psychology, and I wouldn't presume to give you advice in that field. Mine is national defense. I have had thirty years of experience and success, Professor, and I'll ask you not to criticize my judgment."

The professor appealed to Mr. Cuthrell. "Look," he pleaded, "isn't it war and military matters we're all trying to get rid of? Wouldn't it be a whole lot more significant and lots cheaper for me to try moving cloud masses into drought areas, and things like that? I admit I know next to nothing about international politics, but it seems reasonable to suppose that nobody would want to fight wars if there were enough of everything to go around. Mr. Cuthrell, I'd like to try running generators where there isn't any coal or water power, irrigating deserts, and so on. Why, you could figure out what each country needs to make the most of its resources, and I could give it to them without costing American taxpayers a penny."

"Eternal vigilance is the price of freedom," said the general heavily.

Mr. Cuthrell threw the general a look of mild distaste. "Unfortunately, the general is right in his own way," he said. "I wish to Heaven the world were ready for ideals like yours, but it simply isn't. We aren't surrounded by brothers, but by enemies. It isn't a lack of food or resources that has us on the brink of war—it's a struggle for power. Who's going to be in charge of the world, our kind of people or theirs?"

The professor nodded in reluctant agreement and arose from the table. "I beg your pardon, gentlemen. You are, after all, better qualified to judge what is best for the country. I'll do whatever you say." He turned to me. "Don't forget to wind the restricted clock and put the confidential cat out," he said gloomily, and ascended the stairs to his bedroom.

For reasons of national security, Operation Brainstorm was carried on without the knowledge of the American citizenry which was footing the bill. The observers, technicians and military men involved in the activity knew that a test was under way—a test of what, they had no idea. Only thirty-seven key men, myself included, knew what was afoot.

In Virginia, the day for Operation Brainstorm was unseasonably cool. Inside, a log fire crackled in the fireplace, and the flames were reflected in the polished metal cabinets that lined the living room. All that remained of the room's lovely old furniture was a Victorian love seat, set squarely in the center of the floor, facing three television receivers. One long bench had been brought in for the ten of us privileged to watch. The television screens showed, from left to right, the stretch of desert which was the rocket target, the guinea-pig fleet, and a section of the Aleutian sky through which the radio-controlled bomber formation would roar.

Ninety minutes before H hour the radios announced that the rockets were ready, that the observation ships had backed away to what was thought to be a safe distance, and that the bombers were on their way. The small Virginia audience lined up on the bench in order of rank, smoked a great deal, and said little. Professor Barnhouse was in his bedroom. General Barker bustled about the house like a woman preparing Thanksgiving dinner for twenty.

At ten minutes before H hour the general came in, shepherding the professor before him. The professor was comfortably attired in sneakers, gray flannels, a blue sweater and a white shirt open at the neck. The two of them sat side by side on the love seat. The general was rigid and perspiring; the professor was cheerful. He looked at each of the screens, lighted a cigarette and settled back, comfortable and cool.

"Bombers sighted!" cried the Aleutian observers.

"Rockets away!" barked the New Mexico radio operator.

All of us looked quickly at the big electric clock over the mantel, while the professor, a half-smile on his face, continued to watch the television sets. In hollow tones, the general counted away the seconds remaining. "Five . . . four . . . three . . . two . . . one . . . *Concentrate*!"

Professor Barnhouse closed his eyes, pursed his lips, and stroked his temples. He held the position for a minute. The television images were scrambled, and the radio signals were drowned in the din of Barnhouse static. The professor sighed, opened his eyes and smiled confidently.

"Did you give it everything you had?" asked the general dubiously.

"I was wide open," the professor replied.

The television images pulled themselves together, and mingled cries of amazement came over the radios tuned to the observers. The Aleutian sky was streaked with the smoke trails of bombers screaming down in flames. Simultaneously, there appeared high over the rocket target a cluster of white puffs, followed by faint thunder.

General Barker shook his head happily. "By George!" he crowed. "Well, sir, by George, by George, by George!"

"Look!" shouted the admiral seated next to me. "The fleet—it wasn't touched?"

"The guns seem to be drooping," said Mr. Cuthrell.

We left the bench and clustered about the television sets to examine the damage more closely. What Mr. Cuthrell had said was true. The ships' guns curved downward, their muzzles resting on the steel decks. We in Virginia were making such a hullabaloo that it was impossible to hear the radio reports. We were so engrossed, in fact, that we didn't miss the professor until two short snarls of Barnhouse static shocked us into sudden silence. The radios went dead.

We looked around apprehensively. The professor was gone. A harassed guard threw open the front door from the outside to yell that the professor had escaped. He brandished his pistol in the direction of the gates, which hung open, limp and twisted. In the distance, a speeding government station wagon topped a ridge and dropped from sight into the valley beyond. The air was filled with choking smoke, for every vehicle on the grounds was ablaze. Pursuit was impossible.

"What in God's name got into him?" bellowed the general.

Mr. Cuthrell, who had rushed out onto the front porch, now slouched back into the room, reading a penciled note as he came. He thrust the note into my hands. "The good man left this billet-doux under the door knocker. Perhaps our young friend here will be kind enough to read it to you gentlemen, while I take a restful walk through the woods."

> *"Gentlemen,"* I read aloud, *"As the first superweapon with a conscience, I am removing from your national defence stockpile. Setting a new precedent in the behavior of ordnance, I have humane reasons for going off. A. Barnhouse."*

■ ■ ■

Since that day, of course, the professor has been systematically destroying the world's armaments, until there is now little with which to equip an army other than rocks and sharp sticks. His activities haven't exactly resulted in peace, but have, rather, precipitated a bloodless and entertaining sort of war that might be called the "War of the Tattletales." Every nation is flooded with enemy agents whose sole mission is to locate military equipment, which is promptly wrecked when it is brought to the professor's attention in the press.

Just as every day brings news of more armaments pulverized by dynamopsychism, so has it brought rumors of the professor's whereabouts. During the last week alone, three publications carried articles proving variously that he was hiding in an Inca ruin in the Andes, in the sewers of Paris, and in the unexplored lower chambers of Carlsbad Caverns. Knowing the man, I am inclined to regard such hiding places as unnecessarily romantic and uncomfortable. While there are numerous persons eager to kill him, there must be millions who would care for him and hide him. I like to think that he is in the home of such a person.

One thing is certain: at this writing, Professor Barnhouse is not dead. Barnhouse static jammed broadcasts not ten minutes ago. In the eighteen months since his disappearance, he has been reported dead some half-dozen times. Each report has stemmed from the death of an unidentified man resembling the professor, during a period free of the static. The first three reports were followed at once by renewed talk of rearmament and recourse to war. The saber rattlers have learned how imprudent premature celebrations of the professor's demise can be.

Many a stouthearted patriot has found himself prone in the tangled bunting and timbers of a smashed reviewing stand, seconds after having announced that the archtyranny of Barnhouse was at an end.

But those who would make war if they could, in every country in the world, wait in sullen silence for what must come—the passing of Professor Barnhouse.

■ ■ ■

To ask how much longer the professor will live is to ask how much longer we must wait for the blessings of another war. He is of short-lived stock: his mother lived to be fifty-three, his father to be forty-nine; and the life-spans of his grandparents on both sides were of the same order. He might be expected to live, then, for perhaps fifteen years more, if he can remain hidden from his enemies. When one considers the number and vigor of these enemies, however, fifteen years seems an extraordinary length of time, which might better be revised to fifteen days, hours or minutes.

The professor knows that he cannot live much longer. I say this because of the message left in my mailbox on Christmas Eve. Unsigned, typewritten on a soiled scrap of paper, the note consisted of ten sentences. The first nine of these, each a bewildering tangle of psychological jargon and references to obscure texts, made no sense to me at first reading. The tenth, unlike the rest, was simply constructed and contained no large words—but its irrational content made it the most puzzling and bizarre sentence of all. I nearly threw the note away, thinking it a colleague's warped notion of a practical joke. For some reason, though, I added it to the clutter on top of my desk, which included, among other mementos, the professor's dice.

It took me several weeks to realize that the message really meant something, that the first nine sentences, when unsnarled, could be taken as instructions. The tenth still told me nothing. It was only last night that I discovered how it fitted in with the rest. The sentence appeared in my thoughts last night, while I was toying absently with the professor's dice.

I promised to have this report on its way to the publishers today. In view of what has happened, I am obliged to break that promise, or release the report incomplete. The delay will not be a long one, for one of the few blessings accorded a bachelor like myself is the ability to move quickly from one abode to another, or from one way of life to another. What property I want to take with me can be packed in a few hours. Fortunately, I am not without substantial private means, which may take as long as a week to realize in liquid and anonymous form. When this is done, I shall mail the report.

I have just returned from a visit to my doctor, who tells me my health is excellent. I am young, and, with any luck at all, I shall live to a ripe old age indeed, for my family on both sides is noted for longevity.

Briefly, I propose to vanish.

Sooner or later, Professor Barnhouse must die. But long before then I shall be ready. So, to the saber rattlers of today—and even, I hope, of tomorrow—I say: Be advised. Barnhouse will die. But not the Barnhouse Effect.

Last night, I tried once more to follow the oblique instructions on the scrap of paper. I took the professor's dice, and then, with the last, nightmarish sentence flitting though my mind, I rolled fifty consecutive sevens.

Good-by.

ALICE WALKER

Alice Walker's parents were black sharecroppers in Georgia, a fact that has deeply influenced her life and her writing. Born in 1944, she attended Spelman College, Atlanta, and Sarah Lawrence College. She worked for the civil rights movement in Georgia and Mississippi, and in 1967 married a white civil rights lawyer (the marriage was dissolved in 1976). For a time she was employed by the New York City Welfare Department. In 1968 she became a writer-in-residence and a teacher of black studies at Jackson State College, and has subsequently taught at a number of universities across the United States. Her publications include several books of poetry, essays, and novels, including *The Third Life of Grange Copeland* (1970), *Meridian* (1976), *The Color Purple* (1982), winner of a Pulitzer Prize and an American Book Award, and *The Temple of My Familiar* (1989). *The Color Purple* was adapted to film in 1985, directed by Steven Spielberg. Walker's short stories have been gathered in *In Love and Trouble: Stories of Black Women* (1973) and *You Can't Keep a Good Woman Down* (1981). *Anything We Love Can Be Saved* (1997) collects some of what the author calls her "activist," "womanist" prose.

Walker writes from a background of racial, social, and sexual discrimination that has significantly shaped her career as an author. She is particularly concerned with the plight of the black woman in the United States, doubly oppressed by the sexism of her own race and the bigotry of white society. Walker's preoccupation with sexual politics has led some critics to accuse her of stereotyping male characters, but her work rises above simplistic denunciations of male chauvinism to plead for a fulfillment of human potential through a love and an understanding that cross sexual and racial boundaries. As a Southern writer, she has been compared to Faulkner in the evocative richness of her prose, and in her ability to dramatize the sensibility of a naive or uneducated protagonist. In Walker's hands, the ungrammatical syntax of black Americans becomes a powerful, sometimes poetic expression of strong feeling, evoking a history and tradition that are deeply embedded in American consciousness, though often ignored or misrepresented. The uneasy relationship between blacks and whites is subtly explored in "Nineteen Fifty-five" (*You Can't Keep a Good Woman Down*), in which a white rock-'n'-roll singer (clearly modelled on Elvis Presley) achieves fame through a song written by a black woman, but searches in vain for the joy in life that the woman has expressed through the song. It may be noted here that Presley's 1956 hit record "Hound Dog" was first recorded in 1953 by Willie Mae ("Big Mama") Thornton.

Nineteen Fifty-five

1955

The car is a brandnew red Thunderbird convertible, and it's passed the house more than once. It slows down real slow now, and stops at the curb. An older gentleman dressed like a Baptist deacon gets out on the side near the house, and a young fellow who looks about sixteen gets out on the driver's side. They are white, and I wonder what in the world they doing in this neighborhood.

Well, I say to J.T., put your shirt on, anyway, and let me clean these glasses offa the table.

We had been watching the ballgame on TV. I wasn't actually watching, I was sort of daydreaming, with my foots up in J.T.'s lap.

I seen 'em coming on up the walk, brisk, like they coming to sell something, and then they rung the bell, and J.T. declined to put on a shirt but instead disappeared into the bedroom where the other television is. I turned down the one in the living room; I figured I'd be rid of these two double quick and J.T. could come back out again.

Are you Gracie Mae Still? asked the old guy, when I opened the door and put my hand on the lock inside the screen.

And I don't need to buy a thing, said I.

What makes you think we're sellin'? he asks, in that hearty Southern way that makes my eyeballs ache.

Well, one way or another and they're inside the house and the first thing the young fellow does is raise the TV a couple of decibels. He's about five feet nine, sort of womanish looking, with real dark white skin and a red pouting mouth. His hair is black and curly and he looks like a Loosianna creole.

■ ■ ■

About one of your songs, says the deacon. He is maybe sixty, with white hair and beard, white silk shirt, black linen suit, black tie and black shoes. His cold grey eyes look like they're sweating.

One of my songs?

Traynor here just *loves* your songs. Don't you Traynor? He nudges Traynor with his elbow. Traynor blinks, says something I can't catch in a pitch I don't register.

The boy learned to sing and dance livin' round you people out in the country. Practically cut his teeth on you.

Traynor looks up at me and bites his thumbnail.

I laugh.

Well, one way or another they leave with my agreement that they can record one of my songs. The deacon writes me a check for five hundred dollars, the boy grunts his awareness of the transaction, and I am laughing all over myself by the time I rejoin J.T.

Just as I am snuggling down beside him though I hear the front door bell going off again.

Forgit his hat? asked J.T.

I hope not, I say.

The deacon stands there leaning on the door frame and once again I'm thinking of those sweaty-looking eyeballs of his. I wonder if sweat makes your eyeballs pink because his are sure pink. Pink and gray and it strikes me that nobody I'd care to know is behind them.

I forgot one little thing, he says pleasantly. I forgot to tell you Traynor and I would like to buy up all of those records you made of the song. I tell you we sure do love it.

Well, love it or not, I'm not so stupid as to let them do that without making 'em pay. So I says, Well, that's gonna cost you. Because, really, that song never did sell all that good, so I was glad they was going to buy it up. But on the other hand, them two listening to my song by themselves, and nobody else getting to hear me sing it, give me a pause.

Well, one way or another the deacon showed me where I would come out ahead on any deal he had proposed so far. Didn't I give you five hundred dollars? he asked. What white man—and don't even need to mentioned colored—would give you more? We buy up all your records of that particular song: first, you git royalties. Let me ask you, how much you sell that song for in the first place? Fifty dollars? A hundred, I say. And no royalties from it yet, right? Right. Well, when we buy up all of them records you gonna git royalties. And that's gonna make all them race record shops sit up and take notice of Gracie Mae Still. And they gonna push all them other records of yourn they got. And you no doubt will become one of the big name colored recording artists. And then we can offer you another five hundred dollars for letting us do all this for you. And by God you'll be sittin' pretty! You can go out and buy you the kind of outfit a star should have. Plenty sequins and yards of red satin.

I had done unlocked the screen when I saw I could get some more money out of him. Now I held it wide open while he squeezed through the opening between me and the door. He whipped out another piece of paper and I signed it.

He sort of trotted out to the car and slid in beside Traynor, whose head was back against the seat. They swung around in a u-turn in front of the house and then they were gone.

J.T. was putting his shirt on when I got back to the bedroom. Yankees beat the Orioles 10-6, he said. I believe I'll drive out to Paschal's pond and go fishing. Wanta go?

While I was putting on my pants J.T. was holding the two checks.

I'm real proud of a woman that can make cash money without leavin' home, he said. And I said *Umph*. Because we met on the road with me singing in first one little low-life jook after another, making ten dollars a night for myself if I was lucky, and sometimes bringin' home nothing but my life. And J.T. just loved them times. The way I was fast and flashy and always on the go from one town to another. He loved the way my singin' made the dirt farmers cry like babies and the womens shout Honey, hush! But that's mens. They loves any style to which you can get 'em accustomed.

1956

My little grandbaby called me one night on the phone: Little Mama, Little Mama, there's a white man on the television singing one of your songs! Turn on channel 5.

Lord, if it wasn't Traynor. Still looking half asleep from the neck up, but kind of awake in a nasty way from the waist down. He wasn't doing too bad with my song either, but it wasn't just the song the people in the audience was screeching and screaming over, it was that nasty little jerk he was doing from the waist down.

Well, Lord have mercy, I said, listening to him. If I'da closed my eyes, it could have been me. He had followed every turning of my voice, side streets, avenues, red lights, train crossings and all. It give me a chill.

Everywhere I went I heard Traynor singing my song, and all the little white girls just eating it up. I never had so many ponytails switched across my line of vision in my life. They was so *proud*. He was a *genius*.

Well, all that year I was trying to lose weight anyway and that and high blood pressure and sugar kept me pretty well occupied. Traynor had made a smash from a song of mine, I still had seven hundred dollars of the original one thousand dollars in the bank, and I felt if I could just bring my weight down, life would be sweet.

1957

I lost ten pounds in 1956. That's what I give myself for Christmas. And J.T. and me and the children and their friends and grandkids of all description and just finished dinner—over which I had put on nine and a half of my lost ten—when who should appear at the front door but Traynor. Little Mama, Little Mama! It's that white man who sings— — —. The children didn't call it my song anymore. Nobody did. It was funny how that happened. Traynor and the deacon had bought up all my records, true, but on his record he had put "written by Gracie Mae Still." But that was just another name on the label, like "produced by Apex Records."

On the TV he was inclined to dress like the deacon told him. But now he looked presentable.

Merry Christmas, said he.

And same to you, Son.

I don't know why I called him Son. Well, one way or another they're all our sons. The only requirement is that they be younger than us. But then again Traynor seemed to be aging by the minute.

You looks tired, I said. Come on in and have a glass of Christmas cheer.

J.T. ain't never in his life been able to act decent to a white man he wasn't working for, but he poured Traynor a glass of bourbon and water, then he took all the children and grandkids and friends and whatnot out to the den. After while I heard Traynor's voice singing the song, coming from the stereo console. It was just the kind of Christmas present my kids would consider cute.

I looked at Traynor, complicit. But he looked like it was the last thing in the world he wanted to hear. His head was pitched forward over his lap, his hands holding his glass and his elbows on his knees.

I done sung that song seem like a million times this year, he said. I sung it on the Grand Ole Opry, I sung it on the Ed Sullivan show. I sung it on Mike Douglas, I sung it at the Cotton Bowl, the Orange Bowl. I sung it at Festivals. I sung it at Fairs. I sung it overseas in Rome, Italy, and once in a submarine *underseas*. I've sung it and sung it, and I'm making forty thousand dollars a day offa it, and you know what, I don't have the faintest notion what that song means.

Whatchumean, what do it mean? It mean what it says. All I could think was: these suckers is making forty thousand a *day* offa my song and now they gonna come back and try to swindle me out of the original thousand.

It's just a song, I said. Cagey. When you fool around with a lot of no count mens you sing a bunch of 'em. I shrugged.

Oh, he said. Well. He started brightening up. I just come by to tell you I think you are a great singer.

He didn't blush, saying that. Just said it straight out.

And I brought you a little Christmas present too. Now you take this little box and you hold it until I drive off. Then you take it outside under that first streetlight back up the street aways in front of that green house. Then you open the box and see . . . Well, just *see*.

What had come over this boy, I wondered, holding the box. I looked out the window in time to see another white man come up and get in the car with him and then two more cars full of white mens start out behind him. They was all in long black cars that looked like a funeral procession.

Little Mama, Little Mama, what is it? One of my grandkids come running up and started pulling at the box. It was wrapped in gay Christmas paper—the thick, rich kind that it's hard to picture folks making just to throw away.

J.T. and the rest of the crowd followed me out the house, up the street to the streetlight and in front of the green house. Nothing was there but somebody's gold-grille white Cadillac. Brandnew and most distracting. We got to looking at it so till I almost forgot the little box in my hand. While the others were busy making 'miration I carefully took off the paper and ribbon and folded them up and put them in my pants pocket. What should I see but a pair of genuine solid gold caddy keys.

Dangling the keys in front of everybody's nose, I unlocked the caddy, motioned for J.T. to git in on the other side, and us didn't come back home for two days.

1960

Well, the boy was sure nuff famous by now. He was still a mite shy of twenty but already they was calling him the Emperor of Rock and Roll.

Then what should happen but the draft.

Well, says J.T. There goes all this Emperor of Rock and Roll business.

But even in the army the womens was on him like white on rice. We watched in on the News.

Dear Gracie Mae [he wrote from Germany],

How you? Fine I hope as this leaves me doing real well. Before I came in the army I was gaining a lot of weight and gitting jittery from making all them dumb movies. But now I exercise and eat right and get plenty of rest. I'm more awake than I been in ten years.

I wonder if you are writing any more songs?

Sincerely,
Traynor

I wrote him back:

Dear Son,

We is all fine in the Lord's good grace and hope this finds you the same. J.T. and me be out all times of the day and night in that car you give me—which you know you didn't have to do. Oh, and I do appreciate the mink and the new self-cleaning oven. But if you send anymore stuff to eat from Germany I'm going to have to open up a store in the neighborhood just to get rid of it. Really, we have more than enough of everything. The Lord is good to us and we don't know Want.

Glad to here you is well and gitting your right rest. There ain't nothing like exercising to help that along. J.T. and me work some part of every day that we don't go fishing in the garden.

Well, so long Soldier.

Sincerely,
Gracie Mae

He wrote:

Dear Gracie Mae,

I hope you and J.T. like that automatic power tiller I had one of the stores back home send you. I went through a mountain of catalogs looking for it—I wanted something that even a woman could use.

I've been thinking about writing some songs of my own but every time I finish one it don't seem to be about nothing I've actually lived myself. My agent keeps sending me other people's songs but they just sound mooney. I can hardly git through 'em without gagging.

Everybody still loves that song of yours. They ask me all the time what do I think it means, really. I mean, they want to know just what I want to know. Where out of your life did it come from?

Sincerely,
Traynor

1968

I didn't see the boy for seven years. No. Eight. Because just about everybody was dead when I saw him again. Malcolm X, King, the president and his brother, and even J.T. J.T. died of a head cold. It just settled in his head like a block of ice, he said, and nothing we did moved it until one day he just leaned out the bed and died.

His good friend Horace helped me put him away, and then about a year later Horace and me started going together. We was sitting out on the front porch swing one summer night, dusk-dark, and I saw this great procession of lights winding to a stop.

Holy Toledo! said Horace. (He's got a real sexy voice like Ray Charles.) Look *at* it. He meant the long line of flashy cars and the white men in white summer suits jumping out on the drivers' sides and standing at attention. With wings they could pass for angels, with hoods they could be the Klan.

Traynor comes waddling up the walk.

And suddenly I know what it is he could pass for. An Arab like the ones you see in storybooks. Plump and soft and with never a care about weight. Because with so much money, who cares? Traynor is almost dressed like someone from a storybook too. He has on, I swear, about ten necklaces. Two sets of bracelets on his arms, at least one ring on every finger, and some kind of shining buckles on his shoes, so that when he walks you get quite a few twinkling lights.

Gracie Mae, he says, coming up to give me a hug. J.T.

I explain that J.T. passed. That this is Horace.

Horace, he says, puzzled but polite, sort of rocking back on his heels, Horace.

That's it for Horace. He goes in the house and don't come back.

Looks like you and me is gained a few, I say.

He laughs. The first time I ever heard him laugh. It don't sound much like a laugh and I can't swear that it's better than no laugh a'tall.

He's gitting fat for sure, but he's still slim compared to me. I'll never see three hundreds pounds again and I've just about said (excuse me) fuck it. I got to thinking about it one day an' I thought: aside from the fact that they say it's unhealthy, my fat ain't never been no trouble. Mens always have loved me. My kids ain't never complained. Plus they's fat. And fat like I is I looks distinguished. You see me coming and know somebody's *there*.

Gracie Mae, he says. I've come with a personal invitation to you to my house tomorrow for dinner. He laughed. What did it sound like? I couldn't place it. See them men out there? he asked me. I'm sick and tired of eating with them. They don't never have nothing to talk about. That's why I eat so much. But if you come to dinner tomorrow we can talk about the old days. You can tell me about that farm I bought you.

I sold it, I said.

You did?

Yeah, I said, I did. Just cause I said I liked to exercise by working in a garden didn't mean I wanted five hundred acres! Anyhow, I'm a city girl now. Raised in the country it's true. Dirt poor—the whole bit—but that's all behind me now.

Oh well, he said, I didn't mean to offend you.

We sat for a few minutes listening to the crickets.

Then he said: You wrote that song while you was still on the farm, didn't you, or was it right after you left?

You had somebody spying on me? I asked.

You and Bessie Smith got into a fight over it once, he said.

You *is* been spying on me!

But I don't know what the fight was about, he said. Just like I don't know what happened to your second husband. Your first one died in the Texas electric chair. Did you know that? Your third one beat you up, stole your touring costumes and your car and retired with a chorine to Tuskegee. He laughed. He's still there.

I had been mad, but suddenly I calmed down. Traynor was talking very dreamily. It was dark but seems like I could tell his eyes weren't right. It was like some*thing* was sitting there talking to me but not necessarily with a person behind it.

You gave up on marrying and seem happier for it. He laughed again. I married but it never went like it was supposed to. I never could squeeze any of my own life either into it or out of it. It was like singing somebody else's record. I copied the way it was sposed to be *exactly* but I never had a clue what marriage meant.

I bought her a diamond ring big as your fist. I bought her clothes. I build her a mansion. But right away she didn't want the boys to stay there. Said they smoked up the bottom floor. Hell, there were *five* floors.

No need to grieve, I said. No need to. Plenty more where she come from.

He perked up. That's part of what that song means, ain't it? No need to grieve. Whatever it is, there's plenty more down the line.

I never really believed that way back when I wrote the song, I said. It was all bluffing then. The trick is to live long enough to put your young bluffs to use. Now if I was to sing that song today I'd tear it up. 'Cause I done lived long enough to know it's *true*. Them words could hold me up.

I ain't lived that long, he said.

Look like you on your way, I said. I didn't know why, but the boy seemed to need some encouraging. And I don't know, seem like one way or another you talk to rich white folks and you end up reassuring *them*. But what the hell, by now I feel something for the boy. I wouldn't be in his bed all alone in the middle of the night for nothing. Couldn't be nothing worse than being famous the world over for something you don't even understand. That's what I tried to tell Bessie. She wanted that same song. Overheard me practicing it one day, said, with her hands on her hips: Gracie Mae, I'ma sing your song tonight. I *likes* it.

Your lips be too swole to sing, I said. She was mean and she was strong, but I trounced her.

Ain't you famous enough with your own stuff? I said. Leave mine alone. Later on, she thanked me. By then she was Miss Bessie Smith to the World, and I was still Miss Gracie Mae Nobody from Notasulga.

■ ■ ■

The next day all these limousines arrived to pick me up. Five cars and twelve bodyguards. Horace picked that morning to start painting the kitchen.

Don't paint the kitchen, fool, I said. The only reason that dumb boy of ours is going to show me his mansion is because he intends to present us with a new house.

What you gonna do with it? he asked me, standing there in his shirt sleeves stirring the paint.

Sell it. Give it to the children. Live in it on weekends. It don't matter what I do. He sure don't care.

Horace just stood there shaking his head. Mama you sure looks *good*, he says. Wake me up when you git back.

Fool, I say, and pat my wig in front of the mirror.

■ ■ ■

The boy's house is something else. First you come to this mountain, and then you commence to drive and drive up this road that's lined with magnolias. Do magnolias grow on mountains? I was wondering. And you come to lakes and you come to ponds and you come to deer and you come up on some sheep. And I figure these two is sposed to represent England and Wales. Or something out of Europe. And you just keep on coming to stuff. And it's all pretty. Only the man driving my car don't look at nothing but the road. Fool. And then *finally*, after all this time, you begin to go up the driveway. And there's more magnolias—only they're not in such good shape. It's sort of cool up this high and I don't think they're gonna make it. And then I see this building that looks like if it had a name it would be The Tara Hotel. Columns and steps and outdoor chandeliers and rocking chairs. Rocking chairs? Well, and there's the boy on the steps dressed in a dark green satin jacket like you see folks wearing on TV late at night, and he looks sort of like a fat dracula with all that house rising behind him, and standing beside him there's this little white vision of loveliness that he introduces as his wife.

He's nervous when he introduces us and he says to her: This is Gracie Mae Still, I want you to know me. I mean . . . and she gives him a look that would fry meat.

Won't you come in Grace Mae, she says, and that's the last I see of her.

He fishes around for something to say or do and decides to escort me to the kitchen. We go through the entry and the parlor and the breakfast room and the dining room and the servants' passage and finally get there. The first thing I notice is that, altogether, there are five stoves. He looks about to introduce me to one.

Wait a minute, I say. Kitchens don't do nothing for me. Let's go sit on the front porch.

Well, we hike back and we sit in the rocking chairs rocking until dinner.

■ ■ ■

Gracie Mae, he says down the table, taking a piece of fried chicken from the woman standing over him, I got a little surprise for you.

It's a house, ain't it? I ask, spearing a chitlin.

You're getting *spoiled*, he says. And the way he says *spoiled* sounds funny. He slurs it. It sounds like his tongue is too thick for his mouth. Just that quick he's finished the chicken and is now eating chitlins *and* a pork chop. *Me* spoiled, I'm thinking.

I already got a house. Horace is right this minute painting the kitchen. I bought that house. My kids feel comfortable in that house.

But this one I bought you is just like mine. Only a little smaller.

I still don't need no house. And anyway who would clean it?

He looks surprised.

Really, I think some peoples advance *so* slowly.

I hadn't thought of that. But what the hell, I'll get you somebody to live in.

I don't want other folks living 'round me. Makes me nervous.

You *don't*? It *do*?

What I want to wake up and see folks I don't even know for?

He just sits there downtable staring at me. Some of that feeling is in the song, ain't it? Not the words, the *feeling*. What I want to wake up and see folks I don't even know for? But I see twenty folks a day I don't even know, including my wife.

This food wouldn't be bad to wake up to though, I said. The boy had found the genius of corn bread.

He looked at me real hard. He laughed. Short. They want what you got but they don't want you. They want what I got only it ain't mine. That's what makes 'em so hungry for me when I sing. They getting the flavor of something but they ain't getting the thing itself. They like a pack of hound dogs trying to gobble up a scent.

You talking 'bout your fans?

Right. Right. He says.

Don't worry 'bout your fans, I say. They don't know their asses from a hole in the ground. I doubt there's a honest one in the bunch.

That's the point. Dammit, that's the point! He hits the table with his fist. It's so solid it don't even quiver. You need a honest audience! You can't have folks that's just gonna lie right back to you.

Yeah, I say, it was small compared to yours, but I had one. It would have been worth my life to try to sing 'em somebody else's stuff that I didn't know nothing about.

He must have pressed a buzzer under the table. One of his flunkies zombies up.

Git Johnny Carson, he says.

On the phone? asks the zombie.

On the phone, says Traynor, what you think I mean, git him offa the front porch? Move your ass.

■ ■ ■

So two weeks later we's on the Johnny Carson show.

Traynor is all corseted down nice and looks a little bit fat but mostly good. And all the women that grew up on him and my song squeal and squeal. Traynor says: The lady who wrote my first hit record is here with us tonight, and she's agreed to sing it for all of us, just like she sung it forty-five years ago. Ladies and Gentlemen, the great Gracie Mae Still!

Well, I had tried to lose a couple of pounds my own self, but failing that I had me a very big dress made. So I sort of rolls over next to Traynor, who is dwarfted by me, so that when he puts his arm around back of me to try to hug me it looks funny to the audience and they laugh.

I can see this pisses him off. But I smile out there at 'em. Imagine squealing for twenty years and not knowing why you're squealing? No more sense of endings and beginnings than hogs.

It don't matter, Son, I say. Don't fret none over me.

I commence to sing. And I sound——wonderful. Being able to sing good ain't all about having a good singing voice a'tall. A good singing voice helps. But when you come up in the Hard Shell Baptist church like I did you understand early that the fellow that sings is the singer. Them that waits for programs and arrangements and letters from home is just good voices occupying body space.

So there I am singing my own song, my own way. And I give it all I got and enjoy every minute of it. When I finish Traynor is standing up clapping and clapping and beaming at first me and then the audience like I'm his mama for true. The audience claps politely for about two seconds.

Traynor looks disgusted.

He comes over and tries to hug me again. The audience laughs.

Johnny Carson looks at us like we both weird.

Traynor is mad as hell. He's supposed to sing something called a love ballad. But instead he takes the mike, turns to me and says: Now see if my imitation still holds up. He goes into the same song, *our* song, I think, looking at his flaky audience. And he sings it just the way he always did. My voice, my tone, my inflection, everything. But he forgets a couple of lines. Even before he's finished the matronly squeals begin.

He sits down next to me looking whipped.

It don't matter, Son, I say, patting his hand. You don't even know those people. Try to make the people you know happy.

Is that in the song? he asks.
Maybe. I say.

1977

For a few years I hear from him, then nothing. But trying to lose weight takes all the attention I got to spare. I finally faced up to the fact that my fat is the hurt I don't admit, not even to myself, and that I been trying to bury it from the day I was born. But also when you git real old, to tell the truth, it ain't as pleasant. It gits lumpy and slack. So one day I said to Horace, I'ma git this shit offa me.

And he fell in with the program like he always try to do and Lord such a procession of salads and cottage cheese and fruit juice!

One night I dreamed Traynor had split up with his fifteenth wife. He said: *You meet 'em for no reason. You date 'em for no reason. You marry 'em for no reason. I do it all but I swear it's just like somebody else doing it. I feel like I can't remember Life.*

The boy's in trouble, I said to Horace.

You've always said that, he said.

I have?

Yeah. You always said he looked asleep. You can't sleep through life if you wants to live it.

You not such a fool after all, I said, pushing myself up with my cane and hobbling over to where he was. Let me sit down on your lap, I said, while this salad I ate takes effect.

In the morning we heard Traynor was dead. Some said fat, some said heart, some said alcohol, some said drugs. One of the children called from Detroit. Them dumb fans of his on a crying rampage, she said. You just ought to turn on the TV.

But I didn't want to see 'em. They was crying and crying and didn't even know what they was crying for. One day this is going to be a pitiful country, I thought.

RUDY WIEBE

Born in 1934 to a Mennonite family in Fairholme, in the hilly woodlands of northern Saskatchewan, Rudy Wiebe notes in "Passage by Land" that landscape and cultural heritage have always been important to him. Though he did not learn English until he went to school, and did not see a mountain or a plain until he was almost thirteen, he later found language and landscape indissolubly wedded to each other. Encountering the world was a "wandering to find"—a sensibility reiterated in a 1994 book about the Arctic, *A Discovery of Strangers*; and paramount in his work is the sense of wandering that derives from his early experience, expressing itself as a quest for knowledge itself, about ways of knowing. In "Where Is the Voice Coming From?" for example, he does not portray a contrast so much as he enacts one, between the passivity of information and the activity of art.

His Mennonite background features significantly in two of his novels, *Peace Shall Destroy Many* (1964) and *The Blue Mountains of China* (1970); the latter, a modern epic, probes the idealistic impulses behind the sect, traces its spiritual and geographic journeys, and tries to come to terms with the power of the commitment that has impelled so many people to accept its invitation to individual action. His sympathy for human beings takes a different form in *First and Vital Candle* (1966), *The Temptations of Big Bear* (1973), about the Riel Rebellion, and "Where Is the Voice Coming From?" which became the title story of a collection that appeared in 1974. The Aboriginal peoples who appear in these works are admirably realized characters, and Wiebe has endeavoured with great sensitivity to cross the cultural barriers that lie between him and his subject. But he is acutely conscious of the difficulty of being anyone but oneself, of the limitations that one's perspective erects against complete understanding, and of the problems that face the artist and the historian when they try to convey their perceptions of truth or reality. "Where Is the Voice Coming From?" resulted, Wiebe writes, from personal encounters with museum displays and historical accounts of Indian and Royal Canadian Mounted Police history, and from reading in nineteenth-century newspapers and in volume 12 (*Reconsiderations*) of Arnold Toynbee's *A Study of History.* On top of all that is his overpowering urge to "make story," for, as he writes in his introduction to the anthology *The Story-Makers* (1970), a good story seduces "both teller and listener out of their world into its own," illuminating "the world in which teller and listener actually are" and often proving "the more pleasurable as the seduction becomes less immediate: story worth pondering is story doubly enjoyed."

Where Is the Voice Coming From?

The problem is to make the story.

A difficulty of this making may have been excellently stated by Teilhard de Chardin: "We are continually inclined to isolate ourselves from the things and events which surround us . . . as though we were spectators, not elements, in what goes on." Arnold Toynbee does venture, "For all that we know, Reality is the undifferentiated unity of the mystical experience," but that need not here be considered. This story ended long ago; it is one of finite acts, of orders, of elemental feelings and reactions, of obvious legal restrictions and requirements.

Presumably all the parts of the story are themselves available. A difficulty is that they are, as always, available only in bits and pieces. Though the acts themselves seem quite clear, some written reports of the acts contradict each other. As if these acts were, at one time, too well known; as if the original nodule of each particular fact had from somewhere received non-factual accretions; or even more, as if, since the basic facts were so clear perhaps there were a larger number of facts than any one reporter, or several, or even any reporter had ever attempted to record. About facts that are still simply told by this mouth to that ear, of course, even less can be expected.

An affair seventy-five years old should acquire some of the shiny transparency of an old man's skin. It should.

Sometimes it would seem that it would be enough—perhaps more than enough—to hear the names only. The grandfather One Arrow; the mother Spotted Calf; the father Sounding Sky; the wife (wives rather, but only one of them seems to have a name, though their fathers are Napaise, Kapahoo, Old Dust, The Rump)—the one wife named, of all things, Pale Face; the cousin Going-Up-To-Sky; the brother-in-law (again, of all things) Dublin. The names of the police sound very much alike; they all begin with Constable or Corporal or Sergeant, but here and there an Inspector, then a Superintendent and eventually all the resonance of an Assistant Commissioner echoes down. More. Herself: Victoria, by the Grace of God etc. etc. QUEEN, Defender of the Faith, etc. etc. and witness "Our Right Trusty and Right Well-beloved Cousin and Councillor the Right Honorable Sir John Campbell Hamilton-Gordon, Earl of Aberdeen; Viscount Formartine, Baron Haddo, Methlic, Tarves and Kellie, in the Peerage of Scotland; Viscount Gordon of Aberdeen, County of Aberdeen, in the Peerage of the United Kingdom; Baronet of Nova Scotia, Knight Grand Cross of Our Most Distinguished Order of Saint Michael and Saint George etc. Governor General of Canada." And of course himself: in the award proclamation named "Jean-Baptiste" but otherwise known only as Almighty Voice.

But hearing cannot be enough: not even hearing all the thunder of A Proclamation: "Now Hear Ye that a reward of FIVE HUNDRED DOLLARS will be paid to any person or persons who will give such information as will lead . . . (etc. etc.) this Twentieth day of April, in the year of Our Lord one thousand eight hundred and ninety-six, and the Fifty-ninth year of our Reign . . . " etc. and etc.

Such hearing cannot be enough. The first item to be seen is the piece of white bone. It is almost triangular, slightly convex—concave actually as it is positioned at this moment with its corners slightly raised—graduating from perhaps a strong eighth to a weak quarter of an inch in thickness, its scattered pore structure varying between larger and smaller on its perhaps polished, certainly shiny surface. Precision is difficult since the glass showcase is at least thirteen inches deep and therefore an eye cannot be brought as close as the minute inspection of such a small, though certainly quite adequate, sample of skull would normally require. Also, because of the position it cannot be determined whether the several hairs, well over a foot long, are still in some manner attached or not.

The seven-pounder cannon can be seen standing almost shyly between the showcase and the interior wall. Officially it is known as a gun, not a cannon, and clearly its bore is not large enough to admit a large man's fist. Even if it can be believed that this gun was used in the 1885 Rebellion and that on the evening of Saturday May 29, 1897 (while the nine-pounder, now unidentified, was in the process of arriving with the police on the special train from Regina), seven shells (all that were available in Prince Albert at that time) from it were sent shrieking into the poplar bluff as night fell, clearly such shelling could not and would not disembowel the whole earth. Its carriage is now nicely lacquered, the perhaps oak spokes of its petite wheels (little higher than a knee) have been recently scraped, puttied and varnished; the brilliant burnish of its brass breeching testifies with what meticulous care charmen and women have used nationally advertised cleaners and restorers.

Though it can also be seen, even a careless glance reveals that the same concern has not been expended on the one (of two) 44 calibre 1866 model Winchesters apparently found at the last in the pit with Almighty Voice. It also is preserved in a glass case; the number 1536735 is still, though barely, distinguishable on the brass cartridge section just below the brass saddle ring. However, perhaps because the case was imperfectly sealed at one time (though sealed enough not to warrant disturbance now), or because of simple neglect, the rifle is obviously spotted here and there with blotches of rust and the brass itself reveals discolorations almost like mildew. The rifle bore, the three long strands of hair themselves, actually bristle with clots of dust. It may be that this museum cannot afford to be as concerned as the other; conversely, the disfiguration may be something inherent in the items themselves.

The small building which was the police guardroom at Duck Lake, Saskatchewan Territory, in 1895 may also be seen. It had subsequently been moved from its original place and used to house small animals, chicken perhaps, or pigs—such as a woman might be expected to have under her responsibility. It is, of course, now perfectly empty, and clean so that the public may enter with no more discomfort than a bend under the doorway and a heavy encounter with disinfectant. The doorjamb has obviously been replaced; the bar network at one window is, however, said to be original; smooth still, very smooth. The logs inside have been smeared again and again with whitewash, perhaps paint, to an insistent point of identity-defying characterlessness. Within the small rectangular box of these logs not a sound can be heard from the streets of the probably dead town.

Hey Injun you'll get hung for stealing that steer
Hey Injun for killing that government cow you'll get
three weeks on the woodpile Hey Injun

The place named Kinistino has disappeared from the map but the Minnechinass Hills have not. Whether they have ever been on a map is doubtful but they will, of course, not disappear from the landscape as long as the grass grows and the rivers run. Contrary to general report and belief, the Canadian prairies are rarely, if ever, flat and the Minnechinass (spelled five different ways and translated sometimes as "The Outside Hill," sometimes as "Beautiful Bare Hills") are dissimilar from any other of the numberless hills that everywhere block out the prairie horizon. They are not bare; poplars lie tattered along their tops, almost black against the straw-pale grass and sharp green against the grey soil of the plowing laid in half-mile rectangular blocks upon their western slopes. Poles holding various wires stick out of the fields, back down the bend of the valley; what was once a farmhouse is weathering into the cultivated earth. The poplar bluff where Almighty Voice made his stand has, of course, disappeared.

The policeman he shot and killed (not the ones he wounded, of course) are easily located. Six miles east, thirty-nine miles north in Prince Albert, the English Cemetery. Sergeant Colin Campbell Colebrook, North West Mounted Police Registration Number 605, lies presumably under a gravestone there. His name is seventeenth in a very long "list of non-commissioned officers and men who have died in the service since the inception of the force." The date is October 29, 1895, and the cause of death is anonymous: "Shot by escaping Indian prisoner near Prince Albert." At the foot of this grave are two others: Constable John R. Kerr, No. 3040, and Corporal C.H.S. Hockin, No. 3106. Their cause of death on May 28, 1897 is even more anonymous, but the place is relatively precise: "Shot by Indians at Min-etch-inass Hills, Prince Albert District."

The gravestone, if he has one, of the fourth man Almighty Voice killed is more difficult to locate. Mr. Ernest Grundy, postmaster at Duck Lake in 1897, apparently shut his window the afternoon of Friday, May 25, armed himself, rode east twenty miles, participated in the second charge into the bluff at about 6:30 P.M., and on the third sweep of that charge was shot dead at the edge of the pit. It would seem that he thereby contributed substantially not only to the Indians' bullet supply, but his clothing warmed them as well.

The burial place of Dublin and Going-Up-To-Sky is unknown, as is the grave of Almighty Voice. It is said that a Métis named Henry Smith lifted the latter's body from the pit in the bluff and gave it to Spotted Calf. The place of burial is not, of course, of ultimate significance. A gravestone is always less evidence than a triangular piece of skull, provided it is large enough.

Whatever further evidence there is to be gathered may rest on pictures. There are, presumably, almost numberless pictures of the policemen in the case, but the only one with direct bearing is one of Sergeant Colebrook who apparently insisted on advancing to complete an arrest after being warned three times that if he took another step he would be shot. The picture must have been taken before he joined the force; it reveals him a large-eared young man, hair brushcut and ascot tie, his eyelids slightly drooping, almost hooded under thick brows. Unfortunately a picture of Constable R.C. Dickson, into whose charge Almighty Voice was apparently placed in that guardroom and who after Colebrook's death was convicted of negligence, sentenced to two months hard labor and discharged, does not seem to be available.

There are no pictures to be found of either Dublin (killed early by rifle fire) or Going-Up-To-Sky (killed in the pit), the two teenage boys who gave their ultimate fealty to Almighty Voice. There is, however, one said to be of Almighty Voice, Junior. He may have been born to Pale Face during the year, two hundred and twenty-one days that his father was a fugitive. In the picture he is kneeling before what could be a tent, he wears striped denim overalls and displays twin babies whose sex cannot be determined from the double-laced dark bonnets they wear. In the supposed picture of Spotted Calf and Sounding Sky, Sounding Sky stands slightly before his wife; he wears a white shirt and a striped blanket folded over his left shoulder in such a manner that the arm in which he cradles a long rifle cannot be seen. His head is thrown back; the rim of his hat appears as a black half-moon above eyes that are pressed shut in, as it were, profound concentration above a mouth clenched thin in a downward curve. Spotted Calf wears a long dress, a sweater which could also be a man's dress coat, and a large fringed and embroidered shawl which would appear distinctly Doukhobor in origin if the scroll patterns on it were more irregular. Her head is small and turned slightly towards her husband so as to reveal her right ear. There is what can only be called a quizzical expression on her crumpled face; it may be she does not understand what is happening and that she would have asked a question, perhaps of her husband, perhaps of the photographer, perhaps even of anyone, anywhere in the world if such questioning were possible for an Indian lady.

There is one final picture. That is one of Almighty Voice himself. At least it is purported to be of Almighty Voice himself. In the Royal Canadian Mounted Police Museum the Barracks Grounds just off Dewdney Avenue in Regina, Saskatchewan it lies in the same showcase, as a matter of fact immediately beside, that triangular piece of skull. Both are unequivocally labeled, and it must be assumed that a police force with a world-wide reputation would not label *such* evidence incorrectly. But here emerges an ultimate problem in making the story.

There are two official descriptions of Almighty Voice. The first reads: "Height about five feet, ten inches, slight build, rather good looking, a sharp hooked nose with a remarkably flat point. Has a bullet scar on the left side of his face about 1½ inches long running from near corner of mouth towards ear. The scar cannot be noticed when his face is painted but otherwise is plain. Skin fair for an Indian." The second description is on the Award Proclamation: "About twenty-two years old, five feet ten inches in height, weight about eleven stone, slightly erect, neat small feet and hands; complexion inclined to be fair, wavy dark hair to shoulders, large dark eyes, broad forehead, sharp features and parrot nose with flat tip, scar on left cheek running from mouth towards ear, feminine appearance."

So run the descriptions that were, presumably, to identify a well-known fugitive in so precise a manner that an informant could collect five hundred dollars—a considerable sum when a police constable earned between one and two dollars a day. The nexus of the problems appears when these supposed official descriptions are compared to the supposed official picture. The man in the picture is standing on a small rug. The fingers of his left hand touch a curved Victorian settee, behind him a photographer's backdrop of scrolled patterns merges to vaguely paradisaic trees and perhaps a sky. The moccasins he wears make it impossible to deduce whether his feet are "neat small." He may be five feet, ten inches tall, may weigh eleven stone, he certainly is "rather good looking" and, though it is a frontal view, it may be that the point of his long and flaring nose could be "remarkably flat." The photograph is slightly over-illuminated and so the unpainted complexion could be "inclined to be fair"; however, nothing can be seen of a scar, the hair is not wavy and shoulder-length but hangs almost to the waist in two thick straight braids worked through with beads, fur, ribbons and cords. The right hand that holds the corner of the blanket-like coat in position is large and, even in the high illumination, heavily veined. The neck is concealed under coiled beads and the forehead seems more low than "broad."

Perhaps, somehow, these picture details could be reconciled with the official description if the face as a whole were not so devastating.

On a cloth-backed sheet two feet by two and one-half feet in size, under the Great Seal of the Lion and the Unicorn, dignified by the names of the Deputy of the Minister of Justice, the Secretary of State, the Queen herself and all the heaped detail of her "Right Trusty and Right Well Beloved Cousin," this description concludes: "feminine appearance." But the picture: any face of history, any believed face that the world acknowledges as *man*—Socrates, Jesus, Attila, Genghis Khan, Mahatma Gandhi, Joseph Stalin—no believed face is more *man* than this face. The mouth, the nose, the clenched brows, the eyes—the eyes are large, yes, and dark, but even in this watered-down reproduction of unending reproductions of original, a steady look into those eyes cannot be endured. It is a face like an axe.

■ ■ ■

It is now evident that the de Chardin statement quoted at the beginning has relevance only as it proves itself inadequate to explain what has happened. At the same time, the inadequacy of Aristotle's much more famous statement becomes evident: "The true difference [between the historian and the poet] is that one relates what *has* happened, the other what *may* happen." These statements cannot explain the storyteller's activity since, despite the most rigid application of impersonal investigation, the elements of the story have now run me aground. If ever I could, I can no longer pretend to objective, omnipotent disinterestedness. I am no longer *spectator* of what *has* happened or what *may* happen: I am become *element* in what is happening at this very moment.

For it is, of course, I myself who cannot endure the shadows on that paper which are those eyes. It is I who stand beside this broken veranda post where two corner shingles have been torn away, where barbed wire tangles the dead weeds on the edge of this field. The bluff that sheltered Almighty Voice and his two friends has not disappeared from the slope of the Minnechinass, no more than the sound of Constable Dickson's voice in that guardhouse is silent. The sound of his speaking is there even if it has never been recorded in an official report:

hey injun you'll get
hung
for stealing that steer
hey injun for killing that government
cow you'll get three
weeks on the woodpile hey injun

The unknown contradictory words about an unprovable act that move a boy to defiance, an implacable Cree warrior long after the three-hundred-and-fifty-year war is ended, a war already lost the day the Cree watch Cartier hoist his gun ashore at Hochelaga and they begin the retreat west; these words of incomprehension, of threatened incomprehensible law are there to be heard, like the unmoving tableau of the three-day siege is there to be seen on the slopes of the Minnechinass. Sounding Sky is somewhere not there, under arrest, but Spotted Calf stands on a shoulder of the Hills a little to the left, her arms upraised to the setting sun. Her mouth is open. A horse rears, riderless, above the scrub willow at the edge of the bluff, smoke puffs, screams tangle in rifle barrage, there are wounds, somewhere. The bluff is green this spring, it will not burn and the ragged line of seven police and two civilians is staggering through, faces twisted in rage, terror, and rifles sputter. Nothing moves. There is no sound of frogs in the night; twenty-seven policemen and five civilians stand in cordon at thirty-yard intervals and a body also lies in the shelter of a gully. Only a voice rises from the bluff:

We have fought well
You have died like braves
I have worked hard and am hungry
Give me food

but nothing moves. The bluff lies, a bright green island on the grassy slope surrounded by men hunched forward rigid over their long rifles, men clumped out of rifle-range, thirty-five men dressed as for fall hunting on a sharp spring day, a small gun positioned on a ridge above. A crow is falling out of the sky into the bluff, its feathers sprayed as by an explosion. The first gun and the second gun are in position, the beginning and end of the bristling surround of thirty-five Prince Albert Volunteers, thirteen civilians and fifty-six policemen in position relative to the bluff and relative to the unnumbered whites astride their horses, standing up in their carts, staring and pointing across the valley, in position relative to the bluff and the unnumbered Indians squatting silent along the higher ridges of the Hills, motionless mounds, faceless against the Sunday morning sunlight edging between and over them down along the tree tips, down into the shadows of the bluff. Nothing moves. Beside the second gun the red-coated officer has flung a handful of grass into the motionless air, almost to the rim of the red sun.

And there is a voice. It is an incredible voice that rises from among the young poplars ripped of their spring bark, from among the dead somewhere lying there, out of the arm-deep pit shorter than a man; a voice rises over the exploding smoke and thunder of guns that reel back in their positions, worked over, serviced by the grimed motionless men in bright coats and glinting buttons, a voice so high and clear, so unbelievably high and strong in its unending wordless cry.

■ ■ ■

The voice of "Gitchie-Manitou Wayo"—interpreted as "voice of the Great Spirit"—that is, Almighty Voice. His death chant no less incredible in its beauty than in its incomprehensible happiness.

I say "wordless cry" because that is the way it sounds to me. I could be more accurate if I had a reliable interpreter who would make a reliable interpretation. For I do not, of course, understand the Cree myself.

J. Michael Yates

J. Michael Yates was born in Fulton, Missouri, in 1938 and grew up in the United States. He emigrated to Canada as an adult, working in a variety of jobs—writing, editing, and teaching creative writing (he was the founding editor of Sono Nis Press)—and living in a variety of places, from West Vancouver to the Queen Charlotte Islands. The range of backgrounds has had its impact on his writing, which transcends borders both political and generic. He writes poetry, drama, fiction, and meditations on existence that embrace features of several different genres. He does not write sociological documentary. Repeatedly, however, he uses the actual forms of literature to require his reader to see the world—and their roles in it—with abrupt clarity. He manages to do so, Andreas Schroeder writes, in his introduction to *Stories from Pacific & Arctic Canada* (1974), while avoiding the "haven of straight metaphor or fable." Readers may have to suspend the laws of ordinary logic in order to follow Yates's stories, but in doing so they have the opportunity to discover—and surrender to—the inventive logic of the stories themselves.

Among Yates's books are the autobiography *Line Screw* (1993), about his years working as a prison guard, and two collections of fiction, *The Abstract Beast* (1971) and *Fazes in Elsewhen* (1977). "The Sinking of the Northwest Passage" comes from the first of the collections. It coolly portrays a universe of domestic ritual and suburban monomania, whose bizarreness is the more acute for its familiarity.

The Sinking of the Northwest Passage

So many of us, alas, were born with
no Northwest Passage to discover.
We spend our lives carrying that
poignant absence inside us wherever
we go, around and around the earth.

Commodore Eric F.F. Forrer stood in the box of his sailboat, *The Northwest Passage*, near the base of the bowsprit (whose configuration was most personal, most abstract), arms folded over his still large-calibre chest and shouted: "Eric F.F. Forrer, Commodore!" And then he listened to his echo skittering away among the branches and boles of the scrub-pine.

There was no retort. But as if there had been one, as if there had been a challenge, he continued at the top of his basso: "I am Commodore because I say so. Let any man who doubts come forward and say."

The as-if: "In what navy do you serve, sir?"

The Commodore: "None. Such institutions are for ordinary men."

The as-if: "Such titles as 'Commodore' are earned with valor and conferred in formal and elaborate ceremony."

The Commodore: "Ordinary! Ordinary!"

The as-if: "Nevertheless."

The Commodore: " 'Nevertheless' hell! And nuts! Didn't great Caesar place the laurel on his own brow? And what of Tamburlaine? These were great men in history. I am greater than all history!"

The as-if: "Who says so?"

The Commodore: "I say so, you imbecile. Do you doubt it?"

The as-if: "Frankly, yes."

The Commodore: "Frankly, you are a quadrilateral incandescent ordinary gregarious afterbirth of a self-conscious bitch monkey. Why do I waste time talking to you? Name me one, among all past and present commodores, name me one who ever built his own ship with his own hands as I have."

The as-if: "I cannot."

The Commodore: "Of course you can't. I am my own navy, and as head of it, it is fitting and proper that I function as its commodore."

The as-if: "Hmmmmm."

The Commodore: "Further, mister, this may appear an innocuous sailing vessel, but, in fact, it is a cleverly-camouflaged submarine, and if you don't vanish, this instant, I shall cause it to dive, rig for silent running, and sink you with cleverly-concealed torpedos. Do we understand one another?"

The as-if: "Of course, sir. Right away, sir."

The Commodore: "Excellent. Once, while rafting on a lake near Terrace in the wilds of British Columbia, I sank an entire fleet of pleasure craft which annoyed me while I was sun bathing."

Out of the door of the house shuffled a woman hugging herself across her copious bosom against the chill of the northern morning; she yawned, then stood squinting at the tableau of Commodore Eric F.F. Forrer standing in the bow of his sailing ship which stood solid as a monument on its supports in the middle of the smooth asphalt driveway.

"Excellent sailing this morning (pointing to the asphalt of the driveway and the long winding asphalt road which led down the dome toward the town). Not a ripple. But I could wish for more wind, you know?"

"Why all the shouting? There's no one around."

"You'd be surprised, my dear, how many there are around us."

With that he stepped to the port railing and urinated noisily upon the pavement below.

"Oh, don't do that. Someone might see."

"But you just assured me there's no one about."

"Never mind."

He zipped up the fly of his "northern tuxedo" (overalls) with ceremony.

"Come aboard, come aboard, don't just stand there on the surface, can't you see I'm under way?"

She climbed up the ladder still shivering from the chill of the dew-soaked dome.

"Look at that view of Mount Forrer. You can see four hundred miles."

"Yes, it's beautiful. Every day it's the same but not the same."

"Light. Things never look the same on successive days. It's all in how you look at a thing. And every day the light is changing. Wait till you see it up close. We're going to sail right to it, then right up to its summit before we turn again into the Northwest Passage."

"There's no water straight to the mountain."

"Never mind that."

"And you know there's no longer a Northwest Passage to be found."

"Ordinary poppycock. You can come with me, or I'll set you ashore on an island and proceed alone, or leave you here. Whatever you prefer."

"Thank you. We'll think about it again after breakfast. Come on in now."

"Alright. I'll just anchor up now. I won't be a minute."

Over her shoulder she heard the clank of anchor and chain striking the dark asphalt. The boat secured, he followed her into the house.

After his third mug of sourdough wet breakfast (four fingers of over-proof rum, honey, cinnamon, lemon juice, and strong black tea—never mixed in that order) he commented: "This is one of the best houses I ever built. It voyages well. Hardly keels at all in the wind."

"Yes."

"But it won't get through the passage. The passage is quite narrow, you know."

"No, I didn't know. How do you know, if it's never yet been discovered ?"

"I know these things. It is my affair to know them."

"Yes, of course."

"We'll have to have just the right tide, woman, just the right tide. It may be necessary to wait days, days, or even months for just the right tide . . . and even then it'll be handy to have pikepoles starboard and port to push us off if she goes too close to the sides. But at the right tide, at just the right tide, with the big rollers behind us, we should surf right on through."

"I hope so."

"Probably we won't even need any canvas, much less the engine. No engine is really dependable anyway. Trust the natural stuff—wind and water."

"If you say so."

"I do. Truly."

It was a bright summer morning, light tentacles reaching in through the windows and curling about the legs of the furniture—brilliant as only mornings in the long-lit northern summers can be—when the first foreign, altogether indescribable, sound from the driveway filled their ears.

The Commodore leapt to the screen door and scowled out into the dazzling sunlight.

"What is it?"

"Nothing I can see. Ship's riding easily at anchor."

"What a strange noise."

". . . Yes . . . "

The sound again.

"It's coming from the boat."

"Is she breaking up?"

"I built it."

"Silly of me."

"Extremely."

"Why don't you go out and look around?"

"I guess I'd better."

He turned from the door and began placing dishes in a cupboard.

"Then go."

He first withdrew his pocket-watch from the upper left-hand pocket of his overalls and glanced at the time, then replaced it, then gazed slowly around the kitchen and through the doorway to the living room which framed a magnificent view of Mount Forrer, then pushed out the door and strode slowly down the asphalt driveway. She watched from the door and the house slowly filled with her ineffable dread. She could see nothing unusual—only the driveway with the boat on its supports filling it, and Commodore Eric F.F. Forrer nearing the source of the noise which was growing louder and continuous now.

"What do you see? Can you see anything?"

"The ship looks fine."

Then he was bending over examining the supports.

"Is it too heavy for them? Are they breaking?"

"No."

"Then what is it?"

"Eh . . . here!"

He was looking at the cross-members on the pavement.

"What?"

"The supports seem to be sinking through the pavement. Funny they've been here in this same position for such a long time . . . all these years . . . same weight, same conditions . . . wily would they wait until this moment to begin sinking?"

She came up beside him and bent over too, examining. "I don't know. Maybe it's the heat."

"Can't be. It's not hot out."

"It's been much hotter than this on other days and it had no effect. Don't you remember the hot scorcher of a summer we had about nine years ago? If the supports were ever going to sink through the asphalt, they would have done so then."

"Well, it's right in front of your eyes, woman . . . sinking . . . there, look!"

As if on cue, the back cross-member vanished and the stern of the vessel settled to the ground. It gave the whole vehicle a strange lurching look—as if climbing a great swell on the high seas. The lines of the craft had become so familiar to them, and now the deck was almost at a thirty degree angle with the horizon.

"And look under here, the keel's more than halfway submerged."

"Yes."

"Blast it, blast the blasted luck!"

"What now?"

"Quick, help me put those planks over there under the hull."

Soon an assortment of weather-silvered two by sixes and two by eights were neatly formed into a protective bed beneath the middle and forward hull.

"We've got to keep her from keeling over; it'll smash the ribbing and ruin everything. I'll never find yellow cedar of that quality again. They don't even replant that stuff after they cut it."

They braced the boat from pavement to gunwales with four by fours.

"Where are you going?"

"To get jacks, jack her up, and build another platform under the stern."

"How did this happen? Do such things happen?"

"No."

The Commodore was fretfully pulling out hairs of his blonde moustache, a growth that couldn't be seen at a distance greater than a few feet. One could always tell when he enjoyed a book: its pages were full of hairs from his moustache.

"On the other hand, seamanship is a tricky science and a difficult art. There are strange currents, woman, strange currents which sink great ships even in the fairest of surface conditions. Tides change. Sea-floors rearrange themselves. A man can never know too much about navigation—although there are things a man can know far too much about. I'll get the jacks."

Behind him he heard the sound begin again, and even before he turned he knew the bow support and remaining keel had disappeared under the surface of the asphalt.

"Oh dear, now the bow is down."

"I have eyes. I . . . have . . . eyes."

"Will the planks keep it afloat?"

"Who can be certain of such things? No sense trying the jacks now. There's nothing forward or astern skookum enough to take leverage against that weight. I have no intention of cracking ribs and breaking off her railings to get purchase. Better *The Northwest Passage* go down just as I made her, than go down broken and maimed."

"But wouldn't it be better to save even . . . "

"No."

"Can't you do something?"

"Possibly I could tunnel in two places beneath the ship, run belts under, then hire a crane to yard her up while I build new supports under her."

"Yes, do that. But you would have to ruin the driveway, wouldn't you?"

"Yes."

He went in through the screen door then emerged a few minutes later carrying two kitchen chairs.

"What are those for?"

"We'll sit and keep a close watch. She's sailing high and easy now on the planks. Maybe something will occur to us."

"Did you call about the crane?"

"Yes."

"What did they say?"

"Either there is no elevation company listed in the yellow pages, or there is no crane this far north large enough for the job, or it would require two smaller cranes (and likely the two operators couldn't coordinate their lifting: suppose a bee flew into the cab of one of them at a crucial moment. And everyone knows that two machines cannot be perfectly harmonized . . . even by a third machine; there are too many variables). If one failed, not only would all that effort be in vain, but much money would go for nothing; all our money is riding on the planks before us there. If one broke down in mid-lift (even without damage to the vessel, let us hopefully suppose), then where would we be? We would pay for men and machines alike by the hour nevertheless, if we could pay. They would have to send for a mechanic and then for parts which must be flown in from the outside. Or, since all of them are on tracks, it would take a long time to get up here from their present job-sites, if, indeed, they could be spared at all. This is the building season, and all things and all men are under contract. In fact, they wouldn't be allowed to come up here on tracks, they would scar the pavement, and there are ordinances. They would have to bring them on low-beds and it would be necessary to add the cost of the trucks and their drivers. If they came on trucks, there would be far too much weight per axle for the myriad small bridges between the city and this driveway. There are ordinances, always ordinances to protect the forms of civilisation. They aren't fond, you know, of small and extraordinary jobs like this one and avoid them at all costs. Or the line was busy. Or out of order. Or they wouldn't believe me."

"I'd forgotten."

"Why do women forget such things?"

"I'm not women; I'm singular; and I don't know why I forget such things."

"Sit down. I'm sorry."

"Thank you. I'm sorry too. Can you use the ship's radio to call for help?"

"No, there are too many domes and ridges for sending signals from here. And there are no charts for this extremity of north; no one sails here."

"How about sending up a flare?"

"Too dry. The forest fire hazard is too high. I won't risk burning the ship; too much of my life is in her seams."

"I suppose so."

"Believe it."

They sat, she still hugging herself, he with his left arm across the back of her chair, and both gazing at the soft line where the keel touched the pavement.

"Possibly it was only the night air. It might have somehow weakened the supports."

"There was nothing wrong with the supports. They sank without giving way."

"Ah, that's right. But it's not sinking now."

"I'm afraid you're wrong. Since the forward support disappeared, it's been sinking steadily."

"I can't hear it. And it doesn't look like it to me."

"Look closely. Don't you see how the planks we set underneath are gradually floating out beyond the sides?"

"Yes . . . I see it now. But why do we hear nothing?"

"Not all sinking is sensory. It sometimes goes on through the nights and days without our noticing at all. By the time we've grown cognizant of it, there is no bilge-pump strong enough to save us. Probably *The Northwest Passage* began to sink the moment I touched pencil to paper to design her."

"Do you think so?"

"Yes."

"And, knowing this, it made no difference?"

"No."

"I think I wouldn't have gone through with it, if such a suspicion occurred to me."

"I could have preferred things otherwise . . . but without boats to build . . . there wouldn't be anything."

The ship was settling evenly, gracefully, now, toward the waterline. Without sound. Not far away a grouse drummed. A ptarmigan strode across the asphalt road. And a black bear was nosing a blueberry bush absent of berries. High sun strummed through the well-strung rigging of the mast and cross-spars, then darted here and there among the polished brass fittings.

"Soon she'll hit the water-line."

"Yes."

"Then, who knows?"

"Say, I just thought of something. Maybe *The Northwest Passage* simply has a mind of her own and is trying to tell us something by launching herself. She'll stop at the water-line. I think I'll go inside for a bottle of champagne to christen her, just in case."

"That sparkling muscatel?"

"Don't be coarse. It's twenty a magnum."

"Ships should be christened with rum. Bring the rum."

"Where's your sense of ceremony?"

"In my insides—where that rum is going."

She brought the rum.

"There's the water-line!"

"Good. Now we'll see."

"I have the champagne near the door."

"Very well, if she stops at the water-line, you have my leave to ruin my stern varnish with that belly-rot."

"Later you'll be glad I christened her properly."

The mast stood like a sundial, wavering only slightly in the breeze and the almost imperceptible silent settlings below. It marked the passing of high noon and cast its crossed shadows in the direction of evening and the dark which never seems to arrive in the summer north, but suddenly is upon you.

"So much for my water-line." He tossed the empty rum bottle into the bushes which lined the driveway.

"Yes, nothing showing of it at all. I'll only have to pick up that bottle and discard it later."

"So you will. So you will."

Before she could protest, he leapt from his chair, raced to the ladder at the side of the vessel, climbed it, and drew the ladder up on the deck.

"What do you think you can accomplish from up there?"

No answer. He was drawing up the anchor. The anchor secured, he began pacing around the decks, the bill of his sailing cap pulled low against the vanishing rays of the strange northern sun. He paused to check this fitting, then that, gave a turn-buckle a couple of turns, then went inside to his compass, charts, and wheel.

"Don't you think you ought to come down?"

His head appeared around the frame of the cabin door. He glared at her with fraudulent anger.

"I mean, you never know what might happen."

"You never know."

He unlashed the mainsail and pulled it determinedly up the mast, secured the boom, then returned to the wheelhouse. A weak breeze over the dome-top began to luff the canvas erratically. He emerged again quickly, leapt to the bow, cupped his hands, and: "In the name of Boreas and all inspiration . . . MORE GODDAM WIND!!"

And you could hear it in the distant trees like a locomotive nearing.

"There's always breeze in the late afternoon and evening. You know it as well as I do."

"Never mind. Where's my line now?"

"About midway between water-line and gunwale, I guess."

The mainsail was full now. The Commodore went forward and ran up the jib which stiffened until it looked like the blade of a knife held aloft.

"Alright now, alright, we'll see what we'll see." And into the cabin we went again. Below on the driveway she paced round and round the craft, hugging herself against the chill and wind rising. The vessel heaved back and forth in the pavement and the noise had returned—grating and grating of the cedar ribs against the stone layers and permafrost into which it was sinking.

The Commodore again came out of the cabin, and, struggling against the winds mounting to gale force, managed to get the deep green spinnaker up. It required almost super-human effort. The canvas ballooned and burgeoned like the throat-sac of a monster frog.

The noise now was truly stupendous. It overwhelmed even the sound of the careering wind. She stood in the draft of the vessel, but not too close: it pitched now side to side and forward and aft, as if in the highest of seas. Anything might have happened—sails might have split, the boat might have broken up, or might even have rolled free. But these things did not occur; simply the violent motion accelerated the sinking.

Commodore Eric F.F. Forrer stood, legs rooted substantially far apart, knees bending rhythmically to absorb the shocks of the listing and pitching, there in the wheelhouse at the wheel until, at a dramatic moment toward late evening, the bowsprit nosed under and the wind expired as if there had never been wind, and the forward decks were awash with asphalt.

"You see? It didn't work."

The Commodore standing on the slant amidships, cap in his left hand, mopping his brow with his right sleeve: "On the contrary, woman, on the contrary."

Another lurch. The stern and aft decking sank from sight. He sprang to the roof of the cabin. The sails hung limp from their rigging.

"This is the best ship I ever made. See how she sinks evenly instead of going stern or bow first. You can tell the character of a boat by the way she dies."

"I see."

"Plenty of time for all hands to abandon."

"Plenty."

"Better stand back and clear. Sometimes the last suction can be fierce."

"Very well. Have all abandoned?"

"Yes, I gave the order some time ago."

"I didn't hear it."

"Doubtless it was the big wind and the sound of the sinking."

"Yes, I suppose."

The surface of the driveway was now level with the flat roof of the wheelhouse. No wind, and darkness closing like the shutter of a camera.

"I'll get a light."

She returned with a glass lantern, brilliant and hissing.

"Is there any more rum?" he asked as he began climbing the rigging toward the cross-spar.

"No. I'm sorry."

He sat, legs dangling on either side of the mast, and holding the tip of the mast near the flag with one hand.

The light of the lantern lit one side of his profile so brightly that his features seemed almost washed out. The other side of his face, like the moon which had now risen over the scrub-timber at the crest of the dome, erased itself in darkness. Up the mast crept the asphalt like mercury in a barometer. There was little sound now, so smooth was the surface of the mast, save the occasional crinkle of new canvas going under.

When the surface met the corrugated soles of his deck shoes, he stood upon the cross-spar, drew himself to his full height, inhaled the darkness deeply, and shouted:

"Eric F.F. Forrer, Commodore!"

There was no retort. Nor did he begin to polemicize as if there had been one.

She held the light closer as the asphalt gathered in his broad shoulders.

His last words were: "Blow that damned thing out."

She did.

And there was not a trace, not a ripple, not even a small indentation in the dark surface of the driveway. She spent some minutes looking after she re-lit the lamp (not difficult in the windless darkness; there was still plenty of pressure in it).

And then she went inside where the bottle of champagne still stood waiting; she replaced it in the liquor cupboard. She would fetch the empty rum bottle in the morning and throw it in the trash.

As she switched out the lights from room to room and began to prepare for bed, the house rolled a little . . . like a large boat at a calm mooring. But she hardly noticed the motion; miniature earth tremors are so very usual in that precinct of the world.

Acknowledgments

An honest attempt has been made to secure permission for all material used, and if there are errors or omissions, these are wholly unintentional and the Publisher will be grateful to learn of them.

A Civil Peace from *Girls at War and other stories* by Chinua Achebe. Copyright © 1972 by Chinua Achebe. Reprinted by permission of Harold Ober Associates Incorporated.

A Northern Belle from *Hunting the Wild Pineapple* by Thea Astley. 1991. Reprinted by permission of Penguin Australia.

Death by Landscape from *Wilderness Tips* by Margaret Atwood. Copyright © 1991 by O.W. Toad Ltd. Used by written permission from McClelland & Stewart, Inc., *The Canadian Publishers.*

The History of Word War 3 by J.G. Ballard is from the collection WAR FEVER published by Flamingo, an imprint of HarperCollins, London and Farrar Straus, New York. Copyright © 1990 J G Ballard. All rights reserved. Reproduced by permission of the author c/o Margaret Hanbury, 27 Walcot Square, London SE11 4UB.

Report from *Unspeakable Practices, Unnatural Acts*. Copyright © 1968 by Donald Barthelme. Used by permission of the author and The Wylie Agency Incorporated.

Eyes from *A North American Education* by Clark Blaise. Copyright © 1973 by Clark Blaise. Reprinted by permission of the author.

Allal Copyright © 1979 by Paul Bowles. Reprinted from *Collected Stories 1939-1976* with the permission of Black Sparrow Press.

Two Fishermen from *Morley Callaghan's Stories* by Morley Callaghan. Reprinted by the permission of the Estate of Morley Callaghan.

"Do You Love Me?" from *War Crimes* by Peter Carey. Copyright © Peter Carey 1979. Reproduced by permission of the author c/o Rogers, Coleridge & White Ltd., 20 Powis Mews, London W11 1JN.

The Company of Wolves from *The Bloody Chamber & Other Stories* by Angela Carter. Copyright © 1979. Reprinted by permission of the Estate of Angela Carter c/o Rogers, Coleridge & White Ltd., 20 Powis Mews, London W11 1JN.

Ko-ishin-mit and the Shadow People from *Son of a Raven, Son of a Deer*, by George Clutesi. Published by Gray's 1967. Used by permission of the author's estate.

In the Gloaming by Alice Elliott Dark from *The Best American Short Stories of the Century*. Originally published in *The New Yorker*, 1993. Reprinted by permission of Simon & Schuster Inc.

Dry September from *Collected Stories of William Faulkner* by William Faulkner. Copyright © 1950 by Random House Inc. Reprinted by permission of Random House Inc.

Great Falls from *Rock Springs* by Richard Ford. Copyright © 1987 by Richard Ford. Reprinted by permission of the author and Grove/Atlantic, Inc.

The Road from Colonus from *The Collected Tales of E.M. Forster* by E.M. Forster. Published 1947 by Alfred A. Knopf, Inc. Reprinted by permission of The Provost and Scholars of King's College, Cambridge and the Society of Authors as the literary representatives of the E M Forster Estate.

With a Capital T by Mavis Gallant. Reprinted by permission of Georges Borchardt, Inc.

No Place Like from *Livingston's Companions* by Nadine Gordimer. Published 1971 by Viking. Reprinted by the permission of Russell & Volkening as agents for the author. Copyright © 1971 by Nadine Gordimer.

Slow Dissolve from *The Bearded Ladies* by Kate Grenville. Published by University of Queensland Press. Used by permission of the publisher.

Letters from the Samantha *from Ellis Island & Other Stories* by Mark Helprin. © 1976, 1977, 1979, 1980, 1981 by Mark Helprin. Used by permission of Dell Publishing, a division of Random House, Inc.

Hills Like White Elephants from *Men Without Women* by Ernest Hemingway. Reprinted by permission of Simon & Schuster.

Over Here Copyright © Jack Hodgins 1995. First published in *Prism International* 33 No.3 (Spring 1995). Reprinted here by an arrangement of Bella Pomer Agency.

The Washerwoman's Children from *Dear Miss Manfield* by Witi Ihimaera. Copyright © 1989 by Witi Ihimaera. Reprinted by permission of Penguin Books (New Zealand) Ltd.

California Cancer Journeys from *New Orleans is Sinking* by Mark Anthony Jarman. Copyright © 1998 by Mark Anthony Jarman. Reprinted by permission of Oberon Press, Ottawa.

Borders from *One Good Story That One* by Thomas King. Published by HarperCollins Publishers Ltd. Copyright © 1993 by Thomas King. Reprinted by permission of the author and publisher.

My Son the Fanatic by Hanif Kureishi. Reprinted from *Love in Blue Time.* Reprinted by permission of Simon & Schuster Inc.

When Mr. Pirzada Came to Dine from *Interpreters of Maladies* by Jhumpa Lahiri. Copyright © 1999 by Jhumpa Lahiri. Reprinted by permission of Houghton Mifflin Company. All rights reserved.

The Horse Dealer's Daughter from *The Complete Short Stories of D.H. Lawrence.* Copyright © 1922 by Thomas B. Seltzer, Inc., renewed 1950 by Frieda Lawrence. Reprinted by permission of Lawrence Pollinger Limited and the Estate of Frieda Lawrence Ravagli.

The First Contact with the Gorgonids copyright © 1991 by Ursula Le Guin; first appeared in *Omni;* from *A Fisherman of the Inland Sea;* reprinted by permission of the author and the author's agents, the Virginia Kidd Agency, Inc.

The Movers from *Pangs of Love and Other Stories* by David Wong Louie. Copyright © 1991 by David Wong Louie. Reprinted by permission of Alfred A. Knopf, a Division of Random House Inc.

Swimming Lessons from *Tales from Firozsha Baag* by Rohinton Mistry. Copyright © 1987 by Rohinton Mistry. Used by written permission from McClelland & Stewart, Inc., *The Canadian Publishers.*

The Children Stay from *The Love of a Good Woman* by Alice Munro. Copyright © 1998 by Alice Munro. Used by written permission from McClelland & Stewart, Inc., *The Canadian Publishers.*

My Aunt Gold Teeth from *A Flag on the Island* by V.S. Naipaul Copyright © 1999. Reprinted by permission of Gillon Aitken & Associates. Reprinted by permission.

In the Region of Ice from *The Wheel of Love* by Joyce Carol Oates. Copyright © 1970. Reprinted by permission of John Hawkins & Associates, Inc.

A Good Man is Hard to Find from *A Good Man is Hard to Find* by Flannery O'Connor. Copyright © 1953 by Flannery O'Connor and renewed 1981 by Regina O'Connor. Reprinted by permission of Harcourt Brace Jovanovich, Inc.

He from *Flowering Judas and other stories* by Katherine Anne Porter. Copyright © 1930, renewed 1958 by Katherine Anne Porter. Reprinted by permission of Harcourt Brace Jovanovich, Inc.

The Half-Skinned Deer from *Close Range: Wyoming Stories* by Annie Proulx. Published under the Scribner Imprint. Reprinted by permission of Simon & Schuster Inc.

Responsibility from *Young Men* by Russell Smith. 1999. Reprinted by permission of Doubleday Canada Ltd.

The More Little Mummy in the Word from *Ladies and Escorts* by Audrey Thomas. Reprinted by permission of the author.

Giving Blood from *The Music School* by John Updike. Copyright © 1966 by John Updike. Reprinted by permission of Alfred A. Knopf, Inc., a Division of Random House Inc.

Cages from *Man Descending* by Guy Vanderhaeghe. Copyright © 1982 by Guy Vanderhaeghe. Used by written permission from McClelland & Stewart, Inc., *The Canadian Publishers.*

Report on the Barnhouse Effect from *Welcome to the Monkey House* by Kurt Vonnegut Jr., copyright © 1961 by Kurt Vonnegut Jr. Used by permission of Dell Publishing, a Division of Random House Inc.

Nineteen Fifty-five from *You Can't Keep a Good Woman Down* copyright © 1981 by Alice Walker, reprinted by permission of Harcourt Inc.

Where is the Voice Coming From? by Rudy Wiebe is printed in *The Angel of the Tar Sands and Other Stories.* Copyright © Jackpine House Ltd., 1999.

The Sinking of the Northwest Passage from *The Abstract Beast* by J. Michael Yates 1971. Reprinted by permission of the author.